VENUS IN BOSTON

Copyright © 2002 by University of Massachusetts Press
All rights reserved
Printed in the United States of America
LC 2001057396
ISBN 1-55849-325-5 (cloth); 326-3 (paper)

Designed by Jack Harrison
Set in Janson Text with Juniper display type

Library of Congress Cataloging-in-Publication Data

Thompson, George, b. 1823
    Venus in Boston and other tales of nineteenth-century city life / George Thompson;
edited with an introduction by David S. Reynolds and Kimberly R. Gladman.
        p. cm.
    Includes bibliographical references.
    ISBN 1-55849-325-5 (lib. cloth : alk. paper) — ISBN 1-55849-326-3 (pbk. : alk. paper)
    1. Boston (Mass.)—Fiction. 2. New York (N.Y.)—Fiction. 3. City and town life—Fiction.
4. Thompson, George, b. 1823. 5. Authors, American—19th century—Biography.
I. Reynolds, David S., 1948– II. Gladman, Kimberly R., 1968– III. Title
PS3032.T29 V46 2002
813'.3—dc21
                                                                            2001057396

British Library Cataloguing in Publication data are available.

CONTENTS

MY LIFE:
OR THE ADVENTURES OF GEO. THOMPSON

ACKNOWLEDGMENTS

A number of people have been instrumental in bringing this project to fruition. We are especially grateful to Paul Wright, our editor at the University of Massachusetts Press, who has been a supportive and helpful presence at every stage of the process. Carol Betsch, managing editor, and Jack Harrison, design and production manager, were also tireless and meticulous partners in reproducing Thompson's texts. Our text of *City Crimes* would have been incomplete without the kind efforts of Courtney Page of the Tulane University Library and Julie Cobb of the Newberry Library, both of whom supplied us with several passages that were missing or illegible in the microfilmed version of the novel. The library staff of the American Antiquarian Society (AAS), especially Joanne Chaison, Georgia Barnhill, Tom Knoles, Marie Lamoureux, and Dennis Laurie, gave us warm encouragement and invaluable assistance in microfilming *My Life*, researching Thompson, and choosing illustrations for this volume. Dennis Laurie also first alerted us to the existence of *Venus' Miscellany*, which proved so relevant to Thompson's career, and directed us to issues of the paper held at Princeton University, which Margaret Sherry of Princeton's Firestone Library helped us locate. Eugene Zepp and Roberta Zonghi of the Boston Public Library and Alan Jutzi of the Huntington Library facilitated the reproduction of images from *Venus in Boston* and *City Crimes*, respectively. The following people helped us to compile our primary bibliography by confirming their institutions' Thompson holdings: Susan Brady of Yale's Beinecke Library; Clark Evans of the Library of Congress; Lynne Farrington of the Annenberg Rare Book Library at the University of Pennsylvania; and Lisa Libby of the Huntington Library.

We also thank George Thompson of the Bobst Library at New York University for his generous help in researching his namesake on several occasions, as well as Paul Erikson for first pointing us to *Ten Days in the Tombs* and the AAS copy of *Adolene Wellmont*. Finally, we are indebted to Marc Dolan and Donna Dennis for their very useful comments on drafts of the introduction.

D. S. R.
K. R. G.

INTRODUCTION

David S. Reynolds and Kimberly R. Gladman

One of America's earliest and most prolific authors of pulp sensation fiction, George Thompson (1823–ca. 1873) catered to the antebellum public's thirst for sex and violence while exposing hypocrisy and corruption on the part of the nation's ruling class. No one in pre–Civil War America was more successful than he in capturing what was then called "city mysteries," that witches' brew of crime, eroticism, and social protest whose other main American exponent was George Lippard. The title page of Thompson's *City Crimes*, which declares the work simultaneously "a mirror of fashion" and "a picture of poverty" and promises the reader a "startling revelation" of two cities' secrets, is emblematic of the city mysteries genre as a whole, which was centrally concerned with class differences and with the nature of urban experience.

Like much popular literature, city mysteries fiction was long dismissed by critics but can now be seen as a vital part of American literary and social history, of interest to scholars with a wide range of approaches and theoretical perspectives. The now canonical authors of the American Renaissance can be shown to have been influenced by these novels, the study of which can therefore enrich one's understanding of Hawthorne, Melville, Poe, and others. At the same time, city mysteries novels were an important part of antebellum working-class culture: a large number of their readers were workers; many of their authors became involved in working-class politics; and the texts themselves are a valuable source of popular conceptions of class identity and class relations in this period. Scholars concerned with gender, race, and ethnicity, furthermore, can find in these novels a wealth of images of women and female sexuality as well as of a variety of ethnic groups, including African Americans, Jews, and Irish and German immigrants. These images are often sexist, racist, and anti-Semitic; in many cases, however, they demonstrate significant sympathy for oppressed groups in addition to an understanding of social injustice.

The three works reprinted here, the novels *Venus in Boston* and *City Crimes* and Thompson's putative autobiography, *My Life: or the Adventures of Geo. Thompson*, can be read in a variety of ways and can serve as points of entry into discussions of many issues in antebellum literature. This introduction places the works in cultural and historical context, thus making them available for study by students and teachers in many fields.

Historical Background

City mysteries fiction was an internationally popular genre of the mid-nineteenth century. The French author Eugène Sue is considered to have invented it with *Les Mystères de Paris*, a newspaper serial that appeared in 1842–43. Although his title echoed Ann Radcliffe's *The Mysteries of Udolpho* (1794), Sue substituted a malignant cityscape for the haunted countryside of gothic fiction, and replaced the latter's supernatural terrors with the horrors of urban poverty and crime. The novel recounts the adventures of a German prince who wanders the streets of Paris in disguise, performing acts of charity and vigilante justice. Along the way, it vividly depicts the sufferings of the poor and advocates ameliorating them through social and penal reforms, as well as through philanthropy by the rich. The novel was immensely popular both in France and in the rest of Europe, and by 1844 had been translated and imitated many times, inspiring mysteries of places as varied as London, Russia, Brussels, Berlin, Hamburg, Vienna, and Pest.

Les Mystères de Paris did far more than just inaugurate a new genre, however; its admirers and detractors alike considered it a major event in literary history, and its aesthetic and political significance was widely debated. Many literary critics decried it as the start of "industrial literature," that is, literature created as a product for sale, which would spell the death of "true" literature. Others, however, saw it as the beginning of a new type of literary art, both more democratic and more realistic than any that had come before it.

On the political front, some socialist newspapers endorsed the novel, believing that it could spur efforts to improve social conditions, and even advocated some of Sue's suggested reforms. Marx and Engels, however, strongly disagreed with this view in "The Holy Family" (1845), claiming that despite the author's alleged sympathy for socialism, his novel lacked revolutionary potential because it drama-tized particular wrongs done to poor people, not their collective oppression; described only a criminal underworld, not the majority of workers; and depicted the sufferings of the working class from a bourgeois point of view. Nevertheless, three years later, some French critics blamed Sue for the Revolution of 1848.

The American genre began with another controversial best-seller, George Lippard's *The Quaker City; or, the Monks of Monk Hall: A Romance of Philadelphia Life, Mystery, and Crime.*[1] Sold in ten installments between fall 1844 and spring 1845, Lippard's novel was based in part on a famous court case of 1843 in which Singleton Mercer, a well-off Philadelphian, was acquitted after killing the alleged seducer of his sister. It also contained a variety of sensational subplots involving evil, rich hypocrites who exploit poor characters. By the time a few sections of it had appeared, it had divided the city along class lines: many workers became fans of Lippard, while their wealthier fellow citizens objected to his thinly veiled portray-als of local celebrities and denounced his depictions of sex and violence as immoral. In November 1844, a performance of a play based on the novel had to be canceled

---

1. For Lippard, see David S. Reynolds, *George Lippard* (Boston: G. K. Hall, 1982), and *George Lippard: Prophet of Protest: Writings of an American Radical, 1822–1854* (New York: Peter Lang, 1986); Heyward Ehrlich, "The 'Mysteries' of Philadelphia: Lippard's *Quaker City* and 'Urban' Gothic," *ESQ: A Journal of the American Renaissance*, 66 (1st quarter 1972): 50–65.

owing to fears of violence between admirers and opponents of the work. After six months, the first two-thirds of the novel were published in one volume, which sold 48,000 copies; in May 1845, Lippard published a greatly expanded version of the completed novel, which sold 60,000 copies in its first year and 10,000 copies annually during the next decade, making it the most popular work of fiction in the United States before *Uncle Tom's Cabin*.

Lippard's success, like Sue's, encouraged many imitators. Between 1844 and 1860, over fifty novels of American city life appeared claiming to reveal the mysteries—or, as some titles proclaimed, the "mysteries and miseries"—of New York, Boston, Philadelphia, and many smaller cities, including Rochester, St. Louis, New Orleans, and San Francisco.

George Thompson was among the most productive writers of these novels, which typically portrayed a city's powerful elites as corrupt and perverse, and the poor as the victims of their brutality and callousness. They entertained their readers with sensational accounts of sex and violence, as well as raucous humor; at the same time, however, they often included clear diagnoses and denunciations of the economic roots of inequality and injustice.

In Thompson's hands, the city mysteries genre became an expansive medium that incorporated other sensational popular culture phenomena as well. From penny newspapers and true crime pamphlets, Thompson derived images of crime and violence with proven appeal for the American masses. From the exhibitions of Phineas T. Barnum, he inherited an interest in the freakish and bizarre. From British and French pornography, he gleaned erotic themes, such as the sexually voracious woman and the reverend rake, which he reshaped in an urban, antebellum American context. From abolitionist and working-class literature, he adapted plotlines concerning oppressed ethnic and racial minorities and social outcasts.

The works that resulted are filled with gore, sex, and perversity to such a degree that Thompson can be identified as the most shockingly sensational and openly erotic American writer of his day. At the same time, his horrific narratives contain political subtexts with the potential to subvert middle-class mores, unmask hypocrisy, and expose the prevailing fluidity of American life, which particularly victimized the urban poor.

George Thompson's Life and Works

It is impossible to determine exactly how many novels Thompson wrote, but he was unquestionably prolific. In his autobiography Thompson boasts, "I have written a sufficient quantity of tales, sketches, poetry, essays and other literary stock of every description, to constitute half a dozen cartloads." A late nineteenth-century collector of his work seemed to agree, estimating that he had written a hundred books.[2] Today, evidence of more than sixty different titles survives.[3] Most of Thompson's fiction appeared in pamphlets about one hundred pages long and six

2. Henry Spencer Ashbee, *Bibliography of Prohibited Books* (1880; rpt., New York: Jack Brussel, 1962), p. 218.
3. See bibliography of Thompson's works at the end of this volume.

Portrait of George Thompson from the January 22, 1855, issue of *The Broadway Belle*. Courtesy, American Antiquarian Society.

by nine inches in size, bound between paper covers; a number of the novels were also serialized in newspapers. Many of the works soon vanished because they were published in these ephemeral forms, but whole or partial copies of over forty works remain, including more than twenty-five complete novels (all, until now, available only on microfilm or in rare book rooms).

Like some of his fiction, many of the details of Thompson's life have disappeared from view. One of the few sources of information (albeit biased) about his life prior to 1855 is the perfervid autobiography *My Life*, reprinted here for the first time since its publication in Boston in 1854.

My Life contains many of the standard elements of Thompson's novels, including pious hypocrites, adulterous spouses, bleak cityscapes, and violent death of various kinds. The text's sensation mongering certainly casts doubt on its reliability as a biographical document, and most of its details cannot be taken as fact in the absence of independent confirmation. Whether or not it is an accurate depiction of Thompson's private life, however, *My Life* is an invaluable source of information about the image of himself he sought to project to the reading public. The authorial persona constructed in these pages is that of a writer both entertaining and principled, who is aware of and in tune with both contemporary tastes and American history.

Thompson's *Life* is a work of self-promotion which mimics at several moments the paradigmatic American autobiography by Benjamin Franklin. Like Franklin, Thompson relates the story of a boy rising from obscurity to renown and success through his own efforts. Born in New York in 1823 and orphaned soon after, he claims to have rebelled against the authority of his guardians in early adolescence and begun a career first as a printer's apprentice, then as a journalist and fiction author. Unlike the young Franklin, however, this runaway and aspiring writer devotes little thought to the pursuit of virtues such as temperance, tranquillity, or moderation. Instead, he spends many nights in barrooms and theaters and engages in a number of brawls which land him briefly in prison. (It was during one such six-week stint that he wrote *Venus in Boston.*) Yet he highly values justice and honesty, as he frequently demonstrates by aiding those who have been wronged (such as the lovely Mrs. Raymond) and exposing hypocrisy wherever he finds it.

Thompson's account of one particularly zany Fourth of July spent in Boston exemplifies his narrative's mixture of entertaining irreverence and American idealism. The evening before the holiday, Thompson and a group of friends donned Shakespearean costumes (pilfered from a theater) and marched through the Boston streets, drinking themselves into a frenzy and finally spending the night in jail. The next day, however, the author claims he was sober enough to pen for public recitation an Independence Day poem that avoided trite patriotism and dwelt on "the sublime moral spectacle afforded by an oppressed people arising in their might to throw off the yoke of bondage and assert their independence as a nation."

Thompson frequently refers to historical events, places, and people that would have been well known to his readers. For example, he claims to have grown up on Thomas Street in New York City, "very near the famous brothel of Rosina Townsend." The Townsend brothel was notorious as the site of one of the most sensational crimes of the century: the 1836 murder of the beautiful prostitute Helen Jewett by her paramour Richard Robinson, who was later acquitted despite his apparent guilt.

As Patricia Cline Cohen has recently shown, the Jewett murder was a seminal event in the commercialization of the American news media. New York's recently founded penny newspapers boosted their circulation enormously through their competing sensational coverage of the murder investigation and trial, establishing themselves as a major force in the antebellum press. Interest in the murder was also fueled and gratified by lithographs of Jewett, both dead and alive, as well as of Robinson; by cheap pamphlets claiming to describe the victim's history and character; and by novelizations of her tragic story. Treatments of the case continued to appear long after the trial was over, perhaps in part because many people felt that justice had not been done: Robinson's acquittal was widely seen as the result of class and gender prejudice on the part of judge and jury, who gave greater credence to the testimony of the accused, a clerk from a respectable family, than to that of the many prostitutes who testified for the prosecution.[4]

Thompson retells Helen Jewett's story in his own narrative, capitalizing, like so many others before him, on its enduring fascination. By claiming to have grown up in her neighborhood, he also uses her story to demonstrate his long and privileged acquaintance with the seamy underside of city life, as well as his strong sense of justice. As a close neighbor, he says, he had often seen Jewett promenading with Robinson and was among the first visitors who walked through the brothel after she was killed, in order to view the mutilated and "half-burned remains of a once beautiful woman." Robinson's acquittal, he goes on to say, struck him as a shameful "instance of perverted justice," a "striking illustration of the 'glorious uncertainty of the law.'"

Thompson also links himself to real people and publications in and around Boston. Near the end of his narrative, he describes his socializing—like Walt Whitman at Pfaff's restaurant in Manhattan—with a bohemian group of Boston actors and writers who styled themselves the "Uncle and Nephews Club." The group included the black performer Jim Ring, the impersonator of villains Chunkey Munroe, the dancer Sam Lake, the dramatist Charley Saunders, the reporter Ned Wilkings, and many others. He claims in addition to have written for three years for the Charlestown paper the *Bunker Hill Aurora and Boston Mirror*, where his "good original tales and sprightly editorials" greatly increased its popularity, although he never received a byline. After a quarrel with the paper's owner, he says, he finally left this job and began a career as a novelist, eventually gaining substantial recognition.

This last statement is undoubtedly true, as sources outside the autobiography can confirm. Between 1848 and 1854 there appeared, in quick succession, more than two dozen novels by George Thompson,[5] many issued under the pseudonym "Greenhorn." They included the two novels reprinted here, *Venus in Boston* and *City Crimes* (both 1849), as well as other works of urban exposé fiction such as *New York Life: or, The Mysteries of Upper-Tendom Revealed* (1849); lively depictions of the sufferings and adventures of prostitutes, such as *The Countess, or Memoirs of Women of Leisure* (1849) and *The Gay Girls of New York* (1853); an assortment of crime novels, including *Jack Harold* (1850), *Life and Exploits of "Bristol Bill"* (1851), *The Road to Ruin* (1851), and *Harry Glindon, or the Man of Many Crimes* (1854); and other works of sensation fiction such as *Catherine and Clara, or the Double Suicide* (1854) and *Kate Castleton, the Beautiful Milliner; or, the Wife and Widow of a Day* (1853). *Kate Castleton* provides evidence that in at least one instance, Thompson's popularity extended beyond the English-speaking community: the novel was also published in (presumably rough) German translation as *Käthchen Castleton, die schöne Putzmacherin* (the beautiful cleaning woman).

4. See Patricia Cline Cohen, *The Murder of Helen Jewett: The Life and Death of a Prostitute in Nineteenth-Century New York* (New York: Alfred A. Knopf, 1998).

5. See bibliography of Thompson's works for further details. The numbers cited for works published in certain time periods (here, 1848–54; later, 1855–57) are conservative estimates, based on the number of works whose dates could be conclusively determined.

A number of Thompson's novels were serialized in newspapers published by William Berry, who also published some of his works in book form. In 1849 *Venus in Boston* appeared as the "$1000 Prize Tale" in Berry's *Life in Boston Sporting Chronicle, and Lights and Shadows of New England Morals;* this paper also carried Thompson's *Adventures of a Pickpocket* that same year. In 1850 another Berry paper, *Life in Boston and New England Police Gazette,* serialized *Mysteries of Leverett Street Jail,* which Thompson refers to in *My Life,* as well as *Jack Harold, or the Criminal's Career* and *Sharps and Flats; or the Perils of City Life.*[6] In 1851 *The Criminal* and *The Road to Ruin* appeared in the same paper. *City Crimes* seems not to have been serialized in either periodical, but both provide information about that novel's publication history. The September 1, 1849, *Sporting Chronicle* advertised what was presumably the initial publication, "in four numbers," of *City Crimes.* Some eight months later, a notice in the May 18, 1850 *Police Gazette* enthusiastically announced a reprint: "City Crimes! The rapidity with which this REALLY THRILLING NOVEL has disappeared from the counters of periodical dealers, and the still active demand for the work, has induced us to reprint this master work of GREENHORN." This republication was to proceed in two parts, with the first ready around June 1.

Thompson reports having left Boston a year before he wrote *My Life* (presumably in 1853), and his autobiography ends with the conjecture that "I may hereafter continue to write tales for the public amusement." This prediction proved true: between 1855 and 1858, Thompson published at least a dozen new books, offering readers a steady supply of romance, intrigue, and crime, with titles such as *The Mysteries of Bond Street; or, the Seraglios of Upper Tendom* (1857); *Confessions of a Sofa* (1857); *Tom De Lacy, or the Convict's Revenge* (1855); and *The Bridal Chamber, and its Mysteries* (1855) (in which a cuckolded newlywed brands the word "harlot" on his wife's forehead with a hot penknife).

Thompson also continued to write for newspapers. Between 1855 and at least 1858, he intermittently edited *The Broadway Belle, and Mirror of the Times,* a humorous New York weekly. The *Belle*'s offerings included serial novels (many of them by Thompson), cartoons, jokes, amusing anecdotes and news items, as well as advertisements for books by Thompson and other authors in the catalog of Prescott H. Harris, who also published the *Belle.* The paper's inaugural issue of January 1, 1855, vowed that its "main object shall be to avoid dullness as we would shun the devil, and to be always lively. . . . The paper will always be original throughout . . . impartial in its criticisms, fearless in its display of the NAKED TRUTH, witty in its jokes, and spicy without being obscene."[7] In its first month the paper certainly steered clear of dullness, publishing lurid articles about prostitution and crime, satires of New York society, and a play (in installments) called *The Demon of Death: or, The Bandit's Oath!!!* Written by "Green Horn," the *Demon* was said to have won a $500 prize offered by P. T. Barnum for the best original play adapted for performance at his American Museum.[8] The paper was less successful, how-

6. *Sharps and Flats* is not definitely but quite likely by Thompson; see bibliography.
7. *The Broadway Belle, and Mirror of the Times,* January 1, 1855, p. 2.
8. Ibid.

ever, in avoiding charges of obscenity: on January 30, the *New York Daily Tribune* reported that "P. H. Harris, publisher of a vulgar sheet called *The Broadway Belle*, and Geo. Thompson, said to be the editor," had been arrested for publishing "an indecent article, entitled 'Important to Husbands and Wives,' in the last issue of that paper."[9] The offending article was composed almost entirely of excerpts from the work of a writer "who has made matrimonial excesses, and their pernicious consequences, his principal theme."[10] These quotations combine instruction with titillation as they admonish husbands not to overtax their wives sexually. Women's diseases, the reader is advised, are frequently "caused . . . by the frequency, the fury, the almost goatishness, of [their] husband's demands . . . nor do husbands always consider how exceedingly tender, and how liable to consequent inflammation and disease, this [the female] apparatus [is]." Overindulgence in sexual pleasure is also said to cause infertility and female irritability, and any amount of intercourse during pregnancy will both weaken and and pervert the child in the womb, since "it withdraws that vital energy required by [the woman's] precious charge. It also sensualizes that charge—it partaking by sympathy with its mother's feelings." Male self-control is advisable at all times, moreover, since lust is "the concomitant and parent of all other sins. . . . It will drain the last cent, and then pursue its victim night and day until he becomes literally desperate, and is almost compelled to lie, steal, forge, rob ANY AND EVERY thing to procure the wages of this sin."[11]

The controversy over this article is discussed and dismissed in an editorial in the February 12 *Belle* titled "We Live!" "No doubt many of our friends think we are dead or transported ere this," the piece begins, "by the base exaggerated accounts which have filled the papers for the last ten days . . . . That we have ever been arrested is false, and the idea that we have been held to bail is absurd."[12] The "splendid article" just quoted above did, it is true, give offense to "certain would-be moralists," who "entered a complaint at the Mayor's office." When the authorities were informed, however, that the text in question was not an original composition but a series of extracts from a "medical work published by Fowler and Wells," the district attorney entered a complaint against those publishers and withdrew the one against Thompson and Harris.[13] The entire episode is mocked on the front page of this issue of the *Belle*, where a cartoon depicts George Thompson making his way to the Tombs, New York's famous prison, after "seeing by the daily papers the report that he was arrested and held to bail in $500, (being the first he had heard of it)."[14] In the end, the *Belle*'s readers are asked to "appreciate the step taken by our worthy Mayor to suppress all publications bearing an immoral tendency" and assured that "hereafter we shall be very careful that nothing improper, or any unworthy person, is introduced to the Belle."[15]

9. *New York Daily Tribune*, January 30, 1855, p. 7. We thank George Thompson of Bobst Library for this citation.
10. *The Broadway Belle, and Mirror of the Times*, January 29, 1855, p. 2.
11. Ibid.
12. Ibid., February 12, 1855, p. 2.
13. Ibid.
14. Ibid., p. 1.
15. Ibid., p. 2.

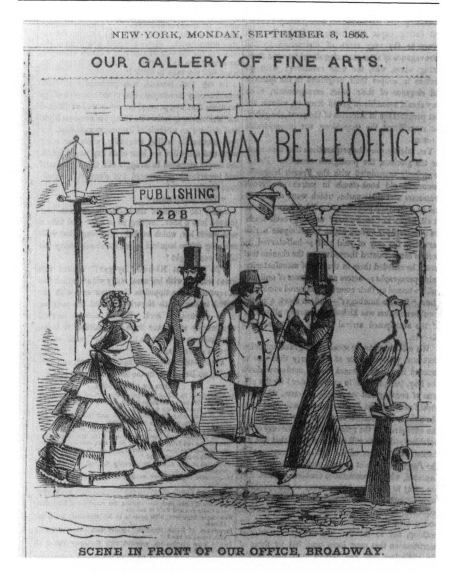

"The stout gentleman in the back ground is George Thompson, the Editor of this paper; the tall gentleman is P. F. Harris, the publisher." From the September 3, 1855, issue of *The Broadway Belle.* Courtesy, American Antiquarian Society.

Top half of the February 12, 1855, issue of *The Broadway Belle*. The cartoon in the center depicts Thompson on his way to the Tombs, after reading of his own arrest. (Original entire front page is 12 inches wide by 15.5 inches long.) Courtesy, American Antiquarian Society.

In fact, the paper seems to have gone on largely as before; but there is no evidence in the remaining issues of any further legal difficulties. The paper seems to have grown in popularity, although the editors' boasts about how much are certainly not to be taken at face value: on one occasion they claimed to have sold out an edition of 17,000 copies.[16] On another, they asserted that a particularly popular serial had boosted circulation to 70,000.[17] Whatever degree of success it enjoyed, however, the weekly was also troubled by repeated conflicts between Thompson and Harris. The two men may have been old friends (in one issue Thompson reminisces about boyhood days, when he used to "sit astride of a hogshead on the wharf, and lick molasses with a straw, in company with P. H.

16. Ibid., October 8, 1855, p. 3. An editorial notice in this issue asserts that "last week we circulated seventeen thousand copies, and had not enough to supply the demand."

17. *The Broadway Belle, and New York Shanghai*, September 10, 1855, p. 2. The serial in question is Thompson's *The Locket*, which had run in the paper earlier.

Harris, Esq."),[18] but their professional relationship was less than idyllic. In the February 12 issue, Thompson is already referred to as "our former editor."[19] On March 5 it becomes clear that the two men are involved in a copyright dispute. "Whereas George Thompson has seen fit to state that 'The Magic Night Cap' and 'The Locket'—two stories written by him for this paper—were *his* property," Harris writes, "I deem it my duty to state that such is false. I have in my possession and own the Copyright of them both. They were written for me by Mr. Thompson, at the time he was writing for me by the week." Harris goes on to say that he bears Thompson no ill will and that their disagreement would never have arisen, had Thompson not "been made the tool of others . . . whose only interest is to accomplish their own end—malice." Indeed, he wishes Thompson "every success," both for "his good and that of his wife" (giving us, in the process, our only clue that Thompson was married).[20] Despite these kind words, in another article on the same page Harris writes that since "Mr. Thompson has dragged us into the field, we are *compelled*, in justice to ourselves, to answer; and, in so doing, we shall make but *one* job of it." In the next issue, he vows, "We shall place his past career before the public in its true light," and tells the readers to "ask yourselves if you could have done more than we have done to lift a poor, degraded being from the gutter . . . [and] if he is justified in the step he has taken."[21] Sadly for those of us who might have liked to hear Harris's version of Thompson's past, the March 12 issue includes, "in place of an article against Mr. Thompson which we promised in our last," a letter from Thompson apologizing for "absurd statements" he made while laboring under an "insane delusion" and being made "a tool and a scape-goat." Thompson announces his intention to go into "the literary business" in Boston, and Harris wishes him well, saying that Thompson's behavior was the result of manipulation by Harris's enemies.[22]

In the September 3 issue (the next one that we could locate) George Thompson is again listed as editor. The paper is now titled *The Broadway Belle, and New York Shanghai;* this change, and Thompson's mention of "old times" and "the former career of the BELLE" suggest that the paper had ceased to appear at some point earlier in the year and was now resuming publication.[23] This arrangement was short-lived, however. The September 17 issue includes the announcement, "With this number of the *Belle* ends George Thompson's connection with this paper."[24] Harris is named editor in the surviving issues from October and November 1855 (in which it is again called *The Broadway Belle, and Mirror of the Times*). That this

18. Ibid.
19. *The Broadway Belle, and Mirror of the Times,* February 12, 1855, p. 1.
20. The *New York Evening Post* for Wednesday, October 9, 1861, carried a notice of the death, on October 8, of Ann Thompson, the 36-year-old wife of George Thompson. She was to be buried in Greenwood Cemetery. Given the commonness of the names, of course, it is impossible to know if this referred to our George Thompson and his wife.
21. *The Broadway Belle, and Mirror of the Times,* March 5, 1855, p. 2. See also cartoon on front page depicting frequently drunk ex-editor.
22. Ibid., March 12, 1855, p.2.
23. *The Broadway Belle, and New York Shanghai,* September 3, 1855, p. 2.
24. Ibid., September 17, 1855, p. 2.

was not the end of the story, however, is evident from an issue of *The Broadway Belle* (without subtitle) which appeared on November 8, 1858, edited by Thompson and published by "Wm. T. Anderson." Referring to the *Belle* of a few years earlier, Thompson writes, "The name of the paper was the same as ours—'The Broadway Belle;' yet how different in character from the 'Belle' of today!" The earlier paper is said to have been damaged by its proprietor (Harris), "who, without one particle of talent, possessed the impudence of the devil, [and] began to lead a particularly gay life," thus neglecting the paper, while the editor (Thompson), "although at that time, as now, leading a life of stern morality and inflexible virtue, was entirely too careless as to the contents of the paper." As he revives the *Belle*, Thompson vows to devote "his industrious pen to the religious instruction and moral improvement of the human race."[25] Lest readers think him grown too tame, however, this issue also features a cartoon of "Our Fighting Editor," with fists at the ready and hair standing on end in rage. A caption warns: "He eats raw Buffalo beef, drinks Jersey lightning calculated to kill at fifty paces and sleeps on a mattress stuffed with the moustaches of the enemies he has slain. Beware!"[26]

Thompson's writings in the various incarnations of the *Belle* are often witty, irreverent, and critical of political and religious authorities as well as economic inequality. They are, however, also often virulently racist. On September 10, 1855, for example, Thompson denounced the attempted formation of an African American military company in Boston, calling it the absurd project of "fanatical abolitionists."[27] *Ten Days in the Tombs*, a novel serialized in the paper under the pseudonym John McGinn (but advertised in a number of issues with Thompson's name as author), contains many passages of intense anti-black and anti-immigrant sentiment. *Ten Days* claims to relate the prison experience of "a certain Fat Philosopher of our acquaintance who is a literary man of some eminence."[28] This character is a portrait of Thompson, who repeatedly refers to his substantial girth in *My Life* and the *Belle*, and who was pictured as rotund in drawings published in the paper. Writing about himself in the third person, Thompson presents himself as a convivial and principled man who was arrested for drunkenness and spent time in jail, like a faster-living, urban Thoreau, instead of paying the fine demanded by the unjust Prohibitory Liquor Law, which disproportionately punished the poor. He also denounces at length and in detail the tyranny of black and Irish convicts over other prisoners, and says that blacks in particular have been "spoiled by sleek-faced abolitionists."[29] Although a number of his novels are ambivalent about racial issues (as we discuss later), and some may even lend themselves to readings subversive of racial hierarchy, it is evident that much of his journalistic work, and some of his fiction, perpetuated the worst racial and ethnic stereotypes of his time.

25. *The Broadway Belle*, November 8, 1858, p.2.
26. Ibid.
27. *The Broadway Belle, and New York Shanghai*, September 10, 1855, p.2.
28. John McGinn [George Thompson], *Ten Days in the Tombs, or, A Key to the Modern Bastile* (New York: P. F. Harris, 1855), p. 16.
29. Ibid., p. 29.

The combination of racism, anti-immigrant prejudice, and sympathy for the white, U.S.- born working poor which Thompson's work displays was typical of the nativist movement in antebellum America (in which Thompson's fellow city mysteries author Ned Buntline played an active part). It is not surprising, then, to find that Thompson endorsed George Law, a contender for the presidential nomination of the Know-Nothing Party in 1856. *The Locket*, a novel Thompson published in 1855, is dedicated to Law, "to whom the eyes of the whole American People now turn as their sole preserver from universal political corruption: to whom we look for salvation from the accursed effects of foreign influence."[30] It is not known, however, whether Thompson was involved, apart from this dedication, in any political activities in the Know-Nothing Party or any other.

The *Belle* was not the only, and certainly not the most transgressive, journalistic venue for Thompson's work in the latter half of the 1850s. He also wrote regularly for another New York paper, *Venus' Miscellany: A Weekly Journal of Wit, Love and Humor*. Published by James Ramerio, the *Miscellany* seems to have begun publication in autumn 1856 and continued at least through summer 1857. (The earliest of the ten surviving issues that we know of is dated January 31, 1857 and is numbered Volume 1, Whole No. 12, which suggests that the inaugural issue appeared the previous November; the last surviving issue is that of July 11, 1857.) Its editors, listed on the editorial page as "Ramerio and Clarke," at one point claimed to have a circulation of 49,000 copies.[31] Although this number may certainly be greatly inflated, the paper does seem to have enjoyed a relatively wide geographic distribution, since (as we discuss below) it contains references to readers and agents in Pennsylvania and Massachusetts.

Neither Thompson's name nor his primary pseudonym, "Greenhorn," is mentioned in the *Miscellany*, but an examination of what remains of the paper clearly indicates that he was one of its most important contributors. The May 9, 1857, issue, for example, carries the final installment of *The Mysteries of Bond Street*, which we know to be by Thompson.[32] In the *Miscellany*, however, this work is attributed to "Appollonius of Gotham." In another issue, Appollonius, who is praised as "one of our favorite writers," is said to be the author of another Thompson title, *La Tour de Nesle; or the Amours of Margurite of Burgundy*, (which was also serialized in the paper).[33] These quotations clearly establish "Appollonius" as one of Thompson's pseudonyms. It is thus possible to attribute to Thompson Appollonius's *Loves of Cleopatra* (serialized beginning in the July 11, 1857, issue) and to surmise that he probably wrote other novels for the paper which have not survived, since Appollonius is listed on the paper's editorial page in each surviving

30. George Thompson, *The Locket: A Romance of New York by George Thompson, Esq.* (New York: P. F. Harris, 1855) , p. 1. For more on Law, see William E. Gienapp, *The Origins of the Republican Party, 1852–1856* (New York: Oxford University Press, 1987), and *A Sketch of Events in the Life of George Law, Published in Advance of his Biography* (New York: J. C. Derby, 1855).

31. *Venus' Miscellany*, May 9, 1857, p. 3.

32. According to the title page of *The Mysteries of Bond Street*, it is "by the author of" *Anna Mowbray*, *Bridal Chamber*, and *Kate Montrose*, which are known to be Thompson's (see bibliography).

33. *Venus' Miscellany*, July 4, 1857, p. 3. Ashbee attributes this work to Thompson.

Advertisements in the May 23, 1857, issue of *Venus' Miscellany*. Thompson's *The Mysteries of Bond-Street*, *The Confessions of a Sofa*, and *Margurite of Burgundy* are advertised, along with "French transparent cards," "French prints," and "cundums." Courtesy, American Antiquarian Society.

issue as one of its "principal writers, the talent of whom is well known to our readers."

Indeed, other features of the paper suggest that Thompson may have been the principal writer working under the aegis of James Ramerio. The second page of each issue includes an advertisement for a list of books published by Ramerio, under the heading "Rich, Rare and Racy Reading." The book list (which does not include authors' names) always contains a large group of titles known to be by Thompson, as well as a number of others which may be his; it is possible that these lists were almost entirely composed of Thompson titles put out by Ramerio.[34] On May 23, 1857, this "rich, rare and racy" list includes *City Crimes, Venus in Boston*, and *My Life*, indicating that all three of the works in this volume were republished by Ramerio in 1857. The paper also frequently contained ads for individual Thompson titles (without any author's name), including *The Mysteries of Bond-Street, Confessions of a Sofa*, and *Margurite of Burgundy*, and serialized at least one additional Thompson novel, *Adventures of Lola Montes*, under yet another pseudonym, "Eugene de Orsay."[35]

In *Venus' Miscellany*, Thompson found an outlet for his work that made the *Broadway Belle* look merely mischievous and charming. In addition to serial fiction by Thompson and others, the *Miscellany*'s standard fare included jokes, anecdotes, advertisements, and correspondence, as well as occasional front-page engravings of bare-breasted, bare-legged women.[36] The journal's central concern, as its title indicates, was love of the most carnal sort. A typical issue might contain riddles such as "Why is the moon called she? Because there's a man *in her*, so folks say. Second— because for the most part she is *horny*"; salacious political commentary, such as the observation that the Mormon leader "Brigham Young cannot be said to rule with a rod of iron, as he emphatically enforces his commands by a pole of flesh! It is *hard*, no doubt, but not fatal"; and lewd anecdotes like the one about the polygamous Indian chief who, when asked what he did with his seven wives, replied, "I f——'em all, f——'em all!"[37] Thompson's novels were advertised between ads for "Cundums . . . [a] great invention . . . to prevent conception in females . . . a long time in general use by the French," and alongside ads for Dr. J. C. Norton's line of sex-related medicines. The latter included aphrodisiacs (the "LOVE NECTAR . . . [for] reviving the drooping energies of nature"), contraceptives (the "Celebrated Preventive" for

34. For example, the July 11 list includes fifteen titles by Thompson (*The Mysteries of Bond-Street, Adventures of Lola Montes, Adventures of a Sofa, Marie de Clairville, Tour de Nesle, Bridal Chamber, Anna Mowbray, Gay Deceiver, Dissipation, Julia King, Adventures of a Libertine, The Countess, Venus in Boston, The Demon of Gold*, and *Kate Montrose*); eight which there is reason to believe may be his (*Harriet Wilson, Madeline the Avenger, Paul the Profligate, Adventures of a Country Girl, Simon the Radical, The Evil Genius, Sharps and Flats*, and *The Lame Devil*) ; and only five others (*The Amours, Intrigues and Adventures of Aaron Burr, Flora Montgomery, Secret Passion, The Wedding Night, or Advice to Timid Bridegrooms*, and an illustrated Aristotle). See bibliography for questions regarding Thompson's authorship of individual works.

35. Ashbee attributes this work to Thompson; it is also listed on the title page of *The Mysteries of Bond-Street*. See bibliography.

36. See, for example, "Rosina's Dream of Bliss," front page of the *Miscellany*, May 16, 1857.

37. *Venus' Miscellany*, July 11 and May 23, 1857.

"married people who do not wish to increase their families"), and abortifacients ("Periodical Pills . . . for unhealthy and delicate females who have neglected to use [Norton's] preventive, and whose strength will not permit childbearing").[38]

Each number also featured letters, most of them supposedly from readers, which one suspects were drafted on the editor's desk. In a number of these, the alleged writers (usually women) express their gratitude to the *Miscellany* for improving their sex lives, and explain in considerable detail how this has occurred. For example, a letter signed "Maria C." begins by asserting that "our pleasures are considerably enhanced by intellect, and the pleasures of sexual intercourse more than any other. The spicy tales, anecdotes and correspondence contained in your sheet . . . increase the mutual pleasure tenfold." Reading the *Miscellany*, she goes on to say, gave her courage to confess to her husband that she was having a lesbian affair with a neighbor, an admission that sent him "into an ecstacy [sic] of delight." ("Had my husband not been a subscriber," she avers, "he would never have had from me the confessions which I have found afforded him so much pleasure.") Predictably, the letter then relates that the man declared "he must be a witness of the scene," and during her next encounter with "Mrs. S.," Maria's husband "crept softly in and assisted me in completing the pleasure." Lest readers puzzle over the women's activities, Maria explains that when he entered, "I had her in such a position, her back to the door, and our heads and tails somehow so mixed that we were laying at reverse ends." Afterward, Mrs. S. felt guilt at betraying her husband, but Maria "told her to make herself easy on that score, as I would before the week was ended have as much from her husband as she just had from mine."[39] Such threesomes were clearly a popular fantasy among readers of the *Miscellany*. In a letter in another issue, a woman (after discoursing on the size of her husband's penis and the joys of her open marriage) reveals that she and her spouse often had encounters with another woman. "We owe much of our enjoyment," she concludes, "to the feelings inspired by the 'Miscellany,' and take this method to thank the editor of that paper for our pleasure." This gratitude is so great, in fact, that "I believe I would make wanton enough of myself to take him between my thighs, in gratitude for his kindness."[40]

Unsurprisingly, *Venus' Miscellany* seems to have had repeated run-ins with the authorities, who considered it obscene. Between May and July 1857 alone, there are mentions in its pages of "ferocious officers of the Police" in Boston having "made another demonstration against some of our agents"; of a reader's having been arrested and imprisoned after police found in his pockets "a copy or two of *Venus' Miscellany*"; and of another reader's having had "much difficulty . . . in obtaining the *Miscellany*, since there has been a regular crusade going on" against it in his city.[41] In the June 20 issue, the editors reprint a notice from a Pittsburgh paper about police in that city having seized "a bundle of obscene papers . . . ordered

38. See, e.g., ibid., May 23, 1857, p. 2.
39. Ibid., July 11, 1857, p. 3.
40. Ibid., May 16, 1857, p. 3.
41. Ibid., May 23, 1857, p. 2, and July 4, 1857, p. 3.

in New York." Among them was *Venus' Miscellany*, which the Pittsburgh paper described as "both vulgar and stupid." "That it should reach the circulation it enjoys here, is a sad commentary on the morals of our citizens," the article went on. The mayor, however, to whom the obscene papers were brought, now "intends bringing to justice any one who may attempt to sell the sheet in this vicinity." The editors of the *Miscellany* reprint this article only to scoff at it, claiming that they have five times the circulation of the paper in which it appeared.[42]

Although the editors at one point claim that "there is nothing in the character of the paper, as it now is, that the law can take offence at," there are indications that they knew they were skirting the boundaries of the permissible.[43] In one issue they refer to plans, since abandoned, to increase the number of their subscribers to ten thousand and then end street sales, so that they might give readers "every delicacy we pleased to serve ... which we could not publish while our paper circulated where it now does." When this proved impracticable, a woman author who had been engaged to write a novel for the more daring subscription sheet was asked to "rewrite, and modulate her production to suit the present state, and tide of the *Miscellany*."[44] In addition, the paper's masthead lists no street address, but only a post office box, and all books advertised could be had only by mail.

We do not know how long *Venus' Miscellany* continued to publish, or how long Thompson continued to write for it, or any other paper or publisher. His autobiography ends with an ominous reference to "many bitter enemies" who "continue to snarl at my heels like mongrel curs." One might surmise that among these enemies were real-life counterparts of the scoundrels and hypocrites who populate his novels, and imagine that he met his end at their hands as dramatically as one of his characters. Unfortunately, no information about the manner or exact date of Thompson's death is available.[45] There is evidence, however, that he died relatively young. The back covers of the Jack Harold series, twelve Thompson novels issued by Frederic A. Brady,[46] bear testimonials to Thompson's work which praise him in the past tense. "The exceeding popularity acquired by this remarkable set of books," the publisher's blurb asserts, "is owing to the fact that the author, GREENHORN, had a thorough knowledge of all grades of criminals." The books, it is claimed, show the spirit of a fearless writer, for "such an [sic] one was GREEN-HORN." The Jack Harold series is undated, but Brady ceased publishing in 1873.[47] Advertisements in the inside covers for books published by Robert M. De Witt of

42. Ibid., June 20, 1857, p. 3.
43. Ibid., May 23, 1857, p. 2.
44. Ibid., May 9, 1857, p. 3.
45. We have searched the *New York Evening Post* death notices for 1857–75, and found only one George Thompson without a middle initial. He is unlikely to have been our author, however, since he died August 1, 1864, at the age of forty-four (when our Thompson would have been forty) and was associated with a business.
46. The twelve novels were *Jack Harold, The Spaniard's Crime, The Criminal, The Outlaw, The Road to Ruin, Life and Exploits of "Bristol Bill," The Brigands, Dashington, The Virgin Wife, Fast Life in London and Paris, Grace Willard: or The High and the Low*, and *Alice Wade, or Guilt and Retribution*.
47. *Dictionary of Literary Biography*, vol. 49. (Detroit: Gale 1986), p. 64.

33 Rose Street date the series more precisely, since De Witt had an office at that address only between 1870 and 1877.[48] This means that the Jack Harold series must have been published between 1870 and 1873, and Thompson must have died by 1873 at the latest. Indeed, he may have died significantly earlier, since no evidence survives of any new text published under his name or pseudonyms between the November 8, 1858, issue of the *Broadway Belle* and the Jack Harold series. This is not conclusive evidence, since some of the surviving works are not dated, and others may have been lost. What one can be sure of, however, is that Thompson's novels retained sufficient popularity to be reissued after the Civil War; and that the author himself, if his presumed birthdate of 1823 is correct, did not live past fifty.

Sensationalism and Irrationalism

"When Novels are extensively read, and the practice continued, Crime will prevail." This quotation from Daniel Webster served as the epigraph to *The Confessions and Experience of a Novel Reader*, an anonymous 1855 book by a Chicago physician which lambasted the kind of pulp fiction Thompson wrote. Although he did not mention Thompson or other American writers by name, the author noted the extraordinary popularity of "Yellow-Jacket Literature," referring to the lurid yellow covers of the pamphlet novels they produced.[49] He estimated that in the United States, with its population of 24 million, there was "an enormous circulation of over 2.5 million volumes, extending their deleterious influence, and diffusing their pernicious principles throughout society." In these novels, he lamented, "the murderer, robber, pirate, swindler, the grog-shop tippler, the lady of fashion, the accomplished rake and libertine, are meritorious characters, held up in a spirit of pride and levity, and surrounded by a 'halo of emulation'." "Vice unmasked, say you," he continued, "but where is virtue portrayed?" Calling attention to the pervasiveness of this fiction, he wrote: "If any one has any doubts as to the fearfully rapid increase of this public poison—a demoralizing literature, the real 'Pandora's box of evil passions'—the flood-gate, from beneath whose slimy jaws runs a stream of pollution, sending forth its pestilential branches to one great ocean of immorality, let such a one take a trip with me through the length and breadth of our land."[50]

This pulp fiction, he found, was everywhere, even in the homes of "professing Christians." He surmised that the "deleterious influence" of yellow-jacket fiction "operates directly upon the minds of very nearly 9,500,000 of our population, and indirectly upon the GREAT MASS." Besides causing a range of mental and physical illnesses, this fiction posed a threat to American society itself. The final effect of such literature, he warned, was to "subvert the purity of our Republican institutions," destroy the elective franchise, and foster "elements of revolution, which, if

48. Ibid., p. 118.
49. *Confessions and Experience of a Novel Reader* (Chicago: William Stacy, 1855), p. 11. Thompson's *My Life* was published in yellow covers.
50. Ibid., pp. 32, 48, 27.

we neglect to elevate the masses" through healthy moral literature, "will crush us in the might and majesty of our fancied security."[51]

The physician was hardly alone in his complaints about pamphlet fiction. The critic Edwin Whipple labeled this fiction the "Romance of Rascality," asserting that "rascality is now the rage. The thief and cut-purse, the murderer and the incendiary, strut and swagger in the sunny land of romance."[52] He elaborated: "Let an author's brain teem with monsters, let him pile horror upon horror, draw aside the 'decent drapery' which covers the nakedness of depravity, and have a pool of blood running and glistening through his compositions, and there are people who will throw up their caps in admiration of his 'power,' and be voluble in praise of his insight."[53] While pointing out that there was nothing intrinsically wrong with portraying criminals—Shakespeare and Goethe, for instance, did so with artistic finesse—Whipple insisted that there is a huge difference between presenting "criminals as they are in themselves, and exhibiting criminals as proper objects of esteem and moral approbation." Although rooted in the French novel and British crime fiction, sensation fiction experienced a sea change when adopted by American authors. "This compound of English ruffianism and French ethics," wrote Whipple, "has invaded the United States in large force, and it comprises at present a considerable portion of the literature which people read."[54] Capitalizing on new printing technology and means of distribution, American publishers had made sensation literature cheap and widely available, purveying what Whipple dubbed "perdition at low prices" and establishing "an equality in evil as well as good."[55] The particularly horrific quality of American cheap literature was a common theme among both foreign and native commentators. The *Foreign Quarterly Review* of London generalized: "The more respectable the city in America, the more infamous, the more degrading and disgusting, we have found to be its Newspaper Press."[56] In the 1850s the *Westminster Review* declared: "Our press is bad enough, but its violence is meekness and even its atrocities are virtue, compared with the system of brutal and ferocious outrage which distinguishes the press of America."[57] The journalist Lambert Wilmer asserted that penny newspapers and pulp novels familiarized American youths with iniquity: "No narrative of human depravity or crime can shock or horrify the American reader. He has studied every phase of profligacy and flagrant villainy in his early childhood." Narratives about "notorious highwayman, burglars, and pickpockets" and about "New York life" in the city's "resorts of prostitution and infamy" were, according to Wilmer, "the most saleable books on the market," since "nothing is read now by young people, but pamphlet novels and the New York weekly papers." In his view, the popular press emitted

---

51. Ibid., pp. 29, 32, 62, 67.
52. Edwin Whipple, *Essays and Reviews* (Boston: Ticknor, Reed, and Fields, 1851), pp. 74, 75.
53. Ibid., pp. 76. 77.
54. Ibid., pp. 79, 84.
55. Ibid., p. 77.
56. *Foreign Quarterly Review* (London), October 1842.
57. Quoted in Lambert A. Wilmer, *Our Press Gang; or, A Complete Exposition of the Corruptions and Crimes of American Newspapers* (Philadelphia: J. T. Lloyd, 1859), p. 261.

"the thickest of all darkness"—mass-oriented writing in which young men learned "atheism, obscenity, contempt and defiance of the law, the arts of the seducer, the mysteries of brothels, the practice of pugilism."[58]

Sensational literature did not escape the notice of the major writers of the period. Walt Whitman, for instance, wrote a newspaper article on the extreme popularity of "blood and thunder romances with alliterative titles and plots of startling interest." He noted "The public for whom these tales are written," "require strong contrasts, broad effects, and the fiercest kind of 'intense' writing generally." He stressed that such writing was "a power in the land, not without great significance in its way, and very deserving of more careful consideration than has hitherto been accorded it."[59]

Despite its popularity and cultural importance, sensational literature was long neglected by critics and historians. There were several reasons for this neglect. To begin with, many examples of the genre disappeared. Most sensational fiction, like the penny papers it was associated with, was designed for rapid reading and disposal. By the same token, not many reviewers found these novels worth discussing in respectable periodicals. Moreover, prudish censors such as Anthony Comstock, hoping to wipe out everything remotely linked to pornography, destroyed the plates of many of these novels. Between 1872 and 1879 alone, Comstock would collect and destroy twenty-four tons of "bad books," among which were doubtless a number by George Thompson.[60]

Another factor in the long neglect of sensational fiction was that it violated traditional canons of critical taste. During the era of the New Criticism, when American literature was struggling to gain viability as a discipline in a largely anglophone university environment, the pulp fiction of the past was hardly an attractive genre to put on display. To be sure, much of this fiction possesses some of the very characteristics—paradox, irony, and ambiguity—the New Critics prized. But the New Critics were powerfully drawn to such writers as Melville, Hawthorne, and Dickinson in whom these qualities were expressed with symbolism and artistry. Only a handful of maverick critics—Alexander Cowie, Frank Luther Mott, Leslie Fiedler, and Janis P. Stout—discussed popular sensational fiction, and even their discussions were spotty and undeveloped.[61]

The rise of new historicism and cultural studies opened the way for serious reconsideration of non-canonical literature. African American literature, Native

58. Ibid., pp. 173, 340, 375.

59. From the *Brooklyn Daily Times*, December 13, 1858, in *The Uncollected Poetry and Prose of Walt Whitman*, ed. Emory Holloway (Gloucester, Mass.: Peter Smith, 1972), 2: 20–21.

60. See Anthony Comstock, *Traps for the Young*, ed. Robert Bremner (1884; rpt., Cambridge, Mass.: Harvard University Press, 1967).

61. See Frank Luther Mott, *Golden Multitudes: The Story of Best Sellers in the United States* (New York: Macmillan, 1947); Alexander Cowie, *The Rise of the American Novel* (New York: American Book Co., 1948); Mary Noel, *Villains Galore: The Heyday of the Popular Story Weekly* (New York: Macmillan, 1954); David Brion Davis, *Homicide in American Fiction* (Ithaca: Cornell University Press, 1957); Leslie Fiedler, *Love and Death in the American Novel*, Rev. ed.; (New York: Stein and Day, 1966); and Janis P. Stout, *Sodoms in Eden: The City in American Fiction before 1860* (Westport, Conn.: Greenwood Press, 1976).

American writing, and fiction and poetry by women (particularly the domestic novel) won the special attention of the early canon expanders. More recently, scholars have come to recognize that the picture of the cultural past remains skewed so long as sensational literature and its contexts are ignored.[62] Sensational fiction was at least as popular and culturally influential as domestic novels—probably more so, given its cheap price and massive distribution. True, certain domestic novels, notably Susan Warner's *The Wide, Wide World* and Maria Cummins's *The Lamplighter*, sold as many copies as Lippard's *The Quaker City* or Thompson's *City Crimes*. But there is good reason why commentators such as Whitman and Whipple saw sensational fiction as an unparalleled cultural force. Whereas the domestic novel generally sold for a dollar (sometimes more) and was designed mainly for the middle-class Victorian parlor, the sensation novel sold for twelve and a half or twenty-five cents and was peddled everywhere: in sidewalk stalls, train stations, and stores. One observer of pamphlet novels commented that in cities, "where the telegraph and railroad converge the rays of glittering wealth, the traveler is met at every corner and proffered, again and again, the public aliment, novels, romances! Romances, novels!"[63] Appreciated by an increasingly mobile readership undergoing rapid lifestyle changes early in the industrial and transportation revolutions, these novels were read and enjoyed on the run.

Some modern critics have echoed nineteenth-century evaluations of sensation fiction as worthless or even pernicious—not, however, because it could incite the revolutionary fervor the Chicago doctor feared, but precisely because it did not. These critics argue that the novels portray some injustices and contain some shocking passages but nevertheless reaffirm the dominant cultural values that they pretend to flout. Christopher Looby has articulated this position specifically with regard to Thompson in a discussion of *The House Breaker*. In that novel, Looby writes, "the private vices of those 'in high places' rather than their systematic economic domination . . . occupy the readers' attention and are construed as the proper objects of their anger"; the excitement and sensation of Thompson's style,

62. See especially Ehrlich, "The 'Mysteries' of Philadelphia"; Adrienne Siegel, "Brothels, Bets, and Bars: Popular Literature as Guidebook to the Urban Underground, 1840–1870," *North Dakota Quarterly*, 44 (Spring 1976): 5–22 and *The Image of the American City in Popular Literature, 1820–1870* (Port Washington, N.Y.: Kennikat Press, 1981); Larzer Ziff, *Literary Democracy: The Declaration of Cultural Independence in America* (New York: Viking, 1981); Michael Denning, *Mechanic Accents: Dime Novels and Working-Class Culture in America* (London: Verso, 1987); David S. Reynolds, *Beneath the American Renaissance: The Subversive Imagination in the Age of Emerson and Melville* (New York: Knopf, 1988). More recent discussions of nineteenth-century sensational literature include Amy Gilman Srebnick, *The Mysterious Death of Mary Rogers: Sex and Culture in Nineteenth-Century America* (New York: Oxford University Press, 1995); Hans Bergmann, *God in the Street: New York Writing from the Penny Press to Melville* (Philadelphia: Temple University Press, 1995); Stuart M. Blumin, "George G. Foster and the Emerging Metropolis," intro. to Foster's *New York by Gas-Light* (1850; rpt., Berkeley: University of California Press, 1990), pp. 1–61; Karen Halttunen, *Murder Most Foul: The Killer and the American Gothic Imagination* (Cambridge, Mass.: Harvard University Press, 1998); and Cohen, *The Murder of Helen Jewett*. For discussions of British sensational literature, see Winifred Hughes, *The Maniac in the Cellar: Sensation Novels of the 1860s* (Princeton: Princeton University Press, 1980). and Randolph Woods Ivy, "The Victorian Sensation Novel: A Study in Formula Fiction" (Ph.D. diss. University of Chicago, 1974).
63. *Confessions of a Novel Reader*, p. 29.

in his view, "depends constitutively upon its fundamental endorsement of the taboos it violates."[64]

It is true that Thompson's fiction sometimes contains elements of conventionality, such as the presence of moral exemplars, and that it often echoes sexist and racist attitudes in antebellum culture. It is also clear that Thompson, as a writer of sensation fiction, made no attempt at a systematic exposition of political principles. Nevertheless, to represent Thompson's fiction as uniformly conventional or reactionary would be to ignore an overwhelming amount of textual evidence to the contrary. When we read his fiction, we realize that there was ample justification for the charges of blasphemy, salaciousness, gratuitous violence, and revolutionary politics that contemporary reviewers such as Whipple leveled at the pulp fiction of this period. Light years distant from conventionality, Thompson's texts subvert much that is associated with bourgeois ideals: domesticity and Christian nurture, the cult of true womanhood, institutional power structures such as the church and big business; white supremacy, the commonsense view of the human mind as rational and guided by ethics, and the notion that literature must teach a clear moral lesson.

It is useful to begin by discussing the last two issues—human rationality and literary didacticism—since they bear most obviously on the question of the subversive potential of Thompson's work. His novels are about sensation and entertainment, and the depiction of good, virtuous people is often dull. This may be the true reason behind his claim, late in *City Crimes*, that few such people even exist: "Have you noticed, reader, while perusing this narrative, that nearly all the characters introduced have been more or less tainted with crime? . . . Alas! human excellence is so very scarce, that had we taken it as the principal ingredient of our book, we should have made a slim affair of it, indeed."

Although a typical Thompson novel does include a rational, ethical character, this character is either marginalized or surrounded by so much suffering and evil that morality is invisible or impotent in most scenes of the novel. A prime example of powerless goodness is Sophia Franklin of *City Crimes*. Sophia is similar to the countless pious, angelic heroines who served as moral exemplars in domestic novels. Unlike the typical moral exemplar, however, she barely appears in the novel, while her murderous, promiscuous mother and sister take center stage. Although Thompson tells us he is including this "excellent young lady" to "illumine our dark pages with a celestial light," Sophia's light is never allowed to shine brightly, since we almost never see her. Indeed, Thompson's moral exemplars seem to exist only to be assaulted with disturbing phenomena. In an ironic reversal of the domestic ideal of family togetherness, Sophia's mother and sister plot to undermine her virtue by accepting money from a rake who attempts to seduce her; only the intervention of the male protagonist, Frank Sydney, prevents the seduction. The fact that Sophia does not save herself differentiates her from the

64. Christopher Looby, "George Thompson's 'Romance of the Real': Transgression and Taboo in American Sensation Fiction," *American Literature*, 65, no. 4 (December 1993): 661.

typical domestic heroine, who, as Nina Baym and others have shown, is actively virtuous.[65] Passivity, not action or efficacy, characterizes Thompson's good heroines. The innocent fruit seller of *Venus in Boston*, Fanny Aubrey, is another virtuous woman who does not act so much as she is acted upon. Like Sophia, she arrives at the brink of moral ruin only to be saved fortuitously by a helpful male character.

Although the positive male figures in Thompson's novels are more aggressive than the model heroines, they are assailed constantly by demonic forces that undermine and largely invalidate their virtue. Frank Sydney of *City Crimes* exemplifies this paradoxical feature of Thompson's fiction. To be sure, the virtuous Frank has a certain moral power in the novel: he prevents the planned robbery of his own house; he brings about the reclamation of two criminals, Clinton Romaine and the Doctor; and he proves victorious in the end over his enemy, the Dead Man. But Frank encounters so much grotesquerie and violence throughout the novel that the reader may feel that Thompson includes this model of probity principally to torment him. At the start of the novel, Frank leaves his comfortable upper-class environment with the worthy aim of doing good to those less fortunate than he. Before long, however, he finds himself entangled in a net of crime and intrigue spun by a bizarre group of thieves, murderers, and prostitutes. He is constantly exposed to the most revolting sights imaginable and is made to endure a succession of horrors and tortures.

It is clear from the texture of Thompson's fiction that the author's real interest lies not in virtuous activity but in the vicious, the degrading, and the disgusting. He was appealing to the same public that feasted on sensational penny newspapers and the gallery of freaks at P. T. Barnum's museum. Penny newspapers, replacing the stodgy six-pennies of the past, had been introduced in the early 1830s by Benjamin Day and James Gordon Bennett. Day's *New York Sun* and Bennett's *Herald* became the first of a string of cheap, mass-oriented papers that thrilled American readers with daily reports of tragedies and crimes. Emerson noted the sensationalism of America's penny papers. "What sickening details in the daily journals!" he wrote. He lamented that even "family newspapers" such as the *New York Tribune* had exceeded crime sheets like the *Newgate Calendar* and the *Pirate's Own Book* "in the freshness as well as the horror of their records of crime," so that the typical American was devoted "to reading all day murders & railroad accidents."[66] Thoreau likewise spoke of the "monstrous and startling events as fill the daily papers."[67] Thompson's crime-filled fiction was the literary equivalent of the penny newspaper.

Another leading influence on Thompson's sensationalism, Phineas T. Barnum,

65. Nina Baym, *Women's Fiction: A Guide to Novels by and about Women in America, 1820–1870* (Ithaca: Cornell University Press, 1978); see also Jane Tompkins, *Sensational Designs: The Cultural Work of American Fiction, 1790–1860* (New York: Oxford University Press, 1985).
66. *Emerson in His Journals*, ed. Joel Porte (Cambridge, Mass.: Harvard University Press, 1982), p. 433.
67. *The Journal of Henry David Thoreau*, ed. Bradford Torrey and Francis H. Allen (New York: Dover, 1962), 267.

had got his start in 1836 with his public exhibition of Joice Heth, a black woman purportedly 161 years old who claimed to have been George Washington's nanny. Barnum became notorious as the era's Prince of Humbug by putting on display at his museum on Broadway oddities and anomalies, both human and animal, that attracted droves of sensation seekers. Thompson expressed a fascinated, if quite critical, view of Barnum on several occasions. In his novel *The Gay Girls of New York*, he describes "a certain gentleman whose name begins with a B, and who, commencing on nothing, has amassed a princely fortune by the exhibition of the most palpable humbugs—some of them confoundedly silly—that ever existed! The Fejee Mermaid—Joice Heath [sic]—the Woolly Horse—the Bearded Lady——oh, thou Spirit of Humbug!" Pondering Barnum's popularity, Thompson writes, "What a singular thing is public curiosity, and how eagerly people will flock and pay money to behold the most repulsive-looking objects, which afford no instruction, produce no agreeable sensations, but which merely gratify a morbid and depraved appetite!"[68]

Thompson also dedicated an entire book to Barnum, a parody of the impressario's best-selling *Life of P. T. Barnum* (1855), titled *Autobiography of Petite Bunkum, the Great Yankee Showman*. This work was advertised in the *Belle* as "the book that Barnum attempted to suppress by an injunction."[69] If it disturbed Barnum, however, it was probably less because of anything uncomplimentary in it than because it appeared before his autobiography and may possibly have competed with it. Thompson's book, a mild satire, was copyrighted in 1854, and a notice at the end refers to the public excitement about Barnum's "forthcoming Autobiography." "The editor," this notice also asserts, "deems it but just to say, that, although the object of this work is playfully to lampoon the great Yankee Showman, P. T. Barnum, he, with the public at large, confesses to a liking for that individual."[70]

Indeed, Thompson was just as intent as Barnum on displaying the repulsive and the bizarre. *The Gay Girls of New York* contains a sequence in which the heroine, Hannah Sherwood, disfigured by vitriol, is exhibited publicly by a Barnumesque showman who advertises her as a "STUPENDOUS ATTRACTION!!! The greatest wonder which the world has ever produced, in the shape of a LIVING WOMAN well-formed and accomplished, who was born with a DEATH'S FACE!!! This extraordinary freak of nature will remain on exhibition for a few days only. Admission one shilling. Call and see!!"[71] This display of the woman with a "Death's Face" is just an open instance of the Barnumesque exhibitionism that governs Thompson's

---

68. *The Gay Girls of New York, or Life on Broadway: Being a Mirror of the Fashions, Follies and Crimes of a Great City* (New York, 1853), pp. 102, 101.

69. *Broadway Belle* (New York), October 15, 1855. The January 1, 1855 issue also cites reviews from the *Boston Transcript*, the *Daily Times*, and the *Herald* which claim that Barnum tried to have the book suppressed by the Supreme Court.

70. *Autobiography of Petite Bunkum, the Great Yankee Showman* (New York: P. H. Harris, 1855); last page.

71. *The Gay Girls of New York*, p. 99.

fiction. The villainous Dead Man of *City Crimes* is a walking freak show, having destroyed his face with acid in order to conceal his criminal past. One of his sons, known as the Image, is a mute, ghoulish dwarf who lives in a black basement. The Dead Man, along with his criminal cronies, occupies Manhattan's subterranean tunnel networks, called in the novel the Dark Vaults, which, in Thompson's portrayal, are a nightmarish version of Barnum's museum. Frank Sydney, who is led into the Vaults, is greeted by the sight of a near-naked man, "seated upon a heap of excrement and filthy straw," devouring a pig's carcass "swollen and green with putrefaction." The man is surrounded by other "starving wretches" who share the decayed meat, which turns them into howling maniacs whose limbs rot until "finally they putrify and die." Later Frank Sydney is exposed to even worse horrors. For a time he is imprisoned in a torture room, the Chamber of Death, at the center of which is a huge table surrounded by skeletons arranged "in all kinds of obscene positions." To escape the chamber, Frank must wade through excrement-filled sewers.

In this and many similar moments in his fiction, Thompson crosses from the Barnumesque to the merely revolting. In the lively competition among antebellum fiction writers to outdo one another's disgusting images, Thompson was the clear winner, with George Lippard a distant second, and Poe, for all his horror, almost out of the running, trailing perhaps a score of anonymous and pseudonymous sensational novelists. A typically gross Thompson scene occurs in Mike Simpson's recounting of his criminal past in *Venus in Boston*. Having murdered his fellow butler, Lagrange, at the behest of the adulterous Lady Hawley, Mike avenges her subsequent betrayal of him by decapitating Lagrange, stuffing his gory remains into a wine cask, and later serving wine from the cask to his mistress and her lover, who praise the wine's rich color and flavor.

Arguably Thompson's most disgusting scene occurs in his novel *The Road to Ruin: or, The Felon's Doom*, in which the criminal-protagonist, Jack Harold, tortures a man who has murdered his daughter and a house guest. Over several days Jack starves, scorches, and brands the man, who is driven mad and, in a grisly effort to feed himself, tears flesh from his own shoulders, eats it, and then chews off parts of his own lips and tongue and swallows them, too. Next, the man is bound and thrown into a basement on top of his two victims' decomposed corpses, which he greedily devours.

The Subversion of Domesticity

Clearly, Thompson himself was trying to tap what he called "public curiosity" over "the most repulsive-looking objects, which afford no instruction, produce no agreeable sensations, but which merely gratify a morbid and depraved appetite."[72] In so doing, he was thumbing his nose at the decorous tone that characterized the period's domestic novels. Typically, domestic novels traced the

72. Ibid., p.102.

success of a virtuous heroine in overcoming personal misfortune and moving toward middle-class marriage, guided by strong Christian faith. In the domestic novel, home is an ideal to be gained, and marriage is a kind of heavenly reward for virtuous behavior.

Thompson's novels move in a very different direction. Domestic bliss is repeatedly revealed as ephemeral. Families are constantly shattered as a result of the perverse, often adulterous activities of one or both spouses. The novels end not with detailed paeans to marital togetherness, like most domestic novels, but with highly disturbing, sensational images. At the end of *City Crimes*, Thompson focuses on two grotesque incidents—the torture and blowing up of the Dead Man and Josephine's deceiving of Thurston into marriage, leading to their suicides after he discovers her facial deformity—rather than on Sophia and Frank's marriage, which is relegated to a brief letter so saccharine it sounds like self-parody. Similarly, he ends *Venus in Boston* not with some didactic denouement but with the ironic suggestion that the novel's villains are still successful by pursuing evil: the Chevalier and the Duchess are continuing their "brilliant career of crime," Mike Simpson is "on a professional tour to the South and West," and Sow Nance has become "the most abandoned prostitute in Ann Street." Even Thompson's novels that seem to end conventionally, such as *The House Breaker*, have an ironic twist. One of the happy marriages in this work is made possible when a man dies of joy upon his wife's giving birth—to the son of a burglar; the latter had slipped into bed in her husband's place one night and so surpassed him in erotic talent that she pretended not to notice the deception.

In addition to ambiguous endings, Thompson's fiction features narratives that repeatedly deconstruct marriage and family. Domestic fiction enforced the notion of Christian nurture: the idea, popularized by the Reverend Horace Bushnell in his widely read book *Christian Nurture* (1848), that religious values communicated from parent to child were the main shaping influences on the child's development. Mark Twain applies his satirical scalpel to this domestic ideal in his portrait of Huck Finn's discomfort with Miss Watson's religious teachings. Thompson uses satire to similar ends, though his satire more closely resembles a sledgehammer than a scalpel.

Instead of Christian nurture, Thompson presents pornographic and criminal nurture. Maria Archer of *City Crimes* tells Frank Sydney how her parents had been exemplars not of religion but of hypocritical lust. Each of her parents, though outwardly pious, was having a secret affair, her mother with the family's clergyman, her father with the maid. The young Maria, a keyhole witness to both affairs, leaves home in disgust and later expresses her "joy at having escaped from such an abode of hypocrisy as my parents' house." Maria's life continues to parody the domestic ideal, when she is inveigled into marriage by a man who proves to be the obverse of the model husband. The dissolute Frederick Archer forces his wife to become a prostitute to support him. Eventually he murders her with a bowie knife when she refuses to give him money.

An even more dramatic reversal of Christian nurture is apparent in the family situation of *City Crimes'* leading villain, the Dead Man. His marriage is a demonic parody of the courtship and marriage of domestic novels. Indeed, he never courts at all, but rather takes possession of a woman after having murdered her husband. Perversely, he cuts out the eyes of her two children and later slashes their throats. The new children he has by her are devilishly distant from the "little men" and "little women" whom authors of domestic fiction such as like Louisa May Alcott would popularize. The deformed Image, more animal than human, receives communications from his parents only through blows and curses. The other child, Jack the Prig, is a living mockery of Christian nurture, since he is trained in crime and atheism. Like the lawless Pearl of *The Scarlet Letter* or the wild Topsy of *Uncle Tom's Cabin*, Jack gives irreverent answers when asked to recite the catechism. But Jack's irreverence goes far beyond Pearl's or Topsy's; moreover, Thompson's adult questioner, unlike Hawthorne's or Stowe's, takes pleasure in it. The Dead Man is delighted when Jack declares that "His majesty, old Beelzebub!" created him and when he answers the question "What is the whole duty of man?" as follows: "To drink, lie, rob, and murder when necessary." The Dead Man has taught Jack to call the Bible "all a cursed humbug!" and to address him as "the d——dest scoundrel that ever went unhung." Proud of Jack's future as a criminal, the Dead Man announces, "The day when he commits a murder will be the happiest day of my life."

Mockery of domesticity appears as well in other bizarre family situations in Thompson's fiction. Mrs. Franklin of *City Crimes* becomes so bored and sexually frustrated by her proper husband, whom she calls a "canting religionist" always "discoursing upon the pleasures of the domestic circle, and such humbugs," that she arranges with her daughter Josephine to have him killed so they can lead a life of shameless promiscuity. Like the Dead Man, Mrs. Franklin exercises parental nurture in a notably un-Christian manner. Not only does she try to arrange the seduction of her good daughter, Sophia, but she also encourages and cultivates Josephine's promiscuity, warning her: "Do not mate yourself in marriage to a man who, when he becomes your husband, will restrict you in the enjoyment of those voluptuous pleasures in which you now take such delight."

Another instance of parodied domesticity is the family background of the procuress Sow Nance in *Venus in Boston*. In a typical moment of Thompson black humor, Sow Nance boasts: "I came from a first-rate family, I did; my father was hung for killing my mother—one of my brothers has also danced a hornpipe in the air, and another is under sentence of death, off South, for beating a woman's brains out with a fire-shovel, and choking her five children with a dishcloth."

Nearly every Thompson novel portrays a family that is violated or ripped apart by some evil force. Like his fellow sensationalist Lippard, Thompson determinedly inverts the pattern of domestic fiction, showing repeatedly the destruction rather than the construction of conventional family life.

Eroticism and Gender Issues

In the perverse homes of Thompson's novels, the characters are surrounded with sexually charged literature and entertainments. Here again he establishes his distance from the domestic novel, in which the heroine reads principally the Bible and religious tracts. Thompson's heroines never pick up the Bible; instead, they feast on pornography. The "Venus" of Boston boasts that she is the author of *Confessions of a Voluptuous Young Lady of High Rank* and the editor of an American edition of John Cleland's *Fanny Hill*. Josephine Franklin and her mother even have an entire room outfitted with "a large number of figures, exquisitely made of wax, representing males and females, in every imaginable variety of posture, a few classical, others voluptuous, and many positively obscene." The Franklins frequently use this room to consummate affairs, using the figures for inspiration: when a spring was touched, Thompson writes, "instantly every wax figure was in motion, imitating the movements of real life with wonderful fidelity." In *The Road to Ruin*, Jack Harold finds his lover reading a "licentious" novel whose erotic scenes he invites her to act out with him; she readily complies, and they spend a day performing the "amorous and bacchanalian revelry" described in the novel. The heroine of *The Mysteries of Bond Street* finds herself in a brothel with a library stocked with *The Lustful Turk, Fanny Hill*, and "the filthy work entitled *The Education of Laura.*"[73]

Thompson's own fiction can be placed firmly in the genre of popular pornography. Steven Marcus long ago brought to light the "Other Victorians"—writers of pornography in nineteenth-century England—and more recently critics are discovering "Other Americans," most notably Thompson.[74] These other Americans were reacting against a middle-class culture that was in some ways absurdly prudish, at least in its pretensions. In polite circles, undergarments were called "inexpressibles," piano legs were covered with frilly stockings, and multilayered ladies' fashions strove to hide as much flesh as possible. The cult of gentility, the behavioral corollary of the cults of domesticity and true womanhood, resulted in such laughable forms of repression as an 1831 art exhibit in Boston where nude statues were decorously draped in dimity aprons.

Repression, as we know, almost inevitably breeds some kind of backlash. Beneath the icy surface of puritanical standards seethed a fascination with pornography and outré sexual activity. As early as 1833 the reformer John McDowall, investigating the popularity of erotic books, prints, snuffboxes, and music boxes, wrote that he was "completely astounded" to find that "our country was flooded with these obscene articles."[75] A federal law of 1842 banning the importation of foreign pornographic images (though not books) ironically may have provoked the development of indigenous pornographic or semipornographic material. The

---

73. *The Mysteries of Bond-Street: or, the Seraglios of Upper Tendom* (New York 1857).

74. Steven Marcus, *The Other Victorians: A Study of Sexuality and Pornography in Mid-Nineteenth-Century England* (New York: Basic Books, 1966).

75. *Memoir and Select Remains of the Late Rev. John R. McDowall, the Martyr of the Seventh Commandment in the Nineteenth Century* (New York: Leavitt, Lord, & Co., 1838), p. 222.

popularity of Hiram Powers's derivative white marble sculpture *The Greek Slave* owed much to the fact that it presented female frontal nudity, although in "chaste" fashion. The late 1840s brought the craze of so-called "model artists" or *tableaux vivants*, theatricals staged both publicly and privately by naked or partially clothed men and women posing in scenes titled "Venus in a Shell," "Eve in Eden," and "Lady Godiva." In the 1840s a surge of racy "sporting" periodicals with titles like *The Sporting Whip, The Rake,* and *The Libertine* provided working-class readers with a steady supply of crime news, sporting reports, and sexual gossip. The most popular and long-lived of all the sporting papers, the *National Police Gazette*, would enjoy an eighty-eight year run thrilling American readers with countless crime reports, many of them sex-related, such as one headlined "Alleged Incest of a Father upon His Daughters—Brutal and Lascivious Attempts upon a Third—Wonderful and Horrible Details."[76] The 1840s and 1850s offered a window of opportunity for pornographers like Thompson, particularly since the early 1830s reform efforts of McDowall had collapsed and Comstock's organized censorship was far in the future.

Of necessity, Thompson's pornography was, by today's standards, of the "soft" variety. Even the mass-oriented publishers and distributors that issued his books (such as Boston's Fedheren & Co., which also sold toothpaste, soap, and medicine) did not publish material that was full of the particulars of sex. But Thompson's work contains scene after scene in which outré sex is suggested, if not described in detail. For instance, in recounting the ménage à trois involving Mrs. Franklin, her daughter Josephine, and a ship's captain, he writes: "And clasping both ladies around the waists, he kissed them alternately, again and again. That night was one of guilty rapture to all the parties; but the particulars must be left to the reader's imagination." Often Thompson claims to be restraining his own desire to tell the reader more, as when in *Jack Harold* he writes about a nude woman being watched by a lecherous Spaniard who later will rape her: "And now we must check the wanton impulses of our rambling pen, which prompts us to glide into all the particulars of that voluptuous scene."[77]

To say that Thompson's pornography is suggestive rather than explicit, however, is not to diminish its adventurousness and transgressiveness, given the era in which it appeared. On the contrary, his fiction constantly surprises with the risks it takes. Among the kinds of sexual activity Thompson depicts are adultery, miscegenation, group sex, incest, child sex, rape, and gay sex. In *City Crimes* he tells us that in the Dark Vaults "the crime of incest is as common . . . as dirt! I have known a mother and a son—a father and a daughter—a brother and a sister—to be guilty of criminal intimacy!"

To a large extent, Thompson's aim is that of most pornographers: arousal of the male reader. His fiction abounds with voyeuristic scenes in which a hidden man watches a woman disrobing, coming out of a bath, standing unclothed before a

76. *National Police Gazette* (New York), May 2, 1846.
77. *Jack Harold, or the Criminal's Career* (1850; rpt., New York : F. A. Brady, 1851), p. 101.

mirror, or the like. Although his descriptions of naked women are never detailed, they are always titillating. Doubtless many male readers of his time were excited by the glimpses he provided of the female anatomy, such as Venus of Boston's "glorious bust, where on two 'hillocks of snow' projected their rose-tinted peaks, in sportive rivalry—revealed, with bewildering distinctness, by the absence of any concealing drapery!"

It is misleading, however, to suggest that sensation fiction like Thompson's and Lippard's was designed only for male readers. The label Leslie Fiedler once gave this fiction—"the male novel"—oversimplifies both its aims and its content.[78] As more recent scholars have shown, no single body of popular literature appealed only to male or female readers. Ronald Zboray has demonstrated that men read domestic novels and women enjoyed adventurous and sensational literature.[79] Women's attraction to the latter was widely noted in the nineteenth century. An article titled "Working Girls and their Literature" explained that since women generally had "dull, monotonous" jobs, "it is but natural that they should plunge into sensational literature, and devour the worst novels that are written"; indeed, women, lamented the essayist, delighted in "the sensational and sickly stories with which our book-stalls teem."[80] Another commentator noted, "there are only two classes of American novels—the 'chaste' and the 'sensational.'" In the "chaste" camp were moral domestic and religious writings, while the "sensational," genre was "generally villainous" and was "read with the greatest avidity" and "found in the boudoir, in the thieves' den, and in the log cabin beyond the Rocky Mountains."[81] This statement brings attention to the oft-noted ubiquity of sensational novels, which were found not only in the faraway "cabin" but also in the middle-class woman's "boudoir."

Women who read Thompson's fiction would have found their sex represented in complex ways. On the one hand, his works contain characters, plotlines, and images that could serve as fodder for female erotic fantasy and quasi-feminist meditation. Many women in his work are portrayed as victims of partriarchal oppression and especially of the sexual double standard, and a woman's right to sexual pleasure is frequently affirmed. On the other hand, not all of his women characters are sympathetic, and many of those who find erotic fulfillment also become terrifyingly violent. In *City Crimes*, for example, the Franklin women conspire to murder their husband and father, and Julia Fairfield unhesitatingly poisons her second husband when he gets in the way of a new affair. Although their sexual frustration sometimes seems to be offered as a mitigating factor in their crimes, these characters are still clearly villains and deserve punishment for their misdeeds. Ultimately, Thompson's women are figures of both fantasy and nightmare. They enact the rejection, and even inversion, of the maternal and nurturing

---

78. Leslie Fiedler, "The Male Novel," *Partisan Review*, 37 (1970): 74–89.
79. Ronald Zboray, *A Fictive People: Antebellum Economic Development and the American Reading Public* (New York: Oxford University Press, 1993).
80. *The Golden Age* (New York), July 29, 1871.
81. Ibid., September 13, 1873.

female roles promoted by the cult of true womanhood, a middle-class ideology which held that women were naturally chaste and good beings with a weak sex drive. In doing so, they explore both the sexual and the aggressive potential that ideology repressed.

In bringing attention to women's powerful sexual urges, Thompson was participating in a small but growing movement of progressive writers and thinkers, including the poet Walt Whitman and his close friend Lorenzo Fowler, the popular phrenologist who later devoted himself to "sexual science."[82] Throughout *Leaves of Grass*, Whitman affirms the power of women's sexuality. In one poem he writes, "Sex contains all, bodies, souls, / Without shame the man I like knows and avows the deliciousness of his sex, / Without shame the woman I like knows and avows hers."[83] Fowler, whose Manhattan publishing firm distributed the first edition of *Leaves of Grass* and published the second, rooted his theory of the female sex drive in phrenology, the pseudoscience which held that among the brain's many segments was "amativeness," or sexual desire, which Fowler insisted was equally strong in men and women. Fowler became the era's leading promoter of the idea that sexual satisfaction was essential to a woman's physical and emotional well-being. He titled a chapter of his book *Sexual Science* "Passion Absolutely Necessary for Woman" and wrote, "The non-participant female is a natural abomination."[84]

Thompson may have shared Whitman's and Fowler's perception of woman's powerful sexual nature. His characters frequently denounce society's double standard, which permitted promiscuity for men but not for women. The Venus of Boston, for example (who was, of course, in no way restrained by societal mores), at one point teases a man by declaring herself envious of him for "belonging to a sex which possesses the exclusive privilege of unrestricted amative enjoyment," whereas she belongs to "those unfortunate mortals called women;—unfortunate because they are women, and because they are even more ardent in their passions than those who have the happiness to be men."

Many other women in Thompson's fiction are unapologetic and open in their declarations of sexual desire. Unrepentantly "fallen," these women take pleasure in promiscuity. While marginalizing chaste heroines like Sophia Franklin, Thompson foregrounds women whose sexual hunger is virtually insatiable. Typical in this regard is Julia Fairfield, the aristocratic, outwardly proper fiancée of Frank Sydney in *City Crimes*. While coyly resisting Frank's tentative premarital advances, Julia is secretly having a torrid affair with her black servant, Nero, by whom she is pregnant. Suspicious of her, Frank consults a phrenologist (almost certainly a

---

82. Lorenzo Fowler's brother, Orson, was one of the publishers whose medical work Thompson and Harris claimed to be quoting in their controversial article in the *Belle*, "Important to Husbands and Wives."

83. Walt Whitman, "A Woman Waits for Me," in *Leaves of Grass: Comprehensive Reader's Edition*, ed. Harold Blodgett and Sculley Bradley (New York: New York University Press, 1965), pp. 101–2.

84. Lorenzo Fowler, *Sexual Science; Including Manhood, Womanhood, and Their Mutual Interrelations* (Philadelphia: National Publishing Co., 1870), p. 680. For a discussion of other progressive thinkers and reformers involved with the issue of sexuality, see Hal D. Sears, *The Sex Radicals: Free Love in High Victorian America* (Lawrence: Regents Press of Kansas, 1977).

fictional rendering of Lorenzo Fowler), who has read her "bumps" and found that she is "of an uncommonly ardent and voluptuous temperament." "Phrenology confirms this," he explains, "for her amative developments are singularly prominent." Frank's suspicions about her are confirmed after he marries her, and finally he casts her off. Far from being hurt or ashamed, however, Julia (who has murdered her mixed-race baby) relishes the prospect of independence and complete sexual freedom. "Now," she declares to him, "I am mistress of my own actions—free to indulge to my heart's content in delightful amours! You cannot understand the fiery and insatiate cravings of my passions. I tell you that I consume with desire—but not for enjoyment with such as you, but for amours that are recherche and unique. Ah, I would give more for one hour with my superb African, than for a year's dalliance with one like you, so ordinary, so excessively common-place!"

In his colorful depictions of Julia and other wives who escape marriage, Thompson not only flouted the cult of domesticity but also may have created for women readers a tantalizing space of sexual imagination. Two heroines who play out a particularly varied array of fantasies are Josephine Franklin and her mother. Having violently severed the domestic tie by murdering Edgar Franklin, these nymphomaniacs devote themselves to using men (and boys) solely for sexual gratification and then disposing of them. For a time Mrs. Franklin takes special delight in her affair with the fifteen-year-old Clinton Romaine. Soon Josephine has a dalliance with the Reverend Sinclair, who overcomes his initial prudery and becomes a regular visitor to her bedroom. Like all their lovers, these men eventually bore the Franklin women, who move on to others, keeping diary records of their sexual conquests. Along the way, they seek out unconventional situations, believing that "an amour must be delicious and unique." Cross-dressing, with overtones of gay sex and pedophilia, is represented in a scene at a masquerade ball in which Josephine, playfully costumed as a boy, is approached by the Spanish ambassador. Fooled by the disguise, he says: "Were you a lady, you would be beautiful, but as a boy you are doubly charming. Be not surprised when I assure you that you please me ten times—aye, ten thousand times, more, as a boy, than as a woman. By heaven, I must kiss those ripe lips!" Mrs. Franklin, as frolicsome as Josephine, at one point joins her, as noted earlier, in a sexual romp with a boat captain. Having aspersed "the insipidity of a domestic life," Mrs. Franklin revels in role reversal, as when she gives the virtuous Sophia this unmotherly advice: "Your sister and I have long since learned to dispose of our persons for pecuniary benefit, as well as for our sensual gratification—for it is as pleasurable as profitable; and you must do the same, now that you are old enough."

The Franklins are extreme examples of the typical Thompson female protagonist, who seeks liberation from entrapment in a dull or unequal marriage. Thompson's plots often reflect, albeit in lurid guise, a central idea of the free love movement: women, given few options for self-support in a male-dominated capitalist society, resort to all kinds of stratagems to stay afloat financially. If one common avenue was prostitution, another was "legalized prostitution," the term free lovers used to describe the conventional marriage. Near the end of the novel,

Julia Fairfield marries an elderly man for his money and discovers on their wedding night that he is impotent. Using free love terms to derogate such unions, Thompson indicates that Julia would be justified if she took on lovers:

> How often do we see old, decrepit men wooing and wedding young girls, purchased by wealth from mercenary parents! Well have such sacrifices to Lust and Mammon, been termed legalized prostitution. And does not such a system excuse, if not justify, infidelity on the part of the wife? His miserable physical incapacity provokes without satisfying the passions of his victim; and in the arms of a lover she secretly enjoys the solace which she cannot derive from her legal owner.

This view of woman as the sexually deprived slave of an impotent husband is reiterated throughout Thompson's fiction. In *Venus in Boston*, Lady Hawley justifies her adulterous affair, saying: "How terrible it is for a young and passionate woman to be linked in marriage to an old, impotent, cold, and passionless being, who claims the name of man, but is not entitled to it! And then she solaces herself with a lover—as she must, or die." Driven by sexual deprivation to detest the word "husband," she asserts that "'tis slavery—'tis madness, to be chained for life to but one source of love, when a thousand streams would not satiate or overflow." Some of Thompson's heroines claim to be driven by unsated lust not only to adultery but to prostitution as well. A novice brothel girl in the same novel, for instance, complains when charged with entertaining a single older gentleman: "When shall I become a courtezan? How long must I remain here, pining for the embraces of fifty men, and enduring the impotent caresses of but one,—and he, bah! A fellow of no more fire or animation, or power, than a lump of ice!"

Just as antebellum free love societies such as Modern Times on Long Island and the community at Berlin Heights, Ohio, offered men and women sexual pleasure outside marriage, so did Thompson create ample space in his fiction for extramarital passion. Julia Hamilton, the heroine of his novel *The Delights of Love; or the Lady Libertine*, is "the widow of an old gentleman, who has left her a vast fortune, and an undisturbed virginity." Removed from the constraints of marriage, she enlists a young actor to teach her "those delights from which the impotence of an aged spouse has hitherto debarred her." Having derived from her Italian mother sexual urges "almost fierce in their ardour and intensity," she has a love bout with the actor that leaves him "astonished and almost terrified at the fury of her passions and the insatiability of her requirement."[85]

Thompson links extramarital sex directly with the free-love movement in *Fanny Greeley; or, Confessions of a Free-love Sister Written by Herself*, whose initially virginal heroine, charmed by a lecturer into desiring to be "openly a follower of the glorious new school," becomes the "queen of love" of a free love group. She then seeks out both men and women for indiscriminate sexual liaisons with others "laboring in the passional spheres."[86]

85. *The Delights of Love; or, the Lady Libertine. Being the Adventures of an Amorous Widow* (New York: J. H. Farrell, n.d.), in Ashbee, *Bibliography of Prohibited Books*, pp. 203, 205.
86. *Fanny Greeley; or, Confessions of a Free-love Sister Wriiten by Herself* (New York: Henry S. G. Smith, n.d.), in Ashbee, *Bibliography of Prohibited Books*, pp. 212, 216.

Race, Ethnicity, and Class

While promoting some radical notions of the free love and temperance movements, Thompson also provided variations on images from antislavery and working-class literature. At first glance, Thompson's treatment of racial and ethnic minorities seems to cater to white working-class prejudices: Jews (such as *Venus in Boston*'s Mike), Irish immigrants, and blacks are frequently portrayed in stereotypical terms. At least in the case of African Americans, however, careful reading of Thompson's work reveals a greater complexity. In his study of blackface minstrel shows in antebellum America, *Love and Theft*, Eric Lott has described minstrelsy as a multivalent form of entertainment through which white working-class men expressed a wide range of attitudes toward African Americans, some aggressively racist, others sympathetic and admiring. He argues that minstrelsy served its audience as a means of maintaining their distance from blacks through ridicule and caricature; but it simultaneously gratified a fascination with black culture and a desire to blur racial identities.[87] Thompson's fiction (whose readership, after all, probably overlapped in large part with the audience for minstrelsy) shows evidence of similar contradictory impulses. His black characters are often described in degrading and brutish terms, but on closer consideration are seen to embody the justified rage of an oppressed minority.

As Melville would do in "Benito Cereno," Thompson conjures up role-reversal situations in which blacks gain temporary dominance over whites. Few issues surrounding race relations frightened antebellum whites more than the possible assumption of power by blacks. White southerners were haunted by a fear of slave revolts which turned to outright terror after John Brown's 1859 raid on Harper's Ferry, Virginia, aimed at inciting massive slave rebellions. Later, the southern effort to disempower blacks would breed the Ku Klux Klan and Jim Crow. In the North, the antebellum period saw a constriction of social and legal rights for blacks, caused largely by fear among whites of blacks' potential ascendancy to power and status.

Such fears may have increased the sensational effect of Thompson's plots in which blacks are assigned influence. Thompson explores a black man's sexual possession of an upper-class white woman in Julia Fairfield's affair with her servant, Nero, describing their fornication in terms of social role reversal:

> She abandoned her person to his embraces, and returned them! She, the well-born, the beautiful, the wealthy, the accomplished lady—the betrothed bride of a young gentleman of honor—the daughter of an aristocrat—the star of a constellation of fashion—yielding herself to the arms of a negro servant.
> Yes, that black fellow covers her exquisite neck and shoulders with lustful kisses! His hands revel amid the glories of her divine and voluptuous bosom; and his lips wander from her rosy mouth, to the luxurious beauties of her finely developed bust.

87. See Eric Lott, *Love and Theft: Blackface Minstrelsy and the American Working Class* (New York: Oxford University Press 1993).

If here a white woman becomes sexually enthralled by a black man, elsewhere in Thompson's fiction blacks exercise other kinds of control over whites. In *Venus in Boston,* two black characters, Pete York and Washington Goode, lock the aggressive white hero Corporal Grimsby into a basement called the Black Hole, while the black cab driver Jonas "enjoys the familiar acquaintance of many white courtezans of beauty and fashion," receives sexual favors from them for bringing them johns, and edits the *Key to the Chambers of Love,* a whorehouse guidebook "extensively patronized by [white] sporting bloods." Yet another strong black figure in the novel is Timothy Tickels's maid, who exhibits furious antiwhite passions. In an effort to subjugate the heroine, Fanny Aubrey, the maid tears off the girl's clothing and beats her savagely with a rope.

These scenes of miscegenation and black-on-white violence clearly contributed to the titillation value of the novels, with the extra frisson that comes from breaking a racial taboo. That the violence, at least, may also be interpreted as justified reprisal against whites for the oppression of racial minorities is made clear in *The Gay Girls of New York,* which features one of the most interesting racially mixed characters in nineteenth-century fiction, Cleopatra (aka Cleo). Half Indian and half black, Cleo has experienced heinous racism and thus dedicates herself to the vengeful punishment of whites. Her Native American father was killed in a skirmish against whites. Her mother, a slave on a South Carolina sugar plantation, died from a brutal flogging at the hands of a cruel overseer, whom Cleo later managed to kill without being discovered. A kind mistress taught Cleo to read, making her a cultured woman. At sixteen, Cleo was impregnated by her master's son—"almost a matter of course" for female slaves, she comments—and had a daughter whom she educated and hoped to marry off to an unbiased white man. But her daughter was raped by her master (who was, of course, her own grandfather) and subsequently drowned herself in shame. Cleo, after being flogged when she complained about the incident, succeeded in killing her master and fleeing north to Manhattan. Having spent eight years as a procuress for a wealthy rake, she now exults in her power over innocent white girls she lures into his den of seduction. To the novel's heroine, Lucy Pembroke, she announces: "White girl, . . . I am your mistress now, if I am black. You are my slave; and if you offend me, I will strip you, tie you up, and whip you until your red blood pours in streams from your white shoulders." Here Thompson pointedly reverses the customary practice in the antebellum South of white masters stripping and flogging their slaves. Making sure that we see Cleo's violence as race-specific retaliation, he has her tell Lucy: "I hate you because you belong to the accursed white race! The sight of that pale face of yours makes my half negro, half Indian blood boil within me; for negroes stolen from Africa and Indians in their own rightful territories, have been oppressed and crushed by your race."[88]

Cleo's explanation of her sufferings is part of a larger pattern in Thompson's work in which oppressed or criminal characters voice social protest. As bad as

88. *Gay Girls of New York,* pp. 43, 41, 42.

Thompson's criminals are, they at least have the virtue of honesty. In contrast, their enemies—aristocrats, politicians, clergymen, judges, manufacturers, merchants, and other established types—are, with few exceptions, corrupt hypocrites. Time and again, Thompson makes use of a common character type in antebellum sensational literature: the justified criminal. In an era of widening class divisions and well-publicized instances of upper-class depravity, writers like Thompson often depicted outcasts and criminals waging war against social injustice.

Frequently his criminal characters interrupt their nefarious activities with declamations against outwardly respectable hypocrites. The murderer Mike Simpson, appalled by the two-faced Lady Hawley and her aristocratic lover, tells them, "You will remember, comrades, that as great a villain as I am, I am no hypocrite, and was never accused of being one. And yet hypocrisy prevails in every department of life." Similarly, the criminal hero of *The Ladies' Garter* claims he has "always scorned the disguise of hypocrisy which I might easily have assumed," insisting, "I never sail under false colors, but always openly display the blood-red flag of the pirate."[89] The leader of a crime band in *Jack Harold* declares, "we are honorable thieves, who recognize no law, except those who govern themselves."[90] His daughter, defending him as a kind of modern Robin Hood, argues that his open villainy is infinitely preferable to the cloaked depravity of the rich; she calls his band "robbers—not mean, paltry, sneaking thieves, who steal trifles, and like cowards deprive poor men of the fruits of their honest toil—but bold and gallant freebooters, who plunder from the rich, and despise them while they do it."[91] The title character of *Harry Glindon, or, the Man of Many Crimes* is driven by "cruelty, a thirst for blood," because, in his words, "society is badly organized, and the world is full of abuses." He cites the "bloated Judge" who, though universally revered, "punishes a culprit for a trivial offence" while being "himself a drunkard, an adulterer, and a villain," the "distinguished statesman" with "his pockets full of bribe-money," and the "inhuman, cruel" rich man who takes "advantage of his position to oppress the poor devils under his control."[92]

The figure of the exploitive rich man was a common one in antebellum protest literature. America's boom-and-bust economy, markedly unstable in a time before government controls, created great insecurity among the nation's poor. The labor theory of value, which equated value with actual work accomplished, generated sympathy for common workers and mistrust of the so-called idle rich. Novelists and pamphleteers lambasted the spoiled "upper ten" while casting pity on the oppressed "lower million." In one poem Whitman typically describes "an aristocrat" as "a smoucher grabbing the good dishes exclusively to himself and grinning at the starvation of others as if it were funny."[93] Between 1825 and 1860, the richest

89. *The Ladies' Garter* (New York: Howland & Co., ca. 1853), p. 63.
90. *Jack Harold, or the Criminal's Career.* (Boston: W. Berry, 1850), p. 18.
91. Ibid., p. 28.
92. *Harry Glindon, or, the Man of Many Crimes: A Startling Narrative of the Career of a Desperate Villain* (New York; 1854), p. 15.
93. Whitman, *Leaves of Grass*, p. 696.

10 percent of free wealth holders owned a staggering 73 percent of the nation's assets; by the Civil War, the poorest half of Americans owned just 1 percent of all assets.[94] Conspicuous opulence among the rich generated resentment among the laboring poor, particularly in cities. Thompson has Jack Harold remark on these contrasts, declaring: "New York is indeed at once a Paradise and a Pandemonium; within it, the extremes of wealth and poverty jostle with each other, while piety and vice are next door neighbors. The millionaire lives in the next street to the mendicant; and the sanctuary of prayer adjoins a brothel."[95]

Thompson is not subtle about his distaste for the wealthy, who almost invariably appear in his novels as cold, superficial double-dealers. At the start of *City Crimes*, he labels the rich person "the oppressor who sets his heel upon the neck of the brother man." Frank Sydney's "false and hollow-hearted" rich friends, with names like Narcissus Nobs and Archibald Slinkey, admire Frank only for his money, abandoning him when his fortunes decline. The Dead Man, for all his wickedness, is presented as being morally superior to the merchant Paul Hartless. Having escaped from prison by hiding in a crate that ends up in Hartless's warehouse, the Dead Man overhears Hartless decrying ordinary workers and singing the praises of cheaper convict labor. Hartless boasts that his labor costs have plummeted since he fired his regular workers and hired convicts. He callously refuses to help the impoverished wife of one of his fired employees and readily donates $100 to the absurdly named Society for Supplying Indigent and Naked Savages in Hindustan with Flannel Shirts. Of this "wealthy proprietor," Thompson writes, "Thou rotten-hearted villain!—morally thou art not fit to brush the cowhide boots of the MAN that thou callest thy servant!" The Dead Man proves himself a justified criminal when he sets fire to Hartless's warehouse, uttering the righteous words, "Your abominable treatment of that poor man is about to meet with a terrible retribution."

Frank Sydney, of course, is the one exception to this rule, a rich man who is good and kind. Nevertheless, he is clearly shown to be a rare specimen who has somehow escaped the corruption and evil that pervade his class. Indeed, although he is rich, he is not linked to a class of similar people. An orphan who lives alone on an inheritance from an uncle, Frank disdains the company of his wealthy acquaintances and seeks companionship, as well as opportunities for doing good, among the poor.

The injustice of class divisions in America is again made clear in the scene of Frank Sydney's arrest, which provides "an idea of the way in which justice is sometimes administered in New York." Frank receives profuse apologies when a policeman discovers he is rich, and leaves "disgusted with the injustice and partiality of this petty minion of the law; for . . . had he himself been in reality nothing more than a poor sailor, as his garb indicated him to be, the three words, 'lock him up,' would have decided his fate for that night; and . . . upon the following

94. Jeffrey G. Williamson and Peter H. Lindert, *American Inequality: A Macroeconomic History* (New York: Academic Press, 1964), pp. 36–37, 101, 141.
95. *Jack Harold*, p. 7.

morning the three words, 'send him over,' would have decided his fate for the ensuing six months."

The Reverend Sinclair has a similar experience when he is arrested for drunk and disorderly behavior. The judge initially intends to put him in prison, saying, "Looks guilty—old offender—thief, no doubt—send him up for six months!" Only after Sinclair whispers a few words to him does the judge recognize him and say, "Dr. Sinclair—humph! sentence is revoked—you're discharged; the devil!— about to send you up for six months—a great mistake, upon my word—ha, ha, ha!" This judge "had himself been drunk the night before," and he takes a cut of the money and property the police steal from the unjustly accused. His corruption is typical, Thompson tells us, of his colleagues, who often "examine" female witnesses in their private chambers with licentious thoroughness. Sinclair witnesses even greater injustice, however, the night before his appearance in court, when he is locked in a cold cell among a crowd of miserable men, one of whom freezes to death before morning. The victim is described as "a poor fellow creature, whose only crime had been his poverty," and Thompson uses the incident to denounce the entire structure of government: "Out upon such justice and such laws, which tolerate such barbarities to one whose misfortunes should be pitied, not visited by the damnable cruelty of the base hirelings of a corrupt misgovernment!"

In addition to corrupt officials, Thompson's fiction also abounds in hypocritical reformers. In this respect it echoed the cases of several real-life reformers who got into serious trouble because of evidence that they secretly took pleasure in the very vices they denounced. For example, the Washingtonian temperance movement came into disrepute in 1845 when its chief promoter, John B. Gough, disappeared for a week, then was found in a whorehouse evidently recovering from a bender, though some of his followers accepted his flimsy story that he had accidentally swallowed drugged cherry soda and was spirited away by prostitutes.

The drunken temperance reformer was an especially common character in Thompson's novels. Mark Twain, who in the 1850s apprenticed in the same Manhattan journalistic circles that produced Thompson, would later immortalize the figure in his portrait of the Duke, who, when he first joins Huck, has been "runnin' a little temperance revival" that had brought in good money until the report spread that he was wont to enjoy "a private jug, on the sly."[96] Twain borrowed this ironic figure from writers such as Thompson, who had previously popularized it. In *City Crimes*, Thompson satirizes John Gough as Samuel Cough, "a distinguished advocate of temperance." He presents Cough swigging brandy, singing "obscene songs," and explaining his whorehouse mishap as

> a bad scrape I got into, in Albany; I got infernally drunk, and slept in a brothel, which was all very well, you know, and nothing unusual—but people found it out! Well, I got up a cock-and-bull story about drinking drugged soda, and some people believe it and some people don't. Now, when I get corned, I keep out of sight.— Ah, temperance spouting is a great business!

96. Mark Twain, *Adventures of Huckleberry Finn* (1885; rpt., New York: W. W. Norton, 1977), p. 99.

Thompson depicted the figure again in *The Countess*, which portrays "a great temperance advocate, and a friend to moral reform" who "never visited the metropolis without the participation of metropolitan pleasures," including drinking and whoring.[97] In *Adventures of a Pickpocket*, the Unitarian reformer Shadbelt drinks himself into a stupor while mouthing temperance truisms: "A drop more, if you—hic—please, Mr. Whanger. The sin of intemperance brings many—many souls within the clutches of—hic—Satan."[98] In another novel Thompson describes an evangelical temperance reformer, the Reverend Helphire Howler, as a "brandy-sucking, psalm-singing, sanctimonious old hypocrite."[99]

Thompson harps so insistently on hypocrisy that he can be identified as an important popularizer of his era's most subversive character type, the oxymoronic oppressor: the outwardly respectable but inwardly corrupt social leader. In antebellum literature this figure had various avatars, including the Christian slaveholder (Thomas Auld of Frederick Douglass's *Narrative*), the churchgoing capitalist (such as the banker Job Joneson in Lippard's *The Quaker City*), and the double-dealing judge (most notably Jaffrey Pynchon of Hawthorne's *House of the Seven Gables*). Although all of these character types appear in Thompson's fiction, it was another version of the oxymoronic oppressor—the reverend rake—that received special attention.

Cases of sexual misconduct were reported regularly in the *National Police Gazette* during the time that Thompson was writing novels. One *Gazette* story, "Incest by a Clergymen on Three Daughters," recounted the investigation of a Massachusetts preacher whose daughters charged him with having raped them many times.[100] Another, "More Religious Hypocrites," described parishioners in a Methodist church on Long Island who were "detected in acts of lasciviousness and beastiality [sic], unequalled in the vilest brothels of The [Five] Points."[101] Similar stories appeared under titles such as "A Reverend Rascal" and "The Reverend Seducer." One of the period's most notorious scandals, reported in the *Gazette* under the heading "A Reverend Wretch," involved the popular preacher John Newland Maffitt, who arranged a mock marriage with a young woman, enjoyed her sexually for ten days, then cast her off, aided in his scheme by two other clergymen. "The reader now may see what some of these preachers are!" editorialized the *Gazette*. "Hypocrisy, cant, espionage, malice, lust, and all uncharitableness pour from their hearts as filth from a corrupted fountain."[102] Public outrage also greeted shocking revelations about the Anglican archbishop of New York, Benjamin T. Onderdonk, who in 1845 was put on trial and then defrocked for having seduced a number of his female parishioners.

97. *The Countess, or Memoirs of Women of Leisure: Being a Series of Intrigues with the Bloods, and a Faithful Delineation of the Private Frailties of Our First Men, Respectfully Dedicated to the Lawyers, Merchants, and Divines of the Day* (Boston: Berry & Wright, 1849), p. 48.
98. *Adventures of a Pickpocket, or, Life at a Fashionable Watering Place* (New York, n. d.), p. 33.
99. *The Ladies' Garter*, p 56.
100. *National Police Gazette*, December 12, 1846.
101. Ibid., January 22, 1848.
102. Ibid., December 9, 1848.

Given the number of such cases, it is perhaps understandable that Thompson generalized that "within the pale of every church, hypocrisy, secret and damning hypocrisy of heart, is a predominating quality," and that "every church wants a purging, a complete cleaning out."[103] In *Venus in Boston* he describes an average preacher: "Look at that venerable looking old gentleman, who every Sabbath stands in his pulpit to declaim against wickedness and fleshly lusts. Mark his libidinous eye, as he follows that painted strumpet to her filthy den." A lecherous criminal in *The Road to Ruin* contemplates satisfying his lust by entering the ministry: "Perhaps I may become a parson—who knows? I have often thought that I possessed brass and licentious inclinations in sufficient quantity to qualify me to become a shining light—a pillar of the church."[104] In *City Crimes* he fictionalizes Maffitt as the Reverend John Marrowfat, who has sexual adventures and drinking sprees with his reformer friend Samuel Cough. Marrowfat is just one of several reverend rakes in *City Crimes*. Others include the Reverend Balaam Flanders and the Rev. Sinclair. Flanders has an affair with one of his parishioners, whose teenaged daughter, knowing him to be a "reverend libertine" and "a consummate scoundrel and hypocrite," tortures him by leading him on when he tries to seduce her as well.

Sinclair is Thompson's most deeply probed religious hypocrite. Though not as multifaceted a character as Arthur Dimmesdale of *The Scarlet Letter*, Sinclair bears comparison with Hawthorne's fallen minister. Just as Dimmesdale is a learned, powerful preacher whose public denunciations of sin cloak his own failings, so Sinclair is a "learned and talented divine" who decries the world's "sins and follies" even though he is privately given to lust. Both ministers are the relatively weak pawns of sexually aggressive women, Dimmesdale of Hester Prynne, who tells him that their union had "a consecration of its own," and Sinclair of Josephine Franklin, who lures him to bed.[105] Like Hawthorne, too, Thompson shows understanding and compassion for his minister's fall from grace. A minister, he writes, is "very often thrown into the society of pretty women of his flock, under circumstances which are dangerously fascinating. The 'sister,' instead of maintaining a proper reserve, grows too communicative and too familiar, and the minister, who is but a man . . . often in an unguarded moment forgets his sacred calling."

Hawthorne's portrait of religious hypocrisy is more morally resonant than Thompson's, for Dimmesdale is conscience-stricken and publicly confesses his sin, whereas Sinclair unrepentantly enjoys his follies and sinks willingly into ignominy. But Thompson's portrait is almost as tragic as Hawthorne's. Sinclair's descent from public renown to lonely wretchedness is harrowing. After being cast off by Josephine Franklin, Sinclair becomes "a wine bibber and a lover of the flesh." Soon he loses his job, his salary, and his home. Now a penniless beggar and street drunkard, he enters a saloon, where, in response to mocking calls for "A sermon!"

103. *The Countess*, p. 19.
104. *The Road to Ruin: or, the Felon's Doom.* (New York: F. A. Brady, ca. 1851), p.12.
105. Nathaniel Hawthorne, *The Scarlet Letter* (1850; rpt., New York: W. W. Norton, 1998) 1: 1411.

he delivers "a wild, incoherent harangue, made up of eloquence, blasphemy, and obscenity," until he is pelted with rotten eggs and driven out into the stormy night. Finally "homeless, shelterless—ragged, dirty, starving," he goes to his former fine home on Broadway, seeking help from its current owner. The latter turns out to be a master printer, Mr. Grump, "one of the miserable whelps who fatten on the unpaid labor of those in their employ." Grump cruelly sends him away, and, dazed and confused, Sinclair stumbles into an unfenced pit and dies.

Mysteries of the American City

The grim fate of Sinclair points to a dark thread that runs through nearly all of Thompson's narratives. Along with sexual adventurousness and social satire, his novels have an undercurrent of ambiguity. His fictional world is one in which goodness often falters and wickedness often succeeds. American society, in his view, is a frighteningly fluid realm of dizzying contrasts and fleeting happiness. Sinclair is just one of many Thompson characters who fall from prominent social peaks, illustrating that people's class positions may be not only arbitrary and unfair but also unstable. Few of Thompson's characters live the American dream of upward mobility; instead, most could be said to enact the American nightmare, an experience of dramatic class descent, in which people fall out of the middle class and are unable to regain their position.

As exaggerated as his fiction may seem, there is some truth to Thompson's claim that he was representing real life. He writes that his aim in *Venus in Boston* is "to adhere as closely as possible to truth and reality, and to depict scenes and adventures which have actually occurred." The instability of his characters' lives reflected the prolonged economic upheavals that beset Americans after the panic of 1837, just as his contrasts between wealth and poverty exposed the nation's growing class divisions. The frequent success of his characters in using disguises and shams to advance themselves mirrored what many were calling the Age of Humbug, the period that produced Barnum, quack medicines, and the confidence man. As we have shown, his treatments of sex and social protest were often anchored in real life.

Even the urban landscape of his novels reflected the social and physical geography of America's cities. Between 1835 and 1860 cities were growing tremendously, at a time when public service departments—sanitary commissions, police and fire departments, park departments, networks of homeless shelters, and the like—were not yet sufficiently organized to aid social outcasts effectively or improve the lives of average citizens. Such departments would arise during and after the Civil War. Before then, America's cities were in many ways chaotic. Public gatherings, unchecked by any trained police force, often degenerated into riots. Fires, fought by eager but undisciplined companies of "b'hoys," regularly became conflagrations consuming entire city blocks. Urban poor districts, particularly New York's Five Points, were infamous for their squalor, unrelieved by the housing projects and shelters that later brought a modicum of order to the slums. Many city streets were unpaved, turning into mud in the winter and dust in the summer.

Garbage, in an age before regulated trash collection, was freely tossed onto the streets, where scavenging pigs were the only reliable means of public waste removal. Historians agree that in the rapid expansion of the 1830s and 1840s, American city dwellers lost social knowledge of and physical contact with one another. The city was suddenly an overwhelming place, and novelists who described urban mysteries depicted this new estrangement with awe.

Thompson hyperbolically but powerfully delineates the instability and squalor of the antebellum urban environment. Later, the literary naturalists would limn city life as a Darwinian contest for survival. Thompson presaged them by depicting its bleakness and impersonality. "All was cold selfishness," he writes of a crowded city hovel. "There was no room in any heart for the holy feeling of human brotherhood. The struggle to live—the fight for existence amidst the dense throngs of such a city as this, had smothered all gentle sensibilities. To each, each seemed a foe, and even the common courtesies of life were submerged in the conflict to exist."[106] *City Crimes*, in particular, is a suggestive evocation of the gloomy side of life in Manhattan. The quintessential city mysteries novel, it offers a view of the urban landscape unlike those found in more mainstream, middle-class literature.

At first glance, the novel's protagonist, Frank Sydney, might seem to be a specimen of what some critics, following Walter Benjamin, have called the *flâneur*: a middle-class urban wanderer who interprets the strange and potentially overwhelming city in a way comprehensible to middle-class readers.[107] However, while Frank does wander the streets and encounter unfamiliar people, his viewpoint is not that of the narrative voice, and his story is not the only one that it follows. The omniscient narrator relates alternately the actions of Frank, Julia, the Franklins, Sinclair, the Dead Man, and others, weaving together a number of stories that repeatedly intersect with one another and then diverge again. Moreover, even when Frank is the focus, we do not necessarily see things through his eyes. In chapters 5 and 6, in fact, he appears in disguise, as a "stranger" who interacts with common men in a bar and then in the Vaults. Only in chapter 7 is it revealed, though most likely "the reader need not be told, that the stranger of the Dark Vaults, and Frank Sydney, were one and the same person."

Furthermore, Frank is not the source of knowledge or interpretation, which instead come most often from working- or criminal-class characters. This is true for information about Frank's personal life—Frank learns about his wife's infidelity from thieves who have stolen her letters—as well as for the larger mysteries of the city and its geography. On repeated descents into the Vaults, he must be led by

106. *Mysteries and Miseries of Philadelphia, by a Member of the Philadelphia Bar* (New York: Williams, n.d.), p. 8.

107. For a discussion of the *flâneur* in antebellum writing, see Hans Bergmann, *God in the Street: New York Writing from the Penny Press to Melville* (Philadelphia: Temple University Press, 1995), and Dana Brand, *The Spectator and the City in Nineteenth-Century American Literature* (New York: Cambridge University Press, 1991). Neither Bergmann nor Brand focuses on the city mysteries genre. See also Walter Benjamin, "On Some Motifs in Baudelaire," in *Illuminations*, ed. Hannah Arendt (New York: Shocken, 1968), pp. 155–200.

members of the Dead Man's gang, and is ultimately able to escape from them only by following the Doctor out through the sewers.

The process of coming to understand the city is represented in *City Crimes* not as gaining an overview or a panoramic picture of the whole, but as learning the secret routes and hidden entrances in a particular part of it. Those who really know the city, it is implied, are not the middle-class people able to traverse a variety of neighborhoods and look at them as distanced observers, but the lower-class denizens of a neighborhood who know what is concealed behind its facades and beneath its streets. In keeping with this conception of knowledge, the novel contains no panoramic vistas or broad cityscapes, but instead abounds in visions of small or enclosed spaces: "the Dark Vaults," the "Infernal Regions," a "subterranean village," small hovels, the forty-foot cave. The Dead Man spends one chapter nailed inside a box; Fred Archer suffocates in a vault; Frank is imprisoned in the Manhattan jail called the Tombs.

City Crimes also lacks any example of what is often considered the prototypical urban scene: a street bustling with crowds of people. When large groups or crowds of strangers do appear, the individuals that make up these crowds are portrayed as pitiable at best, and horrible at worst. For example, in chapter 5 a group of people in a tavern make up a motley crew of about a dozen persons who are variously described as "wretched," "filthy-looking," "villainous-looking," "miserable and ragged," and "overrun with vermin." A similar group confronts Sinclair when he spends the night in jail. There about twenty men are "huddled together in the cold"; they are condemned as "a swarm of felons, vile negroes, vagabonds and loafers—the scum of the city!" Belonging to this crowd has degraded them completely: "made hideous and inhuman by vice and wretchedness," they curse and glare at one another with "savage eyes." The most miserable crowd of all, however, dwells in the subterranean village of the Dark Vaults. There Kinchen and Frank come upon a cave "literally crammed with human beings. Men and women, boys and girls, young children, negroes, and hogs were laying [sic] indiscriminately upon the ground, in a compact mass. These beings were vile and loathsome in appearance, beyond all human conception, every one of them was a mass of rags, filth, disease, and corruption."

To be part of a crowd, in *City Crimes*, is thus to be part of a myriad, a swarm, a motley crew; to be crammed or huddled together in vice or wretchedness, indiscriminate, inhuman, loathsome. Rather than thematizing and conceptually mastering the crowd, as some middle-class fiction did, *City Crimes* negates its existence whenever possible, retaining it only as the ultimate nightmare awaiting those who fall to the absolute bottom of the social structure.

Many of the spaces in Thompson's novels also correspond to actual places in the cities he chose as settings. The Dark Vaults, with tunnels and hidden chambers that provided an impenetrable hiding place for criminals and outcasts, was the fictional correlative of an actual network of tunnels that underlay New York's slums throughout the nineteenth century and beyond. In 1890 Jacob Riis would describe "the big vaulted sewers [which] had long been a runway for thieves—the Swamp

Angels—who through them easily escaped when chased by the police, enormous tunnels in which a man may walk upright the full distance of the block and into the Cherry Street sewers—if he likes the fun and is not afraid of the rats."[108] Several decades later, when the future poet William Carlos Williams was interning as a doctor in Hell's Kitchen, he could note that the area "was said to be honeycombed with interconnecting tunnels from flat to flat so that a man who had taken it on the lam, once he got inside an entry, was gone from the police forever."[109]

In Thompson's fictionalized rendition, the tunnels were more than just a criminal hideout. They epitomized everything degraded in New York life. Thompson generalizes that his aim in the novel is to "drag forth from the dark and mysterious labyrinths of great cities, the hidden iniquities which taint the moral atmosphere, and assimilate human nature to brute creation." Nowhere are these "hidden iniquities" more evident than in the Dark Vaults, a maze of horrors that makes the Paris sewers in Victor Hugo's *Les Miserables* or the underground crypt in Hawthorne's *The Marble Faun* seem tame by comparison. The site of incest, murder, madness, torture, and cannibalism, the Dark Vaults are also—perhaps most horrifically—an extension of the lives of ordinary antebellum New Yorkers. Many of the garbage-devouring pigs familiar on Manhattan's muddy streets, Thompson tells us, ended up in the Dark Vaults. The animals ventured into street sewers "to devour the vegetable matter, filth and offal that accumulate there," and, unable to get out, found their way to the vaults, where they were "killed and eaten by the starving wretches" who lived underground. All the dregs of the unsanitary city seeped into the cavernous vaults, which were connected to the main sewer draining into the East River. The novel's hero, Frank Sydney, is forced to escape his subterranean captors by wading up to his chest through "the dark, sluggish and nauseous stream of the filthy drainings of the vast city overhead," surrounded by rats, reptiles, and rotting corpses.

Frank's plunge into the urban underworld, where he is threatened at every turn, suggests how evanescent is the happiness of even the best-intentioned city dweller. In this hidden realm he encounters the Dead Man, the devilish prince of the Dark Vaults and the very incarnation of city mysteries. Living in unrestrained brutishness, he and his criminal cohorts display the raw ferocity underlying city life, as Thompson views it. The Dead Man torments Frank, cuts out Clinton Romaine's tongue, rapes Julia, torches the Franklins' house, and disfigures Josephine Franklin. A remorseless killer who takes sadistic pleasure in his victims' pain, he declares, "Would that the human race had but one single throat, and I could cut it at a stroke."

More than just a melodramatic villain, he is a cultural symbol, since his amorality stems largely from his experience with a number of social phenomena thematized by Thompson. Having espoused crime in his youth, the Dead Man becomes, in

108. Jacob Riis, *How the Other Half Lives*, excerpted in *Writing New York: A Literary Anthology*, ed. Phillip Lopate (New York: Library of America, 1998), p. 299.
109. William Carlos Williams, "Hell's Kitchen," ibid., p. 731.

rapid succession, a quack doctor, a reverend rake, and a drunken temperance lecturer. As a doctor, he recalls, he was "overrun with patients, none of whom I cured." As a clergymen, he spent most of his time with the "young sisters" of his flock. As a temperance leader, he reports, "for over a year, I lectured in public, and got drunk in private—glorious times! but at last people began to suspect that I was inspired by the spirit of alcohol, instead of the spirit of reform." After thriving as a crowd-pleasing hypocrite, the Dead Man turns gleefully to overt crime.

The Dead Man, then, embodies many of the social oxymorons that, in Thompson's texts, make virtue and vice empty signifiers. Having donned and discarded religious and reform disguises with the ease of Melville's confidence man, the Dead Man is prepared to murder and torture without a twinge of conscience. A pastiche of contradictory elements in American culture, the Dead Man demonstrates the utter moral vacuum that could result when all of these elements were combined in one person. The fact that even this merciless killer is presented as being superior to the wealthy businessman Paul Hartless indicates the depth of Thompson's cynicism.

Though not as given to dark philosophizing as his contemporaries Melville and Hawthorne, Thompson was capable of gloomy meditation. Indeed, the city mysteries genre as a whole is overwhelmingly dark and negative, and offers neither hope nor comfort, except that which comes from a cathartic echo of one's own outrage and fear. "How inexplicable are the affairs of life!"[110] Just as Melville's Pierre, after moving from a rural idyll into a city nightmare, concludes, "Oh, what a vile juggler and cheat is man!" Thompson has a disillusioned city character declare that "the world is only a cheat and a continual lie."[111]

In a sense Thompson's cynicism was even deeper than that of the canonical writers, all of whom were aware of the same cultural paradoxes that informed his fiction. Like Thompson, Hawthorne tapped into such popular stereotypes as the reverend rake involved with a parishioner (*The Scarlet Letter*), the double-dealing judge and justified criminal (*House of the Seven Gables*), and the immoral reformer (*The Blithedale Romance*). Similarly, Melville transformed several stock antebellum characters, including the oxymoronic oppressor (the "ungodly, god-like" Ahab)[112], the well-intentioned hero tormented by city mysteries (Pierre), the rebellious black (Babo), and the confidence man. Whitman, like Thompson, expressed disgust with corruption in high places, as is reflected in his tirade in the 1855 preface to *Leaves of Grass* against the "swarms of cringers, suckers, doughfaces, lice of politics, planners of sly involutions for their own preferment to city offices or state legislatures or the judiciary or congress or the presidency."[113]

These writers forged a number of artistic alternatives to the grim social realities

110. *Adventures of a Pickpocket*, p. 87.
111. Herman Melville, *Pierre; or, The Ambiguities* (1852; rpt., New York: Library of America, 1984), p. 318; *The Mysteries of Bond-Street*, p. 58.
112. Herman Melville, *Moby-Dick; or, The Whale* (1851; rpt., New York: W. W. Norton, 1967), p. 77.
113. Preface to Whitman, p. 18.

that confronted them. In *The Scarlet Letter*, for instance, Hawthorne recast nineteenth-century stereotypes in the context of seventeenth-century Puritanism, investing them with a moral resonance absent in Thompson. Arthur Dimmesdale may be as sinful as Thompson's reverend rakes, Hester as rebellious as his heroines, and Chillingworth as wicked as his villains. But because Hawthorne probes these characters' moral and psychological depths within a fully realized Puritan symbology of guilt and retribution, they achieve true earnestness and profundity. Melville's Ahab is as cruel and overbearing as Thompson's oxymoronic oppressors; but, yoked with mythic archetypes (King Ahab of 1 Kings, Prometheus, Lear) and sent on a voyage that symbolizes truth seeking, he has a philosophical suggestiveness lacking in Thompson's oxymoronic characters. Pierre's plunge into the squalor and criminality of New York life is in the vein of popular city mysteries, but it takes on entirely new dimensions when linked with Melville's own experience as a misunderstood, conflict-ridden author. Whitman, believing that the nation was on the verge of unraveling becasue of political corruption and sectional quarrels, set out in *Leaves of Grass* to encompass all of America and in doing so heal its deepening divisions.

Thompson used none of these artistic strategies to combat the social ills he perceived. Instead these ills were enacted in his fast-paced narratives, populated with semi-grotesques and tormented innocents. Although he can be faulted for not rising above the social mire and introducing a fresh artistic vision, he remains a valuable specimen of nineteenth-century popular culture. If each of the major writers fashioned what Richard Poirier calls an artistic "world elsewhere," apart from American society, Thompson depicted a troubled, often nightmarish "world here," embodying the frustrations and tensions of city life.[114] All too painfully, he perceived cultural contradictions that negated moral effort. Thematically, his novels strip cultural signifiers—religious, reformist, and socioeconomic—of clear signifieds, leaving the reader hovering over a hermeneutic abyss.

In this regard, there is symbolism in the memorable murder of the Dead Man by the Doctor toward the end of *City Crimes*. When fragments of the Dead Man's body are scattered after the explosion of the bomb planted in his stomach, we are reminded of the willfully fragmented messages of the novel as a whole. When alive, the Dead Man, as his name implies, embodied the death of morality. In death, he becomes the emblem of the ultimate dispersal of meaning in the fractured world Thompson so powerfully represented.

---

114. Richard Poirier, *A World Elsewhere: The Place of Style in American Literature* (New York: Oxford University Press, 1966), pp. 3-4.

NOTE ON THE TEXTS

The text of *Venus in Boston; A Romance of City Life* follows a microfilmed copy of the first edition (New York, 1849) in the Boston Public Library. This was originally published under Thompson's primary pseudonym, "Greenhorn." All footnotes in the texts of this work and those following are by the author. Obvious typographical errors have been silently corrected. In a few instances indecipherable words in the original of this text and those following have been indicated thus: [*illegible word*]. The characteristic spelling "extacies" has been left as in the original.

The text of *City Crimes; or Life in New York and Boston* follows a microfilmed copy of the first edition (Boston: W. Berry, 1849) in the Newberry Library, Chicago. As with *Venus in Boston*, this was originally published under Thompson's primary pseudonym, "Greenhorn." Obvious typographical errors have been silently corrected, but the nonstandard spellings "courtezan," "thro'," and "tho'" have been left as in the original. The exclusive use of single quotes, in the original text, even for dialogue within a story told by a character, has also been preserved.

The text of *My Life: or, The Adventures of Geo. Thompson* follows a microfilmed copy of the first edition (Boston: Federhen, 1854) in the American Antiquarian Society, Worcester, Massachusetts. As with the other texts, obvious typographical errors have been silently corrected.

VENUS IN BOSTON;

A ROMANCE OF CITY LIFE.

"Ah, Vice! how soft are thy voluptuous ways!
While boyish blood is mantling, who can 'scape
The fascination of thy magic gaze?
A Cherub-hydra round us dost thou gape,
And mould to every taste, thy dear, delusive shape."

BYRON'S CHILDE HAROLD

{First published 1849}

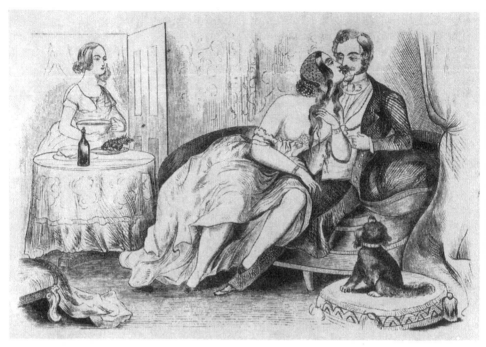

Frontispiece to *Venus in Boston*, 1850 edition. By courtesy of the Trustees of the Boston Public Library.

INTRODUCTION

I conceive it to be a prominent fault of most of the tales of fiction that are written and published at the present day, that they are not sufficiently *natural*—their style is too much exaggerated—and in aiming to produce startling effects, they depart too widely from the range of probability to engage the undivided interest of the enlightened and judicious reader. Believing as I do that the romance of reality—the details of common, everyday life—the secret history of things hidden from the public gaze, but of the existence of which there can be no manner of doubt—are endowed with a more powerful and absorbing interest than any extravagant flight of imagination can be, it shall be my aim in the following pages to adhere as closely as possible to truth and reality; and to depict scenes and adventures which have actually occurred, and which have come to my knowledge in the course of an experience no means limited—an experience replete with facilities for acquiring a perfect insight into human nature, and a knowledge of the many secret springs of human action.

The most favorable reception which my former humble productions have met with, at the hands of a kind and indulgent public, will, I trust, justify the hope that the present Tale may meet with similar encouragement. It certainly shall not prove inferior to any of its predecessors in the variety of its incidents or the interest of its details; and as a *romance of city life*, it will amply repay the perusal of all country readers, as well as those who reside in cities.

With these remarks, preliminary and explanatory, I proceed at once to draw the curtain, and unfold the opening scene of my drama.

CHAPTER I

The blind Basket-maker and his family.

It was a winter's day, and piercing cold; very few pedestrians were to be seen in Boston, and those few were carefully enveloped in warm cloak and great coats, for the weather was of that intense kind that chills the blood and penetrates to the very bone. Even Washington street—that great avenue of wealth and promenade of fashion, usually thronged with the pleasure-seeking denizens of the metropolis—was comparatively deserted, save by a few shivering mortals, who hurried on their way with rapid footsteps, anxious to escape from the relentless and iron grasp of

3

hoary winter. And yet on that day, and in that street, there stood upon the pavement directly opposite the "Old South Church," a young girl of about the age of fourteen years, holding in her hand a small basket of fruit, which she offered to every passer-by. Now there was nothing very extraordinary in this, neither was there anything very unusual in the meek and pleading look of the little fruit girl, as she timidly raised her large blue eyes to the face of every one who passed her—for such humble callings, and such mute but eloquent appeals, are the common inheritance of many, very many of God's poor in large cities, and do not generally attract any great degree of notice from the careless (and too often unfeeling) children of prosperity; —but there was something in the appearance of the pale, sad girl, as, in her scant attire she shivered in the biting wind, not often met with in the humble disciples of poverty—a certain subdued, gentle air, partaking of much unconscious grace, that whispered of better days gone by.

At length the clock in the steeple of the "Old South" pronounced that the dinner hour had arrived—and despite the intense cold, the street soon became alive with people hurrying to and fro; for what weather can induce a hungry man to neglect that important era in the events of the day—his *dinner?* This perfumed exquisite hurried by to fulfil an appointment and dine at Parker's; the more sober and economical citizen hastened on his way to "feed" at some establishment of less pretensions and more moderate prices; while the mass of the diners-out repaired to appease their hunger at the numerous cheap refectories that abound in the neighborhood. But the poor, forlorn little fruit girl stood unnoticed by the passing throng, which like the curtain of a river hurried by, leaving her upon its margin, a neglected, drooping flower.

"Ah," she murmured—"why will they not buy my fruit? I have not taken a single penny to-day, and how can I return home to poor grandfather and my little brother, without food? Good people, could you but see them, your hearts would be softened—." And the tears rolled down her cheeks.

While thus soliloquizing, she had not noticed the approach of a little old man, in a faded, threadbare suit, and with a care-worn, wrinkled countenance. He stopped short when he saw that she was weeping, and in an abrupt, yet not unkind manner, inquired—

"My child, why do you weep?"

The girl looked up through her tears at the stranger, and in a few artless words related her simple story. She was an orphan, and with her little brother, lived with her grandfather. They were very poor, and were wholly dependent upon a small pittance which the grandfather (who was blind) daily earned by basket making, together with the very small profits which she realized by the sale of fruit in the streets. Her grandfather was very ill, and unable to work, and the poor family had not tasted food that day.

"Poor thing!" exclaimed the little old man when she had concluded her affecting narrative. He straightway began fumbling in his pockets, and it seemed with no very satisfactory result, for he muttered—"The devil! I have no money—not a copper; bah! I can give you nothing. But hold! where do you live, my child?"

The girl stated her place of residence, which was in an obscure but respectable section of the city. The little old man produced a greasy memorandum book, and a stump of a pencil, with which he noted down the direction; then, uttering a grunt of satisfaction, but without saying a single word, he resumed his walk, and was soon lost in the crowd.

Evening came, and with it a furious snow-storm. Madly the wind careered through the streets—now fiercely dashing the snow into the faces of such unfortunate travellers as chanced to be abroad in that wild weather—now shaking the roofs of crazy old houses—and now tearing away in the distance with a howl of triumph at its power. The storm fiend was abroad—the elements were at war, and yet in the midst of that furious tumult, the poor fruit girl was toiling on her way towards her humble home. She reached it at last. It was a poor and lowly place, the abode of humble but decent poverty; yet the angel of peace had spread her wings there, and contentment had sat with them at their frugal board. True, it was but a garret; yet that little family, with hearts united by holy love, felt that to them it was a *home*. And then its little window commanded a distant view of a shining river, and green, pleasant fields beyond; and all day long, in fine weather, the cheerful sunshine looked in upon them, casting a gleam of gladness upon their hearts. It had been a happy home to the blind basket-maker and his grandchildren; but alas! sickness had laid its heavy hand upon the aged man, and want and wretchedness had become their portion.

The girl entered with a sad heart, for she brought no relief to the hungering and sorrowing inmates of that lowly dwelling. Without saying a word she seated herself at the bedside of her grandfather, and taking his hand in hers, bedewed it with her tears. The old man turned towards her, and said—

"Thou art weeping, Fanny—what distresses thee? Tears are for the aged and the sorrowing—not for the young. Thou hast not brought us food?—well, well; the will of Heaven be done! I shall soon be in the grave, and then thou and Charley—"

"No, no, grandfather, pray don't say so," cried the poor girl, sobbing as if her heart would break—"what should we do without you? Heaven may spare you many happy years. I can work for you, and—"

"So can I, too," rejoined her brother Charley, a lad eight or nine years of age— "and only to-day I got a promise from Mr. Scott the tailor, that I might, when a little older, run of errands for him, and my wages will be a dollar and a half a week—only think how much money I shall earn!"

"Thou art a brave little man," said the grandfather—"but, my children, let us put our trust in God, and if it is His will that my earthly pilgrimage should end, be it so! Thank Heaven, I owe nothing, and can die at peace with all the world."

It had long been Fanny's custom to occupy an hour of so every evening, in reading to her grandfather. But that evening she did not, as usual, draw up the little table, and open the pages of some well-thumbed, ancient volume, to read, for perhaps the twentieth time, of the valorous deeds of some famed knight of the olden time, or mayhap, of the triumphant death of some famed martyr for religion's sake. For alas! the frugal but wholesome meal which had always preceded the reading of those ancient chronicles, was now wanting; and the little family sat listening to the raging of the pitiless storm without and counting the weary moments as they passed.

The bell in a neighboring steeple had just told the hour of nine, when, as the echo of that last stroke died away in the distance, a heavy step was heard ascending the stairs that led to their humble apartment. As the sound approached nearer, Fanny heard a voice occasionally giving utterance to expressions of extreme irritation and impatience, accompanied by certain sounds indicating that the person, whoever it might be, often stumbled upon the dark, narrow and somewhat dilapidated stair-case. "Blood and bomb-shells!" exclaimed a voice—"I shall never reach the top, and my shins are broken. The devil! there I go again. Corporal Grimsby, thou art an ass, and these stairs are the devil's trap!" And here the luckless unknown paused a moment to breathe, rub his shins, and refresh himself with an emphatic imprecation upon all dark and broken stair-cases in general, but upon *that* one in particular. At this moment, Fanny made her appearance at the landing with a light, and was astonished to behold her new acquaintance of that afternoon, the little old man who had inquired her residence. A most rueful expression sat upon his visage, and he carried upon one arm a huge basket. The friendly light enabled him soon to reach the end of his journey; he entered the little room without ceremony, and depositing his burden upon the table, exclaimed—

"Hark'ee, child, I am an old soldier, am not apt to grumble at trifles, [*illegible word*] and blunderbusses! I never before got into such a snarl.—Mounting the ramparts of the enemy was mere child's play to it!" Here he began to take out the contents of the basket, meanwhile keeping up a running commentary, during which his countenance wore an expression of the most intense ill-humor, in strange contrast with the evident benevolence of his character and intentions. He found fault with everything which he had brought, although, in truth, the articles were all of excellent quality.

"Here," said he, with a growl of dissatisfaction—"is a pair of chickens—starved, skinny imps, for which I paid double their value to that knave of a poultry merchant—bah! And here are some French rolls, that I'll be sworn are as hard as the French cannon balls that were thrown at Austerlitz. These vegetables are well enough, and this pastry hath a savory smell, but pistols and cutlasses! this wine *looks* as sour as General Grouty's face on a grand parade. Let me draw the cork and taste—no, by the nose of Napoleon! it is excellent—fit for the great Frederick himself. Here, child, haste and spread a cloth, for I am hungrier than a Cossack. Powder and shot! we shall have a supper fit for a Field Marshal!"

By this time the eccentric but kind old man had placed upon the table all the materials of an excellent and substantial repast. This done, he turned to the grandfather of Fanny, who had listened to his speech with much astonishment, and exclaimed—

"Cheer thee up, old friend, cheer thee up, and pick a bone with us; here, wash the cobwebs from thy throat by a hearty draught from this flask. I am an old soldier, and love all men; I stand on no ceremony; so fall to, fall to!"

Saying this, he seated himself at the table, and having seen that all were duly supplied with a liberal portion of the edibles, commenced the attack with [*illegible word*] truly surprising. Nor were the others at all backward in emulating so good an example. The grandfather, whose illness had mainly been produced by a lack of those little luxuries so essential to the debilities and infirmities of advanced age, after partaking sparingly of what was set before him, felt himself much bettered and refreshed thereby; and Fanny, who had dried her tears, and satisfied the cravings of hunger, smiled her gratitude upon the kind provider. Little Charley had already become much attached to "good Corporal Grimsby," who had given him such a nice supper—while the latter gentleman, having finished his meal, drew forth an antiquated pipe, having a Turk's head for the bowl and a coiled serpent for the stem, which having lighted, he proceeded to smoke with much gravity and thoughtfulness. Not a word did he utter, but smoked away in silence, until the clock struck ten; then pocketing his pipe, and depositing the now empty flask and dishes in the basket, he announced his intention of departing. The grandfather was cut short in a grateful acknowledgment of the stranger's kindness, by the abrupt exit of that singular personage, who bolted down stairs with a precipitancy that was truly alarming, scarce waiting for Fanny to light him down.

This singular visit was of course the subject of much surprise and conjecture in the little family of the blind basket-maker; but when Fanny related how the stranger had accosted her in the street, and inquired her residence, they concluded that he was some eccentric but benevolent person, who had taken that method of contributing to the relief of their wants.

And who was this queer little old man, so shabby and threadbare—so "full of strange oaths," —so odd in his manner, so kind in his heart—calling himself Corporal Grimsby—who had come forward at that opportune moment to supply a starving family with food? Time will show.

CHAPTER II

Innocence in the Grip of Lust.

The day which succeeded the stormy night described in the last chapter, was an unusually fine one. The sun shone clear and bright, and many people were abroad to enjoy the fine bracing air, and indemnify themselves for having been kept within doors on the preceding day. The streets were covered with an ample garment of snow, and the merry music of the sleigh-bells was heard in every direction.

At an early hour, Fanny Aubrey (for that was the name of our little heroine,) issued from her dwelling, and taking the sunny side of the streets, resumed her accustomed perambulations, with her basket on her arm. Fanny was small for her age, but exceedingly pretty; her eyes were of a dark blue—her hair a rich auburn— her features radiant with the inexpressible charm of youth and innocence. I have said that her air was superior to her condition; in truth, every motion of hers had in it a certain winning grace, and her step was light as a fawn's, although her figure was not without a certain degree of plumpness, which gave ample promise of a speedy voluptuous development. Though plumpness in the female figure is considered to be incompatible with perfect grace, I agree with those who regard it as decidedly preferable to an excessive thinness, though the latter be accompanied with the lightness of a zephyr, and the grace of a sylph.

Dress is sometimes acknowledged to be a sign of character—and the dress of Fanny Aubrey certainly indicated the native refinement of her mind—for though poor in material and faded by long use, it was well put on and scrupulously neat—indeed, there was something almost coquettish in the style of her bonnet and the arrangement of her scanty shawl—too scanty, alas! to shield her adequately from the inclemency of the weather.

As she passed along the street, her beauty and prepossessing appearance attracted the attention of many gay loiterers, who regard her with various feelings of admiration, pity and surprise that one so lovely should pursue so humble an occupation; nor were there wanting many well-dressed libertines, young and old, who gazed with eyes of lustful desire upon the fair young creature, evidently so unprotected and so poor.

Reader, pardon us if for one brief moment we pause to contemplate the black and hideous character of THE SEDUCER. Should the teeming hosts of hell's dominions meet in grand convention, amid the mysterious darkness and lurid flames of their eternal abode—should that infernal conclave of murderers, robbers, monsters of iniquity, perpetrators of damning crimes; possessors of black hearts and polluted souls on earth, whose mighty sins had sunk them in that burning pit—should all those lost spirits select from among their number, *one fiend*, the worst of them all, to represent them *all* on earth—unite within his being *all* the crimes of which they had collectively been guilty—to show mankind how vast and stupendous have been *all* the sins perpetrated since the creation of the globe—*that fiend* could not cast a blacker shadow upon human nature than doth the seducer of female innocence. Oh! if there be one wretch living who deserves to be cast forth from the society of his fellow men—if there be one who deserves to be trod on as a venomous insect, and crushed as the vilest reptile that crawls—it is he who calmly and deliberately sets himself about the hellish task of accomplishing the ruin of a weak, confiding woman—and then, having sipped the sweets and inhaled the fragrance of the flower, tramples it beneath his feet. Will not the thunderbolts of Omnipotent wrath shatter the perjured soul of such a villain?

But to resume. Fanny Aubrey pursued her walk, and was so fortunate as to escape the insults (except such as were conveyed in glances,) of the many libertines who are ever ready to take advantage of a female in a situation like hers. As she was passing a magnificent mansion in a quarter of the city mainly occupied by the residences of the aristocracy, a beautiful young lady alighted from a splendid sleigh, and observing the little fruit girl, beckoned her to approach. Fanny modestly complied, and the young lady, with one of the sweetest smiles imaginable selected an orange from her basket, and taking out a purse, presented her with a bright gold coin.

"I have no change, Miss," said Fanny, in some confusion.

"Keep the money, my poor girl," rejoined the young lady, with a look of deep compassion, as a tear of pity dimmed her bright eyes—"I am sure you need it; you are much too pretty for such an employment. If you will try and pass this way to-morrow at about this time, you may see me again."

Amid Fanny's heartfelt thanks, the young lady entered the mansion, and the door was closed.

Poor Fanny! she resumed her journey with a light heart. She never before had possessed so much money. Five dollars! the sum seemed inexhaustible, and she began to devise a thousand plans to expend it to advantage—and the fact that she herself was not included in any of those plans, was a beautiful illustration of the unselfishness of her character. Not for a moment did she dream of appropriating it to the purchase of a good warm shawl or dress for herself, although, poor girl! she so much needed both. She would buy a nice comfortable rocking-chair for her grandfather; or a thick great-coat for little Charley—she couldn't make up her mind which, she loved them both so much—yet when she thought of the poor, sick, blind old man, a holy pity triumphed over sisterly affection, and she resolved upon the rocking-chair. Then she determined to hasten homewards to communicate her good fortune to her friends; and on her way she could not help thinking of the beautiful young lady who had given her the money, of her sweet smile, and the kind words she had spoken; and wondered if she should really see her again the next day. These thoughts, and the hope of seeing her benefactress again, made her feel very happy; and she was hastening towards her home with a glad heart, when her footsteps were arrested by a crowd of those dissolute young females, who pervade every section of the city, and are universally known as "apple girls."

These girls are usually from ten to fifteen years of age, and are proverbial for their vicious propensities and dishonesty. Under pretence of selling their fruit, they are accustomed to penetrate into the business portions of the city particularly; and in doing this they have two objects in view. In the first place, if on entering an office or place of business, they find nobody in, an opportunity is afforded them for plunder; and it is needless to say they are ever ready to steal and carry off whatever they can lay their hands on. Secondly, these girls have been brought up in vice from their infancy; they are, for the most part, neither more nor less than common prostitutes, and will freely yield their persons to whoever will pay for the same. —Should the merchant, or lawyer, or man of business, into whose office one of these "apple girls" may chance to intrude, solicit her favors (and there are many miscreants, *respectable* ones, too, who do this, as we shall show,) and offer her a small pecuniary reward, he has only to lock his door and draw his curtains, to accomplish his object without the slightest difficulty. Thus, their ostensible employment of selling fruit is nothing but a cloak for their real trade of prostitution and thieving. The profanity and obscenity of their conversation alone, is a sufficient evidence of their true character.

The girls whom we have mentioned as having encountered Fanny on her return home, were a squalid and dirty set, though several of them were not destitute of good looks, as far as form and features were concerned. They surrounded her with many a fierce oath and ribald jest, and it was easy to see that they were jealous of her superior cleanliness of person and respectability of character.

"Ha, ha!" cried one, a dirty-faced wench of thirteen, clutching Fanny fiercely by the arm, while the poor girl stood afraid and trembling in the midst of that elfish crew—"ha, ha! here is my fine lady, with her smooth face and clean gown, who disdains to keep company with us, and do as we do! Let us tear off her clothes, and roll her in the mire!"

They were proceeding to act upon this suggestion, when Fanny, bewildered and speechless with terror, dropped her gold coin, which she held in her hand, upon the ground. It was instantly snatched up by one of the gang, who was immediately attacked by the others, and a fierce struggle ensued, for the possession of the coin, the young wretches tearing, scratching and biting each other like so many wild cats. During this conflict, Fanny made off as fast as she could run, but was followed and overtaken by one of the gang, a large girl of fifteen, who was known among her companions by the pleasing title of "Sow Nance." She was a thief and prostitute of the most desperate and abandoned character, hideously ugly in person, and of a disposition the most ferocious and deceitful.—Laying her brawny hand upon Fanny's shoulder, she said, in a hoarse and croaking voice—

"See here, Miss What's-yer-name, I wants to speak to you, if you please. You needn't be afraid of me, for I won't hurt you. Them thieving hussies has got your money, and you must make up your loss the best way you can. Look at my basket— you see it's empty, don't yer? I've sold all my fruit already, and if you'll go with me, I'll show you a nice gentleman who will buy all the fruit in your little basket, and pay you well, too. It's not far—will you go with me?"

The prospect of effecting a speedy sale of her stock in trade, was too tempting to be resisted by poor Fanny, especially in view of the severe loss she had just sustained, in being robbed of the money which the kind young lady had given her. She therefore gladly consented to accompany Sow Nance to the nice gentleman who would pay her so well for the contents of her basket.

Poor, innocent, unsuspecting Fanny! she little thought that the abandoned creature at her side was leading her into a snare, imminently dangerous to her peace of mind and future happiness! "I will save up money enough to buy grandfather a rocking-chair, after all," thought she, as she gaily trudged onward, while ever and anon Sow Nance would glare savagely at her from the corners of her snake-like eyes. It is one of the worst qualities peculiar to corrupt human nature, the hatred with which the wicked and abandoned regard the innocent and pure. Fanny had never in the slightest degree injured the wretch who was plotting her ruin;—and Sow Nance had no other reason for hating her, than because she herself was a guilty and polluted being, while Fanny she knew to be without stain or blemish.

In about a quarter of an hour they reached a handsome brick house in South street.

"This is the place," said Sow Nance, as she rang the door bell; the summons was immediately answered by an old negro woman, who, exchanging a significant look with Nance, admitted them, and ushered them into a large parlor. The apartment was handsomely furnished, the walls adorned with many pictures, and the floor covered with a very rich carpet.

"Sit down, young ladies, and I will call Mr. Tickels down," said the old negro woman, as she left the room; in a few moments, a gentleman entered, and regarded Fanny with a gaze so piercing, that the poor girl was covered with confusion.

The gentleman was, to all appearances, full sixty years of age; he was a large, portly man, with very gray hair and a very red face: he was attired in a dressing-gown and slippers, and wore a magnificent diamond pin in his shirt frill.

This man was one of those wealthy beasts whose lusts run riot on the innocence of young females—whose crimes outnumbered the gray hairs upon his head, and whose riches were devoted to no other purpose than the procurement of victims for his appetite, and the gratification of his abominable passions.

A vague, strange fear stole over Fanny, while this gentleman thus viewed her so closely—a fear which she could not define, yet which rendered her excessively uneasy. Apparently the survey was satisfactory to the gentleman—for he smiled, and in doing so displayed two rows of teeth not unlike the fangs of a wolf. Then he beckoned Sow Nance to follow him from the room, and held a whispered conversation with her in the passage.

"Who is she, Nance?" asked the gentleman.

"Not *one of us*," was the reply, "she sells fruit, and is poor, but her folks are respectable; —you must pay me well for bringing her here, for she's handsome."

"True; but are you sure she has never—"

"*Sure!*" replied Nance, almost fiercely—"I'll take my oath on it; hasn't she always kept away from us, and ain't all the girls hating her like h——l, 'cause she's virtuous? Don't you suppose *I* know?"

"Good," said the gentleman; and taking a gold coin from his pocket, he gave it to Nance, who, stooping down, secreted it in her stocking; then she noiselessly opened the front door and left the house, singing in a hoarse voice, as she sped on her way towards Ann street, (where she lived,) these barbarous words:—

> The lamb to the wolf is sold, sold, sold;
> No more she'll return to her fold, fold, fold—
> And Sow Nance will dare another to snare,
> And the wolf shall have her for gold, gold, gold!"

The gentleman (I use the word *ironically*, reader,) re-entered the parlor, advanced to where Fanny was seated, and laying his heavy hand upon the young girl's shoulder, glued his polluted lips to her pure cheek. She sprang from his profaning grasp with a cry of terror, and fled towards the door—it was *locked!* The gentleman laughed, and said—

"No, no, my pretty bird, you cannot escape from your cage so easily; and why should you wish to? Your cage shall have golden wires, and you shall be fed on delicacies, my little flutterer—so smooth the feathers of your bright wings, my dear, and sing your sweetest notes!"

Fanny burst into tears, and fell on her knees before the old libertine. —Young and innocent as she was, a dark suspicion of his purpose came like a shadow over her soul, and she cried in piteous accents—

"Pray, good sir, let me go home to my poor grandfather and my little brother—they will be expecting me, and will feel worried at my absence. Surely, sir, you will not have the heart to harm me—I am but a poor fruit girl, without father or mother. Pray let me go, sir."

That appeal, made touching by the youth and innocence of the speaker, and by her profound distress, might have melted a heart of iron—but it moved not the stony heart of the old villain, and he looked upon her with his cold, hard eyes, and his disgusting smile, as he said—

"Your tears make you doubly interesting, my sweet child. I am afraid that your poor grandfather and your little brother, as you call them, will be obliged to wait a long while for your return, let them worry ever so much at your absence. You say truly that I have not the heart to harm you, a poor fruit girl,—no, I will make a lady of you; and as you have, you say, neither father nor mother, I will supply their place, my pretty dear, and be your *lover* into the bargain. Those coarse garments shall be changed for silks and satins,—that shining hair shall be made radiant with gems,—jewels shall sparkle on that fair neck, and on those taper fingers,—you shall ride in a carriage, and have servants to wait on you,—and you shall sleep on a downy bed, and live in a grand house, like this. Say, will not all these fine things be better than selling fruit in the cold streets?"

But the sobbing girl implored him to let her go home. The gentleman ground his teeth with rage.

"Well, well," said he, after a brief pause, and speaking in an assumed tone of kindness, "you *shall* go home, since you wish it." He rang a bell, and the old negro woman appeared, to whom he whispered for a few moments, and then left the room.

"Come, Miss," said the old wench, addressing Fanny, with a grin that was anything but encouraging or expressive of a friendly feeling—"come with me up stairs, and wash the tears from your pretty face; then you shall go home—ha, ha, ha!"

It was a demon's laugh, full of malice and hatred; yet Fanny smiled through her tears, for she saw not the old wretch's malignity, and only thought of her escape from the danger which had menaced her, and anticipated the happiness she should feel when once more in safety beneath her own humble roof, in the society of all she held dear on earth. Joyfully did she follow the old wench up stairs and into an apartment still more handsomely furnished than the one below; but what was her astonishment and affright, when her sable conductress gave her a violent push which threw her violently to the floor, and then quickly left the room and locked the door! A presentiment that she was imprisoned, and for the worst of purposes, flashed through her mind, and she made the apartment resound with her shrieks. But, alas! no help was near—no friendly hand was there to burst open the door of her prison, and rescue her from a house, within whose walls she was threatened with the worst fate that can befall a helpless maiden—the loss of her honor. Her loud shrieks penetrated not beyond the precincts of that massive building—her calls for help were answered only by the taunting laugh of the black hag outside, who loaded her with alternate abuse, threats, and curses. At last, exhausted and despairing, poor Fanny threw herself upon the carpet, and prayed—oh, how earnestly!—that no harm might happen to her, which could call the blush of shame to her cheek, or make her poor grandfather think of her as a lost, polluted thing.

Somewhat relieved by this, (and who shall say that a holy whisper breathed not into her pure heart the assurance that she should pass unscathed through the fiery furnace?) she arose with a calmer spirit, and began to survey the apartment in which she was confined. It was a large room, very elegantly furnished, containing a piano, and a profusion of paintings. On examining one of these, Fanny turned away with a burning cheek—for it was one of those immodest productions of the French school, which show how art and talent can be perverted to the basest uses. She looked at no more of the pictures, but went to a window and looked out. The view from thence was not extensive, but merely included a garden of moderate size, surrounded by a high wall; the prospect was not a pleasant one, for instead of blooming flowers, the appropriate divinities of such a place, nothing was to be seen but a smooth surface of snow, relieved here and there by gaunt trees, whose leafless branches waved mournfully in the breeze, seeming to sing a requiem for the departed summer.

Fanny turned sadly away from this gloomy prospect, and seating herself upon a luxurious sofa, abandoned herself to the melancholy reflections engendered by her situation. Soon the fortitude which she had summoned to her aid, deserted her, and as the increasing darkness of the room betokened the approach of night, a thousand fears chilled her heart. She was alone in that strange house—no friends were near—the treatment she had received from the gentleman and his negro menial, indicated that neither of them would hesitate to do her mischief, if they were so inclined—what if they should murder her—or, dreadful thought! first outrage, and then despatch her! While employed in such terrible meditations as these, the darkness increased; grim shadows hovered around, and dim but terrific shapes seemed to glide towards the trembling girl. She groped her way towards the window, and looked out—there was no moon, and not a star glimmered in the firmament. Soon the darkness grew so intense, that had she held her hand close to her eyes, she could not have seen it.

Every moment augmented her fears; and sinking down in one corner, she pressed her hands to her aching eyes, as if to shut out some hideous spectacle.

Not long had she been thus, when a mortal terror, to which all her other fears were as nothing, seized her; she shivered with horror, and cold perspiration started from every pore of her skin—for her sense of hearing, painfully acute, detected the presence of a *moving object* in the room—she heard the rustle of garments—a footstep—the sound of breathing; she strained her eyes through the intense darkness, but could distinguish nothing. The moving object approaching her, nearer and nearer—it seemed to be groping in search of her—and her blood froze with horror when at last a cold hand touched her cheek, and she beheld a pair of eyes glaring at her through the gloom. A low, mocking laugh—a whispered curse—and the object glided away; then Fanny lost all consciousness.

When she recovered from the swoon into which she had fallen, daylight was shining through the windows. Hours passed away, and no one came to invade the girl's solitude. At about noon, the door was unlocked, and the old negro woman appeared, bearing a plate of provisions and a basket full of clothing. Placing the food before Fanny, the hag bade her eat, a request readily complied with, as she had fasted since the preceding day. While she was eating, the old negress regarded her with a hideous grin, and eyes expressing all the malignity of a serpent; and at the conclusion of the repast, asked her—

"Well, Miss, how did you pass the night?"

Fanny related the fearful visitation she had experienced, and implored to be released from her confinement; the black woman laughed disdainfully.

"No, no, Miss," said she, "my master will never let you go until of your own free will, you become his own little lady, and take him for a lover. Listen to me, girl: I am going to speak for your own good. My master is very fond of young ladies such as you, and goes to every expense to get them into the house; but he never likes to *force* them to his wishes, his delight being to have them *willing* to receive him as a lover—do you understand? But those silly girls who are *not* willing, he shuts up in this room, which is haunted by a fearful spectre, who every night visits the obstinate girl, and sometimes punishes her dreadfully, until she consents to my master's wishes."

Fanny shuddered—and the old black woman continued, in a gentler tone—

"Now won't you, to avoid this fearful spectre, consent to become my master's little lady? I am sure you will, my dear. See—I have brought you some fine clothes to wear, so that you may be fit to receive Mr. Tickels this afternoon, as he intends to visit you. Now, don't fail to be very good and kind to him, for he loves you very much, and will make a fine lady of you. Come, let us take off those old clothes, and put on this beautiful silk dress that has been bought on purpose for you."

We have so far depicted Fanny as a very timid, gentle girl; but she was not destitute of a becoming spirit.—When, therefore, she heard that old wretch so calmly and deliberately talk of her surrendering herself to dishonor and shame, the flush of indignation mantled her cheek; she arose, and boldly confronting her tormentor, said, with spirit and determination—

"I *will not* wear your fine clothes, nor become the slave of your master's will! He is a villain for keeping me here—and you are a wretch, a wicked wretch, for trying to tempt me to do wrong. I am not afraid of the spectre you speak of, for God will protect me, and keep me from harm. You may kill me, if you like, but I will not—*will not* be guilty of the wickedness you wish me to commit; and if ever I get free from this bad place, you and your master shall be made to suffer for treating me so. Remember this, you nasty old black devil—remember this!"

The negress quailed before the young girl, whose singular beauty was enhanced ten-fold by the glow of indignation on her cheek and the sparkle of anger in her eye. Then, without saying a word, she left the room, locking the door after her.

Half an hour elapsed, and the wench again made her appearance; in her hand she carried a short, stout piece of rope. With the fury of a tigress, and a countenance (black as she was) livid with rage, she flew at the young girl, tore every shred of clothing from her person, and then beat her cruelly with the rope, until her fair skin was covered in various places with black and blue marks. In vain poor Fanny implored for mercy; the black savage continued to beat her until obliged to desist by sheer exhaustion. Throwing herself breathless into a chair, she said, with a fierce oath—

"So, Miss—I'm a nasty old black devil, am I? You impudent hussy, how dare you use such language to me? But I'll learn you better. You shall be more civil, and do as my master wishes, and obey me in everything, or I'll not leave a whole bone in your skin. Now put on these new clothes instantly, or I solemnly swear I'll not leave off beating you, until you lie at my feet, a corpse!"

Poor Fanny was obliged to obey—for, apart from the black woman's threat, she had no alternative but to put on the costly garments which had been procured for her, her own clothes being torn to pieces; and of course she did not wish to remain in a state of nudity. She therefore dressed herself—and in truth, the garments were well selected, and fitted her to a charm. Even when attired in her old clothes, she had looked exceedingly pretty; but now, dressed in an elegant costume which displayed her fine shape and budding charms to the best advantage, she was positively beautiful. Even the old black woman could not help smiling with satisfaction at her improved appearance.

"She is a choice tit-bit for my master's appetite," thought she, chuckling to herself; and then she brought water, and made Fanny wash the traces of tears from her face, and arrange her rich auburn hair neatly and tastefully. This done, the negress departed, after telling the young girl to prepare to receive Mr. Tickels in the course of the afternoon.

What must have been the reflections of that poor young creature, while dreading the entrance of the hoary villain who sought her ruin? We can but imagine them: doubtless she thought with agony of her poor grandfather and little Charley, both of whom she knew would suffer all the anguish of uncertainty and fear, with reference to her fate. Then, perhaps, her mind reverted to the happiness she used to enjoy within the hallowed precincts of her humble home—which, humble as it was, and devoid of every luxury, and many comforts, was nevertheless endeared to her by a thousand tender associations, and had been to her as an ark of safety from the storms of life. Her thoughts next dwelt upon the kind young lady, who had given her the gold coin, and whose sweet smile and pitying words still lingered in her heart. And should she ever see those dear relatives or that kind friend again? Or if she did, would she be able to look them in the face as a pure and stainless girl, or would she blush in their presence with a consciousness of degradation? But she was interrupted in these painful meditations by the sound of the key turning in the lock; and a moment afterwards Mr. Tickels entered the room, and advanced towards her. On observing her improved appearance, a smile of intense satisfaction overspread his bloated face and sensual features—and his eyes rested admiringly upon her form, which, though not ripened, was beginning to assume a voluptuous fullness that betokened approaching womanhood. Taking her hand, he drew her to a sofa and seated her by his side. How tumultuously her heart beat with apprehension and fear!—and the old *gentleman's* first words were by no means calculated to allay her alarm.

"My charming little girl," said he, raising her hand to his lips—"how beautiful you look! A *fruit girl!*—by heavens, you are fit to be a duchess! Such sweet blue eyes—such luxuriant hair—such pure Grecian features—such a complexion, the rose blending with the lily—such a snowy breast, expanding into the two "apples of love!" And that little foot, peeping so coquettishly from beneath the skirts of your dress, should ever be encased in a satin slipper, and press naught but rich and downy carpets in the magnificent saloons of aristocratic wealth! Nay, nay, my little trembler, be not afraid, but listen to me: I love you more than words can express—you are the star of my life, and your lustre shall light me on my way to more than celestial felicity. Hear me still further: the world bows the knee to me because I am rich—thus do I kneel to you, my angel, for you are beautiful. You shall dwell with me in a mansion, to which, in point of splendor, this is nothing. I will have a *boudoir* prepared expressly for your use; it shall be lined with pink satin, and in summer the windows will overlook a beautiful garden, full of choice fruits and rare flowers; a sparkling fountain shall play in its centre, and your ears will be ravished with the melody of birds. You shall wander in that garden as much as you choose, and when you are tired, you shall repose in a shady arbor, and dream of love and its thousand blisses. In the winter season, like this, the opera, the ball-room, the theatre, shall minister to your pleasure; and in those places, none shall surpass you in splendor of dress or magnificence of jewels. Say, *belissima*, will you give me your love in exchange for all these things?"

While uttering the above wild rhapsody, (which is given at length in order to show the temptations with which the old libertine sought to allure his intended victim,) he had kneeled at her feet, and, despite her resistance, encircled her waist with his arm.

And did that poor girl—the daughter of poverty—the child of want—whose home was a garret, and who was familiar with the chills of winter and the cravings of hunger,—did she, while listening to the splendid promises of the rich man who knelt at her feet, for a moment waver in her pride of virtue, or even dream of accepting his brilliant offers? No! for even had she no other scruples, a host of holy memories encircled her heart, as a shield of power against the tempter's wiles,—the memory of home, of the two loved beings she had left there, of former happiness in a more elevated sphere; and of a gentle mother, whose beauty and virtues she had inherited, whose counsels she remembered, and who was sleeping in the churchyard.

Disengaging herself from the libertine's embrace, and thoroughly aroused to a sense of her danger, and the necessity of making all the resistance she was capable of, to preserve her chastity and honor, the young girl, losing all sense of fear, poured forth a torrent of indignant eloquence that for the time completely abashed and overcame the hoary and lecherous villain.

"No, sir—I will not, cannot love you; I hate and despise you, old wretch that you are, seeking to tempt a poor child like me to her ruin. Oh! you are rich, and have the manners of a gentleman before the world,—and yet you are more base, mean and cowardly than the commonest ruffian that ever stole a purse or cut a throat! Let me go hence, I command you; you dare not refuse me, for I know there is a law to protect *me*, as well as the richest and the highest, and I will go to those who execute the law, and have you dragged to the bar of justice to answer for this outrage. Do you hear, sir?—let me go from this accursed place, or dread the power of the law and the vengeance of Almighty God!"

The libertine quailed before the flashing eyes and proud scorn of his intended victim; his discomfiture, however, lasted but for a moment. His red face grew black with the passions of rage and lust combined; he muttered a fierce curse, and springing forward, seized her in his vice-like grasp, and forced her towards the sofa, exclaiming—

"Curses on you, little hell-bird, since neither persuasions nor promises will make you mine, it shall be done by force. Nay, if you scream so, by the powers of darkness I'll strangle you!"

In all human probability he would have been as good as his word, for Fanny continued to scream louder and louder; when suddenly Mr. Tickels received a blow on the head that brought him to the ground, and a voice cried out—

"Broad-swords and bomb-shells! I am just in time!"

While the libertine lay sprawling upon the carpet, Fanny turned to thank her deliverer; and what was her astonishment and joy when she beheld the wrinkled, care-worn face, and odd, shabby garments of—Corporal Grimsby.

CHAPTER III

The Rescue.

"By the nose of Napoleon!" cried the worthy Corporal, clasping Fanny in his arms,—"this is fortunate. Attacked the enemy in the rear—drove him from his position,—completely routed him, and left him wounded on the field; and you, my dear child, are the spoils of war!"

Mr. Tickels arose with difficulty from his prostrate position, rubbing his forehead, which was decorated with a token of the Corporal's vigor, in the shape of a huge bump not included in the science of phrenology. Turning fiercely to the latter gentleman, and quivering with rage, he demanded—

"Death and fury, sir! how dare you intrude into this room,—into this house? Who are you, and what in the divil's name brings you here? Speak, you villain, or—"

"Hold!" cried the Corporal, his face crimsoning with anger, for he was a choleric little old gentleman, was the Corporal, and as quick to become enraged as to do a good action; "hold! No man shall call me villain with impunity; I shot two rascally

Dons at Madrid for the same word, and by God, sir, if *you* repeat it, I'll cane you within an inch of your life!"

Mr. Tickels was as great a coward as a scoundrel; and though he was a much more powerful man than the Corporal, he deemed it prudent not to enrage the fierce little old gentleman more than necessary. He therefore adopted a milder tone, and asked,—

"Well, sir, what is your business here?"

"To convey this poor child to her home and friends," replied the Corporal, sternly. "It matters not how I ascertained her whereabouts; 'tis enough to know that I arrived here in time to rescue her from your brutality. You shall pay dearly for this outrage, damn you!" added the Corporal, again getting into a passion, and turning very red in the face. "But come, my child, let us leave the den of this old hyena, and go to your poor grandfather and little Charley."

Mr. Tickels closed the door, and placed his back against it with a determined air.

"You are mistaken, sir," said he, calmly,—"if you suppose that you can thus force yourself into my house, and into my private apartments, and without explanation kidnap or carry off a young person whose presence here is no affair of yours. Do you know me, sir? I am the Honorable Timothy Tickels, ex-member of Congress, men are not in the habit of questioning my motives or interfering with my actions. I am rich, and my influence is unbounded, and, were I so disposed, I could have you severely punished for the assault which you have committed on me. Your dress and appearance indicate poverty, although your language evinces that you have enjoyed more elevated fortunes; I am disposed to be not only merciful, but generous. Come, sir—leave this young person with me, unmolested; depart from this house quietly, and say nothing about what you have seen, and here is a fifty dollar bill for you. When you need more, come to me, and you shall have it."

The Honorable Mr. Tickels drew from his well-filled wallet a bank-note for the amount named, and handed it to the Corporal, who regarded it with a curious smile, and twirled it in his fingers. His smile may have been one of gratification at receiving the money—but it looked very much like a sneer of contempt for the donor and his bribe.

"Now is it not strange," quoth the Corporal, soliloquizing,—"that this dirty little bit of paper—its intrinsic value not one cent, its representative value fifty dollars, —is it not strange, I say, that this flimsy trifle, that an instant's application to the sickly flame of a penny candle would destroy, can procure food for the starving, clothing for the naked, shelter for the homeless? Great is thy power, money!—thou art the key to many of earth's pleasures, —the magic wand, which can summon a host of delights to gild the existence of thy votaries; thou cans't buy roses to strew life's rugged pathway—but thou cans't not, O great deity at whose shrine all men kneel, thou cans't not cleanse the polluted soul, still the troubled conscience, or dim the pure surface of unsullied honor. Nor cans't thou purchase *me*, thou sordid dross. Guns and grappling-irons!" abruptly added the Corporal, abandoning his philosophical strain, and getting into a towering passion,—"would you bribe me to desert my post as a guardian of innocence, and turn traitor to every principle of honor in my heart?—Bah!" and crumpling the bill in his hand, he threw it into the face of the Honorable Mr. Tickels, much to that individual's amazement.

"What do you mean, sir?" he demanded, "do you scorn my gift?"

"Yes!" thundered the little Corporal, "you and your gift may go to the devil together; and hark'ee, sir, perhaps 'tis well that you should know who *I* am, as you have so formally introduced yourself to me; I am—"

The remainder of the sentence was whispered in the ear of his listener, but the effect was magical. The Honorable Mr. Tickels started, and rapidly surveyed the person and countenance of the Corporal; then he reddened with confusion, and began to murmur a broken apology for his conduct, in which he was interrupted rather abruptly.

"Not a word, sir, not a word," said the little old gentleman, all your apologies cannot remove from my mind the impression created by your treatment of this poor child; and, sir," (here the Corporal again lost his temper) "you cannot destroy my conviction that you are the d——dest scoundrel that ever went unhung! Consider yourself fortunate if you are not held legally responsible for your forcible detention of the young girl in your house, and for your attempted outrage on her person,—damn you! Come, my child, this gentleman will no longer oppose our exit from his mansion."

The Corporal was right; the Honorable Mr. Tickels offered not the slightest objection to their departure, but on the contrary ushered them down stairs with great politeness, and held open the street door for them to pass out.

When Fanny found herself once more in the open street, out of the power of her persecutor, and on the way to her home and friends, her gratitude to her deliverer knew no bounds; she thanked the good Corporal a thousand times, and spoke of the approaching meeting with her grandfather and brother with rapture. Soon they reached their place of destination; once more the young girl stood in the humble apartment wherein all her affections were centered; —once more her aged grandfather clasped her in his arms, and again did she receive the fond kiss of fraternal love from the lips of her brother.

As soon as they had left the residence of the Honorable Mr. Tickels, in South street, the gentleman locked himself up in his study, threw himself into a chair, and actually began tearing his hair with rage and vexation.

"Hell and furies!" cried he—"to be thus fooled and baffled at the very moment when my object was about to be accomplished—to have that luscious morsel snatched from my grasp, when I was just about to taste its sweets. The thought is madness! And, in the name of wonder, how came HE to know that she was here, and why does *he* interest himself in her at all? I dare not trifle with *him!* Were some poor, poverty-stricken devil to constitute himself her champion, I might crush him at once; but *he* is above my reach. No matter; she shall yet be mine—I swear it, by all the powers of hell! I care not whether by open violence, or secret abduction, or subtle stratagem; I shall gain possession of her person, and once in my power, not all the angels in heaven, or men on earth, or fiends in hell, shall tear her from my grasp.—Ah, by Beelzebub, well tho't of!—I know the mistress of a house of prostitution (of which house I am the *owner,*) beneath whose den, as she has often told me, there is a secret cellar, which she has had privately constructed, and to which there is no access except through a panel in her chamber—which panel and the method of opening it, are known only to her, and a few persons in whom she can place implicit confidence. —This brothel-keeper told me, too, that she had the cellar made as a safe depository for young females who had been abducted from their homes,—a place of security from the search of friends, and the police. In that subterranean retreat, (which she informed me, is luxuriantly furnished, although the light of day never penetrates there,) these stolen girls are compelled to receive the visits of their lovers; and there, amid the gloom and silence of that underground prison they are initiated in all the mysteries of prostitution. By heaven 'tis the very place for my little fruit girl; she shall be abducted and conveyed there—and once safely lodged in these secret "Chambers of Love," HE who spoiled by sport to-day, shall in vain search for her. Let him come, bringing with him the myrmidons of the law; and let them search my house— then let them, if they choose, go to the brothel, beneath the foundation of which the girl is hidden, and search *that* house, too,—ha, ha, ha! They will search for her in vain. But *how* to abduct her—there's the rub! Tush! when did my ingenuity ever fail me, when appetite was to be fed or revenge gratified? Courage, Timothy Tickels, courage! Thy star, though dim at present, shall soon be in the ascendant!"

Such were the reflections of the old libertine, as he sat in his study after the departure of the Corporal and Fanny; and he was so delighted at the thought of a safe asylum for the latter, that, with restored good humor he applied himself to the discussion of a bottle of wine, and then, stretching himself comfortably on a sofa, fell asleep and dreamed of the subterranean "Chamber of Love," and the little fruit girl.

CHAPTER IV

A night in Ann street.

We proceed now to show how the Corporal discovered the fact that Fanny Aubrey was confined in the mansion of the Honorable Mr. Tickels, in South street.

Great was the consternation and alarm of the blind basket-maker and little Charley, as the day passed away and evening came on, without the return of Fanny. They were agitated with a thousand fears for her safety, for both their lives were bound up in hers, and they doted on her with an affection rendered doubly ardent by their poverty and almost complete isolation from the world. In the midst of their distress, Corporal Grimsby entered, bringing, as on the evening before, a basket of provisions. To him they communicated the intelligence that Fanny had not returned; and the eccentric old man, without waiting to hear the recital of their fears, threw the basket on the table, bolted precipitately down stairs, and walked away towards Ann street with a rapidity that betokened the existence of some fixed purpose in his mind. Meanwhile, his reflections ran somewhat in the following strain, and were half muttered aloud, as he trudged quickly onward, now nearly upsetting a foot passenger and receiving a malediction on his awkwardness, and then bruising his unlucky shins against lampposts and other street fixtures.

"By the nose of Napoleon! what can have become of the little minx? lost or stolen? —most probably the latter, for in this infernal city a pretty girl like her, so unprotected and so poor, can no more traverse the streets with safety, than can a fine fat goose waddle into the den of a wolf unharmed. Curses on these lamp-posts, I am always breaking my neck against them—bah! Well, to consider: but why the devil do I interest myself in this little girl at all? Is it because I am a lonely, solitary old codger, with neither chick nor child to bless me with their love, and whom I may love in return? Bah! no—that can't be; and yet, somehow, there is a vacant corner in my old heart, and the image of that little girl seems to fill it exactly. I am an old fool, and yet—damn you, sir, what d'ye mean by running against me, eh!—and yet, it did me more good to see that hungry family last night, eat the food that I had provided for them, than it did when I, Gregory Grimsby, was promoted to the elevated rank of Corporal. Now about this little girl—I'll bet my three-cornered cock'd hat against a pinch of Scotch snuff that she has been abducted—entrapped into the power of some scoundrel for the worst of purposes. That's the most natural supposition that I can get at. Now display thy logic, Corporal: thy supposed scoundrel must be rich, for poor men can seldom afford such expensive luxuries as mistresses; being rich implies that he is *respectable*— so the world says and thinks—bah! Being respectable, he would not compromise his character by engaging personally in such a low business as entrapping a girl; no—he would employ an *agent*; and such an agent must necessarily be a very low person, whether male or female—if a male, he is a ruffian—if a female, she is a strumpet—and where do ruffians and strumpets, of the *lower orders* (for even in crime there is an aristocracy)* where do they usually reside? why, in a congenial atmosphere—in the lowest section of the city; and what is the lowest section of this city? why, *Ann street*, to be sure. Truly, Corporal Grimsby, thou art an admirable logician! So now I am on my way to Ann street, to explore its dens, in the hope (a vain one, I fear) of finding the supposed agent who was employed by the supposed

---

*The honest Corporal was right; the well-dressed, gentlemanly, speculating, wholesale swindler would scorn to associate with the needy wretch who protracts a miserable existence by small pilferings—and the fashionable courtezan who promenades Washington street and "sees company" at a splendidly furnished brothel, can perceive not the slightest resemblance between her position in society and that of the wretched troll who practises indiscriminate prostitution in some low "crib" in Ann street. And yet philosophy and common sense both level all moral distinction between the two conditions. —A noble murderer once protested against being hung on the same gallows with a chimney-sweep—there was aristocracy with a vengeance! We opine that the lofty and arrogant pretensions of some of our "nabobs," who are often of obscure and sometimes of ignominious birth, are scarcely less ridiculous than the aristocratic notions of a gentlemanly rascal who robs *a la mode* and picks a pocket with gentility and grace!

rich scoundrel to abduct, kidnap, or entrap my little Fanny. Should I be so fortunate as to find that agent, money will readily induce him or her to divulge the place where the girl is hid; for the principle of "honor among thieves" has, I believe, but an imaginary existence."

Leaving the Corporal to explore the intricate labyrinths of Ann street, (in the hope of obtaining some clew to the fate of Fanny Aubry,) thou wilt have the kindness, gentle reader, to accompany us into one of the squalid dens of that great sewer of vice and crime. But first we pause to read and admire the *sign* which decorates the exterior of a "crib" opposite Keith's Alley, and which, with a peculiarity of orthography truly amusing, notifies you that it is a *"Vittlin Sollor."* (This sign remains there to this day.) Passing on, we cannot fail to be impressed with the "mixed" nature of the society of the place; colored ladies and gentlemen (by far the most decent portion of the population) are every where to be seen, thronging the side-walks, indulging in boisterous laughter; loafers of every description are lounging about, whose tattered garments indicate the languishing condition of their wardrobes; great, ruffianly fellows stare at you with eyes expressive of the villainy that prompts to robbery and murder; —miserable men, ghastly women, and dirty children obstruct the pathway, and annoy you with their oaths and ribald jests. Let us descend this steep flight of steps, and enter this cellar. Be not too fastidious in regard to the odor of the place, for *eau de cologne* and otto of rose are not exactly the commodities disposed of here, the place being devoted to the sale of that beverage classically termed "rot-gut," and eatables which, unlike wine, are by no means improved in flavor by age. There is the "bar," and the red-nosed gentleman behind it seems to be one of its best patrons. A wooden bench extends around the apartment, and upon it are seated about twenty persons of both sexes. A brief sketch of a few of the "ladies" of this goodly company may prove interesting, from the fact that the names are real, and belong to prostitutes who even now inhabit the regions of Ann street.

That handsome, finely-formed female, with dark eyes and hair in ringlets, and who is also very neatly dressed, is "Kitty Cling-cling," who has been termed the "belle of Ann street." That lady in a red dress, with hair uncommonly short, (she having only recently dispensed with a wig,) is Joannah Westman, of Fleet street, and Liverpool Jane from the same *respectable* neighborhood. This renowned "Lady" of the town was (and is) distinguished by a huge scar on her left cheek, which seems to be the exact impression of a gin bottle, probably thrown in some brawl in Liverpool, her native place. Then there is Lize Whittaker, from Lowell, who "ties up" at the corner of Fleet and Ann streets. Then we notice two ladies who rejoice in the mellifluous names of "Bald-head" and "Cockroach," and who are both worthy representatives from Keith's Alley. These, with a small sprinkling of ebony lasses and their attendant cavaliers, make up the very respectable assemblage.

And now everybody brightens up, as a couple of colored gentlemen enter the cellar, and seating themselves upon a raised platform termed by courtesy "the orchestra," commence tuning a fiddle and base viol, preparatory to a dance by "all the characters." —Away the musicians glide into the harmonious measures of a gay quadrille—and to say the truth, the music is excellent, for Picayune and Joe are very skillful performers on their respective instruments; and are well qualified to play for a much more select and fashionable auditory. And now the voluptuous Kitty Cling-cling is led to the centre of the festive hall by a sable mariner, and begins to foot it merrily to the dulcet strains; while Bald-head and Cockroach find partners in two African geniuses, whose dress and general appearance would most decidedly exclude them from admission into a fancy ball at Brigham's. Away they go, through all the intricate mazes of the giddy dance. But see—a crowd of well-dressed but dissipated young men enter the cellar, their wild looks and disordered attire plainly indicating that they are on a regular "time." Those young men have been imbibing freely at some fashionable saloon in Court or Hanover street, and have come to consummate the evening's "fun" by having a dance with the fallen goddesses of Ann street. With a facetious perversity, they select as partners the most hideous of the negro women, and "mix in" the dance with a relish that could not be surpassed if their partners were each a Venus, and the cellar a magnificent hall of Terpsichore. The dance concluded, they throw down a handful of silver upon the counter, and invite "all hands to take a drink," but very rarely drink themselves in such a place, well knowing the liquor to be unworthy the palate of men accustomed to the superior beverages of the aristocratic establishments. At the completion of this ceremony, they take their departure, to visit some other "crib," and repeat the same performances.

But let us (supposing ourselves to be invisible) pass from the dance hall and enter the adjoining apartment, which is smaller. Seated around a rough deal table are about thirty men and women, engaged in smoking and drinking. The room is dimly lighted by a couple of tallow candles, stuck in bottles; the walls are black with dust and smoke, and the aforesaid table and a few benches constitute the entire furniture of the room. The general frequenters of the cellar are not admitted to this place, it being especially reserved for the use of those ladies and gentlemen who gain their living on the principle of an equal division of property—or in other words, *thieves*. In this room, secure from being overheard by the uninitiated and vulgar crowd, they could "ply the lush," and "blow a cloud," while they talked over their exploits and planned new depredations. The room was called the "Pig Pen," and the society who resorted there classed themselves under the expressive title of "Grabbers." Although not a regularly organized association, it had a sort of leader or captain whose authority was generally recognized. This gentleman was called "Jew Mike," from the fact of his belonging to the Hebrew persuasion; he was a gigantic, swarthy ruffian, with a long, black and most repulsive features, and was dressed in a style decidedly "flash," his coat garnished with huge brass buttons, and his fingers profusely adorned with jewelry of the same material. He had recently graduated from the State Prison, where he had served a term of ten years for manslaughter, as the jury termed it; although it was universally regarded as one of the most cold-blooded and atrocious murders ever committed. To sum up the character of this man in a few words, he was a most desperate and blood-thirsty villain, capable of perpetrating the most enormous crimes; and dark hints were sometimes thrown out by his associates in reference to his former career; some said that he was an escaped murderer from the South; others that he had been a pirate; while all united in bearing unqualified testimony as to the villainy of his character and the number and blackness of his crimes. He could not plead *ignorance* in extenuation of his manifold enormities, for he possessed an education that would have qualified him to move in a respectable sphere of society, had he been so disposed. Upon his right was seated no less a personage that "Sow Nance," the hideous girl who had that day entrapped poor Fanny Aubry into the power of Mr. Tickels; she was much intoxicated, and by the maudlin fondness which she displayed for Jew Mike, it was easy to surmise the nature of the relation existing between her and him. Included in the company were several other "apple girls," whose proficiency as thieves entitled them to the distinction of being considered as competent "Grabbers;" each one of these wretched young creatures had her lover, of "fancy man," who was generally some low, petty thief—although, among the male portion of the assembly, there were several expert and daring robbers, the most distinguished of whom was Jew Mike himself, whose skill as a burglar had elevated him to the highly honorable position of captain of the "Grabbers."

The "lush" was freely handed round, and the company soon grew "half seas over;" then came wildly exaggerated narratives of exploits in robbery, thieving, and almost every species of crime, interspersed with smutty anecdotes and obscene songs, in which the females of the company were not a whit behind the males. At length Jew Mike himself was vociferously called on for either a song or a story; and not being a vocalist, the gentleman preferred entertaining his friends with the latter; so, clearing his throat by an enormous draught of brandy, he began as follows:

JEW MIKE'S STORY

"You see, lads and lasses, a year or two before I came to this accursed country to be *jugged for a ten spot*, for manslaughter, (it was a clear murder, though, and a good piece of work, too,) I was a nobleman's butler in the great city of London. Ah, *that* was the place for a man to get a living in! No decent "Grabber," would stoop to petty stealing there; beautiful burglaries, yielding hundreds of pounds in silver plate; elegant highway robberies, producing piles of guineas and heaps of diamond watches,—that was the business followed by lads of the cross at that time in England. Well, there's no use in crying over spilt milk, any how; I was obliged to step out of England when the country got too hot to hold me, and if I returned there, by G——! my life wouldn't be worth a moment's purchase. And now to go on with my story. I was a nobleman's butler, and glorious times I had of it—little to do, plenty of pickings and stealings, free access to the pantry and wine-cellar, and enjoying terms of easy intimacy with the prettiest chambermaid in London. The only drawback upon my happiness was Lord Hawley's *valet*, a Frenchman, named Lagrange, who had been in his lordship's service many years, and was regarded as a remarkably honest and faithful man,—and so he was; but those qualities which rendered him valuable to his lordship, of course rendered him devilish obnoxious to me,—for he suspected my real character, and was continually playing the spy upon me, and informing my master of all my little peccadilloes. For instance, his lordship would send for me in his library, and say, sternly,—'Simpson, my valet Lagrange informs me that you are improperly intimate with one of the female domestics; you must stop it, or quit my service.' And perhaps the next day he would again summon me before him, and, with that cursed valet grinning maliciously at me from behind his chair, say to me,— 'Simpson, I hear that you make too free with my wine, and are frequently intoxicated; stop it, or I shall dismiss you.' In short, Lagrange was the bane of my existence, and I secretly swore to be terribly revenged upon him for his tattling propensities. You'll soon see how well I kept my oath.

"My Lady Hawley was a very gay, dissipated and beautiful woman, and I had long been aware that during my master's absence she was in the habit of receiving the clandestine visits of a handsome young officer of dragoons. To tell the truth, I used to admit him to the house, and see that no one was in the way to observe him enter her ladyship's chamber, for which services I received very liberal rewards from both her ladyship, and Captain St. Clair. Lord Hawley doted upon his wife, who was many years younger than himself; and often have I laughed in my sleeve when I thought what a cuckold she made of him. But he suspected nothing of the kind; I was the only person, besides the parties, who knew of the intrigue; even Lagrange, artful spy as he was, did not discover it. My master, who was addicted to gambling, was absent until a late hour every night, at Crockford's; and thus her ladyship had every opportunity to enjoy frequent interviews with her lover. As I knew of her frailty, I had her completely in my power; and often I was tempted to threaten her with exposure, unless she would "come down" handsomely with a thousand pounds or so, and grant me *any other favor* that I might choose to demand, as the price of my silence,—for, as I said before, she was a beautiful woman, and a butler has feelings as ardent as those of a captain of dragoons.

"Well, matters continued very quiet and agreeable, until late one night, after I had gone to bed, I heard a low but hurried knock at the door of my room. I arose, hastily threw on a few garments, and opened the door, when to my astonishment in rushed Lady Hawley, in her night-dress, and threw herself into a chair, breathless with agitation. Almost instantly the thought flashed through my mind that her intrigue had been discovered; cautiously closing the door, I advanced towards her ladyship, and in a respectful manner inquired why she had honored me with a visit so unexpected, and what might be the cause of her evident agitation, at the same time assuring her of my assistance, should she require it. She fixed her proud, beautiful eyes upon my face, and said, in a voice trembling with emotion,—

" 'Good heavens, Simpson, only think of it, my foolish affair with Captain St. Clair is discovered!'

" 'Is it possible, your ladyship?' I cried, 'and may I ask who—'

" 'His lordship's valet, Lagrange, saw me, half an hour ago, conducting the Captain to the private stair-case which leads to the garden,' replied her ladyship, shuddering, and shading her face with her hands.

" 'And might not your ladyship purchase his silence?' I asked. She replied,—

" 'I have just come from his room; you know how obstinate he is,—how entirely devoted to his lordship,—how blindly honest and faithful he has ever been,—how singularly averse to receiving presents from any source whatever, fearing it might have the appearance of bribery. I went to his room, and offered him a hundred guineas if he would solemnly swear never to reveal what he had seen. In a tone of cold indifference he said, 'I must do my duty to his lordship, to whom I am bound by the strongest ties of gratitude, even at the sacrifice of your ladyship's honor.' I entreated him, almost on my knees, to give the required promise; I offered to double, nay, treble the sum that I had named, but no; he turned from me, almost with disdain, (the low-born menial!) and requested me to retire, as I must be aware of the impropriety of such a visit, at such an hour. Perceiving the uselessness of attempting to bribe him to secrecy, I left him, cursing him for his obstinacy, and came direct to you. Heavens!' added her ladyship, drawing her robe over her partially denuded bosom, 'how desperate the fear of exposure has made me, that in this indecent attire I go at midnight to the chambers of male servants!— Simpson, can you help me in this dreadful emergency? You have heretofore proved faithful to me,—do not desert me now. *Lagrange must be silenced!*—do you understand me? At any cost,—at any risk,—his babbling tongue must be hushed, *by you*, for you are the only person whom I can trust in the affair. Yes, he must never speak the word that will proclaim my dishonor to the world!'

" '*At any cost*, your ladyship?' rejoined I, fixing my eyes steadily upon hers, for her despair rendered me bold, and I was not one to suffer an opportunity to slip by unimproved.

" 'I understand you, fellow!' she replied, with a hysterical laugh and a glance of scorn,—'and much as I despise you, I answer yes! at any cost. But, gracious Heavens, what do I say? *you*, a menial, a base-born servitor! But no matter; even *that* is far preferable to exposure. Good God! to think of being cast off by his lordship with loathing and contempt, despised and hated by my relatives,—an eternal blot upon my name,—forever excluded from the sphere of society of which I am the star and centre,—no, that shall never, never be. Silence Lagrange—silence him forever,— then ask of me any favor, and it shall not be denied.'

"I approached her ladyship; she was pale as marble, but how superbly beautiful! Her glossy hair, all disordered, hung in rich masses upon her uncovered shoulders; her seductive night-dress but imperfectly concealed the glories of her divine form,—her heaving bosom, so voluptuous and fair, was more than half disclosed to my gaze. With a palpitating heart I laid my trembling hand upon one of her plump, white shoulders. Never shall I forget the majestic rage and scorn of her look, as she started to her feet, and stood before me in all the pride of her imperial beauty.

" 'Fellow,' she said, with desperate calmness, 'you are bold; but perhaps I ought to have expected this. I perceive that you are disposed to take every advantage of my situation. Be it so, then; but not until you have *earned the reward*, can you claim it. Remember this. Fortunately, his lordship is out of town, and will not return until the day after to-morrow; but oh! how unfortunate that his accursed valet did not accompany him! Lagrange pretended to be ill, and was left behind, and my lord was attended by another servant. No matter,—you will have an opportunity to dispose of this French spy ere the return of his master. I care not what method you take to silence his tongue,—but be secret and sure; and when the work is done, you shall have your reward—not before.'

"Having thus spoken, her ladyship swept out of the room with the air of a queen, leaving me to devise the best method of silencing Lagrange forever. I could not mistake her ladyship's meaning; she wished me to *murder* the man. Now, the fact is, ladies and gentlemen, murder's a devilish ticklish business, any how; not that I ever had any false delicacy in relation to the wickedness of the thing— pshaw! nothing of the kind,—you'll all believe me when I assure you that I'd as soon cut a human throat, as wring the neck of a chicken, for that matter; but then the consequences of a discovery are so ducedly unpleasant, and although I am confident in my own mind that I am destined to terminate my existence ornamented with a hempen cravat, I have never had any desire to hasten that consummation. So I didn't altogether relish the job which her ladyship had given me; but when I thought of her surpassing beauty, my hesitation vanished like mists before the rising sun, and I resolved to do it.

"Several times the next day I tried to provoke Lagrange into a quarrel, but the wily rascal, as if divining my intentions, only shrugged his shoulders and smiled in the cold and sarcastic manner peculiar to him. This enraged me greatly, and after applying the most abusive epithets to him, I finally struck him. But all availed nothing; unlike the majority of his countrymen, the fellow was cold and passionless, even under insults and blows. I had provided myself with a sharp butcher's knife, which I carried in my sleeve, ready to plunge into his heart, had he offered to attack me in return; and thus I hoped to make it appear that I had slain him in self-defence. But his admirable coolness and self-possession defeated that scheme,— and I saw that I would be obliged to slay him deliberately as the first opportunity.

"That opportunity was not long wanting.

"During the afternoon he had occasion to visit the wine vault, of which I alone had the key; I accompanied him thither, and while he was engaged in selecting some malt liquor for the servants' table, I said to him,—

" 'Monsieur Lagrange, you are acquainted with a secret that intimately concerns her ladyship; what use do you intend to make of this knowledge?'

"The Frenchman very coolly intimated that it was none of my business, and continued his employment. His back was towards me; I approached nearer to him, and said, in a low tone—

" 'You infernal, backbiting, sneaking scoundrel, you have often betrayed me to my master, and would now betray her ladyship. You shall not live to do it—die like a dog, as you are!'

"While thus addressing him, I had drawn forth my knife; and as I uttered the last words, I plunged it with all my force into his left side, up to the very handle. The blade passed directly through his heart, and without a groan he fell dead at my feet.

"No remorse—no sorrow for the bloody deed I had committed, found entrance to my soul; on the contrary, I gazed at the corpse with savage exultation. 'That babbling tongue is now forever hushed,' thought I; and then, as a sudden strange thought struck me, I added—'and that tongue shall be my passport to a bliss more exquisite than the joys of Paradise.' With an untrembling hand I cut off the dead man's tongue, secured it about me, and having hid the body behind a row of wine casks, left the cellar, securely locked the door, and then went about my usual avocations, resolving to dispose of the corpse that night in some manner that should avert suspicion from me, for I had every confidence in my own ingenuity.

"Towards evening, I sought and obtained an interview with her ladyship, in private. She advanced to meet me with a hurried step and sparkling eyes.

" 'Simpson, *is it done?*' she asked, in a tone of extreme agitation, and laying her delicate hand on my arm.

" 'It is, your ladyship,' was my reply, producing and holding before her the bloody evidence of the deed—'and here is the tongue of Lagrange,—the tongue that would have proclaimed your shame and effected your ruin, had its owner lived; but he now lies a cold corpse, and this once mischievous member is now as powerless as a piece of carrion beneath a butcher's shamble.'

" 'And the body—how will you dispose of that?' she asked, shuddering, and turning from the sickening spectacle with disgust.

" 'To-night it shall be sunk deep in the waters of the Thames,' I replied; and then, in a more familiar manner than I had as yet ventured to assume, I reminded her ladyship of the *reward* she had promised me, as soon as the job should be completed. Again she shuddered; —and turned deadly pale; and with a bitter smile, which seemed to me to be expressive of hatred and contempt combined, she answered—

" 'You are right, Simpson; you have obeyed my wishes, and merit your reward, —but not now, not now! Come to my chamber at midnight; I shall expect you,— you understand. Go now—leave me; remove all traces of your crime. I shall take care to have a quantity of plate removed form the house to-night, and destroyed, and when his lordship returns to-morrow, he will imagine that Lagrange, despite his supposed faithfulness and integrity, has absconded and stolen the plate,—that will account to him for the valet's sudden disappearance. Leave me.'

" 'Remember, at midnight, your ladyship,' said I, and left her; but when I had closed the door of the apartment, I imagined that I heard her give utterance to a scornful laugh. However, I attributed it to her gratification at the death of Lagrange, and descending to the wine cellar, I busied myself in washing away the stains of blood from the floor. How impatiently I longed for the arrival of midnight! the hour that was to bring with it the reward of my crime!

" 'During the evening, I paid a visit to a noted "*boozing ken*" in St. Giles', which bore the very suitable appellation of the "Jolly Thieves." Here I engaged two desperate fellows of my acquaintance—(for I went on a *crack*, now and then, myself, just to keep my hand in,)—to make away with the body of Lagrange; they were to come to the rear of my master's house, an hour after midnight, provided with a sack and some means of conveyance; and, for a liberal reward, they promised to carry off the corpse, and, having attached a heavy weight to it, sink it in the

Thames,—although I felt assured in my own mind, that, instead of giving it to the fishes, they would make a more profitable disposition of it, by selling it to some surgeon for dissection;—body-snatching being a part of their profession, as well as burglary and murder. Having made this important arrangement, and paid them a good round sum in advance, (for I was well provided with money,) I returned to my master's house, which I reached about eleven o'clock.

" 'At length the welcome midnight hour arrived, and with a beating heart I repaired to the chamber of her ladyship. It was a large apartment, furnished with exquisite taste and elegance,—in fact, a perfect bower of the graces; and, to my somewhat voluptuous mind, not the least attractive feature of it, was a magnificent and luxurious *bed*, mysteriously hidden beneath a profuse cloud of snowy drapery, heavily laden with costly lace. I had already pictured to myself the delights of an amorous dalliance within that bower of Venus, with one whose glorious beauty could not have been surpassed by that of the ardent goddess herself—but how grievously was I doomed to be disappointed, at the very moment when I fancied my triumph certain! But I must not anticipate my story.

"In answer to my respectful, and I must own, somewhat timid, knock at the chamber door, I heard the musical but subdued voice of her ladyship bidding me to 'come in.' I entered, and having softly closed the door, noiselessly turned the key in the lock, and advanced to where she was seated by a table, upon which there stood wine, and materials of a *recherche* supper. Drawing a chair close to her ladyship, I seated myself, and gazed at her long and ardently, while she, apparently unconscious of my presence, seemed to be deeply engaged in perusing a splendid volume of Byron's poems.

"Surprised and not perfectly at ease, in consequence of her silence and abstraction (for she had not even glanced at me,) I at length ventured to observe—

" 'Your ladyship sees that I am punctual; as of course I could not neglect to keep so delightful an appointment.'

"Still she answered nothing, nor even raised her eyes from the book! During the silence of some minutes that ensued, I had an excellent opportunity to feast my eyes upon the seraphic loveliness of her face, and the admirable proportions of her queen-like form. She was dressed with studied simplicity, and in a style half *neglige*, infinitely more fascinating than the most elaborate full dress. A robe of snowy whiteness, made so as to display her plump, soft arms, and fine, sloping shoulders, and entirely without ornament, constituted her attire; and a single white rose alone relieved the jet darkness of her clustering hair. She was seated in a manner that enabled me to view her profile to the best advantage; I was never more forcibly struck with its purely classical and Grecian outlines; and I observed that a soft expression of melancholy was blended with the usual *hauteur* that sat enthroned upon her angelic features.

"As I gazed admiringly upon the beautiful woman, whom I could almost imagine to be a being from a celestial world, I could not help saying to myself—

" 'After all, she is an adulteress and a murderess; and is now about to sacrifice her person to me, the instrument of her murderous wishes. Why, what a devil is here, in the form of a lovely woman, whose beauty would seem to proclaim her a tenant of the skies, while the black depravity of her heart fits her only for the companionship of the fiends below! Why do I hesitate and tremble in her presence? She is in my power—my *slave!* Yet, by heavens, what a superb creature! A thousand passionate devils are dancing in her brilliant eyes—her lips are moist with the honey of love—and her form seems to glow with ardent but hidden fires! Come, let me delay no longer, but speak to her in the language befitting a master to his slave!'

" 'Lady,' said I, in a tone familiar, yet not disrespectful—'why this reserve and silence? You know for what purpose I come thus at midnight to your chamber— it is by your own appointment, and to receive the reward of a difficult and dangerous service which I have performed for you. Nay, I see that you have anticipated my coming, by preparing this delicate and acceptable feast for our entertainment. Is it not so, my charmer? And you have dressed yourself in this bewitching style of chaste simplicity, solely to please me—am I right? But come; though you have not yet spoken or looked at me, sweet coquette that you are, I read in your bright eyes the confirmation of my hopes. Let us first banquet upon the delights of love, and then sip the ruby contents of the sparkling wine-cup, which I'll swear are not one half so sweet as the nectar of your lips, which now I taste.'

"I clasped her in my arms as I spoke, and attempted to imprint a kiss upon her lips; but she hurled me from her with disdain, and said, with an air of lofty dignity—

" 'Dog, how dare you thus intrude into the sanctity of my chamber? and how dared you for a moment presume to think that I intended to keep the promise which, in my eagerness to have Lagrange silenced, I gave you? Know that, sooner than submit to your base and loathsome embraces, I'd brave exposure and even death itself! If *money* will satisfy you, name your sum, and be it ever so great, it shall be paid to you; but presume not to think that Lady Adelaide Hawley can ever so far forget her birth and rank, as to debase herself with such as you.'

" '*Money*, your ladyship, was not what I bargained for,' I boldly replied; for the scorn and contempt with which she treated me, stung me to the quick, and enraged me beyond all measure. 'If your ladyship refuses to perform, honorably and fairly, your part of the contract, you must take the consequences; you shall be proclaimed as an adulteress, and as an accessory to the crime of murder.'

" 'Fool!' she cried—yet her countenance indicated the fear she really felt, notwithstanding the boldness of her words— 'fool! expose me at your peril! You dare not, for your own neck would be stretched in payment for your treachery, while your charges against me, low, miserable menial that you are, would never be believed—never! Such accusations against me, a peeress of the realm, and a lady whose reputation has never been assailed, would but add to the general belief in your own guilt, and the certainty of your fate; such charges would be regarded as a paltry subterfuge, and no one would credit them. Go, fellow—the bat cannot consort with the eagle, nor can such as you aspire to even the most distant familiarity with persons of my rank. Depart, instantly; and to-morrow you shall receive a pecuniary reward that will amply compensate you for the disappointment you now feel.'

"With these words she turned away from me, waving her hand in token that the conference was closed; but I was enraged and desperate, as much by the scorn of her manner as by the disappointment I felt. A hell of passion was burning in my heart; and I said to her, in a low, deep tone—

" 'Woman, you shall be mine, even if I am obliged to commit another murder— I swear it! I hesitated not at perpetrating a deed of blood; nor will I hesitate now to obtain, by violence and even bloodshed, the reward you promised me for that deed! Lady, be wise; we are alone at this silent hour—I am powerful and you are helpless. Consent, then, or—'

"She interrupted me with a scornful laugh, that rendered me almost frantic with fury. Reason forsook me; I lost all self-control, and rushed upon her with the ferocity of a madman, determined to strangle her.

"Ere I could lay my grasp upon her, I was seized with a force that nearly stunned me. I arose with difficulty, and to my astonishment beheld the handsome countenance and glittering uniform of her ladyship's favored lover, Captain St. Clair!

" 'Villain,' said he, in his usual cold and haughty manner, (he was of noble blood, and as proud as Lucifer,) 'you little imagined that I was a witness of the entire scene in which you have played so praiseworthy a part! Upon my honor, you are the most ambitions of butlers! Cooks and chambermaids are not sufficiently delicate for your fastidious taste, forsooth!—but you must aspire to ladies of noble birth! Faith, I should not be surprised to hear of your attempting an intrigue with her gracious Majesty, the Queen! Hark'ee, fellow, begone! and thank my moderation that I do not punish you upon the spot, for your infernal presumption! Yet I would scorn to tarnish the lustre of my good sword with the blood of such a thing as thou!'

" 'Captain,' said I, boldly, (for I am no coward, ladies and gentlemen, as you all know,) 'as you have seen fit to play the spy, it is fair to presume that you are acquainted with the circumstances upon which my claim to the favor of this lady is based. At her instigation, and prompted by her promises of reward, I have murdered Lord Hawley's valet, Lagrange, in order to prevent his revealing to his master, the criminal intimacy existing between you and her ladyship. Now, Captain, I submit it to you as a man of honor—having committed such a deed, and exposed myself to such a fearful risk, am I not entitled to the reward promised by her ladyship? without the hope of which reward, I never would have bedewed my hands in the blood of my fellow servant. And can I justly be blamed for claiming that reward, and even for attempting to obtain it by force, since I have faithfully earned it?"

"The Captain laughed, half in good nature, half in scorn, and said—

" 'Faith, you are a well-spoken knave, and appeal to my honor as if you were my equal; and I am half inclined to pardon your presumption on account of your wit. Now listen, my good fellow; —her ladyship, as a measure of policy, wished to have a certain person removed, who was possessed of a dangerous secret; now you were the only available agent she could employ to effect that removal. But you demanded a certain favor, (which shall be nameless,) as the price of your services, and would accept of no other renumeration. The danger was imminent; what could her ladyship do? The man must be disposed of, even at the sacrifice of truth; her ladyship gave the required promise (*intending never to keep it*,) you performed the service, and very properly, I own, come to receive your reward. Of course, you perceive the impossibility of a compliance with your wishes. No intrigue can exist between the patrician and the plebeian—you are low-born, she of the noblest blood of the kingdom. Are you so blind, man, that you cannot see—or are you so stupid that you cannot comprehend—the repugnance which her ladyship must naturally feel at the very idea of an amorous intimacy existing between a high-born lady and—good heavens!—a *butler?* Here, my food fellow, is a purse, containing fifty guineas—I will double the sum to-morrow. Now go; and remember that you have everything to expect from our generosity, in a pecuniary point of view; but a repetition of your demand for her ladyship's favors, will most assuredly result to your lasting disadvantage.'

"Seeing the folly of attempting to press my claim further, I sneaked out of the room, with very much the air of a disconcerted cur with his tail between his legs, to use a simile more expressive than elegant. The moment I had entered my own chamber, the clock in a neighboring steeple proclaimed the hour of two, and then for the first time I remembered the appointment which I had made with my two particular friends, from the "Jolly Thieves," in reference to the disposal of Lagrange's body. The hour appointed for meeting them, was passed; and suddenly a thought struck me—a strange thought—which had no sooner flashed through my mind, than I resolved to act upon its suggestion. 'Twas a glorious plan of revenge, and one which could only have emanated from my fertile imagination.

" 'The corpse of the Frenchman shall become the instrument of my vengeance," thought I, chuckling with glee. 'I shall not need the assistance of those two fellows now—and, if they are still lurking about the house, I will reward them for their trouble and send them away. Ah, lucky thought—lucky thought!'

"I found my two friends in waiting for me; they grumbled much at my want of punctuality, but their murmurings were hushed when I paid them liberally, and dismissed them, saying that I had discovered a much safer and more convenient method of disposing of the body, than the plan originally proposed, and therefore should not require their assistance.—They departed, rejoicing at their good fortune in being freed from a difficult and dangerous task, and congratulating themselves on having received as much money as they had been promised for its performance.

"Taking with me a dark lantern, I descended noiselessly into the wine vault, and having secured the massive iron door, proceeded to execute my plan of vengeance. Comrades, can you guess what that plan was? No, I'll swear you cannot. But listen, and you shall hear.

"Placing my light in a convenient position, I dragged the dead body of Lagrange from its place of concealment; then I bent over it, and examined the ghastly countenance. The features were pale and rigid, the teeth firmly set, and the glassy eyes wide open and staring. The awful expression of those dead orbs seemed, bold as I was, to freeze my very soul as with the power of a basilisk. For a single moment I repented the deed; but that feeling soon passed, and I rejoiced at it.

"It occurred to me to search the pockets of my victim; I did so, and found a small sum of money, and a sealed letter, addressed to Lord Hawley. The valet had probably intended to despatch that letter to his master that afternoon—which design was frustrated by his sudden death by my hand. Eagerly I broke the seal, and read as follows:—

" 'LONDON.

" 'My lord. —Should your lordship have possibly designed extending your visit to Berkshire beyond the time originally alotted to the same, I entreat your lordship to set aside every consideration—every engagement, however pressing or important its nature may be, and to return immediately to town. Something has occurred, in the conduct of her ladyship, intimately affecting your lordship's honor. To relieve your lordship from any painful uncertainty that may be occasioned by this indefinite announcement, you will pardon me for stating plainly, that I myself saw her ladyship and Captain St. Clair, under circumstances that admitted of but one opinion in reference to the nature of the intimacy existing between them. Simpson, the butler, whom I am persuaded is in the confidence of her ladyship and the Captain, this afternoon questioned me in regard to my knowledge of the affair, and the use I intended to make of that knowledge; and he, not deeming my replies satisfactory, abused and struck me. My duty to your lordship prevented any retaliation on my part; and that duty, (the offspring of humble gratitude for your lordship's many acts of generous kindness to me, both in this country and in France,) now impels me to communicate these unpleasant facts—which I do, with sincere sorrow for her ladyship's indiscretion, and every desire for the preservation of your lordship's honor.

" 'From your lordship's humble servant,
" 'LOUIS LAGRANGE.'

"This letter, so characteristic of the polished, wily and educated Frenchman, was written in the French language, with which I was well acquainted, I therefore easily translated it. After a careful perusal, I placed it in my pocket-book—for I was well aware that it might one day prove a valuable auxiliary to me, should I feel disposed to inform my master of his wife's infidelity, and his lordship then could not doubt the truth of his own favorite and faithful servant, in whom he had the most unbounded confidence.

" 'Oh, scornful Lady Hawley and sarcastic Captain St. Clair!' I could not forbear exclaiming—'ye shall both be caught in a net of your own making, when ye least expect it! My lady will be turned out of doors as an adulteress; and my gentleman will perhaps be shot through the head by the husband he has wronged! Patience, patience, good Simpson; thou shalt yet riot in the very satiety of thy vengeance. But now to put in operation my first method—an ingenious one it is, too—of avenging my wrongs!'

"Among the various wines with which the extensive cellar was abundantly stocked, was a large cask containing a particular kind, of a very rich and peculiar flavor; and of this wine I knew Lady Hawley, who was a luxurious woman, very fastidious in her taste, to be especially fond. Captain St. Clair, too, preferred it above all other kinds; and at the midnight suppers which he so often enjoyed with her ladyship, the ruby contents of this particular cask was most frequently called into requisition, as I well know, for I had been accustomed to carry it from the cellar to the door of the bed-chamber wherein the amorous pair indulged in the joys both of Venus and of Bacchus. The wine had been imported by his lordship, who was a *bon vivant*, from Bordeaux and was particularly valued for its rich color, solid body, and substantial yet delicate flavor, rivalling in these qualities, perhaps, that classic beverage, the famed Greek wine.

" 'I will add to the exquisite flavor of this wine,' said I—'her ladyship and her lover shall banquet on human blood; the corruption of a putrifying corpse shall be mingled with the sparkling fluid that nourishes their unholy passions.'

"With but little difficulty, and less noise, (for I well understood such matters,) I removed the head of the cask, which I found to be about half full. How luxurious was the odor that arose from the dark liquid, fragrant with spices! Taking a small vessel, I drank a bumper—then another. My blood instantly became charged with a thousand fires; my heart seemed to swell with mighty exultation; my brain seemed to swim in a sea of delight. I laughed with mad glee to think of the superb vengeance I was about to wreak on my enemies; then I raised the corpse of Lagrange with Herculean strength, thrust it into the cask, and pressed it into the smallest possible compass; but found to my inexpressible chagrin, that it would be absolutely impossible to re-adjust the head of the cask, unless the body was in some manner made smaller. After a few moments' reflection, a happy thought struck me. I hesitated not a moment, but drew a sharp clasp knife from my pocket, deliberately severed the head from the body, and thrust it into the cask. Then, without the least difficulty, I replaced the top of the cask, and my work was accomplished.

"I repaired to my chamber but slept not, as you may suppose; the events of that day and night had been of a nature too singularly exciting to admit of repose. Shortly after I had retired, I heard Lady Hawley conduct her lover to the back stair-case; there was a sound of kissing, and a whispered appointment made for another meeting, on a night when his lordship would probably be absent. 'Yes, and at that interview, my amorous pair,' thought I, 'shall you taste of the wine which I have improved by an addition which you little suspect, but with which you shall one day be made acquainted.' And then I laughed till the tears rolled down my cheeks.

"Lord Hawley returned at the expected time, and immediately inquired for his valet, Lagrange. The gentleman was, of course, among the missing; and I overheard her ladyship announcing to her husband that the Frenchman had absconded, carrying off plate and jewelry to a considerable amount. Lord Hawley was extremely shocked and grieved on receiving this (false) intelligence; and I heard him mutter, as he retired in great perturbation of mind to his study,—'What, can it be possible?—Lagrange, whom I esteemed to be the most honest and faithful fellow in the world—of whose fidelity I have had so many evidences,—whom I have often benefitted,—can it be that *he* has deserted and robbed me? Then indeed do I believe all mankind to be false as hell!'

"A week passed, and nothing occurred in Hawley House worthy of mention. At the expiration of that time, his lordship went on a short journey, (connected with some political object,) which would occasion him a fortnight's absence from home. Then was her ladyship and the captain in clover! and then was afforded me an opportunity to set before them the wine which I had enriched by my famous *addition!*

"Not deeming it necessary to adopt the usual precautions, my lady feasted, toyed and dallied with her handsome lover in her own private apartments, fearing no detection, as she was certain that her husband would not return before the specified time, and as I was the only person aware of the captain's presence in the house; she feared not, thinking that I dared not betray her, as she imagined that I was completely in her power on account of the murder I had committed. Pretty fool! she little thought of the plan I had formed for her destruction, and that of her haughty and hated paramour.

"I waited on them at table in my humblest and most respectful manner; and I could perceive that they inwardly congratulated themselves on having, as they thought, completely subdued me, and bribed me to eternal silence with regard to their amours.

"At their very first banquet, (for the splendor of their repasts merited that high-sounding title,) I was requested to bring from the cellar a decanter of their *favorite* wine. You may be sure I did not mistake the cask, comrades. I drew from the cask which contained the corpse of Lagrange, a quantity of the wine, and holding it to the light, observed with intense satisfaction that it had assumed a darker tinge—it looked just like blood. For a moment I was tempted to *taste* it; but damn me! bad and blood-thirsty as I was, I could not do *that*. The corpse had been soaking in the wine a full week; I was convinced that the liquid was pretty thoroughly impregnated with the flavor of my scientific improvement; and even my stomach revolted at the idea of drinking wine tainted and reeking with the dead flesh and blood of the man I had murdered.

"I placed the wine on the table before my lady and the Captain; and I am free to confess that I trembled somewhat, in view of the possibility of their detecting, at the first taste, the trick which I had played them. Very nervous was I, when the Captain slowly poured out a wine glass full, and raised it to his lips; but how delighted was I, when he drained every drop of it with evident satisfaction, smacked his lips, and said to the lady—

" 'By my faith, Adelaide, 'tis a drink for the gods! How that wine improves by age! Never before has it tasted so rich, so fruity, so delicious! Observe what a firm body it has—what deep, rich color—a fitting hue for a soldier's beverage, for 'tis red as blood. Allow me to fill your ladyship's glass, that you may judge of its improved and wonderful merits.'

"Her ladyship drank, and pronounced it excellent. I was in silent extacies. 'Drink the blood and essence of the murdered dead, ye fools, and call it sweet as honey to your taste!' I mentally said—'ere many days your souls shall be made sick with the knowledge of *what* ye have drank!'

"The guilty pair were not in the slightest degree reserved in my presence; on the contrary they jested, they talked, they indulged in familiarities before my face, in a manner that astonished me not a little. Comrades, none of you have seen much of fashionable life, I take it; for although you all belong to the very best society in Ann street, you can't reasonably be supposed to have much of an idea of society as 'tis seen in the mansion of an English nobleman. Therefore, if you don't think my yarn already too tedious, (it's as true as gospel, every word of it, upon the unsullied honor of a gentleman!) and if you'd like to know something of the capers of rich and fashionable people in high life, I'll tell you, in as few words as possible, some of the sayings and doings of my lady Hawley and her handsome lover, Captain St. Clair, as witnessed by me, at the time of which I have been speaking, in London."

Jew Mike paused to take breath and "wet his whistle;" while all his listeners eagerly requested him to "go on" with his yarn. During the progress of the narrative, an old, comical looking man, not over well dressed, had entered the room, unnoticed; and seating himself in one corner, he pulled a pipe from his pocket, lighted it, and began to smoke, at the same time taking a keen and intelligent survey of the motley assembly. Jew Mike, having quenched his thirst, resumed his story. [The reader will be good enough to observe, that while we give the substance of this worthy gentleman's narrative, we pretend not to give his precise words. It is highly probable that he adapted his language to the humble capacities of his low and illiterate auditors; and we have taken the liberty to clothe his ideas in words better suited to the more intelligent and refined understandings of our readers.]

"Well, ladies and gentlemen," said Jew Mike—"as I was saying, Lady Hawley and Captain St. Clair got so bad that they never minded my presence a bit, but talked and acted before me with as much freedom as if I were both deaf and blind. My lady would dress herself in the Captain's uniform, which fitted her to a charm, for she was a large, magnificent woman, while he was of no great stature for a man, although exceedingly well-made and handsome. Not was that all: the Captain would attire himself in her splendid garments, and, but for his moustache and imperial, might have passed for a very handsome woman. And, to carry out the idea still further, my lady would pretend to take very bold and improper liberties with her lover, which he would affect to resent with all the indignation proper to his assumed sex. Then they would roll and tumble upon the soft carpet until they were quite spent and breathless; after which the Captain would run into the chamber, and conceal himself beneath, behind, or *in* the bed; she would follow in pursuit, close the chamber door, and—I would apply my eye to the key-hole; but as I am a polite man, and as there are ladies present, (ahem!) you'll excuse me for not entering into particulars.

"So much for their actions, now for their words. I was attending them at supper one night, and to say the truth they were both of them highly elevated in consequence of having too profusely imbibed their favorite wine, seasoned with the *essence of Lagrange*, the name which I had privately given it. The Captain was very slightly attired, and my lady had on nothing but a very *intimate* garment, which revealed rather more than it concealed—for they had just before been playing the very interesting game of "hide and seek," and had not yet resumed all their appropriate garments. I had formerly regarded lady Hawley as the very *beau ideal* of all that was dignified, haughty and majestic; but that night she looked lewd and sensual, in an eminent degree, and appeared utterly reckless of all decency. She exposed her person in a manner that astonished me, and seemed to abandon herself without reserve, to all the promptings of her voluptuous nature. Her appearance, conversation and actions were not without their influence on me, you may be sure; and if ever I envied mortal man, it was that young officer, who could revel at will in the arms of the beautiful wanton at his side.

"The Captain, reclining his head upon her fair bosom, said—

" 'And so Adelaide, in a few days your odious husband will return, and terminate these rapturous blisses. Why in the devil's name don't the accursed old man die of apoplexy, or break his neck, or get shot in a duel, or do something to relieve us of his hated interference with our stolen joys?'

" 'Ah, St. Clair," answered the lady, with a glance of passion—'would that the old man were dead! Since I have tasted the sweets of your society—since I first listened to the music of your voice, and since first this heart beat tumultuously against yours, my whole nature is changed—my blood is turned to fire; my religion is my love for you; my deity is your image, and my heaven—is in your arms. Oh,' she suddenly exclaimed, as the rich blood mantled on her face and neck—'how terrible it is for a young and passionate woman to be linked in marriage to an old, impotent, cold, passionless being, who claims the name of *man*, but is not entitled to it! And then if she solaces herself with a lover—as she must, or die—she is continually agitated with fears of her husband's jealousy, and the dread of discovery. Like the thirsty traveller in a barren waste, her soul yearns for an ocean of delights— and pants and longs in vain. Husband—would that there was no such word, no such relation as it implies—'tis slavery, 'tis madness, to be chained for life to but one source of love, when a thousand streams would not satiate or overflow. Yet the world—the world—disgraces and condemns such as I am, if discovered; it points to my withered husband, and says—'there is your only *lawful* love.' Heavens! the very thought of him sickens and disgusts me; *he* a lover! He is no more to be compared to thee, my St. Clair, than is the withered leaf of autumn to the ripe peach or juicy pomegranate!'

" 'By all the gods of war," exclaimed the Captain, fired with admiration at her beauty and the fervor of her passion for him, and straining her to his breast in a perfect phrenzy of transport—'thy husband shall be no longer a stumbling-block between us, angel of my soul; I will insult him—he will challenge me—we will fight—I am the best shot in Europe, and he will be shot through the heart, if the cold dotard have one. Yet stay—damn it, why not have him disposed of after the manner of the valet? Ha, ha! a good thought! Simpson, what say you? Will you do it for a couple of hundred guineas, and without laying claim to the favors of her ladyship?'

"The last sentence was uttered with a very palpable sneer; it enraged me, for by it I was reminded of the manner in which I had been swindled out of the reward promised for my other murder. Besides, the man's cool villainy, and the woman's shameless lechery, disgusted me, bad as I was; for they belonged to that class which professes all the gentility, refinement and virtue in the world; and to hear the one glorying in adultery, and the other deliberately proposing murder, afforded such a damnable instance of the sublime hypocrisy peculiar to the "upper ten" of society, that I became desperately angry, and answered the Captain in a manner that astonished him.—You will remember, comrades, that as great a villain as I am, I am no hypocrite, and was never accused of being one. And yet hypocrisy prevails in every department of life. Look," continued Jew Mike, getting into a philosophical strain, and stroking his enormous beard with an air of profound complacency—"Look at that venerable looking old gentleman, who every Sabbath stands in his pulpit to declaim against wickedness and fleshy lusts. Mark his libidinous eye, as he follows that painted strumpet to her filthy den. There's hypocrisy. Then turn your eyes toward a sister city, and mark that grey-headed, sanctimonious editor, who every week solemnly prates of honesty, sobriety, and their kindred virtues. 'What an excellent man he is,' exclaim the whole tribe of fat, tea-drinking old women in mob-caps, raising their pious eyes and snuffy noses to heaven. —Ha, ha, ha! Why, ladies and gentlemen, that editor is so cursedly dishonest and so im—*mensely* mean, that his hair wouldn't stay black, but turned to a dirty white before its time—so mean, his food won't digest easy—his shirt won't dry when washed—his clothes won't fit him—the cholera won't have him— musquitoes won't bite him—and if, after his lean carcass is huddled under the turf, his cunning little soul should attempt to crawl through the key-hole of hell's gate, the devil, whose lacky he has ever been, would kick him with as much disgust as this *fraction* once displayed in kicking a poor wretch whom he had beggared, starved and ruined!

"But I see, comrades, that you begin to grow impatient at this moralizing—and well you may, for 'tis always distasteful to look at such reptiles as we have been contemplating. Well, to take up the thread of my yarn, which I shall bring to a close as speedily as possible, for 'tis getting late.—When the Captain proposed that I should murder Lord Hawley, his and her ladyship's hypocrisy enraged me to such an extent, that I boldly looked him in the face, and said to him—

" 'Say, who is the greater villain, you or I? You, who prate of your birth, rank and position in life, and propose a murder, or I, making no pretensions whatever, I that have committed a murder at the instigation of one of your class, in the hope of reward? Look you, Captain; neither you nor your noble strumpet at your side shall bribe me to commit further crime. Wretches that you both are, false in honor and in truth, know that I am already fearfully revenged upon you—and your exposure is at hand. Another murder, indeed!—*have you not both drank blood enough?*'

"This last sentence I uttered with such significance that the Captain started and turned pale. 'What mean you, scoundrel?' he demanded.

" 'Follow me, both of you, to the wine cellar!' I exclaimed in answer, fully determined to reveal the awful truth to them at once. Astonished and subdued by the impressiveness of my manner and the singularity of my words, they obeyed.

Having seized a light from the table, I led the way to the cellar, and advanced to the cask wherein rotted the remains of the murdered Lagrange.

"The scene must have been a striking one, comrades. There was the vast vault, dimly lighted by a single wax taper; around were many black and mouldering casks containing the juice of the grape, some of which was of a great age. Before one of those casks, much larger than the others, stood I, brandishing aloft the implement with which I was about to break open that strange tomb, and disclose its awful secret. Beside me, dressed in the slight garments I have already described, their pale countenances expressive of mingled curiosity and fear, stood Lady Hawley and Captain St. Clair, whom I thus addressed—

" 'This cask, may it please your ladyship and the Captain, contains the wine which you both are so extremely fond of. You have observed, with some surprise, that its flavor has of late much improved. I shall now, with your permission, show you the cause of that improvement, for which —ha, ha, ha! —you are solely indebted to me. The opening of this cask will disclose a mystery that you have never dreamed of. Look!'

"They both strained forward in eager expectation. A few blows sufficed to remove the head of the cask. Horror! a sickening stench arose, and there became visible the headless trunk of a human being. That portion of the body which was not immersed in the wine, was putrid. 'Look here!' cried I, in mad triumph, plunging my arm into the cask, and drawing forth the ghastly head of Lagrange. I held aloft the horrid trophy of my vengeance; there were the dull, staring eyes, the distorted features, and drops of wine oozed from between the set teeth. With a long, loud shriek, her ladyship fell to the ground insensible; muttering fierce curses on me, the Captain turned to raise her, and profiting by the opportunity, I escaped from the cellar and fled from the house. Making the best of my way to the 'Jolly Thieves,' in St. Giles, I sought safety and concealment there, where I had ample leisure to mature my future plans.

"In a day or two I saw it announced in one of the newspapers that a cask had been found floating in the river Thames, which on opening was found to contain the body and head of a man, and a quantity of wine. The circumstance gave rise to the supposition that the body had been procured by some surgeon for dissection, and for some reason had been abandoned and thrown overboard. The cask and its contents had, of course, been thrown into the river through the agency of the Captain; and the affair gave rise to neither excitement nor investigation.

"Meanwhile, Lord Hawley had returned to town. No sooner was I apprised of the fact, than I sent him the following blunt and somewhat rude epistle—for I felt too keen a thirst for vengeance on my enemies to admit of my being very choice or respectful in my language, even to a nobleman:—

" 'My lord,—you are a cuckold. Do you doubt it? I can prove it, beyond the shadow of a doubt. Captain Eugene St. Clair is your lady's lover—she is his mistress. For a long time past, she has, during your absence, received him into her chamber. You are laughed at by the pretty pair, as a withered, impotent old dotard. You know the handwriting of your late valet, Lagrange. Accompanying this is a letter written by him, to you; before he had an opportunity of sending it to you, he was *made away with*, through the instrumentality of your amiable wife, who had every reason to suppose that he would betray her. The tale trumped up by the noble harlot about the Frenchman's having stolen your property and fled, is a lie. My lord, I think you have reason to be grateful to me for exposing the guilty parties; if so, any pecuniary reward which you may see fit to send me, by one of your servants, (I am at the *Jolly Thieves*, in St. Giles,) will be gratefully accepted by

MICHAEL SIMPSON.'

"I thus freely disclosed my place of concealment to his lordship, because I apprehended no danger to myself, knowing that the nobleman was a man of honor, who would not injure the person who had rendered him such an important service as to put him on the track to avenge his wrongs. And I also anticipated receiving a liberal reward for my information; nor was I disappointed,—for that very evening a servant in the Hawley livery called at the *Jolly Thieves*, and presented me with a small package, which on opening I found to contain bank notes to the amount of five hundred pounds, and the following note, which though in his lordship's handwriting, bore neither address nor signature:—

" 'Here is the reward of your information. Accept, also, my thanks. The proof you have furnished of the truth of your statement, admits of no doubt. I know how to punish the w**e and her blackguard paramour. You had better leave the country, for I can surmise what agency *you* had in the affair of Lagrange's disappearance; but as you were the tool of others, I stoop not to molest you. Should the event, however, gain notoriety, *the law* of course, will not prove equally considerate.'

"I was overjoyed! Five hundred pounds, and the certainty of having ruined my enemies! That night I gave a sumptuous supper to all the frequenters of the *Jolly Thieves*; and a jolly time we had of it, I'll assure you, comrades. The most respectable men in London were present at the feast; there were nine cracksmen, five highwaymen, twelve pickpockets, two murderers, three gentlemen who had escaped from transportation, and a smart sprinkling of small workmen, in the way of *fogle hunters*, (handkerchief thieves,) and *body snatchers*, (grave robbers). Full forty of us sat down to a smoking supper of stewed tripe and onions,—ah, how my mouth waters to think of it now! And then the *lush!*—gallons of ale, rivers of porter, and oceans of grog! Every gentleman present volunteered a song; and when it came to be my turn, I gave the following, which, (being something of a poet,) I had myself composed, expressly for the occasion, to the air of the *Brave Old Oak*:—

SONG OF THE JOLLY THIEF.

"A song to the thief, the jolly, jolly thief,
    Who has plied his trade so long;—
May he ne'er come down to the judge's frown,
    Or the cells of Newgate strong.
'Tis a noble trade, where a living's made

By an art so bold and free;
May he never be snug in a cold, stone jug,
Or swing from a two-trunk'd tree!

CHORUS
Then here's to the thief, the jolly thief
Who plies his trade so bold—
May he never see a turnkey's key,
Or sleep in a prison cold!

"This song was received with the most uproarious applause by the jovial crew; and we separated at a late hour, after giving three groans for the new police.

"A few days passed away. I never neglected each morning to carefully peruse all the newspapers; and just as I was beginning to despair of ever seeing any announcement calculated to assure me that my enemies were overthrown, I had the intense satisfaction of reading the following paragraph in the *Times:*—

" 'AN AFFAIR OF HONOR. Yesterday morning, his lordship Viscount Hawley and the Honorable Captain Eugene St. Clair had a hostile meeting in the suburbs of London. Circumstances of a delicate nature, of which we are not at liberty to speak at present, are reported to have led to the difficulty between the noble gentlemen. At the first fire Captain St. Clair fell, and upon examination it was found that he had been shot through the heart. He died instantly. His lordship was uninjured, and immediately departed for the Continent unaccompanied by her ladyship.'

"I danced with delight when I read this paragraph. 'My vengeance is already half accomplished,' thought I. But what had become of Lady Hawley? The newspapers, from day to day and from week to week, were silent with respect to her fate. At length I began to fear that her ladyship, after all, was destined to escape uninjured by my endeavors to effect her ruin. Was I right? You shall see.

"Nearly two years passed away, during which time, with the aid of my five hundred pounds, I had set up a first-rate public house in a populous and respectable neighborhood, and was making money. I have little doubt but that the sign of '*The Red Cask*' is still remembered in that vicinity—for that was the name which, actuated by a strange whim, I had given to my tavern; and the same was illustrated by a huge swinging sign in front, on which was painted the representation of a large cask overflowing with blood—which, I need scarcely tell you, was a sly and humorous allusion to the affair of Lagrange's murder.—Well, one cold, stormy winter's night, when the wind was howling like ten thousand devils around the house, I was seated in my comfortable tap-room, making myself extremely happy over a reeking jarum of hot rum punch. I was alone, for the hour was late, and all my guests had departed; when suddenly, during a pause in the clatter of the elements, I heard a low, timid knock at my outer door, which faced on the street. —Supposing it to be either some thirsty policeman, or a belated traveller anxious to escape from the fury of the storm, I arose and unbarred the door; as I opened it, a fierce gust of wind rushed in, so piercing cold, that it seemed to chill me to the very marrow of my bones; and at the same moment I beheld a human form crouching down under the narrow archway over the door, as if vainly endeavoring to shield herself from the fury of the tempest. I knew it was a woman, for I caught a glimpse at an old bonnet and tattered shawl. She shivered with the cold, which even made my teeth chatter, stout and rugged as I was. 'What do you want?' I demanded roughly—for I was impatient at having been thus unseasonably interrupted while paying my devotions to the mug of hot rum punch, in front of a rousing fire. As she made no immediate reply, I was about to bid her begone and shut the door, when she said, in a faint, yet earnest tone—'Oh, sir, for God's sake, as you hope for mercy yourself hereafter, let me come in for a moment—only a moment—that I may warm my benumbed and freezing limbs!' I paused a moment; I am not naturally hard-hearted, unless there is something to be gained by it; and besides, I felt a kind of curiosity to see what sort of a creature it was who wandered the streets that awful night, destitute and houseless; so I bade her come in, and with difficulty she followed me into the tap-room; placing a seat for her near the fire, I resumed my own, and while leisurely sipping my punch, a good opportunity was afforded me to examine her narrowly. She was probably about twenty years of age, but much suffering had made her look older. Though her features were worn and wasted, and though her cheeks were hollow by the pinchings of want, she was beautiful; her eyes were large, lustrous and eminently expressive, and two or three stray curls of luxuriant hair peeped from beneath her old, weather stained bonnet. Her form was tall, and graceful in its outlines; but what particularly struck me was the singular whiteness and delicacy of her hands, which plainly indicated that she had never been accustomed to labor of any kind. Her dress was wretched in the extreme, and was scarce sufficient to cover her nakedness, much less shield her from the inclemency of the weather,—nay, my inquisitive researches soon convinced me that the miserable gown she wore was, excepting an old shawl, her *only garment*—no under clothing, not even stockings,—and her feet (I noticed that they were small and symmetrical,) were only separated from the cold side-walk by thin and worn-out shoes. —Yet, notwithstanding all her poverty and wretchedness, there was about her a look of subdued pride, which, though in strange contrast with her garb, well became her general air, and regular handsome features. Everything about her, excepting her dress, convinced me that she had fallen from better days, and, somehow, that look of pride struck me as being strangely familiar; yet I racked my brain in vain to recall from the dreamy past some image that I could identify with the female before me, who sat in front of my blazing fire and warmed her chilled limbs with every appearance of the most intense satisfaction.

"Her superior air commanded my involuntary respect. 'Madam,' said I, 'are you hungry?' She eagerly answered in the affirmative; I placed provisions before her, and she ate with an appetite almost ravenous. I then gave her some mulled wine, which seemed to revive her greatly; and she returned me her thanks in a manner so lady-like and refined (a manner, however, which insensibly partook of a peculiar and indirect kind of *hateur*, as remarkable in her tone as in the expression of her features,) that I was more than ever satisfied that she had descended to her present wretched situation, certainly from a respectable, if not from a very superior, order of society.

" 'You have benefitted me greatly, sir, and I thank you,' said she, inclining her head towards me with an air almost condescending. 'I assure you, you have not bestowed your *assistance* (she didn't say *charity*, observe!) upon a habitual mendicant or common person. I am by birth a lady; you will pardon me for declining to state the causes of my present condition. Again I thank you.'

"The devil, comrades! here was a starving, freezing beggar woman whom I had picked out of the street, and warmed and fed, playing the condescending, reserved lady, forsooth! and abashing and humbling me by her d——d lofty, proud looks! Ha, ha, ha! and yet I liked it, mightily; the joke was too good; and so I continued to 'madam' her, until at last I actually detected her on the very point of calling me 'fellow;' but fortunately for her, she checked herself in time to escape being turned into the street forthwith.

"And yet the superiority of her air and the haughtiness of her manner had for me an indescribable charm, no less than her beauty; and I resolved, if possible, to make her my mistress, for I doubted not that when she should become nourished and strengthened by proper food and rest, she would make a very desirable companion for a man of my amorous temperament. However, I did not broach the subject at that time, but contented myself with seeing that she was comfortably provided for that night, under the charge of one of the females of the house, to whom I gave money with which to provide the strange lady with proper and respectable clothing in the morning. The next day I had occasion to go away at an early hour, and did not return until late in the afternoon, and on entering my little parlor, I was surprised at beholding a lady, handsomely dressed, who advanced towards me with an air of dignified politeness. Her rich hair was most tastefully arranged; her neat dress closely fitted a slender but elegant shape, and I was struck with the dazzling fairness and purity of her complexion, and the patrician cast of her features. A second glance told me it was the female whom I had relieved the previous night; and I became aware of the fact that the strange lady was no other than Lady Adelaide Hawley!

"She did not recognize me, for I was much changed, in consequence of having removed the huge beard which I had worn, while in her husband's service. You may imagine my triumph at finding the proud lady an inmate of my house and a dependent on my bounty, under circumstances so humiliating to her and so gratifying to me; and you may well believe that I lost no time in giving her to understand the nature of the reward I expected in return for my hospitality. Would you believe it? She actually repulsed me with scorn, and began to talk of her birth, and the superiority of her rank to mine! Her confounded pride had now become altogether ridiculous; and somewhat enraged, I told her who I was. She started, regarded me for a moment with a scrutinizing look, and burst into tears, saying— 'It is so, indeed! My punishment is just; I am humbled and degraded before the very menial I despised. Take, me, Simpson; do with me as you will; crime levels all ranks. Yet stay; I am still feeble; delay the consummation of your triumph for one week. During that period I shall regain the strength I have lost, and the beauty that has faded; then shall I be a fitting partner for your bed.' I consented; two or three days passed, and I was rejoiced to perceive that she daily grew in strength and beauty, and was fast regaining that voluptuousness of person which had formerly distinguished her. She related to me, at my request, the particulars of her downfall. She had been cast off by her husband and rejected by her relations with scorn and curses, when the fact of her adultery with St. Clair was discovered. —Entirely friendless and without resources, she was compelled to place herself under the protection of a gentleman of fashion and pleasure, who rioted on her luxuriant charms for a brief season, until possession and excess produced satiety, the sure forerunner of disgust—she was then thrown aside as a worthless toy, to make room for some fresh favorite. Rendered desperate by her situation, she became an *aristocratic courtezan*, freely sacrificing her person to every nobleman and gentleman of rank who chose to pay liberally for her favors. In this manner she subsisted for a time in luxury—but at last, her patrons (as is always the case) grew tired of her; she had become

> "Like a thrice-told tale,
> Vexing the dull ears of a drowsy man,"

and was again thrown upon the world without resources. Her indomitable pride still clung to her, through all her misfortunes; and though she plainly saw that her amours with the aristocracy were at an end forever, she disdained to seek meaner lovers among the humbler classes. Every offer made to her by men of medium rank, was spurned by the proud harlot with supreme contempt. 'I am a companion for nobility—not for the grovelling masses,' she would reply, in answer to all such offers; nor did the pinchings of want and hunger even for a moment shake her resolution, or disarm her prejudices. She might, had she been disposed, have still lived in comfort and even splendor, by becoming an inmate of some fashionable brothel; but as in such an establishment she would be required to bestow her favors indiscriminately on men of all ranks, who could pay for the same, she recoiled from the idea with disgust. Thus did the pride of this singular woman triumph over her wants and poverty; when on the very verge of starvation, with the means of relief within her grasp, the thought—'I am of noble birth,' would sustain her, and enable her to resist successfully the longings of hunger and the sufferings incidental to a homeless life. No scrupulous delicacy prevented her from accepting any assistance, pecuniary or otherwise, that might be offered to her; she even did not hesitate to ask for charity, in tones of *affected* humility; but the all-pervading principle, PRIDE OF BIRTH, implanted within her breast, imperiously restrained her from bestowing the favors of her patrician person upon 'vulgar plebeians;' and, in consequence, she had sunk lower and lower in want, destitution and misery, until driven, on that terrible winter's night, to supplicate for a slight and temporary relief at the door of one whom she had formerly so much despised, but on whom she was now so dependent.

"It was a cold evening, and her ladyship and myself were seated before a comfortable fire. An abundance of wholesome food, and every comfort which it was in my power to procure for her, had improved her appearance greatly. Her form had regained much of its natural roundness, and her countenance had recovered all its original beauty. She was gazing pensively into the fire; while I regarded *her* with an eye of admiration, and a heart full of amorous longings. At length I broke the silence. 'To-morrow night, madam,' said I, 'the week for which you stipulated, will have expired.' She sighed deeply, and murmured, in an almost inaudible tone, 'It is so, indeed.' Noticing the sigh which accompanied her words, a frown of displeasure gathered on my brow; but it was almost instantly dispelled, in the delight I felt at my approaching happiness. 'Yes,' I continued, 'to-morrow night I shall be the happiest of men; but madam, why delay until to-morrow night that felicity which may as well be enjoyed to-night? You can never be more beautiful or more voluptuous than you are at this moment.' During the utterance of these words, I had drawn my chair close to hers, and encircled her enchanting waist with my arm; I felt her heart throbbing wildly beneath my hand, which had invaded the snowy regions of her swelling charms—and I took it to be the wild throbbing of passion. We were alone—not a soul was stirring in the house; propitious moment! How longingly I gazed upon her dewy lips, which reminded me of the lines in Moore's *Anacreon*—which, I suppose, is all Latin and Greek to you, comrades:—

> "Her lips, so rich in blisses,
> Sweet petitioners for kisses!
> Pouting nest of bland persuasion,
> Ripely suing Love's invasion."

And they did not long sue in vain; for such vigorous salute as I gave them would have put even Captain St. Clair to the blush. While thus tasting the honey of the sweetest and most luscious pair of lips in the three kingdoms, I fancied that I felt her trembling with delight in my arms; but too soon did I become aware that she was only shuddering with disgust; for by a vigorous effort she struggled from my embrace, and, breathless and panting, said—'Not now, Simpson, not now, I entreat, I implore you! To-morrow night, the week's exemption which I craved, will be completed,—then—then—at this hour—you may—you will find me in my chamber; *then*, so help me God! I will offer no resistance; but now, not now!' I surveyed her ladyship with some surprise; her eyes sparkled like diamonds, and her face, neck and bosom were suffused with a ruddy, glowing hue. 'As you please, madam,' I coldly rejoined, for I was provoked at her violent and unexpected resistance—'as you please; but remember, I am no longer to be trifled with. To-morrow night be it, then; and see that you do not repeat this obstinacy of conduct, for I will then accomplish my object, even if I have to resort to force and violence!' '*I will not then resist you*, I swear it!' said she, with much solemnity of manner, and then added—'one favor I will ask of you: permit me to remain all day to-morrow in my chamber, and do not even attempt to see me, until twelve o'clock to-morrow night, at which hour you will find me waiting for your appearance.' I agreed to this request; and she bade me good-night in a tone almost cheerful, as she left the room to seek her chamber.

"The next day and the next evening passed;—the midnight hour arrived. I closed my house, and repaired to the chamber which had been assigned to the use of my lady guest. Finding the door unlocked, I softly entered the apartment; it was a spacious room, tolerably well furnished, and the bed was shrouded by muslin curtains; a lighted candle stood upon the table; glancing around I saw nobody. 'She is in bed,' thought I, and every nerve in my body thrilled with delight at the thought. I approached the bed, and drew aside the curtain. There she lay—but how very still! 'She sleeps,' thought I, somewhat surprised; and bending over in the dim light of the unsnuffed candle, I kissed her lips—heavens! what made them so very cold—and why was the hand which I had lasciviously laid upon her bosom, dampened with a warm liquid? I rushed to the table, seized the candle, and returned to the bed-side. There she lay—DEAD! The life-blood was welling from an awful gash in her left breast; her right hand grasped a dagger—the instrument of her death; the bed on which she lay was literally soaked with her blood, and my hand was stained with it. Then I comprehended her words—*'I will not then resist you!'* I staggered back, horror-stricken; the shadow of remorse for the first time darkened my soul; I would have wrested the dagger from her lifeless hand, and plunged it into my own heart, but in the agonies of death she had clutched it too firmly to admit of my easily tearing it from her grasp. I turned from the bed, and again placed the candle upon the table; I sat down by it, with the cold perspiration starting from every pore. Ha! what is this? a letter, and addressed to me? I had not observed it before. Eagerly I tore it open, and instantly recognized the elegant handwriting of her ladyship—not a blot, not a misformed letter marred the beautiful chirography of the missive; it was written with the same grace and precision that had in former days characterized her ladyship's notes of invitation to her splendid parties. As near as I can remember, it read as follows:—

"'Death is preferable to the dishonor of your vile embraces. Were you a man of birth, gladly would I accept the protection of your arms; but Lady Adelaide Hawley can never become the mistress of a menial. I welcome death, as it will preserve me from staining the purity of my noble blood by cohabitation with such as *thou* art. May heaven pity and forgive me!'

"After I had read this characteristic note, I reflected deeply upon the tragic event—her suicide. Innocent as I was of her death, might I not be arrested as her murderer?* Circumstances were strong against me; how could I prove my innocence? Many men have been hung on circumstantial evidence less strong. Though I had escaped detection on a murder which I had actually committed, I now feared that I should suffer for a deed of which I was not guilty. The gallows arose before my excited fancy, in all its terrors; my throat seemed encircled by the fatal rope. —I determined to fly the country; instantly acting upon this impulse, I left the chamber, and hastily collected together all my money (which was

---

*Acute and sagacious as Jew Mike was, it did not occur to him, in his trepidation and alarm, that the note which he had just read, and which was in Lady Hawley's own handwriting, would clearly exonerate him from all suspicion of his having murdered her. But guilt is sometimes singularly short-sighted, and Mike, as cunning a villain as he was, threw aside or perhaps destroyed the only evidence he could have possibly produced to substantiate his innocence.

considerable) and valuables. Then I left the house, and seeking a safe asylum in an obscure party of the city, remained there until an opportunity was afforded me to take ship to America. I arrived here—soon spent all my money—was hauled up for a murder—was convicted of manslaughter only, and did the State service for a period of ten years in the stone institution at Charlestown; served out my time— and here I am. Now, comrades, you have heard my story; that it has been a long one, and a dry one, I grant—at all events, the narration of it has made *me* confoundedly dry. Here's a health to jolly thieves all the world over, and confusion to honesty, the law, and the police!"

Jew Mike did honor to his own toast in a bumper of brandy; nor were the others backward in following his example. Sow Nance, who had just awoke from a sound sleep, swore it was the most capital story she had ever heard in her life, which opinion she enforced by many oaths that we need not repeat. 'Charcoal Bill' and 'Indian Marth' were loud in their expressions of delight; and Jew Mike had the satisfaction of perceiving that he had pleased his audience, and made himself the hero of the night. A general conversation followed, which lasted until the Jew, as chairman of the meeting and Captain of the *Grabbers*, called the assembly to order, and announced that Sow Nance had the floor; —whereupon silence was restored, and that lady gave utterance to the following words, in a hoarse voice.— Her remarks were copiously interspersed with oaths, which, out of respect for the reader's feelings and our own credit, we omit:—

"Well, gals and fellers, being as how my Mike here has been a blowin' off his gas, I might as well blow mine. You all know how I first came to be se-duced, don't yer? It was a rich State street lawyer wot first did it, when I was 'leven years old. Ha, ha, ha! a jolly old cock he was, with a bald head and a face all over red pimples— he used to be mighty fond of us girls, I tell yer. Maybe I didn't use to suck the money out of him, by threatenin' to *blow* on him—well, I did! Yer all know how I had a young-'un, and how—ha, ha, ha!—the brat was found, the next day after it was born, dead in the *Black Sea*; it never died no nat'ral death that young-'un didn't, yer can bet yer life; the old Cor'ner wasn't far out of the way when he said in his werdict that the child had been strangled! The State street lawyer was its father, I believe, tho' I can't say for certain, I had so many partick'lar friends; for if I *ain't* werry good-looking, I've got winnin' ways. I came from a first-rate family, I did; my father was hung for killing my mother—one of my brothers has also danced a horn pipe in the air, and another is under sentence of death, off South, for beating a woman's brains out with a fire shovel, and choking her five children with a dishcloth. He's one of the true breed, he is. I ain't no dishonor to my family, either; for besides that strangling business, (mind, I didn't say *I* did it!) I once pitched a drunken sailor down stairs, which accidentally broke his neck, after I had lightened his pockets of what small change he had about him. —To tell the honest truth, I'm rather too ugly to make much money by doing business myself; so I've gone into the business of picking up young, good-looking gals, coaxing them off, and getting them into the houses of my regular customers, who pay me well, at so much a head. My best customer is the rich Mr. Tickels, who lives in

South street; many's the young gal I've carried to him, and many's the dollar I've earned by it. Look here—do you see this five dollar gold piece? I earned it this morning by coaxing a gal to go with me to Mr. Tickel's house; she was a little beauty, I tell yer, and I'll bet she won't come out of that house the same as she went in, no how. She was a fruit gal, but she wasn't one of us; her name, I believe was Fanny—"

"Blood and battering-rams!"

This singular exclamation was made by the comical looking old man, who had entered the "Pig Pen" unperceived, and had been seated in the corner unnoticed by any of the company. He had arisen from his seat, and stood in an attitude which betokened profound interest and great astonishment. For a moment the whole gang, male and female, regarded him with surprise and suspicion; then Jew Mike sprang forward, seized him by the throat, shook him strongly, and in a rough, fierce voice, demanded:—

"Death and the devil, old scoundrel, how came you here? Who are you?—are you a police spy—one of Marshal Threekey's gang? Speak, d——n you, before I break every bone in your accursed old carcass!"

It was a singular contrast, between the great, powerful ruffian, and the little old man—nevertheless, the latter individual (who, the reader need scarcely be told, was no other than our eccentric friend, the Corporal,) did not tamely submit to such rough treatment; extricating himself, with much agility, from the grasp of the Jew, he dealt that worthy such a quick and stinging blow in the region of his left ear, that it laid him sprawling on the floor, at the same moment exclaiming—

"Skulls and skeletons! do you take me for a child? Nay, come on again, if you are so disposed, and by the nose of Napoleon! I'll beat you to a jelly!"

It is difficult to say what might have been the fate of the gallant Corporal, had a second encounter taken place, for the Jew arose from the floor with a howl of rage, his dark face livid with passion. But, fortunately for our friend, at this crisis there stepped forward a big, brawny, double-jointed Irishman, with a fist like a shoulder of mutton; this gentleman gloried in the title of 'Cod-mouth Pat,' in humorous allusion to the peculiar formation of his 'potato trap,' an aperture in his head which might have been likened either to a cellar door or a coal scuttle.

"Och, be the powers, Misther Jew Mike," said Pat, placing himself between the Corporal and his gigantic antagonist—"be asy, and lave the owld gintlman alone; he's a brave little man intirely, and it's myself that'll fight for him. Whoop! show me the man that 'od harm my friend, and be the holy poker, and that's a good oath, I'll raise a lump on his head as big as the hill of Howth, and that's no small one!"

The good-hearted Irishman's interference saved the Corporal from a severe beating, if not from being killed outright—for the Jew dared not engage in a personal conflict with a man of Pat's resolution and strength. Yet any ordinary observer could not have failed to notice the look of deadly vengeance that gleamed in his eyes, indicating that he would not soon forget or forgive the blow he had received.

At that moment, a loud noise resembling the crash of decanters and glasses, mingled with loud oaths and yells of defiance, which sounds proceeded from the adjoining dance cellar, plainly indicated that one of those "bloody rows" for which Ann street is famous, had commenced. Such a scene was too much the element of Cod-mouth Pat for him to remain tranquil during its progress; with an unearthly yell he grasped a short, thick cudgel which he always carried, and leaving the "Pig Pen," plunged into the thickest of the fight. Many a black eye and broken head attested the vigor of his arm; but the glory of his achievements did not screen him from being borne to the watchhouse, nor did his valor prevent the magistrate in the morning from inflicting upon him a very decent fine, which drew from him the indignant remark that—" 'Tis a great country, any how, where a man can't have a ginteel bit of a fight without paying for it!"

The Corporal's case again looked desperate, when Pat left the "Pig Pen," for he was then without a protector from the vengeance of Jew Mike. But the Jew did not appear inclined to assail the old man personally, though his ferocious eyes still gleamed with rage. Standing apart, he held a whispered conversation with Sow Nance, during which the Corporal could occasionally overhear the words—'spy,' 'danger,' 'police,' 'murder,' and the like. At last they seemed to arrive at some definite conclusion; for the Jew came forward, and said—

"Old fellow, whoever you are, you have heard too much of our private discourse, for our safety. —We must confine you, until such time as you may succeed in convincing us that you meant no foul play in thus intruding into our secret rendezvous."

The Corporal began to speak, but the Jew fiercely commanded him to be silent. Meanwhile, Sow Nance had procured a rope, and ere the old man was aware of her intention, she had seized and pinioned his arms with great dexterity.

"Into the *Black Hole* with him!" shouted the Jew. The poor Corporal was hurried from the room, through a low, narrow door, along a dark, winding passage, and soon found himself in a spacious cellar, crowded with negroes, who were drinking "blue ruin" and smoking vile cigars. This resort of the "colored society" was a place of the most degraded and vicious kind, frequented by the lowest of the black population of Ann street. At that period, respectable public houses for the exclusive accommodation of the colored aristocracy, were very rare; and it is only recently that the enterprise and public spirit of Mr. William E. Ambush has established a *recherche* and elegant Saloon in Belknap street, bearing the poetical cognomen of "*The Gazelle.*" We allude to this latter place for the purpose of showing that however degraded may be the colored denizens of Ann street, and however low their resorts, there are nevertheless those of the same complexion who are elevated in their notions of propriety, and strictly exclusive in their associations.

"Hallo, here—where's Pete York?" demanded the Jew, looking around upon the sable assembly with an air of authority.

A small, very black and hideous looking negro stepped forward in answer to the name, with a grin that would not have disgraced the very devil himself.

"Dat's me, master," said he. (It may be as well to remark here, that this negro was soon afterwards sentenced to be hung for an atrocious murder, in Ann street. His sentence was, however, commuted by the Governor to imprisonment for life. He is now comfortably located in the Charlestown State Prison.)

"Well, then, you black scorpion, I wish you to take charge of this old fellow, and let him not escape, as you value your life. Keep him here safely for a day or two, and I'll reward you well for your trouble. Sooner than let him escape, *kill him*—do you hear?"

The negro *did* hear, and perfectly comprehended, also. He replied not in words, but in expressive pantomime. Drawing a knife from his belt, he passed his finger approvingly along its glittering edge—then he drew it lightly across his own throat, in the immediate vicinity of his windpipe; by which actions he meant to intimate that should the old gentleman, with whose guardianship he had the honor to be entrusted, manifest the least inclination to "give him the slip," he, Mr. Peter York, would, in the most scientific manner, merely cut his throat from ear to ear, as a particular token of his warm personal regard. Jew Mike appeared perfectly satisfied with the assurance thus eloquently conveyed, and, accompanied by Sow Nance, left the cellar, leaving the Corporal to the tender mercies of as desperate a band of villains and cut-throats as ever prowled about in the dark alleys and underground dens of Ann street.

"Now, my good fellow," said the old gentleman, addressing the negro whose prisoner he now was—"you had better instantly unbind me, and suffer me to take my departure from this infernal trap. Give me my liberty, and I will pay you ten times the sum that your Jew friend can afford to give you for detaining me here. What say you?"

"Oh, you shut up!" responded Pete York—"you s'pose I'm going to b'lieve any such gas as dat? You look like paying more money than Jew Mike, and not a decent coat on your back! Hush up your mouf, or you'll get this knife a-twixt your ribs in less than no time."

The black ruffian, in order to convince his prisoner that he meant what he said, pressed the sharp point of his knife so closely to the Corporal's breast, that it penetrated the skin. Mr. York, having thus practically admonished his victim to preserve silence, (which the Corporal thought it best to do, under the circumstances,) called to another negro, who was indulging in deep potations at the bar, in company with his "ladye love," a wench whose personal attractions consisted of a knotty head, flat nose, and mouth of immoderate dimensions—and that she *was* attractive to her lover, was afterwards manifested by the fact that in a fit of jealousy he murdered a rival in her affections; for which amusement he was hung in the yard of the Leverett street jail on the 25th day of May, 1849, in the presence of a very jovial party, who were highly delighted with the exhibition.

"Wash Goode," cried Mr. Peter York, addressing that gentleman with a familiar abbreviation of his patriotic Christian name—"look yeah, a moment, will you nigger?"

Mr. Washington Goode crossed the cellar, and desired to know in what way he could be serviceable to his particular friend and boon companion, Mr. Peter York. The latter gentleman explained himself in a few words.

"Jew Mike has put this old white man under my charge," said he, "for a few days, and I don't know where the h——l to keep him. What shall I do with the old son of a ———?"

"Why, put him in de coal-hole, to be sure," replied the other, with a boisterous laugh at his own ingenious suggestion.

Mr. York signified his approval of this plan, and dragging the poor Corporal into the dark passage which he had traversed in going to the cellar, he seized a large iron ring, opened a trap door, and violently pushed his victim into the dark and yawning chasm. Then he shut down the trap door, securely fastened it and departed.

The unfortunate Corporal fell a distance of about eight feet, and landed upon a soft, damp bed of earth, with but little personal injury. It will be recollected that his arms had been pinioned by Sow Nance; but, by a desperate effort, the old man succeeded in freeing himself from his bonds. He then essayed to examine and explore the dismal pit into which he had been thrown—which, in the intense darkness that prevailed, was a task of no little danger. However, he cautiously began to grope about, and soon became satisfied that the place was of considerable extent.

It will readily be inferred that our friend Corporal Grimsby was a man of dauntless courage; but, notwithstanding this, a thrill of terror nearly paralysed his limbs, when, while exploring the dungeon into which he had been thrown, his feet came in contact with an object, which, on examination, he discovered to be a human skeleton. The dread of being left to starve and perish in that dismal den, in such awful company, well nigh overcame both his philosophy and courage; and seating himself upon the damp earth, he abandoned himself to those feelings of despondency naturally engendered by his situation.

A man placed in such circumstances, in the midst of intense darkness, can "take no note of time." An hour of horror will sometimes seem an age, while a week of unalloyed pleasure will often glide by seemingly with the same rapidity as a few fleeting moments. It may have been one hour—it may have been ten—that the Corporal sat on the floor of his dungeon; when suddenly he was startled by the noise of the trap-door above his head being opened, and looking up, he beheld Sow Nance gazing down upon him, holding in her hand a lantern. After regarding him intently for a few moments, she thus addressed him:—

"Say, old chap, what'll yer give me if I help yer to 'scape from this hole? Yer don't look as if yer had any money—but if yer have, pay me well, and I'll get you out."

"Lower down a ladder or a rope, and raise me from this infernal trap, and you shall have this purse—see, 'tis full of gold!" replied the Corporal, at the same time producing from his pocket a purse which was evidently well lined with the "needful."

Nance uttered an exclamation of surprise and pleasure, and then disappeared; in a few minutes she returned and lowered a ladder into the pit; the Corporal rapidly ascended, and soon stood at the side of his deliverer, whom he could not avoid thanking warmly, as he gave her the purse. Bidding him follow her, she conducted him through the dark passage; they entered the "Pig Pen," which was empty—passed through the dance cellar without attracting any attention, and to the intense joy of the Corporal, he found himself standing in the open air, with the sun shining brightly, and no one to hinder his departure from those corrupt regions of sin and horror.

He distinctly remembered that Sow Nance had boasted of having enticed a young girl to the abode of Mr. Tickels in South street. Now this latter individual was known to him as a libertine and a villain; and inwardly praying that he might not be too late to rescue his fair young friend (for he doubted not it was Fanny Aubrey,) from the power of such a monster, in season to preserve her virtue undefiled, he made the best of his way to South street. The reader knows how he rushed into the room just as Tickels was preparing to consummate the outrage, and how he laid the villain sprawling upon the floor, exclaiming—

"Broad-swords and bomb-shells! I am just in time!"

We have now seen the manner in which Corporal Grimsby discovered the whereabouts of Fanny Aubrey: and the mystery of his having arrived at a moment so very opportune, is explained.

CHAPTER V

The Chevalier and the Duchess.

A period of six months elapsed, and it was now the month of June—voluptuous June, clad in the gorgeous livery of summer. A great change had taken place in the circumstances of several of the most prominent characters of our narrative. The grandfather of Fanny—the blind old basket-maker—had been "gathered to his fathers," and was sleeping in a humble but honorable grave. The excellent old Corporal, having seen the remains of his aged friend consigned to its kindred dust, had procured a comfortable and delightful asylum for the two orphans in the family of a valued friend of his—an elderly gentleman whom we shall call Mr. Goldworthy; he was a retired merchant, possessing an ample fortune, and was a widower, having an only daughter, with whom he resided in a splendid mansion in Howard street. Miss Alice Goldworthy, (then in her eighteenth year,) was one of those rare creatures who seldom bless this grovelling earth with their bright presence. She was truly an admirable combination of excellent personal and mental qualities, and possessed in an eminent degree that beautiful art (so seldom attained) of making all who came within the sphere of her genial influence, *perfectly happy*. But her most amiable characteristic was her good heart, which prompted her to entirely overlook every consideration of self, in her desire to benefit others. We have now, in our mind's eye, the exquisite original from whom we imperfectly draw this beautiful character; her pure soul looks gently forth from the azure depths of her soft eyes; lovely in her smile, for it is the glad sunshine of a happy heart—but has that heart ne'er known affliction or grief? Ah, yes; the harsh world hath, in former times, bruised that gentle sanctuary of all womanly virtue, by its rude contact; but an o'er-ruling Providence would not suffer the blighting storms of life to crush the sweet flower that bent resignedly to the blast—for the angels in heaven are not more pure and holy than she. Peace be with her, now and forever! and should her eyes e'er encounter these humble lines, she will pardon their unknown author for having ventured to gild his pages with her beautiful character— for he has gazed upon her as upon a star, shipping with a serene and softened lustre from the blue vault of heaven.

Her domestic accomplishments were not inferior to her social virtues. In the charming (because truthful) words of an unpretending but excellent poet—

> "She had read
> Her father's well-filled library with profit,
> And could talk charmingly; then she could sing
> And play, too, passably, and dance with spirit;
> Yet she was knowing in all needle-work,
> And shone in dairy and kitchen, too
> As in the parlor."

When Fanny Aubrey was ushered into the presence of this amiable young lady, she started with surprise and pleasure—for she instantly recognized in her the kind young lady who had presented her with the gold coin on the memorable day when she was entrapped by Sow Nance into the house of Mr. Tickels. The recognition was mutual; Miss Alice instantly remembered the pretty fruit girl whose appearance had so much interested her; and warmly did she welcome both the young orphans, as future inmates of her family. Fanny had never before lived in such a grand house, surrounded by every appliance of luxurious wealth; yet the unbounded kindness of Miss Alice and her worthy father soon placed her perfectly at her ease. Excellent teachers were provided for her and her brother Charles— and, under the fostering care of their generous patrons, they promised to become ornaments to the elevated sphere of society in which they were probably destined to move.

Time passed on, and nothing occurred to interrupt the smooth current of Fanny's existence, until it was deemed advisable to engage a person properly qualified to give her instructions on that indispensable fixture to a fashionable parlor—the piano-forte. A teacher of some reputed talent was employed for this purpose; he was a Mr. Price, of Charlestown—and has since rendered himself somewhat famous for his amours in the above city with a married lady whom we shall call Mrs. Stout; he had for some time been giving her lessons on the piano—but the husband suspected that he was in the habit of imparting to her secrets more profound than those of music; he accordingly placed himself in a position to observe the operations of the parties—and soon detected them under circumstances of a very unequivocal character. Rushing in, he severely castigated the gay Lothario, who, laboring under the great disadvantage of having his costume seriously disarranged, could only

implore for mercy, while he assumed the abject posture so faithfully depicted by a
talented artist, in the engraving which accompanies this chapter. Long previous
to this humorous event, Mr. Price was, as we have stated, engaged to instruct the
pretty Fanny Aubrey in the science and mystery of the noble instrument of which
he was a well-known professor; but he soon began to indulge in such alarming
familiarities with his fair pupil, that she acquainted her friends with his conduct,
and the consequence was that Mr. Price received a very dishonorable dismissal
from the house. Nature has been very miserly of her favors to this amorous music
teacher: his countenance resembles that of an unwashed charcoal merchant, while
his manners are utterly devoid of anything like gentlemanly refinement.—We are
no great critic of the art of piano teaching; but we opine that it is rather unnecessary,
in the first stages of the instruction, to clasp a lady's waist, or even to bring one's
mouth in too close proximity to her rosy lips. It leads a sensitive female, or a
fastidious gentleman to suspect the existence of a strong desire to enjoy a more
familiar intimacy with a feminine pupil, and is apt to result in the teacher's
ignominious ejection from the house and family which he attempts to dishonor.

With the exception of Mr. Price's insults, (from which she easily escaped by
appealing to her kind patrons for protection,) Fanny's life passed on happily and
quietly for some time; until one evening, on entering the parlor, she was startled
by seeing no less a person than the Hon. Timothy Tickels, of South street, in
familiar and friendly conversation with Mr. Goldworthy and Miss Alice. Mr. Tickels
himself started and turned pale on beholding the maid whom he had attempted to
dishonor under circumstances of such peculiar atrocity; however, he quickly
recovered himself, and bowed low as Mr. Goldworthy presented her to him,
saying—

"Mr. Tickels, this is Miss Aubrey, the young lady whom I spoke to you about, as
having recently come to reside with me. Fanny, this is an old and much esteemed
friend of mine, who has expressed a great desire to see you, and whom, I am sure,
you will love and respect for his piety and moral excellence!"

Fanny coldly returned the salutations of the lecherous old hypocrite, whom
she had such a good reason to hate and despise; it was evident to her that he had
imposed on her worthy patrons, who really believed him to be a man of un-
blemished moral and religious character. During the evening, other company came
in, and Tickels, having placed himself at Fanny's side, whispered in her ear—

"My dear young lady, I see you recognize me; I also knew you instantly; for
God's sake do not expose me! I am sincerely sorry for the wrong I meditated
against you—I have since repented in sackcloth and ashes. Promise me, I entreat
you, that you will not whisper a word in regard to that infamous affair to Miss
Alice or her father—or, indeed, to any one else; promise me, angel that you are—
will you not?"

Fanny reflected a few moments, during which she asked herself—"What is the
right course for me to pursue in this matter? It will be very wrong for me to ruin
this man by exposing him, if he has sincerely repented. The Bible tells us to forgive
our enemies—ought I not to forgive him? Yes, I will; my heart and conscience tell
me it will be right to do so. Mr. Tickels," she added, aloud—"I forgive you for

having tried to injure me, and, if you have truly repented, I will never say anything about the affair which you wish to have kept secret."

How artlessly and ingenuously she pronounced those words of forgiveness, to a man who had tried to inflict upon her the greatest injury that can befall woman—a man who, even at that moment, in the black hypocrisy of his heart, gloated upon her youthful charms as the wolf doth feast his savage eyes upon the innocent lamb! Yes, and even at that moment, too, his polluted soul was hatching an infernal plan to get her again in his power, in a place where no aid was ever likely to wrest her from his grasp—a place established for purposes of lust and outrage, to which he had alluded, (in his soliloquy after the rescue of Fanny by the Corporal,) as the "Chambers of Love."

"Ah, my young paragon of virtue," said the old hypocrite to himself—"it is all very well for you to prate of forgiveness; but I'll have you in the 'Chambers' in less than a month—then see if you can again escape me! In that luxurious underground retreat, from whose mysterious recess no cry can reach the ears of prying mortals above—there, amid the sumptuousness of an Oriental palace, will I riot on those charms of thine, which now I dare but gaze upon! I'll make thee a slave to every extravagant caprice of my passion; I'll become a god of pleasure, and thou, my beautiful blonde, shalt be my ministering angel; for me shalt thou fill the glittering wine-cup with the sparkling gem of the grape; for me shalt thou sing at the banquet, and preside as Venus at the rosy couch of love."

Such were the thoughts that passed through the mind of the disgusting old voluptuary, while his lying tongue gave utterance to words like the following:—

"A thousand thanks, my kind young lady, for that promise! Ah, if you only knew how beautiful you are, you would not so much blame me for my folly—my wickedness. But I'll say no more, as such language seems to pain you. I have, by long fasting and sincere prayer, succeeded in cleansing my heart from every impure desire—I can now view you with the holy feelings—the passionless regard, of a father for his daughter. My dear child, forget not your promise to refrain from exposing an erring fellow mortal; and may Heaven bless you!"

Poor, unsuspecting Fanny!—could she have seen the black heart of the smooth villain who addressed her with such pious humility, how well she might have exclaimed, with Byron—

> "Thy love is lust, thy friendship all cheat,
> Thy smiles hypocrisy, thy words deceit."

Mr. Tickels continued to visit the Goldworthys frequently; and they, far from suspecting his real character, always received him with the familiarity of an old friend. They noticed that Fanny treated him with marked coolness and reserve; this they thought but little of, however, merely regarding it as an excess of diffidence.

It is now necessary that we introduce a new character on the stage. This was a gentleman who bore the rather aristocratic title of the "Chevalier Duvall," and was supposed to be a foreigner of distinguished birth; and if noble lineage ever indicated itself by splendid personal or mental gifts, then was the Chevalier entitled to the fullest belief when he declared himself to have descended from one of the noblest families of France—for a man of more superb and commanding beauty never won the heart of a fair lady. We confess ourselves rather opposed to the prevailing tastes of authors, who make all their heroes and heroines perfect paragons of personal beauty—but, in the present instance, we are dealing, not with an imaginary creation, but with an actual character. The Chevalier, then, was a man of a thousand; elegant in his carriage, superbly graceful in every movement, possessing a form of perfect symmetry, and a countenance faultlessly handsome, no wonder that he captivated the hearts of many lovely damsels, and made no unfavorable impression upon the mind of the fair Alice Goldworthy, whom he had casually met in polished society, and whose admiration he had enlisted, as much by the charms of inimitable wit as by the graces of his matchless person. What wonder that the gentle girl, all unskilled as she was in the ways of the world, should receive his frequent visits with pleasure; and when her kind father intimated to her that her lover was a man possessing no visible resources, and was besides very unwilling to allude to his former history, which was involved in much obscurity, what wonder that she made herself his champion, and assured her father that he (the Chevalier) was everything that the most fastidious could desire. And the good old man, never very inquisitive or meddlesome in what he considered the affairs of others, and satisfied that his daughter's views of her lover must be correct, forbore to pain her further by any insinuations derogatory to the Chevalier's character, and made no objections to his oft-repeated visits.

Delicious was that dream of love to the pure-hearted maiden! Her lover was to her the *beau ideal* of manhood; so delicate in his attentions, so uniformly respectful in his behavior. What if mystery *did* exist in reference to his history and resources?—when did Love ever stop to make inquiries relative to descent or dollars? As long as she believed Duvall to be an honorable and good man, she would have deserted her luxurious home and shared poverty and exile with him, if necessary. Ah, how often does Love, in the best and purest natures, triumph over filial affection and every consideration of worldly or pecuniary advantage.

"My Alice," said Duvall, as they were seated in Mr. Goldworthy's luxurious parlor, at that most delightful period of the day—twilight—bewitching season, when day softly melts into the embrace of night!—"My Alice, there is much connected with my name and fortunes that must be to you a profound mystery; but, believe me, my name is untainted with dishonor, and my fortunes are free from disgrace. A solemn vow prevents me from explaining myself further, until the blissful moment when I can call you wife; then, idol of my soul, shall you know all. Behold this right hand; it has never committed an action that could make this cheek blush with shame. And now, fairest among women, when shall I claim this soft hand as my own lawful prize?"

The day was named, and the happy Alice was for the first time clasped to the bosom of her lover.

*   *   *   *   *

At the hour of noon, on the next day, a gentleman might have been seen standing on the steps of the Tremont House, gazing with an eye of abstraction upon the passing throng. The age of this gentleman might have been a matter of dubious inquiry; he was not young, you'd swear at the first glance, and yet, after you had gazed two minutes into his superb countenance, you would be as ready to swear that he was not over thirty, or thirty-five at most. In truth, he was one of those singular persons whose external appearance defies you to form any opinion as to their age, with any hope of coming within twenty years of the truth. Not a single gray hair could be seen among the glossy curls that fell over his noble forehead— not a wrinkle disfigured the smooth surface of his dark, beautiful skin—and yet there was *something* that we cannot define or describe, in the expression of his eyes, which now flashed with all the fire of youth, and then grew almost dim as with the shadows of advancing age—a something that indicated to any acute observer that the elegant stranger had passed the prime of manhood.

He was dressed with tasteful simplicity. A splendid black suit set off his fine form to advantage; yet his attire was utterly devoid of ornament. Many were the bright eyes that glanced admiringly at his handsome person; yet he seemed unconscious of the admiration he excited, and gazed upon the passing crowd with all the calm complacency of a philosopher.

This gentleman was the Chevalier Duvall. Not long had he been standing upon the steps of the Tremont House, when he was accosted by an elderly gentleman of a portly appearance, whom he cordially greeted with every token of familiar friendship.

The portly old gentleman was the Honorable Timothy Tickels; he and the Chevalier had long been intimate friends, having frequently met at the house of Mr. Goldworthy. After the usual compliments, Mr. Tickels remarked to his friend—

"By the way, my dear Chevalier, you remember that you long since promised to introduce me to a sister of yours, whose charms you highly extolled. I am anxious to see if she really merits your somewhat extravagant praise. I have a few hours of leisure to-day, and if you will present me to her, I shall be delighted."

"Certainly, my good sir, certainly," rejoined the Chevalier—"the distance is but trifling, and if you will do me the honor to accompany me, to my humble abode, you shall be made acquainted with the most beautiful woman in Boston. My sister is called the *Duchess*, and as mystery is the peculiar characteristic of myself and family, you will have the kindness to address her by that title."

Mr. Tickels expressed his thanks; and the two gentlemen proceeded to Somerset street, wherein stood the residence of the Chevalier. It was a house of modest exterior, very plain but respectable in appearance; yet the interior was furnished very handsomely. On entering the house, Duvall directed a servant to inform the Duchess that he had brought a gentleman to be introduced to her; and in about a quarter of an hour the lady sent word that she was prepared to receive her brother and his friend in her *boudoir*. Accordingly, the gentlemen ascended to that apartment; and on entering, Mr. Tickels stood for a few moments rooted to the floor with astonishment.

It was a small chamber, but furnished with every indication of the most exquisite taste. Fresh flowers, smiling from beautiful vases, scented the air with their delicious perfume; classic statuary adorned every corner, and gorgeous drapery at the windows excluded the glare of day, producing a kind of soft twilight. Voluptuous paintings, with frames superbly carved and gilded, ornamented the walls; and the footsteps fell noiseless on the rich and yielding Turkish carpet. A splendid harp and piano evinced the musical taste of the tenant of that elegant retreat.

But it was not the fragrance of flowers, or the beauties of sculpture, or the divine skill of the painter, that enthralled the senses of Mr. Tickels, and caused him to pause as if spell-bound in the centre of the room. No—his gaze was riveted upon a female form that reclined upon a sofa; and now we are almost inclined to throw down our pen in despair, for we are conscious of our inability to describe such a glorious perfection of womanly beauty as met the enraptured gaze of a man, whose sensual nature amply qualified him to appreciate such charms as she possessed.

She was not what the world calls a *young* woman; yet thirty years—thirty summers—had not dim'd the lustre of her beauty. Truly, she was the VENUS OF BOSTON! A brow, expansive and intellectual—hair of silken texture, that fell in massive luxuriance from beneath a jewelled head-dress which resembled the coronet of a duchess—cheeks that glowed with the rosy hue of health and a thousand fiery passions—eyes that sparkled with that peculiar expression so often seen in women of an ardent, impetuous nature, now languishing, melting with tender desires, now darting forth arrows of hate and rage—these were the characteristics of the Duchess! There she lay, the very personification of voluptuousness—large in stature, full in form, and exquisitely beautiful in feature! Her limbs (once the model of a renowned sculptor at Athens,) would have crazed Canova, and made Powers break his "Greek Slave" into a thousand fragments; and those limbs—how visible they were beneath the light, transparent gauze which but partially covered them! Her leg, with its exquisite ankle and swelling calf,— faultless in symmetry,—was terminated by a tiny foot which coquettishly played with a satin slipper on the carpet,—a slipper that would have driven Cinderella to the commission of suicide. Her ample waist had never been compressed by the wearing of corsets, or any other barbarous tyranny of fashion; yet it was graceful, and did not in the least degree approach an unseemly obesity; and how magnificently did it expand into a glorious bust, whereon two "hillocks of snow" projected their rose-tinted peaks, in sportive rivalry—revealed, with bewildering distinctness, by the absence of any concealing drapery! When she smiled, her lips, like "wet coral," parted, and displayed teeth of dazzling whiteness, and when she laughed, she did so *musically*. Her hand would have put Lord Byron in extacies, and her taper fingers glittered with costly gems. Such was the glorious creature who entranced the senses of the Honorable Timothy Tickels on entering her luxurious *boudoir*.

She greeted her brother the Chevalier with a smile, and his friend with a graceful inclination of her head; but she did not arise, for which she apologized by stating that she was afflicted with a slight lameness caused by a recent fall. Then she glided into a discourse so witty, so fascinating, that Mr. Tickels was charmed beyond expression.

"I must really chide you, Chevalier," said she, turning to her brother—"for not having afforded me the gratification of an earlier introduction to your friend; for I now have the honor of making his acquaintance under extremely unfavorable circumstances; —almost an invalid, and arrayed in this slovenly *dishabille*. "My dear Mr. Tickels," she added, "you must not look at me, for I am really ashamed of having been caught in this deplorable plight."

Admirable stroke of art! —to apologize to an accomplished libertine, for liberally displaying to his amorous gaze charms that would have moved a marble statue!

"Magnificent Duchess," quoth Mr. Tickels, drawing nearer to her, and eagerly surveying the exposed charms of her splendid person—offer no apology for feasting my eyes on beauty such as yours. I am no fulsome flatterer when I declare to you, that you are the queen and star of all the beautiful women it has ever been my lot to behold! You are not offended at my familiarity?"

The Duchess only said "fie!" and pouted for a moment, so as to display her ripe lips to advantage; and then her face became radiant with a smile that made Mr. Tickels' susceptible heart beat against his ribs like the hammer on a blacksmith's anvil.

The Chevalier rose. "You must excuse me, both of you," said he, as he took up his hat—"I have got an engagement which will oblige me to deprive myself of the pleasure of your agreeable company for the present. So *au revoir*—make yourself perfectly at home, my dear Mr. Tickels; and it will be your own fault if you do not ripen the intimacy which has this day commenced between yourself and the Duchess."

The Chevalier departed, and Mr. Tickels was alone with the magnificent Duchess.

The old libertine spoke truly when he declared that he had never before seen such a beautiful woman. Accustomed as he was to the society of ladies, in whose company he always assumed a degree of familiarity that was almost offensive, he was nevertheless so awed and intoxicated by the divine loveliness of the Duchess, that, when he found himself alone with her, he completely lost his usual self-possession, and could only declare his admiration by his glances—not by words. For a few minutes she coquettishly toyed with her fan—then she carelessly passed her jewelled hand over her queenly brow to remove the clustering hair; and finally, with an arch glance, she complimented Mr. Tickels on his taciturnity, and laughingly enquired if he was always thus silent in the society of ladies?

"Madam," replied Mr. Tickels—"I am struck dumb by your unsurpassable beauty. Forgive me, but my tongue is mute in the presence of such a divinity."

"Fie, sir! I must scold you if you flatter me," responded the Duchess, as her cheeks were suffused with a charming blush—"and yet I find it very hard to be angry with you, for your compliments are clothed in language so elegant, that they are far from being odious. Here is my hand, in token of my forgiveness."

She gave him her hand—a hand so white, so soft, so exquisitely delicate, that its touch thrilled through the entire frame of Mr. Tickels. Involuntarily he raised it to his lips, and knelt down before her;—then suddenly recollecting himself, he arose, murmuring a confused apology for his rudeness. Her brilliant eyes were turned upon his, with a soft expression, like that of languishing desire; and partly rising from the sofa, she made room for Mr. Tickels to seat himself at her side. This action she accompanied by a gesture of invitation; and eagerly did the old gentleman sink down upon the soft and yielding sofa. At first he sat at a respectful distance from her; but gradually he edged closer and closer, until their persons touched. Still she manifested not the slightest displeasure; and at last, maddened by his close proximity to such matchless charms—for lust very often triumphs over prudence—he ventured to steal his arm around her voluptuous waist. To his inexpressible delight, she did not repulse him; and then how wildly palpitated his heart, as he gazed down into those swelling regions of snow, within whose mysterious depths a score of little Cupids might have nested! Bolder and bolder grew the excited old voluptuary, as he found that she did not resist his amorous advances; her fragrant breath fanned his cheek, and the glances of her lustrous eyes dazzled his senses. Her ripe lips were provokingly near to his—why not taste their nectar? He pressed her closer to him, and she turned her charming face full towards him, and seemed, with an arch smile, to challenge him to bear off the prize. One little inch alone intervened between her rosy mouth and his own *watering* one; in a moment 'twas done! He had stolen a kiss, and received in return a playful tap with her fan. Who, that has once ravished a kiss from the divine lips of a lovely woman, does not feel inclined to repeat the offence? Again and again he kissed her; and finally, almost beside himself with rapture, he glued his hot lips to her neck, her shoulders, her bosom. Then Mr. Tickels became sensible that he had gone too far—for she disengaged herself from his embrace, and said, with an air of offended dignity—

"You seem to forget yourself, sir; my foolish complacency to the friend of my brother has, I fear, led me to permit liberties, which have engendered in your breast desires injurious to my honor. I confess that I was, for a moment, overcome by certain feelings which I possess, in common with all others of the human family; nay, I will even admit that I am of a nature peculiarly ardent and susceptible; and your refined gallantry, and my close contact with your really very agreeable person, aroused my passions, and caused me to forget my prudence until your liberties became so intimate that I feared for the safety of my honor. I must not forget my position as a lady of character and birth; and I trust that you will remember your pretensions to the title of a gentleman."

"Forgive me, beautiful Duchess," cried Tickels, in tones the most abject—"on my bended knees I implore your pardon. What man, possessing heart and soul, could view such heavenly charms as thine, without being betrayed into an indiscretion? But forgive me, and I will ask no greater favor than to be allowed to kiss that beauteous hand."

"I am not angry with you," said the Duchess, giving him her hand, which he raised reverently to his lips, "for I can fully appreciate the feelings which prompted your conduct; therefore, I willingly forgive,—and now that we are good friends again, you may come and sit by my side, provided you will promise to be very good, and neither kiss me or clasp my waist with your arm. So, sir, that is very well—but why do you gaze so intently at my pretty shoulders and —but, good heavens! until this moment I was unconscious of my almost naked condition; if you will persist in looking at me, I must positively cover myself with a shawl."

"Charming Duchess, that would be worse sacrilege than to cover a costly jewel with tow-cloth," rejoined Tickels; and the lady smiled at his gallantry, as she remarked—

"Nevertheless, naughty man, you must not take advantage of my negligent and slight attire to devour my person with your eyes. Besides, I am too *em bon point* for either grace or beauty, and am naturally anxious to conceal that defect."

"Defect!" exclaimed Tickels,—"if there is one single defect in your glorious person, then is Venus herself a pattern of ugliness. The voluptuous fullness of your form is your most delightful attribute."

A silence of some minutes ensued, during which the old libertine continued his longing gaze, while the lady took up and fondly caressed a beautiful little lap-dog, whose snowy fleece was prettily set off by a silver collar, musical with bells. How Tickels envied the little animal, when its mistress placed it in her bosom, and bestowed upon it every epithet of tender endearment!

"Poor Fido!" at length said the lady, with a soft sigh,—"thou art the sole companion of my solitude. You would scarcely believe, Mr. Tickels, how devotedly I am attached to this little creature, and how much he loves me in return. He will only take his food from my hand, and I feed him on the most delicate custards. Every morning I wash him carefully in rose water, and he is my constant bed-fellow at night. ('Lucky dog!' sighed Tickels.) I have only his society to dispel the *ennui* of my solitude; —but, now I think of it, I have other sources of amusement: for there are my books, my music, my flowers. By the way, are you fond of music? Yes, I know you are; for you are a gentleman of too much elegant refinement of mind, not to love the divine harmony of sweet sounds. And now I shall put your gallantry to the test by requesting you to bring my harp hither; and to reward you for your trouble, you shall hear a song."

The instrument was placed before her, and she sang, with exquisite feeling and pathos, the beautiful song commencing with—

"'Twere vain to tell thee all I feel,
Or say for thee I sigh."

Tickels, to do him justice, was a true connoisseur in music; and warmly did he express his gratification at the performance, particularly as the Duchess accompanied the words by glances expressive of every tender emotion.

"Heigho! what can have become of the Chevalier? Devoted as he is to the erratic pursuits of a man of fashion, he is seldom at home, and consequently I see but little of him." Thus spoke the Duchess, after a long pause which had begun to be embarrassing.

"Do you long for his return?" asked Tickels—"will not my society compensate for his absence?"

"Oh, yes!" laughingly replied the lady—"you are gallant and agreeable; whereas my brother is often moody and abstracted. Besides, you know, a *brother* cannot of course be such a pleasant companion to a lady, as—as—I had almost said a *lover.* In truth, I am willing to confess that you are a dear, delightful old gentleman, and I am half in love with you already. Nay, don't squeeze my hand so, or I shall repent having made the declaration."

"You are a sweet creature," rejoined Tickels—"and very cruel for having afforded me a glimpse of heaven, and then shut out the prospect from my longing gaze. But tell me, how is it that you and your brother are so completely isolated in society? Certainly you must have relatives and many friends; yet you complain of solitude. If my question is not impertinent, will you tell me?—for a woman of your extraordinary beauty and accomplishments never finds it difficult to surround herself with a circle of admirers, and loneliness is an evil with which she never need be afflicted. To say merely that I feel interested in you, would fail to express the degree of admiration with which I regard you; and it would afford me an unspeakable pleasure to hear the history of your life, from those rosy lips."

"Alas!" exclaimed the Duchess, as a tear dim'd for a moment the lustre of her fine eyes—"my story is but a short and sad one. Such as it is, however, you shall have it. I was born beneath the fair skies of sunny France; my parents were noble and rich—my father, the Duke D'Alvear, could even boast of royal blood in his veins, while my mother was closely allied to several of the most aristocratic families in the kingdom. Reared in the lap of luxury, my childhood passed like a pleasant dream, with nothing to disturb its quiet, until I had reached my fifteenth year, at which period I lost both my parents by a catastrophe so sudden, so dreadful, that when you hear its particulars, you will not blame me for weeping as I do now." Here the lady's voice was broken by many sobs—but she soon recovered her composure, and continued her narrative.

"My mother was beautiful but frail—which was in her case peculiarly unfortunate, for my father was the most jealous of men. He had reason to suppose that a handsome young Count was too intimate with her; keeping his suspicions profoundly secret, he made preparations for a long journey, and having announced his intention of remaining abroad several months, he departed from Paris. That very night, at midnight, he abruptly returned, proceeded directly to my mother's chamber, and found the Count St. Cyr in her arms. The guilty pair were taken too much by surprise to attempt resistance or escape, and both were slain on the spot by my father, who had provided himself with weapons for that purpose. The Duke then went to his own chamber—the report of a pistol was heard soon afterwards, and the unfortunate man was found dead, with his brains scattered over the carpet. Thus in one fatal night were my only brother and myself made orphans—nor was this our only misfortune, for the notary who had the charge of our joint patrimony, absconded, and left us penniless. Why need I dwell on the painful details of our poverty and its attendant miseries? Suffice it to say that I resisted a hundred offers from men of rank and wealth, who would have maintained me in luxury had I consented to part with the priceless gem of my virtue. Yes—I resisted each tempting proposal, for poverty itself was sweeter to me than dishonor. We came to America, and finally to Boston; the Chevalier, by giving private lessons in the sword exercise, supports us both in a style of quiet comfort—but I charge you, sir, never let that fact be known, for the gossiping world must never learn that the son of France's proudest noble has so degenerated as to *labor* for his support. Of course, with our modest means, we can mix but little in the gay and fashionable world—as for myself, I prefer to remain at home, and see but few persons except my brother and such of his intimate friends as he occasionally brings home with him. My retired habits have preserved me from the matrimonial speculations of gentlemen, of which I am very glad, for I do not think I shall ever marry; and the seclusion of my life has also saved me from the dishonorable proposals of amorous gentlemen, who are ever ready to insult a good-looking woman provided she is poor, and they are wealthy. Unfortunately for me, I have a constant craving for male society; and when thrown into the company of an agreeable man, be he young or old, passions which have never been gratified will assert their supremacy in my breast, and I often tremble lest, in a moment of delirium, I surrender my person unresisting to the arms of a too fascinating seducer. This weakness of my ardent nature has already several times nearly brought me to ruin; and when your arms just now encircled me, and your lips were pressed to mine, the dizzy delight which I experienced would, in a few moments, have made me your victim, had I not, by a powerful effort, overcome that intoxication of my senses which was fast subduing me; I escaped from your arms, and thank heaven! my honor is preserved. Now, sir, I have frankly told you all; you certainly will not censure me for my misfortunes—and I trust you will not blame me for those propensities of nature to which we are all subject, and which are so peculiarly strong in me as to render their subjection an act of heroic self-denial."

Thus ended the narrative of the Duchess; and it may well be imagined that her words inflamed the passions of her listener more than ever. To have that splendid creature sit by his side, and candidly confess to him that the ardor of her soul yearned for enjoyments which cold prudence would not permit her to indulge in,—what could have been more provoking to his already excited feelings? Mr. Tickels gazed earnestly at her for a few minutes, and his mind was decided; he resolved, if possible, to *reason* her into a compliance with his wishes.

"Madam," said he, assuming a tone of profound respect—"you are an educated and accomplished lady; your mind is of the most elevated and superior order. You can reflect, and reason, and view things precisely as they are, without any exaggeration. Look abroad upon the world, and you will see all mankind engaged exactly alike— each man and woman is pursuing that course which he or she deems best calculated to promote his or her happiness; and happiness is the essence of *pleasure*. Your miser hoards gold—that is *his* source of pleasure; your vain woman seeks pomp, and display, and adorns her person with many jewels—from all of which she derives *her* pleasure; and as the child is pleased with its rattle, so is the musty antiquarian with his antique models—so is the traveller with his journeyings and explorations—so is the soldier with glory—and so is the lady of warm impulses with her secret amours. All seek to extract pleasure from the pursuit of some darling object most congenial with their passions, their tastes, their preferences. Why, then, should any one seek to set aside the order of things universal—the routine of nature? As consistently might we disturb the harmonious operation of some complex machinery, as to act in opposition to the great fundamental law of human nature—viz: *that every created being, endowed with a ruling passion, should seek its legitimate gratification.* By legitimate gratification, I mean, that indulgence which interferes not with the enjoyments or interests of others. The miser should not accumulate his gold at the expense of another; the libertine should not revel in beauty's arms, by force; the lady must make a willing sacrifice—thus nobody is injured—and thus the pleasure is *legitimate;* though bigoted churchmen and canting hypocrites may declaim on the sin of carnal indulgences unsanctioned by the priest and his empty ceremonies. Fools! NATURE, and her laws, and her promptings, and her desires, spurn the trammels of form and custom, and reign triumphant over the hollow mummery of the parson and his pious foolery.

"Now, dear madam," continued the artful logician, (whose words belied his own sentiments, and his own belief,) "supposing that you admit all these premises; what do we next arrive at? Let me be plain, since you have been so candid with me. You have admitted that the prevailing and all-absorbing passion of your nature is—an intense desire to enjoy that delicious communion which had its origin in the garden of Eden. Why deprive yourself of the gratification you long for? Why do you hunger for the fruit which is within your reach? Why disregard the promptings of nature? Why obstinately turn aside from a bliss which is the rightful inheritance of every man and woman on the face of the earth? And, lastly, why are you so cruel to me, whom you have been pleased to pronounce agreeable? Answer me, charming Duchess, and answer me as your own generous heart and good sense shall dictate."

The Duchess was silent for a short time, and appeared to reflect profoundly; then she said, in a tone and manner singularly earnest—

"Listen to me, my friend—for that you are such, I am very sure. I do not deprive myself of the pleasures of which you speak, in consequence of any scruples, moral or religious. I have no respect for the institution of matrimony, or its obligations; I laugh at the doctrines of those who speak of the crime of an indulgence in Love's pleasures, without the sanction of the church. I agree with you that we all have derived from nature the *right* to feed our diversified passions according to their several cravings; but while we are authorized, by the very laws of our being, to seek those delights of sense for which we yearn, a perverted and ridiculous PUBLIC OPINION prohibits such indulgences, unless under certain restrictions, and accompanied by certain forms. Now, though this public opinion undoubtedly *is* ridiculous and perverted, it must nevertheless be respected, particularly by a lady; otherwise the world, (which is public opinion,) calls her a harlot—points at her the finger of scorn—excludes her from all decent society, and she is forever disgraced and ruined. I must preserve my reputation and position as a lady, no matter at what cost, or what sacrifice; ardently as I long for the delights of love, I shall never, to enjoy them, surrender my personal freedom by marriage, or my character by yielding to the solicitations of a lover, —unless, in the latter case, I should unfortunately, while in the intoxication of excited passion, grant the favors which he asks; which I pray heaven may never happen to me! It is all very well, sir," continued the Duchess, assuming a tone of arch vivacity—"it is all very well for you *men* to be in such continual readiness to indulge in the joys of Venus, whenever opportunity presents itself; for this odious public opinion is very lenient with you, gay deceivers that you are, and kindly pardons and even smiles at your amorous frailties; but we poor women, good heavens! must not swerve six inches from the straight path of rectitude marked out for us, under pain of eternal condemnation and disgrace; and thus we are either driven into matrimony, or are obliged to deprive ourselves of a bliss (to use your own language) which is the rightful inheritance of every man and woman on the face of the earth. Well," added the Duchess, in a tone of mock melancholy which was irresistibly charming,—"poor *I* must submit to the stern decree, as well as the rest of those unfortunate mortals called women;—unfortunate because they *are* women, and because they are even more ardent in their passions than those who have the happiness to be men. Let me congratulate you, sir, on your felicity in belonging to a sex which possesses the exclusive privilege of unrestricted amative enjoyment; and I am sure you will not refuse to sympathize with me on my misfortune, in having been born one of those wretched beings who are doomed to be forever shut out from a Paradise for which they long,—a Paradise whose bright portals are guarded by the savage monster, Public Opinion, which ruthlessly denies the admission within its flowery precincts, of every poor daughter of Eve."

Mr. Tickels had listened with breathless attention to the words of the Duchess; he plainly saw that she was not to be subdued by *argument*. "Her only vulnerable point lies though the avenue of the passions," thought he—"for according to her own confession, she was intoxicated with rapture when encircled by my arms, and when receiving my ardent kisses; and only escaped the entire surrender of her person to me, by a powerful effort. My course, then, is plain—I must delicately and gradually venture on familiarities which are best calculated to arouse her sensibilities, without incurring her suspicions as to my ultimate object. I must—I shall succeed; for, by heaven! if I should fail to make this exquisite creature mine, I'll eat my own heart with vexatious disappointment!"

"My dear madam," said he, taking the unresisting hand of the Duchess in both of his, and gently pawing it in a manner that would have been disgusting to a spectator—"what can I say, after your candid avowal? Simply, that you are the most ingenuous, the most delightful creature in the world. I love you to distraction; and yet I will not urge you to depart from the course which you seem determined to pursue, though by adhering to that course you deprive me, as well as yourself, of the most exquisite delights this world can afford. Nevertheless, let us be friends, if we cannot be lovers. See, my hair is gray; I am old enough to be your father; will you not confer upon me a daughter's love? Ah, that bewitching smile is a token of assent. Thanks, sweet one; now, you know, a father should be the recipient of all his daughter's little joys and sorrows—he should be made acquainted with all her pretty plans and all her naughty wishes; is it not so, my charming daughter?* Again your soft smile answers, yes. And when the daughter thus bestows her confidence upon her father, she leans her head upon his bosom, and his protecting arm embraces her lovely waist—thus, as I now do yours. He places his venerated hand in her fair breast—thus—and feels the pulsations of her pure heart; ah! methinks this little heart of thine, sweet one, beats more violently than comports with its proper freedom from fond and gentle longings; thy father must reprove thee, thou delightful offender—yet he forgives thee with this loving kiss—nay, start not, for 'tis a father's privilege. How dewy are thy lips, my daughter, and thy breath is fragrant with the odor of a thousand flowers—'tis thy father tells thee so! Pretty flutterer, why dost thou tremble? I will not harm thee. Ah, is it so?—dost thou tremble with the bliss of being held in a father's arms, and pressed to his heart? Why doth this bosom heave—why do thine eyes sparkle as if with fire, and thy cheeks glow with the rosy hue of a ripe peach? What meaneth that longing, languishing, earnest, voluptuous look? Doth my daughter yearn after the soft joys of Venus?—Confess it, and I'll forgive thee; for thou art a passionate darling, and such desires as now swell within my breast become thee well, for they are nature's promptings, and enhance thy beauty. Ah, ha! that blush, glowing like a cloud at sunset, assures me that I am not mistaken. Yes, hide thy radiant face in my bosom, and let me gather thee closer to my heart—my life—my treasure! Let me no longer play the father; let me be thy lover—thy all—thy own Timothy—thy chosen Tickels! Ah, my bird, have I caught thee at last?—thou art mine—mine— mine—"

Every circumstance of position and the lady's compliance seemed about to confer upon Mr. Tickels the boon which he so eagerly desired, when at that critical moment the Duchess uttered a piercing scream, and pointed frantically upward to a large mirror that hung directly over the sofa upon which they were partially

---

*As an apology for the insertion of this silly, sickening rhapsody of the old libertine, the author begs to state that he introduced it, (as well as other speeches of a like character,) for the purpose of painting, in strong colors, the disgusting lechery of a man, whose primal passions had degraded him to the level of a brute. He would also assure the reader that the character of old Tickels is drawn from a living original, whose real name sounds very much like the curious cognomen that has been assigned him. It will readily be observed that during the entire scene between him and the Duchess, the latter makes him her complete tool—encouraging him to take the very liberties which she affects to resent, and even while declaring her firm intention of remaining virtuous, using language most calculated to inspire him with the thought of being able to enjoy her charms in the end. Her object in all this will be shown towards the conclusion of the chapter. It has been the author's design to portray, in the character of the Duchess, an accomplished, artful, fascinating and totally depraved woman, possessing the beauty of an angel, and the heart of a devil—precisely such a one as could not fail to enslave and victimize such a sensual old wretch as Mr. Tickels; how far this design has been successful, the intelligent and discerning reader is left to judge. In the Chevalier Duvall will be recognized one of those splendid villains, whose superb rascality is cloaked beneath the mantle of a fine person, elegant address, and the assumption of every quality likely to interest and please the credulous people whom he *honors* with his patronising friendship.

reclining; the old libertine glanced hurriedly up at the mirror, and to his horror he saw there reflected the figure of the Chevalier Duvall, standing in the centre of the room. He had entered abruptly and noiselessly, and was contemplating the scene before him with every appearance of astonishment and rage.

The Duchess hid her face in her hands, and sobbed violently, as if overcome with shame and affright; while old Tickels, pale and trembling with fear, (for he was a most detestable coward,) fell upon his knees, and gazed upon the Chevalier with an expression of countenance that plainly indicated the terror which froze his blood, and rendered him speechless—for the position in which he and the Duchess had been detected, would, he well knew, admit of no explanation—no equivocation.

"God of heaven!" said Duvall, in a voice whose calmness rendered it doubly impressive and terrible—"am I the sport of some delusion—some conjuror's trick? Do I dream—or do these eyes actually behold that which appalls my soul? Speak, Duchess—for sister I will not call you—and you, white-faced craven—what is the meaning of this scene?"

But neither the Duchess nor Mr. Tickels could utter one word in reply.

"Damnation!" exclaimed the Chevalier, drawing a pistol from his pocket, and cocking it—"answer me, one of you, and that quickly, or there will be blood spilled here!"

This brought Mr. Tickels to his senses; he arose from his knees and stammered forth—

"My dear sir—don't shoot, for God's sake—put up that pistol, and I'll explain all. I—that is—you know, my dear Chevalier—as a man of the world—beautiful woman—strong temptation—"

"Hold, sir!" cried the Chevalier—"say no more, in that strain, or you die upon the instant. Duchess, tell me the meaning of all this."

The lady raised her tearful eyes imploringly to the stern face of her brother, and said, in a voice rendered indistinct by her sobs—

"Oh, brother! pardon your erring sister, who, in a moment of weakness, forgot her proud and unsullied name! You know the fire and passion of my nature; and you know the resolution with which I have heretofore struggled against it. I am inexperienced—unused to the ways of the world—unaccustomed to the artifices of wicked men. Debarred as I am from male society, what wonder that, in the company of a male, I should be overcome by the weakness of a woman's nature? Forgive me, Chevalier, I implore you—indeed, my honor is preserved; your timely intervention prevented the consummation of my ruin."

"Sister," rejoined Duvall, gazing at her with a softened aspect—"I *do* forgive you, your honor being still undefiled; I know the power of your passions, notwithstanding your many excellent qualities; and I can scarcely wonder at your momentary weakness, when an accomplished villain tempts you to ruin. Hereafter, dear sister, govern those unruly passions with a rod of iron; remember the grandeur of our ancestral house and name, and let that remembrance be your safeguard. — As for you, sir," continued the Chevalier, turning savagely towards Mr. Tickels, while his magnificent features grew dark with terrible rage—"as for you, sir, you have betrayed my confidence and abused my hospitality; I introduced you into this house, supposing you to be a man of honor and a friend. You have attempted the seduction of my sister; you have basely tried to take advantage of the weakness of an inexperienced and unsuspecting woman; but more than all this, sir—and my blood boils with fury at the thought! —you would have tarnished the unstained name and honor of a kingly race! Look you, sir, these wrongs demand instant reparation—one or both of us must die. Here are two pistols; take your choice; place yourself at the distance of six paces from me, and let impartial Fate decide the issue!"

"But, my dear sir," cried the old villain, almost beside himself with terror—"I can't—I don't want to be killed—my God, sir, I never fired a pistol in all my life. Can't we settle this matter in some other way? Will not *money*—"

"Money!" exclaimed the Chevalier, scornfully—"fool, can money heal a wounded honor, or wipe away the odium of your insults? Choose your weapon, sir!"

"Mercy—mercy!" cried the dastard, falling on his knees before his stern antagonist—"I am rich, let me depart in safety, and I'll give you a cheque for a hundred—"

The Chevalier cocked a pistol.

"Five hundred—," groaned Tickels.

The pistol was raised, and pointed at his head.

"A thousand dollars!" yelled the victim, his face streaming with a cold perspiration, his hair bristling, and his teeth chattering with fright.

The Chevalier paused, and said, after a few moments' reflection—

"After all, to make such men as you disgorge a portion of their wealth, is a punishment as severe as any that I can inflict upon you. You are a coward and dare not fight; I wish not to murder you in cold blood. I will content myself with exposing your infamous conduct to the world—publishing your rascality in every newspaper, and you will be kicked like a dog from all decent society; this will I do, unless you immediately fill me out a cheque for the sum of five thousand dollars."

"Five thousand devils!" growled Tickels, gaining courage as he believed his life to be in no imminent danger—"what! five thousand dollars for only having kissed and toyed a little with a pretty woman, without having reaped any substantial benefit? No, no, my friend—you can't come it; you are, to use a vulgar phrase, cutting it rather fat; I'm not so precious green as you think. I don't mind giving you a couple of hundred, or so, for what fun I've had, but five thousand—whew! rather a high price for the amusement, considering what a remarkably free-and-easy lady your sister is!"

"No more of this!" thundered the Chevalier, in a tone that made Mr. Tickels leap two feet into the air—"instantly give me a cheque for the sum that I demand, or by my royal grandfather's beard, (an oath I dare not break,) I'll blow your head into fragments! —Look at that clock; it now lacks one minute of the hour; that minute I give you to decide; if, at the expiration of that period, you do not consent to do as I request, you die!"

The muzzle of the pistol was placed in very close proximity to the victim's head; there was no alternative—life was exceedingly sweet to Mr. Tickels, although the wickedness of half a century rested heavily on his soul; in a few seconds more, unless he consented to give up a portion of his basely acquired wealth, he had every reason to fear that soul would be ushered into a dark and unfathomable eternity. No wonder, then, that he tremulously said—

"Put up your weapon; I will do as you require."

Writing materials were soon brought, and in a few minutes the Chevalier was the possessor of a cheque on a State street bank, bearing the substantial autograph of Timothy Tickels.

"Now, sir," said Duvall, depositing the valuable document in his pocket-book— "you are at liberty to depart. I am confident that you will, for your own sake, keep this affair a profound secret; and so far as myself and much-injured sister are concerned, you may rest assured that nothing shall ever be said calculated to compromise your reputation. I cannot avoid expressing my regret that a man of your advanced age, and high standing in society, should descend so low as to manifest such base and grovelling sensuality—such unprincipled libertinism— especially towards a lady who has heretofore regarded you as a friend. Go, sir, and seek some other victim, if you will—but confine your amours to your own class, and do not again aspire to the favors of a lady in whose veins flows the noblest blood of France!"

Mr. Tickels took his leave of the indignant brother and his much-injured sister, with a very ill grace; and bent his steps towards his own house, grinding his teeth with impotent rage. The loss of his money, and the mortifying disappointment he had experienced, rendered him furious, and he muttered as he strode thro' the streets with hasty and irregular steps—

"Eternal curse on my ill fortune! Five thousand dollars gone at one fell swoop— but hah! the money's nothing, when I think of my being cheated out of the enjoyment of such celestial charms as those possessed by that splendid enchantress! —At the very critical moment—when she lay panting and unresisting in my arms— with all her glorious beauties spread out before me, like the delicious materials of a dainty feast—just as the cup of joy was raised to my eager lips, and I was about to quaff its bewildering contents, to be balked by the unexpected entrance of that accused Chevalier. Confusion! —I shall go mad with vexation. * * * * Well, 'tis of no use to grumble about what can't be helped; let me rather turn my attention to future joys, concerning which there can be no disappointment. My plans are all arranged; in a few days my pretty Fanny Aubrey will be an inmate of the luxurious "Chambers of Love." Ha, ha! *that* thought almost reconciles me to the loss of the Duchess—though, egad! *she* is a luscious piece, all fire, all sentiment, all enthusiasm! But oh! five thousand dollars, five thousand dollars! * * * But let me see: where is the infernal trap of that scoundrel, *Jew Mike*, whom Sow Nance recommended as a fellow well qualified to abduct my pretty Fanny, and convey her to the "Chambers?" Ah, good; his address is in my memorandum book: '*Inquire for the Pig Pen, No.—Ann street, any night after midnight.*' Ugh! I don't like this venturing among cut-throats and thieves, at such untimely hours; but nothing risk, nothing have; and anything for love!"

The reader's attention is now summoned to the scene which transpired between the Chevalier and the Duchess, immediately after the departure of Mr. Tickels from the house.

The Duchess, who had been sitting upon the sofa, bathed in tears and sobbing as if her heart would break, jumped up, bounded across the carpet in a series of graceful pirouettes, and then, throwing herself upon the floor, indulged in a peal of silvery laughter that made the room fairly echo, exclaiming—

"What a d——d old fool that man is! Oh, I shall die—I shall positively suffocate with mirth!"

The Chevalier, throwing aside every appearance of indignation and dignity, placed himself in that humorous and rather vulgar position, sometimes adopted by jocose youths, who wish to intimate to their friends the fact that any individual has been most egregiously "sucked in." Fearing that the uninitiated may not readily comprehend this pantomimic witticism, we may as well state, for their enlightenment, that it is accomplished by applying the thumb to the tip of the nose, and executing a series of gyrations with the open hand; the whole affair being a very playful and ingenious invention, much practised by newsboys, cabmen, second-hand clothes dealers, and sporting gentlemen.

"A cool five thousand!" shouted the Chevalier, abandoning this comic picture, and "squaring off" at his reflection in the mirror, in the most approved style of the pugilistic art—as if he were about to give himself a "punch in the head," for being such a funny, clever dog; "bravo! I'll go and get the cheque cashed at once; and then hurrah for a brilliant season of glorious dissipation! But, my Duchess, how the devil did you mange to get the old fool so infatuated—so crazy with passion? for I stood over ten minutes looking at both of you through the key-hole, before I entered the room, and I never before saw a man act so extravagantly ludicrous; it was only with extreme difficulty that I could keep myself from laughing outright. And you, witch that you are, looked as if you were panting and dying with amorous desires. By my soul, 'twas admirably done!"

The Duchess smiled with gratification at the praise; and arising from the carpet, on which she had been literally *rolling* in the excess of her mirth, threw herself upon the sofa in an attitude of voluptuous abandonment; and while complacently viewing her matchless leg, she said—

"For your especial entertainment, my Chevalier, I will relate all that transpired between me and the old goat, after your departure. At first, he assailed me with a profusion of silly, sickening compliments on my beauty; I blushed, (you know how well I *can* blush, when I try,) and assured him that his praises were divine—so eloquent, so elegantly conveyed—and yet I thought them intolerably stupid. Then I gave him my hand to kiss; and its contact with his lips made him as amorous as I could possibly desire. He knelt at my feet; then arose, apologizing for his rudeness. I threw all my powers of fascination into my looks, and permitted him to take a seat by my side, on the sofa. At first, he sat apart from me; but at last, gaining courage, he moved close to me, and gently placed his arm around my waist; of course, I did not repulse him. With secret joy I observed the eagerness with which he regarded such parts of my person as were exposed—and I took good care to reveal it liberally; how the odious old wretch gloated upon this bust, which you, my Chevalier, pronounce so charming! At last, he kissed me—ugh! how horribly the old creature's breath smelt! But I pretended to be more pleased than angry; and from my lips his nauseous mouth wandered to my neck, my shoulders, my bosom. I fairly shuddered as he besmeared me with his disgusting kisses; and thinking that he had gone far enough, for that time, I burst from his embrace, and reproached him (but not too severely,) for his rude behavior—taking good care, however, to fan his passions into a still fiercer flame, by telling him that my reason for particularly dreading such familiarities, was, that they had a tendency to excite my own desires to a degree that was dangerous to my honor. As I foresaw, this artful assurance was received by him with ill-concealed delight. He begged my pardon; it is needless to say, I forgave him, and suffered him to resume his seat at my side, on condition that he would take no further liberties, knowing very well that he could not long keep his promise. Then came more compliments; I sang and played for him, and he was beyond measure delighted. After a short conversation on the secluded manner in which I lived, and the loneliness which I felt, I confessed to him that I was half in love with him; while at the same time I thought him the most disgusting old brute in existence. In return for my pleasing lie, he pressed my hand fervently, and requested me to relate to him the story of my life, from "my own rosy lips," as he said. My Chevalier, you know what splendid powers of imagination, and what a rich, prolific fancy I possess; and well I may— for am I not a leading contributor to a fashionable ladies' magazine, besides being the authoress of "Confessions of a Voluptuous Young Lady of High Rank," and also the editress of the last edition of the "Memoirs of Miss Frances Hill?" Well, I entertained my aged admirer with a pretty little impromptu "romance," "got up expressly for the occasion," as the playbills have it; and he religiously believed every word of it—though, of course, it contained not one single word of truth in it. I told him that *my brother* and myself—ha, ha!—were the children of some Duke Thingumby, (whose name I have forgotten already,) who was one of the greatest nobles in France; yes, faith—our venerable papa had royal blood in his veins, while our mamma, bless her dear soul, was 'closely allied to several of the most aristocratic families in the kingdom.' Then I trumped up a cock-and-bull story about papa killing mamma in a fit of jealousy, having caught her in a naughty fix with the young Count Somebody-or-other, whom he also slew, and then, to wind up the fun, went to his own chamber and shot himself—great booby as he was! Next, the notary who had charge of our princely fortune, "stepped out," as they say, and left us, poor orphans, without the price of a penny roll. I was intensely virtuous, of course, resisted a hundred tempting offers to become the kept mistress of men of wealth and rank—we came to America, and settled in Boston, where you now obtain for us a comfortable subsistence by privately teaching the use of the small sword. Ah, my Chevalier, wasn't that brought in well? Then I went on to lament that my passions were so fiery that I could not enjoy the society of an agreeable man without danger to my honor; and concluded my story by hinting to Mr. Tickels that my virtue had never been in such peril, as when his arms had embraced me—for, said I, my senses were fast becoming intoxicated; and in a few moments more I should have been your victim, had I not, by a powerful effort, escaped from the sweet delirium which was stealing over my soul. Thus you will see, Chevalier, that my story and its accompanying remarks were both judicious and appropriate; my victim manifested the most intense interest during the recital, and I could plainly perceive the exciting effect which the concluding words of my narrative had upon him.

> "My story being done,
> He gave me for my pains a world of sighs."

"After the completion of my delightful little romance," continued the Duchess,"the venerable goat attempted to subdue me by the force of *argument*; and, to do him justice, I must say that his philosophy, if not very rational, was at least very profound. He went over the entire field of moral subtleties, and proved himself an excellent sophist. He argued that as nature had given me passions, I was justified in gratifying them, despite the opinions of the world and the prohibitions of decent society. Much more he said that I have forgotten; but the drift of his remarks was, that as I had admitted him to be the most charming and agreeable person in the world, I could not do a better thing than to throw myself into his arms, and enjoy with him, as he said, "the rightful inheritance of every man and every woman on the face of the earth."

"In reply to his specious reasoning, I assured him that I couldn't think of complying with his wishes, as I should thereby lose my reputation and position in society, as a lady—which was, I added, the only consideration that restrained me from testing those joys which he had so eloquently depicted; for as to any scruples, moral or religious, I had none whatever. Then I congratulated him on his happiness in belonging to a sex having the privilege of amative delights, with almost perfect impunity; and deplored my own hard fate—for, said I, am I not a woman, and are not women sternly prohibited from tasting the joys of love unsanctioned by the empty forms of matrimony, under pain of having their names and characters forever blasted and disgraced?"

"Well, my Chevalier, the old wretch, seeing that he was not likely to accomplish his object by argument, adopted a new plan. Instantly, he dropped the lover, and became the fond and doting father, in which sacred capacity he proceeded to take liberties to which his former familiarities were as nothing. He began by reminding me of his gray hair and advanced age; then he asked permission to regard me as a daughter, to which I made no objection, as I wished to see how far he would operate during the personation of that character—though I shrewdly suspected that his actions would be anything but fatherly. Therefore, when he again clasped my waist, and made me lean against him, I did not repulse him, for his conduct was in furtherance of *our* plans; and I also permitted him, (though with extreme disgust on my part,) to toy with my breasts, and kiss me again and again, all of which he did under cover of his holy privileges as a father! The moment had then arrived for *me* to play *my* part; and though the old rascal's conduct and person were loathsome to me in the extreme, I affected all the languor, flutter, and ardor of passionate longings; which he perceived with the most extravagant demonstrations of delight—"

"I know all the rest," interrupted the Chevalier, almost suffocated with laughter, in which the merry Duchess joined him—"I applied my eye to the key-hole just at that moment, and saw the old goat, as you properly term him, hugging you with the ferocity of a bear; I heard him say—'Let me no longer play the father; let me be thy lover—thy all—thy own Timothy—thy chosen Tickels!' Ha, ha, ha! was anything so richly ludicrous. And, by Jove, how admirably you acted, my Duchess! You appeared absolutely dying with rapture—your eyes seemed to express a thousand soft wishes—your face glowed as if with the heat of languishing desire; how wildly you seemed to abandon your person to his lascivious embraces! and yet I know the disgust which you must have felt towards him, at that very moment; for he was anything but a comely object, with his gray hair disordered, his bloated countenance red as fire, and his dress indecently disarranged. At that moment I noiselessly stole into the room; and just at the very instant when the old fool thought himself sure of his prey, you screamed, and pointed to my reflection in the mirror. The result was precisely as I expected; too cowardly to fight, afraid of his life, and anxious to preserve his reputation, he preferred giving me the handsome sum of five thousand dollars—which money we very much needed, and which will last us a long time, provided we exercise a reasonable degree of economy. That last five hundred, which we extracted from the parson, lasted us but little over a month; let us be more discreet hereafter, my Duchess—we may live splendidly, but not extravagantly; for old age will come on us by-and-by, and your beauty will fade—then what is to become of us, unless we have a snug competency in reserve? And really, my dear, you must curtail your personal expenditures; you recollect but a week ago you gave two hundred dollars for that diamond coronet you have on—and you are constantly purchasing costly dresses and superb shawls. Do you not observe the plainness of my attire? Believe me, an elegant simplicity of dress is far more attractive to men of taste, than gaudy apparel can possibly be."

"Have you done sermonizing?" cried the Duchess, good-humoredly—"really, you would make an admirable parson; and a far better one, I am sure, than the reverend gentleman whom we wheedled out of the five hundred dollars. But go at once and get the cheque cashed; you shall give me exactly one half, and we both shall have the privilege of expending our several portions as we choose."

"Agreed," said the Chevalier,—"but I have a little business to transact in my *workshop*, before I go to the bank. What are you laughing at?"

"Oh," answered the Duchess—"I cannot help thinking of that amusing old goat, Mr. Tickels. The recollection of that man will certainly kill me! The idea of your passing me off as your sister was so rich; he little suspected that for years we have been tender lovers and co-partners in the business of fleecing amorous gentlemen out of their money. And then to represent myself as the daughter of a French nobleman!—Why, my father gained a very pretty living by going around

the streets with a hand-organ, on which he played with exquisite skill, and was
accompanied in his perambulations by a darling little monkey named Jacko—
poor Jacko! he came to his death by being choked with a roasted potato. My
mother, rest her soul! was an excellent washerwoman, but her unfortunate fondness
for strong drink resulted in her being provided with bed and board in the alms
house, in which excellent institution she died, having first conferred upon the
world the benefit of bringing me into existence; therefore, instead of having first
seen the light within the marble walls of a French palace, I drew my first breath in
the sick ward of a pauper's home. At ten years of age I was a *ballet girl* at the
theatre; at fourteen, my Chevalier, it was my good fortune to meet you; you initiated
me, not only into the mysteries of love, but into the art of making money with far
greater facility than as a *figurante* in the opera. You christened me 'Duchess,' —
took the title of 'Chevalier,' and together we have led a life of profit, of pleasure,
and of charming variety."

"And I," rejoined the Chevalier, "can boast of a parentage as distinguished as
your own. My father was an English thief and pickpocket; he took pains to teach
me the science of his profession, and I will venture to affirm that I can remove a
gentleman's watch or pocket-book as gracefully as could my venerated sire himself,
whose career was rather abruptly terminated one fine morning in consequence of
a temporary valet having tied his neckcloth too tightly: he was hung in front of
Newgate jail, for a highway robbery, in which he acquired but little glory and less
profit, —for he only shot an old woman's poodle dog, and stole a leather purse full
of halfpence. My mother was a very pretty waiting woman at an ordinary tavern;
one night she abruptly stepped out and sailed for America, carrying with her my
unfinished self, and the silver spoons. I saw you—admired you—made you my
mistress, and partner in business, the profitable nature of which is proved by our
being now possessed of the very pretty sum of five thousand dollars, the result of
three hours' operation."

"You have yet one grand stroke of art to accomplish, which will place us both
on the very pinnacle of fortune," said the Duchess. "I allude, of course, to your
approaching marriage with Miss Alice Goldworthy."

The Chevalier's brow darkened, and his handsome features assumed an
expression of uneasiness.

"That," said he, "is the only business in which I ever faltered. Poor young lady!
she is so good, so pure, so confidingly affectionate, that my heart sinks within me
when I the think of the ruin which her marriage with me will bring upon her.
When I gaze into her lovely countenance, and hear the tones of her gentle voice,
remorse for the wrong that I contemplate towards her, strikes me to the soul, and
I feel that I am a wretch indeed."

"Pooh!" exclaimed the Duchess, her lips curling with disdain—"you grow very
sentimental indeed! Perhaps you really *love* this girl?"

"No, Duchess, no—but I pity her; a devil cannot love an angel. There was a
time when my soul was unstained with guilt or crime—then might I have aspired
to the bliss of loving such a divine creature as Alice; but now—villain as I am—

there can be no sympathy between my heart and hers. Well, well—the die is cast; I will wed her, for I covet the splendid fortune which she will inherit on the death of her father. You know that the wedding day will soon arrive; but how I dread its approach! for I fear that ere I can embrace my bride within the sacred nuptial couch, she will discover that which I can never remove or entirely conceal—that *fatal mark*, the brand of crime, which I carry upon my person. She loves me; but her love would be changed to hate, were she to see that horrid emblem of guilt."

"You must conceal it from her view," rejoined the Duchess, shuddering—"or it will spoil all. The marriage would be annulled by the discovery of that detestable mark."

"Let us trust to fortune," said the Chevalier. —"I must leave you now, and shut myself up for an hour or so in my *workshop*. Afterwards, I shall go and convert the cheque into substantial cash."

Duvall left the room, and ascended to the highest story in the building. Here he entered a small apartment, which contained many curious and remarkable things. A small printing press stood in one corner; in another was a pile of paper, and other materials; tools of almost every description lay scattered about, among which were the necessary implements for robbery and burglary. An experienced police officer would have instantly pronounced the place a secret den for the printing of counterfeit bank-notes—and so it was. The gallant Chevalier was the most expert and dangerous counterfeiter in the country.

Seating himself at a trunk, on which stood writing materials, he drew forth the cheque which Mr. Tickels had given him. Having examined it long and narrowly, he took a pen and paper, and wrote an exact copy of it; this he did so admirably, that Mr. Tickels himself would have been puzzled to point out the original and genuine cheque which he had written.

"This will do," said the Chevalier, communing with himself—"to-day I will draw five thousand dollars; and within a week I will *send* and draw five thousand more; and it shall be done so adroitly, that I will never be suspected. Hurrrah! Chevalier Duvall, thy star is on the ascendant!"

That afternoon the gentleman presented the cheque at the bank; it was promptly paid, and he returned to the Duchess, with whom he celebrated the brilliant success of the operation, by a magnificent supper.

CHAPTER VI

*The Stolen Package. — The Midnight Outrage. — The Marriage,
and Awful Discovery.*

A very merry party were assembled in the elegant parlor of Mr. Goldworthy's superb mansion in Howard street about two weeks after the events described in the last chapter. There was Fanny Aubrey herself, looking prettier than ever, with her splendid hair tastefully braided, her graceful, *petite* form set off to advantage by an elegant dress, and her lovely countenance radiant with the hues of health and happiness. Then there was her friend and benefactress, Miss Alice, looking very beautiful, her face constantly changing from smiles to blushes—for the next day was to witness her marriage with the Chevalier Duvall. At her side was seated her lover and affianced husband, his dark, handsome features lighted up with an expression of proud triumph, almost amounting to scorn. Then there was Corporal Grimsby, very shabby, very sarcastic, and very droll; near him sat the Honorable Timothy Tickels, wearing upon his sensual countenance a look of uneasiness, and occasionally betraying a degree of nervous agitation that indicated a mind ill at ease. At intervals he would glance suspiciously and stealthily at the Chevalier—for that was their first meeting since his scandalous adventure with the Duchess, and he was not without a fear that he might be exposed, in the presence of that very respectable company, in which case his reputation would be forever ruined; but his fears were groundless—the Chevalier had not the remotest idea of exposing him, having his own reasons for keeping the affair profoundly secret; and he saluted and conversed with Mr. Tickels with as much composure and politeness as though nothing had ever happened to disturb the harmony of their friendship. Mr. Goldworthy himself was present, and also a nephew of his—a handsome youth of nineteen, named Clarence Argyle; he was studying the profession of medicine at a Southern University, and was on a visit at his uncle's house. It was evident, by the assiduity of his attentions to Fanny Aubrey, that the mental and personal charms of the fair maid were not without their effect upon him; and it was equally evident by the pleased smile with which she listened to his entertaining conversation—addressed to *her* ear alone—that the agreeable young stranger had impressed her mind by no means unfavorably. Fanny's brother, Charles, completed the party.

It will be necessary to explain here, that the old Corporal had never exposed the rascally conduct of Mr. Tickels towards Fanny, in consequence of the young lady's having earnestly entreated him not to do so. He had never before met the old libertine at the house of Mr. Goldworthy; and (until informed of the fact by Fanny,) was ignorant that he (Tickels) was in the habit of visiting there, as a friend of the family. He treated him with coldness and reserve; but otherwise gave no indication of the contempt which he felt for the unprincipled old wretch.

As Mr. Goldworthy surveyed, with a smiling aspect, the sociable group which surrounded him, little did he suspect that the man who on the morrow was to become his son-in-law—who was to lead to the altar his only child, that pure and gentle girl—little, we say, did he suspect that the Chevalier Duvall was in reality a branded villain of the blackest dye—a man whose soul was stained by the commission of almost every crime on the dark catalogue of guilt. And as little did he think that his warm political and personal friend, the Honorable Timothy Tickels—the man of ample wealth, of unbounded influence, of exalted reputation—was at heart an abandoned and licentious scoundrel, who had basely tried to accomplish the ruin of a poor orphan girl, and was even at that very moment gloating over an infernal plan which he had formed, for getting her completely in his power, where no human aid was likely to reach her.

"To-morrow, my Alice," whispered the Chevalier in the ear of the blushing object of his villainous designs—"to-morrow, thou are mine! Oh, the devotion of a life-time shall atone to you for the sacrifice you make, in wedding an unknown stranger, whose birth and fortunes are shrouded in a veil of mystery."

"Thy birth and fortunes are nothing to me," responded Alice, softly, as a tear of happiness trembled in her eyes—"so long as thy heart is faithful and true."

What wonder that the Chevalier's false heart grew cold in his breast, at the simple words of the confiding, gentle, unsuspecting creature whom he designed to ruin? But still he hesitated not; "her father's gold is the glittering prize which I shall gain by this marriage," thought he; and the vile, sordid thought stimulated him on, despite the remonstrances of his better nature.

"When I return to the University, we will write to each other often, will we not?" said Clarence Argyle to Fanny, in a tone that could not be overheard by the others of the party; and the fair girl yielded a blushing consent to the proposal, so congenial to her own inclination. The whisper and the blush were both observed by old Tickels, who said to himself—

"Humph! 'tis easy to see that those two unfledged Cupids are already over head and ears in love with each other. Have a care, Master Argyle—thy pretty mistress may be lost to thee to-morrow; go back to thy books and thy studies—for she is not for thee. Ah, the devil! I like not the look which that impertinent old fellow, who calls himself Corporal Grimsby, fastens upon me— it seems as if he read the secret thoughts of my soul! He has once already snatched from my grasp my destined prey; let him beware how he interferes a second time, for Jew Mike is in my employ, and his knife is sharp and his aim sure!"

"That d——d scoundrel, Tickels, meditates mischief, I am convinced," thought the Corporal, whose keen and penetrating gaze had been for some time riveted upon the old libertine—"and I feel convinced that my pretty Fanny is the object of his secret machinations. Beware, old Judas Iscariot! —you'll not get off so easy the next time I catch you at your tricks."

"And so, my dear Mr. Tickels, you are again a candidate for Congress," remarked Mr. Goldworthy, during a pause in the conversation.

"I again have that distinguished honor," was the pompous reply. "My party stands in great need of my services and influence in the House at the present crisis."

"No doubt," dryly observed the Corporal—"I would suggest that your first public act be the introduction of a bill for the punishment of seduction, and the protection of poor orphan girls."

Mr. Tickels writhed beneath the sarcasm, and turned deadly pale, although he and his tormentor were the only persons present who comprehended the secret meaning of the words—for Fanny was too much engrossed in conversation with Argyle, to heed the remark.

"And, my good sir," rejoined the Chevalier, who was resolved to improve so good an opportunity to wound the old reprobate to the quick, (although he was ignorant of the application of the Corporal's words,)—"do not, I beseech you, neglect to insert a clause in your bill, providing also for the punishment of those respectable old wretches who bring ruin and disgrace upon families, by the seduction of wives—of daughters—or of *sisters!* I confess myself interested in the passage of such an act, in consequence of a wealthy old scoundrel having once dared to insult grievously a near female relative of mine. The name of this old wretch—"

Tickels cast an imploring look at the Chevalier, and the latter was silent—but upon his lips remained an expression of withering scorn; for villain as he himself was, he detested the other for his consummate hypocrisy. The vicious frequently hate others for possessing the same evil qualities that characterise themselves. The character of the Chevalier was doubtless hypocritical in its nature; but *his* hypocrisy was, in our opinion, far less contemptible than that of Tickels; the former was a hypocrite for pecuniary gain; the latter, for the gratification of the basest and most grovelling propensities that can disgrace humanity.

"Gentlemen—gentlemen!" cried Mr. Goldworthy, amazed at the turn which the conversation had taken, and comprehending neither of the allusions—"I beg you to remember that there are ladies present."

"Blood and bayonets!" exclaimed the Corporal—"you are right: I forgot the ladies, my worthy host, and crave your pardon and theirs, for my indiscreet (though I must say, *devilish appropriate*) remarks!"

The Chevalier also apologized, though with less circumlocution than the worthy Corporal; and nothing further occurred to disturb either the harmony of the company, or the equanimity of Mr. Tickels, until Mr. Goldworthy, with a countenance full of astonishment and alarm, announced to his guests that he had, during the evening, lost from his pocket a package of bank-notes and valuable papers, amounting to some thousands of dollars, which he had procured for investment the following day in an extensive mercantile speculation—for although retired from active business, he still frequently ventured large sums in operations which were generally successful.

For half an hour previous to making his fearful discovery, he had been in private and earnest conversation with the Chevalier, concerning some arrangements relative to the approaching marriage.

"It is indeed astonishing—what can have become of it?" cried the old gentleman, searching every pocket in vain for the missing package. "I am certain that 'twas safely in my possession scarce one hour ago," continued he; and summoning a couple of servants, he commanded a diligent search to be made in every part of the room—but still in vain; no package was to be found.

Everybody present, with but one exception, expressed their concern and astonishment; that exception was Fanny Aubrey; she was much agitated, and pale as death.

It was suggested by the Chevalier and several others, that he must have dropped the package in the street, as it could not be found in the house. In reply to this, Mr. Goldworthy said—

"No, no, my friend—I will swear that I lost it in this very room, within an hour. Plague on it! what particularly vexes me, is, that it comprised all my present available capital—and to have it disappear in such a d——d unaccountable, mysterious manner! Why, curse it," cried the old gentleman, getting more and more angry— "if I didn't know the thing to be impossible, I should suspect that there was an accomplished pickpocket in the room!"

"So should I," dryly observed the Corporal; and so said the Hon. Mr. Tickels, also.

The Chevalier arose, and said, with calm dignity—

"Gentlemen, I conceive that an insinuation has been made, derogatory to our honor. Mr. Goldworthy, your words indirectly imply a suspicion; I must request you, sir, to explain your words, and to state distinctly whether or no you suppose that any person present has robbed you. I also suggest that all here be carefully searched."

"Good heavens, my dear Chevalier!" cried Mr. Goldworthy, much excited— "can you think for a moment that I suspect you or these gentlemen, of an act so base and contemptible? Pardon my hasty words; vexation at my great loss (a serious one, I assure you,) for a moment overcame my temper. Let the package go to the devil, sooner than its loss should occasion the least uneasiness to any of us. Come, my dear friends, let's say no more about it."

Harmony was once more restored; but still Fanny Aubrey looked so pale and agitated, that Miss Alice, crossing over to where she sat, anxiously inquired if she were unwell? The poor girl essayed to reply, but could not; it was evident to her friend, that she was struggling with feelings of the most painful nature. She pressed Alice's hand, burst into tears, and abruptly left the room.

"The poor girl is either very unwell, or very much troubled about something," whispered Alice to her cousin Clarence—"I will go and comfort her;" and having made her excuses to the company, she left the room, and followed Fanny to her chamber.

Her departure was the signal for the guests to take their leave of their worthy host. Mr. Goldworthy warmly pressed the Chevalier's hand at parting, and said to him—

"To-morrow, my dear sir, you will by my son-in-law. Be kind to my Alice, she is a good girl, and worthy of you. God bless you both! I did intend to advance you a sum of money, sufficient to enable you to begin housekeeping in handsome style; but the loss of that large sum of money to-night will, I fear, place it out of my power to assist you much, at present. However, I shall endeavor to raise a respectable sum for you, in the course of a few days. Meantime, you and Alice must be my guests; and I am not sure but that I shall insist upon your continually residing beneath my roof—for I am a lonely old man, and so accustomed to the kind attentions and sweet society of my only daughter, that to part with her would deprive me of half my earthly joys. Farewell—may you and her be happy together!"

Tears stood in the eyes of the good old man, as he uttered these words; and again the conscience of the Chevalier upbraided him for his contemplated villainy— but still he paused not nor faltered in carrying out his diabolical schemes.

Meanwhile, the following scene occurred in Fanny's chamber, to which Alice had repaired for the purpose of ascertaining the cause of the young girl's agitation and tears.

"What is the matter, my dear sister? For such I will call you," said Alice, clasping her arms around the weeping girl, who had thrown herself upon the bed without undressing.

"Oh, my friend, my benefactress!" cried Fanny—"how can I help feeling so distressed, when I know that your happiness is about to be destroyed forever?"

"My happiness destroyed!" cried Alice, surprised and alarmed—"what mean you! Do you allude to my marriage to-morrow with the Chevalier Duvall? Yes, I see you do. Silly girl, that marriage will render me the happiest of women; what reason have you for supposing otherwise? The Chevalier loves me, and I sincerely reciprocate his affection; so dry your tears, for you know you are to be bridesmaid, and smiles better become you than tears."

These words were spoken in the kindest and gentlest tone; but Fanny exclaimed—

"Miss Alice, you are cruelly deceived in that man."

"Deceived!" cried the young lady—"what mystery is hidden in your words? Oh, if you love me, Fanny—and you have often told me that you did—instantly explain the meaning of your dreadful declaration."

"Listen to me, Miss Alice," said Fanny, with a calmness that strangely contrasted with her previous agitation—"and I will tell you plainly what I have seen, and what I think. To you I owe everything: the comforts of a home, the kindness of a friend, and the benefits of a superior education, now enjoyed by my brother and myself—two poor orphans, who, but for your benevolence, would be dependent upon the world's cold charity. My gratitude I can never express; my heart alone can feel it—but oh! believe me, I would gladly lay down my life to promote your happiness. How, then, can I see future years of misery awaiting you, without tears of anguish—without feeling an intense anxiety to preserve you from a fate ten times worse than death?"

"Do not interrupt me, I pray you," continued Fanny, seeing that Alice was about to speak—"To-morrow you are engaged to be married to the man calling himself the Chevalier Duvall. When I first saw him, I was struck with his beauty and accomplishments—his brilliant wit, and graceful manners; and when, in sisterly confidence, you informed me that he was your affianced husband, you know how warmly I congratulated you on having won the affections of a man who, as I then believed, was in every way calculated to make you happy.

"Alice, I tell you that man is a villain!" cried Fanny, with startling emphasis—"I saw him pick your father's pocket of the money that was lost; yes, I alone saw him do it; *that* was the cause of my agitation and tears. Do not marry him, for he is a robber and a scoundrel!"

"Say no more, Miss Aubrey," said Alice, rising with an air of cold dignity, which plainly indicated her entire disbelief of the statement she had just heard—"Say no more: you have mistaken your position, when you seek to prejudice me against a gentleman whom I am so soon to call my husband. Nay, not a word more—I will not listen to you. The Chevalier Duvall is the very soul of honor; and to accuse *him*—how can I say it?—of the crime of *theft*, is so preposterous that it would be ludicrous under any other circumstances. Fanny, I can scarcely believe that you have been actuated by *jealousy* in telling this dreadful story; I will try to think that your eyes deceived you, and that you really *thought* that you saw the Chevalier do as you have said. But oh! how mistaken you are, unhappy girl! when you impute such a crime to one of the noblest and best of men."

"But, Miss Alice," cried Fanny, almost angrily—for she was certain of the truth of her statement—"I tell you that I am not mistaken; I saw—"

"Silence, I entreat—I command you!" cried the young lady, now thoroughly indignant at the disgraceful accusation which had been brought against her lover—"speak not another word to me on this odious subject, or you forfeit my friendship forever. Good night; learn in future to be more discreet."

So saying, Alice left the unhappy young girl to her bitter tears. Soon wearied nature asserted her rights, and she sobbed herself to sleep. But her slumbers were disturbed by hideous dreams: in fancy she again saw the magnificent Chevalier dexterously abstract the package of money from Mr. Goldworthy's pocket—then she thought that the brilliant stranger stood over her, and surveyed her with an expression of fearful menace. The scene again changed; she was alone, in a vast and splendid apartment, reclining upon a sumptuous couch; delicious music, from invisible minstrels, soothed her soul into a sort of dreamy and voluptuous trance; an unearthly happiness filled her heart—her senses were intoxicated with delight. Suddenly, in the dim distance, she saw a Hideous Object, and the blood went tingling through her veins with terror; it had the form of a gigantic reptile; slowly it crawled towards the couch on which she lay; dim grew the light from the sparkling chandeliers—heavy grew the air with noxious odors; the Hideous Object crouched beneath the bed; she heard its deep breathing—its heavy sighs; then it reared its awful form above her, and then approached its ghastly head to hers; she felt its foul breath upon her cheek—its green dragon-like eyes penetrated her soul, and made her brain dizzy—it fanned her by the flapping of its mighty wings. It breathed into her ear vile whispers, tempting her to crime. It placed its huge vulture's claw upon her heart, as if to tear it from her breast. She awoke.

Gracious heavens! there—there—at her bedside, stood a human form, its countenance dark and threatening—the savage features almost totally concealed by masses of black and shaggy hair. A rough, hard hand rested upon her breast, and a pair of fierce, cruel eyes struck terror to her soul.

She uttered one piercing scream, and fainted. The report of a pistol was heard; then hasty footsteps descended the stair-case; the hall was rapidly traversed—the street door was opened and shut with a loud noise—and all was still.

In a few minutes the affrightened inmates of the mansion, half dressed, were hastening to the scene of the late tumult; Mr. Goldworthy and his daughter Alice were among them. What was the astonishment and dismay of the startled group, on discovering that Fanny Aubrey was nowhere to be found, while at her chamber door, wounded and bleeding, lay the insensible form of Clarence Argyle!

They raised the young gentleman, and placed him upon the bed; a physician, who fortunately resided next door, and was almost instantly upon the spot, pronounced the wound severe, but not dangerous. He had been shot in the breast; the ball was with some difficulty extracted, and the patient rendered as comfortable as possible.

But where was the clue to all this fearful mystery? What had become of Fanny Aubrey? Who had dared to enter that house at midnight, and after nearly murdering one of the inmates, carry off a young lady? What was the *object* of the perpetrator of the outrage? These were the questions uttered by everybody present; but no one could answer them.

Both Mr. Goldworthy and Alice watched over the sufferer during that night. Towards morning, he revived sufficiently to tell them all he knew of the dreadful occurrence which had taken place. His chamber adjoined that of Fanny; he had been aroused from his slumbers by her piercing scream; instantly leaping from his bed, he rushed into the young lady's apartment, and saw a tall, black-visaged ruffian standing over her apparently insensible form, in the act of dragging her from the couch. The villain turned suddenly, drew a pistol upon the young gentleman, and fired. Clarence fell, severely wounded, and remained unconscious of everything, until he found himself stretched upon a bed of pain, with his uncle and cousin watching him with affectionate solicitude.

On learning that poor Fanny had disappeared—undoubtedly carried off by the ruffian whom he had seen in her chamber—the grief and rage of Clarence knew no bounds. Regardless of his wound and sufferings, he would have arisen from his bed and gone in pursuit of the ravisher, had he not been restrained by his more considerate relatives, who represented to him the folly and danger of his undertaking such a hopeless task, in his precarious state of health. Overcome by their united persuasions, as well as by a consciousness of his own bodily weakness, he contented himself with his uncle's assurance that every effort would immediately be made to discover the whereabouts of poor Fanny, and restore her to her friends.

Early the next morning, Corporal Grimsby, as being the friend and guardian of the missing girl, was apprised of the fact of her abduction. It is needless for us to repeat all the singular oaths with which the eccentric, good old man expressed his honest indignation, when he received the alarming intelligence; suffice it to say, he swore by the nose of Napoleon, and by his own whiskers, (an oath which he used only on very solemn occasions,) never to rest until he had discovered Fanny, his darling *protege*, and severely punished her rascally kidnapper.

A dark suspicion crossed his mind that the villain Tickels was at the bottom of the business; acting upon the first impulse of the moment, he instantly proceeded to the residence of the old libertine, forced his way into his presence, and boldly accused him of the deed. Mr. Tickels was perfectly on his guard, for he had expected such a visit; with cool politeness he assured the Corporal that until that moment he knew nothing of the matter; he was sorry that his *friend* should suspect him of any participation in such a piece of rascality; he had long since cleansed and purified himself of the wicked and silly passion which he at one time felt for Miss Aubrey;

he sincerely hoped that nothing unpleasant would befall her; he'd do all in his power to seek her out; and concluded by coolly inviting the Corporal to breakfast with him.

"Breakfast with the devil!" cried the old man, indignantly—"sooner would I sit down to table in social companionship with—with *Jew Mike* himself!" and as he uttered these words, he gazed keenly into the other's countenance. Tickels started, and turned deadly pale; the Corporal, with a sarcastic smile, bowed with mock politeness, and withdrew.

"Swords and carving-knives! I thought so," he muttered, after he had left the house—"a masterly stroke, that; a masterly stroke! This villain Jew Mike is the *cher amie* of Sow Nance, as she is called; and Nance is in the confidence of Tickels; what wonder that the dirty slut recommended her *pal* and paramour to the old libertine, as a fit agent to abduct my poor Fanny—and what wonder that he was employed to accomplish that object? But first, I'll hasten to Mr. Goldworthy's house, and question the young man who was wounded; if his description of the villain corresponds with the appearance of Jew Mike, then there can be no further doubt on the subject, and I shall know what course to pursue. Egad! how old Tickels changed color when I mentioned Jew Mike! His confusion alone indicated his guilt. 'Sdeath; I have no time to lose; may heaven preserve and guard that poor, persecuted orphan girl!'"

On reaching Mr. Goldworthy's house, he requested to be conducted immediately to Clarence's chamber. In answer to his inquiries, the young man stated that the villain who had wounded him was a tall, powerfully built person, his face almost entirely concealed by a profusion of black hair. The Corporal rubbed his hands with glee.

"Jew Mike, by the bones of the great Mogul!" he exclaimed—"and now that I am on the right scent, I shall soon ferret out the ravenous wolves that have carried my poor lamb to their infernal den. Ah, Corporal Grimsby, thou art a cunning dog!" So saying, he departed on his benevolent errand of endeavoring to rescue Fanny Aubrey from the power of her enemies.

*   *   *   *   *

That evening, from every window of Mr. Goldworthy's princely mansion in Howard street, shone brilliant lights. It was the eve appointed for the marriage of Alice and the Chevalier Duvall.

In consequence of the melancholy and startling events which took place in the house on the preceding night—the severe wounding of Clarence, and the abduction of Fanny—it had been suggested by both Alice and her father, that it would be proper to defer the performance of the ceremony for a short time, or until the fate of the missing girl could be ascertained; the Chevalier, however, strongly opposed this proposition, and assuming the authority of an accepted suitor, delicately but firmly insisted that the marriage should take place that evening, as had been previously arranged "for," said he, "to defer the consummation of our happiness will not assist in the recovery of Miss Aubrey. When I become your husband, my Alice, I can with far more propriety aid in seeking the lost one, for were we to remain unmarried, my interest in the poor young lady might be imputed to improper or even dishonorable motives."

This reasoning had the desired effect; it was decided that the marriage ceremony should not be postponed.

Alice had not communicated to the Chevalier the story which Fanny had told her, concerning the affair of the lost package of money—for as she utterly disbelieved the tale, (imputing it to the effects of an excited imagination,) she had no desire to wound the feelings of her lover by acquainting him with the absurd charge (as she thought) which had been brought against him. How blind is love to the imperfections, the faults, and even the crimes of the object of its adoration! We believe it is Shakespeare who says:

"Love looks not with the eye, but with the mind,
And therefore is wing'd Cupid painted blind."

The folding doors which separated the two spacious parlors in Mr. Goldworthy's house were thrown open, forming a vast hall, brilliantly illuminated by superb chandeliers, and decorated with every appliance of modern elegance and taste. About a dozen relatives and friends of the family had assembled to witness the ceremony; among them were several of the wealthiest members of the Boston aristocracy. There was the gray-headed millionaire, who has made his name famous by the magnificence of his donations to public institutions which are already wealthy enough; but then such liberal gifts are heralded in the newspapers, and his name is blazoned forth as the great philanthropist; and —it really is so troublesome to give to the suffering poor; besides, the world seldom hears of deeds of unostentatious charity. Now, we are one of those plain people who like to look at things in the light of common reason, without regard to high-sounding titles, or lofty associations; and it is our unpretending opinion that the God of charity and mercy looks down with much greater approbation upon the act of feeding a starving family, or comfortably clothing a few of His naked little ones, than upon the bestowal of twenty or thirty thousand dollars on this or that University, for the purpose of endowing a Professor of Humbugonomy, that he may initiate a class of learned blockheads into the mysteries of star-gazing, patient-killing, legal fleecing, or cheating the devil by turning parson.

Besides the gray-headed millionaire, to whom we have thus particularly alluded, there was the young lady who boasts of being heiress to hundreds of thousands of dollars; consequently, of course, she is unanimously voted to be "charming— divine—perfection!" Her beauty is pronounced angelic; her accomplishments are the theme of universal admiration. "Oh, she is an unsurpassable creature!" exclaim the whole tribe of contemptible, sycophantic, brainless calves in broadcloth, who are ever ready to fall down and worship the golden emblem of themselves. And yet she is pug-nosed, freckle-faced, and red-headed; insolent to her equals, coarsely familiar with her inferiors; her vulgarity is without wit, her affectation is devoid of elegance or grace; ignorant and stupid, the meanest kitchen wench would suffer by a comparison with her. In striking contrast with this ludicrous specimen of degraded aristocracy, there were several young ladies present who were really lovely and accomplished women. These were the personal friends of Alice; they had come to witness her nuptials with the magnificent Chevalier.

Precisely as the clock struck eight, Duvall entered the apartment, and saluted the company with that exquisite and gentlemanly grace for which he was distinguished. With difficulty could the assembled guests refrain from expressing their admiration aloud; for his appearance was singularly grand and imposing. In his dress, not the slightest approach to foppery could be detected; all was faultless elegance. In his dark eyes and on his proud features an observer could read the lofty triumph which he felt; for was not he, an unknown and perhaps penniless adventurer, about to wed the beautiful and accomplished daughter of one of Boston's "merchant prices?"

Soon the clergyman arrived, and Alice was summoned to take her part in the solemn ceremony which was about to be performed. She was dressed in simple white, her only ornaments consisting of a few natural flowers among the rich clusters of her shining hair.

She was very beautiful; the flush of happiness suffused her cheeks—her eyes sparkled with ineffable joy. Oh, terrible sacrifice!

The ceremony proceeds; the solemn words are spoken. 'Tis all over—friends crowd around with their congratulations—there are smiles, and blushes, and tears; but a deep sense of happiness pervades every heart. Alice is the wife of Duvall, by the sacred rites of the church, in the sight of Heaven, and before men. The Chevalier pressed her madly to his heart, while

"Unto the ground she cast her modest eye,
And, ever and anon, with rosy red,
The bashful blush her snowy cheeks did dye."

Then came music, and the merry dance—and finally, a repast, that rivalled in luxury the banquet of an emperor. In the midst of the supper, in obedience to the secret signal of one of her bridesmaids, Alice stole away, and was conducted by a charming *coterie* of her female friends, to Hymen's sacred retreat, the nuptial chamber—which nothing should induce us to invade, gentle reader, were it not necessary to do so in order to develop a scene in our narrative, which cannot possibly be omitted.

It was an apartment of but moderate size; yet it was a gem of luxurious comfort. Everything was in the most perfect taste; and it was evident by a certain refined delicacy in all the arrangements, that the fair Alice herself had superintended the preparations. Happy the man who should bestow the first chaste kiss of wedded love, upon the pure lips of a lovely bride, within that soft bower of voluptuousness!

She is disrobed; from her virgin limbs are removed the snowy garments; she is coquettishly arrayed in the seductive costume of bewitching night! She blushes, and is almost painfully embarrassed; for never before have her glowing charms been contemplated thus, even by female eyes. She finds herself at last reclining within the luxurious folds of the magnificent nuptial couch; then her kind friends kiss her—bid her a smiling good-night—and leave her to await the coming of her husband. For the first time, her bosom heaves tumultuously with emotions which she acknowledges to be delightful, though she cannot comprehend them.

But where, meanwhile, is the happy bridegroom? He is at the head of the splendid board, responding to the many toasts which are proposed in his honor, and that of his lovely and expectant bride. Again and again he fills the goblet, and quaffs the foaming champagne. He fascinates everybody by his rare eloquence—his inimitable wit; Mr. Goldworthy congratulates himself on his good fortune in having secured so charming—so talented a son-in-law. The dark eyes of the Chevalier sparkle almost fearfully; his superb countenance is flushed with wine and passion. This rosy god of the grape has nearly conquered him; he is more than half intoxicated. Losing his habitual caution, he launches forth into the recital of the most brilliant and daring adventures in intrigue, fraud and robbery, he relates these events with a gusto that would seem to indicate his having taken a leading part in them himself. The guests are startled, and view him with an admiration mixed with fear. The Chevalier drinks deeper and deeper. Wilder and more exciting grow his narratives; he tells strange tales of the Italian banditti—of pirates upon the Spanish main—of dashing French pickpockets—of bold English highwaymen—of desperate American burglars, and of expert counterfeiters. Mr. Goldworthy, at last, begins to regard him with a feeling akin to suspicion. "Who can this man be," he mentally asks himself—"that talks so familiarly of every species of crime and villainy? Is he a fitting husband for my pure and gentle daughter? Can he have been a participant in those lawless adventures which he so eloquently describes? I like not the dark frown upon his brow, nor the fierce glances of his eyes. But tush! of what am I thinking? I must not harbor unjust suspicions against the husband of my child; he is merely somewhat excited by the generous wine, and probably derived his knowledge of these matters from the romances of the day. 'Tis best that he should drink no more at present; I will therefore hint to him that it is high time for a loyal bridegroom to retire to the arms of his expectant bride. He surely will not disregard so tempting a suggestion, for my Alice is very like her mother, and egad! on *my* wedding night, twenty years ago, I needed no second hint to induce me to fly eagerly to *her* arms. Ah, I was young then, and old age plays sad havoc with us!"

The worthy old gentleman whispered a few moments in the ear of the Chevalier. The latter arose with a flushed cheek and a flashing eye.

"Thanks for the hint, good father-in-law," he cried, draining another goblet of wine—"I have paid my devoirs to Bacchus; now will I worship at the shrine of Venus!"

With rather an unsteady gait he left the apartment, and, under the guidance of two lovely, blushing, tittering damsels, sought the nuptial chamber. At the door of that sacred retreat, his fair guides left him. He entered—and the black-hearted villain, stained with a thousand crimes, stood in the presence of angel purity.

And now, fain would we draw a curtain over what followed—but if we did so, our task would be incomplete. We therefore pass over the delicate details with as much rapidity as the nature of the case will admit.

The Chevalier advanced to the couch, and viewed his bride; evading his ardent gaze, she turned away, her maiden cheek glowing with blushes. Upon the snowy pillow, in rich masses, lay her luxuriant hair; her modestly veiled bosom, whose voluptuousness of outline no drapery could entirely conceal, heaved tumultuously with gushing joy, and holy happiness, and pure passion, and maidenly fear. Her small, exquisite hand, on whose taper fore-finger glittered a magnificent diamond ring, (her husband's gift,) rested upon the gorgeous counterpane, like a snow-flake upon a cluster of roses.

Still the Chevalier profanes not that pure form with his unhallowed touch; perchance some unseen power, the guardian of spotless innocence, restrains him. Placing himself before the splendid mirror, he begins to remove his superb garments with a deliberation and a composure that astonishes even himself.

As each article of dress is successively thrown aside, the magnificent symmetry of that man's unrivalled form becomes more and more apparent. Though of a build unusually powerful, his limbs possess all the grace and suppleness of the Apollo Belvedere. He is one of those rare combinations of strength and beauty, so often represented by classic statuary, yet so seldom seen in a living model.

His task is at length completed; he is in the primeval costume of nature. Complacently he surveys his reflection in the mirror; for he is fully conscious of his great personal advantages, and, in the vanity of his heart, he wishes to display them to the enraptured gaze of his bride. And she—who will say that she does not stealthily contemplate his symmetrical proportions with secret satisfaction—for what woman could, under such peculiar circumstances, be indifferent to the physical advantages possessed by the man of her choice?

Alas! how suddenly did poor Alice's golden dream of happiness vanish forever!

For there—upon her husband's naked breast—in black characters of damning distinctness—is *branded* the ghastly, hideous words—"CONVICTED FELON!!"

Alice uttered one piercing scream, and fainted.

The marriage guests below had not yet departed. They heard that awful cry, which seemed to be the very concentration of all human anguish. Mr. Goldworthy started to his feet, and his cheeks grew ashy pale.

"My friends," said he, in a low tone—"there is something wrong with my child. Remain here, and I will ascertain the cause of this strange outcry."

Having armed himself with a pistol, he repaired to his daughter's chamber, which he entered without ceremony; for when does a father stand on ceremony, when he believes the safety of his only child to be in danger? There, in the centre of the room, confused and abashed, stood the nude form of the Chevalier; and there, upon his breast, did Mr. Goldworthy behold the accursed brand of crime which had horrified his daughter, and elicited her piercing scream.

"*Convicted felon!*" gasped the old gentleman, almost disbelieving the evidence of his own senses. "Good God! am I dreaming, or do I actually behold that awful badge of infamy branded upon the flesh of the husband of my child! Almighty heaven, thy judgments are inscrutable, but this blow is too much—too much!"

He buried his face in his hands, and wept bitterly. The Chevalier, by a powerful effort, recovered his accustomed assurance and presence of mind.

"Come, my good sir," said he—"don't get in such a bad way about a few insignificant letters which are stamped upon me. I pledge you my honor 'twas merely done in jest, in a thoughtless moment. Pray retire, and leave me to console my bride for her silly fright."

"Liar and villain!" cried the old man—"would'st thou, with a red-hot iron, brand such words as *those* upon thee, in jest? Thou are a convicted scoundrel—an imposter—a murderer, for aught I know. Thou hast no claim upon my poor girl, who now lies there, insensible; the marriage is null and void!"

"Pooh—nonsense!" said the Chevalier, very coolly—"you make a devil of a fuss about a very small matter. This brand is but the consequence of a youthful folly—crime, if you will—of which I have long since repented, I assure you. A ruffled shirt will always conceal it from the world's prying gaze; your daughter and yourself are the only persons who will ever know of its existence; why, then, should it interfere with our matrimonial arrangements?"

"Dare you parley with me, villain?" cried Mr. Goldworthy, growing more and more indignant at the other's impudent assurance. "Hark'ee, sir," he continued, "the mystery which has always surrounded you, has been anything but favorable to your reputation, for *honest* men are seldom reluctant to disclose all that concerns their past career and present pursuits. But your damnable effrontery, and the accursed fascination of your manners, overcame all our suspicions relative to you; you were regarded as an honorable man, and a gentleman. Unfortunately, my Alice loved you, and in an evil moment I consented to your union. This evening, at the wine table, when you discoursed so learnedly and eloquently upon the exploits of daring villains, the thought struck me that you must have derived your knowledge of them from personal intimacy; but I instantly discarded the suspicion as unworthy of myself and unjust to you. But now—now your guilt can no longer be questioned, for its history is written there, upon your breast! Scoundrel, I might hand you over to the iron grasp of the law, but I will not; resume your garments, and leave this chamber—for your vile presence contaminates the very atmosphere, and 'tis no place for you!"

"No, you will not hand me over to the law, neither will you expose me," said the Chevalier, his lip curling with proud disdain. "Listen to me, old man: you are right—I *am* a villain—nay, more; I glory in the title. Am I not candid with you?—and yet you, yourself, will be as anxious as I can be, to keep the world ignorant of the fact that I am a villain,—for will the aristocratic Mr. Goldworthy consent that the public shall know that his beautiful daughter Alice is married to a branded criminal? Being perfectly safe, what need is there of concealment on my part? Know, then, that I am an escaped convict from Botany Bay, to which colony I was transported from England, for an atrocious crime. This brand upon my breast was placed there as a punishment for having attempted to murder one of my guards. I have been a pirate, a robber, a highwayman, a burglar, and (but let me whisper this word in your ear,) a *murderer!* Ha, ha, ha! how do you like your son-in-law now?"

"Monster, out of my sight!" cried the old man, shuddering.

"Softly, softly," said the Chevalier, with imperturbable calmness—"you have not heard all yet; of my skill as a pickpocket, you yourself have had ample proof, for 'twas I who relieved you of the valuable package last night; yet you dare not prosecute me—for am I not your son-in-law? But curses on my own indiscretion, in allowing wine to overcome my habitual prudence! For had I not been partially intoxicated, think you this mark of guilt would have been so easily discovered? No, believe me—"

"Silence, villain!" thundered Mr. Goldworthy, no longer able to contain his indignation at the cool effrontery of the Chevalier—"I have bandied words with you too long already; you see this pistol?—you are unarmed; I give you five minutes to dress yourself and leave the house; if you are not gone at the end of that time, I swear by the living God to shoot you through the head."

These last words were pronounced with a calmness that left no doubt of their sincerity on the mind of the Chevalier. Villain as he was, he was brave even to desperation; yet he had no particular wish to be hurried into eternity so unceremoniously. He therefore commenced dressing himself, while Mr. Goldworthy stood with the pistol cocked and pointed at his head with a deadly aim.

Meanwhile, the unfortunate Alice recovered from her swoon. Starting up in bed, she cast a hurried glance at her father and the discomfited Chevalier. That glance was sufficient to reveal to her the true state of affairs; and covering her face with her hands, she wept bitterly.

Who can comprehend the depth and devotedness of woman's love? Could it be possible that there still lingered in her crushed heart a single atom of affection for that branded villain, who had so cruelly deceived her? Philosophy may condemn her—human reason itself may scoff at her—but from her pure heart could not utterly be obliterated the sincere and holy love which she had conceived for that unworthy object. To her might have been applied the beautiful words of the poet Campbell:

> "Let the eagle change his plume,
> The leaf its hue, the flower its bloom,
> But ties around that heart were spun
> Which would not, could not be undone."

Before the expiration of the prescribed five minutes, the Chevalier was dressed, and ready to depart. Turning towards Alice, he regarded her with a look which was eloquently expressive of grief, remorse and sorrow. His breast heaved convulsively; he was evidently struggling with the most powerful emotions. A single tear rolled down his cheek—he hastily wiped it away—murmured, "Farewell, Alice, forever!" —and reminded by an imperious gesture from her father that the scene could continue no longer, he turned calmly and walked out of the room. Mr. Goldworthy followed him to the street door, and saw him depart from the house; then, with a deep-drawn sigh, he returned to his guests, who were naturally eager to know the nature of the difficulty. In answer to their inquiries, the old gentleman said-

"My dear friends, do not, I entreat you, press me for an explanation of this most melancholy affair. Suffice it for me to say, the Chevalier Duvall has proved himself to be utterly unworthy of my daughter. The marriage which has taken place, though not legally void, is *morally* so. I beg of everyone present to respect my feelings as a father and as a man, so far as to preserve a strict silence in reference to this painful matter. The Chevalier Duvall has departed from the house, and will never see my daughter more."

The required promise was given, and the guests took their leave, experiencing feelings of a far different nature from those which had animated them at the commencement of the evening. They had come in the happy anticipation of witnessing the consummation of a beloved friend's felicity; they went away oppressed by a painful uncertainty as to the nature of the difficulty which had arisen in reference to the husband, and chilled by a fear that the earthly happiness of poor Alice was destroyed forever.

The Chevalier returned to the Duchess, to apprise her of the total ruin of his matrimonial schemes, in consequence of the *fatal brand* upon his person having been discovered; and we return to Fanny Aubrey, who had been conveyed by Jew Mike to the *"Chambers of Love,"* in obedience to the directions given him by the Hon. Timothy Tickels.

CHAPTER VII

Showing the operations of Jew Mike and his coadjutors. — The necessity of young ladies looking beneath their beds, before retiring to rest.

We have seen in what manner Jew Mike escaped from the house of Mr. Goldworthy, bearing off the insensible form of Fanny Aubrey; but as the reader may be curious to learn how the ruffian gained entrance to the house, and to the chamber of the young lady, we shall briefly explain.

In the first place, it is perhaps understood that old Tickels applied to Sow Nance for assistance in the business of abducting Fanny, and conveying her to that den of iniquity called the "Chambers of Love," —which place will be hereafter described. Nance, on being applied to, informed her employer that she had a *"love cull,"* (paramour,) who was exactly suited to the business, and who would, for a proper compensation, engage to do the job. Tickels was delighted with the proposal, and eagerly desired to have an early interview with her accommodating lover. But there was a difficulty; Jew Mike had an invincible repugnance to going abroad under any circumstances, inasmuch as he had recently been engaged in a heavy burglary, and the pleasure of his company was earnestly sought after by police officer Storkfeather and other indefatigables. He was safely housed in the "Pig Pen," and regarded it as decidedly unsafe to venture out, even to execute a piece of work as profitable as the one which Mr. Tickels wished him to perform. It was finally arranged that the latter gentleman would call on Mike at the "Pen," on a certain evening. This was done; and the result of that interview was, that Mike, for and in consideration of receiving the sum of one hundred dollars, agreed to carry off Fanny Aubrey, and deposit her safely in the "Chambers of Love."

To obviate the possibility of Mike's being overhauled by his old friends the police officers, it was arranged that a cab should be at his entire disposal; the same vehicle would serve to convey the young lady with secrecy and rapidity to the place destined for her imprisonment. Tickels engaged to have Mike privately introduced into the house of Mr. Goldworthy, and it was effected in this manner.

On the night previous to the abduction, at about the hour of nine, a cab was driven through Ann street, and halted in front of the dance cellar which communicated with the "Pig Pen." The driver of this vehicle was a sable individual, who has since attained some notoriety under the cognomen of "Jonas." He is intimately acquainted with the location and condition of every house of prostitution in Boston, and enjoys the familiar acquaintance of many white courtezans of beauty and fashion, not a few of whom (so 'tis said,) testify their appreciation of his valuable services in bringing them profitable custom, by freely granting him those delightful privileges which are usually extended to white patrons only, who can pay well for the same. Jonas has lately become the editor and proprietor of that valuable periodical known as the "Key to the Chambers of Love," which is a *card* containing a list of almost every bower of pleasure in Boston, with the names of their keepers. It is a document which is extensively patronized by the sporting bloods. This fortunate darkey it was, then, who was employed in the delicate matter, the progress of which we are now describing.

He had no sooner halted his cab, as we have stated, than there cautiously issued from the cellar an individual carefully concealed from observation by a huge slouched hat and cloak. This, it is almost needless to say, was Jew Mike himself. Having greeted Jonas with the assurance of "all right," he quickly entered the cab, and the sable driver started his horse towards Howard street at a slapping pace.

In the neighborhood of the Athenaeum, the cab paused, and Mike got out. He was instantly joined by the Hon. Mr. Tickels, who said to Jonas—

"Drive away, and be on this spot again, with your horse and cab, precisely at twelve o'clock. Remain here until one; if by that time Mike does not make his appearance, you will know that the job can't be done to-night, and you need wait no longer. To-morrow night, be on this spot again, at twelve, and remain until one—and don't fail to repeat this every night until Mike appears with the young woman he is to carry off. For every night that you come here, you shall be paid five dollars. Do you understand?"

"Yes, indeed, ole hoss," replied the delighted Jonas, displaying his mouthful of dominoes—"dat five dollars ebery night will 'nable dis colored person to shine at de balls of de colored society dis winter; perhaps be de manager—yah, yah, yah!" When giving utterance to his peculiar laugh, Jonas makes a noise as if he were undergoing the process of being choked to death by a fat sausage. Having thus given vent to his satisfaction, he mounted his cab and drove off. When he had departed, Tickels drew Mike within the dark shadow of a building, and, in whispered tones, thus addressed him:—

"I have, as you are aware, succeeded in bribing one of Goldworthy's servants to admit you into the house, and conceal you until the favorable moment arrives for you to bear off the prize. Whether you do it to-night, or to-morrow night, or the next, you must be sure to do it only between the hours of twelve and one, for only during that interval of time will Jonas and his cab be in waiting for you. When the time for action arrives, you must satisfy yourself that all is still in the house—that all have retired. I have ascertained that Goldworthy and his household almost invariably retire to rest at ten o'clock; therefore, it is reasonable to suppose that they are all asleep by twelve. At that hour, if you think the coast is clear, steal cautiously forth from your place of concealment, and noiselessly enter the young lady's chamber; this you will have no difficulty in doing, for I have taken the pains to ascertain that she never takes the precaution to lock the door."

"But," interrupted Jew Mike—"in that large mansion, containing so many apartments, how shall I know for certainty which particular room the young woman sleeps in?"

"I have anticipated and provided for that difficulty," rejoined Tickels—"although the servant whom I have bribed, could doubtless direct you to the chamber. Here, on this sheet of paper, I have drawn a diagram of the entire building; by studying it for a few minutes, you will readily be enabled to find your way to any part of the house. —To resume: you will enter the chamber, and assure yourself that the young lady is sleeping; this is an important point, because, if she should chance to be awake, and observe you, she would naturally scream with affright, which would ruin everything. Well, having satisfied yourself, beyond a doubt, that she is fast asleep, you will softly approach the bed, and, in the twinkling of an eye, *bind and gag her!* so that she will be utterly incapable of voice or motion. Then take her in your arms, steal noiselessly down stairs, and make your exit by the front door, which will be left unlocked for that purpose. Having reached the street, leap with your precious burden into the cab, and Jonas will drive you with all speed to the 'Chambers.' Take off your shoes when in the house, and your footsteps will be less liable to be heard. Now, Mike, I have one request to make: I know the laxity of your principles with respect to the virtue of honesty, and admire your system of appropriation—but steal nothing, not even the merest trifle, in the house. I will tell you why I require this of you; when the young lady is missed, if property is also missed, they will naturally suppose that both she and the valuables have been carried off by some marauder; for they could never believe *her* to be guilty of theft; and their affection for her would prompt them to make every effort for her recovery. If, on the contrary, no property disappears with her, they may possibly think that she has voluntarily eloped, and will be apt to trouble themselves very little about her, for her supposed ingratitude will arouse their indignation. Do you not perceive and acknowledge the force of my argument?"

Jew Mike replied that he certainly did, and assured his worthy employer that he would, for the first time in his life, refrain from stealing, even where he had an excellent opportunity.

"This heroic self-denial on your part is worthy of the highest commendation," said Mr. Tickels. "I have but one more observation to make, and then I will detain you no longer. If it should unfortunately happen that you are detected in this business, for God's sake don't bring my name in connection with it. Tell them that your design was to rob the house; they will send you to jail, and no matter how many charges may be brought against you, I have money and influence sufficient to procure your liberation. Now, my good fellow, do you consent to this?"

Mike answered affirmatively; and the two proceeded towards Mr. Goldworthy's house. Fortunately for their operations, there was no moon, and the night was intensely dark; therefore, they were by no means likely to be observed by any prying individual or inquisitive Charley—besides, the gentlemen who belong to the latter class, prefer rather to indulge in a comfortable doze on some door-step, than to go prowling about, impertinently interfering with the business of enterprising burglars and others, who "prefer darkness rather than light."

The Hon. Mr. Tickels and Jew Mike, having reached Mr. Goldworthy's house, stationed themselves in front of the door, and after a short pause, to assure themselves that all was right, the former worthy gave utterance to three distinct coughs, which were, however, rendered in a very low tone. The signal was answered almost immediately; the door was softly opened, and a man made his appearance; this was the unfaithful servant who had been bribed to admit a villain into his master's house.

"Is everything all right, Cushing?" asked Tickels, in a whisper.

"Yes, sir," replied the fellow, in the same tone—"there's no one stirring in the house except myself, as Mr. Goldworthy and the ladies have gone to the theatre, and have not yet returned; and as to the other servants, they have all gone to bed."

"That's well," remarked Tickels—"now, Mike, this man will conceal you in some safe place. If the business can be done to-night, do it; if not, defer it until a favorable opportunity presents itself. You know all the arrangements; therefore I need not repeat them. Fulfil your contract, and come to me for your reward. Good night."

He departed. Cushing desired Jew Mike to follow him into the house; the latter obeyed, and was conducted into a small room, which the servant gave him to understand was his sleeping chamber.

"Is this to be my place of concealment?" demanded Jew Mike, glancing around with a growl of dissatisfaction—"damn it, you couldn't hide a mouse here without its being discovered."

"That's true enough," rejoined Cushing—"you can't hide here, that's certain. I confess I am at a loss where to put you. There's no time to be lost, for I expect my master and the ladies to return every instant. Hell and furies, there's the carriage now! they have come!"

It was true; a carriage stopped at the door, and they could hear the voices and footsteps of people entering the house.

"We are lost!" cried Cushing, pale with fear—"yet stay; there is but one way of escaping immediate detection. Have you the courage to hide in—in—"

"Courage!" exclaimed Mike, in great rage—"show me a place of concealment, and I'll stow myself in it, if it be hell itself! Our enterprise must not fail by my being discovered here."

"Quick, then—this way—follow me—softly, softly," whispered the other, conducting Mike up a flight of stairs, and into a handsomely furnished bed-chamber.

"This," said Cushing—"is the room in which Miss Fanny Aubrey sleeps; the young lady whom you are to carry off. It is the best place in the world for you to conceal yourself in, for your victim will be almost within your grasp. Quick—stow yourself *under the bed*, in the farthest corner. She will not discover you, if you keep perfectly quiet, for you will be screened from view by the thick curtains of the bed. If you cannot do the job to-night, you must remain in your hiding-place all day to-morrow—and indeed, you must not think of stirring forth, until the moment arrives for you to carry off Miss Fanny. I will contrive to supply you with food and drink. Hark!—by God, somebody is coming up-stairs. I must be off—under the bed with you—quick, quick!"

In a twinkling was Jew Mike snugly ensconced beneath the bed, while Cushing hastily left the chamber, and repaired to his own room.

Within the space of one minute afterwards, Fanny Aubrey entered her chamber, accompanied by a maid-servant bearing a light.

"You may set down the candle, Matilda, if you please, dear," said Fanny, in her sweet, gentle voice—"and leave me, for I shall not need your assistance to undress me."

"Indeed, Miss, axing your pardon, I shall do no such thing," responded Matilda, who was a buxom, good-humored, and rather good-looking young woman; and with a kind of respectful familiarity, she began to perform upon her young mistress the delicate and graceful duties of a *femme de chambre*. "You are very silly, Matilda, thus to insist on waiting on *me*; I, that am as poor as yourself, and was brought up as nothing but a fruit girl."

"Lor, Miss!" cried Matilda, holding up her hands with a sort of pious horror—"how can you compare yourself with the likes of me? You were born to be a lady, and I am so happy to be your servant—your own ladies' maid! You will have a fine husband one of these days, Miss. Now, if I might make so bold, there is that pretty young gentleman, Miss Alice's cousin, Master Clarence—"

"Hush, Matilda," interrupted Fanny, blushing deeply—"what has Master Clarence to do with me? you are a silly creature. Make haste and undress me, since you will do it, for I am *so* tired and sleepy!"

Matilda did as she was desired, but being, like all other ladies' maids, very talkative, kept up a 'running commentary' on the charms of her young mistress, as ladies' maids are very apt to do.

"What beautiful hair!" quoth the abigail, in an under tone, as if she were merely holding a sociable chat with herself—"for all the world like skeins of golden thread; and what a fair skin! just like a heap of snow, or a newly washed sheet spread out to bleach. Patience alive! this pretty arm beats Mrs. Swelby's wax-work all hollow; and these beautiful—"

"You vex me to death with your nonsense, Matilda," cried Fanny—"how tiresome you are! Pray be silent."

Thus rebuked, the ladies' maid continued her task in silence. When the young lady was disrobed, and about to retire to bed, she was startled by a sudden exclamation of Matilda's—

"Bless me, Miss! what noise was that? It sounded as if somebody was hid somewhere in this very chamber."

They both paused and listened; all was again still. Fanny, as well as her maid had certainly heard a slight noise, which seemed to have been produced by a slow and cautious movement, and sounded like the rustling of a curtain.

"'Twas nothing but the noise of the night-breeze agitating the window curtains," remarked Fanny, at length, with a smile.

Ah! neither she, nor her maid, saw the two fearful eyes that were glaring at them from among the intricate folds of the curtain, beneath the bed!—Neither saw they the dark and hideous countenance of the ruffian that lay concealed there.

"Well, Miss," said Matilda, not over half re-assured by the words of her mistress—"it may be nothing, as you say; but, for my part, I never go to bed a single night in the year, without first *looking under the bed* to see that nobody is hid away there. And I advise you to do the same, Miss; and I am sure you would, if you only knew what happened to my cousin Bridget."

"And what was that, pray?" asked Fanny, as she got into bed, and settled herself comfortably, in order to listen to what happened to cousin Bridget—all her fears in regard to the noise which she had heard, having vanished.

"Why, you see, miss," said Matilda, seating herself at the bed-side, —"cousin Bridget was cook in a gentleman's family in this city, and a very nice body she was, and is to this day. In the same family there lived a young man as was a coachman, very good-looking, and very attentive to Biddy, as we call her for shortness, miss. But, though he was desperate in love with my cousin, she would give him no encouragement, and the poor fellow pined away, and neglected his wittles, and grew thin in flesh, until, from being called Fat Tom, he got to be nicknamed the 'Natomy, which means a skeleton. It was in vain, miss, that poor 'Natomy threatened to take to hard drinking, or pizen himself with Prooshy acid, unless she took pity on him—not a smile, or a kiss, or a hope could he get from cousin Biddy. Now, between ourselves, I really think she had a sort of a sneaking notion after him; you know, miss, that we women folks like to tease the men, by making them think that we hate 'em, when all the time we are dead in love with 'em. Well, matters and things went on pretty much as I have said, for some times; until something happened that made a great charge in the feelings of cousin Biddy towards Tom the coachman. Biddy slept in a nice little bed-room in the attic—all by herself; and Tom slept in another nice little bed-room in the attic—all by *himself*, too. Well, miss, one night Biddy went to a fancy ball in Ann street, given in honor of her brother's wife's second cousin, Mrs. MacFiggins, having been blessed with three twins at a birth; she danced very late, and drank a great deal of hot toddy, which made her so nervous that she had to go home in a hackney-coach. She went to bed, but the toddy made her feel so very uncomfortable, that she had to get up again, during the night; and she happened, by accident, to reach her hand under the bed—and what do you think, miss? her hand caught hold of something—she pulled it towards her, out from under the bed—and oh, my gracious! what must have been the feelings of the poor body, when she found that she had taken hold of a man's—*nose!* and, what was worse than all, that nose belonged to Tom, the coachman! My poor cousin Biddy, on making this awful discovery, gave a low scream, and fainted; and then—and then, miss—in about half an hour, when she came to her senses, on finding that nobody, except Tom, had heard her scream, she felt so kind of *put out* about the whole matter, that she agreed to marry Tom, if he would promise never to say nothing about it. He agreed, and in a few weeks afterwards they were man and wife. I heard this story, miss, from Biddy's own lips, and it's as true as gospel. So that is the reason why I look under my bed every night, to see if anybody is hid away there; because the very idea of having a man *under* a body's bed, is so awful! But bless me, miss—you are fast asleep already, and I dare say you haven't heard half of my story."

Matilda was right; Fanny had fallen asleep at the most interesting point of the foregoing narrative, and she was therefore in blissful ignorance of the catastrophe by which cousin Biddy became the wife of Tom the coachman. The ladies' maid, muttering her indignation at the very little interest manifested in her story, by her young mistress, left the chamber, and took herself off to bed, leaving the candle burning upon the table.

Half an hour passed; all throughout the house was profoundly still. The deep and regular breathing of Fanny indicated that she slept soundly. A small clock in the chamber proclaimed the hour of midnight. Scarce had the tiny sounds died away in silence, when the hideous head of Jew Mike cautiously emerged from beneath the bed. The ruffian noiselessly crept forth from his place of concealment, and stood over the fair sleeper. Having satisfied himself of the soundness of her slumbers, he drew from his pocket the handkerchief and cord with which he intended to gag and bind her.

At that moment, Fanny stirred, and partially awoke; quick as lightning, Jew Mike crouched down upon the carpet, and crawled beneath the bed. To his inexpressible mortification and rage, the young lady arose from the couch, advanced to the table, and having snuffed the candle, and thrown a shawl over her shoulders, seated herself, and taking up a book, began to read. The truth is, she felt herself rather restless and unwell, and determined to while away an hour or so by perusing a few chapters in the work of a favorite author.

The clock struck one, and then Jew Mike knew that his villainous plans could not be carried out that night. A few minutes afterwards, the negro Jones, who had, since twelve o'clock, been waiting with his horse and cab near Mr. Goldworthy's house in Howard street, drove off—the sable genius muttering, as he urged his 'fast crab' onward—

"Five dollars for to-night, and five dollars more for to-morrow night—dat I'm sure of, any how; gorry, dis nigger's in luck."

After the lapse of fifteen or twenty minutes, Fanny Aubrey closed her book, and again retired to bed. Again she slept; and for that night, she was safe. Mike knew that the cab had departed, and was obliged to defer the execution of his scheme until the next night, or even for a longer period, if a favorable opportunity did not then occur.

Poor Fanny! during the remainder of that night her slumbers were attended by peaceful and pleasant dreams. What if she had known that beneath her couch there lurked a desperate and bloody ruffian, impatiently awaiting the hour when he could bear her off to a fate worse than death!

Slowly wore the night away; and at length the cheerful rays of the morning sun, shining upon the beautiful countenance of the fair sleeper, awoke her from her slumbers. She arose—gracefully as a young fawn did she spring from the chaste embraces of her luxurious couch, and caroling forth a gay air—the gushing gladness of her happy heart—she proceeded to perform the duties of her toilet. Now, like a naiad at a fountain, does she lave that charming face and those ductile limbs in the limpid and rose-scented waters of a portable bath, sculptured in marble and supported by four little Cupids with gilded wings; then, like the fabled mermaid, does she arrange her shining hair in that style of beautiful simplicity which is so becoming, and so seldom successfully accomplished, even by women of undoubted taste. The amorous mirror glowingly reflects her young and budding charms, as she coquettishly admires the loveliness of her delicious little person, half-blushing at the sight of her own voluptuous nudity. Little does she suspect that the savage eyes of a concealed ruffian are gloating with lecherous delight upon her exposed form!

In happy unconsciousness of this hideous scrutiny, the young lady having completed the preliminary arrangements of her toilet, proceeded to array herself in a charming and delicate morning costume. Although it could not be said that

> "Her snowy breast was bare to ready spoil
> Of hungry eyes,"

yet these lines from *Thomson's Seasons* might be applied to her, with peculiar force:—

> "Her polished limbs
> Veil'd in a simple robe, their best attire,
> Beyond the pomp of dress; for loveliness
> Needs not the foreign aid of ornament,
> But is, when unadorn'd, adorn'd the most."

She was scarcely dressed, when the breakfast bell sounded its welcome peal; and she hastened below to take her place at the hospitable family table.

During the whole of that day, Jew Mike did not venture to stir once from his retreat. In the forenoon, a female domestic came and arranged the bed, without discovering him; after a while, Fanny came into the chamber, to dress for dinner, which being done, she withdrew without suspecting the presence of the villainous Jew Mike, who again had an opportunity of feasting his eyes on her denuded charms. Late in the afternoon, much to the joy of the ruffian, who was half starved, Cushing stole into the chamber, bringing with him some provisions and a bottle of wine; those he hastily passed under the bed, and abruptly retired, for he was apprehensive of being detected in the room, which would have ruined all.

Night came on. Mike was a witness of the scene which took place between Alice Goldsworthy and Fanny, wherein the latter charged the Chevalier with having stolen the packet of money. The reader knows how Fanny was afterwards awakened from her sleep by a horrid dream, and how she discovered the form of a man bending over her—that man was, of course, Jew Mike. It will be recollected that the young girl screamed and fainted; that Clarence Argyle rushed into the chamber, and was instantly shot down by Mike—and that the ruffian made his escape from the house, bearing off the unfortunate girl in his arms.

Jonas was waiting at a short distance from the house; Mike hastily entered the cab with his burden, and the negro drove rapidly towards Warren street, wherein was located the "Chambers of Love."

The vehicle halted before a house of decent exterior; Jew Mike came out, bearing the still insensible girl; the door of the house opened, and he entered; then the door closed, and all was still. With a low chuckle of satisfaction, Jonas whipped his horse into a gallop, and away he rattled through the silent and deserted streets.

CHAPTER VIII

The Chambers of Love. — Conclusion.

On entering the house in Warren street with his burden, Jew Mike passed through a dark passage, and entered a large, well-lighted and well-furnished room. Here he was received by a rather stout and extremely good-looking female, the landlady of the house, who rejoiced in the peculiar title of Madame Hearthstone. Notwithstanding the lateness of the hour, several courtezans of the ordinary class were lounging about, or indolently conversing with a few intimate male friends, who were probably their private lovers, or *pimps*.

"Well," said Madame Hearthstone, with a smile of satisfaction—"you have caught the bird at last, I see; but she must not remain here, for when she recovers from her swoon, she may take it into her head to scream, or make a disturbance, which might be heard in the street. We will carry her below to the *Chambers*, and there she may make as much noise as she pleases—there's no possibility of her ever being overheard by people above ground!"

In obedience to her directions, Jew Mike again took the young girl in his arms, and followed Madame out of the room, while she bore a light. She led the way into a bed-chamber on the second floor, which apartment was furnished with that luxury so invariably found in the bowers of land-ladies of pleasure, who care but little for the comfort of their *boarders*, so long as they themselves are "in clover."

The walls of Madame's chamber were beautifully adorned with fancy paper, representing panels in gilded frames, decorated with wreaths of flowers. The lady advanced towards one of these panels, and kneeling down upon the floor, touched a secret spring; instantly a door, which had previously been invisible, sprang open, revealing an aperture large enough to admit a person standing upright.

The reader must not be surprised that the landlady should thus expose to Jew Mike the means of entering her private rendezvous; for Mike was perfectly in her confidence, having often before been employed to convey victims to that den, and being already well acquainted with the mystery of the secret panel.

They entered the aperture—the landlady bearing the light, and the ruffian carrying the unconscious form of Fanny Aubrey. Having carefully closed the panel behind them, they began to descend a long flight of steps, so steep and narrow, that extreme care was necessary to enable them to preserve their footing.

Down, down they went, seemingly far into the bowels of the earth. At length they arrived at the bottom, and a stout oaken door intercepted their further progress. The landlady produced a key, and the door swung back upon its massive hinges; they entered a vast apartment, fitted up in a style of splendor almost equal to the fabled magnificence of a fairy palace.

The hall was of circular shape, surmounted by a dome, from which hung a superb chandelier, which shed a brilliant light over the gilded ornaments and voluptuous paintings that adorned the walls. In the centre stood a table, laden with fruits and wines, around which were seated half a dozen young females, all very beautiful, and several of them nearly half naked. Two of these girls, who were more modestly dressed than the others, seemed sad and dispirited; their four companions, however, appeared vicious and reckless in the extreme.

"Girls," said the landlady, addressing them—"I have brought you a new sister; she has come to learn the delightful mysteries of Venus. Give her all the instruction in your power, and learn her the arts and ways of a finished courtezan."

Jew Mike laid Fanny upon a sofa; the girls crowded around her, and regarded her with looks of interest and joy.

"She is very pretty," said one of them, a bold, wanton looking young creature, of rare beauty, her seductive form wholly revealed beneath a single light gauze garment, such as are worn by ballet girls—"I will become her teacher; I will show her how to turn the brains of men crazy with passion, and bring the proudest of them grovelling at her feet. Oh, 'tis delightful to humble the lords of creation, as they call themselves, and make them whine for our favors like so many sick spaniels!"

"You are a girl of spirit, Julia," said the landlady, regarding her with a look of admiration—"and will make a splendid courtezan."

"But," cried Julia, with sparkling eyes and a heaving breast—"when *shall* I become a courtezan? How long must I remain here, pining for the embraces of fifty men, and enduring the impotent caresses of but one, and *he*, bah! a fellow of no more fire or animation, of *power*, than a lump of ice!"

"Have patience, my love," rejoined the landlady—"Mr. Lawyer may be a poor lover, but he is a profitable patron; so long as he pays liberally for your exclusive favors in these 'Chambers,' you must receive him, for you will share the profits, when you 'turn out.' And now see what you can do in the way of restoring this new comer, for her *owner* will be here soon, to see her. Carry her into the *Satin*

Chamber, which is to be her room, and when she revives, make her partake of some refreshments."

The landlady and Jew Mike left the hall; the massive door was relocked, and ascended to the upper regions of the house, leaving Fanny Aubrey to the care of the inmates of the luxurious Chambers below.

The Satin Chamber was an apartment of moderate dimensions, which adjoined the principal hall. It was completely lined throughout with white satin, which produced an effect so voluptuous as to defy description. Into this gorgeous bower of lust the girls carried Fanny, and laid her down upon a soft and yielding couch.

Restoratives were applied, and she was speedily brought to a state of consciousness. Her wonder and astonishment may easily be imagined, when, on starting up, she found herself in that strange place, surrounded by a group of showily dressed females, some of them indecently nude.

Without answering her eager inquiries, as to where she was, and how she came there, they brought her wine and other refreshments, of which they compelled her to partake.

"You are in a place of safety, and among friends," said one of them, a beautiful brunette of sixteen, whose glossy hair fell in rich masses upon her naked shoulders and bosom. —This abandoned young creatures was a Jewess, named Rachel; her own wild, lascivious passions had been the cause of her being brought to the 'Chambers,' rather than the arts of the man who was at that time enjoying her delectable favors.

"Yes, dear," chimed in the voluptuous Julia—"we are your sisters, and it will be our task to teach you the delights of love, while you remain among us.—But come, girls; let us leave our sister to repose; she is a little Venus, and will dream of Cupid's pleasures, and when she awakes from her soft slumbers, she may find herself in the arms of an impetuous lover. —Happy girl! I envy her the bliss which she is soon to experience, because it is to her, as yet, a bliss *untasted*."

Each of the embryo Cyprians kissed the intended victim; some did it almost passionately, as if their libidinous natures derived a gratification even in kissing one of their own sex; some did it laughingly, with whispered words of encouragement and congratulation; but one of them, less hardened than the rest, dropped a tear of pity on her cheek, and in a gentle, yet faltering voice, murmured— "Poor girl, I am sorry for you!" They departed, and Fanny was left alone—alone with her tears, her troubled thoughts, and a thousand fears; for she remembered having seen the ruffian at her bed-side, and although she recollected nothing of what had subsequently occurred, still she doubted not that she had been carried to the place where she found herself, for some terrible purpose.

The six 'daughters of Venus' returned to the principal hall, and had scarcely resumed their places at the table, when the door was opened, and an old gentleman entered. He was a very tall, erect, slim personage, dressed in blue broadcloth, his neck neatly enveloped in a white cravat, garnished with a shirt collar of uncommon magnitude. Judging from appearances, he might formerly have been an individual of rather comely presence; but, strange to say, he was almost entirely destitute of a *nose*—the place formerly occupied by that important feature, being now supplied by a stump of flesh little larger than an ordinary pimple. This deformity gave his face an aspect extremely ludicrous, if not positively disgusting; and was the result of an indiscreet amour in former times, which not only communicated the fiery brand of destruction to his nasal organ, but also effectually disqualified him from any further direct indulgence in the amorous gambols of Venus. Thus painfully afflicted, 'Tom Lawyer,' as he has always been familiarly called, was obliged to content himself with such enjoyments as lay within the limited range of his physical powers—enjoyments which, though rather unsatisfactory, were nevertheless expensive; yet his immense wealth enabled him to command them. To explain: he would maintain in luxury some beautiful young female, with whom he would pass a portion of his leisure time in harmless dalliance—therefore was he the *patron* of the voluptuous Julia, whom he kept strictly secluded in the 'Chambers,' fearing that her unsatisfied passions would seek their 'legitimate gratification,' were an opportunity afforded her to do so.

As he entered, Julia affected the utmost delight at seeing him, and rushing into his arms, almost devoured him with kisses; and then she followed him into an adjoining chamber, her beautiful countenance wearing an expression of ill-concealed disgust.—They entered—the door was closed, and—we dare not describe what followed.

* * * * *

At an early hour, on the morning succeeding these events, Jew Mike called on the Hon. Mr. Tickels, for the purpose of receiving the one hundred dollars, which had been promised him as the reward of his villainy in abducting Fanny Aubrey.

On learning that the infamous project had been crowned with complete success, the old libertine was overjoyed beyond measure; but when Mike demanded the one hundred dollars, his face lengthened—for he was avaricious as well as villainous, and his recent loss of five thousand dollars, in favor of the Chevalier and the Duchess, made him exceedingly loth to part with a cool hundred so easily.—Not exactly knowing the sort of a man he had to deal with, he assumed a stern tone and aspect, and said—

"One hundred dollars, for two nights' work! Do you take me for a fool? Here, fellow, is twenty dollars for you, and I consider you are well paid for your trouble."

"But sir," remarked Mike—"you know you promised—"

"Pooh!—promises are nothing; when a man wants to get possession of a pretty girl, he'll promise anything; when she is once in his power, he is not so liberal. Here, take your twenty dollars, and be off!"

"And this is my reward and thanks for the risk I have run!" demanded Jew Mike, bitterly.

"I've no time to waste words with you," rejoined Tickels, haughtily—"I know you; you're an old offender, and I could send you to prison, if I chose, without paying you a cent.—Once more, take the money, or leave it."

"Then you would break your contract with me? Be it so—keep your money; but, by God! I'll drink your heart's blood for this! My name is Jew Mike, and I have said it. Farewell, till we meet again!"

He rushed from the house, leaving Tickels divided by joy at having saved a hundred dollars, and fear, in consequence of the ruffian's savage threat.

Five minutes after Mike's departure, Corporal Grimsby entered, announced the abduction of Fanny Aubrey from the house of her friends, on the preceding night, and boldly accused Tickels of having been the cause of that outrage. The details of this interview are related in the sixth chapter of this narrative; it is consequently unnecessary to repeat them.

Satisfied in his own mind that old Tickels was at the bottom of the business, and that Jew Mike was the agent employed, the Corporal made the best of his way to Ann street, resolved to find the Jew, and prevail upon him, by bribes, to disclose the place where Fanny had been carried. During the whole of that day, he searched in vain; Mike was nowhere to be found; —towards evening, however, as the old gentleman was about to abandon the search in despair, he was informed by 'Cod-mouth Pat,' whom he had enlisted in his service, that Mike had just been seen to enter the 'Pig Pen.' With some difficulty, our friend contrived to gain an entrance to that 'crib,' where he had the satisfaction to find the object of his anxious search brooding over a half pint of gin. The ruffian instantly recognised in the Corporal, the person who had escaped from the 'Coal Hole,' some time previously, but every hostile feeling vanished, when the old man announced the object of his visit to be the discovery of Fanny Aubrey, and the punishment of the villain Tickels.

Without entering into details which might prove tedious, suffice it to say that Jew Mike agreed to conduct the Corporal to the place where Fanny was confined, on condition that the punishment of old Tickels should be left entirely to him, (Mike). This was assented to, and the pair instantly set out, in a cab, for the 'Chambers of Love,' in Warren street—the Corporal, eager to rescue poor Fanny from the power of her persecutors, and the Jew thirsting to revenge himself upon his employer, for having refused to give him the stipulated reward.

That same evening, at about the hour of seven, the Hon. Timothy Tickels issued from his residence in South street, and proceeded towards Warren street, which having reached, he entered the mansion of Madame Hearthstone. That lady, with a significant smile, conducted him to her chamber, and opened the secret panel; they descended the steps, and Mr. Tickels was ushered in the grand hall of the 'Chambers of Love.' The landlady pointed to the door of the apartment to which Fanny Aubrey had been conveyed; the old libertine opened the door, and entered.

In a few moments a piercing scream is heard—then another; but alas! those sounds could not be heard above, from the depths of that voluptuous tomb. But hark!—there is a noise without—nearer and nearer comes the tumult—the great door is burst open with a tremendous crash, and Jew Mike rushes in, followed by

Corporal Grimbsy. "This way!" shouts the Jew—"Forward!" responds the gallant Corporal. They reach the door of the *Satin Chamber*—they open it.

"Brick-bats and paving-stones! just in time again!"

There, upon a satin couch, her dress disordered and torn, her face flushed, her hair in wild disorder, her bosom naked and bleeding, lay Fanny Aubrey, panting, writhing, fiercely struggling in the ruffian grasp of the villain Tickels, who savagely turned and confronted the intruders. In an instant, he was stunned by a powerful blow from the gigantic fist of Jew Mike, and Fanny was folded in the arms of her preserver, the brave old Corporal.

They left that underground hell—the Corporal, bearing the now overjoyed Fanny in his arms, and Jew Mike, half carrying, half dragging the insensible form of old Tickels. They reached the chamber above, and emerged from the secret panel; the affrightened inmates of the house offered no resistance; they entered the cab which was in waiting, and were driven to the residence of the Corporal, who, with his fair young *protege*, alighted, and entered the house; then Jew Mike and his victim were driven to Ann street, and the vehicle halted before the cellar which led to the 'Pig Pen.'

The night was very dark, and no one observed the Jew, as, issuing from the cab, he descended into the cellar, bearing in his powerful arms the unconscious form of Tickels. Fortunately for him, he passed through the cellar and 'Pig Pen,' without exciting much notice, as the hour was too early for the usual revellers of the place to assemble, and those who saw him, merely supposed that he was carrying some drunken friend to a place of safety from the police—a sight common enough in that region. Mike needed no light to guide his footsteps, he traversed the dark passage, he seized the iron ring, and drew up the trap door of the 'Coal Hole,' from which the Corporal so providentially escaped. Then, with a deep curse, he cast the old libertine into the dark abyss, closed the entrance, and departed.

When Tickels revived, and found himself in that loathsome place, he rent the air with his cries and supplications; but no aid came to the crime-polluted wretch, and in a few days he sank beneath the combined effects of despair, starvation, and the foetid atmosphere, and miserably perished.

CONCLUSION

The Conclusion of a Tale is like the end of a journey: the Author throws aside his pen and foolscap as the tired traveller does the dusty garments of the road, and stretching himself at ease, looks back upon the various companions of his erratic ramblings.

The curiosity of the reader is doubtless highly excited to know who "Corporal Grimsby" is. Circumstances, we regret to say, will not permit us to state definitely— but should a guess be made that the worthy old Corporal, and a certain Capt.

S——, commander of a Revenue Cutter, were one and the same person, we will venture to say that the conjecture would not be far removed from the actual truth.

The "Chevalier Duvall" and the "Duchess" still continue in their brilliant career of crime, in Boston. We regret that the limits of the present work have not permitted us to record more fully their extraordinary operations in voluptuous intrigue and stupendous fraud.

Fanny Aubrey is again a happy inmate of the family of Mr. Goldworthy. Poor Alice, although a shade has been cast over her pure life by the dark villainy of the Chevalier, has been restored to a state of comparative felicity by the constant kindness and sympathy of her relatives and friends.

"Jew Mike" has gone on a professional tour to the South and West. "Sow Nance" has become the most abandoned prostitute in Ann street.

Dear reader, thanking thee for the patience with which thou hast accompanied us in our devious wanderings, and hoping that thou hast not always found us to be a dull companion, we bid thee farewell.

City Crimes;

OR
LIFE IN NEW YORK AND BOSTON.
A VOLUME FOR EVERYBODY:
BEING A MIRROR OF FASHION,
A PICTURE OF POVERTY,
AND A STARTLING REVELATION
OF THE SECRET CRIMES
OF GREAT CITIES

{First published 1849}

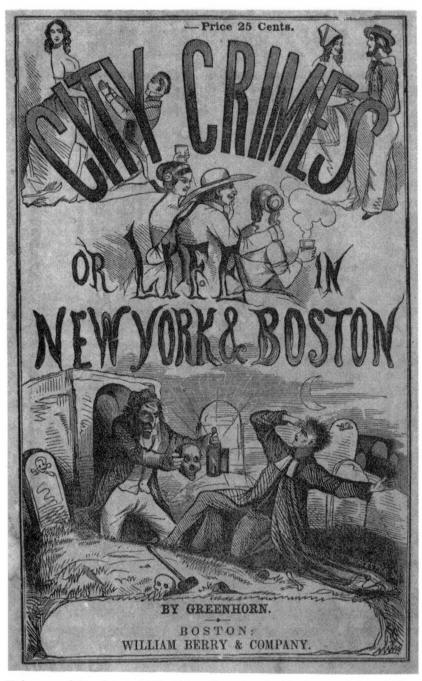

Title page of *City Crimes*, 1849 edition. Reproduced with the permission of The Huntington Library, San Marino, California.

CHAPTER I

*A Young Gentleman of Wealth and Fashion—a noble resolve—the flatterers—
the Midnight Encounter—an Adventure—the Courtezan—
Temptation triumphant—how the Night was passed.*

'What a happy dog I ought to be!' exclaimed Frank Sydney, as he reposed his slippered feet upon the fender, and sipped his third glass of old Madeira, one winter's evening in the year 18—, in the great city of New York.

Frank might well say so; for in addition to being as handsome a fellow as one would be likely to meet in a day's walk, he possessed an ample fortune, left him by a deceased uncle. He was an orphan; and at the age of twenty-one, found himself surrounded by all the advantages of wealth, and at the same time, was perfect master of his own actions. Occupying elegant apartments at a fashionable hotel, he was free from any of those petty cares and vexations which might have annoyed him, and he kept an establishment of his own; while at the same time he was enabled to maintain, in his rooms, a private table for the entertainment of himself and friends, who frequently repaired thither, to partake of his hospitality and champagne suppers. With such advantages of fortune and position, no wonder he exclaimed, as at the beginning of our tale—'What a happy dog I ought to be!'

Pursuing the current of his thought Frank half audibly continued—

'Yes, I have everything to make me truly happy—health, youth, good looks and wealth; and yet it seems to me that I should derive a more substantial satisfaction from my riches were I to apply them to the good of mankind. To benefit one's fellow creatures is the noblest and most exalted of enjoyments—far superior to the gratification of sense. The grateful blessings of the poor widow or orphan, relieved by my bounty, are greater music to my soul, than the insincere plaudits of my professed friends, who gather around my hearth to feast upon my hospitality, and yet who, were I to lose my wealth, and become poor, would soon cut my acquaintance, and sting me by their ingratitude. To-night I shall have a numerous party of these *friends* to sup with me, and this supper shall be the last one to which I shall ever invite them. Yes! My wealth shall be employed for a nobler object than to pamper these false and hollow-hearted parasites. From this night, I devote my time, my energies and my affluence to the relief of deserving poverty and the welfare of all who need my aid with whom I may come in contact. I will go in person to the squalid abodes of the poor—I will seek them out in the dark alleys and obscure lanes of this mighty metropolis—I will, in the holy mission of charity, venture into the vilest dens of sin and iniquity, fearing no danger, and shrinking not

107

from the duty which I have assumed. —Thus shall my wealth be a blessing to my fellow creatures, and not merely a means of ministering to my own selfishness.'

Noble resolve! All honor to thy good and generous heart, Frank Sydney! Thou hast the true patent of nature's nobility, which elevates and ennobles thee, more than a thousand vain titles or empty honors! Thou wilt keep thy word, and become the poor man's friend—the liberal and enlightened philanthropist—the advocate of deserving poverty, and foe to the oppressor, who sets his heel upon the neck of his brother man.

The friends who were to sup with him, arrived, and they all sat down to a sumptuous entertainment. Frank did the honors with his accustomed affability and care; and flowing bumpers were drunk to his health, while the most flattering eulogiums upon his merits and excellent qualities passed from lip to lip. Frank had sufficient discernment to perceive that all this praise was nothing but the ebullitions of the veriest sycophants; and he resolved at some time to test the sincerity of their protestations of eternal friendship.

'Allow me, gentlemen,' said Mr. Archibald Slinkey, a red-faced, elderly man, with a nose like the beak of a poll-parrot—'to propose the health of my excellent and highly esteemed friend, Frank Sydney. Gentlemen, I am a plain man, unused to flattery, and may be pardoned for speaking openly before the face of our friend— for I will say it, he is the most noble hearted, enlightened, conscientious, consistent, and superlatively good fellow I ever met in the course of my existence.'

'So he is,' echoed Mr. Narcissus Nobbs, a middle-aged gentleman, with no nose to speak of, but possessing a redundancy of chin and a wonderful capacity of mouth—'so he is, Slinkey; his position—his earning—his talent—his wealth—'

'Oh, d——n his wealth,' ejaculated Mr. Solomon Jenks, a young gentleman who affected a charming frankness and abruptness in his speech, but who was in reality the most specious flatterer of the entire party. Mr. Jenks rejoiced in the following personal advantages: red hair, a blue nose, goggle eyes, and jaws of transparent thinness.

'D——n his wealth!' said Jenks—'who cares for *that?* Sydney's a good fellow— a capital dog—an excellent, d——d good sort of a whole-souled devil—but his *wealth is* no merit. If he lost every shilling he has in the world, why curse me if I shouldn't like him all the better for it! I almost wish the rascal would become penniless tomorrow, in order to afford me an opportunity of showing him the disinterestedness of my friendship. I would divide my purse with him, take him by the hand and say—Frank, my boy, I like you for yourself alone, and d——n me if you are not welcome to all I have in the world—That's how I would do it.'

'I thank you gentlemen, for your kind consideration,' said Frank; 'I trust I may never be necessitated to apply to any of my friends, for aid in a disagreeable emergency—but should such ever unfortunately be the case, be assured that I shall not hesitate to avail myself of your generous assistance.'

'Bravo—capital—excellent!' responded the choir of flatterers, in full chorus, and their glasses were again emptied in honor of their host.

It was midnight ere these worthies took their departure. When at length they were all gone, and Frank found himself alone, he exclaimed— 'Thank heaven, I am at last rid of those miserable and servile fellows, who in my presence load me with the most extravagant praise and adulation, while behind my back they doubtless ridicule my supposed credulity. I have too long tolerated them—henceforth, I discard and cast them off.'

He approached the window, and drawing aside the curtain, looked forth into the streets. The moon was shining brightly; and its rays fell with dazzling lustre upon the snow which covered the ground. It was a most lovely night, altho' excessively cold; and Sydney, feeling not the least inclination to retire to rest, said to himself:

'What is to prevent me from beginning my career of usefulness and charity to-night? The hour is late—but misery sleeps not, and 'tis never too late to alleviate the sufferings of distressed humanity. Yes, I will go forth, even at the midnight hour, and perchance I may encounter some poor fellow-creature worthy of my aid, or visit some abode of poverty where I can minister to the comfort of its wretched inmates.'

He threw on an ample cloak, put on a fur cap and gloves, and taking his sword-cane in his hand, left the hotel, and proceeded at a rapid pace thro' the moon-lit and deserted streets. He entered the Park, and crossed over towards Chatham street, wishing to penetrate into the more obscure portions of the city, where Poverty, too often linked with Crime, finds a miserable dwelling-place. Thus far, he had not encountered a single person; but on approaching the rear of the City Hall, he observed the figure of a man issue from the dark obscurity of the building, and advance directly toward him. Sydney did not seek to avoid him, supposing him to be one of the watchmen stationed in that vicinity, but a nearer view satisfied him that the person was no watchman but a man clothed in rags, whose appearance betokened the extreme of human wretchedness. He was of a large and powerful build, but seemed attenuated by want, or disease—or perhaps, both. As he approached Sydney, his gestures were wild and threatening: he held in his hands a large paving-stone, which he raised, as if to hurl it at the other with all his force.

Sydney, naturally conceiving the man's intentions to be hostile, drew the sword from his cane, and prepared to act on the defensive, at the same time exclaiming:

'Who are you, and what do you wish?'

'Money!' answered the other, in a hollow tone, with the stone still upraised, while his eyes glowed savagely upon the young man.

Sydney, who was brave and dauntless, steadily returned his gaze, and said, calmly:

'You adopt a strange method, friend, of levying contributions upon travellers. If you are in distress and need aid, you should apply for it in a becoming manner— not approach a stranger in this threatening and ruffianly style. Stand off—I am armed, you see—I shall not hesitate to use this weapon if—'

The robber burst into a wild, ferocious laugh:

'Fool!' he cried. 'What can your weak arm or puny weapon do, against the strength of a madman? For look you, I am mad with *hunger!* For three days I have not tasted food—for three cold, wretched nights I have roamed thro' the streets of this Christian city, homeless, friendless, penniless! Give me money, or with this stone will I dash out your brains.'

'Unfortunate man,' said Sydney, in accents of deep pity—'I feel for you, on my soul I do. Want and wretchedness have made you desperate. Throw down your weapon, and listen to me; he who now addresses you is a man, possessing a heart that beats in sympathy for your misfortunes. I have both the means and the will to relieve your distress.'

The robber cast the stone from him, and burst into tears. 'Pardon me, kind stranger,' he cried, 'I did intend you harm, for my brain is burning, and my vitals consumed by starvation. You have spoken to me the first words of kindness that I have heard for a long, long time. You pity me, and that pity subdues me. I will go and seek some other victim.' 'Stay,' said Sydney, 'for heaven's sake give up this dreadful trade of robbery. Here is money, sufficient to maintain you for weeks— make a good use of it—seek employment—be honest, and should you need further assistance, call at ——— Hotel, and ask for Francis Sydney. That is my name, and in me you will ever find a friend, so long as you prove yourself worthy.'

'Noble, generous man!' exclaimed the robber, as he received a fifty dollar note from the hands of Frank. 'God will reward you for this. Believe me, I have not always been what I now am—a midnight ruffian, almost an assassin. No—I have had friends, and respectability, and wealth. But I have lost them all—all! We shall meet again—farewell!'

He ran rapidly from the spot, leaving Frank to pursue his way alone, and ponder upon this remarkable encounter.

Leaving the Park, and turning to the left, Frank proceeded up Chatham street towards the Bowery. As he was passing a house of humble but respectable exterior, he observed the street door to open, and a female voice said, in a low tone—'Young gentleman I wish to speak to you.'

Frank was not much surprised at being thus accosted, for his long residence in New York had made him aware of the fact that courtezans often resorted to that mode of procuring 'patronage' from such midnight pedestrians as might happen to be passing their doors. His first impulse was to walk on without noticing the invitation—but then the thought suggested itself to his mind: 'Might I not possibly be of some use or benefit to that frail one? I will see what she has to say.'

Reasoning thus, he stepped up to the door, when the female who had accosted him took him gently by the hand, and drawing him into the entry, closed the door. A lamp was burning upon a table which stood in the passage, and by its light Frank perceived that the lady was both young and pretty; she was wrapped in a large shawl, so that the outlines of her form were not plainly visible, yet it was easy to be seen that she was of good figure and graceful carriage.

'Madame, or Miss,' said Frank, 'be good enough to tell me why—'

'We cannot converse here in the cold,' interrupted the lady, smiling archly. 'Pray, sir, accompany me up-stairs to my room, and your curiosity shall be satisfied.'

Frank (who had his own reasons) motioned her to lead the way; she took the lamp from the table, and ascended the staircase, followed by the young gentleman. The lady entered a room upon the second floor, in which stood a bed and other conveniences denoting it to be a sleeping chamber; a cheerful fire was glowing in the grate. The apartment was neatly and plainly furnished, containing nothing of a character to indicate that its occupant was other than a perfectly virtuous female. No obscene pictures or immodest images were to be seen—all was unexceptionable in point of propriety.

The lady closed and locked the chamber door; then placing two chairs before the fire, she seated herself in one, and requested Frank to occupy the other. Throwing off her shawl, she displayed a fine form and voluptuous bust—the latter very liberally displayed, as she was arrayed in nothing but a loose dressing gown, which concealed neither her plump shoulders, nor the two fair and ample globes, whiter than alabaster, that gave her form a luxurious fullness.

'You probably have sufficient discrimination, sir, to divine my motive in inviting you into this house and chamber,' began the young lady, not without some embarrassment. 'You will readily infer, from my conduct, that I belong to the unfortunate class—'

'Say no more,' said Frank, interrupting her, 'I can readily guess why you accosted me, and as readily comprehend your true position and character. Madame, I regret to meet you in this situation.'

The lady cast down her eyes, and made no immediate reply, but for some minutes continued to trace imaginary figures upon the carpet, with the point of her delicate slipper. Meanwhile, Frank had ample leisure to examine her narrowly. His eyes wandered over the graceful, undulating outlines of her fine form, and lingered admiringly upon the exposed beauties of her swelling bosom; he glanced at her regular and delicate features which were exceedingly girlish and pretty, for she certainly was not much over sixteen years of age. When it is remembered that Frank was a young man of an ardent and impulsive temperament, the reader will not be surprised that the loveliness of this young creature began to excite within his breast those feelings and desires which are inherent in human nature. In fact, he found himself being gradually overcome by the most tumultuous sensations: his heart palpitated violently, his breath grew hurried and irregular, and he could scarcely restrain himself from clasping her to his breast with licentious violence. His passions were still further excited, when she raised her eyes to his face, and glanced at him with a soft smile, full of tenderness and invitation. Frank Sydney was one of the best fellows in the world, and possessed a heart that beat in unison with every noble, generous and kindly feeling; but he was not an angel. No, he was *human*, and subject to all the frailties and passions of humanity. When, therefore, that enticing young woman raised her eyes, swimming with languishing desire, to his face, and smiled so irresistibly, he did precisely what ninety-nine out of every one hundred young men in existence would have done, in the same circumstances—he encircled her slender waist with his arm, drew her to his throbbing breast, and tasted the nectar of her ripe lips, which so plainly invited the salute. Ah Frank, Frank! thou hast gone too far to retract now! Thy hand plays with those ivory globes—thy lips kiss those rounded shoulders, and that beauteous neck—thy brain becomes dizzy, thy senses reel, and thy amorous soul bathes in a sea of rapturous delight!

* * * * *

Truly, Frank Sydney, thou art a pretty fellow to prate about sallying forth at midnight to do good to thy fellow creatures! —Here we find thee, within an hour after thy departure from thy home, on an 'errand of mercy,' embraced in the soft arms of a pretty wanton, and revelling in the delights of voluptuousness. We might have portrayed thee as a paragon of virtue and chastity; we might have described thee as rejecting with holy horror the advances of that frail but exceedingly fair young lady—we might have made a saint of thee, Frank. But we prefer to depict human nature *as it is* not *as it should be;* —therefore we represent thee to be no better than thou art in reality. Many will pardon thee for thy folly, Frank, and admit that it was natural—very natural. Our hero did not return to his hotel until an hour after daybreak. The interval was passed with the young lady of frailty and beauty. He shared her couch; but neither of them slumbered, for at Frank's request, his fair friend occupied the time in narrating the particulars of her history, which we repeat in the succeeding chapter.

CHAPTER II

The Courtezan's story, showing some of the Sins of Religious Professors—A carnal Preacher, a frail Mother, and a lustful Father—a plan of revenge.

'My parents are persons of respectable standing in society; —they are both members of the Methodist Episcopal church, and remarkably rigid in their observance of the external forms and ceremonies of religion. Family worship was always adhered to by them, a well as grace before and after meals. They have ever been regarded as most exemplary and pious people. I was their only child; and the first ten years of my life were passed in much the same manner as those of other children of my sex and condition. I attended school, and received a good education; and my parents endeavored to instill the most pious precepts into my mind, to the end, they said, that I might become a vessel of holiness to the Lord. When I reached my twelfth year, a circumstance occurred which materially diminished my belief in the sanctity and godliness of one of my parents, and caused me to regard with suspicion and distrust, both religion and its professors.

'It was the custom of the pastor of the church to which my parents belonged, to make a weekly round of visits among the members of his congregation. These visits were generally made in the middle of the forenoon or afternoon, during the absence of the male members of the various families. I observed that 'our minister' invariably paid his visits to our house when my father was absent at his place of business. Upon these occasions, he would hold long and private conferences with my mother, who used to declare that these interviews with that holy man did her more substantial *good* than all his preaching. 'It is so refreshing to my soul,' she would say, 'to pray in secret with that good man—he is *so* full of Christian love—so tender in his exhortations—so fervent in his prayers! O that I could meet him every day, in the sanctity of my closet, to strengthen my faith by the outpourings of his inexhaustible fount of piety and Christian love!'

'The *wrestlings with the Lord* of my maternal parent and her holy pastor, must have been both prolonged and severe, judging from the fact that at the termination of these pious interviews, my mother sometimes made her appearance with disordered apparel and disarranged hair; while the violence of her efforts to strengthen her faith was further manifest from the flushed condition of her countenance, and general peculiarity of aspect.

'One afternoon the Reverend Mr. Flanders—for that was the name of our minister—called to see my mother, and as usual they retired together to a private room, for 'holy communion.' Young as I was, my suspicions had long been excited in regard to the nature of these interviews; I began to think that their true object partook more largely of an earthly and carnal character, than either the pastor or my mother would care to have known. Upon the afternoon in question, I determined to satisfy myself on this point;—and accordingly, as soon as they entered the room and closed the door, (which they always locked,) I stole noiselessly up-stairs, and stationed myself in the passage, on the outside of the room, and listened intently. I had scarcely taken up my position, when my ear caught the sound of *kissing;* and applying my eye to the key-hole, I beheld the Rev. Mr. Flanders bestowing the most fervent embraces upon my mother, which she returned with compound interest. The pious gentleman, clasping her around the waist with one arm, proceeded to take liberties which astonished and disgusted me: and my mother not only permitted the revered scoundrel to do this, but actually seemed to encourage him. Soon they placed themselves upon a sofa, in full view of my gaze; and I was both mortified and enraged to observe the wantonness of my mother, and the lasciviousness of her *pious* friend. After indulging in the most obscene and lecherous preliminaries, the full measure of their iniquity was consummated, I being a witness to the whole disgraceful scene. Horrified, and sick at heart, I left the spot and repaired to my own room, where I shed many bitter tears, for the dishonor of my mother and the hypocrisy of the minister filled me with shame and grief. From that moment, I ceased to love and respect my mother, as formerly; but she failed to perceive any alteration in my conduct towards her, and at that time was far from suspecting that I had witnessed the act of her dishonor and disgrace.

'I had always regarded my father as one of the best and most exemplary of men; and after my mother's crime, I comforted myself with the reflection that *he*, at least, was no hypocrite! but in every sense a good and sincere Christian. Nothing happened to shake this belief, until I had reached my fourteenth year; and then, alas! I became too painfully convinced that all *his* professions of piety and holiness were but a cloak to conceal the real wickedness of his heart. It chanced, about this time, that a young woman was received into our family, as a domestic: this person was far from being handsome or in the slightest degree interesting, in countenance—yet her figure was rather good than otherwise. She was a bold, wanton-looking wench; and soon after she came to live with us, I noticed that my father frequently eyed her with something sensual in his glances. He frequently sought opportunities of being alone with her; and one evening, hearing a noise in the kitchen, I went to the head of the stairs, and listened—there was the sound of a tussle, and I heard Jane (the name of the young woman,) exclaim—'Have done, sire—take away your hands—how dare you?' And then she laughed, in a manner that indicated her words were not very seriously meant. My father's voice next reached me; what he said I could not clearly distinguish; but he seemed to be remonstrating with the girl, and entreating her to grant him some favor; what that favor was, I could readily guess; and that she *did* grant it to him, without much further coaxing, was soon evident to my mind, by certain unmistakable sounds. But I preferred *seeing* to *hearing;* creeping softly down the kitchen stairs, I peeped in at the door, which was slightly ajar, and beheld my Christian papa engaged in a manner that reflected no credit on his observance of the seventh commandment.

'Thus having satisfied myself as to the nature and extent of *his* sanctity and holiness, I softly ascended the stairs, and resumed my seat in the parlor. In less than ten minutes afterwards, the whole family were summoned together around the family altar, and then my excellent and pious father poured out his pure spirit in prayer, returning thanks for having been 'preserved from temptation,' and supplicating that all the members of his household might flee from fleshy lusts, which war against the soul; to which my chaste and saint-like mother responded in a fervent 'Amen.' From that evening, the kitchen wench with whom my father had defiled himself, assumed an air of bold insolence to every one in the house; she refused to perform any of the menial services devolving upon her, and when my mother spoke of dismissing her, my father would not listen to it; so the girl continued with us. She had evidently obtained entire dominion over my father, and did not scruple to use her power to her own advantage; for she flaunted about in showy ribbons and gay dresses, and I had no difficulty in surmising who furnished her with the means of procuring them.

'I still continued to attend the church of the Rev. Mr. Flanders. He used to preach excellent sermons, so far as composition and style of delivery were concerned; his words were smooth as oil; his manner full of the order of sanctity; his prayers were fervid eloquence. Yet, when I thought what a consummate scoundrel and hypocrite he was at heart, I viewed him with loathing and disgust.

'I soon became sensible that this reverend rogue began to view me with more than an ordinary degree of interest and admiration; for I may say, without vanity, that as I approached my fifteenth year, I was a very pretty girl; my form had begun to develop and ripen, and my maiden graces were not likely to escape the lustful eyes of the elderly roues of our 'flock,' and seemed to be particularly attractive to that aged libertine known as the Rev. Balaam Flanders.

'So far from being flattered by the attentions of our minister (as many of our flock were,) I detested and avoided him. Yet his lecherous glances were constantly upon me, whenever I was thrown into his society; even when he was in the pulpit, he would often annoy me with his lustful gaze.

'A bible class of young ladies was attached to the church, of which I was a member. We assembled at the close of divine service in the evening, for the study and examination of the Scriptures. Mr. Flanders himself had charge of this class, and was regarded by all the young ladies (myself excepted) as a 'dear, good man.' When one of us was particularly apt in answering a question or finding a passage, he would playfully chuck the good scholar under the chin, in token of his commendation; and sometimes, even, he would bestow a fatherly kiss upon the fair student of holy writ.

'These little tokens of his amativeness he often bestowed on me; and I permitted him, as I considered such liberties to be comparatively harmless. He soon however went beyond these 'attentions' to me—he first began by passing his hand over my bust, outside my dress, and, growing emboldened by my suffering him to do this, he would slide his hand into my bosom, and take hold of my budding evidences of approaching womanhood. Once he whispered in my ear—'My dear, what a delicious bust you have!' I was by no means surprised at his conduct or words, for his *faux pas* with my frail mother convinced me that he was capable of any act of lechery. I also felt assured that he lusted after me with all the ardor of his lascivious passions, and I well know that he waited but for an opportunity to attempt my seduction.—I hated the man, both for his adultery with my mother, and his vile intentions towards myself—and I determined to *punish him* for his lewdness and hypocrisy—yes, punish him through the medium of his own bad passions, and in a manner that would torture him with alternate hope and despair; now inspiring him with rapture by apparently almost yielding to his wishes, and then maddening him by my resistance—at the same time resolving not to submit to his desires in any case. This was my plan for punishing the hoary libertine, and you shall see how well I carried it out.

'I did not discourage my reverend admirer in his amorous advances, but on the contrary received them in such a manner as might induce him to suppose that they were rather pleasing to me than otherwise. This I did in order to ensure the success of my scheme—I observed with secret satisfaction that he grew bolder and bolder in the liberties which he took with my person. He frequently accompanied me home in the evening after prayer meeting; and he always took care to traverse the most obscure and deserted streets with me, so as to have a better opportunity to indulge in his licentious freedoms with me, unobserved. Not content with thrusting his hand into my bosom, he would often attempt to pursue his investigations elsewhere: but this I always refused to permit him to do. He was continually embracing and kissing me—and in the latter indulgence, he often disgusted me beyond measure, by the excessive libidinousness which he exhibited—I merely mention these things to show the vile and beastly nature of this man, whom the world regarded as a pure and holy minister of the gospel. Though old enough to be my grandfather, the most hot blooded boy in existence could not have been more wanton or eccentric in the manifestations of his lustful yearnings. In fact, he wearied me almost to death by his unceasing persecution of me; yet I bore it with patience, so as to accomplish the object I had in view.

'I have often, upon the Sabbath, looked at that man as he stood in the pulpit; how pious he appeared, with his high, serene forehead, his carefully arranged gray hair, his mild and saint-like features, his snow-white cravat, and plain yet rich suit of glossy black! How calm and musical were the tones of his voice!—How beautifully he portrayed the happiness of religion, and how eloquently he prayed for the repentance and salvation of poor sinners! Yet how black was his heart with hypocrisy, and how polluted his soul with lust!

'One New Year's evening—I remember it well—my parents went to pay a visit to a relative a short distance out of the city, leaving me in charge of the house; the servants had all gone to visit their friends, and I was entirely alone. I had good reason to suppose that the Rev. Mr. Flanders would call on me that evening, as he knew that my parents would be absent. I determined to improve the opportunity, and commence my system of torture. Going to my chamber, I dressed myself in the most fascinating manner, for my wardrobe was extensive; and glancing in the mirror, I was satisfied of my ability to fan the flame of his passions into fury. I then seated myself in the parlor, where a fine fire was burning: and in a few minutes a hurried knock at the door announced the arrival of my intended victim. I ran down stairs and admitted him, and he followed me into the parlor, where he deliberately took off his overcoat, and then wheeling the sofa in front of the fire, desired me to sit by him. This I did, with apparent hesitation, telling him there was nobody in the house, and I wasn't quite sure it was right for me to stay alone in his company. This information, conveyed with a well assumed maiden bashfulness, seemed to afford the old rascal the most intense delight; he threw his arm around me, and kissed me repeatedly, then his hand began the exploration to which I have alluded. I suffered him to proceed just far enough to set his passions in a blaze; and then, breaking from his embrace, I took my seat at the further end of the sofa, assuring him if he approached me without my permission, I should scream out. This was agony to him; I saw with delight that he was beginning to suffer. He begged, entreated, supplicated me to let him come near me; and at last I consented; upon condition that he should attempt to take no further liberties. To this he agreed, and seating himself at my side, but without touching me, he devoured me with lustful eyes. For some minutes neither of us spoke, but at length he took my hand, and again passed his arm around my waist. I did not oppose him, but remained passive and silent. 'Dear girl,' he whispered, 'pressing me close to him—'why need you be so cruel as to deny me the pleasure of love? Consider, I am your minister, and cannot sin: it will therefore be no sin for you to favor me.'

'Oh, sir,' I answered, 'I wish you were a young man—then I could almost—'

'Angelic creature!' he cried passionately—'true, I am not young, but Love never grows old—no, no, no! Consent to be mine, sweet delicious girl, and —'

'Ah, sir!' I murmured—'you tempt me sorely—I am but a weak giddy young creature; do not ask me to do wrong, for I fear that I may yield, and how very, very wicked that would be!'

'The reverend gentleman covered my cheeks and lips with hot kisses, as he said—'Wicked—no! Heaven has given us passions, and we must gratify them. Look at David—look at Solomon—both good men;—they enjoyed the delights of love, and are now saints in Heaven, and why may not we do the same? Why, my dear, it is the special privilege of the ministry to—'

'Ruin us young girls, sir?' I rejoined, smiling archly. 'Ah, you have set my heart in a strange flutter! I feel almost inclined—if you are sure it is not wicked—very sure—then I—'

'You are mine!' he exclaimed in a hoarse whisper, with frenzied triumph gleaming in his eyes. I never saw anybody look so fearful as he did then; his form quivered with intense excitement—his features appeared as if convulsed—his eyes, almost starting from their sockets, were blood shot and fiery. I trembled, lest in the madness of his passions, he might forcibly overcome me. He anticipated no resistance, imagining that he had an easy prey; but, at that very instant when he thought he was about to intoxicate his vile soul with the delicious draught of sensual delight, I spurned him from me as I would have spurned the most loathsome reptile that crawls amid the foetid horrors of a dungeon vault. —That was the moment of my triumph; I had led him step by step, until he felt assured of his ultimate success: I had permitted him to obtain, as it were, glimpses of a Paradise he was never to enjoy; and at the very moment he thought to have crossed the golden threshold, to enter into the blissful and flowery precincts of that Paradise, he was hurled from the pinnacle of his hopes, and doomed to endure the bitter pangs of disappointment, and the gnawings of a raging desire, never to be appeased!

'Thus repulsed, my reverend admirer did not resume his attempt, for my indignation was aroused, and he saw fierce anger flashing from my eyes. I solemnly declared, that had he attempted forcibly to accomplish his purpose, I would have dashed out his brains with the first weapon I could have laid my hand to!

'Humbled and abashed, he retired to a corner of the room, where he seated himself with an air of mortified disappointment. Yet still he kept his eyes upon me; and as I knew that his desires were raging as violently within him as ever (tho' he dare not approach me,) I devised the following method of augmenting his passions, and inflicting further torture upon him: —In my struggle with him, my dress had become somewhat disarranged and torn; and standing before a large mirror which was placed over the mantle-piece, I loosened my garments, and while pretending to examine the injury which had been done to them, I took especial pains to remove all covering from my neck, shoulders and bosom, which were uncommonly soft and white, as you, my dear, can testify. The sight of my naked charms instantly produced the desired effect upon the minister, who watched my slightest movement with eager scrutiny: he ceased almost to breathe, but panted—yes, absolutely *panted*—with the intensity of his passions.—Oh, how my heart swelled with delight at the agony he was thus forced to endure! Affecting to be unconscious of his presence, I assumed the most graceful and voluptuous attitudes I could think of—

and he could endure it no longer; for—would you believe it?—he actually fell upon his knees before me, and groveled at my feet, entreating me, in a hoarse whisper, to kill him at once and end his torments, or else yield myself to him!

'My revenge was now accomplished, and I desired no more. I requested him to arise from his abject posture, and listen to me. Then I told him all I knew of his hypocrisy and wickedness—how I had become aware of his criminal intercourse with my mother, which, combined with his vile conduct and intentions in regard to myself, had induced me to punish him in the manner I had done, by exciting his passions almost to madness, and then repulsing him with disdain. I added, maliciously, that my own passions were warm and ardent, and that my young blood sometimes coursed thro' my veins with all the heat of sensual desire—and that were a man, young and handsome, to solicit my favors, I *might possibly yield*, in a thoughtless moment: but as for *him*, (the minister) sooner than submit to *his* embraces, I would permit the vilest negro in existence, to take me in his arms, and do with me as he pleased.

'All this I told the Rev. Mr. Flanders, and much more; and after listening in evident misery to my remarks, he took himself from the house. After this occurrence, I discontinued my attendance at his church and bible class. When my parents asked me the reason of my nonattendance, I refused to answer them; and at length they became enraged at what they termed my obstinacy, and insisted that I should not fail to attend church on the following Sabbath.—When the Sabbath came, I made no preparation for going to church; which mother perceiving, she began to apply the most reproachful and severe language to me. This irritated me; and without a moment's reflection, I said to her angrily:

'I can well conceive, madam, the reason of your great partiality to the Rev. Mr. Flanders; your many *private interviews* with him have wonderfully impressed you in his favor!'

'Wretch, what do you mean?' stammered my mother in great confusion, and turning pale and red alternately.

'You know very well what I mean, vile woman!' I cried, enraged beyond all power of restraining my speech, and perfectly reckless of the consequences of what I was saying. 'I was a witness of your infamous adultery with the hypocritical parson, and—'

'As I uttered these words, my mother gave a piercing scream, and flew at me with the fury of a tigress. She beat me cruelly, tore my hair and clothes, and being a large and powerful woman, I verily believe she would have killed me, had not my father, hearing the noise, rushed into the room, and rescued me from her grasp. He demanded an explanation of this extraordinary scene, and, in spite of the threatening looks and fierce denial of my mother, I told him all. He staggered and almost fell to the floor, when I thus boldly accused her of the crime of adultery; clinging to a chair for support, he faintly ejaculated—'My God, can this be true?'

'It is false—I call Heaven to witness, it is false!' exclaimed my wretched and guilty mother—then, overcome by the terrors of the situation, she sank insensible upon the carpet. My father summoned a servant to her assistance; and then bade me follow him into another room. Carefully closing the doors, he turned to me with a stern aspect, and said, with much severity of tone and manner:

'Girl, you have made a serious charge against your mother; you have impugned her chastity and her honor. Adultery is the most flagrant crime that can stain the holy institution of marriage. If I believed your mother guilty of it, I would cast her off forever!'

'I laughed scornfully as he said this, whereupon he angrily demanded the cause of my ill-timed mirth; and as I detested his hypocrisy, I boldly told him that it ill became *him* to preach on the enormity of the crime of adultery, after having been guilty of that very offence with his kitchen wench! He turned deadly pale at this unexpected retort, and stammered out—'Then you know all—denial is useless.' I told him how I had witnessed the affair in the kitchen, and reproached him bitterly for the infamous conduct. He admitted the justness of my rebuke, and when I informed him that Mr. Flanders had attempted to debauch me, he foamed with rage, and loaded the reverend libertine with epithets which were decidedly uncomplimentary. Still, he doubted the story of my mother's crime—he could not believe *her* to be guilty of such baseness; but he assured me that he should satisfy himself of her innocence or guilt, then left me, after having made me promise not to expose him in reference to his affair with the servant girl in the kitchen.

'Upon leaving me, my father immediately sought an interview with my mother, who by this time had recovered from her swoon. She was in her chamber; but as I was naturally anxious to know what might pass between my parents, under such unusual circumstances, I stationed myself at the door of the room, as soon as my father had entered, and heard distinctly all that was said.

CHAPTER III

Domestic Troubles—A Scene, and a Compromise—an Escape—various matters amative, explanatory and miscellaneous, in the Tale of the Courtezan.

'Well, madam,' said my father, in a cold, severe tone—'this is truly a strange and serious accusation which our daughter has brought against you. The crime of adultery, and with a Christian minister!'

'Surely,' rejoined my mother, sobbing—'you will not believe the assertions of that young hussy. I am innocent—indeed, indeed I am.'

'I am inclined to believe that you *are* innocent, and yet I never shall rest perfectly satisfied until you *prove* yourself guiltless in this matter,' rejoined my father, speaking in a kinder tone. 'Now listen to me,' he continued. 'I have thought of a plan by which to put your virtue, and the purity of our pastor, to the test. I shall invite the reverend gentleman to dinner this afternoon, after divine service; and when we have dined, you shall retire with him to this room, for private prayer. You shall go first, and in a few minutes he shall follow you; and I shall take care that no secret communication is held between you, in the way of whispering or warnings of any kind, whether by word or sign. I will contrive means to watch you narrowly, when you are with him in the chamber; and I caution you to beware of giving him the slightest hint to be on his guard, for that would be a conclusive evidence of your guilt. He will of course conduct himself as usual, not knowing that he is watched. If you are innocent, he will pray or converse with you in a Christian and proper manner; but if you ever *have* had criminal intercourse with him, he will, in all human probability, indicate the same in his language and actions. This is most plain; and I trust that the result will clear you of all suspicion.'

'My mother knew it would be useless to remonstrate, for my father was unchangeable, when once he had made up his mind to anything. She therefore was obliged to submit. Accordingly, Mr. Flanders dined with us that day: once, during the meal, happening to look into his face, I saw that he was gazing at me intently, and I was startled by the expression of his countenance: for that expression was one of the deadliest hate. It was but for an instant, and then he turned away his eyes; yet I still remember that look of bitter hatred. As soon as dinner was over, my mother withdrew, and a few minutes afterwards my father said to the minister:

'Brother Flanders, I am going out for a short walk, to call upon a friend; meantime, I doubt not that Mrs. —— will be happy to hold sisterly and Christian communion with you. You will find her in her chamber.'

'It is very pleasant, my brother,' responded the other—'to hold private and holy communion with our fellow seekers after divine truth. These family visits I regard as the priceless privilege of the pastor; by them the bond of love which unites him to his flock, is more strongly cemented. I will go to my sister and we will pray and converse together.'

'Saying this, Mr. Flanders arose and left the room; he had scarcely time to ascend the stairs and enter my mother's chamber, when my father quickly and noiselessly followed him, and entered an apartment adjoining. He had previously made a small hole in the wall, and to this hole he applied his eye. So rapid had been his movements, that the minister had just closed the door, when he was at his post of observation; so that it was rendered utterly impossible for my mother to whisper a word or make a sign, to caution her paramour against committing both her and himself. I lost no time in taking up my position at the chamber door, and availed myself of the keyhole as a convenient channel for both seeing and hearing. I saw that my mother was very pale and seemed ill at ease, and I did not wonder at it, for her position was an extremely painful and embarrassing one. She well knew that my father's eye was upon her, watching her slightest movement; she knew, also, that the minister was utterly unaware of my father's *espionage*, and she had good reason to fear that the reverend libertine would, as usual, begin the interview by amorous demonstrations. Oh, how she must have longed to put him on his guard, and thereby save both her honor and her reputation!—But she dare not.

'The minister seated himself near my unhappy mother, and opened the conversation as follows:

'Well, my dear Mrs. ——, I am sorry to inform you that I have tidings of an unpleasant nature to communicate to you. *We are discovered!'*

'These fatal words were uttered in a low whisper; but yet I doubt not that my father had heard them. I could see that my mother trembled violently—yet she spoke not a syllable.

'Yes,' continued the minister, all unconscious of the disclosure he was making to my father—'Your daughter knows all. She suspected, it seems, the real object of our last interview, when, you recollect, we indulged in a little amative dalliance.— On New Year's evening, during your absence, I called here and saw your daughter, when she reproached me for having debauched you, stating in what manner she had seen the whole affair. Since then, I have had no opportunity of informing you that she knew our intimacy.'

'Still my mother uttered not a single word!'

'This girl,' continued the minister, 'must be made to hold her tongue, somehow or other: it would be dreadful to have it reach your husband's ears. But why are you so taciturn to-day, my dear? Come, let us enjoy the present, and dismiss all fear for the future. But first we must make sure that there are no listeners *this* time,' and he approached the door.

'I retreated precipitately, and slipped into another room, while he opened the chamber; seeing no-one on the outside, he closed it again, and locked it. I instantly resumed my station; and I saw the minister approach my mother, (who appeared spell-bound,) and clasp her in his arms. He was about to proceed to the usual extreme of his criminality when my father uttered an expression of rage; I instantly ran into the room which had before served me as a hiding place, and in a moment more my father was at the door of my mother's chamber, demanding admission. After a short delay, the door was opened; and then a scene ensued which defies my powers of description.

' 'Tis needless to dwell upon the particulars of what followed. My father raved, the pastor entreated, and my mother wept. But after an hour or so, the tempest subsided; the parties arriving at the reasonable conclusion, that what was done could not be undone. Finally it was arranged that Mr. Flanders should pay my father a considerable sum of money, upon condition that the affair be hushed up.— My mother was promised forgiveness for her fault—and as I was the only person likely to divulge the matter, it was agreed that I should be placed under restraint, and not suffered to leave the house, until such time as I should solemnly swear never to reveal the secret of the adultery.— Accordingly, for one month I remained a close prisoner in the house, and at the end of that period, not feeling inclined to give the required pledge of secrecy, I determined to effect my escape, and leave my parents forever.—The thought of parting from them failed to produce the least impression of sadness upon my mind, for from the moment I had discovered the secret of their guilty intrigues, all love and respect for them had ceased. I knew it would be no easy matter for me to depart from the house unperceived, for the servant wench, Janet, was a spy upon my actions; but one evening I contrived to elude her observation, and slipping out of the door, walked rapidly away. What was to become of me, I knew not, nor cared, in my joy at having escaped from such an abode of hypocrisy as my parents' house—for of all the vices which can disgrace humanity, I regard *hypocrisy* as the most detestable.

'Fortunately, I had several dollars in my possession; and I had no difficulty in procuring a boarding house. And now as my story must be getting tedious by its length, I will bring it to a close in as few words as possible. I supported myself for some time by the labor of my needle; but as this occupation afforded me only a slight maintenance, and proved to be injurious to my health, I abandoned it, and sought some other employment. It was about that time that I became acquainted with a young man named Frederick Archer, whose manners and appearance interested me exceedingly, and I observed with pleasure that he regarded me with admiration. Our acquaintance soon ripened into intimacy; we often went to places of amusement together, and he was very liberal in his expenditures for my entertainment. He was always perfectly respectful in his conduct towards me, never venturing upon any undue familiarity, and quite correct in his language. One evening I accompanied him to the Bowery Theatre, and after the play he proposed that we should repair to a neighboring 'Ladies Oyster Saloon,' and partake of refreshments. We accordingly entered a very fashionable place, and seated our-selves in a small room, just large enough to contain a table and sofa. —The oysters were brought, and also a bottle of champagne; and then I noticed that my companion very carefully locked the door of the room. This done, he threw his arms around me, and kissed me. Surprised at this liberty, which he had never attempted before, I scolded him a little for his rudeness; and he promised not to offend again. We then ate our oysters, and he persuaded me to drink some of the wine. Whether it contained a stimulant powder, or because I had never drank any before, I know not; but no sooner had I swallowed a glass of the sparkling liquid, than a strange dizzy sensation pervaded me—not a disagreeable feeling, by any means, but rather a delightful one. It seemed to heat my blood, and to a most extraordinary degree. Rising, I complained of being slightly unwell, and requested Frederick to conduct me out of the place immediately. Alas, sir, why need I dwell upon what followed? Frederick's conquest was an honest one; I suffered him to do with me as he pleased, and he soon initiated me into the voluptuous mysteries of Venus. I confess, I rather sought than avoided this consummation—for my passions were in a tumult, which could only be appeased by full unrestrained gratification.

'From that night my secret frailties with Frederick became frequent. I granted him all the favors he asked; yet I earnestly entreated him to marry me. This he consented to do, and we were accordingly united in the bonds of wedlock. My husband immediately hired these furnished apartments, which I at present occupy; and then he developed a trait in his character, which proved him a villain of the deepest dye. How he made a livelihood, had always to me been a profound mystery; and as he avoided the subject, I never questioned him. But how he intended to live, after our marriage, I soon became painfully aware. *He resolved that I should support him in idleness, by becoming a common prostitute.* When he made this debasing and inhuman proposition to me, I rejected it with the indignation it merited; where-upon he very coolly informed me, that unless I complied, he should abandon me to my fate, and proclaim to the world that I was a harlot before he married me. Finding me still obstinate, he drew a bowie knife, and swore a terrible oath, that unless I would do as he wished, he would kill me! Terrified for my life, I gave the required promise; but he made me swear upon the Bible to do as he wished. He set a woman in the house to watch me during the day, and prevent my escaping, and in the evening he returned, accompanied by an old gentleman of respectable appearance, whom he introduced to me as Mr. Rogers. This person surveyed me with an impertinent stare, and complimented me on my beauty; in a few minutes, Frederick arose and said to me—'Maria, I am going out for a little while, and in the meantime you must do your best to entertain Mr. Rogers.' He then whispered in my ear—'Let him do as he will with you, for he has paid me a good price; now don't refuse him, or be in the least degree prudish, or by G—— it shall be worse for you!' Scarcely had he taken his departure, when the old wretch, who had *purchased* me, clasped me in his palsied arms, and prepared to debauch me; in reply to my entreaties to desist, and my appeals to his generosity, he only shook his head, and said—'No, no, young lady, I have given fifty dollars for you, and you are mine!' The old brute had neither shame, nor pity, nor honor in his breast; he forced me to comply with his base wishes, and a life of prostitution was for the first time opened to me.

'After this event, I attempted no further opposition to my husband's infamous scheme of prostituting myself for his support. Almost nightly, he brought home with him some *friend* of his, who had previously paid him for the use of my person. The money he gains in this way he expends in gambling and dissipation; allowing me scarcely anything for the common necessaries of life, and I am in consequence obliged to solicit private aid from such gentlemen as are disposed to enjoy my favors. My husband rarely sleeps at home, and I see but very little of him; this is a source of no regret to me, for I have ceased to feel the slightest regard for him.

'And now, sir, you have heard the particulars of my history. You will do me the justice to believe that I have been reduced to my present unfortunate position, more through the influence of circumstances, than on account of any natural depravity.—True, I am now what is termed a woman of the town—but still I am not entirely destitute of delicacy or refinement of feeling. I am an admirer of it in others. My parents I have never seen, since the day I quitted their house; but I have heard that my mother has since given birth to a fine boy, the very image of the minister; and also that Jane, my father's paramour, has become the mother of a child bearing an astonishing resemblance to the old gentleman himself!

'If you ask me why I do not escape from my husband, and abandon my present course of living, I would remind you that, as society is constituted, I never can regain a respectable standing in the eyes of the world. No, my course is marked out, and I must adhere to it. I am not happy, neither am I completely miserable; for sometimes I have my moments of enjoyment. When I meet a gentlemanly and intelligent companion, like yourself, disposed to sympathize with the misfortunes of a poor and friendless girl, I am enabled to bear up under my hard lot with something like cheerfulness and hope.'

Thus ended the Courtezan's Tale; and as it was now daylight, Frank Sydney arose and prepared for his departure, assuring her that he would endeavor to benefit her in some way, and generously presenting her with a liberal sum of money, for which she seemed truly grateful. He then bade her farewell, promising to call and see her again ere long.

CHAPTER IV

A Fashionable Lady—the Lovers—the Negro Paramour—astounding developments of Crime in High Life—the Accouchement—Infanticide— the Marriage—a dark suspicion.

The scene changes to that superb avenue of fashion, Broadway; the time, eleven o'clock in the morning, and the place, one of the noblest mansions which adorn that aristocratic section of the city.

Miss Julia Fairfield was seated in a luxurious apartment, lounging over a late breakfast, and listlessly glancing over the morning newspapers.

This young lady was about eighteen years of age, a beauty, an heiress, and, per consequence, a *belle*. She was a brunette; her beauty was of a warm, majestic, voluptuous character; her eyes beamed with the fire of passion, and her features were full of expression and sentiment. Her attire was elegant, tasteful, and unique, consisting of a loose, flowing robe of white satin, trimmed with costliest lace; her hair was beautifully arranged in the best Parisian style; and her tiny feet were encased in gold-embroidered slippers. The peculiarity of her dress concealed the outlines of her form; yet the garment being made very low in the shoulders, the upper portions of a magnificently full bust were visible.

For some time she continued to sip her chocolate and read in silence; but soon she exclaimed, in a rich, melodious voice—

'Very well, indeed!—and so those odious editors have given the full particulars of the great ball last night, and have complimented me highly on my grace and beauty! Ah, I never could have ventured there in any other costume than the one I wore. These loose dresses are capital things—but my situation becomes more and more embarrassing every day.'

At this moment a domestic announced Mr. Francis Sydney, and the announcement was followed by the entrance of that gentleman.

'My dear Julia,' said Frank, seating himself—'you will pardon my intrusion at this unfashionable hour, but I was anxious to learn the state of your health, after the fatigues of last night's assembly.'

'No apology is necessary, my dear Frank,' replied the lady, with a bewitching smile, at the same time giving him her hand, which he tenderly raised to his lips. 'I am in excellent health this morning, although dreadfully bored with *ennui*, which I trust will be dispelled by the enlivening influence of your presence.'

'What happiness do I derive from the reflection, my sweet girl,' said Frank, drawing his chair closer to hers, 'that, in one short month, I shall call you mine! Yes, we shall then stand before the bridal altar, and I shall have the felicity of wedding the loveliest, most accomplished, and purest of her sex!'

'Ah, Francis,' sighed the lady—'how joyfully will I then bestow upon you the gift of this hand!—my heart you have already.'

'These words were said with so much tenderness, and with such a charming air of affectionate modesty, that the young man caught her to his breast and covered her lips with kisses. Struggling from his ardent embrace, Julia said to him, in a tone of reproach,—

'Francis, this is the first time you ever forgot the respect due to me as a lady; but do not repeat the offense, or you will diminish my friendship for you—perhaps, my love also.—When we are *married*,' she added, blushing—'my person will be wholly yours—but not till then.'

'Pardon me, dear Julia,' entreated Frank, in a tone of contrition—'I will not offend again.'

The lady held out her hand, and smiled her forgiveness.

'Now that we are good friends again,' said she —'I will order some refreshments.' She rang a silver bell, and gave the necessary order to a servant, and in a few minutes, cake and wine were brought in by a black waiter, clad in rich livery. The complexion of this man was intensely dark, yet his features were good and regular and his figure tall and well-formed. In his demeanor towards his mistress and her guest, he was respectful in the extreme, seldom raising his eyes from the carpet, and when addressed, speaking in the most servile and humble tone.

After having partaken of the refreshments, and enjoyed half an hour's conversation, Frank arose and took his leave.

As soon as he had gone, an extraordinary scene took place in that parlor.

The black waiter, having turned the key within the lock of the door, approached Miss Fairfield, deliberately threw his arms around her, and kissed her repeatedly! And how acted the lady—she who had reproved her affianced husband for a similar liberty—how acted she when thus rudely and grossly embraced by that black and miscreant menial? Did she not repulse him with indignant disgust,—did she not scream for assistance, and have him punished for the insolent outrage?

No; she abandoned her person to his embraces, and returned them! She, the well-born, the beautiful, the wealthy, the accomplished lady—the betrothed bride of a young gentleman of honor—the daughter of an aristocrat—the star of a constellation of fashion—yielding herself to the arms of a negro servant!

Oh, woman! how like an angel art thou in thy virtue and goodliness! how like a devil, when thou art fallen from thy high estate!

Yes, that black fellow covers her exquisite neck and shoulders with lustful kisses! His hands revel amid the glories of her divine and voluptuous bosom; and his lips wander from her rosy mouth, to the luxurious beauties of her finely developed bust.

'My beautiful mistress!' said the black, 'how kind in you to grant me these favors! What can I do to testify my gratitude?'

'Oh Nero,' murmured the lady 'what if our intimacy should be discovered? yet you are discreet and trustworthy; for from the night I first hinted my desires to you, and admitted you into my chamber, you have behaved with prudence and caution. Yet you are aware of my situation; you know that I am *enciente* by you; all our precautions have failed to prevent that result of our amours. I dress myself in such a way as to keep my condition from observation; no one suspects it. In a month, you know, I am to be married to Mr. Sydney; but I hope to give birth to the child in less than a week from the present time, so that, with good care and nursing, assisted by my naturally robust constitution, I shall recover my health and strength in sufficient time to enable my marriage to pass on without suspicion. I will endeavor to adopt such artifices and precautions as will completely deceive my husband, and he will never know that I am otherwise than he now supposes me. After my marriage, we can continue our intrigues as before, provided we are extremely cautious. Ah, my handsome African, how dearly I love you.'

The guilty and depraved woman sank back upon a sofa, and her paramour clasped her in his arms.

Let no one say that our narrative is becoming too improbable for belief, that the scenes which we depict find no parallel in real life. Those who are disposed to be skeptical with reference to such scenes as the foregoing had better throw this volume aside; for crimes of a much deeper dye, than any yet described, will be brought forward in this tale: crimes that are daily perpetrated, but which are seldom discovered or suspected. We have undertaken a difficult and painful task, and we shall accomplish it; unrestrained by a false delicacy, we shall drag forth from the dark and mysterious labyrinths of great cities, the hidden iniquities which taint the moral atmosphere, and assimilate human nature to the brute creation.

Five days after the occurrences just described, in the middle of the afternoon, Miss Julia Fairfield rode out in her carriage alone, driven by the black, Nero. The vehicle stopped before a house of respectable exterior, in Washington street, and the young lady was assisted to alight; entering the house, she was received by an elderly female, who immediately conducted her to a private room, which contained a bed and furniture of a neat but unostentatious description. The carriage drove away, and Julia remained several hours in the house. At about nine o'clock in the evening, the carriage returned, and she was assisted to enter, being apparently in a very feeble and unwell condition. She reached her own dwelling, and for over a week remained in her chamber, under plea of severe indisposition. When at length she made her appearance, she looked extremely pale, and somewhat emaciated; yet, for the first time in several months, she wore a tight-fitting dress, and her father, unconscious of her crimes, good-naturedly expressed his joy at seeing her 'once more dressed like a Christian lady, and not in the loose and slatternly robes she had so long persisted in wearing.'

The next morning after her visits to the house on Washington Street, the newspapers contained a notice of the discovery of the body of a newborn mulatto child, in the water off the Bowery. That child was the offspring of Miss Julia and the black; it had been strangled, and its body thrown into the water.

About three weeks after her secret accouchement, Julia became the wife of Frank Sydney. An elegant establishment had been prepared for the young couple, in Broadway. Here they repaired after the performance of the marriage ceremony; and now being for the first time alone with his beautiful bride, Frank embraced her with passionate ardor, and was not repulsed.

Ah, happy bridegroom, how little thou knowest the truth! Thou dost not suspect that the lovely woman at thy side, dressed in spotless white, and radiant with smiles—thou dost little think that she, whom thou hast taken to be thy wedded wife, comes to thy arms and nuptial bed, not a pure and stainless virgin, but a wretch whose soul is polluted and whose body is unchaste, by vile intimacy with a negro menial!

The hour waxes late, and the impatient husband conducts his fair bride to the nuptial chamber—Love's hallowed sanctuary.

Two hours afterwards, that husband was pacing a parlor back and forth, with uneven strides, his whole appearance indicative of mental agony. —Pausing, he exclaimed—

'My God, what terrible suspicions cross my mind! I imagined Julia to be an angel of purity and virtue yet now I doubt her! Oh, horrible, horrible! But may not my doubts be facts without any foundation? I will tomorrow consult a physician on the subject. Pray heaven my suspicions may prove to be utterly groundless!'

He was startled by the sound of an approaching foot-step; the door opened, and his wife entered, bearing a light. How seductive she looked, in her white night-dress! how tenderly she caressed him, as with affectionate concern she inquired if he were unwell.

'Dearest Frank,' she said, 'I had fallen into the most delicious slumber I have ever enjoyed;—doubly delicious, because my dreams were of you. Awaking suddenly, I missed you from my arms, and hastened hither to find you. What is the matter, love?'

'Nothing, Julia,' answered the husband; 'I had a slight head-ache, but it is over now. Return to your chamber, and I will follow you in a few moments.'

She obeyed, and Frank was alone. 'Either that woman is as chaste as Diana,' he said to himself, 'or she is a consummate wretch and hypocrite. But let her not be too hastily condemned. My friend, Dr. Palmer, shall give me his opinion, and if he thinks that she could have been *as she was*, and still be chaste, then I will discard my suspicions; but if, on the contrary, the doctor deems such a condition to be incompatible with chastity, then will I cast her off forever. I cannot endure this fearful state of suspense, would that it were morning!'

Morning came at last, and Sydney sought the residence of Dr. Palmer, with whom he held a long and private consultation. The result of this interview was not very satisfactory to the husband, for the doctor's concluding remarks were as follows:-

'My dear sir, it is impossible for any physician, however great may be his professional knowledge and experience, to decide with positive certainty upon such a matter. Nature has many freaks; the condition of your lady *might* be natural—yet pardon me if, in my own private opinion, I doubt its being so! I have heard of such cases, where the chastity of the lady was undoubted; yet such cases are exceedingly rare. Your position, Mr. Sydney, is a peculiarly embarrassing and delicate one. I cannot counsel you as a physician; yet, as *a friend*, permit me to advise you to refrain from acting hastily in this matter. Your wife may be innocent; you should consider her so, until you have ocular or other positive evidence of her guilt. Meanwhile, let her not know your suspicions, but watch her narrowly; if she were frail before marriage, she needs but the opportunity to be inconstant afterwards. I have attended upon the lady several times, during slight illness, in my capacity as a physician, and I have had the opportunity to observe that she is of an uncommonly ardent and voluptuous temperament. Phrenology confirms this; for her amative developments are singularly prominent.—Candidly, her physical conformation strongly impresses me with the belief, that moral principle will scarcely restrain her from unlawful indulgence, when prompted by inclination.'

'The devil!' muttered Frank, as he retraced his steps home—'I am about as wise as ever! A pretty opinion Dr. Palmer expresses of her, truly! Well, she shall have the benefit of a doubt, and I shall try to look upon her as an innocent woman, until I detect her in an act of guilt. Meanwhile, she shall be watched narrowly and constantly.'

Frank's suspicions with reference to his newly-made wife, did not prevent his carrying out the plan of benevolence which he formed in the first chapter of this narrative. Adopting various disguises, he would penetrate into the most obscure and dangerous quarters of the city, at all hours of the day and night. The details of many of these secret adventures will be hereafter related.

CHAPTER V

A Thieves' Crib on the Five Points—Bloody Mike—Ragged Pete—
the Young Thief, and the stolen Letters—The Stranger—a general Turn-out—
Peeling a Lodger—the 'Forty-Foot Cave.'

It was a dreary winter's night, cold, dark, and stormy. The hour was midnight; and the place, the *'Five Points.'*

The narrow and crooked streets which twine serpent-like around that dreaded plague spot of the city were deserted; but from many a dirty window, and through many a red, dingy curtain, streamed forth into the darkness rages of ruddy light, while the sounds of the violin, and the noise of Bacchanalian orgies, betokened that the squalid and vicious population of that vile region were still awake.

In the low and dirty tap-room of a thieves' *crib* in Cross street, are assembled about a dozen persons. The apartment is twenty feet square, and is warmed by a small stove, which is red-hot; a roughly constructed bar, two or three benches, and a table constitute all the furniture. Behind the bar stands the landlord, a great, bull-necked Irishman, with red hair, and ferocious countenance, the proprietor of the elegant appropriate appellation of 'Bloody Mike.' Upon the table are stretched two men, one richly dressed, and the other in rags—both sound asleep. Beneath the table lay a wretched-looking white prostitute, and a filthy-looking negro—also asleep. The remainder of the interesting party are seated around the stove, and sustain the following dialogue:

'Well, blow me tight,' said one, 'if ever I seed such times as these afore! Why, a feller can't steal enough to pay for his rum and tobacco. I haven't made a cent these three days. D——n me if I ain't half a mind to knock it off and go to work!'

The speaker was a young man, not over one and twenty years of age; yet he was a most wretched and villainous looking fellow. His hair was wild and uncombed; his features bloated and covered with ulcers; his attire miserable and ragged in the extreme; and sundry sudden twitchings of his limbs, as well as frequent violent scratchings of the same, indicated that he was overrun with vermin. This man, whose indolence had made him a common loafer, had become a petty thief; he would lurk around back yards and steal any article he could lay his hands to—an axe, a shovel, or a garment off a line.

'What you say is true enough, Ragged Pete,' said a boy of about fourteen, quite good looking, and dressed with comparative neatness. 'A *Crossman* has to look sharp now-a-days to make a *boodle*. And he often gets deceived when he thinks he has made a raise. Why the other day I cut a rich looking young lady's reticule from her arm in Broadway and got clear off with it; but upon examining my prize, I found it contained nothing but a handkerchief and some letters. The *wipe* I kept for my own use; as for the letters, here they are —they are not worth a tinker's d——n, for they are all about love.'

As he spoke, he carelessly threw upon the table several letters, which were taken up and examined by Ragged Pete, who being requested by others to read aloud, complied, and opening one, read as follows:—

'*Dear Mistress,*--Since your marriage, I have not enjoyed any of those delicious private *tete-a-tetes* with you, which formerly afforded us both so much pleasure. Send me word when I can find you alone, and I will fly to your arms.

'Your ever faithful   Nero'

'By Jesus!' exclaimed Bloody Mike —'it's a mighty quare name me gentleman signs himself, any how. And it's making love to another man's wife he'd be, blackguard! Devil the much I blame him for that same, if the lady's continted !'

'Here,' said Ragged Pete, taking up another letter, 'is one that's sealed and directed, and ain't been broke open yet. Let's see what it says.'

Breaking the seal, he read aloud the contents, thus:-

'*Dear Nero,*—I am dying to see you, but my husband is with me so constantly that 'tis next to impossible. He is kind and attentive to me, but oh! how infinitely I prefer *you to him! I* do not think that he has ever suspected that before my marriage, *I * * * Fortunately for us,* Mr. Sydney has lately been in the habit of absenting himself from home evenings, often staying out very late. Where he goes I care not, tho' I suspect he is engaged in some intrigue of his own; and if so, all the better for us, my dear Nero.

'Thus I arrange matters; when he has gone, and I have reason to think he will not soon return, a light will be placed in my chamber window, which is on the extreme left of the building, in the third story. Without this signal, do not venture into the house. If all is favourable my maid, Susan (who is in our secret,) will admit you by the back gate, when you knock thrice. Trusting that we may meet soon, I remain, dear Nero,

'Your loving and faithful   JULIA.'

'Hell and furies!' exclaimed one of the company, starting from his seat, and seizing the letter; he ran his eye hastily over it, and with a groan of anguish, sank back upon the bench.

The person who manifested this violent emotion, was a young man, dressed in a mean and tattered garb, his face begrimed corresponding with that of the motley crew by which he was surrounded. He was a perfect stranger to the others present, and had not participated in their previous conversation, nor been personally addressed by any of them.

Bloody Mike, the landlord, deeming this a fit opportunity for the exercise of his authority, growled out, in a ferocious tone—

'And who the devil may ye be, that makes such a bobbaboo about a letter that a *kinchen* stales from a lady's work bag? Spake, ye blasted scoundrel; or wid my first, (and it's no small one) I'll let daylight thro' yer skull! And be what right do ye snatch the letter from Ragged Pete? Answer me *that* ye devil's pup!'

All present regarded the formidable Irishman with awe, excepting the stranger, who gazed at him in contemptuous silence. This enraged the landlord still more, and he cried out—

'Bad luck to ye, who are ye, at all at all ? Ye're a stranger to all of us—ye haven't spint a pinney for the good of the house, for all ye've been toasting yer shins furnist the fire for two hours or more! Who knows but ye're a police spy, an officer in disguise, or—'

'Oh, *slash yer gammon*, Bloody Mike,' exclaimed the stranger, speaking with a coarse, vulgar accent—'I know you well enough, tho' you don't remember *me*. Police spy, hey? Why, I've just come out of *quod* myself, d'y see—and I've got *tin* enough to stand the rum for the whole party. So call up, fellers—what'll ye all have to drink?'

It is impossible to describe the effect of these words on everybody present. Bloody Mike swore that the stranger was a 'rare gentleman', and asked his pardon; Ragged Pete grasped his hand in a transport of friendship; the young thief declared he was 'one of the b'hoys from home;' the negro and the prostitute crawled from under the table, and thanked him with hoarse and drunken voices; the vagabond and well-dressed man on the table, both rolled off, and 'called on.' And the stranger threw upon the counter a handful of silver, and bade them 'drink it up.'

Such a scene followed! Half pints of 'blue ruin' were dispensed to the thirsty throng, and in a short time all, with two or three exceptions, were extremely drunk. The negro and the prostitute resumed their places under the table; the well-dressed man and his ragged companion stretched themselves upon their former hard couch; and Ragged Pete ensconced himself in the fireplace, with his head buried in the ashes and his heels up the chimney, in which comfortable position he vainly essay'd to sing a sentimental song, wherein he [*illegible word*] to deplore the loss of his 'own true love.' (The only sober persons were the stranger, the young thief and the Irish landlord.) The two former of these, seated in one corner, conversed together in low whispers.

'See here, young feller, 'said the stranger—'I've taken a fancy to them two letters, and if you'll let me keep 'em, here's a dollar for you.' The boy readily agreed, and the other continued:

'I say, there's a rum set o' coves in this here crib, ain't there? Who is that well-dressed chap on the table?'

'That,' said the boy, 'is a thief who lately made a large haul, since which time he has been cutting a tremendous swell—but he spent the whole thousand dollars in two or three weeks, and his fine clothes is all that remains. In less than a week he will look as bad as Ragged Pete.'

'And what kind of a cove is the landlord, Bloody Mike?' asked the stranger.

'He is the best friend a fellow has in the world, as long as his money lasts,' replied the boy. 'The moment that is gone, he don't know you. Now you'll see in a few moments how he'll clear everybody out of the house except such as he thinks has money. And, 'twixt you and me, he is the d——dst scoundrel out of jail, and would as lief kill a man as not.'

At this moment, Bloody Mike came from behind the counter and took a general survey of the whole party. At length his eye settled upon the form of Ragged Pete, in the fireplace; muttering something about 'pinnyless loafers,' he seized that individual by the heels, and dragging him to the door, opened it, and thrust the poor wretch forth into the deep snow and pelting storm! All the rest with the exception of the stranger, the boy thief, and the well dressed man, shared the same fate. But Mike was not done yet; he swore that the well dressed personage should pay for his lodgings, and deliberately he stripped the man of his coat, vest and boots, after which summary proceeding he ejected him from the house, as he had the others.

'Suppose we take up our quarters in some other 'crib',' whispered the boy to the stranger; the latter assented, and they both arose to depart. The landlord invited them to remain and partake of 'something hot,' but they declined this hospitality, and sallied forth into the street.

It was now about two o'clock, and snowing heavily. The stranger, placing himself under the guidance of the boy, followed him around into Orange street. Pausing before a steep cellar, exceedingly narrow, dark and deep, the young thief whispered—

'This is *the forty-foot cave*—the entrance into the *dark vaults.** You have been down, I suppose?'

The stranger answered in the negative.

'Then come on, if you are not afraid,' said the boy—and followed by his companion, he cautiously began to descend into the dark and dreary chasm.

* It is a fact by no means generally known that there was, beneath the section of New York called the 'Five Points,' a vast subterranean cavern, known as the *dark vaults*. There mysterious passages run in many directions, for a great distance, far beneath the foundations of the houses. Some have supposed that the place was excavated in time of war, for the secretion of ammunition or stores, while others think it was formerly a deep sewer of the city. In these dark labyrinths *daylight* never *shone*: an eternal night prevailed. Yet it swarmed with human beings, who passed their lives amid its unwholesome damps and gloomy horrors. It served as a refuge for monstrous crimes and loathsome wretchedness. The Police rarely ventured to explore its secret mysteries—for Death lurked in its dark passages and hidden recesses. The horrors of this awful place have never heretofore been thoroughly revealed; and now the author of this work will, for the first time, drag forth the ghastly inmates of this charnel-house into the clear light of day.

CHAPTER VI

*The Dark Vaults—Scenes of Appalling Horror—The Dead Man—
The Catechism—arrangements for a Burglary.*

Down, down, they went, far into the bowels of the earth; groping their way in darkness, and often hazarding their necks by stumbling upon the steep and slippery steps. At length the bottom of the 'forty-foot cave' was reached; and the boy grasping the hand of his follower, conducted him thro' a long and circuitous passage. Intense darkness and profound silence reigned; but after traversing this passage for a considerable distance, lights began to illumine the dreary path, and that indistinct hum which proceeds from numerous inhabitants, became audible. Soon the two explorers emerged into a large open space, having the appearance of a vast vault, arched overhead with rough black masonry, which was supported by huge pillars of brick and stone. Encircling this mighty *tomb*, as it might be properly called, were numerous small hovels, or rather *caves*, dug into the earth; and these holes were swarming with human beings.

Here was a *subterranean village*! Myriads of men and women dwelt in this awful place, where the sun never shone; here they festered with corruption, and died of starvation and wretchedness—those who were poor; and here also the fugitive murderer, the branded outlaw, the hunted thief, and the successful robber, laden with his booty, found a safe asylum, where justice *dare not* follow them—here they gloried in the remembrance of past crimes, and anticipated future enormities. Men had no secrets here;—for no treachery could place them within the grasp of the law, and every one spoke openly and boldly of his long-hidden deeds of villainy and outrage.

'Come', said the boy to the stranger—'let us go the rounds and see what's going on.'

They drew nigh a large, shelving aperture in the earth, on one side of the vault, and looking in saw a man, nearly naked; seated upon a heap of excrement and filthy straw. A fragment of a penny candle was burning dimly near him, which showed him to be literally daubed from head to foot with the vilest filth. Before him lay the carcase of some animal which had died from disease—it was swollen and green with putrefaction; and oh, horrible! we sicken as we record the loathsome fact—the starved wretch was ravenously devouring the carrion! Yes, with his finger nails, long as vultures' claws, he tore out the reeking entrails, and ate them with the ferocity of the grave-robbing hyena! One of the spectators spoke to him, but he only growled savagely, and continued his revolting meal.

'Oh, God!' said the stranger, shuddering—'this is horrible!'

'Pooh!' rejoined the boy—'*that's* nothing at all to what you will see if you have the courage and inclination to follow me wherever I shall lead you, in these vaults.'

In another cavern an awful scene presented itself. It was an Irish *wake*—a dead body lay upon the table, and the relations and friends of the deceased were howling their lamentations over it. An awful stench emanating from the corpse, indicated

132

that the process of decomposition had already commenced. In one corner, several half-crazed, drunken, naked wretches were fighting with the ferocity of tigers, and the mourners soon joining in the fray, a general combat ensued, in the fury of which, the table on which lay the body was overturned, and the corpse was crushed beneath the feet of the combatants.

Leaving this appalling scene, the boy and the stranger passed on, until they stood before a cave which was literally crammed with human beings. Men and women, boys and girls, young children, negroes, and *hogs* were laying indiscriminately upon the ground, in a compact mass. Some were cursing each other with fierce oaths; and horrible to relate! negroes were lying with young white girls, and several, unmindful of the presence of others, were perpetrating the most dreadful enormities. These beings were vile and loathsome in appearance, beyond all human conception; every one of them was a mass of rags, filth, disease, and corruption. As the stranger surveyed the loathsome group, he said to his guide, with a refinement of speech he had not before assumed—

'Had any one, two hours ago, assured me that such a place as this, containing such horrible inmates, existed in the very heart of the city, I would have given him the lie direct! But I see it for myself, and am forced to believe it.'

'These wretches,' said the boy—'are many of them related to each other. There are husbands and wives there; mothers and children; brothers and sisters. Yet they all herd together, you see, without regard to nature or decency. Why the crime of *incest* is as common among them as dirt! I have known a mother and her son—a father and his daughter—a brother and sister—to be guilty of criminal intimacy! Those wretched children are many of them the offspring of such unnatural and beastly connections. In my opinion, those hogs have as good a claim to humanity, as those brutes in human form!'

'And how came those hogs to form part of the inhabitants of this infernal place?' asked the stranger.

'You must know,' replied the boy, 'that these vaults communicate with the common street *sewers* of the city; well, those animals get into the sewers, to devour the vegetable matter, filth and offal that accumulate there; and, being unable to get out, they eventually find their way to these vaults. Here they are killed and eaten by the starving wretches. And would you believe it?—these people derive almost all their food from these sewers. They take out the decayed vegetables and other filth, which they actually eat; and the floating sticks and timber serve them for fuel. You remember the man we saw devouring the dead animal; well, he took that carcase from the sewer.'

'And what effect does such loathsome diet produce upon them?' asked the other.

'Oh,' was the reply—'it makes them insane in a short time; eventually they lose the faculty of speech, and howl like wild animals. Their bodies become diseased, their limbs rot, and finally they putrify and die.'

'And how do they dispose of the dead bodies?' asked the stranger.

'*They throw them into the sewer,*' answered the boy, with indifference. His listener shuddered.

'Come,' said the young guide—'you have only seen the wretched portion of the Dark Vaults. You are sick of such miseries, and well you may be—but we will now pay a visit to a quarter where there are no sickening sights. We will go to the *Infernal Regions!*'

Saying this, he led the way thro' a long, narrow passage, which was partially illumined by a bright light at the further end. As they advanced loud bursts of laughter greeted their ears; and finally they emerged into a large cavern, brilliantly illuminated by a multitude of candles, and furnished with a huge round table. Seated around this were about twenty men, whose appearance denoted them to be the most desperate and villainous characters which can infest a city. Not any of them were positively ragged or dirty; on the contrary, some of them were dressed richly and expensively; but there was no mistaking their true characters, for villain was written in their faces as plainly as though the word was branded on their faces with a hot iron.

Seated upon a stool in the centre of the table was a man of frightful appearance: his long, tangled hair hung over two eyes that gleamed with savage ferocity; his face was the most awful that can be imagined—long, lean, cadaverous and livid, it resembled that of a corpse. No stranger could view it without a shudder; it caused the spectator to recoil with horror. His form was tall and bony, and he was gifted with prodigious strength. This man, on account of his corpse-like appearance was known as 'the Dead Man.' He never went by any other title; and his real name was unknown.

The stupendous villainy and depravity of this man's character will appear hereafter. Upon the occasion of his first introduction in this narrative, he was acting as president of the carousals; he was the first one to notice the entrance of the boy and the stranger; and addressing the former, he said—

'How now, *Kinchen*—who have you brought with you? Is the cove *cross* or *square*—and what does he want in our *ken?*'

'He is a *cross cove*,' answered the boy—'he is just from *quay*; and wishes to make the acquaintance of the knights of the Round Table.'

'That being the case,' rejoined the Dead Man,' he is welcome, provided he has the blunt to pay for the *lush* all round.'

The stranger, understanding the import of these words, threw upon the table a handful of money; this generosity instantly raised him high in the estimation of all present. He was provided with a seat at the table, and a bumper of brandy was handed him, which he merely tasted, without drinking.

The boy seated himself at the side of the stranger, and the Dead Man, addressing a person by the name of the 'Doctor,' requested him to resume the narration of his story, in which he had been interrupted by the two newcomers.

The 'Doctor,' a large, dark man, very showily dressed, complied, and spoke as follows:—

'As I was saying, gentlemen, I had become awfully reduced—not a cent in my possession, not a friend in the world, and clothed in rags. One night, half-crazed with hunger, I stationed myself at the Park, having armed myself with a paving stone, determined to rob the first person that came along, even if I should be obliged to dash out his brains.—After a while, a young gentleman approached my lurking place; I advanced towards him with my missile raised, and he drew a sword from his cane, prepared to act on the defensive—but when I mentioned that three days had elapsed since I had taken food, the generous young man, who might easily have overcome me, weak and reduced as I was—took from his pocket a fifty dollar bill, and gave it to me. This generous gift set me on my legs again, and now here am I, a Knight of the Round Table, with a pocket full of rocks, and good prospects in anticipation. Now, the only wish of my heart is to do that generous benefactor of mine a service; and if ever I can do a good action to him, to prove my gratitude, I shall be a happy fellow indeed.'

'Posh!' said the Dead Man, contemptuously—'don't talk to me of gratitude— if a man does *me* a service I hate him for it ever afterwards. I never rest till I repay him by some act of treachery or vengeance.'

As the hideous man gave utterance to this abominable sentiment, several females entered the apartment, one of whom led by the hand a small boy of five years of age. This woman was the wife of the Dead Man, and the child was his son.

The little fellow scrambled upon the table, and his father took him upon his knee, saying to the company—

'Pals, you know the blessed Bible tells us to 'train up a child in the way he should go;' very good—now you will see how well I have obeyed the command with this little *kid*. Attend to your catechism, my son. What is your name?

'Jack the Prig,' answered the boy without hesitation.

'Who gave you that name?'

'The Jolly Knights of the Round Table.'

'Who made you?' asked the father.

'His Majesty, old Beelzebub!' said the child.

'For what purpose did he make you?'

'To be a bold thief all my life, and die like a man upon the gallows!'

Immense applause followed this answer.

'What is the whole duty of man?'

'To drink, lie, rob, and murder when necessary.'

'What do you think of the Bible?'

'It's all a cursed humbug!'

'What do you think of me—now speak up like a man!'

'You're the d——dest scoundrel that ever went unhung,' replied the boy, looking up in his father's face and smiling.

The roar of laughter that followed his answer was perfectly deafening, and was heartily joined in by the Dead Man himself, who had taught the child the very words—and those words were true as gospel. The Dead Man knew he was a villain, and gloried in the title. He gave the boy a glass of brandy to drink, as a reward for his cleverness; and further encouraged him by prophesying that he would one day become a great thief.

Room was now made at the table for the women, several of whom were young and good-looking. They were all depraved creatures, being common prostitutes, or very little better; and they drank, swore, and boasted of their exploits in thieving and other villainy, with as much gusto as their male companions. After an hour of so spent in riotous debauchery, the company, wearied with their excesses, broke up, and most of them went to their sleeping places; the Dead Man, the boy and the stranger, together with a man named Fred, remained at the table; and the former, addressing the stranger, said to him—

'And so, young man, you have just come out of *quod*, hey? Well, as you look rather hard up, and most likely haven't a great deal of blunt on hand, suppose I put you in the way of a little profitable business—eh?'

The stranger nodded approvingly.

'Well, then,' continued the Dead Man—'you must know that Fred Archer here and myself *spotted* a very pretty *crib* on Broadway, and we have determined to *crack* it. The house is occupied by a young gentleman named Sydney, and his wife—they have been married but a short time. We shall have no difficulty in getting into the crib, for Mr. Sydney's butler, a fellow named Davis, is bribed by me to admit us into the house, at a given signal. What say you—will you join us?'

'Yes—and devilish glad of the chance,' replied the stranger, gazing at Fred Archer with much interest. Fred was a good looking young man, genteelly dressed, but with a dissipated, rakish air.

'Very well—that matter is settled,' said the Dead Man. 'Three of us will be enough to do the job, and therefore we shan't want your assistance, *Kinchen*,' he added, addressing the boy. 'It must now be about six o'clock in the morning—we will meet here to-night at eleven precisely. Do not fail, for money is to be made in this affair.'

The stranger promised to be punctual at the appointed hour; and bidding him good night (for it was always night in that place), Fred and the Dead Man retired, leaving the *Kinchen* and the stranger alone together.

'Well,' said the *Kinchen*—'so it seems that you have got into business already. Well and good—but I must caution you to beware of that Dead Man, for he is treacherous as a rattlesnake. He will betray you, if anything is to be gained by it— and even when no advantage could be gained, he will play the traitor out of sheer malice. He is well aware that I, knowing his real character, would not join him in the business, and therefore he affected to think that my assistance was unnecessary.'

'I will look out for him,' rejoined the stranger—and then added, 'I will now thank you to conduct me out of this place, as I have matters to attend to elsewhere.'

The *Kinchen* complied, and in ten minutes they emerged into the street above, by the same way they had entered.

Here they parted, the stranger having first presented the boy with a liberal remuneration for his services as guide, and made an appointment to meet him on a future occasion.

CHAPTER VII

The false wife, and the dishonest servant—scene in the Police Court— capture of the Burglars, and threat of vengeance.

Mr. Francis Sydney and his lady were seated at dinner, in the sumptuously furnished dining parlor of their elegant Broadway mansion. The gentleman looked somewhat pale and ill at ease, but the lady had never looked more superbly beautiful.

The table was waited upon by Davis, the butler, a respectable looking man of middle age, and Mr. Sydney, from time to time, glanced furtively from his wife to this man, with a very peculiar expression of countenance.

'My love,' said Mrs. Sydney, after a pause of several minutes—'I have a little favor to ask.'

'You have but to name it, Julia, to ensure it being granted,' was the reply.

'It is this,' said the lady;—'our present footman is a stupid Irishman, clumsy and awkward; and I really wish him to be discharged. And, my dear, I should be delighted to have the place filled by my father's black footman, who is called Nero. He is civil and attentive, and has been in my father's family many years. Let us receive him into our household.'

'Well Julia,' said the husband, 'I will consider on the subject. I should not like to part with our present footman, Dennis, without some reluctance—for though uncouth in his manners, he is an honest fellow, and has served me faithfully for many years. *Honest* servants are exceedingly scarce now-a-days.'

As he uttered these last words, Davis, the butler, cast a sudden and suspicious look upon his master, who appeared to be busily engaged with the contents of his plate, but who in reality was steadfastly regarding him from the corner of his eyes.

As soon as dinner was over, the lady retired to her *boudoir;* Davis removed the cloth and Mr. Sydney was left alone. After taking two or three turns up and down the room, he paused before the fireplace and soliloquized thus:

'Curses on my unhappy situation! My wife is an adulteress, and my servants in league with villains to rob me! These two letters confirm the first—and my last night's adventure in the Dark Vaults convinced me of the second. And then the woman just now had the damnable effrontery to request me to take her rascally paramour into my service, in place of my faithful Dennis! She wishes to carry on her amours under my very nose! And that scoundrel Davis—how demure, how innocently he looks—and yet how suspiciously he glanced at me, when I emphasized *honest* servants! He is a cursed villain, and yet not one-tenth part so guilty as this woman, whom I espoused in honorable marriage, supposing her to be pure and untainted and yet who was, previous to our marriage, defiled by co-habitation with a vile negro—and now *after* our marriage, is still desirous of continuing her beastly intrigues. Davis is nothing but a low-born menial, without education or position, but Julia is by birth a lady, the daughter of a man of reputation and honor, moving in a brilliant sphere, possessing education and talent, admired as much for her beauty as for her accomplishments and wit—and for her to surrender her person

137

to the lewd embraces of *any man*—much more a negro menial—is horrible! And then to allow herself to be led to the altar, enhanced her guilt tenfold; but what caps the climax of her crimes, is this last movement of hers, to continue her adulterous intercourse! Heavens!—what a devil in the form of a lovely woman! But patience, patience! I must set about my plan of vengeance with patience.'

The reader of course need not be told, that the stranger of the Dark Vaults, and Frank Sydney, were one and the same person. The adventure had furnished him with the evidences of his wife's criminality and his servant's dishonesty and perfidy.

That same afternoon, the young gentleman sallied forth from his mansion, and took his way to the police office. On his way he mused thus:

'By capturing these two villains, the Dead Man and Fred Archer, I shall render an important service to the community. It is evident that the first of these men is a most diabolical wretch, capable of any crime; and the other, I am convinced, is the same Frederick Archer who is the husband of the unfortunate girl with whom I passed the night not long since, at which time she related to me her whole history. He must be a most infernal scoundrel to make his wife prostitute herself for his support; and he is a *burglar* too, it seems. Society will be benefited by the imprisonment of two such wretches—and this very night shall they both lodge in the Tombs.'

When Frank arrived at the police office, he found a large crowd assembled; a young thief had just been brought in, charged with having abstracted a gentleman's pocket-book from his coat pocket, in Chatham Street. What was Frank's surprise at recognizing in the prisoner, the same boy who had been his companion in the Dark Vaults, on the proceeding night! The lad did not know Frank, for there was no similarity between the ragged, vagabond looking fellow of the night before, and the elegantly dressed young gentleman who now surveyed him with pity and interest depicted in his handsome countenance.

It was a clear case—the young offender was seen in the act, and the pocket-book was found in his possession. The magistrate was about to make out his commitment, when Frank stepped forward, and required what amount of bail would be taken on the premises?

'I shall require surety to the amount of five hundred dollars, as the theft amounts to grand larceny,' replied the magistrate.

'I will bail him, then,' said Frank.

'Very well, Mr. Sydney,' observed the magistrate, who knew the young gentleman perfectly well, and highly respected him

'You will wait here in the office for me, until I have transacted some business, and then accompany me to my residence,' said Frank—'I feel interested in you, and, if you are worthy of my confidence hereafter, your future welfare shall be promoted by me.'

Frank had a long private interview with the magistrate. After having made arrangements for the capture of the two burglars, the young man urged the police functionary to take immediate measures for the breaking up of the band of desperate villains who lurked in the Dark Vaults, and the relief of the miserable wretches who found a loathsome refuge in that terrible place. The magistrate listened with attention and then said—

'I have long been aware of the existence of the secret, subterranean Vaults of which you allude, and so have the officers of the police; yet the fact is known to very, very few of the citizens generally. Now you propose that an efficient and armed force of the police and watch, make a sudden descent into the den, with the view of capturing the villains who inhabit it. Ridiculous!—why, sir, the thing is impossible: they have a mysterious passage, unknown to any but themselves, by which they can escape and defy pursuit. The thing has been attempted twenty times, and as often failed. So much for the *villains* of the den;—now in regard to the wretched beings whom you have described, if we took them from that hole, what in the world should we do with them? Put them in the prisons and almshouse, you say. That would soon breed contagion throughout the establishments where they might be placed, and thus many lives would be sacrificed thro' a misdirected philanthropy. No, no—believe me, Mr. Sydney, that those who take up their abode in the Vaults, and become diseased, and rot, and die there, had much better be suffered to remain there, far removed from the community, than to come into contact with that community, and impart their disease and pollution to those who are now healthy and pure. Those vaults may be regarded as the moral sewers of the city—the scum and filth of our vast population accumulate in them. With reference to the desperadoes who congregate there, their living is made by robbery and outrage throughout the city; and all, sooner or later, are liable to be arrested and imprisoned for their offences.'

'I admit the force of your reasoning,' said Frank—'yet I cannot but deeply deplore the existence of such a den of horrors.'

'A den of horrors indeed!' rejoined the magistrate. 'Why, sir, there are at this moment no less than six murderers in the Vaults—one of whom escaped from his cell the night previous to the day on which he was to be hung. The gallows was erected in the prison yard—but when the sheriff went to bring the convict forth to pay the penalty of his crime, his cell was empty; and upon the wall was written with charcoal,—'*Seek me in the Dark Vaults!*' The police authorities once blocked up every known avenue to the caverns, with the design of starving out the inmates; but they might have waited till doomsday for the accomplishment of that object, as the secret outlet which I have mentioned enabled the villains to procure stores of provisions, and to pass in and out at pleasure. I am glad that your scheme, Mr. Sydney, will tonight place in the grip of the law, two of these miscreants, one of whom, the Dead Man, has long been known as the blackest villain that ever breathed. He is a fugitive from justice, having a year ago escaped from the State Prison, where he had been sentenced for life, for an atrocious murder; he had been reprieved from the gallows, thro' the mistaken clemency of the Executive. He will now be returned to his old quarters, to fulfil his original sentence, and pass the remainder of his accursed life in imprisonment and exclusion from the world, in which he is not fit to dwell.'

Frank now took leave of the magistrate, and, accompanied by the young pickpocket, returned to his own residence. It was now about five o'clock, and growing quite dark; a drizzly rain was falling intermingled with snow. Frank conducted the boy to his library, and having carefully closed and locked the door, said to him—

'*Kinchen*, don't you know me?'

The boy started, and gazed earnestly at him for a few moments, and then shook his head.

'Wait here a short time, and I will return,' said Frank, and he stepped into a closet adjoining the library, and shut the door.

Ten minutes elapsed; the closet door opened, and a ragged, dirty looking individual entered the library. The boy jumped to his feet in astonishment, and exclaimed—

'Why, old fellow, how the devil came *you* here?'

'Hush,' said Frank—'I am the man who accompanied you thro' the Vaults last night, and I am also the gentleman who bailed you to-day. Now listen; you can do me a service. You know that the Dead Man, Fred Archer and myself are to enter this house to-night; the two burglars little think that I am the master of the house. It is my intention to entrap those two villains. Take this pistol; conceal yourself in that closet, and remain quiet until you hear the noise of a struggle; then rush to the scene of the conflict, and aid me and the officers in capturing the two miscreants. Rather than either of them should escape, shoot him thro' the head. I am inclined to think that you will prove faithful to me; be honest, and in me you have secured a friend. But I must enlist another person in our cause.'

He rang a bell, and Dennis, the Irish footman, made his appearance. This individual was not surprised to see his master arrayed in that strange garb, for he had often assisted him in similar disguises. Dennis was a large, raw-looking Hibernian, yet possessing an honest open countenance.—Frank explained to him in a few words the state of the case, and the nature of the service required of him; and honest Dennis was delighted with the opportunity of displaying his personal prowess, and fidelity to his master.

'Och, be the powers!' he exclaimed—'it's nather a swerd nor a pistol I want at all, but only a nate little bit of shillalab in my fist, to bate the thieves of the worruld, and scatter them like the praste scatters the divil wid holy water.'

'Very well,' said Frank—'now, *Kinchen*, you will take your station in the closet, for fear you should be seen by the servants, and you, Dennis, will bring him up some refreshments, and then attend to your ordinary duties as usual. Say not a word to anybody in regard to this affair, and give the other servants to understand that I have gone out, and will not return until tomorrow morning. I shall now leave the house, and at about midnight you may expect me, accompanied by the burglars.'

Saying this, Frank quitted the mansion by a private stair-case. Turning into Canal street, he walked towards the Bowery, and not far from where that broad thoroughfare joins Chatham street, he ascended the steps of a dwelling-house, and knocked gently at the door; it was soon opened by the young courtezan with whom Frank had passed the night at the commencement of this tale. She did not recognize the visitor in his altered garb, until he had whispered a few words in her ear, and then uttering an exclamation of pleasure, she requested him to follow her up-stairs.

Frank complied, and after seating himself in the well-remembered chamber, related to the young woman, as briefly as possible, the circumstances under which he had met her husband, Fred Archer, and the share he was to take in the burglary. He concluded by saying—

'I am sure, Mrs. Archer, that you will rejoice in the prospect of getting rid of such a husband. Once convicted and sent to the State Prison, he has no further claim upon you. You will be as effectually separated from him as though you were divorced.'

'I shall be most happy,' said Mrs. Archer—'to escape from the tyrannical power of that bad man. He has used me brutally of late, and I have often suffered for the common necessaries of life. Oh, how gladly would I abandon the dreadful trade of prostitution and live a life of virtue!'

'And so you shall, by Heavens!' cried Frank, in the warmth of his generous nature. 'Take courage, madam, and after the affairs of tonight are settled, your welfare shall be my special care. I will endeavor to procure you a comfortable home in some respectable family, where—'

At this moment the street door was opened, and some one was heard ascending the stairs.

'It is my husband!' whispered Mrs. Archer, and pointing to the bed, she requested Frank to conceal himself behind the curtains; he did so, and in a moment more, Fred Archer entered the room, and threw himself into a chair.

'Well, by G——!' he exclaimed—'it seems impossible for a man to make a living these times! Here I am, without a cursed cent in my pocket. Maria, what money have you in the house?'

'I have no money, Frederick,' replied his wife.

'No money—you lie, cursed strumpet! What do you do with the gains of your prostitution?'

'As God is my witness,' replied the wretched woman, bursting into tears—'I have not received a cent for the past week; I have even suffered for food; and the lady threatens to turn me out of doors this very night, if the rent is not paid. I know not what to do.'

'Do!—why, d——n you, do as other w——s do; go and parade Broadway, until you pick up a flat—ha, ha, ha!' and the ruffian laughed brutally. After a pause, he added—

'Well, I've got an appointment tonight, at eleven o'clock; a little job is to be done, that will fill my pocket with shiners. But don't you expect to get a farthing of the money—no, d——n you, you must earn your living as other prostitutes earn it. Good bye—I'm off.'

He departed, and Frank emerged from his hiding place. 'What a beastly scoundrel that fellow is!' he thought, as he gazed with pity at the weeping and wretched wife. He was about to address her with some words of comfort, when a loud knocking was heard on the chamber door. Mrs. Archer started, and whispered to Frank that it was the landlady, come to demand her rent—she then in a louder tone, requested the person to walk in.

A stout, vulgar looking woman entered the room and having violently shut the door and placed her back to it, said—

'I've come, Missus, or Miss, or whatever you are, to see if so be you can pay me my rent, as has now been due better nor four weeks, and you can't deny it, either.'

'I am sorry to say, madam,' replied Mrs. Archer, 'that I am still unable to pay you. My husband has left me no money, and —'

'Then you will please to bundle out of this house as soon as possible, retorted the woman, fiercely. 'What am I to let my furnished rooms to a lazy, good-for-nothing hussy like you, as is too proud to work and too good to go out and look for company in the streets, and can't pay me, an honest, hard-working woman, her rent! Am I to put up with—'

'Silence, woman!' interrupted Frank—'do not abuse this unfortunate female in this manner! Have you no sympathy—no pity?'

'And who are *you*, sir?' demanded the virago, dreadfully enraged—'how dare *you* interfere, you dirty, ragged, vagabond? Come, tramp out of this, both of you, this very instant, or I shall call in them as will make you!'

Frank made no reply, but very composedly drew from his pocket a handful of silver and gold; at the sight of the money, the landlady's eyes and mouth opened in astonishment—and her manner, from being most insufferably insolent, changed to the most abject servility.

'Oh, sir,' she said, simpering and curtsying—'I am sure I always had the greatest respect for Mrs. Archer, and I hope that neither you nor her will think hard of me for what I said—I only meant—'

'That will do,' cried Frank, contemptuously—and having inquired the amount due, paid her, and then desired her to withdraw, which she did, with many servile apologies for her insolent rudeness.

The young gentleman then prevailed upon Mrs. Archer to accept of a sum of money sufficient to place her beyond immediate want, and promised to call upon her again in a few days and see what could be done for her future subsistence. She thanked him for his kindness with tears in her eyes; and bidding her farewell, he left the house, and proceeded towards the Five Points.

He had no difficulty in finding the 'forty-foot cave,' the entrance of the Dark Vaults; but, previous to descending, curiosity prompted him to step into the *crib* of Bloody Mike, to see what was going on. He found the place crowded with a motley collection of vagrants, prostitutes, negroes and petty thieves; Ragged Pete was engaged in singing a shocking obscene song, the others joined in the chorus. Clothed in filthy rags, and stupidly drunk, was the man whom Frank had seen the night before so handsomely dressed; Bloody Mike, who had 'peeled' his coat, had since become the possessor of all his other genteel raiment, giving the poor wretch in exchange as much 'blue ruin' as he could drink, and the cast-off garments of a chimney-sweep!

Bloody Mike welcomed Frank with enthusiasm, and introduced him to the company as the 'gintleman that had thrated all hands last night.' At this announcement, the dingy throng gave a loud shout of applause, and crowded about him to shake his hand and assure him how glad they were to see him. These demonstrations of regard were anything but pleasing to our hero, who threw a dollar upon the counter, inviting them all to drink; and, while they were crowding around the bar to receive their liquor, he made his escape from the *crib*, and sought the entrance to the Dark Vaults. Having reached the bottom of the 'forty-foot cave' in safety, he proceeded cautiously along the dark passage which he had before traversed, and passing thro' the first Vault, soon emerged into the cavern of the desperadoes. Here he was met by Fred Archer and the Dead Man, who had been waiting for him.

'Ah, old fellow,' said the latter worthy—'here you are; it's somewhat before the appointed time, but so much the better. Put it down and drink a bumper of brandy to the success of our enterprise.'

The three seated themselves at the table, and remained over an hour drinking, smoking and conversing. Frank partook very sparingly of the liquor, but the others drank freely. At last the Dead Man arose, and announced that it was time to go. He then began to make his preparations.

Retiring for a short time to an inner cavern, he returned with his arms full of various articles. First, there were three large horse pistols, two of which he gave to his companions, retaining one for himself; then he produced three cloaks to be worn by them, the better to conceal any booty which they might carry off. There was also a dark lantern, and various implements used by burglars. The Dead Man then proceeded to adjust a mask over his hideous face, which so completely disguised him, that not one of his most intimate acquaintances would have known him. The mask was formed of certain flexible materials, and being colored with singular truthfulness to nature, bore a most wonderful resemblance to a human face. The Dead Man, who, without it, carried in his countenance the loathsome appearance of a putrefying corpse, with it was transformed into a person of comely looks. All the preparations being now complete, the party took up their line of march, under the directions of the Dead Man. To Frank's surprise, that worthy did not lead the way out of the cavern by means of the 'forty-foot cave,' but proceeded in a different course, along a passage, dark and damp, its obscurity but partially dispelled by the dim rays of the dark lantern, which was carried by the leader. After traversing this passage for a considerable distance, the Dead Man suddenly paused, and said to Frank—

'You are not acquainted with the Secret Outlet to these Vaults—and as you are not yet a Knight of the Round Table, I dare not trust you, a stranger, with the knowledge of it, until you join us, and prove yourself to be trustworthy. Therefore, we must blindfold you, until we reach the streets above. This is a precaution we use by every stranger who goes out this way.'

'But why do you not leave the Vaults by the 'forty-foot cave' thro' which I entered?' demanded Frank, who was fearful of some treachery.

'Because,' answered the Dead Man—'there are police officers in disguise constantly lurking around the entrance of that cave, ready to arrest the first suspicious character who may come forth. You were not arrested last night, because you were unknown to the police—but I, or Fred here, would be taken in a jiffy.'

'How would they know *you* in the disguise of that mask?' asked Frank.

'They might recognise me by my form—my gait—my air—my speech—damn it, they would almost know me by my smell! At all events, I prefer not to risk myself, while there is a safe outlet here. But, if you hesitate, you can return the way you came, and we will abandon the undertaking.'

'No,' said Frank—'I will proceed.'

The Dead Man bound a handkerchief tightly over Frank's eyes, and led him forward some distance; at length he was desired to step up about a foot, which he did, and found himself standing upon what appeared to be a wooden platform. The other two took their places beside him, and then he heard a noise similar to that produced by the turning of an iron crank; at the same time he became sensible that they were slowly ascending. Soon a dull, sluggish sound was heard, like the trickling of muddy water; and a foetid odor entered the nostrils, similar to the loathsome exhalations of a stagnant pool. Up, up they went, until Frank began to think that they must have attained a vast height from the place whence they had started; but at last the noise of the crank ceased, the platform stood still, and the Dead Man, after conversing for a short time in whispers with some person, took hold of Frank's arm, and led him forward thro' what appeared to be an entry. A door was opened, they passed out, and Frank, feeling the keen air, and snow beneath his feet, knew that they were in the open streets of the city. After walking some distance, and turning several corners the bandage was removed from his eyes, and he found himself in Pearl street, the Dead Man walking by his side, and Fred following on behind.

They soon turned into Broadway, and in less than ten minutes had reached the mansion of Mr. Sydney. The streets were silent and deserted for the hour was late; and the Dead Man whispered to his companions—

'We can now enter the house unobserved. In case of surprise, we must not hesitate to *kill*, sooner than be taken. I will now give the signal.'

He gave a low and peculiar whistle, and after the lapse of a few moments, repeated it. Instantly, the hall door was noiselessly opened by a person whom Frank recognized as Davis, the butler. The Dead Man beckoned the two others to follow him into the hall, which they did, and the door was closed.

Five minutes after they had entered the house two men who had been concealed behind a pile of bricks and rubbish on the opposite side of the street, crossed over, and passing around to the rear of the house, obtained access to the garden thro' the back gate which had been purposely left unfastened for them. These two men were police officers, who had been for some time on the watch for the burglars. They entered the house thro' the kitchen window, and stationed themselves upon the stairs, in readiness to rush to the assistance of Frank, as soon as he should give the appointed signal.

Meantime, the Dead Man had raised the slide of his dark lantern, and by its light he led the way into the back parlor, followed by the others. Davis had not the remotest suspicion that one of the men, whom he supposed to be a burglar, and whose appearance was that of a ruffian, was his master! No—he looked him full in the face without recognizing him in the slightest degree.

The Dead Man, approaching a side-board, poured out a bumper of wine and tossed it off, after which he drew from his pocket a small iron bar, (called by thieves a *jimmy*,) and applying it to a desk, broke it open in an instant. But it contained nothing of value; —and the burglar, addressing the others, said:

'We must disperse ourselves over the house, in order to do anything. I will rummage the first story: you, Fred, will explore the second, and our new friend here can try his luck in the third. As for you, Davis, you must descend into the kitchen, and collect what silver ware and plate you can find. So now to work.'

At this instant Frank threw himself upon the Dead Man, and exclaimed, in a loud voice:

'Yield, villain!'

'Damnation, we are betrayed!' muttered the ruffian, as with a mighty effort he threw Frank from him, and drew his horse pistol; —levelling it at the young man with a deadly aim, he was about to draw the fatal trigger, when Dennis, the Irish footman, who had been concealed beneath a large dining table, sprang nimbly behind him, and felled him to the carpet with a tremendous blow of his thick cudgel, crying:

'Lie there, ye spalpeen, and rest asy.'

Fred Archer and Davis instantly made for the door, with the intention of escaping—but they were seized by the two policemen, who now rushed to the scene of uproar; the butler and burglar, however, struggled desperately, and one of the policemen was stunned by a heavy blow on his head, with the butt of a pistol, dealt by the hand of Archer, who, thus freed from the grasp of his antagonist, dashed thro' the hall and effected his escape from the house. Davis, however, was quickly overpowered by the other officer, who slipped hand-cuffs upon his wrists, and thus secured him.

All these occurrences took place within the space of two minutes; and the *Kinchen*, who had been secreted in the library upstairs, arrived, pistol in hand, at the scene of action, just as the conflict had terminated.

The Dead Man lay motionless upon the carpet, and Frank began to fear that he was killed; but upon approaching and examining him, he discovered that he still breathed, though faintly. The blow from Dennis' cudgel had apparently rendered him insensible, and blood was flowing from a severe but not serious wound in his head.

The policeman who had been stunned was speedily brought to, by proper treatment;—and it was found that he had sustained but a trifling injury. Frank now approached Davis, and regarding him sternly, said—

'So, sir, you have leagued yourself with burglars, it seems. What induced you to act in this treacherous manner?'

'The promise of a liberal reward,' replied the man, sulkily.

'Your reward will now consist of a residence of several years in the State Prison,' observed his master as he walked away from him.

The noise of the conflict had aroused the inmates of the house from their slumbers, and much alarm prevailed among them, particularly the females, whose screams resounded throughout the building. To quiet them, Dennis was despatched as a messenger, with assurances that the robbers were in safe custody, and no cause for alarm existed. On passing the chamber of his mistress, that lady called to him, desiring to know the cause of the uproar; and when she had learned the details of the affair, she expressed her gratification at the result.

Frank ordered refreshments to be brought up, and while the whole party gathered around the table to partake of a substantial collation, he congratulated the two officers on having secured so desperate and dangerous a villain as the Dead Man. The form of that miscreant was still stretched upon the carpet directly behind Frank, who stood at the table; and as he was supposed to be insensible, from the effect of the heavy blow which he had received, no one deemed it necessary to bestow any attention upon him. But while the officers and others were eating and conversing, the *Kinchen* suddenly uttered an exclamation of alarm, and seizing a wine bottle which stood upon the table, dashed it at the head of the Dead Man, who had arisen upon his knees, and held in his hand a sharp, murderous-looking knife, which he was just on the point of plunging into the side of the unsuspecting Frank! The bottle was broken into shivers against the ruffian's head, and ere he could recover himself, he was disarmed and handcuffed by the officers, one of whom tore the mask from his face; and the spectators shrunk in horror at the ghastly and awful appearance of that corpse-like countenance! Turning his glaring eye upon Frank, he said, in tones of deepest hate—

'Sydney, look at me—*me*, the *Dead Man*—dead in heart, dead in pity, dead in everything save *vengeance!* You have won the game; but oh! think not your triumph will be a lasting one. No, by G——! there are no prison walls in the universe strong enough to keep me from wreaking upon you a terrible revenge! I will be your evil genius; I swear to follow you thro' life, and cling to you in death; yes—I will torture you in hell! Look for me at midnight, when you deem yourself most secure; I shall be in your chamber. Think of me in the halls of mirth and pleasure, for I shall be at your elbow. In the lonely forest, on the boundless sea, in far distant lands, I shall be ever near you, to tempt, to torture, and to drive you mad! From this hour you are blasted by my eternal curse!'

* * * * *

Half an hour afterwards, the Dead Man and Davis the butler were inmates of the 'Egyptian Tombs.'

CHAPTER VIII

The Subterranean Cellar—Capture and Imprisonment of the Black—the Outcast Wife—The Villain Husband—the Murder and Arrest.

The next day after the occurrence of the events detailed in the last chapter, Frank Sydney caused to be conveyed to the negro footman, Nero, the letter which his wife had addressed to him—which letter it will be recollected, had been stolen from the lady, in her reticule, by the young thief, who had sold it and another epistle from the black, to Frank, at the *crib* of Bloody Mike.

The plan adopted by the much injured husband for the punishment of his guilty wife and her negro paramour, will be developed in the course of the present chapter.

The black, upon receiving the letter, imagined that it came direct from the lady herself; and much rejoiced was he at the contents, resolving that very night to watch for the signal in the chamber window of the amorous fair one.

Beneath the building in which Frank resided, was a deep stone cellar, originally designed as a wine vault; it was built in the most substantial manner, the only entrance being protected by a massive iron door—the said door having been attached in order to prevent dishonest or dissolute servants from plundering the wine. In the course of the day upon which he had sent the letter to Nero, Frank paid a visit to this cellar, and having examined it with great care, said to himself—'This will answer the purpose admirably.'

He then summoned Dennis and the *Kinchen*— the latter of whom he retained in his service—and desired them to remove the few bottles and casks of wine which still remained in the cellar and deposit them elsewhere.—This being done, a quantity of straw was procured and thrown in one corner, and then the arrangements were complete.

'Now listen,' said Frank, addressing Dennis and the *Kinchen*; 'a certain person has injured me—irretrievably injured me—and it is my intention to confine him as a prisoner in this cellar. The matter must be kept a profound secret from the world; you must neither of you breathe a syllable in relation to it, to a living soul. My motive for confiding to you the secret, is this: I may at times find it necessary to be absent from home for a day or so, and it will devolve upon you two to supply the prisoner with his food. Be secret—be vigilant, and your faithfulness shall be rewarded.'

Both of his listeners expressed their willingness to serve him in the matter, and Frank dismissed them, with instructions to await his further orders.

Mrs. Sydney, having lost the letter which she had addressed to Nero (never dreaming that it had fallen into the hands of her husband,) that afternoon, while Frank was engaged in the wine cellar, wrote *another letter* to the black, couched in nearly the same language as her former one, and making precisely the same arrangement in reference to an interview with him in her chamber. This letter she gave to her maid, Susan, to convey privately to the black. It so happened that Frank,

147

who had just finished his business in the wine cellar, encountered the girl as she was emerging from the rear of the house; she held her mistress' letter in her hand, and, confused at meeting Mr. Sydney so unexpectedly, thrust it hastily into her bosom. Frank saw the action, and suspecting the truth, forced the letter from her, broke the seal, and hastily glanced over the contents. It instantly occurred to him that, if he permitted this letter to reach its intended destination, the negro would naturally suspect something wrong, from the fact that he had received that morning a precisely similar letter; and thus Frank's plan might be frustrated. On the other hand, it was necessary for Mrs. Sydney to believe that the letter was safely delivered, in order that she might still suppose her husband to be ignorant of her amour with the black. In view of these considerations, Frank put the letter in his pocket, and then turning to the trembling Susan, said to her, sternly—

'Woman, your agency in this damnable intrigue is known to me, and if you would save yourself from ruin, you will do as I command you. Remain concealed in the house for half an hour, and then go to your mistress and tell her that you have delivered the letter to the black; and say to her that he sends word in reply, that *should the signal be given to-night, he will come to her chamber.* And do you, when you hear him knock thrice upon the gate, admit him, and conduct him to your mistress's chamber. Do this, and you are forgiven for the part you have taken in the business; but if you refuse, by the living God you shall die by my hand!'

'Oh, sir,' sobbed the girl, frightened at the threat, 'I will do all you wish me to.'

'Then you have nothing to fear—but remember, I am not to be trifled with.'

Half an hour afterwards, Susan went up to the chamber of her mistress, and said—

'Well, ma'am, I gave the letter to Nero.'

'And did he send any message?' asked the lady.

'Yes, ma'am,' replied the girl, in obedience to the instructions of Frank—'he said that if the signal is given to-night, he will come to your chamber.'

'Very well, Susan—you are a good girl, and here is a dollar for you,' said the lady, and then added—'you will be sure to admit him when he knocks?'

'Oh, yes, ma'am,' replied the maid; and thanking her mistress, she withdrew.

Left alone, the guilty, adulterous woman fell into a voluptuous reverie, in which she pictured to herself the delights which she anticipated from her approaching interview with her sable lover. The possibility of her husband's remaining at home that evening, thereby preventing that interview, did not once obtrude itself upon her mind—so regularly had he absented himself from home every night during the preceding two or three weeks; and as he had never returned before midnight, she apprehended no difficulty in getting her paramour out of the house undiscovered by him.

The conduct of this woman will doubtless appear very extraordinary and unaccountable to those who have not studied human nature very deeply; while the eccentricity of her passion, and the singular object of her desires, will excite disgust. But to the shrewd and intelligent observer of the female heart and its many impulses, the preferences of this frail lady are devoid of mystery. They are readily accounted for—pampered with luxury, and surrounded by all the appliances of a voluptuous leisure, a morbid craving for *unusual indulgences* had commingled with her passions—a raging desire, and mad appetite for a *monstrous* or *unnatural* intrigue—and hence her disgraceful *liaison* with the black.

Were we disposed, what astounding disclosures we could make, of beastly amours among the sons and daughters of the aristocracy! We have known many instances of unnatural births, unquestionably produced by unnatural cohabitations! We once visited the private cabinet of an eminent medical practitioner, whose collection comprised over a hundred half-human monstrosities, preserved; —and we were assured that many were the results of the most outrageous crimes conceivable.—But why dwell upon such a subject, so degrading to humanity? We will pursue the loathsome theme no longer.

Evening came, and after supper Mrs. Sydney retired to her chamber. To her surprise, her husband joined her there; but her surprise increased, and her annoyance was extreme, when he announced his intention of remaining with her that evening, at home!

Disguising her real feelings, and affecting a joy which was a stranger to her heart at the moment, she only smiled as if in approval of his determination. But in her heart she was most painfully disappointed.

'At all events,' she said to herself, 'I will not place a light in my window, which was the signal I arranged with Nero—so I am safe, at least.'

What was her astonishment and dismay, when her husband deliberately took the lamp from the table, and placed it in the window!

Amazed and trembling, she sat for some minutes in silence, while Frank, having lighted a cigar, began smoking with the utmost coolness. At length the conscience-stricken lady ventured to say—

'My dear, why do you place the light in the window?'

'Because it is my whim to do so,' replied Frank.

'It is a singular whim,' remarked his wife.

'Not so singular as the whim of a white lady of my acquaintance, who amalgamates with a negro,' said her husband.

'What do you mean?' demanded the guilty woman, ready to faint with terror and apprehension.

'I mean this, woman—that you are a vile adulteress!' exclaimed Frank, now thoroughly enraged—'I mean that your abominable conduct is known to me— your true character is discovered. Before your marriage you were defiled by that negro footman, Nero—and since our marriage you have sought the opportunity to renew the loathsome intimacy.'

'What proof have you of this?' murmured the wretched woman, ready to die with shame and terror.

'These letters—this one, addressed to you by the black, and this, which you wrote to him this very afternoon; but it did not reach its destination, for I intercepted it. The one which you wrote a few days ago, and which was stolen from you in your reticule, came into my possession in a manner almost providential—

that letter I sent to the place this morning, and he, supposing it came from you, will come to-night to keep the appointment. He will observe the signal agreed upon, and will be admitted into the house, and conducted to this chamber, little imagining who is waiting for him. So you see, madam, both you and your *friend* are in my power.'

It is impossible to describe the expression of despair and misery which overspread the countenance of Mrs. Sydney during the utterance of these words. She attempted to speak, but could not articulate a single syllable—and in another moment had fallen insensible upon the carpet.

Frank raised her and placed her upon the bed; he had scarcely done so, when he heard some one stealthily ascending the stairs, and in another moment the door softly opened, and Nero, the African footman, entered.

Great was his astonishment and alarm on beholding the husband of the lady whom he had come to debauch. His first impulse was to retreat from the room and endeavor to make his escape from the house; but his design was frustrated by Frank, who rushed forward and seized him by the throat, exclaiming, in a tone of furious rage—

'Eternal curses on you, black ruffian, how dare you enter this house?'

The African, recovering somewhat his presence of mind, struggled to release himself from the fierce grasp of Frank, and would probably have succeeded, had not the *Kinchen* entered, and, seizing a chair, dealt him a blow with it which knocked him down. He then drew from his pocket a stout cord, and, with Frank's assistance, bound the negro's arms securely with it.

Nero, though a black, was both educated and intelligent; he knew that he was now in the power of the man who had been so foully wronged, and he conceived that there was but one way to extricate himself from the difficulty—namely, by promises and entreaties.

'Mr. Sydney,' said he, in an humble, submissive tone—'it is evident that you have discovered my intimacy with that lady, by what means I know not. You have just cause to be indignant and enraged; but I throw myself upon your mercy—and consider, sir, the lady made the first advances, and was I so much to blame for acceding to the wishes of such a lovely woman? Now, sir, if you will suffer me to depart, I promise to leave the city of New York forever, and never will I breathe to another ear the secret of my intimacy with your wife.'

'Think not, accursed miscreant, thus to escape my vengeance,' replied Frank. 'That you are less guilty than that adulterous woman who lies there,' he added, pointing to the bed, 'I admit, and her punishment shall be greater than yours, for she shall endure the pangs of infamy and disgrace, while you only suffer the physical inconvenience of a lengthened imprisonment. I cannot suffer you to go at large after this outrage on my honor as a husband and a man. Attempt no further parley— it is useless, for your fate is sealed.'

Frank took from a bureau drawer a brace of pistols, and commanded the negro to follow him, threatening to shoot him through the head if he made the least noise or resistance.—Nero obeyed, trembling with apprehension and dread. Descending the stairs, Frank conducted him to the cellar, and unlocking the massive iron door, bade him enter; the poor wretch began to supplicate for mercy, but his inexorable captor sternly ordered him to hold his peace, and having unbound his arms, forced him into the dark and gloomy vault, closed the door, and locked it. He then gave the key to the *Kinchen*, requesting him to use the utmost vigilance to prevent the escape of the prisoner, and to supply him every day with sufficient food and water.

'You perceive, my boy,' said Frank, 'that I am disposed to place the utmost confidence in your integrity and faithfulness. From the moment I first saw you, I have been impressed with the belief that you possess a good heart, and some principles of honor. Destitution and bad company have led you astray—but I trust that your future conduct will prove your sincere repentance. I will see the gentleman from whom you attempted to take the pocket-book, and I will compromise the matter with him, so that it shall never come to trial. Be honest—be faithful—be true—and in my house you shall ever have a home, and in me you shall ever have a steadfast friend.'

'Oh, sir,' said the *Kinchen*, his eyes filling with tears—'your kindness and generosity have made me a different being from what I was. I now view my former life with abhorrence, and sooner would I die than return to it. Ah, it is delightful to lead an honest life, to have a comfortable home, and a kind friend like you, sir. My faithful devotion to your interests will prove my gratitude. I should like, sometime, to tell you my history, Mr. Sydney; and when you have heard it, I am sure that you will say that I deserve some pity, as well as blame.'

'I shall be pleased to hear your story,' replied Frank. 'As you are now regularly in my service, you shall be no longer designated as *Kinchen*,* for that name is associated with crime. What is your own proper name?'

'Clinton Romaine,' replied the boy.

'Well, Clinton, you shall hereafter be called by that name. To-morrow I will give you an order on my tailor for a new and complete wardrobe. You had better now retire to bed; as for myself,' he added, gloomily—'I shall probably enjoy but little rest or sleep to-night.'

Clinton bade his patron good night, and retired; Frank ascended to the chamber of his wife, and found that she had recovered from her swoon, though she was still pale from apprehension and shame. Averting her eyes from her husband's gaze, she sat in moody silence; after a pause of several minutes, Frank said—

'Julia, it is not my intention to waste my breath in upbraiding you—neither will I allude to your monstrous conduct further than to state it has determined me to cast you off forever. You are my wife no longer; you will leave this house to-night, and never again cross its threshold. Take with you your maid Susan, your wardrobe, your jewels—in short, all that belongs to you; you must relinquish the name of Sydney—cease to regard me as your husband, and never, never, let me see your face again.'

*The term *Kinchen*, in the flash language of the thieves, signifies a boy thief.

These words, uttered calmly and solemnly, produced an extraordinary effect upon the lady; so far from subduing or humiliating her, they aroused within her all the pride of her nature, notwithstanding her recent overwhelming shame. A rich color dyed her cheeks, her eyes sparkled, and her bosom heaved, as she arose, and boldly confronting Frank, said, in passionate tones—

'You cast me off forever!—I thank you for those words; they release me from a painful thralldom. Now am I mistress of my own actions—free to indulge to my heart's content in delightful amours!—I will not return to my father's house—no, for you will doubtless proclaim there the story of my shame, and my father would repulse me with loathing; and even if 'twere not so, I prefer liberty to follow my own inclinations, to the restraint of my parent's house.'

'Wretched woman,' exclaimed Franks—'are you indeed so lost—so depraved?'

'Fool!' returned the frail lady—'you cannot understand the fiery and insatiate cravings of my passions. I tell you that I consume with desire—but not for enjoyment with such as *you*, but for delicious amours which are *recherche* and unique! Ah, I would give more for one hour with my superb African, than for a year's dalliance with one like you, so ordinary, so excessively common-place! Now that the mask is torn from my face, reserve is needless. Know then that I have been a wanton since early girlhood. What strange star I was born under, I know not; but my nature is impregnated with desires and longings which you would pronounce absurd, unnatural, and criminal. Be it so: I care not what you or the world may say or think—my cravings must be satisfied at all hazards. As for relinquishing the name of Sydney, I do so with pleasure—that name has no pleasure for me; I never loved you, and at this moment I hate and despise you. Do you ask me wherefore?— Because you had wit enough to detect me in my intrigues. I shall leave your house tonight, and we meet no more. My future career is plainly marked out: I shall become an abandoned and licentious woman, yielding myself up unreservedly to the voluptuous promptings of my ardent soul. I part from you without regret, and without sorrow do I now bid you farewell forever.'

'Stay a moment,' said Frank, as she was about to leave the room—'I would not have you to be entirely destitute: I will fill you out a check for a sum of money sufficient to keep you from immediate want.'

He wrote out and signed a check for one thousand dollars, which he gave her, and then left her without saying another word. She received the donation with evident satisfaction, and immediately began to make her preparations for departure. Her maid, Susan, assisted her; and also informed her in what manner Frank had compelled her to assist in entrapping Nero into the house. Susan, herself being unobserved, had seen the African conveyed to the cellar, and locked in; this fact she also communicated to her mistress, who heard it with much pleasure, as she had anticipated that her paramour would meet with a worse fate than mere confinement.— She determined to effect his release, if possible, although she knew that some time must necessarily elapse before she could hope to accomplish that object.

When all was ready, Julia and her maid seated themselves in a hackney coach which had been procured, and were rapidly driven from that princely mansion, of which the guilty woman had so recently been the proud mistress, but from which she was now an outcast forever.

That night, Frank, in the solitude of his chamber, shed many bitter tears. He mourned over the fallen condition of that beautiful woman, whom, had she been worthy, he would have cherished as his wife, but who had proved herself not only undeserving of his affection, but depraved and wicked to an astonishing degree. Until the fatal moment when he was led to suspect her chastity, he had loved her devotedly and sincerely. How cruelly had he been deceived!

And that night, in the solitude and darkness of his cold and gloomy dungeon, Nero, the African, swore a terrible oath of vengeance upon the white man who had shut him up in that subterranean cell.

Within a week after the capture of the Dead Man and David the butler, those two villains were inmates of the State Prison at Sing Sing—the former to fulfil his original sentence of imprisonment for life, and the latter to undergo an imprisonment for five years, for his participation in the attempted robbery of Mr. Sydney.

Fred Archer, on escaping from the officer in the manner which we have described, made his way to the Dark Vaults, where he remained concealed for several days, not venturing to appear abroad. At the end of a week he began to grow impatient of the restraint, and, conceiving that no great danger would be incurred if he left his place of refuge in the darkness of night, he resolved to do so; moreover, he was destitute of money, and entertained some hope of being able to extort a sum from his unfortunate wife, whom he had driven to prostitution. Accordingly, at about eight o'clock in the evening, he left the Vaults by means of the secret outlet before alluded to and gaining the street, proceeded at a rapid pace towards the Bowery. In the breast of his coat he carried a huge Bowie knife, with which to defend himself in case any attempt should be made to arrest him.

That very day, Frank Sydney, mindful of his promise, had succeeded in obtaining a situation for Mrs. Archer, in the family of an old lady, an aunt of his, who required the attendance of a young woman as a companion and nurse, she being an invalid. In the afternoon, Mrs. Archer received a visit from the boy, Clinton, who came to announce to her the joyful intelligence of a good home having been secured for her; he then placed the following brief note from Frank in her hands:—

'Mrs. Archer,—Madame: I shall this evening call upon you, to confirm the words of my messenger. The unfortunate career which you have followed, is now nearly ended. Extortion and oppression shall triumph no longer.   F.S.'

It was about eight o'clock in the evening when Frank knocked at the door of the house in which Mrs. Archer resided, and he was admitted by the mercenary landlady who figured not very creditably upon a former occasion. She immediately recognized the young gentleman, who was dressed in the garments of a laborer; and very civilly informing him that the young lady was at home, requested him to walk upstairs to her room.

Our hero assumed a disguise upon that occasion, for this reason: he did not know but that the house was publicly regarded as a brothel; and he therefore did not wish to hazard his reputation by being recognized either while entering or leaving the place.

He ascended the stairs and knocked gently at the chamber, which was immediately opened by Mrs. Archer, who pressed his hand with all the warmth of a grateful heart, and placed a chair for him near the fire.—Glancing around the room, Frank saw that she had made every arrangement for her departure: bandboxes and trunks were in readiness for removal, and all her little effects were heaped together in one corner. She herself was dressed with considerable elegance and taste; a close fitting dress of rich silk displayed the fine proportions of her symmetrical form to advantage.

'I know not how to thank you, Mr. Sydney,' she said, seating herself—'for your generous interest in my welfare; but oh! believe me, I am grateful for your kindness.'

Frank assured her that he had derived much satisfaction from what services it had been in his power to render, tending to her benefit. He then related to her all that had occurred on the night of the attempted robbery at his house—how her husband had made his escape, and was probably lurking in the Dark Vaults.

'Then he is still at large,' said Mrs. Archer, shuddering—'and I am not yet safe.'

'Fear nothing,' said her benefactor—'he dare not intrude into the respectable and quiet asylum where you are to be placed. No harm can reach you there.'

'God grant it may be so!' fervently ejaculated the young lady; and at that instant some one was heard stealthily ascending the stairs. 'It is Frederick!' she whispered—'you had better conceal yourself, to avoid useless altercation.' Frank quickly secreted himself behind the curtains of the bed, his former hiding place: and in another moment Fred Archer entered the room, and closed the door with extreme caution. 'Maria,' he said, roughly—'I must have money from you to-night; the affair which I spoke to you about, when I was last here, failed most infernally. One of the very fellows who were to assist me in the job, proved to be the owner of the house which we were going to plunder. He had a trap prepared for us, and two of my pals were taken, while I escaped just by a miracle. I dare not go abroad in daylight, for fear of being arrested; and I need money—give it to me!'

'Frederick,' said his wife, mildly—'I have but a few dollars, and you are welcome to them. I leave this house to-night; I am going to live hereafter a life of honesty and virtue.'

'Indeed!' exclaimed Archer, now observing for the first time the preparations for removal—'and may I ask where the devil you're going?'

'I do not wish to tell you, Frederick,' replied the lady—'I shall have a good and comfortable home; let that suffice. I will always pray for your welfare; but we must part forever.'

'Ha! is it so?' he hissed from between his clenched teeth, while the hot blood of anger mantled on his face, and his eyes were lit up with the fires of demoniac passions—'do you think to desert me and cast me off forever?'—As he spoke, his right hand was thrust into the breast of his coat.

'We must part; my resolution is fixed,' she replied firmly. 'Your treatment of me—'

She paused in affright, for her husband had seized her violently by the arm; then he plucked the gleaming Bowie knife from its sheath, and ere she could scream out, the murderous blade was buried in her heart!

From his place of concealment behind the curtains of the bed, Frank saw the atrocious deed perpetrated. The villain had struck the fatal blow ere he could rush forth and stay his murderous arm. The poor victim sank upon the floor, the lifeblood streaming from her heart.—Ere the horrified witness of the crime could seize the murderer, he had fled from the house with a celerity which defied pursuit.

Frank, overwhelmed with grief at the tragic fate of that erring but unfortunate woman, raised her body in his arms and placed it upon a sofa. He then drew from her bosom the reeking blade of the assassin, and as he did so, the warm blood spouted afresh from the gaping wound, staining his hands and garments with gore.

He bent over the corpse, and contemplated the pallid features with profound sorrow. As he thus gazed mournfully at the face of the dead, holding in his hand the blood-stained knife, the chamber door opened, and the landlady entered the room.

On beholding the awful scene—the bleeding, lifeless form stretched upon the sofa, and the young man standing with a gory knife grasped in his hand—the landlady made the house resound with her shrieks and cries of 'Murder!'

The street door below was forced open and men with hurried footsteps ascended the stairs—in a moment more the chamber was filled with watchmen and citizens.

'Seize the murderer!' exclaimed the landlady, pointing towards Frank. Two watchmen instantly grasped him by the arms, and took from him the bloody knife.

Frank turned deadly pale—he was speechless—his tongue refused its office, for then the dreadful conviction forced itself upon him, that he was regarded as the murderer of that young woman. And how could he prove his innocence? The weight of circumstantial evidence against him was tremendous and might produce his conviction and condemnation to an ignominious death!

Several persons present recognized him as the rich and (until then) respectable Mr. Sydney; and then they whispered among themselves, with significant looks, that he was *disguised!*—clad in the mean garb of a common laborer!

Now it happened that among the gentlemen who knew him, were two of the flatterers who supped with him in the first chapter of this narrative—namely, Messrs. Narcissus Nobbs and Solomon Jenks: the former of whom it will be recollected, was enthusiastic in his praises of Frank, upon that occasion, while the latter boisterously professed for him the strongest attachment and friendship. The sincerity of these worthies will be manifested by the following brief conversation which took place between them, in whispers—

'A precious ugly scrape your friend has got himself into,' said Mr. Nobbs.

'*My* friend, indeed!' responded Mr. Jenks, indignantly—'curse the fellow, he's no friend of mine! I always suspected that he was a d——d scoundrel at heart!'

'I always *knew* so,' rejoiced Mr. Nobbs.

Oh, hollow-hearted Jenks and false-souled Nobbs! Ye fitly represent the great world, in its adulation of prosperous patrons—its forgetfulness of unfortunate friends!

Frank Sydney was handcuffed, placed in a coach and driven to the Tombs. Here he was immured in the strong cell which had long borne the title of the 'murderer's room.'

Fred Archer was safely concealed in the secret recesses of the Dark Vaults.

CHAPTER IX

The Masquerade Ball—the Curtain raised, and the Crimes of the Aristocracy exposed.

Mrs. Lucretia Franklin was a wealthy widow lady, who resided in an elegant mansion in Washington Place. In her younger days she had been a celebrated beauty; and though she was nearly forty at the period at which we write, she still continued to be an exceedingly attractive woman. Her features were handsome and expressive, and she possessed a figure remarkable for its voluptuous fullness.

Mrs. Franklin had two daughters: Josephine and Sophia. The former was eighteen years of age, and the latter sixteen. They were both beautiful girls, but vastly different in their style of beauty; Josephine being a superb brunette, with eyes and hair dark as night, while Sophia was a lovely blonde, with hair like a shower of sunbeams, and eyes of the azure hue of a summer sky.

In many other respects did the two beautiful sisters differ. The figure of Josephine was tall and majestic; her walk and gestures were imperative and commanding. Sophia's form was slight and sylph-like; her every movement was characterized by exquisite modesty and grace, and her voice had all the liquid melody of the Aeolean harp.

In mind and disposition they were as dissimilar as in their personal qualities. Josephine was passionate, fiery and haughty to an eminent degree; Sophia, on the contrary, possessed an angelic placidity of temper, and a sweetness of disposition which, like a fragrant flower, shed its grateful perfume upon the lowly and humble, as upon the wealthy and proud.

Mrs. Franklin's husband had died two years previous to the date of this narrative; he had been an enterprising and successful merchant, and at his death left a large fortune to his wife. Upon that fortune the lady and her two daughters lived in the enjoyment of every fashionable luxury which the metropolis could afford; and they moved in a sphere of society the most aristocratic and select.

Mr. Edgar Franklin, the lady's deceased husband, was a most excellent and exemplary man, a true philanthropist and a sincere Christian. He was scrupulously strict in his moral and religious notions—and resolutely set his face against the least departure from exact propriety, either in matters divine or temporal. The austerity of his opinions and habits was somewhat distasteful to his wife and eldest daughter, both of whom had a decided predilection for gay and fashionable amusements. Previous to his death, they were obliged to conform to his views and wishes; but after that event, they unreservedly participated in all the aristocratic pleasures of the 'upper ten': and their evenings were very frequently devoted to attendance at balls, parties, theatres, the opera, and other entertainments of the gay and wealthy inhabitants of the 'empire city.'

Mr. Franklin's death had occurred in a sudden and rather remarkable manner. He had retired to bed in his usual good health, and in the morning was found dead by the servant who went to call him.

The body was reclining upon one side in a natural position, and there was nothing in its appearance to indicate either a violent or painful death. Disease of the heart was ascribed as the cause of his sudden demise; and his remains were deposited in the family tomb in St. Paul's churchyard. Many were the tears shed at the funeral of that good man; —for his unaffected piety and universal benevolence had endeared him to a large circle of friends.

The grief of the bereaved widow and eldest daughter was manifested by loud lamentations and passionate floods of tears; but the sorrow of the gentle Sophia, though less violent, was none the less heart-felt and sincere.

There was little sympathy between the haughty, imperious Josephine and her mild, unobtrusive sister. Their natures were too dissimilar to admit of it; and yet Sophia loved the other, and at the same time feared her—she was so cold, so distant, so formal, so reserved. Josephine, on her part, viewed her sister as a mere child— not absolutely as an inferior, but as one unfitted by nature and disposition to be her companion and friend. Her treatment of Sophia was therefore marked by an air and tone of patronizing condescension, rather than by a tender, sisterly affection.

Mrs. Franklin loved both her daughters, but her preference manifestly inclined to Josephine, whose tastes were in exact accordance with her own. Sophia had little or no inclination for the excitement and tumult of fashionable pleasures; and therefore she was left much to herself, alone and dependent upon her own resources to beguile her time, while her mother and sister were abroad in the giddy whirl of patrician dissipation.

But upon the Sabbath, no family were more regular in their attendance at church than the Franklins. Punctually every Sunday morning, the mother and daughter would alight from their splendid carriage opposite St. Paul's church, and seating themselves in their luxuriously cushioned and furnished pew, listen to the brilliant eloquence of Dr. Sinclair, with profound attention. Then, when the pealing organ and the swelling anthem filled the vast dome with majestic harmony, the superb voice of Josephine Franklin would soar far above the rolling flood of melody, and her magnificent charms would become the cynosure of all eyes. Few noticed the fair young creature at her side, her golden hair parted simply over her pure brow, and her mild blue eyes cast modestly upon the page of the hymn-book before her.

Having now introduced Mrs. Lucretia Franklin and her two daughters to the reader, we shall proceed at once to bring them forward as active participants in the events of our history.

It was about three o'clock in the afternoon; in a sumptuous chamber of Franklin House (for by that high-sounding title was the residence of the wealthy widow known,) two ladies were engaged in the absorbing mysteries of a singular toilet.

One of these ladies was just issuing from a bath. Although not young, she was very handsome; and her partially denuded form exhibited all the matured fullness of a ripened womanhood. This lady was Mrs. Lucretia Franklin.

Her companion was her daughter Josephine. This beautiful creature was standing behind her mother; she had just drawn on a pair of broadcloth pants, and was in an attitude of graceful and charming perplexity, unaccustomed as she was to that article of dress. The undergarment she wore had slipped down from her shoulders, revealing voluptuous beauties which the envious fashion of ladies' ordinary attire, usually conceals.

Upon the carpet were a pair of elegant French boots and a cap, evidently designed for Miss Josephine. Various articles of decoration and costume were scattered about: upon a dressing-table (whereon stood a superb mirror,) were the usual luxurious trifles which appertain to a fashionable toilet—perfumes, cosmetics, &c.—and in one corner stood a magnificent bed.

This was the chamber of Josephine; that young lady and her mother were arraying themselves for a grand fancy and masquerade ball to be given that night, at the princely mansion of a *millionaire.*

By listening to their conversation, we shall probably obtain a good insight into their true characters.

'I am thinking, mamma,' said Josephine—'that I might have selected a better costume for this occasion, than these boys' clothes. I shall secure no admirers.'

'Silly girl,' responded her mother—'don't you know that the men will all run distracted after a pretty woman in male attire? Besides, such a costume will display your shape so admirably.'

'Ah, that is true,' remarked the beautiful girl, smiling so as to display her brilliant teeth; and removing her feminine garment, she stood before the mirror to admire her own distracting and voluptuous loveliness.

'And this costume of an Oriental Queen—do you think it will become me, my love,' asked her mother.

'Admirably,' replied Josephine—'it is exactly suitable to your figure. Ah, mamma, your days of conquest are not over yet.'

'And yours have just begun, my dear. Yours is a glorious destiny, Josephine; beautiful and rich, you can select a husband from among the handsomest and most desirable young gentlemen in the city. But you must profit by *my* experience: do not be in haste to unite yourself in marriage to a man who, when he becomes your husband, will restrict you in the enjoyment of those voluptuous pleasures in which you now take such delight. *I* 'married in haste and repented at leisure;' after my union with your father, I found him to be a cold formalist and canting religionist, continually boring me with his lectures on the sins and folly of 'fashionable dissipation,' as he termed the elegant amusements suitable to our wealth and rank and discoursing upon the pleasures of the domestic circle, and such humbugs. All this was exceedingly irksome to me, accustomed as I was to one unvarying round of excitement; but your father was as firm as he was puritanical—and obstinately interposed his authority as a husband, to prevent my indulging in my favorite entertainments. This state of affairs continued, my dear, until you attained the age of sixteen, when you began to feel a distaste for the insipidity of a domestic life, and longed for a change.—Our positions were then precisely similar: we both were debarred from the delights of gay society, for which we so ardently longed. One obstacle, and one only, lay in our way; that obstacle was your father—my husband. We were both sensible that we never could enjoy ourselves in our own way, while *he lived*; his death alone would release us from the condition of thralldom in which we were placed—but as his constitution was robust and his health invariably good, the agreeable prospect of his death was very remote—and we might have continued all our lives under the despotic rules of his stern morality, had we not rid ourselves of him by—'

'For Heaven's sake, mother,' said Josephine, hastily—'don't allude to *that!*'

'And why not,' asked the mother, calmly. 'You surely do not regret the act which removed our inexorable jailer, and opened to us such flowery avenues of pleasure? Ah, Josephine, the deed was admirably planned and skillfully executed. No one suspects—'

'Once more, mother, I entreat you to make no further allusion to that subject; it is disagreeable—painful to me,' interrupted the daughter, impatiently. 'Besides, sometimes the walls have ears.'

'Well, well, child—I will say no more about it. Let us now dress.'

Josephine, having arranged her clustering hair in a style as masculine as possible, proceeded to invest herself in the boyish habiliments which she had provided. First, she drew on over her luscious charms, a delicately embroidered shirt, of snowy whiteness, and then put on a splendid cravat, in the tasteful fold of which glittered a magnificent diamond. A superb Parisian waistcoat of figured satin was then closely laced over her rounded and swelling bust; a jacket of fine broadcloth, decorated with gold naval buttons and a little cap, similarly adorned, completed her costume. The character she was supposed to represent was that of 'the Royal Middy;' and her appearance was singularly captivating in that unique and splendid dress.

Mrs. Franklin, when attired as the Sultana or Oriental Queen, looked truly regal—the rich and glittering Eastern robes well became her voluptuous style of beauty.

The labor of the toilet being completed, the ladies found that it still lacked an hour or so of the time appointed for them to set out; and while they partook of a slight but elegant repast, they amused themselves and beguiled the time by lively and entertaining chat.

'These masquerade balls are delightful affairs; one can enjoy an intrigue with so much safety, beneath the concealing mask,' remarked Mrs. Franklin.

'And yet last Sabbath, you recollect, Dr. Sinclair denounced masquerades as one of Satan's most dangerous devices for the destruction of souls,' said Josephine.

'True—so he did,' assented her mother—'but he need never know that we attend them.'

'The Doctor is very strict—yet he is very fascinating,' rejoined her daughter;— 'do you know, mamma, that I am desperately enamored of him? I would give the world could I entice him into an intrigue with me.' And as she spoke, her bosom heaved with voluptuous sensations.

'Naughty girl,' said Mrs. Franklin, smiling complacently—'I cannot blame you for conceiving a passion for our handsome young pastor. To confess the truth, I myself view him with high admiration, not only as a talented preacher, but also as one who would make a most delightful lover.'

'Delightful indeed!' sighed Josephine—'but then he is so pure, so strict, so truly and devotedly religious, that it would be useless to try to tempt him by any advances; I should only compromise myself thereby.'

'Well, my dear,' remarked Mrs. Franklin, 'there are other handsome young men in the world, besides our pastor—many who would grovel at your feet to enjoy your favors. By the way, who is your *favored one* at present?'

'Oh, a young fellow to whom I took a fancy the other day,' replied Josephine. 'he is a clerk, or something of the kind—respectable and educated, but poor. I encountered him in the street—liked his fresh, robust appearance—dropped my glove—smiled when he picked it up and handed it to me—encouraged him to walk me home—invited him in, and made him, as well as myself, extremely happy by my kindness. I permitted him to call frequently, but of course I soon grew tired of him—the affair lacked zeal, romance, piquancy; so, this morning when he visited me, I suffered him to take a last kiss, and dismissed him forever, with a twenty-dollar bill and an intimation that we were in future entire strangers. Poor fellow! he shed tears—but I only laughed, and rang the bell for the servant to show him out. Now, mamma, you must be equally communicative with me, and tell me who has the good fortune to be the recipient of *your* favors at present.'

'My dear Josey,' said Mrs. Franklin—'I must really decline according you the required information; you will only laugh at my folly.'

'By no means, mamma,' rejoined the young lady—'we have both at times been strangely eccentric in our tastes, and must not ridicule each other's preferences, however singular.'

'Well then, you must know that my lover is a very pretty youth of about fifteen, who reciprocates my passion with boyish ardor. You will acknowledge that to a woman of my age, such an amour must be delicious and unique. For a few days past I have not seen the youthful Adonis, who, by the bye, bears the very romantic name of Clinton Romaine. I first met him under very unusual and singular circumstances.'

'Pray, how was that, mamma?' asked Josephine.

'You shall hear,' replied her mother. 'The occurrence which I am about to relate took place a month ago. I was awakened one night from a sound sleep by a noise in my chamber, and starting up in affright, I beheld by the light of a lamp which was burning near the bed, a boy in the act of forcing open my *escritoire*, with a small instrument which caused the noise. I was about to scream for assistance, when the young rogue, perceiving that he was discovered, advanced to the bed, and quieted me by the assurance that he intended me no personal harm, and implored me to suffer him to depart without molestation, promising never to repeat his nocturnal visit. He then placed upon the table my watch, purse, a casket of jewels, which he had secured about his person—and, in answer to my inquiry as to how he had obtained an entrance into my chamber he informed me that he had climbed into the window by means of a ladder which he had found in the garden. While he was speaking, I regarded him attentively, and was struck with his boyish beauty; for the excitement of the adventure and the danger of his position had caused a flush upon his cheeks and a sparkle in his eyes, which captivated me. I found it impossible to resist the voluptuous feelings which began to steal over me—and I smiled tenderly upon the handsome youth; he, merely supposing this smile to be an indication of my having forgiven him, thanked me and was about to depart in the same manner in which he came, when I intimated to him my willingness to extend a much greater kindness than my pardon. In short, his offence was punished only by sweet imprisonment in my arms; and delighted with his precocity, I blessed the lucky chance which had so unexpectedly furnished me with a youthful and handsome lover. Ere daylight he departed; and has since then frequently visited me, always gaining access to my chamber by means of the gardener's ladder. To my regret he has of late discontinued his visits, and I know not what has become of my youthful gallant. And now my dear, you have heard the whole story.'

'Very interesting and romantic,' remarked Josephine, and consulting her gold watch, she announced that the hour was come for them to go to the masquerade.

The mother and daughter enveloped themselves in ample cloaks, and descending the stairs, took their seats in the carriage which was in readiness at the door. A quarter of an hour's drive brought them to the superb mansion wherein the entertainment was to be given. Alighting from the carriage, they were conducted by an obsequious attendant to a small ante-room, where they deposited their cloaks, and adjusted over their faces the sort of half-mask used on such occasions. A beautiful boy, dressed as a page, then led the way up a broad marble stair case, and throwing open a door, they were ushered into a scene of such magnificence, that for a moment they stood bewildered and amazed, tho' perfectly accustomed to all the splendors of fashionable life.

A fine-looking elderly man, without a mask and in plain clothes, advanced towards the mother and daughter; this gentleman was Mr. Philip Livingston, the host—a bachelor of fifty, reputed to be worth two millions of dollars. The page who had waited upon the two ladies, *whispered* their names in Mr. Livingston's ear; and after the usual compliments, he bowed, and they mingled with the glittering crowds which thronged the rooms.

We feel almost inadequate to the task of describing the wonders of that gorgeous festival; yet will make the attempt, for without it, our work would be incomplete.

Livingston House was an edifice of vast dimensions, built in the sombre but grand Gothic style of architecture. Extensive apartments communicated with each other by means of massive folding doors, which were now thrown open, and the eye wandered through a long vista of brilliantly lighted rooms, the extent of which seemed increased ten-fold by the multitude of immense mirrors placed on every side. Art, science and taste had combined to produce an effect the most grand and imposing; rare and costly paintings, exquisite statuary, gorgeous gildings, were there, in rich profusion. But the most magnificent feature of Livingston House was its *conservatory*, which was probably the finest in the country, second only in beauty to the famous conservatory of the Duke of Devonshire in England. A brief description of this gem of Livingston House may prove interesting to the reader.

Leaving the hall through an arch tastefully decorated with flowers and ever-greens, the visitor descended a flight of marble steps, and entered the conservatory, which occupied an extensive area of ground, and was entirely roofed with glass. Though the season was winter and the weather intensely cold, a delightful warmth pervaded the place, produced by invisible pipes of heated water. The atmosphere was as mild and genial as a summer's eve; and the illusion was rendered still more complete by a large lamp, suspended high above, and shaped like a full moon; this lamp, being provided with a peculiar kind of glass, shed a mild, subdued lustre around, producing the beautiful effect of a moonlit eve! On every side rare exotics and choice plants exhaled a delicious perfume; tropic fruits grew from the carefully nurtured soil;—orange, pomegranate, citron, &c. Gravelled walks led through rich shrubbery, darkened by overhanging foliage. Mossy paths, of charming intricacy, invited the wanderer to explore their mysterious windings. At every turn a marble statue, life-sized, met the eye: here the sylvan god Pan, with rustic pipes in hand—here the huntress Diana, with drawn bow—here the amorous god Cupid, upon a beautiful pedestal on which was sculptured these lines, said to have been once written by Voltaire under a statue of the heathen divinity:

'Whoe'er thou art, thy master see;—
He *was*, or *is*, or *is to be.*'

In the centre of this miniature Paradise was an artificial cascade, which fell over a large rock into a lake o'er whose glassy waters several swans with snow white plumage were gliding; and on the brink of this crystal expanse, romantic grottos and classic temples formed convenient retreats for the weary dancers from the crowded halls. In short, this magnificent conservatory was furnished with every beautiful rarity which the proprietor's immense wealth could procure, and every classic and graceful adornment which his refined and superior taste could suggest.

Mrs. Franklin and her daughter, who had come on purpose to engage in amorous intrigues, agreed to separate, and accordingly they parted, the mother remaining in the ball room, while Josephine resolved to seek for adventures amid the mysterious shades of the conservatory.

Over five hundred persons had now assembled in the halls appropriated to dancing; and these were arrayed in every variety of fancy and picturesque costume possible to be conceived. The grave Turk, the stately Spanish cavalier, the Italian bandit and the Grecian corsair, mingled together without reserve;—and the fairer portion of creation was represented by fairies, nuns, queens, peasant girls and goddesses.

Mrs. Franklin soon observed that she was followed by a person in the dress of a Savoyard; he was closely masked, and his figure was slight and youthful. Determined to give him an opportunity to address her, the lady strolled to a remote corner of the hall, whither she was followed by the young Savoyard, who after some apparent hesitation, said to her—

'Fair Sultana, pardon my presumption, but methinks I have seen that queenly form before.'

'Ah, that voice!' exclaimed the delighted lady—'thou art my little lover, Clinton Romaine.'

'It is indeed so,' said the boy, gallantly kissing her hand. The lady surveyed him with wanton eye.

'Naughty truant!' she murmured, drawing him towards her—'why have you absented yourself from me so long? Do you no longer desire my favors?'

'Dear madam,' replied Clinton—'I am never so happy as when in your arms; but I have recently entered the service of a good, kind gentleman, who has been my benefactor; and my time is devoted to him.'

'Come with me,' said the lady, 'to a private room, for I wish to converse with you without being observed.'

She led the way to a small anteroom, and having carefully fastened the door to prevent intrusion, clasped the young Savoyard in her arms.

*　*　*　*　*

Half an hour afterwards, the boy and his aristocratic mistress issued from the ante-room, and parted. Clinton wandered thro' the halls, and descending into the conservatory, entered a temple which stood upon the margin of the little lake, threw himself upon a luxurious ottoman, and abandoned himself to his reflections.

'How ungrateful I am,' he said half aloud—'to engage in an intrigue with that wicked, licentious woman, while my poor master, Mr. Sydney, is languishing in a prison cell, charged with the dreadful crime of murder! And yet I know he is innocent. I remember carrying his note to Mrs. Archer on the fatal day; I knew not its contents, but I recollect the words which he instructed me to say to her—they were words of friendship, conveying to her an assurance that he had procured for her a situation with his aunt. Surely, after sending such a message, he would not go and murder her! And his aunt can testify that such an arrangement was made, in reference to Mrs. Archer. Oh, that I could obtain admission to the cell of my poor master, to try to comfort him, to whom I owe so much! But alas! the keepers will not admit me; they remember that I was once a thief, and drive me from the prison door with curses.

'I am persuaded in my own mind,' continued Clinton, following the course of his reflections—'that Fred Archer is the murderer of that woman. I know he secretes himself in the Dark Vaults, but I dare not venture there to seek him, for my agency in the arrest of the Dead Man is known to the 'Knights of the Round Table,' and were I to fall in their power, they would assuredly kill me. Now, what has brought me here to-night?—Not a desire for pleasure; but a faint hope of encountering amid the masked visitors, the villain Archer; for I know that he, as well as the other desperadoes in the Vaults, frequently attends masquerade balls, in disguise, on account of the facilities afforded for robbery and other crimes. Oh that I might meet him here to-night—I would boldly accuse him of the murder, and have him taken into custody, trusting to chance for the proofs of his guilt, and the innocence of my master.'

It may be well here to observe that it was comparatively easy for such characters as Archer and his companions to gain admission to such a masquerade ball as we are describing. In the bustle and confusion of receiving such a large company, they found but little difficulty in slipping in, unnoticed and unsuspected.

'And that horrible Dead Man,' continued Clinton—'thank God, *he* is now safe within the strong walls of the State Prison, there to pass the remainder of his earthly existence. How awfully he glared upon me, on the night of his capture! Oh, if he were at large, my life would be in continued danger; I should not sleep at night, for terror; I should tremble lest his corpse-like face should appear at my bedside, and his bony fingers grapple me by the throat! Yes, thank God—he is deprived of the power to injure me; I am safe from his fiend-like malice.'

At this moment, Clinton heard foot-steps approaching, and presently some one said—

'Let us enter this little temple, where we can talk without being overheard.'

The blood rushed swiftly through Clinton's veins, and his heart beat violently; for these words were spoken in the well-known voice of Fred Archer! With great presence of mind he instantly crept beneath the ottoman on which he had been lying; and the next moment two persons entered the temple, and seated themselves directly above him.

'It was, as you say,' remarked Archer to his companion in a low tone—'a most extraordinary piece of good luck for me that Sydney was taken for that murder which I committed; suspicions are diverted from me, and he will swing for it, that's certain. I'm safe in regard to that business.'

'And yet, I almost regret, Fred,' said the other, speaking in an almost inaudible whisper—'that Sydney is in the grip of the Philistines; my vengeance upon him would have been more terrible than a thousand deaths by hanging. Well, since it is so, let him swing, and be d——d to him!'

A long conversation here followed, but the two men spoke in such a low tone, that Clinton could only hear a word now and then. He was, however, certain as to the identity of Fred Archer; and he determined not to lose sight of that ruffian without endeavoring to have him taken into custody.

At length the two men arose and quitted the temple, followed at a safe distance by the boy.

At the bottom of the marble steps which led to the halls above, Fred Archer and his companion paused for a few moments, and conversed in whispers; then the two parted, the former ascending the steps, while the latter turned and advanced slowly towards Clinton.

The boy instantly started in pursuit of Archer; but as he was about to pass the person who had just quitted the company of that villain, his progress was arrested by a strong arm, and a voice whispered in his ear—'Ah, *Kinchen*, well met!—come with me!'

Clinton attempted to shake off the stranger's grasp—but he was no match for his adversary, who dragged him back into the little temple before mentioned, and regarded him with a terrible look.

'Who are you—and what means this treatment of me?' demanded the boy, trembling with affright.

The mysterious unknown replied not by words—but slowly raised the mask from his face. Clinton's blood ran cold with horror; for, by the dim and uncertain light, he beheld the ghastly, awful features of THE DEAD MAN!

'Said I not truly that no prison could hold me?—vain are all stone walls and iron chains, for I can burst them asunder at will! I had hoped to avenge myself on that accursed Sydney, in a terrible appalling manner; but the law has become the avenger—he will die upon the gallows, and I am content. Ha, ha, ha! how he will writhe, and choke while I shall be at liberty, to read the account of his execution in the papers, and gloat over the description of his dying agonies! But I have an account to settle with *you*, Kinchen; you recollect how you hurled the wine-bottle at my head, as I was about to stab Sydney on the night of my capture—thereby preventing me from securing a speedy and deadly revenge at that time? Now, what punishment do you deserve for that damnable piece of treachery to an old comrade?'

Thus spoke the terrible Dead Man, as he glared menacingly upon the affrighted and trembling Clinton, whose fears deprived him of all power of utterance.

'Sydney will hang like a dog,' continued the hideous miscreant, the words hissing from between his clenched teeth—'My revenge in *that* quarter shall be consummated, while you, d——d young villain that you are, shall—'

'Sydney shall *not* suffer such a fate, monster!' exclaimed Clinton, his indignation getting the better of his fears, as he looked the villain boldly in the face—'there are two witnesses, whose testimony can and will prove his innocence.'

'And who may those two witnesses be?' demanded the Dead Man scornfully.

'I am one—and Sydney's aunt, Mrs. Stevens, who resides at No.—Grand Street, is the other,' replied Clinton.

'And what can *you* testify to in Sydney's favor?' asked the other in a milder tone.

'I can swear that Mr. Sydney sent me with a note to the lady who was murdered, and desired me to inform her that he had procured a good situation for her with his aunt—thus plainly showing the friendly nature of his feelings and intentions towards her,' replied Clinton.

'And this aunt—what will be the nature of *her* testimony?' inquired the Dead Man, with assumed indifference.

'Mrs. Stevens can testify that the nephew Mr. Sydney strongly recommended her to receive the poor unfortunate lady into her service—and that arrangements were made to that effect,' answered the boy, unsuspiciously.

The Dead Man seemed for a moment lost in deep thought. 'So it appears that there are two witnesses whose testimony *might* tend to the acquittal of Sydney,' he thought to himself. 'Those two witnesses must be put out of the way; one of them is now in my power—*he* is done for; I am acquainted with the name and residence of the other, and by G——d, *she* shall be done for, too!—*Kinchen*,' he said aloud, turning savagely to the boy—'You must accompany me to the Dark Vaults.'

'Never,' exclaimed Clinton, resolutely—'rather will I die here. If you attempt to carry me forcibly with you, I will struggle and resist—I will proclaim to the guests in the ball room your dread character and name; the mask will be torn from your face, and you will be dragged back to prison, from whence you escaped.'

For the second time did the Dead Man pause, and reflect profoundly. He thought somewhat in this wise: —'There is no possible means of egress from this place, except thro' the ball room, which is crowded with guests. True, I might bind and gag the *Kinchen*, but his struggles would be sure to attract attention—and my discovery and capture would be the result. It is evident, therefore, that I cannot carry him forcibly hence, with safety to myself. Shall I *murder* him? No, damn it, 'tis hardly worth my while to do that—and somehow or other, these murders almost invariably lead to detection. The devil himself couldn't save my neck if I were to be hauled up on another murder—yet, by hell, I must risk it in reference to that Mrs. Stevens, whose testimony would be apt to save her accursed nephew, Sydney, from the gallows. Yes, I must slit the old lady's windpipe; but the *Kinchen*— what the devil shall I do to keep *him* from blabbing, since I can't make up my mind to kill him?'

Suddenly, a horrible thought flashed through the villain's mind.

'*Kinchen*,' he whispered, with a fiend-like laugh—'I have thought of a plan by which to *silence your tongue forever.*'

He drew a huge clasp-knife from his pocket. Ere Clinton could cry out for assistance, the monster grasped him by the throat with his vice-like fingers—the poor boy's tongue protruded from his mouth—and oh, horrible! the incarnate devil, suddenly loosening his hold on the throat, quick as lightning caught hold of the tongue, and forcibly drew it out to its utmost tension—then, with one rapid stroke of his sharp knife, he *cut it off*, and threw it from him with a howl of savage satisfaction. 'Now, d——n you,' exclaimed the Dead Man—'see if you can testify in court!'

The victim sank upon the floor, weltering in his blood, while the barbarian who had perpetrated the monstrous outrage, fled from the conservatory, passed through the ball room and proceeded with rapid strides towards the residence of Mrs. Stevens, Sydney's aunt, in Grand Street, having first put on the mask which he wore to conceal the repulsive aspect of his countenance. He found the house without difficulty, for he remembered the number which poor Clinton had given him; and ascending the steps, he knocked boldly at the door.

The summons was speedily answered by a servant who ushered the Dead Man into a parlor, saying that her mistress would be down directly. In a few moments the door opened and Mrs. Stevens entered the room.

This lady was a widow, somewhat advanced in years, and in affluent circumstances. Her countenance was the index of a benevolent and excellent heart; and in truth she was a most estimable woman.

'Madam,' said the Dead Man—'I have called upon you at the request of your unfortunate nephew, Francis Sydney.'

'Oh, sir,' exclaimed the old lady, shedding tears—'how is the poor young man—and how does he bear his cruel and unjust punishment?—for unjust it is, as he is innocent of the dreadful crime imputed to him. Alas! the very day the poor lady was murdered, he called and entreated me to take her into my service, to which I readily consented. Oh, he is innocent, I am sure.'

'Mrs. Stevens,' said the villain—'I have something of a most important nature to communicate, relative to your nephew; are we certain of no interruption here? —for my intelligence must be delivered in strict privacy.'

'We are alone in this house,' replied the unsuspecting lady. 'The servant who admitted you has gone out on a short errand, and you need fear no interruption.'

'Then, madam, I have to inform you that—'

While uttering these words, the Dead Man advanced towards Mrs. Stevens, who stood in the centre of the apartment; he assumed an air of profound mystery, and she, supposing that he was about to whisper in her ear, inclined her heard toward him. That movement was her last on earth; in another instant she was prostate upon the carpet, her throat encircled by the fingers of the ghastly monster; her countenance became suffused with a dark purple—blood gushed from her mouth, eyes and nostrils—and in a few minutes all was over!

The murderer arose from his appalling work, and his loathsome face assumed, beneath his mask, an expression of demoniac satisfaction.

' 'Tis done!' he muttered—'damn the old fool, she thought I was a *friend* of her accursed nephew's. But I must leave the corpse in such a situation that it may be supposed the old woman committed suicide.'

He tore off the large shawl which the poor lady had worn, and fastened it about her neck; then he hung the body upon the parlor door, and placed an overturned chair near its feet, to lead to the supposition that she had stood upon the chair while adjusting the shawl about her neck and then overturned it in giving the fatal spring. This arrangement the Dead Man effected with the utmost rapidity and then forcing open a bureau which stood in the parlor, he took from the drawer various articles of value, jewelry, &c., and a pocket-book containing a considerable sum of money—forgetting, in his blind stupidity, that the circumstances of a robbery having taken place, would destroy the impression that the unfortunate old lady had come to her death voluntarily by her own hands.

The murderer then fled from the house and that night he and Archer, in the mysterious depths of the Dark Vaults, celebrated their bloody exploits by mad orgies, horrid blasphemy, and demoniac laughter.

We left Clinton weltering in his blood upon the floor of the temple in the

conservatory. The poor mangled youth was discovered in that deplorable situation
shortly after the perpetration of the abominable outrage which had deprived him
of the blessed gift of speech forever. He was conveyed to the residence of Dr.
Schultz, a medical gentleman of eminent skill, who stopped the effusion of blood,
and pronounced his eventual recovery certain. But oh! who can imagine the
feelings of the unfortunate boy, when returning consciousness brought with it the
appalling conviction that the faculty of expressing his thoughts in words was gone
forever, and henceforward he was hopelessly *dumb*! By great exertion he scrawled
upon a piece of paper his name and residence; a carriage was procured, and he was
soon beneath the roof of his master, Mr. Sydney, under the kind care of honest
Dennis and the benevolent housekeeper.

And Sydney—alas for him! Immured in that awful sepulchre of crime, the
Tombs—charged with the deed of murder, and adjudged guilty by public opinion—deserted by those whom he had regarded as his friends, suffering from
confinement in a noisome cell, and dreading the ignominy of a trial and the horrors
of a public execution—his fair fame blasted forever by the taint of crime—what
wonder that he, so young, so rich, so gifted with every qualification to enjoy life,
should begin to doubt the justice of divine dispensation, and, loathing existence,
pray for death to terminate his state of suspense and misery!

But we must not lose sight of Josephine Franklin; her adventures at the
masquerade hall were of too amorous and exciting a nature to be passed lightly over,
in this mirror of the fashions, follies and crimes of city life.— Our next chapter will
duly record the particulars of the fair lady's romantic intrigues on that brilliant and
memorable occasion.

CHAPTER X

The Amours of Josephine — The Spanish Ambassador, and the Ecclesiastical Lover.

Josephine, dressed as the 'Royal Middy,' entered the conservatory, and strolled
leisurely along a gravelled walk which led to a little grotto composed of rare
minerals and shells. Entering this picturesque retreat, she placed herself upon a
seat exquisitely sculptured from marble, and listened to the beautiful strains of
music which proceeded from the ball room.

While thus abandoning herself to the voluptuous feelings of the moment, she
observed that a tall, finely formed person in the costume of a Spanish cavalier,
passed the grotto several times, each time gazing at her with evident admiration.
He was masked, but Josephine had removed her mask, and her superb countenance
was fully revealed. The cavalier had followed her from the ball-room, but she did
not perceive him until he passed the grotto.

'I have secured an admirer already,' she said to herself, as a smile of satisfaction parted her rosy lips. 'I must encourage him, and perhaps he may prove to be a desirable conquest.'

The cavalier saw her smile and, encouraged by that token of her complaisance, paused before the grotto, and addressed her in a slightly foreign accent:—

'Fair lady, will you suffer me to repose myself for a while in this fairy-like retreat?'

'I shall play off a little prank upon this stranger,' thought Josephine to herself— 'it will serve to amuse me.' And then she burst into a merry laugh, as she replied—

'I have no objection in the world, sir, to your sharing this grotto with me; but really, you make a great mistake—you suppose me to be a lady; but I'm no more a lady than you are, don't you see that I'm a *boy*?'

'Indeed!—a *boy*!' Exclaimed the stranger, surveying Josephine with great interest. 'By heaven, I took you for a female; and though you are a boy, I will say that you are an extremely pretty one.'

He entered into the grotto, and seated himself at her side. Taking her hand, he said—

'This hand is wonderfully fair and soft for a boy's. Confess, now—are you not deceiving me?'

'Why should I deceive you?' asked Josephine—'if my hand is fair and soft, it is because I have been brought up as a gentleman, and it has never become soiled or hardened by labor.'

'And yet,' rejoined the stranger, passing his hand over the swelling outlines of her bosom, which no disguise could entirely conceal—'there seems to me to be something feminine in these pretty proportions.'

'You doubtless think so,' replied Josephine, removing his hand—'but you greatly err. The fact is, my appearance is naturally very effeminate, and sometimes it is my whim to encourage the belief that I am a female. I came here to-night, resolved to produce that impression; and you see with what a successful result—you yourself imagined me to be a lady dressed in male attire, but again I assure you that you never were more mistaken in your life. The fullness of my bosom is accounted for, when I inform you that my vest is very skillfully *padded*. So now I hope you will be no longer skeptical in regard to my true sex.'

'I no longer doubt you, my dear boy,' said the stranger, gazing at Josephine with increased admiration. 'Were you a lady, you would be beautiful, but as a boy you are doubly charming. Be not surprised when I assure you that you please me ten times—aye, ten thousand times more, as a boy, than as a woman. By heaven, I must kiss those ripe lips!'

'Kiss *me*!' responded Josephine, laughing—'come, sire, this is too good—you must be joking.'

'No, beautiful boy, I am serious,' exclaimed the stranger, vehemently—'you may pronounce my passion strange, unaccountable, and absurd, if you will—but 'tis none the less violent or sincere. I am a native of Spain, a country whose ardent souls confine not their affections to the fairest portion of the human race alone, but—'

'What mean you?' demanded Josephine, in astonishment. The stranger whispered a few words in her ear, and she drew back in horror and disgust.

'Nay, hear me,' exclaimed the Spaniard, passionately—'it is no low-born or vulgar person who solicits this favor; for know,' he continued, removing his mask—'that I am Don Jose Velasquez, ambassador to this country from the court of Spain; and however high my rank, I kneel at your feet and—'

'Say no more, sir,' said Josephine, interrupting him, and rising as she spoke—'it is time that you should know that your first supposition in reference to me was correct. I am a woman. I did but pretend, in accordance with a suddenly conceived notion, to deceive you for a while, but that deception has developed an iniquity in the human character, the existence of which I have heard before, but never fully believed till today. Your unnatural iniquity inspires me with abhorrence; leave me instantly and attempt not to follow me, or I shall expose you to the guests, in which case *His Excellency* Don Jose Velasquez, ambassador to this country from the court of Spain, would become an object of derision and contempt.'

The Spaniard muttered a threat of vengeance and strode hastily away. Josephine put on her mask, and leaving the grotto, was about to return to the ball-room, when a gentleman, plainly but richly attired in black velvet, and closely masked, thus accosted her in a respectful tone—

'Lady—for your graceful figure and gait betray you, notwithstanding your boyish disguise—suffer me to depart so far from the formality of fashionable etiquette as to entreat your acceptance of me as your *chaperon* through this beautiful place.'

This gentleman's speech was distinguished by a voice uncommonly melodious, and an accent peculiarly refined; he was evidently a person of education and respectable social position. The tones of his voice struck Josephine as being familiar to her; yet she could not divine who he was, and concluded that there only existed an accidental resemblance between his voice and that of some one of her friends. His manner being so frank, and at the same time so gentleman-like and courteous, that she replied without hesitation—

'I thank you, sir—I will avail myself of your kindness.' She took his proffered arm, and they began slowly to promenade the principal avenue of the conservatory, engaged at first in that polite and desultory discourse which might be supposed to arise between a lady and gentleman who meet under such circumstances.

At length, becoming fatigued, they entered a pretty little arbor quite remote from observation, and seated themselves upon a moss-covered trunk. After a few commonplace observations, the gentleman suddenly addressed Josephine in a start of ardent passion.

'Lady,' he exclaimed, taking her hand and pressing it tenderly, 'pardon my rudeness; but I am overcome by feelings which I never before experienced. Although your face is concealed by your mask, I know you are beautiful—the rich luxuriance of your raven hair, and the exquisite proportions of this fair hand, are proofs of the angelic loveliness of your countenance. Am I presumptuous and bold—does my language give you offence?—if so, I will tear myself from your side, though it will rend my heart with anguish to do so. You do not speak—you are offended with me; farewell, then—'

'Stay,' murmured Josephine—'I am not offended, sire—far from it; you are courteous and gallant, and why should I be displeased?' The gentleman kissed her hand with rapture.

'Oh,' said he, in a low tone—'I am entranced by your kindness. You will be surprised when I assure you that I am but a novice in the way of love; and yet I most solemnly declare that never before have I pressed woman's hand with passion—never before has my heart beat with the tumult of amorous inclination—never before have I clasped woman's lovely form as I now clasp yours.' And he encircled the yielding form of Josephine with his arms.

'Why have you been such a novice in the delights of love?' she asked, permitting him to clasp her passionately to his breast.

'Dear lady,' he replied—'my position in life is one that precludes me in a great measure from the enjoyment of sensual indulgences; and I have heretofore imagined myself impervious to the attacks of Venus; but ah! you have conquered me. My leisure moments have been devoted to study and contemplation; I ventured here to-night to be a spectator of the joys of others, not designing to participate in those joys myself. The graceful voluptuousness of your form, developed by this boyish costume, fired my soul with new and strange sensations, which, so help me heaven! I never experienced before. Ah, I would give half of my existence to be allowed to kiss those luscious lips!'

'You can have your wish at a far less expense,' murmured the lady, her bosom heaving with passionate emotions.

'But first remove that mask,' said the gentleman, enraptured at the success of the first intrigue of his life.

'I have no objection to uncover my countenance, provided you bestow upon me a similar favor,' replied Josephine.

'I am most anxious to preserve my *incognito*,' said the gentleman, in a tone of hesitation. 'My standing and peculiar occupation in life are entirely incompatible with such a festival as this, and my reputation would be dangerously compromised, if not utterly ruined. Nay, then, since you insist upon it, fair creature, I will unmask, trusting to your honor as a lady to keep my secret.'

He uncovered his face, and Josephine was thunderstruck when she recognized in the amorous stranger, no less a personage than Dr. Sinclair, the pious and eloquent rector of St. Paul's.

Yes—that learned and talented divine, who had so often denounced the sins and follies of the fashionable world, and declaimed particularly against the demoralizing influences of masquerade balls—that young and handsome preacher, whose exalted reputation for sanctity and holiness had induced the amorous Josephine and her licentious mother to suppose him inaccessible to their lustful glances, and far removed from the power of temptation—that model of purity and virtue was now present at this scene of profligate dissipation, gazing into the wanton eyes of a beautiful siren, his face flushed with excitement, and his heart palpitating with eager desire!

For a few moments Josephine sat overcome by astonishment, and could not utter a single syllable.

'You seem surprised, dear lady,' said Dr. Sinclair—'may I ask if you have ever seen me before?'

'You can read in my countenance an answer to your question,' replied Josephine, taking off her mask.

'Heavens, Miss Franklin!' exclaimed the divine. It was now his turn to be astonished.

'We meet under extraordinary circumstances,' said Dr. Sinclair after a short and somewhat embarrassing pause. 'Had I known that you are one who every Sabbath sits under my ministration, no earthly consideration would have induced me to disclose myself—not even the certainty of enjoying your favors. However, you know me now, and 'tis impossible to recall the past; therefore, beautiful Miss Franklin, do not withhold from the preacher that kindness which you would have granted to the private gentleman. —Let us religiously preserve our secret from the knowledge of the world: when we meet in company, let it be with the cold formality which exists between persons who are almost strangers; but now let us revel in the joys of love.'

The superb but profligate Josephine needed no urgent persuasion to induce her to become a guilty participator in a criminal *liaison* with the handsome young rector whom she had so long regarded with the eyes of desire;—*hers* was the conquest, that unprincipled lady of fashion; and *he* was the victim, that recreant fallen minister of the gospel.

Humbled and conscience-stricken, Dr. Sinclair left Livingston House and returned to his own luxurious but solitary home; while Josephine was driven in her carriage to Franklin House, the flush of triumph on her cheeks and her proud, guilty heart reeling with exultation.

CHAPTER XI

The Condemnation to Death—the Burglar's Confession and Awful Fate in the Iron Coffin.

The arrest of Frank Sydney for the murder of Maria Archer created an immense excitement throughout the whole community. —His wealth, standing in society, and former respectability caused many to believe him innocent of the dreadful crime imputed to him; but public opinion generally pronounced him guilty. The following article, extracted from a newspaper published at that period, will throw some light upon the views held in reference to the unhappy young man, and show how the circumstances under which he was arrested operated prejudicially to him:—

'ATROCIOUS MURDER. Last night, about nine o'clock, cries of murder were heard proceeding from the house No.— Bowery. The door was forced open by several citizens and watchmen, who, on entering a room on the second story, found the body of a young woman named Maria Archer stretched upon a sofa, her throat cut in a horrible manner, and standing over the corpse a young gentleman named Francis Sydney, holding in his hand a large Bowie knife, covered with blood. The landlady, Mrs. Flint, stated that Maria had that afternoon announced her intention to remove from the house in the evening; at about eight o'clock, Mr. Sydney called, *disguised*, and went up into the room of the deceased; —after a while, she (the landlady), being surprised that Maria did not begin to remove, went up to her room, and on opening the door, saw the young woman lying upon the sofa, her throat cut, and Mr. Sydney standing over her with the knife in his hand. On seeing this she screamed for assistance, and her cries had brought the watchman and citizens into the house, as we have stated.

'Mr. Sydney is a very wealthy young man, and has heretofore been highly respected. There can be no doubt of his guilt. He had probably formed a criminal connection with Mrs. Archer, whose character for chastity did not stand very high; it is supposed that it was in consequence of this intimacy that Mrs. Sydney recently separated from her husband. It is also presumed that a quarrel arose between Sydney and his paramour in consequence of his refusal to supply her with what money she demanded. This belief is predicated upon the following note, in the handwriting of Sydney, which was found upon the person of his murdered victim:—

'Mrs. Archer.—Madam: I shall this evening call upon you to confirm the words of my messenger. The unfortunate career which you have followed, is now nearly ended. Extortion and oppression shall triumph no longer.   F.S.'

'This note, it will be perceived, accuses her of extortion and contains a threat, &c. Alarmed at this, the poor young woman determined to leave the house that night—but was prevented by her paramour who barbarously slew her.

'The prisoner, whose appearance and behavior after his arrest proved his guilt, was conveyed to the Tombs, to await his trial for one of the most atrocious murders that has stained our criminal courts for many years.'

Thus it will be seen that poor, innocent Frank was regarded as the murderer.

It is needless for us to enter into the particulars of his trial: suffice it to say, he was convicted of the murder and sentenced to death. The evidence, though entirely circumstantial, was deemed positive against him. Mrs. Flint testifying that he was the only person who had entered the house that evening, and the situation in which she had discovered him, the murderous weapon in his hand, and his clothes stained with blood, admitted not a doubt of his guilt in the minds of the jury, who did not hesitate to bring in their fatal verdict, conscientiously believing it to be a just one.

A few days previous to his trial, the public were astounded by the intelligence that Mrs. Stevens, the prisoner's aunt, had committed suicide by hanging; and her nephew's disgrace and peril were supposed to have been the cause of the rash act. But when it came to be discovered that a robbery had been committed in the house, and it was stated by the servant that a strange man had sought and obtained an interview with the unfortunate old lady that evening, the public opinion took a different turn, and the belief became general that she had been murdered by some unknown miscreant, whose object was to plunder the house. No one suspected that she had been slain to prevent her from giving favorable testimony at the trial of her nephew Francis Sydney.

The diabolical outrage perpetrated upon the boy Clinton at the masquerade ball soon became noised abroad, and gave rise to many surmises, and much indignation; tho' no one as yet imagined that any connection existed between that horrible affair and the brutal murder of Mrs. Stevens.

After his conviction and condemnation to death, Sydney was placed in irons, and treated with but little indulgence by the petty officials who have charge of the Tombs. An application on his behalf was made to the Governor, in the hope of either obtaining a pardon, or a commutation of his sentence to imprisonment, but the executive functionary refused to interfere, and Frank prepared for death.

The day before that fixed upon for his execution, a lady applied for admission to the prisoner's cell, her request was granted, and Frank was astonished by the entrance of Julia, his guilty and discarded wife!

Did she come to entreat his forgiveness for her crime, and to endeavor to administer consolation and comfort to him in this his last extremity?

No, the remorseless and vindictive woman had come to exult over his misfortunes, and triumph over his downfall!

'So, miserable wretch,' she said, in a tone of contempt—'You are at last placed in a situation in which I can rejoice over your degradation and shame! A convicted, chained murderer, to die to-morrow—ha, ha, ha!' and she laughed with hellish glee.

'Accursed woman,' cried Frank, with indignation—'why have you come to mock my misery? Have you the heart to rejoice over my awful and undeserved fate?' and the poor young man, folding his arms, wept bitterly, for his noble and manly nature was for the time overcome by the horror of his situation.

'Yes, I have come to gloat upon your misery,' replied the vile, unfeeling woman. 'To-morrow you will die upon the gallows, and your memory will be hated and condemned by those who believe you to be guilty. I am convinced in my own mind that you are innocent of the murder; yet I rejoice none the less in your fate. Your death will free me from all restraint; I can adopt an assumed name, and removing to some distant city, entrap some rich fool into a marriage with me, whose wealth will administer to my extravagance, while I secretly abandon myself to licentious pleasures. Sydney, I never loved you—and when you discovered my intimacy with my dear African, I hated you—oh, how bitterly! When you cast me off, I vowed revenge upon you; but my vengeance will be satisfied to-morrow, when you pay the forfeit of another's crime. And now in the hour of your disgrace and death, I spit upon and despise you!'

'Begone, vile strumpet that you are,' exclaimed Frank, starting to his feet— 'taunt me no more, or you will drive me to commit an actual murder, and send your blackened soul into the presence of your offended Creator!'

'Farewell, forever,' said Julia, in a tone of indifference, and she left her poor, wronged husband to his own bitter reflections. Shortly after her departure, a clergyman entered the cell, and remained with the prisoner until long after midnight, preparing him for the awful change he was to undergo on the morrow.

*　*　*　*　*

That very night Fred Archer issued from the secret outlet of the Dark Vaults, and bent his steps in the direction of Wall street.

This street is the great focus around which all the most extensive financial operations of the great metropolis are carried on. It is occupied exclusively by banks, brokers' and insurance offices, and establishments of the like character.

It was midnight when Archer turned into Wall street from Broadway. The moon was obscured by clouds, and the street was entirely deserted. He paused before a large, massive building in the neighborhood of the Exchange, and glanced around him in every direction to assure himself that he was unobserved. Seeing no one, he ascended the marble steps, drew from his pocket a huge key, and with it unlocked the door; he entered, and closing the door after him, carefully re-locked it.

'So far all is well,' muttered the burglar, as he ignited a match and lighted a piece of wax candle which he had brought with him. 'It's lucky that I obtained an impression of that lock in wax, and from it made this key, or I might have had the devil's trouble in getting in.'

He advanced along the passageway, and opening a large door covered with green baize, entered a commodious apartment, containing a long table covered with papers, a desk, chairs, and other furniture, suitable to a business office. In one corner stood an immense safe, six feet in height and four in depth; this safe, made of massive plates of iron and protected by a door of prodigious strength, contained the books, valuable papers, and cash belonging to the ——— Insurance Company. Archer advanced to the safe, and took from his pocket a piece of paper, on which some words were written; this paper he examined with much attention.

'Here,' said he, 'I have the written directions, furnished me by the locksmith who made the lock attached to the safe, by which I can open it. Curse the fellow, a cool hundred dollars was a round sum of money to give him for this little bit of paper, but without it I never could see the interior of his iron closet, tho' I have an exact model of the key belonging to it, made from an impression in wax, which I bribed the clerk to get for me.'

Pursuing the directions contained in the paper, he touched a small spring concealed in the masonry adjoining the safe, and instantly a slide drew back in a panel of the door, revealing a key-hole. In this he inserted a key, and turned it, but found that he could not unlock it; he therefore had recourse to his paper a second time, which communicated the secret of the only method by which to open the door. Following those directions implicitly, he soon had the satisfaction of turning back the massive bolts which secured the door; a spring now only held it fast, but this was easily turned by means of a small brass knob, and the heavy door swung back upon its gigantic hinges, to the intense delight of the burglar, who anticipated securing a rich booty.

Nor was he likely to be disappointed; for upon examination he found that the safe contained money to a large amount. A small tin cash box was full of bank-notes of various denominations; and in a drawer were several thousands of dollars in gold.

'My fortune is made, by G———d!' exclaimed the burglar, as he stood within the safe, and began hastily to transfer the treasures to his pockets. The light of his candle, which he held in his hand, shed a faint glow upon the walls and ceiling of the apartment.

'The devil!' muttered Archer—'my success thus far must not destroy my prudence. If that light were to be seen from these windows, suspicion would be excited and I might be disagreeably interrupted.'

Reaching out his arm, he caught hold of the door of the safe, and pulled it violently towards him so that the light of his candle might not betray him. The immense mass of iron swung heavily upon its hinges, and closed with a sharp *click*; the spring held it fast, and on the inside of the door there was no means of turning back that spring. Like lightning the awful conviction flashed through the burglar's mind that he was *entombed alive!*

Vain, vain were his efforts to burst forth from his iron coffin; as well might he attempt to move the solid rock! He shrieked aloud for assistance—but no sound could penetrate through those iron walls! He called upon God to pity him in that moment of his awful distress—but that God, whom he had so often blasphemed, now interposed not His power to succor the vile wretch, thus so signally punished.

No friendly crevice admitted one mouthful of air into the safe, and Archer soon began to breathe with difficulty; he became sensible that he must die a terrible death by suffocation. Oh, how he longed for someone to arrive and release him from his dreadful situation, even though the remainder of his days were passed within the gloomy walls of a prison! How he cursed the money, to obtain which he had entered that safe, wherein he was now imprisoned as securely as if buried far down in the bowels of the earth! With the howl of a demon he dashed the banknotes and glittering gold beneath his feet, and trampled on them. Then, sinking down upon the floor of the safe, he abandoned himself to despair.

Already had the air of that small, confined place become fetid and noisome; and the burglar began to pant with agony, while the hot blood swelled his veins almost to bursting. A hundred thousand dollars lay within his grasp—he would have given it all for one breath of fresh air, or one draught of cold water.

As the agonies of his body increased, the horrors of his guilty conscience tortured his soul. The remembrance of the many crimes he had committed arose before him; the spirit of his murdered wife hovered over him, ghastly, pale and bloody. Then he recollected that an innocent man was to be hung on the morrow, for that dreadful deed which *he* had perpetrated; and the thought added to the mental tortures which he was enduring.

A thought struck the dying wretch; it was perhaps in his power to make some atonement for his crimes—he might save an innocent man from an ignominious death. No sooner had that thought suggested itself to his mind, than he acted upon it, for he knew that his moments were few; already he felt the cold hand of death upon him. He took a piece of chalk from his pocket, and with a feeble hand traced the following words upon the iron door of the safe:—

'My last hour is come, and I call on God, in whose awful presence I am shortly to appear, to witness the truth of this dying declaration. I do confess myself to be the murderer of Maria Archer. The young man Sydney is innocent of that crime. God have mercy—'

He could write no more; his brain grew dizzy and his senses fled. It seemed as if his iron coffin was red-hot, and he writhed in all the agony of a death by fire. Terrible shapes crowded around him, and the spirit of his murdered wife beckoned him to follow her to perdition. A mighty and crushing weight oppressed him; blood gushed from the pores of his skin; his eyes almost leaped from their sockets, and his brain seemed swimming in molten lead. At length Death came, and snapped asunder the chord of his existence; the soul of the murderer was in the presence of its Maker.

* * * * *

Morning dawned upon the doomed Sydney, in his prison cell; the glad sunbeams penetrated into that gloomy apartment, shedding a glow of ruddy light upon the white walls. That day at the hour of noon, he was to be led forth to die—he, the noble, generous Sydney, whose heart teemed with the most admirable qualities, and who would not wantonly have injured the lowest creature that crawls upon the Creator's footstool—he to die the death of a malefactor, upon the scaffold!

The day wore heavily on; Frank, composed and resigned, was ready to meet his fate like a man. He had heard the deep voice of the Sheriff, in the hall of the prison, commanding his subordinates to put up the scaffold; he had heard them removing that cumbrous engine of death from an unoccupied cell, and his ear had caught the sound of its being erected in the prison yard. Then he knelt down and prayed.

His hour had come. They came and removed his irons; they clothed him in the fearful livery of the grave. His step was firm and his eye undaunted as he passed into the prison yard, and stood beneath the black and frowning gallows.

The last prayer was said; the last farewell spoken; and many a hard-hearted jailer and cruel official turned aside to conceal the tears which would flow, at the thought that in a few moments that fine young man, so handsome, so talented and so noble to look upon, would be strangling and writhing with the tortures of the murderous rope, and soon after cut down, a ghastly and disfigured corpse.

The Sheriff adjusted the rope, and there was an awful pause; a man was tottering on the verge of eternity!

But oh, blessed pause—'twas ordained by the Almighty, to snatch that innocent man from the jaws of death! At that critical moment, a confused murmur was heard in the interior of the prison; the Sheriff, who had his hand upon the fatal book, which alone intervened between the condemned and eternity, was stopped from the performance of his deadly office, by a loud shout that rent the air, as a crowd of citizens rushed into the prison yard, exclaiming—

'Hold—stay the execution!'

The Mayor of the city, who was present, exchanged a few hurried words with the foremost of the citizens who had thus interrupted the awful ceremony; and instantly, with the concurrence of the Sheriff, ordered Sydney to be taken from the gallows, and conducted back to his cell, there to await the result of certain investigations, which it was believed would procure his entire exoneration from the crime of which he had been deemed guilty, and his consequent release from imprisonment.

It appeared that an officer connected with the ———— Insurance Company, on opening the safe that morning at about half-past eleven o'clock, discovered the dead body of the burglar, the money scattered about, and the writing upon the door. The officer, who was an intelligent and energetic man, instantly comprehended the state of affairs, and hastened with a number of other citizens to the Tombs, in order to save an innocent man from death. Had he arrived a few moments later, it might have been too late; but as it was, he had the satisfaction of rescuing poor Sydney from a dreadful fate, and the credit of saving the State from the disgrace of committing a judicial murder.

A dispatch was immediately sent to the Governor, at Albany, apprising him of these facts. The next day a letter was received from His Excellency, in which he stated that he had just perused the evidence which had produced the conviction of Mr. Sydney, and that evidence, besides being merely circumstantial, was, to his mind, vague and insufficient. The pressure of official business had prevented him from examining the case before, but had he reviewed the testimony, he would assuredly have granted the prisoner a reprieve. The dying confession of the burglar, the husband of the murdered woman, left not the slightest doubt of Mr. Sydney's innocence; and His Excellency concluded by ordering the prisoner's immediate discharge from custody.

Sydney left the prison, and, escorted by a number of friends, entered a carriage and was driven to his residence in Broadway. Here he was received with unbounded joy and hearty congratulations by all his household, including honest Dennis, and poor, dumb Clinton, who could only manifest his satisfaction by expressive signs.

'I will avenge thee, poor boy,' whispered Frank in his ear, as he cordially pressed his hand.

A tall man, wrapped in a cloak, had followed Frank's carriage, and watched him narrowly as he alighted and entered his house. This man's eyes alone were visible, and they glared with a fiend-like malignity upon the young gentleman; turning away, he muttered a deep curse, and a momentary disarrangement of the cloak which hid his face, revealed the horrible lineaments of the DEAD MAN!

CHAPTER XII

Showing how the Dead Man escaped from the State Prison at Sing Sing.

The New York State Prison is situated at Sing Sing, a village on the banks of the Hudson river, a few miles above the city. Being built in the strongest manner, it is deemed almost an impossibility for a prisoner to effect his escape from its massive walls. The discipline is strict and severe, and the system one of hard labor and unbroken silence, with reference to any conversation among the convicts—though in respect to the last regulation, it is impossible to enforce it always, where so many men are brought together in the prison and workshops attached to it.

The Dead Man, (who it will be recollected formerly made his escape from the prison,) on being returned there, after his capture by the two officers at Sydney's house, was locked in one of the cells, and left to his own not very agreeable reflections. He had been sentenced to imprisonment for life; and as his conduct and character precluded all hope of his ever being made the object of executive clemency, he was certain to remain there during the rest of his days, unless he could again manage to escape; and this he determined to do, or perish in the attempt.

For three days he was kept locked in his solitary cell, the only food allowed him being bread and water. On the third day he was brought out, stripped, and severely flogged with the *cats*, an instrument of torture similar to that used (to our national disgrace be it said,) on board of the men-of-war in our naval service. Then, with his back all lacerated and bleeding, the miscreant was placed at work in the shop where cabinet making was carried on—that having been his occupation in the prison, previous to his escape; an occupation which he had learned, while a boy, within the walls of some penitentiary.

The convict applied himself to his labor with a look which only bespoke a sullen apathy; but in his heart there raged a hell of evil passions. That night when he was locked in his cell, he slept not, but sat till morning endeavoring to devise some plan of escape.

The next day it chanced that he and another convict employed in the cabinet-maker's shop were engaged in packing furniture in large boxes to be conveyed in a sloop to the city of New York. These boxes, as soon as they were filled and nailed up, were carried down to the wharf, and stowed on board the sloop, which was to sail as soon as she was loaded. It instantly occurred to the Dead Man that these operations might afford him a chance to escape; and he determined to attempt it, at all hazards.

Upon an elevated platform in the centre of the shop (which was extensive) was stationed an overseer, whose duty it was to see that the convicts attended strictly to their work, and held no communication with each other. This officer had received special instructions from the Warden of the prison, to watch the Dead Man with all possible vigilance, and by no means to lose sight of him for a single moment, inasmuch as his former escape had been accomplished through the inattention of the overseer who had charge of him. Upon that occasion, he had watched for a favorable moment, slipped out of the shop unperceived, entered the Warden's dwelling house (which is situated within the walls of the prison) and helping himself to a suit of citizen's clothes, dressed himself therein, and deliberately marched out of the front gate, before the eyes of half a dozen keepers and guards, who supposed him to be some gentleman visiting the establishment, his hideous and well-known features being partially concealed by the broad-brimmed hat of a respectable Quaker.

To prevent a repetition of that maneuver, and to detect any other which might be attempted by the bold and desperate ruffian, the overseer kept his eyes almost constantly upon him, being resolved that no second chance should be afforded him to 'take French leave.' The Dead Man soon became conscious that he was watched with extraordinary vigilance; he was sagacious as well as criminal, and he deemed it to be good policy to assume the air of a man who was resigned to his fate, knowing it to be inevitable. He therefore worked with alacrity and endeavored to wear upon his villainous face an expression of contentment almost amounting to cheerfulness.

Near him labored a prisoner whose countenance indicated good-nature and courage; —and to him the Dead Man said, in an almost inaudible whisper, but without raising his eyes from his work, or moving his lips:—

'My friend, there is something in your appearance which assures me that you can be trusted; listen to me with attention, but do not look towards me. I am sentenced here for life: I am anxious to escape, and a plan has suggested itself to my mind, but you must assist me—will you do it?'

'Yes, poor fellow, I will, if it lies in my power, provided you were not sent here for any offence which I disapprove of,' replied the other, in a similar tone. 'I was sentenced here for the term of seven years, for manslaughter; a villain seduced my daughter, and I shot him dead—the honor of my child was worth a million of such accursed lives as his. —I consider myself guilty of no crime; he sacrificed my daughter to his lust, and then abandoned her—I sacrificed him to my vengeance, and never regretted the deed. The term of imprisonment will expire the day after to-morrow, and I shall then be a free man; therefore, I can assist you without running any great risk of myself. But you shall not have my aid if you were sent here for any deliberate villainy or black crime—for, thank God! I have a conscience, and that conscience permits me, though a prisoner, to call myself an honest man.'

'Be assured,' whispered the Dead Man, perceiving the necessity of using a falsehood to accomplish his ends—'that I am neither a deliberate villain nor hardened criminal; an enemy attacked me, and in *self defense* I slew him, for which I was sentenced here for life.'

'In that case,' rejoined the other—'I will cheerfully assist you to escape from this earthly hell—for self-defense is Nature's first law. Had you been a willful murderer, a robber, or aught of that kind, I would refuse to aid you—but the case is different.—But what is your plan?'

'I will get into one of these boxes, and you will nail on the cover, and I shall be conveyed on board the sloop, which will sail in less than an hour hence. When the vessel arrives at New York I shall perhaps have an opportunity to get on shore unperceived, and escape into the city, where I know of a place of refuge which the devil himself could not find,'—and the Dead Man chuckled inwardly as he thought of the Dark Vaults.

'The plan is a good one, and worthy of a trial,' said the other. 'But the overseer has his eye constantly upon you—how can you escape his vigilance?'

'There's the only difficulty,' replied the Dead Man—and his subtle brain was beginning to hatch some plan of surmounting that difficulty, when a large party of visitors, among whom were several ladies, entered the shop.

Now the overseer was a young man, and withal a tolerably good-looking one;

and among the ladies were two or three whose beauty commended them to his gallant attentions.

He therefore left his station on the platform, and went forward to receive them, and make himself agreeable.

'Now's my time, by G——d!' whispered the Dead Man to his fellow prisoner; instantly he lay down in one of the boxes, and the other nailed on the cover securely. A few moments afterwards, the box which contained the Dead Man was carried down to the wharf, by two convicts, and placed on board the vessel.

Meanwhile, the overseer had become the oracle of the party of ladies and gentlemen who had visited the shop; surrounded by the group, he occupied half an hour in replying to the many questions put to him, relative to the prison discipline, and other matters connected with it. In answer to a question addressed to him concerning the character of those under his charge, the overseer remarked in a tone of much self-complacency:

'I have now in this shop a convict who is the most diabolical villain that ever was confined in this prison. He is called the Dead Man, from the fact that his countenance resembles that of a dead person. He was sentenced here for life, for a murder, but contrived to escape about a year ago. However, he was arrested on a burglary not long since, sent back here, and placed under my particular care. I flatter myself that he will not escape a second time. Step this way, ladies and gentlemen, and view the hideous criminal.'

With a smirk of satisfaction, the overseer presented his arm to a pretty young lady, whose dark eyes had somewhat smitten him, and led the way to the further end of the shop, followed by the whole party.

The Dead Man was nowhere to be seen!

'Hullo, here! where the devil is that rascal gone?' cried the overseer, in great alarm, gazing wildly about him. 'Say, you fellows there, where is the Dead Man?'

This inquiry, addressed to the convicts who were at work in that part of the shop, was answered by a general 'don't know, sir.'

With one exception they all spoke the truth; for only the man who had nailed the Dead Man in the box, was cognizant of the affair, and he did not choose to confess his agency in the matter. An instant search was made throughout the premises, but without success—and the officers of the prison were forced to arrive at the disagreeable conclusion that the miscreant had again given them the slip. Not one of them had suspected that he was nailed up in a box on board the sloop which was then on her way to New York. The Warden sent for the luckless overseer who had charge of the escaped convict, and sternly informed him that his services were no longer needed in that establishment; he added to the discomfiture of the poor young man by darkly hinting his suspicions that he (the overseer) had connived at the escape of the prisoner—but, as the reader knows, this charge was unfounded and unjust.

The distance between Sing Sing and the city is not great: wind and tide both being favorable, the vessel soon reached her place of destination, and was attached to one of the numerous wharves which extend around the city. The boxes of furniture on board were immediately placed upon carts, for conveyance to a large warehouse in Pearl street.

The tightness of the box in which the Dead Man was placed, produced no small inconvenience to that worthy, who during the passage was nearly suffocated; however, he consoled himself with the thought that in a short time he would be free. The box was about six feet in length; and two in breadth and depth; and in this narrow compass the villain felt as if he were in a coffin. He was greatly rejoiced when the men who were unloading the vessel raised the box from the deck and carried it towards one of the carts.

But oh, horrible! unconscious that there was a man in the box, they stood it upon one end, and the Dead Man was left *standing upon his head.* The next moment the cart was driven rapidly over the rough pavement, towards the warehouse.

There were but two alternatives left for him—either to endure the torments of that unnatural position until the box was taken from the cart, or to cry out for some one to rescue him, in which case, clothed as he was in the garb of the prison, he would be immediately recognized as an escaped convict, and sent back to his old quarters. This latter alternative was so dreadful to him that he resolved to endure the torture if possible; and he could not help shuddering when he thought that perhaps he might be placed in the same position in the warehouse!

The drive from the wharf to Pearl street occupied scarce five minutes, yet during that brief period of time, the Dead man endured all the torments of the damned. The blood settled in his head, and gushed from his mouth and nostrils; unable to hold out longer, he was about to yell in his agony for aid, when the cart stopped, and in a few moments he was relieved by his box being taken down and carried into the warehouse, where, to his inexpressible joy, it was placed in a position to cause him no further inconvenience. The warehouse being an extensive one, many persons were employed in it; and he deemed it prudent to remain in his box until night, as the clerks and porters were constantly running about, and they would be sure to observe him if he issued from his place of concealment then.

As he lay in his narrow quarters, he heard the voices of two persons conversing near him, one of whom was evidently the proprietor of the establishment.

'We have just heard from Sing Sing,' said the proprietor—'that the villain they call the Dead Man made his escape this morning, in what manner nobody knows. I am sorry for it, because such a wretch is dangerous to society; but my regret that he has escaped arises principally from the fact that he is an excellent workman, and I, as contractor, enjoyed the advantages of his labor, paying the State a trifle of thirty cents a day for him, when he could earn me two dollars and a half. This system of convict labor is a glorious thing for us master mechanics, though it plays the devil with the journeymen. Why, I formerly employed fifty workmen, who earned on an average two dollars a day; but since I contracted with the State to employ its convicts, the work which cost me one hundred dollars a day I now get for *fifteen* dollars.' And he laughed heartily.

'So it seems,' remarked the other, 'that you are enriching yourself at the expense of the State, while honest mechanics are thrown out of employment.'

'Precisely so,' responded the proprietor—'and if the *honest mechanics*, as you call them, wish to work for me, they must commit a crime and be sent to Sing Sing, where they can enjoy that satisfaction—ha, ha, ha.'

Just then, a poor woman miserably clad, holding in her hand a scrap of paper, entered the store, and advanced timidly to where the wealthy proprietor and his friend were seated.

The former, observing her, said to her in a harsh tone—

'There, woman, turn right around and march out, and don't come here again with your begging petition, or I'll have you taken up as a vagrant.'

'If you please, sir,' answered the poor creature, humbly—'I haven't come to beg, but to ask if you won't be so kind as to pay this bill of my husband's. It's only five dollars, sir, and he is lying sick in bed, and we are in great distress from want of food and fire-wood. Since you discharged him he has not been able to get work, and—'

'Oh, get out!' interrupted the wealthy proprietor, brutally—'don't come bothering *me* with your distress and such humbug. I paid your husband more than he ought to have had—giving two dollars a day to a fellow, when I now get the same work for thirty cents! If you're in distress, go to the Poor House, but don't come here again—d'ye hear?'

The poor woman merely bowed her head in token of assent, and left the store, her pale cheeks moistened with tears. The friend of the wealthy proprietor said nothing, but thought to himself, 'You're a d——d scoundrel.' And, reader, we think so too, though not in the habit of swearing.

She had not proceeded two dozen steps from the store, when a rough-looking man in coarse overalls touched her arm, and thus addressed her:

'Beg your pardon, ma'am, but I'm a porter in the store of that blasted rascal as wouldn't pay your poor husband's bill for his work, and treated you so insultingly; I overheard what passed betwixt you and him, and I felt mad enough to go at him and *knock blazes* out of him. No matter—every dog has his day, as the saying is; and he may yet be brought to know what poverty is. I'm poor, but you are welcome to all the money I've got in the world—take this, and God bless you.'

The noble fellow passed three or four dollars in silver into her hand, and walked away ere she could thank him.

The recording angel above opened the great Book wherein all human actions are written, and affixed another *black mark* to the name of the wealthy proprietor. There were many black marks attached to that name already.

The angel then sought out another name, and upon it impressed the stamp of a celestial seal. It was the name of the poor laborer.

Oh, laborer! Thou art uncouth to look upon: thy face is unshaven, thy shirt dirty, and lo! thy overalls smell of paint and grease; thy speech is ungrammatical, and thy manners unpolished—but give us the grasp of thy honest hand, and the warm feelings of thy generous heart, fifty, yes a million times sooner than the mean heart and niggard hand of the selfish cur that calls itself thy master!

And oh, wealthy proprietor how smooth and smiling is thy face, how precise thy dress and snow-white thy linen! thy words (except to the poor,) are well-chosen and marked with strict grammatical propriety.—The world doffs its hat to thee, and calls thee 'respectable,' and 'good.' Thou rotten-hearted villain! —morally thou art not fit to brush the cowhide boots of the MAN that thou callst thy servant! Out upon ye, base-soul'd wretch!

The countenance of the wealthy proprietor, which had assumed a severe and indignant expression at the woman's audacity, had just recovered its wonted smile of complacency, when a gentleman of an elderly age and reverend aspect entered the store. He was attired in a respectable suit of black, and his neck was enveloped in a white cravat.

'My dear Mr. Flanders,' said the proprietor, shaking him warmly by the hand, 'I am delighted to see you. Allow me to make you acquainted with my friend, Mr. Jameson—the Rev. Balaam Flanders, our worthy and beloved pastor.'

The two gentlemen bowed, and the parson proceeded to unfold the object of his visit.

'Brother Hartless,' said he to the proprietor, 'I have called upon you in behalf of a most excellent institution, of which I have the honor to be President; I allude to the 'Society for Supplying Indigent and Naked Savages in Hindustan with Flannel Shirts.' The object of the Society, you perceive, is a most philanthropic and commendable one; every Christian and lover of humanity should cheerfully contribute his mite towards its promotion—Your reputation for enlightened views and noble generosity has induced me to call upon you to head the list of its patrons—which list,' he added in a significant whisper, 'will be published in full in the *Missionary Journal and Cannibal's Friend*, that excellent periodical.'

'You do me honor,' replied Mr. Hartless, a flush of pride suffusing his face; then, going to his desk, he wrote in bold characters, at the top of a sheet of paper—

   '*Donations in aid of the Society for Supplying Indigent and Naked Savages in Hindustan with Flannel Shirts.*
   —Paul Hartless. $100.00'

This document he handed to the parson, with a look which clearly said 'What do you think of that?' and then, producing his pocket-book, took from thence a bank-note for one hundred dollars, which he presented to the reverend gentleman, who received the donation with many thanks on behalf of the 'Society for Supplying, &c.' and then left.

All this time the Dead Man lay in his box, impatiently awaiting the arrival of evening, when the store would be closed, and an opportunity afforded him to emerge from the narrow prison in which he was confined. Once, he came very near being discovered; for a person chanced to enter the warehouse accompanied by a dog, and the animal began smelling around the box in a manner that excited some surprise and remark on the part of those who observed it. The dog's acute powers of smell detected the presence of some person in the box: fortunately, however, for the Dead Man, the owner of the four-legged inquisitor, having transacted his business, called the animal away, and left the store.

Mr. Hartless, in the course of some further desultory conversation with Mr. Jameson, casually remarked—

'By the way, my policy of insurance expired yesterday, and I meant to have it renewed to-day; however, to-morrow will answer just as well. But I must not delay the matter, for this building is crammed from cellar to roof with valuable goods, and were it burnt down to-night, or before I renew my insurance, I should be a beggar!'

The Dead Man heard this, and grinned with satisfaction. The day wore slowly away, and at last the welcome evening came; the hum of business gradually ceased, and finally the last person belonging to the warehouse, who remained, took his departure, having closed the shutters and locked the door; then a profound silence reigned throughout the building.

'Now I may venture to get out of this accursed box,' thought the escaped convict:—and he tried to force off the cover, but to his disappointment and alarm, he found that it resisted all his efforts. It had been too tightly nailed on to admit of its being easily removed.

'Damnation!' exclaimed the Dead Man, a thousand fears crowding into his mind,—'it's all up with me unless I can burst off this infernal cover.' And, cursing the man who had fastened it on so securely, he redoubled his efforts.

He succeeded at last; the cover flew off, and he arose from his constrained and painful position with feelings of the most intense satisfaction. All was pitch dark, and he began groping around for some door or window which would afford him egress from the place. His hand soon came in contact with a window; he raised the sash, and unfastened the shutters, threw them open, when instantly a flood of moonlight streamed into the store, enabling him to discern objects with tolerable distinctness. The window, which was not over five feet from the ground, over-looked a small yard surrounded by a fence of no great height; and the Dead Man, satisfied with the appearance of things, proceeded to put into execution a plan which he had formed while in the box. The nature of that plan will presently appear.

After breaking open a desk, and rummaging several drawers without finding anything worth carrying off, he took from his pocket a match, and being in a philosophical mood, (for great rascals are generally profound philosophers,) he apostrophized it thus:

'Is it not strange, thou little morsel of wood, scarce worth the fiftieth fraction of a cent, that in thy tiny form doth dwell a Mighty Power, which can destroy thousands of dollars, and pull down the great fabric of a rich man's fortune? Thy power I now invoke, thou little minister of vengeance; for I hate the aristocrat who expressed his regret at my escape, because, forsooth! my services were valuable to him!—and now, as the flames of fire consume his worldly possessions, so may the flames of eternal torment consume his soul hereafter!'

Ah, Mr. Hartless! that was an unfortunate observation you made relative to the expiration of your term of insurance. Your words were overheard by a miscreant, whose close proximity you little suspected. Your abominable treatment of that poor man is about to meet with a terrible retribution.

The Dead Man placed a considerable quantity of paper beneath a large pile of boxes and furniture; he then ignited the match, and having set fire to the paper, made his exit through the window, crossed the yard, scaled the fence, and passing through an alley gained the street, and made the best of his way to the Dark Vaults.

In less than ten minutes after he had issued from that building, fierce and crackling flames were bursting forth from its doors and windows. The streets echoed with the cry of *Fire*—the deep-toned bell of the City Hall filled the air with its notes of solemn warning and the fire engines thundered over the pavement towards the scene of conflagration. But in vain were the efforts of the firemen to subdue the raging flames; higher and higher they rose, until the entire building was on fire, belching forth mingled flame, and smoke, and showers of sparks. At length the interior of the building was entirely consumed, and the tottering walls fell in with a tremendous crash. The extensive warehouse of Mr. Paul Hartless, with its valuable contents, no longer existed, but had given place to a heap of black and smoking ruins!

The reader is now acquainted with the manner of the Dead Man's escape from Sing Sing State Prison, and the circumstances connected with that event.

CHAPTER XIII

The African and his Mistress—the Haunted House—Night of Terror.

Nero, the African, still remained a prisoner in the vault beneath Sydney's house. He was regularly supplied with his food by Dennis, who performed the part of jailer, and was untiring in his vigilance to prevent the escape of the negro under his charge.

One afternoon a boy of apparently fifteen or sixteen years of age called upon Dennis and desired to speak with him in private. He was a handsome lad, of easy, graceful manners, and long, curling hair; his dress was juvenile, and his whole appearance extremely prepossessing.

The interview being granted, the boy made known the object of his call by earnestly desiring to be permitted to visit the imprisoned black.

'Is it the *nager* ye want to see?' exclaimed Dennis—'and how the devil did ye know we had a nager shut up in the cellar, any how?'

'Oh,' replied the boy, 'a lady of my acquaintance is aware of the fact, and she sent me here to present you with this five dollar gold piece, and to ask your consent to my delivering a short message to the black man.'

'Och, be the powers, and is that it?' muttered Dennis, half aloud, as he surveyed the bright coin which the boy had placed in his hand—'I begin to smell a rat, faith; this gossoon was sent here by Mr. Sydney's blackguard wife, who has such a hankering after the black divil—not contented with her own lawful husband, and a decent man he is, but she must take up wid that dirty nager, bad luck to her and him! My master gave me no orders to prevint any person from seeing the black spalpeen; and as a goold yankee sovereign can't be picked up every day in the street, faith it's yerself Dennis Macarty, that will take the responsibility, and let this good-looking gossoon in to see black Nero, and bad luck to him!'

Accordingly, the worthy Irishman produced a huge key from his pocket, and led the way to the door of the vault, which he opened, and having admitted the youth, relocked it, after requesting the visitor to knock loudly upon the door when he desired to come out.

'Who is there?' demanded the negro in a hollow voice, from a remote corner of the dungeon.

'Tis I, your Julia!' answered the disguised woman, in a soft whisper—for it was no other than Sydney's guilty wife.

'My good, kind mistress!' exclaimed the black, and the next moment he had caught the graceful form of his paramour in his arms. We shall not offend the reader's good taste by describing the disgusting caresses which followed. Suffice it to say, that the interview was commenced in such a manner as might have been expected under the circumstance.

The first emotions of rapture at their meeting having subsided, they engaged in a long and earnest conversation.

We shall not weary the reader's patience by detailing at length what passed between them; suffice it to say, they did not separate until a plan had been arranged for the escape of Nero from that dungeon vault.

When Julia left the abode of her husband, in the manner described in Chapter VIII, she took apartments for herself and her maid Susan at a respectable boarding house near the Battery. Representing herself to be a widow lady recently from Europe, she was treated with the utmost respect by the inmates of the establishment, who little suspected that she was the cast-off wife of an injured husband, and the mistress of a negro! She assumed the name of Mrs. Belmont; and, to avoid confusion, we shall hereafter designate her by that appellation.

Mrs. Belmont was very well satisfied with her position, but she was well aware that she could not always maintain it, unless she entrapped some wealthy man into an amour or marriage with her; for her pecuniary resources, though temporarily sufficient for all her wants, could not last always. In this view of the case, she deemed it expedient to hire some suitable and genteel dwelling-house, where she could carry on her operations with less restraint than in a boarding-house. She accordingly advertised for such a house; and the same day on which her advertisement appeared in the paper, an old gentleman called upon her, and stated he was the proprietor of just such a tenement as she had expressed a desire to engage.

'This house, madam,' said the old gentleman, 'is a neat three-story brick edifice, situated in Reade street. It is built in the most substantial manner, and furnished with every convenience; moreover, you shall occupy it upon your own terms.'

'As to that,' remarked Mrs. Belmont, 'if the house suits me, you have but to name the rent, and it shall be paid.'

'Why, madam,' replied the old gentleman, with some embarrassment of manner—'it is my duty to inform you that a silly prejudice exists in the minds of some people in the neighborhood of the house, and that prejudice renders it somewhat difficult for me to procure a tenant. You will smile at the absurdity of the notion, but nevertheless I assure you that a belief generally prevails that the house is *haunted*.'

'Are there any grounds for each a supposition?' inquired the lady, with an incredulous smile, yet feeling an interest in the matter.

'Why,' replied the owner, 'all who have as yet occupied the house have, after remaining one to two nights in it, removed precipitately, declaring that the most dreadful noises were heard during the night, tho' none have positively affirmed that they actually *saw* any supernatural visitant. These tales of terror have so frightened people that the building has been unoccupied for some time; and as it is a fine house, and one that cost me a good sum of money, I am extremely anxious to get a tenant of whom only a very moderate rent would be required. The fact is, I am no believer in this *ghost* business; the people who lived in the house were probably frightened by pranks of mischievous boys, or else their nervous, excited imaginations conjured up fancies and fears which had no reasonable foundation. Now, madam, I have candidly told you all; it remains for you to decide whether you will conform to a foolish prejudice, or, rising above the superstitions of the vulgar and ignorant, become the occupant of my *haunted* house—which, in my belief, is haunted by naught but mice in the cupboards and crickets in the chimneys.'

Mrs. Belmont reflected for a few moments, and then said—

'If the house suits me upon examination, I will become your tenant, notwithstanding the ghostly reputation of the building.'

'I am delighted, my dear madam,' rejoined the old gentleman, with vivacity, 'to find in you a person superior to the absurd terrors of weak-minded people. If you will do me the honor to accompany me to Reade street, I will go over the house with you, and if you are pleased with it, the bargain shall be completed upon the spot.'

This proposal was acceded to by Mrs. Belmont, who, after putting on her cloak and bonnet, took the arm of the old gentleman and proceeded with him up Broadway. A walk of little more than ten minutes brought them to Reade street, into which they turned; and in a few moments more the old gentleman paused before a handsome dwelling-house, standing about twenty feet back from the line of the street. The house did not adjoin any other building, but was located upon the edge of an open lot of considerable extent.

'This is the place,' said the guide as he took a key from his pocket; then, politely desiring the lady to follow him, he ascended the steps, unlocked the front door, and they entered the house. The rooms were of course entirely empty, yet they were clean and in excellent condition.—The parlors, chambers and other apartments were admirably arranged and Mrs. Belmont, after going all over the house, expressed her perfect satisfaction with it, and signified her wish to remove into it the next day. The terms were soon agreed upon; and Mr. Hedge (for that was the name of the landlord,) after delivering the key into her hands, waited upon her to the door of her boarding-house, and then took his leave.

The next morning, at an early hour, Mrs. Belmont began making preparations to occupy her new abode. From an extensive dealer she hired elegant furniture sufficient to furnish every apartment in the house; and, by noon that day, the rooms which had lately appeared so bare and desolate, presented an aspect of luxury and comfort. The naked walls were covered with fine paintings, in handsome frames; rich curtains were hung in the windows, and upon the floors were laid beautiful carpets.—The mirrors, sofas, chairs and cabinets were of the costliest kind; a magnificent piano was placed in the parlor, and the lady took care that the chamber which she intended to occupy was fitted up with all possible elegance and taste. A voluptuous bed, in which Venus might have revelled, was not the least attractive feature of that luxurious sleeping apartment. Every arrangement being completed, and as it was still early in the afternoon, Mrs. Belmont resolved to carry out a plan which she had formed some days previously—a plan by which she could enjoy an interview with Nero the black. The reader is already aware that she disguised herself in boys' clothes, and accomplished her object without much difficulty.

That evening, Mrs. Belmont was seated in the comfortable parlor of her new abode, before a fine fire which glowed in the ample grate, and diffused a genial warmth throughout the apartment. She had just partaken of a luxurious supper; and the materials of the repast being removed, she was indulging in reflections which were far more pleasing at that moment, than any which had employed her mind since her separation from her husband.

She was attired with tasteful simplicity; for although she expected no company that evening, she had taken her usual pains to dress herself becomingly and well, being a lady who never neglected her toilet, under any circumstances—a trait of refinement which we cannot help admiring, even in one so depraved and abandoned as she was.

As she lounged indolently upon the sofa, complacently regarding her delicate foot, which, encased in a satin slipper, reposed upon the rich hearth-rug, her thoughts ran somewhat in the following channel—:

'Well—I am now not only mistress of my own actions, but also mistress of a splendidly furnished house. Ah, 'twas a fortunate day for me when I separated from that man I once called husband! Yet with what cool contempt he treated me on the night when he commanded me to leave his house forever! How bitterly I hate that man—how I long to be revenged upon him. Not that he has ever injured me—oh, no—'tis I that have injured him; therefore do I hate him, and thirst for revenge! And poor Nero, whom I visited this afternoon in his dungeon—how emaciated and feeble has he become by close confinement in that gloomy place! His liberation must be effected, at all hazards; for strange as it is, I love the African passionately. Now, as regards my own position and affairs: I am young, beautiful, and accomplished—skilled in human nature and intrigue. Two distinct paths lie before me, which are equally desirable: as a virtuous widow lady, I can win the love and secure the hand of some rich and credulous gentleman, who, satisfied with having obtained a pretty wife, will not be too inquisitive with reference to my past history. In case of marriage, I will remove to Boston with my new husband: for not being divorced from Sydney, (how I hate that name!) I should be rendered liable to the charge of bigamy, if the fact of my second marriage should transpire.—On the other hand, leaving marriage entirely out of the question: As a young and lovely woman, residing alone, and not under the protection of male relatives, I shall attract the attention of wealthy libertines, who will almost throw their fortunes at my feet to enjoy my favors. Selecting the richest of these men, it will be my aim to infatuate him by my arts, to make him my slave, and then to deny him the pleasure for which he pants, until he gives me a large sum of money; this being done, I can either surrender myself to him, or still refuse to afford him the gratification he seeks, as suits my whim. When he becomes wearied of my perverseness and extortion, I will dismiss him, and seek another victim. Those with whom I shall thus have to deal, will be what the world calls respectable men—husbands, fathers— perhaps professedly pious men and clergymen—who would make any sacrifice sooner than have their amours exposed to their wives, families, and society generally. Once having committed themselves with me, I shall have a hold upon them, which they never can shake off;—a hold which will enable me to draw money from their well-filled coffers, whenever my necessities or extravagances require it. I may practice whatever imposition or extortion on them I choose, with perfect impunity; they will never dare to use threats or violence towards me, for the appalling threat of *exposure* will curb their tempers and render them tamely submissive to all my exactions and caprices. Thus will I reap a rich harvest from those wealthy votaries of carnal pleasure whom I may allure to my arms, while at the same time I can for my own gratification unrestrainedly enjoy the embraces of any lover whom I may happen to fancy. Ah, I am delightfully situated at present, and have before me a glorious and happy career!'

We have devoted considerable space to the above reflections of this unprincipled woman, because they will serve to show her views in reference to her present position, and her plans for the future.

The agreeable current of her meditations was interrupted by the entrance of her maid Susan.

'Well, ma'am,' said the abigail, 'I have obeyed all your orders; I have locked all the doors, and fastened all the shutters, so that if the ghost *should* pay us a visit, it will have to get in through the keyhole. But oh! my gracious! how terrible it is for you and I, ma'am, two poor weak women, as a body might say, to be all alone together in a house that is haunted!'

'Sit down, Susan,' said Mrs. Belmont, who was herself not altogether devoid of superstitious fears. 'Are you so foolish as to believe in *ghosts*? Do you think that the spirits of dead people are allowed to re-visit the earth, to frighten us out of our wits? No, no—we have reason to fear the *living*, but not those who are dead and buried.'

'But, if you please, ma'am,' rejoined Susan, in a solemn tone, 'I once seed a ghost with my own eyes, and not only seed it, but *felt* it, too.'

'Indeed—and pray how did that happen?' inquired her mistress.

'I'll tell you all about it, ma'am,' replied Susan, who, by the way, was rather a pretty young woman, though she was, like all ladies' maids, a prodigious talker. 'You see, ma'am, I once went to live in the family of a minister, and a very excellent man he was, as prayed night and morning, and said grace afore meals. Oh, he was a dreadful clever gentleman, 'cause he always used to kiss me when he catch'd me alone, and chuck me under the chin, and tell me I was handsome. Well, Saturday the minister's wife and family went to pay a visit to some relations in New Jersey, and was to stay for two or three days; but the minister himself didn't go with them, 'cause he was obliged to stay and preach on Sunday.—Now comes the dreadful part of my story, ma'am, and it is true as gospel.—That Saturday night, about twelve o'clock, I was awoke by hearing the door of my little attic bed-room softly open; and by the light of the moon I seed a human figger, all dressed in white, come into the room, shut the door, and then walk towards my bed. Oh, I was dreadfully frightened, to be sure; and just as I was going to scream out, the ghost puts his hand upon me and says—'*hush!*' which skeer'd me so that I almost fainted away. Well, ma'am, what does the ghost do next but take ondecent liberties with me, and I was too much frightened to say, 'have done, now!' And then the awful critter did what no ghost ever did before to me, nor man neither.—Oh, I actually fainted away two or three times; I did indeed. After a while it went away, but I was in such a flutter that I couldn't sleep no more that night. The next morning I up and told the minister how I had seed a ghost, and how it had treated me; and the minister he smiled, and said he guessed I'd get over it, and gave me some money, telling me not to say anything more about it, 'cause it might frighten the folks. Now, ma'am, after that, you needn't wonder that I believe in ghosts.'

Mrs. Belmont was highly amused by this narration of her maid's experience in supernatural visitation; and the hearty laughter in which she indulged at the close of the story, dispelled in a great measure those unpleasant feelings which had begun to gain the ascendancy over her. While under the influence of those feelings, she had intended to request Susan to sleep with her in her chamber; but as such an arrangement would betray *fear* on her part, while she was most anxious to appear bold and courageous, she concluded to occupy her sleeping apartment alone. Susan herself would have been very glad to share the room of her mistress; but as a suggestion to that effect, coming from her, might have seemed presumptuous and impertinent, she said nothing about it. Accordingly, when the hour for retiring arrived, Mrs. Belmont retired to her chamber, where she dismissed her maid, saying that she should not want her services any more that night; and poor Susan was obliged to ascend to her solitary apartment, which she did with many fearful misgivings, and the most dreadful apprehensions in regard to ghosts, coupled with much painful reflection relative to the unpleasantness of sleeping *alone*—in a haunted house.

Mrs. Belmont disrobed herself, yet ere she retired to her couch, she paused before a large mirror to admire her own naked and voluptuous beauty. While he was surveying herself, she gave utterance to her thoughts in words:—

'Ah, these charms of mine will procure me friends and fortune. What man could resist the intoxicating influence of such glorious loveliness of face and person as I possess!'

Scarcely had she uttered these words, when her ear was greeted by a low sound, which bore some resemblance to a laugh. Terrified and trembling, she cast a rapid glance around the room, but could see nobody; she then examined a small closet which adjoined the chamber and looked under the bed, not knowing but that some person might be concealed there—but she could uncover nothing to account for the noise which she had heard. It then occurred to her to open the door of her chamber; but as she was about to do so, an appalling thought flashed thro' her mind.

'What if some terrible being is now standing at the outside of that door?' and she shrank from opening it. She deeply regretted that she had not requested her maid Susan to sleep with her, as she crept into bed, leaving a candle burning on the table.

For about a quarter of an hour she listened intensely, but the sound which had alarmed her was not repeated; and she began to reason with herself upon the absurdity of her fears. Finally she succeeded in persuading herself that she had in reality heard nothing, but had been deceived by her own imagination. Still, she could not entirely dissipate her fears; she recollected that the house had the reputation of being 'haunted'—and, though she was naturally neither timid nor superstitious, a vague and undefinable dread oppressed her, as she lay in that solitary chamber, where reigned a heavy gloom and profound stillness.

It was an hour after midnight when she awoke from an uneasy slumber into which she had fallen: and the first object which met her gaze, was a human figure, enveloped from head to toe in white drapery, standing near her bed!

Yes, there it stood, with the upper part of a ghastly face alone visible, pointing at her with its finger, and freezing her soul with the steady glare of its eyes.

Long, long stood that dreadful apparition; its attitude seemed to be either menacing or warning. The terrified woman, under the influence of a painful fascination, could not avert her gaze from it; and the spectre stood until the candle was entirely consumed, and the room was wrapped in profound darkness. Then the Form glided to the bedside, and laid its cold hand upon her brow. *'Thou shalt see me again!'* it whispered, and then passed noiselessly from the room.

Mrs. Belmont gave one loud and piercing scream, and then sank into a state of insensibility.

CHAPTER XIV

A Glimpse of the Crimes and Miseries of a Great City.

After his narrow escape from an ignominious death, Frank Sydney resumed his nocturnal wanderings thro' the city, in disguise, in order to do deeds of charity and benevolence to those who needed his aid. One night, dressed in the garb of a sailor, and wearing an immense pair of false whiskers, he strolled towards the Five Points, and entered the 'crib' of Bloody Mike. That respectable establishment was filled as usual with a motley collection of gentlemen of undoubted reputation— thieves, vagabonds, homeless wretches, and others of the same stamp, among whom were some of the most miserable looking objects possible to be conceived.

At the moment of Frank's entrance, Ragged Pete was engaged in relating the particulars of a horrible event which had occurred upon the preceding night on the 'Points.' The incident is a *true* one, and we introduce it here to show what awful misery exists in the very midst of all our boasted civilization and benevolence:—

'You see, fellers,' said Ragged Pete, leisurely sipping a gill of *blue ruin*, which he held in his hand—'the victim was a woman of the town, as lived upstairs in Pat Mulligan's crib in this street. She had once been a decent woman, but her husband was a drunken vagabond, as beat and starved her to such an extent, that she was obliged to go on the town to keep herself from dying of actual starvation. Well, the husband he was took up and sent to quod for six months, as a common vagrant; and the wife she lived in Mulligan's crib, in a room as hadn't a single article of furniture in it, exceptin' a filthy old bed of straw in one corner. A week ago, the poor cretur was taken ill, and felt herself likely to become a mother, but the brutes in the house wouldn't pay no attention to her in that situation, but left her all to herself. What she must have suffered during that night and the next day, you can imagine; and towards evening Pat Mulligan goes to her room, and finds her almost dead, with her poor child in her arms, wrapped up in an old blanket. Well, what does Pat do but ax her for his rent, which she owed him; and because the poor woman had nothing to pay him, the Irish vagabond (axing your pardon, Bloody Mike,) bundles her neck and crop into the street, weak and sick as she was, with a hinfant scarce a day old, crying in her arms. The weather was precious cold, and it was snowing, and to keep herself and child from freezing to death, as she thought, she crept into a hog-pen which stands in Pat's yard. And this morning she was found in the hog-pen, stone dead, and the hogs were devouring the dead body of the child, which was already half ate up! I'll tell you what, fellers,' exclaimed Ragged Pete, dashing a tear from his eye, and swallowing the remainder of his gin—'I'm a hard case myself, and have seen some hard things in my time, but d——n me if the sight of that poor woman's corpse and the mutilated body of her child, didn't set me to thinking that this is a great city, where such a thing takes place in the very midst of it!'

'Three groans for Pat Mulligan!' roared a drunken fellow from beneath the table.

The groans were rendered with due emphasis and effect; and then one of the drunken crowd proposed that they should visit the 'crib' of Mr. Mulligan, and testify their disapprobation of that gentleman's conduct in a more forcible and striking manner.

This proposal was received with a shout of approbation by the drunken crew, and was warmly seconded by Bloody Mike himself, who regarded Mr. Patrick Mulligan as a formidable rival in his line of business, and therefore entertained feelings strongly hostile to his fellow-countryman. Then forth sallied the dingy crowd, headed by Ragged Pete, (who found himself suddenly transformed into a hero,) and followed by Frank Sydney, who was desirous of seeing the issue of this strange affair.

The house occupied by Mulligan was an old, rotten tenement, which would undoubtedly have fallen to the ground, had it not been propped up by the adjoining buildings; and as it was, one end of it had settled down, in consequence of the giving away of the foundation, so that every room in the house was like a steep hill. The lower room was occupied as a groggery and dance-hall, and was several feet below the level of the street.

Into this precious den did the guests of Bloody Mike march, in single file. It had been previously agreed between them, that Ragged Pete would give the signal for battle, by personally attacking no less a person than Mr. Mulligan himself. Frank also entered, and taking up a secure position in one corner, surveyed the scene with interest.

Seated in the corner, upon an inverted wash-tub, was an old negro, whose wool was white as snow, who was arrayed in a dirty, ragged, military coat which had once been red. This sable genius rejoiced in the lofty title of 'the General;' he was playing with frantic violence on an old, cracked violin, during which performance he threw his whole body into the strangest contortions, working his head, jaws, legs and arms in the most ludicrous manner. The 'music' thus produced was responded to, 'on the floor,' by about twenty persons, who were indulging in the 'mazy dance.' The company included old prostitutes, young thieves, negro chimney-sweeps, and many others whom it would be difficult to classify.

The room being small and very close, and heated by an immense stove, the stench was intolerable.—Behind the bar was a villainous looking Irishman, whose countenance expressed as much intellect or humanity as that of a hog. This was Pat Mulligan, and he was busily engaged in dealing out the delectable nectar called 'blue ruin' at the very moderate rate of one penny per gill.

A *very* important man, forsooth, was that Irish 'landlord,' in the estimation of himself and customers.—None dare address him without prefixing a deferential '*Mr.*' to his name; and Frank Sydney was both amused and irritated as he observed the brutal insolence with which the low, ignorant ruffian treated the poor miserable wretches, from whose scanty pence he derived his disgraceful livelihood.

'Mr. Mulligan,' said a pale, emaciated woman, whose hollow cheek and sunken eye eloquently proclaimed her starving condition—'won't you trust me for a sixpenny loaf of bread until to-morrow? My little girl, poor thing, is dying, and I have eaten nothing this day.' And the poor creature wept.

'Trust ye!' roared the Irishman, glaring ferociously upon her—'faith, it's not exactly *trust* I'll give ye; but I'll give ye a beating that'll not leave a whole bone in your skin, if ye are not out of this place in less time than it takes a pig to grunt.'

The poor woman turned and left the place, with a heavy heart, and Ragged Pete, deeming this a good opportunity to begin hostilities, advanced to the bar with a swagger, and said to the Irishman,—

'You're too hard upon that woman, Pat.'

'What's that to you, ye dirty spalpeen?' growled Mulligan, savagely.

'This much,' responded Pete, seizing an immense earthen pitcher which stood on the counter, and hurling it with unerring aim at the head of the Irishman. The vessel broke into a hundred pieces, and though it wounded Mulligan dreadfully, he was not disabled; for, grasping an axe which stood within his reach, he rushed from behind the bar, and swinging the formidable weapon aloft, he would have cloven in twain the skull of Ragged Pete, had not that gentleman evaded him with much agility, and closing with him, bore him to the floor, and began to pummel him vigorously.

No sooner did the customers of Pat Mulligan see their dreaded landlord receiving a sound thrashing, then all fear of him vanished; and, as they all hated the Irish bully, and smarted under the remembrance of numerous insults and wrongs sustained at his hands, they with one accord fell upon him, and beat him within an inch of his life. Not content with this mode of retaliation, they tore down the bar, demolished the glasses and decanters, spilled all the liquor, and in short caused the flourishing establishment of Mr. Pat Mulligan to assume a very forlorn appearance.

While this work of destruction was going on, the alarm was given that a body of watchmen had assembled outside the door, and was about to make an advance upon the 'crib.' To exit the house now became the general intent; and several had already beaten a retreat through the rear of the premises, when the watchman burst into the front door, and made captives of all who were present. Frank Sydney was collared by one of the officials, and although our hero protested that he had not mingled in the row, but was merely a spectator, he was carried to the watch-house along with the others.

When the party arrived at the watch-house, (which is situated in a wing of the 'Tombs,') the prisoners were all arrayed in a straight line before the desk of the Captain of the Watch, for that officer's examination. To give the reader an idea of the way in which justice is sometimes administered in New York, we shall detail several of the individual examinations, and their results:—

'What's your name?' cried the Captain, addressing the first of the prisoners. 'Barney McQuig, an' plaze yer honor,' was the reply, in a strong Hibernian accent.

A sort of under-official, who was seated at the desk, whispered in the ear of the Captain of the Watch—

'I know him, he's an infernal scoundrel, but he *votes our ticket*, and you let him slide, by all means.'

'McQuig, you are discharged,' said the Captain to the prisoner.

'Why, sir, that man was one of the worst of the rioters, and he is, besides, one of the greatest villains on the Points,' remarked a watchman, who, having only been recently appointed, was comparatively *green*, and by no means *au fait* in the method of doing business in that 'shop.'

'Silence, sir!' thundered the Captain—'how dare you dispute my authority? I shall discharge whom I please, damn you; and you will do well if you are not discharged from your post for your interference.'

The indignant Captain demanded the name of the next prisoner, who confessed to the eccentric Scriptural cognomen of 'Numbers Clapp.'

'I know *him*, too,' again whispered the under-official—'he is a common and notorious thief, but he is useful to us as a *stool pigeon*,* and you must let him go.'

'Clapp, you can go,' said the Captain; and Mr. Numbers Clapp lost no time in conveying himself from the dangerous vicinity of justice; though such *justice* as we here record, was not very dangerous to *him*.

---

*A *stool pigeon* is a person who associates with thieves, in order to betray their secrets to the police officers, in reference to any robbery which has been committed, or which may be in contemplation. As a reward for furnishing such information, the *stool pigeon* is allowed to steal and rob, *on his own account*, with almost perfect impunity.

'Now, fellow, what's *your* name?' asked the Captain of a shabbily dressed man, whose appearance strongly indicated both abject poverty and extreme ill health.

'Dionysus Wheezlecroft,' answered the man, with a consumptive cough.

'Do you know him?' inquired the Captain, addressing the under-official, in a whisper.

'Perfectly well,' replied the other—'he is a poor devil, utterly harmless and inoffensive, and is both sick and friendless. He was formerly a political stump orator of some celebrity; he worked hard for his party, and when that party got into power, it kicked him to the devil, and he has been flat on his back ever since.'

'What party did he belong to?—*ours?*' asked the Captain.

'No,' was the reply; and that brief monosyllable of two letters, sealed the doom of Dionysus Wheezlecroft.

'Lock him up,' cried the Captain—'he will be *sent over* for six months in the morning.' And so he was—not for any crime, but because he did not belong to *our party*.

Several negroes, male and female, who could not possibly belong to any party, were then summarily disposed of; and at last it came to Frank's turn to be examined.

'Say, you sailor fellow,' quoth the Captain, 'what's your name?'

Frank quietly stepped forward, and in as few words as possible made himself known; he explained the motives of his disguise, and the circumstances under which he had been induced to enter the house of Pat Mulligan.—The Captain, though savage and tyrannical to his inferiors, was all smiles and affability to the rich Mr. Sydney.

'Really, my dear sir,' said he, rubbing his hands, and accompanying almost every word with a corresponding bow, 'you have disguised yourself so admirably, that it would puzzle the wits of a lawyer to make out who you are, until you should *speak*, and then your gentlemanly accent would betray you. Allow me to offer you ten thousand apologies, on behalf of my men, for having dared to subject you to the inconvenience of an arrest; and permit me also to assure you that if they had known who you were, they would not have molested you had they found you demolishing all the houses on the Points.'

'I presume I am at liberty to depart?' said Frank; and the Captain returned a polite affirmative. Our hero left the hall of judgment, thoroughly disgusted with the injustice and partiality of this petty minion of the law; for he well knew that had he himself been in reality nothing more than a poor sailor, as his garb indicated, the three words, 'lock him up,' would have decided his fate for that night; and that upon the following morning the three words, 'send him over,' would have decided his fate for the ensuing six months.

When Frank was gone, the Captain said to the under official:

'That is Mr. Sydney, the young gentleman who was convicted of murder a short time ago, and whose innocence of the crime was made manifest in such an extraordinary manner, just in time to save his neck. He is very rich, and of course I could not think of locking *him* up.'

The Captain proceeded to examine other prisoners, and Frank went in quest of other adventures, in which pursuit we shall follow him.

As he turned into Broadway, he encountered a showily dressed courtezan, who, addressing him with that absence of ceremony for which such ladies are remarkable, requested him to accompany her home.

'This may lead to something,' thought Frank; and pretending to be somewhat intoxicated, he proffered her his arm, which she took, at the same time informing him that her residence was in Anthony street. This street was but a short distance from where they had met; a walk of five minutes brought them to it, and the woman conducted Frank back into a dark narrow court, and into an old wooden building which stood at its further extremity.

'Wait here a few moments, until I get a light,' said the woman; and entering a room which opened from the entry, she left our hero standing in the midst of profound darkness.—Hearing a low conversation going on in the room, he applied his ear to the key-hole, and listened, having good reason to suppose that he himself was the object of the discourse.

'What sort of a man does he appear to be?' was asked, in a voice which sent a thrill through every nerve in Frank's body—for it struck him that he had heard it before. It was the voice of a man, and its tones were peculiar.

'He is a sailor,' replied the woman—'and as he is somewhat drunk now, the powder will soon put him to sleep, and then—'

The remainder of the sentence was inaudible to Frank; he had heard enough, however, to put him on his guard; for he felt convinced that he was in one of those murderous dens of prostitution and crime, where robbery and assassination are perpetrated upon many an unsuspecting victim.

In a few minutes the woman issued from the room, bearing a lighted candle; and requesting Frank to follow, she led the way up a crooked and broken stair-case, and into a small chamber, scantily furnished, containing only a bed, a table, a few chairs, and other articles of furniture, of the commonest kind.

Our hero had now an opportunity to examine the woman narrowly.—Though her eyes were sunken with dissipation, and her cheeks laden with paint, the remains of great beauty were still discernible in her features, and a vague idea obtruded itself, like a dim shadow, upon Frank's mind, that this was not the *first* time he had seen her.

'Why do you watch me so closely?' demanded the woman, fixing her piercing eyes upon his countenance.

'Ax yer pardon, old gal, but aren't you going to fetch on some grog?' said our hero, assuming a thick, drunken tone, and drawing from his pocket a handful of gold and silver coin.

'Give me some money, and I will get you some liquor,' rejoined the woman, her eyes sparkling with delight, as she saw that her intended victim was well supplied with funds. Frank gave her a half dollar, and she went down stairs, promising to be back in less than ten minutes.

During her absence, and while our hero was debating whether to make a hasty retreat from the house, or remain and see what discoveries he could make tending to throw light on the character and practices of the inmates, the chamber door opened, and to his surprise a small boy of about five years of age entered, and gazed at him with childish curiosity.

'Surely I have seen that little lad before,' thought Frank; and then he said, aloud—

'What is your name, my boy?'

'*Jack the Prig,*' replied the little fellow.

Frank started; memory carried him back to the Dark Vaults, where he had heard the Dead Man *catechise* his little son, and he recollected that the urchin had, on that occasion, made the same reply to a similar question. By referring to the sixth chapter of this work, the reader will find the questions and answers of that singular catechism.

Resolving to test the matter further, our hero asked the boy the next question which he remembered the Dead Man had addressed to his son, on that eventful night:—

'Who gave you that name?'

'*The Jolly Knights of the Round Table,*' replied the boy, mechanically.

'By heavens, 'tis as I suspected!' thought Frank—'the child's answers to my questions prove him to be the son of the Dead Man; the voice which I heard while listening in the passage, and which seemed familiar to me, was the voice of that infernal miscreant himself: and the woman whom I accompanied hither, and whom I half fancied I had seen before—that woman is his wife.'

The boy, probably fearing a return of his mother, left the room; and Frank continued his meditations in the following strain:—

'The mystery begins to clear up. This house is probably the one that communicates with the *secret outlet* of the Dark Vaults, through which I passed, blindfolded, accompanied by those two villains, Fred Archer, and the Dead Man. The woman, no doubt, entices unsuspecting men into this devil's trap, and after *drugging* them into a state of insensibility, hands them over to the tender mercies of her hideous husband, who, after robbing them, casts them, perhaps, into some infernal pit beneath this house, there to die and rot!—Good God, what terrible iniquities are perpetrated in the very heart of this great city—iniquities which are unsuspected and unknown! And yet the perpetrators of them often escape their merited punishment, while I, an innocent man, came within a hair's breadth of perishing upon the scaffold for another's crime! But I will not question the divine justice of the Almighty; the guilty may elude the punishment due their crimes, in this world, but vengeance will overtake them in the next. It shall, however, henceforth be the great object of my life, to bring one stupendous miscreant to the bar of human justice—the Dead Man whose escape from the State Prison was followed by his outrage upon Clinton Romaine, by which the poor boy was forever deprived of the faculty of speech; and 'tis my firm belief that 'twas by his accursed hand my aunt was murdered; she was too elevated in character, and too good a Christian, to commit suicide, and *he* is the only man in existence who could slay such an excellent and honorable woman! Yes—something tells me that the Dead Man is the murderer of my beloved relative, and never will I rest till he is in my power, that I may wreak upon him my deadly vengeance!'

Hearing a footstep on the stairs, he assumed an attitude and expression of countenance indicative of drowsiness and stupidity. A moment afterwards, the woman entered, and placed upon the table a small pitcher containing liquor. Taking from a shelf two tumblers, she turned her back towards Frank, and drew from her bosom a small box, from which she rapidly transferred a few grains of fine white powder into one of the tumblers; then going to a cupboard in on corner, she put a teaspoonful of loaf sugar into each of the tumblers, and placing them upon the table, requested our hero to 'help himself.'

Frank poured some liquor into the tumbler nearest him, and looking askance at the woman as he did so, he saw that her features wore a smile of satisfaction; she then supplied her own glass, and was about to raise it to her lips, when our hero said, in a gruff, sleepy tone—

'I say, old woman, you haven't half sweetened this grog of mine. Don't be so d—d stingy of your sugar, for I've money enough to pay for it.'

The woman turned and went to the closet to get another spoonful of the article in question; when Frank, with the rapidity of lightning, *changed the tumblers*, placing the deadly dose designed for him, in the same spot where the woman's tumbler had stood. This movement was accomplished with so much dexterity, that when she advanced to the table with the sugar, she failed to notice the alteration.

'Well, old gal—here's to the wind that blows, the ship that goes, and the lass that loves a sailor!' And delivering himself of this hackneyed nautical toast, the pretended seaman drank off the contents of his glass, an example which was followed by the female miscreant, who responded to Frank's toast by uttering aloud the significant wish—

'May your sleep to-night be sound!'

'Ay, ay, I hope so, and yours, too,' grumbled our hero, placing an enormous quid of tobacco in his cheek, in order to remove the unpleasant taste of the vile liquor which he had just drank.

There was a pause of a few minutes; when suddenly the woman grasped Frank convulsively by the arm, and gazed into his countenance with wildly gleaming eyes.

'Tell me,' she gasped, like one in the agonies of strangulation—'tell me the truth, for God's sake—*did you change those tumblers?*'

'I did,' was the answer.

'Then I am lost!' she almost shrieked—'lost, lost!' The liquor which I drank contained a powder which will within half an hour sink me into a condition of insensibility, from which I shall only awake a raging maniac! I am rightly served—for I designed that to be *your* fate!'

'Wretched woman, I pity you,' said Frank, in a tone of commiseration.

'I deserve not your pity,' she cried, writhing as if in great bodily torment—'my soul is stained with the guilt of a thousand crimes—and the only reparation I can make you, to atone for the wrong I intended, is to warn you to fly from this house

as from a pestilence! This is the abode of murder—it is a charnel-house of iniquity;
fly from hence, as you value your life—for an hour after midnight my husband, the
terrible Dead Man, will return, and although you frustrated me, you cannot escape
his vengeance, should he find you here. Ah, my God! my brain burns—the deadly
potion is at work!'

And thus the miserable woman continued to rave, until the powerful drug which
she had taken fully accomplished its work, and she sank upon the floor in a state of
death-like insensibility.

'Thou art rightly served,' thought Frank, as he contemplated her prostrate
form—'now to penetrate into some of the mysteries of this infernal den!' Taking
the candle from the table, he began his exploration in that fearful house.

In the apartment which adjoined the chamber he discovered little 'Jack the Prig,'
fast asleep in bed. In the restlessness of slumber, the boy had partially thrown off
the bed-clothes, and he exhibited upon his naked breast the picture of a gallows, and
a man hanging! This appalling scene had been drawn with India ink, and pricked
into the flesh with needles, so that it never could be effaced. It was the work of the
boy's hideous father, who, not contented with training up his son to a life of crime,
was anxious that he should also carry upon his person, through life, that fearful
representation of a criminal's doom.

'Would it not be a deed of mercy,' thought our hero—'to take the poor boy from
his unnatural parents, and train him up to a life of honesty and virtue? If I ever get
the father in my power, I will look after the welfare of this unfortunate lad.'

Frank left the room, and descending the stairs, began to explore the lower
apartments of the house. In one, he found a large collection of tools, comprising
every implement used by the villains in their depredations. There were dark
lanterns, crowbars, augers, London *jimmies*, and skeleton keys, for burglary; also,
spades, pickaxes, and shovels, which were probably used in robbing graves, a crime
which at that period was very common in New York. A large quantity of clothing
of all kinds hung upon the walls, from the broadcloth suit of the gentleman down
to the squalid rags of the beggar; these garments Frank conjectured to be *disguises*,
a supposition which was confirmed by the masks, false whiskers, wigs and other
articles for altering the person, which were scattered about.

In a small closet which communicated with this room, our hero found dies for
coining, and a press for printing counterfeit bank-notes; and a table drawer, which
he opened containing a quantity of false coin, several bank-note plates, and a
package of counterfeit bills, which had not yet been signed.

Having sufficiently examined these interesting objects, Frank passed into the
next room, which was of considerable extent. It was almost completely filled with
goods of various kinds, evidently the proceeds of robberies. There were overcoats,
buffalo robes, ladies' cloaks and furs, silk dresses, shawls, boxes of boots and shoes,
cases of dry goods, and a miscellaneous assortment of articles sufficient to furnish
out a large store. The goods in that room were worth several thousands of dollars.

'I shall now seek to discover the *secret outlet* of the Dark Vaults,' thought Frank,
as he descended into the cellar of the house. Here he gazed about him with much

interest; the cellar was damp and gloomy and his entrance with the light disturbed a legion of rats, which went scampering off in every direction, from a corner in which they had collected together; as the young man approached that corner, a fetid, sickening odor saluted his nostrils and a fearful thought flashed across his mind; a moment afterwards, his blood curdled with horror, for before him lay the dead body of a man, entirely naked, and far advanced in state of decomposition; and upon that putrefying corpse had the swarm of rats been making their terrible banquet!

Sick with horror and disgust, Frank precipitately retreated from the loathsome and appalling spectacle, satisfied that he had beheld one of the Dead Man's murdered victims; and he shuddered as he thought that such might have been *his* fate!

In the centre of the cellar an apparatus of singular appearance attracted his notice; and approaching it he instantly became convinced that this was the *secret outlet* for which he sought. Four strong, upright posts supported two ponderous iron crossbars, to which were attached four ropes of great thickness and strength, these ropes were connected with a wooden platform, about six feet square; and beneath the platform was a dark and yawning chasm.

Closely examining this apparatus, our hero saw that by an ingenious contrivance, a person standing on the platform could, by turning a crank, raise or lower himself at will. He cautiously approached the edge of the chasm, and holding down the light, endeavored to penetrate through the darkness; but in vain—he could see nothing, though he could faintly hear a dull, sluggish sound like that produced by the flowing of a vast body of muddy water, and at the same time an awful stench which arose from the black gulf, compelled him to return a short distance.

'The mystery is solved,' he thought—'that fearful hole leads to the subterranean sewers of the city, and also to the Dark Vaults beyond them. By means of that platform, the villains of the *Infernal Regions* below, can pass to and from their den with facility and safety.'

At this moment he heard the vast bell of the City Hall proclaiming the hour of midnight; and he remembered that the woman had told him that her husband, the Dead Man, would return in an hour from that time. At first it occurred to him to await the miscreant's coming, and endeavor to capture him—but then he reflected that the Dead Man might return accompanied by other villains, in which case the plan would not only be impracticable, but his own life would be endangered.

'And even were the villain to come back alone,' thought Frank, 'were I to spring upon him, he might give some signal which would bring to his aid his band of desperadoes from the Vaults below. No—I must not needlessly peril my own life; I will depart from the house now, satisfied for the present with the discoveries I have made, and trusting to be enabled at no distant time to come here with a force sufficient to overcome the hideous ruffian and all his band.'

Leaving the cellar, he traversed the entry and attempted to open the front door; but to his surprise it was securely locked, nor could all his efforts push back the massive bolts which held it fast. He re-entered the room, and examining the windows, found them furnished with thick iron bars like the windows of a prison, so that to pass through them was impossible; and further investigation resulted in the unpleasant conviction that he was a prisoner in that dreadful house, with no immediate means of escape.

He again descended into the cellar, and began seriously to reflect upon the realities of his situation. He was a young man of determination and courage: yet he could not entirely subdue those feelings of uneasiness and alarm which were natural under the circumstances. He was alone, at midnight, in that abode of crime and murder; near him lay the corpse of an unfortunate fellow creature, who had without a doubt fallen by the hand of an assassin; he was momentarily expecting the return of that arch-miscreant, who would show him no mercy; a deep, unbroken silence, and an air of fearful mystery, reigned in that gloomy cellar and throughout that awful house—and before him, dark and yawning as the gate of hell, was that black and infernal pit which led to the subterranean caverns of the Dark Vaults, far below.

'I will sell my life dearly, at all events,' thought our hero, as he drew a bowie knife from his breast, and felt its keen, glittering edge; then impelled by a sudden thought, he advanced to the mouth of the pit, and cut the four ropes, which sustained the wooden platform, so nearly asunder, that they would be almost sure to break with a slight additional weight.

He had scarcely accomplished this task, when a strange, unnatural cry resounded throughout the cellar—a cry so indescribably fearful that it chilled his blood with horror. It was almost instantly followed by a low and melancholy wail, so intense, so solemn, so profoundly expressive of human misery, that Frank was convinced that some unfortunate being was near him, plunged in deepest anguish and distress.

In a few moments the sound entirely ceased, and silence resumed its reign; then Frank, actuated by the noble feelings of his generous nature, said, in a loud voice—

'If there is any unhappy creature who now hears me, and who needs my charitable aid, let him or her speak, that I may know where to direct my search.'

No answer was returned to this request; all was profoundly silent. Frank, however, was determined to fathom the mystery; accordingly, he began a careful search throughout the cellar, and finally discovered in an obscure corner an iron door, which was secured on the outside by a bolt—to draw back this bolt and throw open this door, was but the work of a moment; and our hero was about to enter the cell thus revealed, when a hideous being started from the further end of the dungeon, and with an awful yell rushed out into the cellar, and hid itself in a deep embrasure of the wall.

Whether this creature were human or not, the rapidity of its flight prevented Frank from ascertaining, he cautiously advanced to the place where it had concealed itself, and by the dim light of the lamp which he carried, he saw, crouching down upon the cold, damp earth, a *living object* which appalled him; it was a human creature, but so horribly and unnaturally deformed, that it was a far more dreadful object to behold than the most loathsome of the brute creation.

It was of pygmy size, its shrunk limbs distorted and fleshless, and its lank body covered with filthy rags; its head, of enormous size, was entirely devoid of hair; and the unnatural shape as well as the prodigious dimensions of that bald cranium, betokened beastly idiocy. Its features, ghastly and terrible to look upon, bore a strange resemblance to those of the *Dead Man!* and its snake-like eyes were fixed upon Frank with the ferocity of a poisonous reptile about to spring upon its prey.

'Who art thou?' demanded our hero, as he surveyed the hideous object with horror and disgust.

It answered not, but again set up its low and melancholy wail. Then with extraordinary agility, it sprang from its retreat, and bounding towards the dungeon, entered, and crouched down in one corner, making the cellar resound with its awful shrieks.

''Tis more beast than human,' thought Frank—'I will fasten it in its den, or it may attack me;' and closing the door, he secured it with the bolt. As he did so, he heard the deep-toned bell peal forth the hour of—*one!*

'It is the hour appointed for the return of the Dead Man!' said our hero to himself, with a shudder; and instantly it occurred to him that he might have descended to the Dark Vaults and escaped that way, had he not cut the ropes which supported the platform. But then he reflected that on reaching the Vaults he would be almost certain to fall into the power of the villains assembled there; and he ceased to regret having cut the ropes.

His attention was suddenly arrested by observing the platform descend into the abyss, moved by an unseen agency; for the apparatus was so contrived, that a person in the Vaults below could lower or raise the platform at will, by means of a rope connected with it.

Frank had anticipated that the Dead Man would enter the house through the front door; but he now felt convinced that the miscreant was about to ascend on the platform from the Vaults; and he said to himself—

''Tis well—these almost severed ropes will not sustain the villain's weight, and if he attains to any considerable height, and then falls, his instant death is certain.'

The platform reached the bottom of the abyss—a short pause ensued, and then it began slowly to ascend; higher, higher it mounted, until our hero, fearing that the rope might not break, was about to cut it again, when a yell of agony reached his ear from the depths of the pit, and at the same moment the slackened condition of the rope convinced him that the platform had fallen. He listened, and heard a sound like the plunging of a body into water; then all was silent as the grave.

'The villain has met with a just doom,' thought Frank; and no longer apprehensive of the return of his mortal enemy, he left the cellar, and entering the room above, in which the stolen goods were deposited, threw himself upon a heap of clothes and garments, and fell into a deep slumber.

It was broad daylight when he awoke; and starting up, his eyes rested upon an object which caused him to recoil with horror. The woman whom he had left insensible from the effects of the powerful drug which she had taken, was standing near him, her eyes rolling with insanity, her hair dishevelled, her clothes torn to rags and her face scratched and bleeding, she having in her own madness inflicted the wounds with her own nails.

'Ha!' she exclaimed—'had'st thou not awakened, I would have killed thee! Thy heart would have made me a brave breakfast, and I would have banqueted on thy life-blood! Go hence—go hence! thou shalt not unfold the awful mysteries of this charnel-house! —Ye must not behold the murdered man who lies rotting in the cellar, nor open the dark dungeon of the deformed child of crime! —'tis the hideous offspring of hideous parents—my child and the Dead Man's! 'Twas a judgement from Heaven, that monstrous being; we dare not kill it, so we shut it up from the light of day. Go hence—go hence, or I will fly at thee and tear thine eyes out!'

Frank left the room, and ascended to the chamber, hoping to find a key which would enable him to unlock the front door; and in a table drawer he discovered one, which he doubted not would release him from his imprisonment. Before departing, he wrote the following words on a scrap of paper:—

'If the villain known as the *Dead Man* still lives, he is informed that he is indebted to *me* for his unexpected fall last night. Let the miscreant tremble—for I have penetrated the mysteries of this infernal den, and my vengeance, if not ordinary justice, will speedily overtake him!

SYDNEY.'

Leaving the note upon the table, Frank descended the stairs, unlocked the door, and departed from that abode of crime and horror.

CHAPTER XV

Showing the pranks played in the Haunted House by the two Skeletons.

When Mrs. Belmont awoke from the swoon into which she had fallen, at sight of the terrible apparition which had visited her, daylight was shining through the windows of her chamber. She immediately recalled to mind the events of the preceding night, and resolved to remove without delay from a house which was troubled with such fearful visitants.

Her maid Susan soon entered, to assist her in dressing; and she learned that the girl had neither seen nor heard anything of a mysterious or ghostly nature, during the night. But when the lady related what *she* had seen, the terror of poor Susan knew no bounds, and she declared her determination not to sleep alone in the house another night.

While at breakfast, a visitor was announced, who proved to be the landlord, Mr. Hedge. The old gentleman entered with many apologies for his intrusion, and said—

'To confess the truth, my dear madam, I am anxious to learn how you passed the night. Were you disturbed by any of the goblins or spectres which are supposed to haunt the house?'

Julia related everything which had occurred, and Mr. Hedge expressed great astonishment and concern.

'It is singular—very singular, and fearful,' said he musingly—'a terrible blot seems to rest upon this house; I must abandon the hope of ever having it occupied, as I presume you now desire to remove from it, as a matter of course?'

'Such *was* my intention,' replied Julia, 'but you will be surprised when I assure you that within the last hour I have changed my mind, and am now resolved to remain here. To me there is a charm in mystery, even when that mystery, as in the present instance, is fraught with terror. I think I need entertain no apprehension of receiving personal injury from these ghostly night-walkers, for if they wished to harm me, they could have done so last night. Hereafter, my maid shall sleep in my chamber with me; I shall place a dagger under my pillow, with which to defend myself in case of any attempted injury or outrage—and I shall await the coming of my spectral friend with feelings of mingled dread and pleasure.'

'I am delighted to hear you say so,' rejoined the old gentleman, as he surveyed the animated countenance and fine form of the courageous woman with admiration. In truth, Julia looked very charming that morning; she was dressed in voluptuous *dishabille*, which partially revealed a bust whose luxurious fullness and exquisite symmetry are rarely equalled by the divine creations of the sculptor's art.

'She is very beautiful,' thought the old gentleman; and the sluggish current of his blood began to course thro' his veins with something of the ardor of youth.

Mr. Hedge was a wealthy old bachelor; —and like the majority of individuals, who belong to that class, he adored pretty women, but had always adored them *at a distance*. To him, woman was a divinity; he bowed at her shrine, but dared not presume to taste the nectar of her lips, or inhale the perfume of her sighs. He had always regarded such familiarity as a type of sacrilege. But now, seated *tete-a-tete* with that charming creature, and feasting his eyes upon her voluptuous beauty, his awe of the divinity merged into a burning admiration of the woman.

Julia knew that Mr. Hedge was rich. 'He admires me,' thought she,—'he is old, but wealthy; I will try to fascinate him, and if he desires me to become either his wife or mistress, I will consent, for a connection with him would be to my pecuniary advantage.'

And she *did* fascinate him, as much by her sparkling wit and graceful discourse, as by her charms of person. She related to him a very pleasing little fiction entirely the offspring of her own fertile imagination, which purported to be a history of her own past life. She stated that she was the widow of an English gentleman; she had recently come to America, and had but few acquaintances, and still fewer friends; she felt the loneliness of her situation, and admitted that she much desired a friend to counsel and protect her; the adroit adventuress concluded her extemporaneous romance by adroitly insinuating that her income was scarcely adequate to her respectable maintenance.

Mr. Hedge listened attentively to this narrative, and religiously believed every word of it. While the lady was speaking, he had drawn his chair close to hers, and taken one of her small, delicate hands in his. We must do him the justice to observe, that though her beauty had inspired him with passion, he nevertheless sincerely sympathised with her on account of her pretended misfortunes—and, supposing her to be strictly virtuous, he entertained not the slightest wish to take advantage of her unprotected situation.

'My dear young lady,' said he—'although I have known you but a very short time, I have become exceedingly interested in you. I am an old man—old enough to be your father; and as a father I now speak to you.—What I am about to say, might seem impertinent and offensive in a young man, but you will pardon it in me. You have unconscientiously dropped a hint touching the insufficiency of your income to maintain you as a lady should be maintained. I am rich—deign to accept from me as a gift—or as a loan, if you will—this scrap of paper; 'tis valueless to me, for I have more money than I need. The gift—or loan—shall be repeated as often as your necessities require it.'

He squeezed a bank-note into her hand—and when she, with affected earnestness, desired him to take it back, assuring him that she needed no immediate pecuniary aid, he insisted that she should retain it; and shortly afterwards he arose and took his leave, having easily obtained permission to call upon her the next day.

'Egad, she would make me a charming wife—if she would only have me,' thought the old gentleman, as he left the house.

'Five hundred dollars!' exclaimed Julia, as she examined the bank-note which he had given her—'how liberal! I have fairly entrapped the silly old man; he is too honorable to propose that I should become his mistress, and he will probably offer me his hand in marriage. I will accept him at once—and to avoid detection, I shall remove with my venerable husband to Boston, which I have heard is a charming city, where a woman of fashion and intrigue can lead a glorious and brilliant career.'

That night she retired early to rest, and her maid Susan shared her chamber— an arrangement highly satisfactory to the abigail, who was glad of company in a house where ghosts were in the habit of perambulating during the night.

Neither mistress nor maid closed an eye in slumber—but midnight came, and they had not seen nor heard anything of a ghostly nature. Yet strange events were taking place in the house,—events which will throw light upon the fearful mysteries of the place.

It was about an hour after midnight, when a large stone among those of which the foundation of the house was built, turned slowly upon pivots, revealing an aperture in the wall, and at the same instant the glare of a lantern shone into the cellar.

From the aperture emerged two persons of frightful appearance, one of whom carried the lantern; they were both dressed in tight-fitting garments of black cloth, upon which was daubed in white paint the figure of a skeleton; and each of their faces had been blacked, and then drawn over with the representation of a skull. Seen by an imperfect light, they exactly resembled two skeletons.

'By Jesus!' exclaimed one of them, in a tone which was anything but hollow or sepulchral—'let's put for the pantry and see what there is to *ate*, for be the powers I'm starved wid hunger!'

'That's the talk, Bloody Mike—so we will,' responded the other worthy, who was no other than our old friend Ragged Pete, though his nearest relatives would never have recognized him in the disguise he then wore.

Mike and Pete ascended to the pantry, and began a diligent search after provisions.

'Glory to ould Ireland, here's grand illigant ham!' exclaimed the first mentioned individual, as he dragged from a shelf a large dish containing the article he had named.

'And blow me tight if here isn't a cold turkey and a pan of pudding,' rejoined Pete, whose researches had also been crowned with success.

'Faith, it's ourselves, Peter, dear, that'll have a supper fit for the bishop of Cork, an' that's a big word,' remarked Mike, as he triumphantly placed upon a table the savory viands above mentioned, and 'fell to' with surpassing vigor, an example in which he was followed by his comrade.

'This playing the ghost is a good business, by jingo!' said Pete, with his mouth full of ham.

'True for ye!' replied the Irish skeleton, his articulation rendered indistinct by the masses of turkey which were fast travelling down his throat to his capacious stomach.

The repast was not finished until they had devoured every atom of the provisions; and then Pete went in quest of something to 'wash the wittles down with,' as he expressed it.

Upon a sideboard in the adjoining room he found wines and liquors of excellent quality, which he and his companion were soon engaged in discussing, with as much ease and comfort as if they were joint proprietors of the whole concern.

The two gentlemen grew quite cosey and confidential over their wine, and as their conversation mainly referred to matters in which the reader perhaps feels an interest, we shall so far intrude upon their privacy as to report the same.

'I've news to tell you, Mike,' said Pete—'the Dead Man has somehow or other found out that the lady who moved into this house yesterday, is the wife of Mr. Sydney, the rich chap that he hates so infernally 'cause he had him arrested once. Well, you know that last night some one cut the ropes that hoists the platform from the Vaults, so that the Dead Man fell and came nigh breaking his neck; and as it is, he's so awfully bruised that he won't have the use of his limbs for some time to come—besides, he fell into the sewers, and would have been drowned, if I hadn't heerd him, and dragged him out. The chap wot played him that trick was this same Sydney; for a note was found this morning in Anthony street crib, bragging about it, and signed with his name. Now it seems that his wife that lives in this house, and who we are trying to skeer out of it, as we have done all the others that ever lived here—it seems that *she* hates Sydney like thunder and wants to be revenged on him for something—and that the Dead Man found that out, too. So 'our boss' thinks he'll try and set up a partnership with this Mrs. Belmont, as she calls herself—and with her aid he calculates to get Mr. Sydney into his power. If the lady and him sets up business together, our services as ghosts won't be wanted any longer; and I'm very sorry for it, because we've had glorious times in this house, frightening people, and making them believe the place was haunted.'

As this long harangue rendered Pete thirsty, he extinguished his eloquence for a few moments in a copious draught of choice Burgundy.

'That row at Pat Mulligan's last night was a divilish nate affair,' remarked Mike.

'Yes,' said Pete—'and we all got bundled off to the watch-house; but the Captain let me go—he always does, because I vote for his party. After I got clear, I came here, wrapped in a great sheet, and went up into Mrs. Belmont's chamber; after frightening the poor woman almost to death, I goes up to the bed, puts my hand on her face, and tells her that she'd see me agin—whereupon she gives a great shriek, and I cut my puck through the hole in the cellar.'

'Be the powers,' remarked Bloody Mike—'it's a great convenience entirely, to have thim secret passages from the Vault into intarior of houses; there's two of thim, one under the crib in Anthony street, and the other under this dacent house in *Rade* street.'

'Yes, you're right,' said Pete—'but come, let's do our business and be off—it's near three o'clock.'

The two worthies mounted the stairs with noiseless steps, and pausing before Mr. Belmont's chamber, Ragged Pete gave utterance to an awful groan. A stifled shriek from the interior of the room convinced them the inmates were awake and terribly frightened.

Pete's groan was followed by a violent *hiccuping* on the part of Bloody Mike— for, to confess the truth, that convivial gentleman had imbibed so freely that he was, in vulgar parlance, most essentially drunk.

'Stop that infernal noise, and follow me into the room,' whispered Pete, who, having confined himself to wine instead of brandy, was comparatively sober.

'Lade on, I'm after ye!' roared the Irish skeleton. Pete, finding the door locked gave it a tremendous kick, and it burst open with a loud crash.

Julia and her maid screamed with horror and affright, as they beheld two hideous forms resembling skeletons come rushing into the room.

Ragged Pete advanced to the bedside of Mrs. Belmont, and threw himself into an approved pugilistic attitude, as if challenging that lady to take a 'set to' with him; while Bloody Mike stumbled over the prostrate form of the lady's maid, who occupied a temporary bed upon the floor. Forgetting his assumed part, he yelled out for something to drink, and forthwith began to sing in tones of thunder, the pathetic Hiberian ballad commencing with—

> 'A sayman courted a farmer's daughter,
> That lived convenient to the Isle of Man.'

'The devil!—you'll spoil all,' muttered Pete, as he seized Mike, and with difficulty dragged him from the room. 'Ain't you a nice skeleton, to get drunk and sing love songs,' he whispered contemptuously, pulling his inebriated comrade downstairs after him: 'No dacent ghost ever gets as corn'd as you be,' he added, as they entered the 'hole in the wall;' after which the stone was turned into its place, which it fitted so exactly, that the most critical eye could not have discovered anything to indicate that it had ever been moved at all.

Mrs. Belmont was now fully satisfied in her own mind that there was nothing supernatural about the nocturnal intruders, but that they were in reality substantial flesh and blood, and though she could not divine how they had entered the house, she was much relieved and comforted by the assurance that it was with *living* men she had to deal— a conviction which was amply confirmed the next morning, when the havoc done to the eatables and drinkables was announced to her by the indignant Susan.

In the afternoon Mr. Hedge called upon her as appointed, and dined with his interesting and fascinating tenant.

After dinner, Julia caused the sofa to be wheeled in front of the glorious fire which glowed in the grate (for the weather was intensely cold) and seating herself, invited the old gentleman to place himself at her side.

Then she exerted all her fine powers of discourse to increase his admiration, and draw from him a declaration of love, and an offer of marriage.

Wine was brought in, and gradually their spirits became enlivened by the sparkling genii of the grape. The old man felt the fires of youth careering through his veins, and his withered cheek was suffused with a flush of passion.

'Beautiful Julia,' said he—'I observe that you have a magnificent piano; will you favor me with an air?'

She smiled an assent, and her aged admirer conducted her to the instrument with the most ceremonious politeness. After a brilliant prelude, executed with artistic delicacy and skill, she dashed off into a superb Italian air, which raised her listener (who was passionately devoted to music,) into the seventh heaven of ecstasy.

'Glorious!—grand!' were his exclamations of delight, when she had finished the air and she needed no urgent persuasion to induce her to favor him with another.

Artfully and admirably did she compose an extempore song, adapted to immediate circumstances, beginning —'I love no vain and fickle youth,' and beautifully depicting the love of a young woman for a man advanced in years. She sung it with a most touching air, and threw into her countenance and style an expression of melting tenderness.

Ere she had terminated, the old gentleman was kneeling at her feet; and pressing her fair hand to his lips.

'Divine creature,' he murmured—'can you pardon the presumption and foolishness of an old man, who dares to love you? Your beauty and your fascinations have conquered and bewildered me. I know that the proposal coming from me, is madness—I know that you will reject my suit with disdain—yet hear me Julia; I am an old, rich and solitary man—I need some gentle ray of sunshine to gild my few remaining years—I need some beautiful creature, like yourself, to preside over my gloomy household, and cheer me in my loneliness by her delightful society and the music of her voice. Boundless wealth shall be at your command; no restraint shall ever be placed upon the number of your servants, the splendor of your carriages and equipages, the costliness of your jewels; and the magnificence of your amusements. Speak—and seal my destiny.'

And Julia *did* speak, and became the affianced wife of Mr. Hedge. Her operations thus far had been crowned with triumphant success.

It was arranged that their marriage should take as privately as possible in one month, from that day.—Julia suggested that, immediately after their union, they should remove to Boston, and take up their permanent residence in that city, to which proposal the old gentleman gave a cheerful consent.

'And if you have no objection, my dear Julia,' said he, 'we will be united by Dr. Sinclair, the young and excellent rector of St. Paul's, to which church I belong.'

Julia signified her compliance with the arrangement. She had both seen and admired the young rector, and thought him handsome—very handsome.

Previous to Mr. Hedge's departure that evening, he presented her with a large sum of money, to defray, he said, the expenses necessary to be incurred in her preparations for the marriage. Then the enamored old gentleman kissed her hand, and took his leave.

When he was gone, Julia abandoned herself to the pleasing thoughts engendered by her present brilliant prospects. While in the midst of these agreeable meditations, she was interrupted by the sound of a footstep behind her; and turning, she beheld a man of an aspect so hideous and revolting, that she screamed with terror.

'Hush! be silent, madam—I mean you no harm,' said the man, as he closed the door, and seated himself at her side upon the sofa. Julia gazed on him with surprise and dread. His face, which at best was the most loathsome and horrible ever worn by man, was mangled and bruised as if by some severe and terrible injury; he moved with evident pain and difficulty, and carried one of his arms in a sling.

'Our interview shall be brief, and to the point,' said the mysterious visitor. 'I am he who is called the *Dead Man*, and I am not disposed to quarrel with the title, for I like it.—You and your history are known to me; it matters not how I obtained my information; you are styled Mrs. Belmont, a widow—but you are the discarded wife of Francis Sydney, and half an hour ago you engaged yourself in marriage to Mr. Hedge, the owner of this house.'

Julia started with alarm, for she felt that she was in the power of that terrible man.

'What is the object of your visit?' she asked.

'Listen and you shall know. I have a secret subterranean cavern which communicates with the cellar of this building, and 'twas by that means I entered the house to-night. Myself and friends often find it convenient to carry stolen goods through this house into our den; and in order to have the place all to ourselves, we have heretofore frightened away the people who have come here to live; thus the house is reputed to be haunted. 'Twas our design to frighten you away, also; but having discovered *who and what you are*, I've concluded to explain the mystery, and set up a copartnership with you.'

'And in what business can *we* possibly be connected together?' asked Julia, with ill-concealed disgust.

'In the business of *vengeance!*' thundered the Dead Man, foaming with rage. 'Tell me, woman—do you hate Sydney?'

'I do!—and would sell my soul to be revenged upon him,' she replied with flashing eyes.

'Enough!' cried the other, with triumphant joy—'I knew you would join me in my plan of vengeance. Now, madam, from this moment we are friends—*partners,* rather let me say—and there's my hand upon it.' And he gripped her hand almost fiercely, while she shuddered at the awful contact. It seemed as if she were touching a corpse.

'Hereafter,' continued the miscreant,—'you shall rest at night securely in this house, undisturbed by pretended ghosts. Do you see these wounds and bruises?—for them I am indebted to Sydney; my wife is a raging maniac, and I am also indebted to him for *that*—and by eternal hell! when I get him in my power, he shall die by inches; he shall suffer every slow torture which my ingenuity can devise; his brain shall burn, and when death shall end his torments, I have sworn to eat his heart; and by G——, *I'll do it!*'

'But how will you get him into your power?' asked Julia, delighted with the prospect of revenging herself upon poor Frank.

'I will contrive some means of deluding him into this house; and once in here, he shall never again behold the light of day,' replied the Dead Man, as he arose to withdraw.

'Stay a moment,' said Julia, with some embarrassment—'there is also a colored man in Sydney's house, and—'

'I know it—he shall be liberated,' interrupted the Dead Man, and added—'you shall see me again to-morrow—farewell.'

He left the room, descended to the cellar, and passed through the secret passage to the Dark Vaults.

That night at about the hour of twelve, the dark figure of a man crossed the garden in the rear of Frank Sydney's house, and approached the iron door of the wine-vault wherein Nero, the African, was imprisoned. By the aid of skeleton keys he unlocked the door, and bade the prisoner come forth.

The negro obeyed, surprised and delighted at his unexpected deliverance.

'To whom am I indebted for this friendly act?' he asked.

'I have no time to answer questions,' replied the Dead Man, for it was he. 'Hasten to your mistress at No.—Reade street, and remember your motto as well as mine must be—'Vengeance on Sydney!' '

'Yes—vengeance on Sydney,' muttered the black, from between his clenched teeth, as he hurried away in the direction of Reade street.

'He will be another agent to assist me in torturing my enemy,' said the Dead Man to himself, as he bent his rapid footsteps towards the Dark Vaults.

Nero soon reached the residence of Mrs. Belmont, in Reade street. He was admitted into the house by Susan, who informed him that her mistress had not yet retired. The black quickly mounted the stairs, and entering the room, was about to rush forward and clasp the lady in his arms, when she checked him by a movement of disgust, desired him not to approach her, and pointing to a chair in a distant corner, coldly requested him to seat himself there.

Why did that unprincipled and licentious woman thus repulse the former partner of her guilty joys—he who had so long been the recipient of her favors, and the object of her unhallowed love? Was it because he was emaciated, filthy and in rags, the results of his long imprisonment in a loathsome dungeon? No—that was not the reason of her repulsing him.

Julia was a woman wildly capricious in her nature; she was a creature of sudden impulses—her most passionate love would often instantly change to bitterest hate. In this instance, her love for the African had entirely and forever ceased, and she now viewed him with contemptuous disgust, wondering that she could ever have had such a *penchant* for him.

"'Tis strange,' she thought, 'that I ever could descend to an intrigue with that vile negro. Heavens! I loathe the very sight of him!'

Nero, on his part, was astounded at this unexpected reception; he had anticipated a night of voluptuous bliss with his former paramour, and he could not divine the cause of her sudden rejection of him.

'My dear Julia, why this coldness? —what have I done to offend you?' he demanded, after a short pause.

'Presume not to call me *your dear Julia*, fellow,' she replied scornfully. 'You have done nothing to offend me, but the days of our familiarity are over. The liberties which I permitted you to take, and the indulgences which I formerly granted to you, can never be repeated. I will not condescend to explain myself farther than to remark, that all my former regard for you has ceased, and I now view you not only with indifference, but with positive dislike. I procured your liberation from that dungeon merely because it was on my account you were placed there. You can, if you choose, re-enter my service as footman, and your wages shall be the same as those of any other servant of your class; but remember—henceforth I am the mistress, and you the menial, and any presumption on your part, or attempt at familiarity, shall be instantly followed by your discharge. Clean yourself of that filth, and begin your duties to-morrow, as a respectful, orderly and obedient servant. You can go now.'

Nero left the room, humbled and crest-fallen, inwardly resolved to revenge himself upon that proud and abandoned woman, should the opportunity ever present itself.

Gentlest of readers, we now invite thee to accompany us to view other scenes and other characters in our grand drama of human life, and its many crimes.

CHAPTER XVI

Showing the Voluptuous Revellings of the Rector and the Licentious Josephine, and illustrating the Power of Temptation over Piety and Morality.

Alas, for Dr. Sinclair! the masquerade ball, and the triumph of Josephine Franklin, were but the commencement of a career of folly and crime on his part. From that fatal night in after years of remorse and misery, he dated his downfall.

He became a frequent visitor at the Franklin House, and continued his guilty amour, with unabated zeal. Yet neither his own idolizing congregation, nor the admiring world, suspected his frailty; he was regarded as the most exemplary of Christians, and the best of men. When in the pulpit, it was often remarked that he seemed absent-minded, and ill at ease; he did not preach with his usual fluent and fervid eloquence, nor pray with his accustomed earnest devotion. In person, too, he was changed; his eyes were red, as if with weeping; his cheeks were pale and haggard, and the rosy hue of health was gone. His dress was frequently neglected and disordered, and he even sometimes appeared with his hair uncombed, and his face unshaved. These indications of mental and personal irregularity were much noticed and commented upon by his congregation, comprised as it was of people the most aristocratic and particular.

'Our dear pastor is ill,' said they, with looks of concern and sympathy; but in answer to the numerous questions addressed to him in reference to the state of his health, he denied the existence of all bodily ailment.

'Then he must be affected with some mental disquietude,' said they, and forthwith he was beset by a tribe of comforters; one of whom had at last the audacity to affirm that the Doctor's breath smelt unpleasantly of wine!

This insinuation was received with contempt, for the brethren and sisters of the congregation would not believe anything discreditable to the beloved rector, and he continued to enjoy their confidence and esteem, long after they had begun to observe something very singular in his conduct and appearance.

But in truth, Dr. Sinclair had fallen from his high estate, and become a wine bibber and a lover of the flesh. His stern integrity, his sterling piety, and his moral principle, were gone forever; the temptress had triumphed and he was ruined.

Why are ministers of the gospel so prone to licentiousness? is a question often asked, and is often answered thus—Because they are a set of hypocritical libertines. But we say, may not we see the reason in this: the female members of a church are apt to regard their minister with the highest degree of affectionate admiration— as an idol worthy to be worshipped. They load him with presents—they spoil him with flattery—they dazzle him with their glances, and encourage him by their smiles. Living a life of luxurious ease, and enjoying a fat salary, he cannot avoid experiencing those feelings which are natural to all mankind. He is very often thrown into the society of pretty women of his flock, under circumstances which are dangerously fascinating. The 'sister,' instead of maintaining a proper reserve, grows too communicative and too familiar, and the minister, who is but a man, subject to all the weaknesses and frailties of humanity, often in an unguarded moment forgets his sacred calling, and becomes the seducer—though we question if literal *seduction* be involved, where the female so readily *complies* with voluptuous wishes, which perchance, she responds to with as much fervor as the other party entertains them. Therefore, we say that licentiousness on the part of ministers of the gospel is produced in *very many* cases by the encouragements held out to them by too admiring and too affectionate sisters.

One evening, Dr. Sinclair repaired to Franklin House at an early hour, for he had engaged to dine with Josephine. He was admitted by a tall, fresh-looking country lad, who had recently entered the house in the capacity of footman, having been selected for that station by Mrs. Franklin herself, as the lady had conceived a strong admiration of his robust form and well-proportioned limbs.

The Doctor found Josephine in her *boudoir*, voluptuously reclining upon a damask ottoman, and languidly turning over the leaves of a splendid portfolio of engravings.

'Ah, my dear Doc,' she exclaimed, using a familiar abbreviation of Doctor, 'I am devilish glad to see you, for I am bored to death with *ennui.* Heigho!'

'And if I may presume to inquire, Josey,' said the Doctor—'what have you there to engage your attention?'

'Oh, views from nature,' she laughingly replied, handing him the portfolio for his inspection.

Turning over the leaves, the Doctor found, somewhat to his astonishment, that the engravings were of rather an obscene character, consisting principally of nude male figures; —and upon these specimens of a perverted art had she been feasting her impure imagination. The time had been, when the Doctor would have turned with pain and disgust from such an evidence of depravity; but he had lately become so habituated to vice, that he merely smiled in playful reproach, and leisurely examined the pictures.

'I commend your taste,' said he, at length. Our preferences are both strictly classical; you dote upon the Apollo Belvedere, while in you I worship a Venus.'

'Yes—*you* are my Apollo,' she rejoined, with a glance of passion, encircling him with her arms.

*   *   *   *   *

Dinner was magnificently served in an apartment whose splendor could scarce have been surpassed in a kingly palace.

They dined alone; for Mrs. Franklin was invisible—and so, also, was the comely young footman!

After dinner, came wine—bright, sparkling wine, whose magical influence gilds the dull realities of life with the soft radiance of fairy land! How the foaming champagne glittered in the silver cup, and danced joyously to the ripe, pouting lip of beauty, and the eloquent mouth of divinity! How brilliant became their eyes, and what a glorious roseate hue suffused their cheeks!

Again and again was the goblet drained and replenished, until the maddening spell of intoxication was upon them both. Hurrah! away with religion, and sermonizing, and conscience! Bacchus is the only true divinity, and at his rosy shrine let us worship, and pledge him in brimming cups of the bright nectar, the drink of the gods!

Then came obscene revels and libidinous acts. The depraved Josephine, attired in a superb robe of lace, her splendid bust uncovered, and her cheeks flushed with wine, danced with voluptuous freedom, while the intoxicated rector, reeling and flourishing a goblet, sang a lively opera air, in keeping with her graceful but indelicate movements. Then—but we will not inflict upon the reader the disgusting details of that evening's licentious extravagances.

Midnight came and the doctor, tipsy as he was, saw the necessity of taking his departure; for though urged by Josephine to pass the night with her, he dared not comply, knowing that his absence from home all night would appear strange and suspicious to his housekeeper and domestics, and give rise to unpleasant inquiries and remarks. He therefore sallied forth, and though he staggered occasionally, he got along tolerably well, until he encountered a watchman standing half asleep in a doorway, muffled up in his huge cloak; and then, with that invincible spirit of mischief which characterizes a drunken man, the Doctor determined to have a 'lark' with the night guardian, somewhat after the fashion of the wild, harem-scarem students at the University at which he had graduated—in which pranks he had often participated.

Leaning against a lamp-post support, he began singing, in a loud and boisterous manner—

'Watchman—hic—tell us of the—hic—night.'

Now it happened that the watchman was one of those surly ruffians who never stop to remonstrate with a poor fellow, in whom wine has triumphed over wit. Instead of kindly inquiring his address, and conducting the unfortunate gentleman to his residence, the self-important petty official adopted the very means to irritate him and render him more boisterous. In a savage, brutal manner, he ordered the doctor to 'stop his d——d noise, and move on, or he'd make him!'

'Nay, friend, thou art insolent,' remarked the young gentleman, who drunk as he was, could not brook the insults of the low, vulgar ruffian.

'Insolent, am I?'—take that, and be d——d to you!' cried the fellow, raising a heavy bludgeon, and dealing the poor Doctor a blow on the head which felled him senseless to the ground, covered with blood.

'That'll teach you genteel chaps not to meddle with us *officers*,' growled the watchman. 'I wonder what he's got about him—perhaps some dangerous weapon—let's see.' Thrusting his hand into the pockets of his victim, he drew forth a valuable gold watch, and a purse containing a considerable sum of money. Why did he so rapidly transfer these articles to this own pockets? Was if for the purpose of restoring them to the owner, on the morrow? We shall see.

'I 'spose I'd better lug him to the watch-house,' said the 'officer'—and he struck his club three times on the pavement, which summoned another 'officer' to his assistance. The two then raising the wounded man between them, conducted him towards the Tombs.

The Doctor, awaking from his unconsciousness, and feeling himself in the grasp of the watchman, instantly comprehended the state of affairs, and shuddered as he thought of his exposure and ruin. The fumes of the wine which he had drunk, had entirely subsided; but he felt himself weak from loss of blood, sick from his recent debauch, while the wound on his head pained him terribly. Oh, how bitterly he deplored his connection with that depraved woman, who had been the cause of his downfall!

The awful dread of exposure prompted him to appeal to the mercy of his captors.

'Watchman,' said he, 'pray conduct me to my home, or suffer me to go there myself, for with shame I confess it, I am a gospel minister, and wish to avoid exposure.'

The two fellows laughed scornfully. 'Don't think to come that gammon over us,' said they. 'A minister indeed!—and picked up blind drunk in the street at midnight!'

'But I have money about me, and will pay you well,' said the Doctor.

The man who had struck him with the club, knowing that he had no money, affected to be indignant at this attempt to 'bribe an officer,' and refused to release him.

Oh, hapless fate!—truly the 'way of transgressors is hard.' The learned and eloquent Dr. Sinclair—the idol of his aristocratic and fashionable congregation—whose words of piety and holiness were listened to with attention by admiring thousands every Sabbath day—was incarcerated in the watch-house! Yes—thrust into a filthy cell, among a swarm of felons, vile negroes, vagabonds and loafers—the scum of the city!

The cell was about twenty feet square; one half of it was occupied by a platform, at a height of four feet from the floor. This platform was called the '*bunk*,' and it was covered with the prostate forms of about twenty men, including the ragged beggar, the raving drunkard, and the well-dressed thief—all huddled together, and shivering with the cold, which was intense. The stone floor of the cell was damp and covered with filth; yet upon it, and beneath the *bunk*, several wretched beings were stretched, some cursing each other and themselves, others making the place resound with hideous laughter, while one was singing, in drunken tones, a shockingly obscene song.

Into this den of horrors was Dr. Sinclair rudely thrust; for no one believed his statement that he was a clergyman, and indeed his appearance, when undergoing the examination of the Captain of the Watch, was anything but clerical. His face was covered with blood, his clothes soiled and disordered, his hat crushed, and his manner wild and incoherent. It is more than probable that, had the Captain known who he was, he would have ordered his immediate discharge.

Groping his way along the damp, cold walls of his cell, which was in profound darkness, the Doctor stumbled over a person who was lying upon the floor, writhing in the agonies of *delirium tremens*. In frantic rage, this miserable creature seized the rector's leg, and bit it horribly, causing him to utter a cry of agony, which was responded to by roars of laughter from the hellish crew. Extricating himself with difficulty from the fierce clutch of the maniac, the unhappy gentleman seated himself upon a large iron pipe which ran through the cell, and prayed for death.

Slowly passed the dreadful night away; and the first faint rays of morning, struggling through the narrow aperture in the wall, revealed an appalling sight. Men made hideous and inhuman by vice and wretchedness lay stretched amid the filth and dampness of that dungeon, glaring at each other with savage eyes. And soon the awful discovery was made, that one of their number had, during the night, been frozen to death! Yes—there, beneath the *bunk*, cold and ghastly, lay the rigid corpse of a poor fellow creature, whose only crime had been his poverty! Out upon such justice and such laws, which tolerate such barbarities to one whose misfortunes should be pitied, not visited by the damnable cruelty of the base hirelings of a corrupt misgovernment!

It is not our wish to devote much time to the relation of unimportant particulars; suffice it to say, that Dr. Sinclair was brought before the police for drunkenness, and was also charged with having violently assaulted Watchman Squiggs, who had taken him in custody!

'You see, yer honor, I was going my rounds, when up comes this ere chap and knocks me down, and would have killed me, if I hadn't hit him a light tap on the head with my club. Then I rapped for help, and —'

'That's enough!' growled the magistrate, who had himself been drunk the night before, and was made irritable by a severe headache—'that's enough—he struck an officer—serious offence—looks guilty—old offender—thief, no doubt—send him up for six months!'

The Doctor whispered a few words in the ear of the magistrate, who rubbed his eyes and regarded him with a look of astonishment, saying—

'Bless my soul, is it possible? Dr. Sinclair—humph! Sentence is revoked—you're discharged; the devil! —about to send you up for six months—a great mistake, upon my word—ha, ha, ha!'

The rector turned to watchman Squiggs, and said to him, sternly—

'Fellow, when I fell into your infernal clutches, I had a watch and money about me; they are now missing; can you give any account of them?'

The watchman solemnly declared he knew nothing about them! The Doctor felt no inclination to bandy words with the scoundrel; he paused a moment to reflect upon the best course to pursue, under the disagreeable circumstances in which he found himself placed. A feasible plan soon suggested itself, and leaving the police office, he stepped into a hackney coach, and requested the driver to convey him with all despatch to Franklin house. Arrived there, he dismissed the vehicle, and ascending to Josephine's chamber, explained to her the whole affair, and threw himself upon a sofa to obtain a few hours' necessary repose.

As soon as he had left the police office, the magistrate whispered to the watchman—

'Squiggs, I know very well that you took that gentleman's watch and money. Don't interrupt me—I say, *I know you did*. Well, you must share the spoils with me.'

'I'll take my oath, yer honor—'

'*Your oath!*—that's a good one!' cried the magistrate, laughing heartily. '—'d'ye think I'd believe you on oath? Why, man, you just now perjured yourself in swearing that Parson Sinclair assaulted you—whereas *you* beat him horribly with your club, with little provocation, and stole his watch and money. I know you, Squiggs; you can't gammon me. Once for all, will you share the booty with me?'

The rascal dared not hesitate any longer; so with great reluctance he drew the plunder from his pocket, and divided it equally with 'his honor,' who reserved the watch for himself, it being a splendid article, of great value.

Is any one disposed to doubt the truth of this little sketch? We assure the reader it is not in the least degree exaggerated. The local magistracy of New York included many functionaries who were dishonest and corrupt. Licentiousness was a prominent feature in the characters of some of these unworthy ministers of justice. Attached to the police office was a room, ostensibly for the private examination of witnesses. When a witness happened to be a female, and pretty, 'his honor' very often passed an hour or so in this room with her, carefully locking the door to prevent intrusion; and there is every reason to suppose that his examination of her was both close and searching.

We remember an incident which occurred several years ago, which is both curious and amusing. A beautiful French girl—a fashionable courtezan—was taken to the police office, charged with stealing a lady's small gold watch. Her accuser was positive that she had the article about her; her pocket, reticule, bonnet, hair, and dress were searched without success. The rude hand of the officer invaded her voluptuous bosom, but still without finding the watch. 'Perhaps she has it in her mouth,' suggested the magistrate; but no, it was not there. 'Where can she have hidden it? I am certain she has it somewhere on her person,' remarked the accuser. 'I will examine her in private,' quoth the magistrate, and he directed the girl to follow him into the adjoining room. His honor locked the door, and said to the fair culprit—'My dear, where have you concealed the watch?' In the most charming broken English imaginable, Mademoiselle protested her innocence of the charge, with such passionate eloquence, that his honor began to think the accuser must be mistaken. 'At all events,' thought he, 'she is a sweet little gipsy;' and he forthwith honored her with a shower of amorous kisses, which she received with the most bewitching *naivete*; but when he began to make demonstrations of a still more decided nature, she resisted, though unsuccessfully, for his honor was portly and powerful, and somewhat 'used to things.' But lo! to his astonishment, he *discovered the watch!*—and in *such* a place! French ingenuity alone could have devised such a method of concealment, and legal research alone could have discovered it.

We left Dr. Sinclair in the chamber of Josephine, at Franklin House, reposing after the exciting and disagreeable adventures of the preceding night. He awoke at noon, somewhat refreshed, and entered a bath while Josephine sent a servant to purchase a suit of clothes, as those which he had worn were so soiled and torn as to be unfit for further service.

Reclining luxuriously in the perfumed water of the marble bath, the Doctor experienced a feeling of repose and comfort. He had long learned to disregard the 'still, small voice' of his own conscience; and, provided he could reach his home and answer all inquiries without incurring suspicion—provided, also, his having been incarcerated in the watch-house should not be exposed—he was perfectly contented.

His clothes being brought him, he dressed himself, and joining Josephine in the parlor, partook of a refreshing repast; then, bidding farewell to his 'lady-love,' he took his departure, and proceeded to his own residence. In answer to the earnest inquiries of the members of his household, he stated that he had passed the night with a friend in Brooklyn; and entering his study, he applied himself to the task of writing his next Sunday's sermon.

CHAPTER XVII

Illustrating the truth of the proverb that 'Murder will out,' and containing an Appalling Discovery.

Two or three days after the above events, Dr. Sinclair was sent for by a woman lying at the point of death. He found her occupying the garret of an old, crazy tenement in Orange street; she was stretched upon a miserable bed, covered only by a few rags, and her short breathings, sunken cheeks, and lustreless eyes, proclaimed that the hand of death was upon her. Though young in years, her appearance indicated that she had passed through much suffering, destitution and sin.

'Are you the clergyman?' she asked in a faint voice.

'I am; what can I do for you, my good woman?' said the Doctor, seating himself on a rickety stool at the bedside.

'Oh, sir,' cried the invalid, evidently in great mental distress, 'I want you to pray for me. Do you think there is any hope for such a sinner as I have been? I am dying, and my soul is lost—forever!'

In his own heart, the rector felt his unfitness to administer comfort in such a case, considering his own wickedness; yet he strove to quiet the uneasiness of the poor creature, by assuring her that there was hope for the 'chief of sinners.' At her request he prayed with her; and then she addressed him as follows:—

'There is something on my mind which I must make confession of, or I shall not die easy—something that will make you shrink from me, as from a guilty wretch, who deserves no mercy. I am a *murderess!*'

'A murderess!' echoed the Doctor, starting back with horror; after a few moments' pause, he added—'proceed with your confession.'

'I will, sir. Four years ago, I entered the service of Mrs. Lucretia Franklin, in Washington Place.'

The Doctor started again—this time with surprise; and he listened with attentive interest to the woman's narrative.

'Mrs. Franklin's husband,' she resumed, 'was a very rich man, and very religious and strict; his daughter Sophia took after him much, and was a very good girl; but his wife and daughter Josephine were exactly contrary to him, for they were very giddy and gay, always going to theatres, and balls, and such like places, keeping late hours, and acting so dissipated like, that at last Mr. Franklin was determined to put a stop to it entirely, and make them stay at home. So he told them that he shouldn't allow them to go on as they had any longer; and having once said the word, he stuck to it. My lady and Miss Josephine were both very much dissatisfied with Mr. Franklin, on account of his being so strict with them; and I could plainly see that they began to hate him. It is now about two years ago, and Josephine was in her sixteenth year (ah, sir, I have good reason to remember the time,) when I found myself in the way to become a mother, having been led astray by a young man, who deceived me under a promise of marriage, and then deserted me. Well, sir, my

219

situation was at last noticed by my lady and her daughter, and one evening they called me up into a chamber, and accused me of being a lewd girl. Falling on my knees, I acknowledged my fault, and implored them to pity and forgive me, and not turn me off without a character. Then Miss Josephine spoke harshly to me, and asked me how I dared do such a thing, and bring disgrace upon their house and family; and her mother threatened to send me to jail, which frightened me so that I promised to do anything in the world if they would forgive me. *'Will you do any thing we command you to do*, if we forgive you?' asked Mrs. Franklin; and I said that I would. *'You must swear it,'* said Miss Josephine; and getting a Bible, they made me swear a dreadful oath to do as they bid me. They then told me that there was one thing I must do, and they would give me as much money as I wanted; they said I must *kill Mr. Franklin!* On hearing such a horrible request, I almost fainted; and told them that I never would do such a dreadful thing. But they reminded me of my oath, and at last threatened and frightened me so, that I consented to do the awful deed. *'It must be done to-night!'* said Miss Josephine, and her eyes seemed to flash fire; then she gave me some brandy to drink, which flew into my brain, and I felt myself able to do anything, no matter how wicked it might be.—They staid with me until midnight, and made me drink brandy until I was almost crazy. You must know, sir, that Mr. Franklin slept in a separate room from my lady, ever since their disagreement; upon that dreadful night he retired to bed at about ten o'clock. Well—but oh, my God! how can I tell the dreadful truth!—yet I must nerve myself to confess the whole matter. At midnight, Mrs. Franklin brought into the room a small copper cup, which contained a small quantity of *lead*; this cup she held over the lamp until the lead was melted as thin as water; and then she handed it to me, and told me to go softly into her husband's room, and *pour the lead into his ear!* I DID IT! Yes, as God is my Judge, I did it!—The poor gentleman was lying on his side, in a sound sleep; with a steady hand I poured the liquid metal into his ear—*it did not awake him!* he merely shuddered once, and died.—The next morning he was found by his servant, stiff and cold. Some people talked of 'disease of the heart,' others, of 'apoplexy,' many, of 'the visitation of God,' while some shrugged their shoulders, and said nothing. But *I* knew the secret of his death! He was buried with great pomp in the family tomb in St. Paul's churchyard. My confession is made. After the funeral, my lady and Josephine gave me plenty of money. 'Go,' said they, 'to some other city, and take up your abode; you will never the mention the manner in which Mr. Franklin came to his death, for such a disclosure would bring your own neck to the halter, without injuring us—*your hand* alone did the deed!' I went to Boston, and gave birth to a stillborn child; my money soon went and I became a common prostitute.—Disease soon overtook me—but why dwell upon the misfortunes and wanderings of a wretch like me? A week ago, I found myself again in New York, the inmate of this garret; to-day I felt myself dying, and sent for a clergyman to hear my dying confession. I am exhausted; I can say no more—God have mercy on me!'

'One word more,' cried the rector; 'by what name were you known to the Franklins?'

'Mary Welch,' she replied, faintly.

The wretched creature soon afterwards breathed her last.

The Doctor left a sufficient sum of money with the inmates of the house to defray the expenses of the woman's funeral, and took his departure from that scene of wretchedness. As he retraced his steps to his own dwelling, his thoughts were of the most painful nature; the woman's confession, implicating Josephine and her mother in the crime of murder, horrified him, and gave rise to the most terrible reflections. In his own heart he could not doubt the truth of the wretched woman's statement, made as it was on her death-bed, and just as she was about to be ushered into the presence of her Maker.

'My God!' thought the rector, entering his study, and throwing himself distractedly into a seat—'to what a dreadful disclosure have I listened—Josephine the murderess of her father! Mrs. Franklin the murderess of her husband! Can it be possible?—Alas, I cannot doubt it; for why should that woman, at the awful moment of her dissolution, tell a falsehood? I remember now the circumstances of Mr. Franklin's death; it was sudden and unaccountable, and privately spoken of with suspicion, as to its cause; yet those suspicions never assumed any definite shape.—The poor gentleman was buried without any post mortem examination, and the singular circumstances of his death were gradually forgotten. But now the awful mystery is revealed to me; he met his death at the hands of that miserable woman, at the instigation of Josephine and her mother.'

But the Doctor's most painful thoughts arose from the reflection that he had formed a criminal connection with such a vile, guilty creature as Josephine. He had learned to tolerate her licentiousness and her consummate hypocrisy; he had loved her with passionate fervor, while he had only regarded her as a frail, beautiful woman, who, having become enamored of him, had enticed him to her arms. But now she stood before him as a wretch capable of any crime—as the murderess of her own father; and all his love and admiration for her were turned into a loathing hate; and while he had no intention of denouncing her and her mother to the authorities of justice, he determined to have but one more interview with her, and at that interview to reproach her for her crime, and cast her off forever.

'But previous to that interview,' thought he, 'I will make assurance doubly sure; I will find means to enter the vault wherein Mr. Franklin's body was interred; I will examine the remains, and as my knowledge of human anatomy is considerable, I shall have no difficulty in discovering the evidences of foul play, if such evidences exist. Having thus satisfied myself beyond the shadow of a doubt that Mr. Franklin was murdered, I can with confidence accuse Josephine and her mother of the deed; and from that moment, all connection between me and that wicked woman shall cease forever. I have been infatuated and enslaved by her seductive beauty and her fascinating favors; but thank God, I am myself again, and resolved to atone for the past, by leading a life of purity and virtue for the future.'

That night the Doctor was called on to perform the marriage ceremony at the house of a friend, at a distant part of the city; and it was late when he set out to return to his own home.

It was a dismal night, dark and starless; the sky was laden with impending storm, and the rector shuddered as he looked forward into the gloom, and contrasted it with the scene of light and gaiety which he had just left. His heart was oppressed with a heavy weight; for he could not shake off the dreadful thought that Josephine—beautiful and accomplished Josephine—whom he had loved with a fervent though unholy passion—was a *murderess!*

While hurrying on with rapid strides, his mind tortured by such painful reflections, a tall figure suddenly stood before him, and a voice whispered—

'Deliver your money, or die!'

The rector perceived that the robber had his arm raised, and that he held in his hand a large knife, ready to strike in case of resistance or alarm. Dr. Sinclair was no coward; had there been a single chance in his favor, he would have grappled with the robber, rather than yield to his demand; yet he was slender and by no means powerful—he was also unarmed; and besides, the idea flashed through his mind that the desperado might be of use to him, and these considerations prompted him to speak in a conciliatory tone and manner:—

'Friend,' said he, 'unfortunately for you I am but a poor parson, and have only about me a few dollars, which I have just received as my fee for uniting a happy couple in the holy bonds of wedlock. What I have you are welcome to; here is my purse.'

The robber took the purse, and was about to move off, when the rector called to him and said,—

'Stay, friend; you are the very man I want to assist me in a dangerous enterprise— one that requires courage, and strength, and skill; if you engage to aid me, your reward shall be liberal—what say you?'

'You must first tell me what it is you want done,' replied the robber.

'I want to break open a tomb in St. Paul's churchyard, and examine a dead body; and to do this I shall require an assistant,' said the Doctor, in a low tone.

'That is all well enough,' rejoined the robber; 'but how do I know that you are not laying a plan to entrap me into the clutches of the law, for having robbed *you?*'

'Pshaw!' exclaimed the Doctor, disdainfully, 'why should I seek to entrap you? You have only relieved me of a few dollars, and what care I for that! Draw near, and examine me closely; do I look like a man who would tell a base lie, even to bring a robber to justice?—have I not the appearance of a gentleman? I pledge you my sacred word of honor, that I meditate no treachery against you.'

'Enough—I am satisfied,' said the robber, after having scrutinized the Doctor as closely as the darkness would admit of—'when is this thing to be done?'

'To-morrow night will probably be stormy, and suitable for the purpose,' replied Dr. Sinclair. 'Meet me precisely as the clock strikes the hour of midnight, at the great gate on the lower extremity of the Park; you must come provided with such tools as will be necessary to effect an entrance into the tomb, which is probably secured by a strong padlock; also bring with you a lantern, and the means of lighting it. My object in thus disturbing the repose of the dead, is of no consequence to you; it will be sufficient for you to understand that you are hired to perform a service, which is to be well paid for when completed—you comprehend me?'

'I do,' said the robber, 'and shall not fail to meet you at the time and place appointed; if you have no more to say to me, I will now bid you good night.'

'Good night,' said the Doctor; 'and pray, my good friend, do not menace any other belated traveller with that ugly knife of yours.'

The robber laughed, and turning on his heel, strode away in the darkness, while the rector continued on his way towards his residence. When he reached his house, and had entered the door, a person emerged from the darkness, and by the light of a street lamp which was near, read the name upon the door-plate.—The Doctor had been followed home by the robber.

'All right,' muttered the latter worthy, as he walked away—'he lives in that house, and his name is Dr. Sinclair. Men of his class don't generally play the spy or traitor; so I can safely keep the appointment. He is not a physician or surgeon; therefore what in the devil's name should he want to break into a tomb for? No matter; to-morrow night will explain the mystery.' And the robber's form was lost in the darkness.

As the Doctor had predicted, the night which followed the adventure just related, was stormy; the snow fell thick and fast, and the darkness was intense. As the clock struck the hour of midnight, a figure muffled in a cloak slowly emerged from the lower extremity of the Park, and paused at the great gate which forms the Southern angle of that vast enclosure. He had waited there but a few minutes, when he was joined by another person, who asked him—

'Well, Sir Robber, is it you?'

'All right, sir; you see I am punctual,' replied the robber. The other person was of course the rector.

Without any further conversation, the two proceeded down Broadway, until they stood before the magnificent church of St. Paul's. This splendid edifice, of Grecian architecture, was situated on the border of an extensive burying ground, which with the church itself, was surrounded by an iron railing of great height. Finding the front gate secured by a massive lock, the robber applied himself to the task of picking it, with an instrument designed for that purpose. This was soon accomplished, and entering the enclosure, the two passed around the rear of the church, and stood among the many tomb-stones which marked the last resting place of the quiet dead.

The rector, being well acquainted with the arrangements of the ground, had no difficulty in finding the tomb he wished to enter. A plain marble slab, upon which was sculptured the words 'Franklin Family,' denoted the spot. It required the united strength of both the men to raise this slab from the masonry on which it rested. This being done, they stepped into the aperture, descended a short flight of stone steps, and found their further progress arrested by an iron door, secured by an immense padlock.

'It will now be necessary to light my lantern; I can do so with safety,' said the robber. And igniting a match, he lighted a dark lantern which he had brought with him. Dr. Sinclair then, for the first time, distinctly beheld the features of his midnight companion; and he started with horror—for the most diabolically hideous countenance he had ever seen or dreamed of in his life, met his gaze. The robber observed the impression he had made upon his employer, and grinned horribly a ghastly smile.

'You don't like my looks, master,' said he, gruffly.

'I certainly cannot call you handsome,' replied the Doctor, trying to smile—'but no matter—you will answer my purpose as well as a comelier person. Let us proceed with our work; can you break or pick this padlock?'

The robber made no reply, but drew from his pocket a bunch of skeleton keys, with which he soon removed the padlock; and the heavy iron door swung upon its rusty hinges with a loud creaking noise.

'D——n and blast that noise!' growled the robber.

'Silence, fellow!' cried the rector, authoritatively; 'you are standing in the chamber of the dead, and such profanity is out of place here—no more of it.'

This reproof was received with a very ill grace by the robber, who glared savagely upon his reprover, and seemed almost inclined to spring upon him and strangle him on the spot—no difficult thing for him to do, for the Doctor was of slender build, while he himself possessed a frame unusually muscular and powerful.

They entered the vault, and the feeble rays of the lantern shone dimly on the damp green walls, and on the few coffins which were placed upon shelves.

An awful odor pervaded the place, so loathsome, so laden with the effluvia of death and corruption, that the rector hesitated, and was more than half inclined to abandon the undertaking; but after a moment's reflection—

'No,' he said, mentally—'having gone thus far, it would ill become me to retreat when just on the point of solving the terrible mystery; I will proceed.'

He advanced and examined the coffins, some of which were so much decayed, that their ghastly inmates were visible through the large holes in the crumbling wood. At length he found one, in a tolerable state of preservation, upon which was a gold plate bearing the name of Edgar Franklin. Satisfied that this was the one he was in search of, he desired the robber to come forward and assist in removing the lid, which being done, a fleshless skeleton was revealed to their view.

'Now, fellow,' said the Doctor, 'I am about to make a certain investigation, of which you must not be a witness; therefore, you will retire to the outer entrance of the tomb, and wait there until I call you. Your reward shall be in proportion to your faithful obedience of my orders.'

Casting a look of malignant hate at the young gentleman, the robber withdrew from the vault, shutting the iron door behind him; and as he did so, he muttered a deep and terrible curse.

'Now may Heaven nerve me to the performance of this terrible task!' exclaimed the rector, solemnly; and bending over the coffin, he held the lantern in such a position as enabled him to gaze into the interior of the skull, through the eyeless sockets.

But oh, horrible—within that skull was a mass of live corruption—a myriad of grave worms banquetting upon the brains of the dead!

The Doctor reeled to the iron door of the vault, threw it open, and eagerly breathed the fresh air from above. This somewhat revived him, and he called on his assistant to come down. The robber obeyed, and was thus addressed by his employer—

'Friend, I have overrated my own powers—perhaps your nerves are stronger, your heart bolder than mine. Go to that coffin which we opened, search the interior of the skull, and if you find anything in it singular, or in the least degree unusual, bring it to me.—Here is a pocket-book containing money to a large amount; take it and keep it, but do as I have requested.'

The robber took the pocket-book and went into the vault. Horror could not sicken *him*; the terrors of death itself had no terror for him.

After the lapse of a few moments, he exclaimed—'I have found something!' and advancing to the door, he handed to the doctor a small object, having first wiped it with an old handkerchief.

Overcoming his repugnance by a powerful effort, the doctor walked back into the vaults towards the lantern, which still remained upon the coffin-lid.

Upon examining the article which had been taken from the skull, he found it to be *a piece of lead*, of an irregular shape and weighing nearly two ounces.

'My belief in the guilt of Josephine and her mother is confirmed,' thought he. 'Shall I deliver them into the hands of justice? that must be decided hereafter; at all events, I will accuse them of the crime, and discontinue all connection with the wretched Josephine forever.'

Having carefully placed the piece of lead in his pocket, he advanced to the door, with the intent of leaving the robber to fasten on the lid of the coffin. To his surprise and horror he discovered that the door was locked! He knocked frantically against it, but was only answered by a low laugh from the outside.

'Wretch—villain!' he exclaimed. 'What mean you by this trick? Open the door instantly, I command you!'

'Fool!' cried the robber, contemptuously. 'I obey your commands no longer. You shall be left in this tomb to rot and die. You spoke to me with scorn, and shall now feel my vengeance. Think not, that I am ignorant of your true object in entering this tomb;—there has been a *murder* committed, and you sought for evidence of the crime. That evidence is now in your possession; but the secret is known to me, and I shall not fail to use it to my advantage. I shall seek out the Franklins, and inform them of the discovery which places them completely in my power. Farewell, parson—; I leave you to your agreeable meditations, and to the enjoyment of a long, sound sleep!'

The miserable rector heard the sound of the ruffian's departing footsteps; with a wild cry of anguish and despair he threw himself against the iron door, which yielded not to his feeble efforts, and he sank exhausted upon the floor, in the awful conviction that he was buried alive!

Soon the horrors of his situation increased to a ten-fold degree—for he found himself assailed by a legion of rats. These creatures attacked him in such numbers that he was obliged to act on the defensive; and all his exertions were scarce sufficient to keep them from springing upon him, and tearing his flesh with their sharp teeth.

To his dismay he observed that the light of the lantern was growing dim and came near to being exhausted; darkness was about to add to the terrors of the place. Nerved to desperation, though faint and sick with the awful stench of that death vault, he searched about for some weapon with which to end his miserable existence. While thus engaged, he stumbled over a heavy iron crowbar which lay in one corner and seizing it with a cry of joy, applied it with all his force to the door of his loathsome prison.

It yielded—he was free! for the slab had not been replaced over the tomb, owing to the robber's inability to raise it. Falling on his knees, the rector thanked God for his deliverance; and ascending the steps, stood in the burial-ground, just as the lamps in the tomb below had become extinguished.

He was about to make his way out of the grave-yard, when he heard the sound of approaching footsteps, and low voices; and just as he had concealed himself behind a tall tomb-stone, he saw, through the thick darkness, two men approach the uncovered tomb from which he emerged only a few minutes before.

"'Twas fortunate I met you, Ragged Pete,' said one; 'for without your aid I never could have lifted this stone into its place; and if it were left in its present position, it would attract attention in the morning, and that cursed parson might be rescued from the tomb. Take hold, and let's raise it on.'

'Werry good—but are you sure that the chap is down there still?' demanded Ragged Pete; 'hadn't we better go down and see if he hasn't took leg bait?'

'Pshaw, you fool!' rejoined the first speaker, angrily; 'how could he escape after I had locked him in? There's an iron door, fastened with a padlock as big as your head; so hold your tongue, and help me raise the stone to its place.'

This was done with considerable difficulty; and the two men sat down to rest after their labor.

'The parson won't live over night; if he is not devoured by the rats, he is sure to be suffocated,' remarked the man who had fastened the doctor in the tomb.

'Somehow or other,' said Ragged Pete, 'whoever offends you is sure to be punished in some dreadful and unheard-of manner. By thunder, I must try and keep in your good graces!'

'You will do well to do so,' rejoined his companion, 'my vengeance is always sure to overtake those who cross my path. Pete, I have led a strange life of crime and wickedness, from my very cradle, I may say, up to the present time. See, the storm is over, and the stars are shining brightly. It lacks several hours of daybreak; and as I feel somewhat sociably inclined, suppose I tell you my story? I have a flask of brandy in my pocket, and while we are moistening our clay, you shall listen to the history of one whose proudest boast is, he never did a good action, but has perpetrated every enormity in the dark catalogue of crimes.'

Ragged Pete expressed his desire to hear the story; and even Dr. Sinclair, in his place of concealment, prepared to listen with attention. Probably the reader has already guessed that the robber was no other than the terrible *Dead Man*; such was indeed the case; it was that same villain, who has occupied so prominent a place in the criminal portions of our narrative. We shall devote a separate chapter to his story.

CHAPTER XVIII

The Dead Man's story; being a tale of many Crimes.

'I never knew who my parents were; they may have been saints—they may have been devils; but in all probability they belonged to the latter class, for when I was three weeks old, they dropped me upon the highway one fine morning near the great city of Boston, to which famous city belongs the honor of my birth! Well, I was picked up by some Samaritans, who wrapped me up in red flannel, and clapped me in the Alms House. Behold me, then, a pauper!

'I throve and grew; my constitution was iron—my sinews were steel, and my heart a lion's. Up to the age of twelve, I was as other children are—I cried when I was whipped, and submitted when oppressed. At twelve, I began to reason and think; I said to myself, —Before me lies the world, created for the use of all its inhabitants. I am an inhabitant and entitled to my share—but other inhabitants, being rogues and sharpers, refuse to let me have my share. The world plunders me—in turn, I will plunder the world!

'At fourteen, I bade adieu to the Alms House, without the knowledge or consent of the overseer. I exchanged my grey pauper suit for a broadcloth of a young nabob, which I accidentally found in one of the chambers of a fashionable hotel, in Court street. Behold me, then, a gentleman! But I had no money; and so took occasion to borrow a trifling sum from an old gentleman, one night, upon one of the bridges which lead from Boston to Charleston. Do you ask how he came to give me credit? Why, I just tapped him on the head with a paving stone tied up in the corner of a handkerchief, after which delicate salutation he made not the slightest objection to my borrowing what he had about him. The next day it was said that a man's body had been found on the bridge, with his skull severely smashed—but what cared I?

'Gay was the life I led; for I was young and handsome. You laugh—but I was handsome then—my features had not the deathlike expression which they now wear. By and by you shall learn how I acquired the hideousness of face which procured for me the title of the *Dead Man*.

'One day I made too free with a gentleman's gold watch on the Common; and they shut me up for five years in the Stone University, where I completed my education at the expense of the State. At twenty I was free again. Behold me, then, a thoroughly educated scoundrel! I resolved to enlarge my modes of operation, and play the villain on a more extensive scale.

'Hiring an office in a dark alley in Boston, I assumed the lofty title of Doctor Sketers. My shelves were well stocked with empty phials and bottles—my windows were furnished with curtains, upon which my assumed name was painted in flaming capitals. The columns of the newspapers teemed with my advertisements, in which I was declared to be the only regular advertising physician—one who had success-fully treated twenty-five millions of cases of delicate unmentionable complaints. Certificates of cure were also published by thousands, signed by people who never existed. Having procured an old medical diploma, I inserted my borrowed name, and exhibited it as an evidence of my trustworthiness and skill. The consequence of all this was, I was overrun with patients, none of whom I cured. My private entrance for ladies often gave admission to respectable unmarried females, who came to consult me on the best method of suppressing the natural proofs of their frailty. From these I would extract all the money possible and then send them to consult the skillful agent of Madam R****. A thriving, profitable business, that of quackery! From it I reaped a golden harvest, and when that became tiresome, I put on a white neckcloth, and became a priest.

'Behold me a deacon, and a brother beloved! Who so pious, so exemplary, so holy as I! I lived in an atmosphere of purity and prayer; prayer seasoned my food before meals, and washed it down afterwards; prayer was my nightcap when I went to bed and my eye opener in the morning. At length I began to pray so fervently with the younger and fairer sisters of the flock, that the old ones, with whom I had no desire to pray, began to murmur—so, growing tired of piety, I kicked it to the devil, and joined the ranks of temperance.

'For over a year I lectured in public, and got drunk in private—glorious times! But at last people began to suspect that I was inspired by the spirit of alcohol, instead of the spirit of reform. A committee was appointed to wait on me and smell my breath—which they had no sooner done than they smelt a rat—and while some were searching my heart, others searched my closet, and not only discovered a bottle of fourth-proof, but uncovered a pile of counterfeit bank notes, there concealed. Reacting like a man of genius, my conduct was both forcible and striking; I knocked three of the brethren down, jumped out of the back window, scaled a fence, rushed through an alley, gained the street and was that afternoon on a steamboat bound for New York.

'On the passage, I observed a gentleman counting a pile of money; he was a country merchant, going to purchase goods. The weather was intensely warm, and many of the passengers slept on deck; among these was the country merchant. He lay at a considerable distance from the others and the night was dark. I stole upon him, and passed my long Spanish knife through his heart. —He died easy—a single gasp and all was over. I took his money, and threw his body over to the fishes. 'Twas my second murder—it never troubled me, for I never had a conscience. I entered New York, for the first time, with a capital of three thousand dollars, got by the murder of the country merchant; and this capital I resolved to increase by future murders and future crimes.

'I will now relate a little incident of my life, which will serve to show the bitterness of my hatred towards all mankind. For several years I had lived in various families, in a menial capacity, my object, of course, being robbery, and other crimes. It chanced that I once went to live in the family of a wealthy gentleman, whose wife was the most beautiful woman I ever saw; and her loveliness inspired me with such passion, that one day, during her husband's absence, I ventured to clasp her in my arms—struggling from my embrace, she repelled me with indignant scorn, and commanded me to leave the house instantly. I obeyed, swearing vengeance against her, and her family; and how well that oath was kept! About a week after my dismissal from the family, being one night at the theatre, I saw Mr.

Ross, the husband of the lady whom I had insulted, seated in the boxes. Keeping my eye constantly upon him, I saw him when he left the theatre, and immediately followed him, though at such a distance as to prevent his seeing me. Fortunately his way home lay through a dark and lonely street; in the most obscure part of that street, I quickened my steps until I overtook him—and just as he was about to turn around to see who followed him, I gave him a tremendous blow on his right temple with a heavy slung shot, and he fell to the earth without a groan. I knew that I had killed him and was glad of it—it was my third murder. After dragging his body into a dark alley, so that he might not be found by the watchman, I rifled his pockets of their contents, among which was the night-key of his house, which I regarded as a prize of inestimable value.

'Leaving the corpse of Mr. Ross in the alley, I went straight to his house in Howard street, and admitted myself by means of the night-key which I had found in his pocket. A lamp was burning in the hall; I extinguished it and groped my way up stairs to the chamber of Mrs. Ross with the situation of which I was well acquainted. On opening the chamber door, I found to my intense delight that no light or candle was burning within; all was in darkness. Approaching the bed, I became convinced that the lady was in a sound sleep; this circumstance added greatly to my satisfaction. Well, I deliberately stripped myself and got into bed; still she awoke not. Think you I was troubled with any remorse of conscience, while lying at the side of the wronged woman whose husband had just been slain by my hand? Not a bit of it; I chuckled inwardly at the success of my scheme, and impatiently waited an opportunity to take every advantage of my position. At last she awoke; supposing me, of course, to be her husband, she gently chided me for remaining out so late; I did not dare suffer her to hear the sound of my voice, but replied to her in whispers. She suspected nothing—and I completed my triumph! Yes, the proud, beautiful woman who had treated me with such scorn, was then my slave. I had sacrificed her honor on the altar of my duplicity and lust!

'Morning came, and its first beams revealed to my victim the extent of her degradation—she saw through the deception, and with a wild cry, fell back senseless. Hastily dressing myself, I stepped into an adjoining room where the two children of Mrs. Ross were sleeping; they were twins, a boy and a girl, three years of age, and pretty children they were. I drew my pocket knife, to cut their throats; just then they awoke, and gazed upon me with bright, inquiring eyes—then recognizing me, their rosy cheeks were dimpled with smiles, and they lisped my name. Perhaps you think their innocence and helplessness touched my heart—hah! no such thing; I merely changed my mind, and with the point of my knife cut out their beautiful eyes! having first gagged them both, to prevent their screaming. Delicious fun, wasn't it? Then I bolted down stairs, but was so unfortunate as to encounter several of the servants, who had been aroused by their mistress's shriek. Frightened at my appearance, (for I was covered with the children's blood,) they did not arrest my flight, and I made good my escape from the house. That scrape was my last for some time; for people were maddened by the chapter of outrages committed by me on that family—the murder of the husband, the dishonor of the wife, and the blinding of those two innocent children. I was hunted like a wild beast from city to city; large rewards were offered for my apprehension, and minute descriptions of my entire person flooded every part of the country. But my cunning baffled them all; for two months I lived in the woods, in an obscure part of New Jersey, subsisting upon roots, and wild herbs, and wild berries, and crawling worms, which I dug from the earth. One day in my wanderings, I came across a gang of counterfeiters, who made their rendezvous in a cave; these were congenial spirits for me—I told them my story, and became one of them. The gang included several men of superior education and attainments, among whom was a celebrated chemist.

'This man undertook to procure for me a certain chemical preparation which he said would alter and disfigure my features so that I never could be recognized, even by those who were most intimately acquainted with me. He was as good as his word; he furnished me with a colorless liquid, contained in a small phial, directing me to apply it to my face at night, but cautioning me particularly to avoid getting any of it into my eyes. His directions were followed by me, to the very letter;—during the night, my face seemed on fire, but I heeded not the torture. Morning came—the pain was over; I arose, and rushed to a mirror. Great God! I scarce knew myself, so terribly changed was my countenance. My features, once comely and regular, had assumed the ghastly, horrible and death-like appearance they now wear. On, how I hugged myself with joy when I found myself thus impenetrably disguised! Never did the face of beauty have half the charms for me, that my blanched and terrific visage had! 'I will go forth into the great world again—no one will ever recognize me!' thought I; and bidding adieu to my brother counterfeiters, I returned to New York. Ha, ha, ha! how people shrank from me! how children screamed at my approach; how mothers clasped their babes to their breasts as I passed by, as though I were the destroying angel! The universal terror which I inspired was to me a source of mad joy. Having ample means in my possession, I began a career of lavish expenditure and extravagant debauchery, until the eye of the police was fastened upon me with suspicion; and then I deemed it prudent to act with more caution. —About that time I became aware of the existence of the Dark Vaults, and the 'Jolly Knights of the Round Table.' Soon after my meeting with that jovial crew, the law put its iron clutch on me for a murder—a mere trifle; I passed my knife between a gentleman's ribs one night in the street, just to tickle his heart a bit, and put him in a good humor to lend me some money, but the fool died under the operation, having first very impolitely called out *Murder!* which resulted in my being captured on the spot by two of those night prowlers known as watchmen. Well, my ugly face was against me, and I could give no good account of myself—therefore they (the judge and jury) voted me a hempen cravat, to be presented and adjusted one fine morning between the hours of ten and twelve. But his Excellency the Governor, (a particular friend of mine,) objected to such a summary proceeding, as one calculated to deprive society of its brightest ornament; he therefore favored me with a special permit to pass the rest of my useful life within the walls of a place vulgarly termed the State Prison—a very beautiful edifice when viewed from the outside. I did not long remain there, however, to partake of the State's hospitality—

to be brief, I ran away, but was carried back again, after being a year at liberty, through the instrumentality of Sydney, whom may the devil confound! But again I escaped—you know in what manner; and you are well acquainted with most of my adventures since—my cutting out the boy Kinchen's tongue, my murder of Mrs. Stevens, and other matters not necessary for me to repeat.'

'But,' said Ragged Pete, with some hesitation, 'you haven't told me of your wife, you know.'

'Wife—ha, ha, ha!' and the Dead Man laughed long and loud; there was something in his laugh which chilled the blood, and made the heart beat with a nameless terror.

'True, Pete, I have not yet told you about my wife, as you call her. But you shall hear. What would you say if I told you that Mrs. Ross, the lady whose husband I murdered, whose children I blinded, and whom I so outrageously deceived herself—what would you say if you were told that the woman who passes for my wife, is that same lady?'

'I should say it was a thing impossible,' replied Pete.

'It is true,' rejoined the Dead Man.—'Listen:—when I left my counterfeiting friends in New Jersey, and returned to New York with my new face, I learned by inquiry that Mrs. Ross was living with her blind twins in a state of poverty, her husband's property, at his death, having been seized upon by his creditors, leaving her entirely destitute. I found her in an obscure part of the city, subsisting upon the charity of neighbors, the occupant of a garret. The woman's misfortunes, through me, had ruined her intellect;—she had grown fierce and reckless,—as wild as a tigress. I sat down and conversed with her; she knew me not. 'You are hideous to look upon,' said she, 'and I like you for it. The world is fair, but it has robbed me of husband, honor and taken away my children's eye-sight. Henceforward, all that is hideous I will love!' I saw that her brain was topsy-turvy, and it rejoiced me. Her children were still pretty, though they were blind; and it almost made me laugh to see them grope their way to their mother's side, and turning their sightless eyes toward her, ask, in childish accents, —'Mamma, what made the naughty man put out our eyes?' Well, the woman, with a singular perversity of human nature, liked me, and commenced to place herself under my protection. She could be of service to me; but her children were likely to prove a burden—and so I got rid of them.'

'What did you do with them—no harm, I hope?' asked Pete.

'Certainly not—the Dark Vaults were not a fit place of abode for the blind babes, and so I sent them to take up their abode in another place, and that was heaven; to explain, I cut their throats, and threw their bodies into the sewers.'

'Monster—inhuman villain!' was the involuntary exclamation of Dr. Sinclair, in his hiding-place behind the tomb-stone.

'Ha—who spoke?' cried the Dead Man, jumping to his feet, and gazing eagerly about him. Pete, did you hear anything?'

'I heerd a noise, that's certain—but perhaps 'twas only the wind a whistling among these old tomb-stones,' answered Pete.

'Most probably it was,' rejoined the other—'for who the devil could be here to-night, besides ourselves? Well, to resume my story: after I had made away with the children, their mother never asked for them; she seemed to have forgotten that she ever had children at all. She manifested a strange unnatural liking for me; not love, but the fierce attachment of a tigress for her keeper. She obeyed me in everything; and finding her such an easy instrument in my hands, I took pains to instruct her in all the mysteries of city crimes. By parading the streets like a woman of the town, she enticed men to my Anthony street crib (which you know communicates with the Vaults,) and by the aid of the drugging powder our victims were soon made unresisting objects of robbery and murder. You know how she allured Sydney into the house, disguised as a sailor, and how the rascal caused her to swallow the dose intended for him—also how he cut the ropes of the platform the same night, which nearly cost me my life. Ever since the woman took the powder, she has been a raging maniac, and I am deprived of her valuable services. May the devil scorch that Sydney!'

'You have had two children by her,' remarked Pete.

'Yes, the first one, that infernal dwarf, whom I call my Image; we kept him shut up in the cellar, in Anthony street. Our second child, whom I have christened Jack the Prig, takes after his mother, and a smart little fellow he is. Why man, he can pick a pocket in as workmanlike a manner as either of us. He will make a glorious thief, and will shed honor on his father's name. The day when he commits murder will be he happiest day of my life.'

Ragged Pete, having imbibed the greater part of the contents of the brandy flask, now suggested to his companion that they should take their departure. The Dead Man assented and the worthy pair took themselves off, little thinking that every word which had been said, was heard by him whom they supposed to be imprisoned in the tomb below.

The rector emerged from his place of concealment, and went to his home with a heavy heart. Though he had himself become, in a measure, depraved and reckless of his moral and religious obligations, still he was horrified and astounded at the awful evidences of crime which had been revealed to him that night.—The miscreant's tale of murder and outrage, told with such cool indifference, and with an air of sincerity that left no doubt of its perfect truth, appalled him; and the proof he had obtained of the guilt of Josephine and her mother struck his soul with horror. Ere he sought his couch, he prayed long and earnestly for the forgiveness of his past transgressions, and for strength to resist future temptations.

CHAPTER XIX

Showing how Mrs. Belmont was pursued by a hideous ruffian.

The time appointed for the marriage of Mr. Hedge to Mrs. Belmont approached. The enamored old gentleman paid her frequent visits, and supplied her liberally with funds, nor did he neglect to make her most costly presents. Julia's position and prospects, with reference to her contemplated marriage, were certainly very gratifying to her; yet there was one thing which troubled her exceedingly and was a source of constant apprehension and dread.

The uneasiness proceeded from the fact that she was completely in the power of the Dead Man, who knew that she was the cast-off wife of Sydney—cast off for the crime of adultery with a black—and who could at any time, by exposing her true character to Mr. Hedge, ruin her schemes in that quarter forever. She knew too well that the deadly villain was as deceitful as he was criminal; and she knew not at what moment he might betray her to her intended husband.

The Dead Man was disposed to take every advantage in his power over her. The secret passage into the cellar admitted him into the house at all hours of the day and night; and his visits were frequent. At first his treatment of her was more respectful than otherwise; but gradually he grew familiar and insolent, and began to insinuate that as she had formerly granted her favors to a negro, she could not object to treat HIM with equal kindness. This hint she received with disgust; and assuming an indignant tone, bade him relinquish all thought of such a connection, and never recur to the subject again.

But the villain was not to be repulsed; each time he visited her he grew more insulting and audacious, until at last his persecutions became almost unbearable to the proud and beautiful woman, who viewed him with loathing and abhorrence.

One afternoon, about a fortnight previous to the time fixed on for her marriage, she was seated in her chamber, engaged in reflections which partook of the mingled elements of pleasure and pain. The day was dark and gloomy, and the wind sighed mournfully around the house, and through the leafless branches of the trees which fronted it. Suddenly the door of the chamber was opened, and the Dead Man entered. Julia shuddered, for the presence of that terrible man inspired her with a nameless dread. He seated himself familiarly at her side—and on glancing at him, she perceived, to her alarm, that he was much intoxicated. His eyes rolled wildly, and his loathsome features were convulsed and full of dark and awful meaning.

'Well, my bird,' said he in an unsteady voice—'by Venus and by Cupid, I swear thou art beautiful today! Nay, thou need'st not shrink from me—for I have sworn by Satan to taste thy ripe charms within this very hour!'

He attempted to clasp her in his arms, but she pushed him from her with a look of such disgust, that he became enraged and furious. Drawing a sharp knife from his pocket, he seized her by her arm, and hissed from between his clenched teeth—

'Hark'ee, woman, I have borne with your d——d nonsense long enough, and now if you resist me I'll cut that fair throat of yours from ear to ear—I will by hell!'

She would have screamed with affright, but he grasped her by the throat, and nearly strangled her.

'Silly wench,' he cried, as he released her and again placed himself at her side—'why do you provoke me into enmity, when I would fain be your lover and friend? Mine you must be—mine you shall be, if I have to murder you!'

Miserable Julia! thy wickedness has met with a terrible retribution; thou art a slave to the lust and fury of a monster more dreadful than the venomous and deadly cobra di capello of the East!

Ye who revel in guilty joys, and drink deep of the nectar in the gilded cup of unhallowed pleasures—beware! Though the draught be delicious as the wines of Cypress, and though the goblet be crowned with flowers, fragrant as the perfume of love's sighs—a coiled serpent lurks in the dregs of the cup, whose deadly fang will strike deep in the heart and leave there the cankering sores of remorse and dark despair. Ye who bask in the smiles of beauty, and voluptuously repose on the soft couch of licentiousness—beware! That beauty is but external; beneath the fair surface lie corruption, disease, and death!

The ruffian, having accomplished his triumph, developed a new trait in the fiendish malignity of his nature. He would have the wretched lady become his menial—he would have her perform for him the drudgery of a servant. He ordered her to bring him wine, and wait upon him; and enforced the command with a blow, which left a red mark upon her beautiful white shoulder.

'Henceforward,' cried he, with an oath, 'I am your master, and you are my slave. Hesitate to obey me in any thing which I may desire you to do, and I will denounce you to Mr. Hedge as a vile adulteress and impostor, unworthy to become his wife, even if you had no husband living. Dare to refuse my slightest wish, and I will prevent your marriage under pain of being sent to the State Prison for the crime of bigamy.'

By these and other threats did the ruffian compel the unhappy Julia to obey him. She brought him wine and waited upon him; and was obliged to submit to every species of insult and degradation. Nor was this the only refinement of cruelty which only his own infernal ingenuity could have devised; he resolved that Nero, the black, should be a witness of her humiliation; and accordingly he rang the bell, and ordered the negro to be sent up. Nero entered the room, and observing the triumphant chuckle of the Dead Man, and the dejected look of his mistress, with his natural acuteness instantly comprehended the true state of affairs. The contempt with which Julia had treated him was still fresh in his memory, and led him to view that lady with hatred; he therefore determined to add to her chagrin and hatred on the present occasion, by enjoying the scene as much as possible.

'Sit down, Nero,' said the Dead Man, with a sardonic grin—'this beautiful lady, who formerly showered her favors upon you, has transferred her kindness to me; I have just tasted the joys of heaven in her arms. Is she not a superb creature?'

'Divinely voluptuous,' replied the African, rubbing his hands and showing his white teeth.

'She is so,' said the other—'but the virtue of obedience is her most prominent and excellent quality. Mark how she will obey me in what I order her to do: Julia, love, my shoes are muddy; take them off my feet, and clean them.'

The high-born lady was about to give utterance to an indignant refusal, when a terrible glance from her tyrant assured her that resistance would be useless. His savage brutality—the blow he had given her—her forced submission to his loathsome embraces—and the consciousness that she was completely in his power, compelled her to obey the degrading command.

Yes—that lovely, educated and accomplished lady actually took off the vile ruffian's dirty shoes, with her delicate hands; then with an elegant pearl handled pen-knife, she scraped off the filth, and afterwards, at the orders of her *master*, washed them with rose-water in a china ewer, and wiped them with a cambric handkerchief—and all in the presence of her negro footman.

This task being completed, the Dead Man requested Nero to retire; and then he inflicted new and nameless indignities upon his poor victim. Once, when she shudderingly refused to obey some horrible request, he struck her violently in the face, and the crimson blood dyed her fair cheek.

To be brief, the stupendous villain, in the diabolical malignity of his nature, derived a fierce pleasure from ill-treating and outraging that frail, but to him inoffensive woman. Her defenceless situation might have excited compassion in the breast of a less brutal ruffian; but when had his stony heart ever known compassion?

Nero entered the room to inform his mistress that Mr. Hedge was below, having called on his accustomed evening visit.

'Wash the blood from your face, then go and receive him,' said the Dead Man. 'I shall station myself in the adjoining room, to see and hear all that passes between you.'

Poor Julia removed from her face the sanguinary stains, and endeavoring to arrange her hair so as to conceal the wound which had been inflicted upon her; all in vain, however, for Mr. Hedge noticed it the first moment she entered the room.

'My own dear Julia,' said he, in a tone of much concern, and taking her hand— 'what has caused that terrible bruise upon your cheek? And my God! you look pale and ill—speak, dearest, and tell me what is the matter.'

She could not reply; but burst into tears; the old gentleman's kindness of manner, contrasted with the savage cruelty of her persecutor, had overcome her. Mr. Hedge strove to comfort her, as a father might comfort a distressed child; and his kindness filled her soul with remorse, in view of the great deceit she was practising upon him. Still, she could not muster sufficient resolution to confess that deceit. Considering herself just on the eve of securing a great prize, she could not bring herself to ruin all by a confession of her true character. In answer to his renewed inquiries, she stated that her wound had been caused by a severe fall; but she assured him that it was nothing serious. The Dead Man grinned with satisfaction, as, with his ear applied to the key-hole, he heard her thus account for the wound inflicted by his own villainous hand.

Mr. Hedge did not remain long that evening: but ere his departure he presented Julia with a magnificent set of diamonds, which had cost him near a thousand dollars.

'Wear these, my dear Julia, for my sake,' said he—'and though they cannot increase your charms, they may serve to remind you of me when I am absent. A fortnight more, and I shall claim you for my own bride; then, in the beautiful city of Boston, we will be enabled to move in that sphere of society and fashion which your loveliness and accomplishments so eminently qualify you to adorn.'

After Mr. Hedge had taken his leave, the Dead Man entered the room with a smile of satisfaction.

'By Satan,' cried he—'Mrs. Belmont, as you call yourself, that old gallant of yours is devilish liberal, and there's no reason why I should not come in for a share of his generosity. These diamonds I shall carry off with me, and you can tell him that you were robbed—and so you are; ha, ha, ha! So you're going to Boston after you're married—hey? Well, I'll go to Boston too; and you must always keep me plentifully supplied with cash to insure my silence with regard to matters that you don't wish to have known. I'll leave you now; but listen:—to-morrow I intend to make a grand effort to get Francis Sydney into my power. Does that intelligence afford you pleasure?'

'Yes,' replied Julia, forgetting in her hatred of Sydney, the cruelty of the Dead Man—'yes, it does; give me but the opportunity to see him writhe with agony, and I forgive your barbarous treatment of me to-day.'

'That opportunity you shall have,' rejoined the ruffian—'come, I am half inclined to be sorry for having used you so; but d——n it, 'tis my nature, and I cannot help it. My heart even now hungers after outrage and human blood—and Sydney—Sydney shall be the victim to appease that hunger!'

Saying this, he quitted the room, leaving Julia to her own reflections, which were of the most painful nature. The only thought which shed a gleam of joy into her heart, was the prospect of soon gratifying her spirit of revenge upon Sydney, whom she unjustly regarded as the author of her troubles.

CHAPTER XX

Frank Sydney in the Power of his Enemies—his incarceration in the Dark Dungeon, with the Dwarf.

The next day after the occurrence just related, Frank Sydney, as was his custom, took a leisurely stroll down the most fashionable promenade of the metropolis— Broadway; this magnificent avenue was thronged with elegantly dressed ladies and gentlemen, who had issued forth to enjoy the genial air of a fine afternoon.

At one of the crossings of the street, our hero observed an old woman, respectfully dressed, but nearly double with age and infirmity, and scarcely able to crawl along, in great danger of being run over by a carriage which was being driven at a furious rate. Frank humanely rushed forward, and dragged the poor creature from the impending danger, just in time to save her from being dashed beneath the wheels of the carriage. She faintly thanked her deliver, but declared her inability to proceed without assistance. On inquiring where she resided, he learned that it was in Reade street, which was but a short distance from where they then stood; and he generously offered her the support of his arm, saying that he would conduct her home, an offer which was thankfully accepted. They soon reached her place of abode, which was a house of genteel appearance, and at the invitation of the old lady, Frank entered, to rest a few moments after his walk.

He had scarcely seated himself in the back parlor, when he was horrified and astounded at what he saw.

The old woman, throwing off her cloak, bonnet and mask, stood before him, erect and threatening; and our hero saw that he had been made the dupe of the *Dead Man!*

'Welcome, Sydney, welcome!' cried the miscreant, his features lighted up with a demon's triumph—'at last thou art in my power. Did I not play my part well? Who so likely to excite thy compassion as an old lady in distress; 'twas ably planned and executed. Thou hast fallen into the trap, and shall never escape. But there are others who will be gratified to see thee, Frank. Nero—Julia—the bird is caught at last!'

These last words were uttered in a loud tone; and were immediately responded to by the entrance of Julia and the black. The woman's eyes flashed fire when she beheld the object of her hate; she advanced towards him and spat in his face, saying—

'May the fires of hell consume thee, heart and soul, detested wretch—thou didst cast me from thee, friendless and unprotected, when a kind reproof might have worked my reformation. Through thee I have become the victim of a ruffian's lust, the object of his cruelty; I have been struck like a dog, (look at this mark upon my cheek,) and I have been compelled to minister to the disgusting and and unnatural lechery of a monster—all through thee, thou chicken-hearted knave, who even now doth tremble with unmanly terror!'

'Woman, thou art a liar!' exclaimed our hero, rising and boldly confronting his three enemies—'I do tremble, but with indignation alone! Dare you charge your misfortune upon me? Did you not dishonor me by adultery with this vile negro? —and then to talk to me of kind reproof! Pshaw, thou double-eyed traitorous w***e! —I had served thee rightly had I strangled thee on the spot, and thrown thy unclean carcase to the dogs!'

'Silence, curse ye, or I'll cut out your tongue as I did the *Kinchen's!*' roared the Dead Man, drawing his knife. 'Nero, what cause of complaint have you against this man?'

'Cause enough,' replied the black—'he shut me up in a dark dungeon for having gratified the wishes of his licentious wife.'

'Enough,' cried the Dead Man—'I will now state my grounds of complaint against him. Firstly—he played the spy upon me, and was the cause of my being returned to the State Prison, from which I had escaped. Secondly—he discovered the secrets of my Anthony street crib, and administered a drug to my wife which has deprived her of reason. And thirdly he is my mortal foe, and I hate him. Is that not enough?'

'It is—it is!' replied Julia and the African. The Dead Man continued:

'Now, Sydney, listen to me: you behold the light of day for the last time. But 'tis not my wish to kill you at once—no, that would not satisfy my vengeance. You shall die a slow, lingering death; each moment of your existence shall be fraught with a hell of torment; you will pray for death in vain; death shall not come to your relief for years. Each day I will rack my ingenuity to devise some new mode of torture.

To increase the horrors of your situation, you shall have a companion in your captivity—a being unnatural and loathsome to look upon—a creature fierce as a hyena, malignant as a devil. Ha, you turn pale; you guess my meaning. You are right; you shall be shut up in the same dungeon with my Image! the deformed and monstrous dwarf, whom Heaven (if there is one,) must have sent as a curse and a reproach to me; he shall now become your curse and punishment!'

Poor Frank heard this awful doom pronounced which he could not repress. He could have borne any ordinary physical torture with fortitude; but the thought of being shut up in that noisome dungeon with a being so fearful and loathsome as the Image, made him sick and faint; and when the Dead Man and the negro seized him in their powerful grasp, in order to convey him to the dungeon, he could make no resistance, even if resistance had been of any avail. Julia did not accompany them, but contented herself with a glance of malignant triumph at her husband.

They descended to the cellar, and entered the secret passage, which they traversed in profound darkness. This passage communicated directly with the cellar of the house in Anthony street; a walk of ten minutes brought them to it, and when they had entered it, the Dead Man ignited a match and lit a lamp.

The appearance of the cellar was precisely the same as when Frank had last seen it. —There was the same outlet and the moveable platform; there, in that dim and distant corner, lay the putrefying corpse; and there, too, was the iron door of the dungeon, secured on the outside by the massive bolt.

At that moment the fearful inmate of that dungeon set up its strange, unnatural cry.

'Hark—my Image welcomes you, Sydney,' whispered the Dead Man, and, assisted by the African, he hurried his victim towards the dungeon door.

'In God's name,' said Frank, imploringly—'I beseech you to kill me at once, rather than shut me up with that fearful creature—for death is preferable to that!'

But the two ruffians only laughed—and drawing back the bolt, they opened the iron door, and thrust their victim into the dungeon; then closing the door, they pushed the bolt into its place, and left him to an eternal night of darkness and horror.

He heard the sound of their department footsteps; groping his way to a corner of the dungeon, he sat down upon the cold stone floor. Had he been alone he could have reconciled himself to his situation; but the consciousness of being in such fearful company, froze his blood with horror.

Soon his eyes became accustomed to the darkness; and as a very faint glimmer of light stole in over the door of the dungeon, he was enabled to see objects around him, though very indistinctly. With a shudder, he glanced around him; and there, cowering in one corner, like some hideous reptile, its green eyes fixed upon him, sat the Image of the Dead Man—the terrible Dwarf!

Hour after hour did that mis-shapen thing gaze upon our hero, until a strange feeling of fascination over him—his brain grew dizzy, and he felt as if under the influence of a horrible dream. Then it uttered its strange, unnatural cry, and with the crawling motion of a snake, stole to his side. He felt its breath, like the noisome breath of a charnel-house, upon his cheek; he felt its cold, clammy touch, and could not thrust it from him; it twined its distorted, fleshless arms around him, and repeated its awful yell. Then Sydney fell prostrate upon the floor, insensible.

When he recovered from his swoon, (in which he had lain for many hours) he felt numbed with cold, sick with the foetid atmosphere of the place, and faint with hunger. The dwarf was ferociously devouring some carrion which had been thrown into the dungeon; and the creature made uncouth signs to our hero, as if inviting him to eat. But on examining the food he found it to be so repulsive, that he turned from it in disgust, and resolved, sooner than partake of it, to let starvation put an end to his misery.

CHAPTER XXI

Josephine and Mrs. Franklin receive two important Visits.

Josephine Franklin and her mother were languidly partaking of a late breakfast, and indolently discussing the merits of the Italian opera, to which they had both been on the preceding night.

It not being the hour for fashionable calls, both ladies were attired with an extreme negligence which indicated that they anticipated seeing no company. And yet, to the eyes of a true connoisseur in beauty, there was something far more seductive in those voluptuous dishabilles, than there could have been in the most magnificent full dress. The conversation in which they were engaged, was characteristic of them both:—

'I think, mamma,' said Josephine—'that the most captivating fellow on the stage last night, was the Signor Stopazzi, who played the peasant. Ah, what superb legs! what a fine chest! what graceful motions! I am dying to get him for a lover!'

'What, tired of the handsome Sinclair already?' asked Mrs. Franklin with a smile.

'Indeed, to confess the truth, mamma,' replied Josephine—'the Doctor is becoming somewhat *de trop*—and then, again, those Italians make such delightful lovers; so full of fire, and passion, and poetry; and music, and charming romance—ah, I adore them!'

'Apropos of Italian lovers,' said her mother. 'I once had one; I was then in my sixteenth year, and superbly beautiful. My Angelo was a divine youth, and he loved me to distraction. Once, in a moment of intoxicating bliss, he swore to do whatever I commanded him, to test the sincerity of his life; and I playfully and thoughtlessly bade him go and kill himself for my sake. The words were forgotten by me, almost as soon as uttered. Angelo supped with me that night, and when he took his leave, he had never seemed gayer or happier. The next day, at noon, I received a beautiful bouquet of flowers, and a perfumed billet-doux; they were from Angelo. On opening the missive, I found that it contained the most eloquent assurance of his sincere love—but, to my, horror, in a postscript of two lines he expressed his intention of destroying himself ere his note could reach me, in obedience to my command. Almost distracted, I flew to his hotel; my worst fears were confirmed. Poor Angelo was found with his throat cut, and quite dead, with my miniature pressed to his heart.'*

'Delightfully romantic!' exclaimed Josephine—'how I should like to have a lover kill himself for my sake!'

But the brilliant eyes of her mother were suffused with tears. Just then a servant in livery entered and announced—

'Dr. Sinclair is below, and craves an audience with Mrs. Franklin and Miss Josephine.'

'Let him come up,' said Josephine, with a gesture of some impatience; for, in truth, she was beginning to be tired of the rector, and longed for a new conquest.

Dr. Sinclair entered with a constrained and gloomy air.

'My dear Doc,' cried Josephine, with affected cordiality—'how opportunely that you called! I was just now wishing that you would come.'

'Ladies,' said the Doctor, solemnly—'I have recently made a terrible, a most astonishing discovery.'

'Indeed! and pray what is it?' cried both mother and daughter.

'It is that Mr. Edgar Franklin, whose death was so sudden and unaccountable, was basely murdered!'

The mother and daughter turned pale, and losing all power of utterance, gazed at each other with looks of wild alarm.

'Yes,' resumed the Doctor—'I have in my possession evidence the most conclusive, that he met his death by the hands of a murderess, who was urged to commit the deed by two other devils in female shape.'

'Doctor—explain—what mean you?' gasped Josephine, while her mother seemed as if about to go into hysterics.

'In the first place I will ask you if you ever knew a woman named Mary Welch?' said the Doctor; then after a pause, he added—'your looks convince me that you have known such a person; that woman recently died in this city, and on her death-bed she made the following confession.'

The rector here produced and read a paper which he had drawn up embodying the statement and confession which the woman Welch had made to him, just before her death. As the reader is acquainted with the particulars of that confession it is unnecessary for us to repeat them.

Having finished the perusal of this document, the rector proceeded to relate an account of his visit to the tomb of Mr. Franklin, and concluded his fearfully interesting narrative by producing the lump of lead which had been taken from the skull of the murdered man.

It is impossible to describe the horror and dismay of the two wretched and guilty women, when they saw that their crime was discovered. Falling on their knees

---

*A fact, derived by the Author from the private history of a fashionable courtezan.

before the rector, they implored him to have mercy on them and not hand them over to justice.—They expressed their sincere repentance of the deed, and declared that sooner than suffer the ignominy of an arrest, they would die by their own hands. Josephine in particular did not fail to remind Dr. Sinclair of the many favors she had granted him and hinted that her exposure would result in his own ruin, as his former connection with her would be disclosed, if herself and mother were arrested and brought to trial.

'Were I inclined to bring you to justice, the dread of my own exposure would not prevent me; for no personal consideration should ever restrain me from doing an act of justice, provided the public good would be prompted thereby. But I do not see the necessity of bringing you to the horrors of a trial and execution; much rather would I see you allowed a chance of repentance. Therefore, you need apprehend no danger from me; the secret of your crime shall not be revealed by me. But I warn you that the secret is known to another, who will probably use his knowledge to his own advantage; the matter lies between you and him. I shall now leave this house, never again to cross its threshold; but ere I depart, let me urge you both before God to repent of your sins. Josephine, I have been very guilty in yielding to your temptations; but the Lord is merciful, and will not refuse forgiveness to the chief of sinners. Farewell—we shall meet no more: for I design shortly to retire from a ministerial life, of which I have proved myself unworthy; and shall take up my abode in some other place, and lead a life of obscurity and humble usefulness.'

With these words the Doctor took his departure, leaving the mother and daughter in a state of mind easier to be imagined than described. Josephine was the first to break the silence which succeeded his exit from the house:—

'So our secret is discovered,' said she.—'Perdition! who would have thought that our crime could ever be found out in that manner? Mother, what are we to do?'

'I know not what to say,' replied Mrs. Franklin. 'One thing, however, is certain; that whining parson will never betray us. He said that the dread of his own folly would not deter him from denouncing us, but he lies—that dread of being exposed will alone keep his mouth shut. Yet, good Heavens! he assures us that the secret is known to another person, who will not scruple to use the knowledge to his advantage. Who can that person be? And what reward will he require of us, to ensure his silence?'

'Mother,' said Josephine, in a decided tone—'We must quit this city forever. We can dwell here no longer with safety. Let us go to Boston, and dwell there under an assumed name. I have heard that Boston is a great city, where licentiousness and hypocrisy abound, in secret; where the artful dissimulator can cloak himself with sanctity, and violate with impunity every command of God and man. Yes, Boston is the city for us.'

'I agree with you, my dear,' rejoined her mother—'it is the greatest lust market of the Union. You will be surprised to learn that several of my old schoolmates are now keeping fashionable boarding house for courtezans in that city and from the business derive a luxurious maintenance. There is my friend Louisa Atwill, whose history I have often narrated to you and there, too, is Lucy Bartlett, and Rachel

Pierce, whose lover is the gay and celebrated Frank Hancock, whom I have often seen—nor must I omit to mention Julia Carr, whose establishment is noted for privacy, and is almost exclusively supported by married men. All these with whom I occasionally correspond testify to the voluptuous temperament of the Bostonians, among whom you will be sure to make many conquests.'

We merely detail this conversation for the purpose of showing the recklessness and depravity of these two women. They had just acknowledged themselves guilty of the crime of murder; and could thus calmly converse on indifferent and sinful topics, immediately after the departure of their accuser, and as soon as their first excitement of fear had subsided.

While thus arranging their plans for the future, the servant in livery again entered, to announce another visitor.

'He is a strange looking man,' said the servant, 'and when I civilly told him that the ladies received no company before dinner, he gave me such a look as I shall never forget, and told me to hold my tongue and lead the way—good Lord, here he comes now!'

The terrified servant vanished from the room, as a tall figure stalked in, wrapped in a cloak. The ladies could scarce repress a shriek, when throwing aside his hat and cloak, the stranger exhibited a face of appalling hideousness; and a fearful misgiving took possession of their minds, that this was the other person who was in the secret of their crime.

'You are the two Franklin ladies I presume—mother and daughter—good!' and the stranger glanced from one to the other with a fierce satisfaction.

'What is your business with us?' demanded Josephine, haughtily.

'Ha! young hussey, you are very saucy,' growled the stranger savagely—'but your pride will soon be humbled. In the first place, are we alone, and secure from interruption?'

'We are—why do you ask?' said Mrs. Franklin.

'Because your own personal safety demands that our interview be not over-heard,' replied the man. 'As you are fashionable people, I will introduce myself. Ladies, I am called the Dead Man, and have the honor to be your most obedient servant. Now to business.'

The Dead Man proceeded to relate those circumstances with which the reader is already acquainted, connected with his visit to the tomb of Mr. Franklin, and the manner in which he had come to the knowledge of that gentleman's murder. He omitted, however, to state that he had shut up the rector in the tomb, for he firmly believed in his own mind that Dr. Sinclair had perished.

'You perceive,' said he, when he had finished these details—'it is in my power to have you hung up at any time. Now, to come to the point at once—what consideration will you allow me if I keep silent in regard to this affair?'

'Of course you require money,' remarked Josephine, who was disposed to treat the matter in as business-like a manner as possible.

'Why—yes; but not money alone,' replied the Dead Man, with a horrible leer; —'you are both devilish handsome, and I should prefer to take out a good portion of my reward in your soft embraces. You shudder ladies; yet would not my arms around those fair necks of yours be pleasanter than an ugly rope, adjusted by the hands of the hangman? You will one day admit the force of the argument; at present I will not press the matter, but content myself with a moderate demand on your purse. Oblige me with the loan—ha, ha!—of the small trifle of one thousand dollars.'

After a moment's consultation with her daughter, Mrs. Franklin left the room to get the money from her escritoire. The door had scarcely closed upon her, when the Dead Man advanced to Josephine, caught her in his arms, despite her resistance, imprinted numberless foul kisses upon her glowing cheeks, her ripe lips, and alabaster shoulders. It was a rare scene; Beauty struggling in the arms of the Beast!

The lecherous monster did not release her until he heard her mother returning. Mrs. Franklin handed to him a roll of bank-notes, and said—

'There is the amount you asked for and you must grant that you are liberally paid for your silence. I trust that you will consider the reward sufficient, and that we shall see you no more.'

'Bah!' exclaimed the ruffian, as he deposited the money in his pocket—'do you think I will let you off so cheaply? No, no, my pretty mistress—you may expect to see me often; and at my next visit I must have something besides money—a few little amative favors will then prove acceptable, both from you and your fair daughter, whose lips, by Satan! are as sweet to my taste as human blood. I know very well you will attempt to run away from me, by secretly removing from the city; but hark'ee— though you remove to hell, and assume the hardest name of Beelzebub's family of fourth cousins—I'll find you out! Remember, I have said it. Adieu.'

And bowing with mock politeness, the miscreant took his departure from the house.

'Good heavens!' exclaimed Mrs. Franklin—'we are completely in the power of that dreadful man. We must leave the city, without delay, for Boston; yet we will spread the report that we are going to Philadelphia, in order to escape from that monster, if possible.'

'A monster indeed!' said Josephine shuddering—'during your absence from the room, he took the most insolent liberties with me, and besmeared me with his loathsome kisses. How horrible it will be, if he ever finds us out, and compels us to yield our persons to his savage lust!'

'True,' said her mother—'and yet, for my own part, sooner than pay him another thousand, I would yield to his desires; for the manner in which we have squandered money, during the last two years, has fearfully diminished my fortune, and there is but a very small balance of cash in my favor at the bank. This house must be sold, together with all our furniture, in order to replenish our funds. Now, my dear, we must make preparations for our instant departure for Boston.'

Mrs. Franklin summoned her servants, paid them their wages, and discharged them all, with the exception of her handsome footman, whom she determined to leave in charge of the house, until it was sold, after which he was privately requested to join his mistress in Boston; he was particularly directed to state, in answer to all inquiries, that the family had gone to Philadelphia. Simon, (for this was the footman's name) promised implicit obedience to these orders; and was rewarded for his fidelity by a private tete-a-tete with his fair patron, during which many kisses were exchanged, and other little tokens of affection were indulged in; after which she gave him the keys of the house, charging him not to visit the wine-cellar too often, and by all means not to admit a woman into the house, under pain of her eternal displeasure.

That same afternoon, the two ladies took passage in a steamer for Boston. They were received on board by the handsome and gentlemanly Captain, who, being somewhat of a fashionable man, had some slight acquaintance with the aristocratic mother and her beauteous daughter. He courteously insisted that they should occupy his own state-room; and they accordingly took possession of that elegant apartment, where they ordered tea be served; and, at their invitation, the Captain supped with them. The repast over, he apologized to the ladies for his necessary absence; and sent the steward to them with a bottle of very choice wine.

The state-room was divided into two apartments by a curtain of silk; and in each of these apartments was a magnificent bed. The floor was handsomely carpeted, and the walls were adorned with superb mirrors and pictures. The Captain was a man of taste, and his cabin was a gem of luxury and splendor.

As the stately steamer ploughed her way through the turbid waters of the Sound, many were the scenes which took place on board of her, worthy to be delineated by our pen. Though it is our peculiar province to write of city crimes, we nevertheless must not omit to depict some of the transactions which occurred during the passage, and which may be appropriately classed under the head of steamboat crimes.

At the hour for retiring, the ladies' cabin was filled with the feminine portion of the passengers, who began to divest themselves of their garments in order to court the embraces of the drowsy god. There was the simpering boarding-school miss of sixteen; the fat wife of a citizen with a baby in her arms, and another in anticipation; the lady of fashion, attended by her maid; the buxom widow, attended by a lap-dog, musical with silver bells, and there, too, was the elderly dame, attended by a host of grandchildren, to the horror of an old maid, who declares she 'can't BEAR young ones,' which is true enough, literally.

Now it is a fact beyond dispute, that ladies, among themselves, when no males are present, act and converse with more freedom from restraint, than a company of men; and the fact was never more forcibly illustrated than upon this occasion. The boarding-school miss, *en chemise*, romped with the buxom widow, who was herself in similar costume. The citizen's fat wife lent her baby to the old maid, who wanted to know how it seemed; and was rewarded for her kindness by a token of gratitude on the baby's part, which caused the aforesaid old maid to drop the little innocent like a hot potato. The fashionable lady, who dressed for bed as for a ball, was arrayed in a very costly and becoming night-dress, ornamented with a profusion of lace and ruffles; and standing before a mirror, was admiring her own charms; yet she painted, and had false teeth—defects which were atoned for by a fine bust and magnificent ankle. Her maid, a stout, well-looking girl, was toying with a very pretty boy of eight or nine years of age, and when unobserved, embraced and kissed him with an ardor which betokened a good share of amative sensibility on her part.

'The men are such odious creatures, I positively cannot endure them,' remarked the old maid.

'And yet they are very *useful*, and sometimes agreeable,' said the buxom widow, with an arch smile, (she was handsome, if she *was* a widow,) and glancing significantly at the citizen's fat wife.

'Pooh!' exclaimed the old maid, climbing into her berth, and privately taking off her wig, (she was bald,)—'I can take my pick of ten thousand men, yet I wouldn't have one of them.' (She had been pining for an offer twenty years!)

The buxom widow got into her berth, which she shared with her lapdog; and as the little animal dove under the bed-clothes and became invisible, it is difficult to conjecture in what precise locality he stowed himself! The fashionable lady 'turned in' after the most approved manner; and as the berths were somewhat scarce, her maid generously offered to share her couch with little Charley, an offer which that interesting youth at first declined, saying he was afraid of her, she 'squeezed him so,' but his scruples were overcome by her assurances that the offence should not be repeated, and Charley concluded to accept the offer.

Those scenes did not pass unwitnessed for two men were standing outside, looking thro' one of the windows, from which the curtain had been partially drawn. Both these men were respectably dressed, and both were over sixty years of age; yet they viewed the unconscious and undressed ladies with lecherous delight.

'But, deacon,' said one—'do look at that one standing before the glass; what breasts—what legs—what a form—what—heavens! I shall go crazy if I look much longer!'

'Now, in my way of thinking,' said the deacon—'that young thing of sixteen is the most delicious little witch of the entire lot;—what a fair skin—what elastic limbs—what wantonness in every look and movement! There's a youthfulness and freshness about her, which render her doubly attractive.'

'Ah, they are all going to retire, and we shall lose our sport. —By the way, deacon, what kind of a set are they that I'm going to preach to, in Boston?' asked the Rev. John Marrowfat—for it was that noted hero of pulpit oratory, amours and matrimony!

'Oh, they're a set of soft-pated fools,' replied deacon Small, 'preach hell-fire and brimstone to 'em, they'll swallow everything you say, and give you a devilish good salary into the bargain.'

A young man, small and thin, and well dressed, now approached, and grasped the deacon by the hand.

'Why, this is an unexpected pleasure,' said the young man—'who would have thought of seeing you here?'

'I am happy to meet you, brother,' said the deacon—'brother Marrowfat, allow me to introduce you to Samuel Cough, a distinguished advocate of temperance.'

'What are you going to do in Boston, Sam?' asked deacon Small.

'Oh, going to astonish the natives a little, that's all,' replied Mr. Cough. 'That was a bad scrape I got into, in Albany; I got infernally drunk, and slept in a brothel, which was all very well, you know, and nothing unusual—but people *found it out!* Well, I got up a cock-and-bull story about drinking drugged soda, and some people believe it and some don't. Now, when I get *corned,* I keep out of sight.—Ah, temperance spouting is a great business! But come, gentlemen—it won't do for us to be seen drinking at the bar; I've got a bottle of fourth-proof brandy in my pocket; let's take a swig all around.'

And producing the article in question, Mr. Cough took a very copious *swig,* and passed the bottle to the others, who followed his example. We shall now leave this worthy trio, with the remark that they all got very comfortably drunk previous to retiring for the night. Mr. Cough turned into his berth with his boots on and a cigar in his mouth; Mr. Marrowfat sung obscene songs, and fell over a chair; and deacon Small rushed into the gentleman's cabin, and offered to fight any individual present, for a trifling wager. He was finally carried to bed in the custody of the boot-black.

Among the passengers was a very handsome lad, twelve or fourteen years of age, whose prepossessing appearance seemed to attract the attention of a tall gentleman, of distinguished bearing, enveloped in a cloak.—He wore a heavy moustache, and his complexion was very dark. He paid the most incessant attention to the boy, making him liberal presents of cake and fruit, and finally gave him a beautiful gold ring, from his own finger.

This man was a foreigner—one of those beasts in human shape whose perverted appetites prompts them to the commission of a crime against nature. Once before, in the tenth chapter of this narrative, we took occasion to introduce one of those fiends to the notice of the reader; it was at the masquerade ball, where the Spanish ambassador made a diabolical proposal to Josephine Franklin, whom he supposed to be a boy. It is an extremely delicate task for a writer to touch on a subject so revolting; yet the crime actually exists, beyond the shadow of a doubt, and therefore we are compelled to give it place in our list of crimes. We are about to record a startling fact—in New York, there are boys who *prostitute* themselves from motives of gain; and they are liberally patronized by the tribe of genteel foreign vagabonds who infest the city. It was well known that the principal promenade for such cattle was in the Park, where they might be seen nightly; and the circumstance had been more than once commented upon by the newspapers.—Any person who has resided in New York for two or three years, knows that we are speaking the truth. Nor is this all. There was formerly a house of prostitution for that very purpose, kept by a foreigner, and splendidly furnished; here lads were taken as apprentices, and regularly trained for the business;—they were mostly boys who had been taken from the lowest classes of society, and were invariably of comely appearance. They were expensively dressed in a peculiar kind of costume; half masculine and half feminine; and were taught a certain style of speech and behaviour calculated to attract the beastly wretches who patronize them. For a long time the existence of this infernal den was a secret; but it eventually leaked out, and the proprietor and his gang were obliged to beat a hasty retreat from the city, to save themselves from the summary justice of Lynch law.

But to return to the steamboat. The foreigner called the lad aside, and the following conversation ensued:—

'My pretty lad, this cabin is excessively close, and the bed inconvenient. I have a very nice state-room, and should be happy to have you share it with me.'

'Thank you, sir,' answered the boy—'if it would cause you no inconvenience—'

'None whatever; come with me at once,' said the other, and they ascended to the deck, and entered his state room. It is proper to observe, that the youth was perfectly innocent, and suspected not the design of his new *friend*. Half an hour afterwards he dashed from the state room with every appearance of indignation and affright; seeking one of the officers of the boat he told his story, and the result was that the foreign gentleman and his baggage were set ashore at a place destitute of every thing but rocks, and over ten miles from any house; very inconvenient for a traveller, especially at night, with a storm in prospect. The miserable sodomite should have been more harshly dealt with.

To return to Josephine and her mother, whom we left in the Captain's elegant state room.

We must here remark that Sophia Franklin, the gentle, angelic sister of the depraved Josephine, had gone to spend a month or so with an aunt, (her father's sister,) in Newark, N.J., which circumstance will account for not accompanying her mother and sister in their flight from New York. It may be as well to add that she was in blissful ignorance of her father having been murdered, and of course, knew nothing of the discovery of that fact by Dr. Sinclair.

'Thank heaven,' cried Josephine, raising the wine glass to her vermilion lips—'we are at last clear of that odious New York! I feel as if just liberated from a prison.'

'The feeling is natural, my dear,' rejoined her mother—'you are no longer in constant dread of that horrible fellow who is so savagely amorous with regard to both of us. We have fairly given him the slip, and it will be difficult for him to find us.'

'Don't you think, mamma,' asked the young lady—'that the Captain, who so politely surrendered this beautiful cabin for our accommodation, is a splendid fellow? Really, I am quite smitten with him.'

'So am I,' remarked her mother—'he is certainly very handsome, and it is hard that he should be turned out of his cabin on our account. Why cannot we all three sleep here? I am sure he needs but a hint to make him joyfully agree to such an arrangement.'

'I understand you mamma,' said Josephine, her eyes sparking with pleasure—'you will see what a delicate invitation I'll give him; but I won't be selfish—you shall enjoy as much benefit from the arrangement as myself. Hark! somebody knocks—it must be the Captain.'

And so it was; he had come to inquire if the ladies were comfortable, and on receiving an affirmative answer, was about to bid them good night and depart, when Josephine invited him to sit down and have a glass of wine with them. It was not in the nature of the good Captain to decline an invitation when extended by a pretty woman. The mother and daughter, tastefully attired in superb evening dresses, looked irresistibly charming—the more so, perhaps, because their cheeks were suffused with the rosy hues of wine and passion.

'I have been thinking, Captain,' said Josephine, casting her brilliant eyes upon the carpet—'that it is unjust for us to drive you from your cabin, and make you pass the night in some less comfortable place. Mother and I have been talking about it, and we both think you had better sleep in here, as usual.'

'What—and drive you ladies out?' cried the Captain—'couldn't think of it, upon my honor.'

'Oh, it doesn't necessarily follow that *we* must be driven out,' said Josephine, raising her eyes to his face, and smiling archly—'you silly man, don't you see that we want to be very kind to you?'

'Is it possible?' exclaimed the Captain, almost beside himself with joy—'dear ladies, you cannot be jesting, and I accept your offer with gratitude and delight. Good heavens, what a lucky fellow I am!'

And clasping both ladies around the waists, he kissed them alternately, again and again. That night was one of guilty rapture to all the parties; but the particulars must be supplied by the reader's own imagination.

*   *   *   *   *

And now, behold Mrs. Lucretia Franklin and her daughter Josephine, in the great city of Boston! The same day of their arrival they hired a handsome house, already furnished in Washington street: and the next day they made their *debut* in that fashionable thoroughfare, by promenading, in dresses of such magnificence and costliness, that they created a tremendous excitement among the bucks and belles who throng there every fine afternoon.

'Who can they be?' was asked by every one, and answered by no one. The dandy clerks, in high dickies and incipient whiskers, rushed to the doors and windows of their stores, to have a glimpse of the two beautiful *unknowns*; the mustachioed exquisites raised their eye-glasses in admiration, and murmured, 'dem foine,' the charming Countess, the graceful Cad, and the bewitching Jane B——t, were all on the *qui vive* to ascertain the names, quality and residence of the two fair strangers, who were likely to prove such formidable rivals in the hearts and purses of the lady-loving beaux of the city.

That evening they went to the opera, and while listening to the divine strains of Biscaccianti, became the cynosure of a thousand admiring glances. And that night, beneath the windows of their residence, a party of gallant amateurs, with voice and instrument, awoke sounds of such celestial harmony, that the winged spirits of the air paused in their aerial flight to catch the choral symphony that floated on the soft breezes of the moon-lit night!

CHAPTER XXII

Showing the Desperate and Bloody Combat which took place
in the Dark Vaults.

'You will pray for death in vain; death shall not come to your relief for years,' were the words of the miscreant who had shut up poor Frank in that loathsome dungeon; —and like a weight of lead, that awful doom oppressed and crushed the heart of our hero, as he lay stretched upon the stone floor of the cell, with the maniac Dwarf gibbering beside him, and staring at him with its serpent-like and malignant eyes.

While lying there, weak with hunger, and his soul filled with despair, a wild delirium took possession of his senses, and in his diseased mind horror succeeded horror. First, the misshaped Dwarf seemed transformed into a huge vulture, about to tear him to pieces with its strong talons; then it became a gigantic reptile, about to discharge upon him a deluge of poisonous slime; then it changed to the Evil One, come to bear him to perdition. Finally, as the wildest paroxysms of his delirium subsided, the creature stood before him as the Image and spirit of the Dead Man, appointed to torture and to drive him mad.

'Die, thou fiend incarnate!' he exclaimed, in a phrenzy of rage and despair; and starting from the ground, he rushed upon the creature and attempted to strangle it. But with an appalling yell, it struggled from his grasp, and leaping upon his shoulders bore him to the earth with a force that stunned him; and then it fastened its teeth in his flesh and began to drink his blood.

But the fates willed that Sydney was not thus to die; for at that moment the iron door was suddenly thrown open, and the glare of a lantern shone into the dungeon; then there entered a person whose features were concealed by a hideous mask, and the dwarf quitted its hold of the victim, and flew screaming into a corner.

'He must be revived ere he is brought to judgement,' said the Mask; and he raised Sydney in his arms, carried him out of the dungeon, and fastened the door.

Then the Mask stepped upon the platform with his burden, and descended into the dark abyss. When Frank recovered his senses, he found himself in a sort of cavern which was lighted by a lamp suspended from the ceiling. He was lying upon a rude bed; and near him, silent and motionless, sat a masked figure.

'Where am I—and who art thou?' demanded our hero, in a feeble tone, as a vague terror stole over him.

The Mask replied not, but rising, brought him a cup of wine and some food, of which he partook with eagerness. Much refreshed, he sank back upon his pillow, and fell into a long, deep slumber. When he awoke, he found himself in the same cavern, on the same bed, and guarded as before by the mysterious Mask, who now spoke for the first time.

'Arise and follow me,' said he.—Sydney obeyed, and followed the Unknown through a long passage, and into a vast hall or cavern, brilliantly lighted. Glancing around him, he saw at once that he was in the Dark Vaults, in that part called the

'Infernal Regions,' the rendezvous of the band of miscreants known as the 'Jolly Knights of the Round Table.'

Seated around that table was a company of men, to the number of about fifty, all so hideously masked, that they seemed like a band of demons just released from the bottomless pit. They sat in profound silence, and were all so perfectly motionless that they might have been taken for statues rudely chiseled from the solid rock.

In the centre of the table, upon a coffin, sat the Judge of that awful tribunal, arrayed from head to foot in a blood-red robe: he wore no mask—why need he? What mask could exceed in hideousness the countenance of the Dead Man?

Sydney was compelled to mount the table, and seat himself before his Judge, who thus addressed him:—

'Prisoner, you are now in the presence of our august and powerful band,—the Knights of the Round Table, of which I have honor to be the Captain. I am also Judge and Executioner.—The charges I have against you are already known to every Knight present. It but remains for them to pronounce you guilty, and for me to pass and execute sentence upon you. Attention, Knights! those of you who believe the prisoner to be guilty, and worthy of such punishment as I shall choose to inflict upon him, will *stand up!*'

Every masked figure arose, excepting *one!* and that one remained silent and motionless. To him the judge turned with a savage scowl.

'How now, Doctor!' he cried in a voice of thunder—'do you dare dissent from the decision of your comrades? Stand upon your feet, or by G—— I'll spring upon you and tear you limb from limb!'

But the Doctor stirred not.

'By hell!' roared the Dead Man, foaming with rage—'dare you disobey the orders of your Captain? Villain, do you seek your own death?'

'*Dare?* exclaimed the Doctor, tearing off his mask, and confronting his ruffian leader with an unquailing eye—'*dare!* Why, thou white-livered hound, I dare spit upon and spurn ye! And forsooth, ye call me a villain—you coward cut-throat, traitor, monster, murderer of weak women and helpless babes! I tell you, Dead Man, your Power is at an end in these Vaults. There are robbers, there may be murderers here—although thank God, *I* never shed human blood—but bad as we are, your damnable villainy, your cruelty and your tyranny have disgusted us. I for one submit to your yoke no longer; so may the devil take you, and welcome!'

Sydney now for the first time recognized in the speaker, the same individual who sought to rob him one night in the Park, and whose gratitude he had won by presenting him with a fifty dollar bill.

The Dead Man glared from some moments in silence upon the bold fellow who thus defied him. At length he spoke—

'Fool! you have presumed to dispute my authority as Captain of this band, and your life is forfeit to our laws. But, by Satan! I admire your courage, and you shall not die without having a chance for your life. You shall fight me, hand to hand— here to-night, at once; the Knights shall form a ring, and we will arm ourselves with

Bowie knives; *cut and slash* shall be the order of the combat; no quarters shall be shown; and he who cuts out his adversary's heart, and presents it to the band on the point of his knife, shall be Captain of the Round Table. Say do you agree to this?'

'Yes!' replied the Doctor, much to the disappointment of his challenger, who would have been glad had the offer been rejected. However, there was no retracting, and instant preparations were made for the combat. Sydney was placed in charge of two men, in order to prevent his escape; and the Knights formed themselves into a large ring, while the combatants prepared for the encounter. Both men stripped to the skin; around their left arms they wrapped blankets to serve as shields; and in their right hands, they grasped long, sharp Bowie knives, whose blades glittered in the brilliant light of the many candles. All was soon ready, and the adversaries entered the ring, amid profound silence.—Poor Sydney contemplated the scene with painful interest; how sincerely he prayed that the Doctor might prove victorious in the combat!

Gaunt and bony, the Dead Man looked like a skeleton; yet the immense muscles upon his fleshless arms, indicated prodigious strength. He looked terribly formidable, with his livid face, deadly eye and jaws firmly set—his long fingers clutching his knife with an iron grasp, and his left arm raised to protect himself.—The Doctor was a large, dark-complexioned, handsome man—an Apollo in beauty and a Hercules in strength, presenting a singular contrast to the hideous, misshapen being with whom he was about to engage in deadly conflict.

Cautiously they advanced towards each other, with knives upraised. Standing scarce five feet apart, they eyed each other for two minutes; not a muscle moved; with a howl like that of a hyena, the Dead Man sprang upon his enemy, and gave him a severe gash upon his shoulder; but the Doctor, who was an accomplished pugilist, knocked his assailant down, and favored him with a kick in the jaw that left its mark for many a day, and did not enhance his beauty.

The Dead Man arose, grinding his teeth with passion, but advancing with extreme caution. By a rapid and dexterous movement of his foot, he tripped the Doctor down, and having him at that disadvantage, was about to bury his knife in his heart, when several of the band rushed forward and prevented him, exclaiming—

'When you were down, the Doctor suffered you to regain your feet, and you shall allow him the same privilege. Begin again on equal terms, and he who gets the first advantage, shall improve it.'

'Curses on you for this interference,' growled the ruffian, as he reluctantly suffered the Doctor to arise. The combat was then renewed with increased vigor on both sides. Severe cuts were given and received; two of the Doctor's fingers were cut off, and Sydney began to fear that he would be vanquished, when, rallying desperately, he closed with the Dead Man, and with one tremendous stroke, severed the miscreant's right hand from his wrist! Thus disabled, he fell to the ground, bathed in blood.

'I'll not take your life, miserable dog,' cried the Doctor, as he surveyed his fallen adversary with a look of contempt—'as I have deprived you of that murderous hand, you shall live. You are now comparatively harmless—an object of pity rather than of fear. I am a surgeon, and will exert my skill to stop the effusion of blood.'

The Dead Man had fainted. He was laid upon the Round Table, and the Doctor dressed the wound. Then he turned to his comrades, and said, 'Gentlemen of the Round Table, you will admit that I have fairly conquered our leader; I have spared his life not in the hope that he will ever become a better man, for that is impossible—but that he may be reserved for a worse fate than death by my knife. He shall live to die a death of horror.'

The band crowded around the Doctor, clapping their hands, and exclaiming— 'Hail to our new Captain!'

'Not so,' cried the Doctor—'to-night I leave this band forever. Nay, hear me, comrades—you know that I am not a bad man by nature—you are aware that I have been driven to this life by circumstances which I could not control. You are satisfied that I never will betray you; let that suffice. Should any of you meet me hereafter, you will find in me a friend, provided you are inclined to be honest.—I have a word to say in regard to this prisoner; he is my benefactor, having once supplied my wants when I was in a condition of deep distress. I am grateful to him, and wish to do him a service. He has been brought before you by the Captain, for some private wrongs, which have not affected you as a band. Say, comrades, will you set him free?'

Many of the band seemed inclined to grant this favor; but one, who possessed much influence, turned the current of feeling against Sydney, by saying—

'Comrades, listen to me. Though our Captain is conquered, we will not do him injustice. This man is his prisoner, captured by his hand, and *he* alone can justly release him. Let the Doctor depart, since he wishes it; but let the prisoner be kept in custody; to be disposed of as our Captain may see proper.'

This speech was received with applause by the others. The Doctor knew it would be useless to remonstrate; approaching Sydney, he whispered—

'Have courage, sir—in me you have a friend who will never desert you. I shall be constantly near you to aid you at the first opportunity. Farewell.'

He pressed Sydney's hand, bade adieu to his comrades, and left the Vaults.

The Dead Man slowly revived; on opening his eyes, his first glance rested upon his prisoner, and a gleam of satisfaction passed over his ghastly visage. At his request, two of the band raised him from the table, and placed him in a chair; then, in a feeble voice, he said—

'Eternal curses on you all, why have you suffered the Doctor to escape? Hell and fury—my right hand cut off!—But no matter; I shall learn to murder with the other. Ha, Sydney! you are there, I see; the Doctor may go, in welcome, since *you* are left to feel my vengeance. I am too weak at present to enjoy the sight of your torture, and the music of your groans. Back to your dungeon, dog; yet stay—the dwarf may kill you, and thus cheat me of my revenge; it is not safe to confine you with him any longer. Maggot and Bloodhound, take Sydney and shut him up in the *Chamber of Death*.'

Two of the worst villains of the gang, who answered to the singular names of Maggot and Bloodhound, seized Sydney by his arms, and dragged him along one of the dark passages which branched off from the Vault. The Dead Man himself followed, bearing a lantern in his only remaining hand.

They arrived at a low iron door, in which was a grating formed of thick bars of the same metal. This door being opened, the party descended a flight of stone steps, and entered an apartment of great extent where the damp, chill air was so charged with noxious vapours, that the light of the lantern was almost extinguished. The stone walls and floor of this dungeon were covered with green damp; and from the ceiling in many places dripped a foul moisture. The further extremity of the place was involved in a profound darkness which could not be dissipated by feeble rays of the lamp.

'Here,' said the Dead Man, addressing his prisoner—'you will be kept in confinement for the rest of your life—a confinement varied only by different modes of torture which I shall apply to you, from time to time. This dungeon is called the Chamber of Death—for what reason you will ere long find out. It is built directly under the sewers of the city, which accounts for the liquid filth that oozes through the ceiling. Many persons have been shut up in this place, for offences against our band and against me; and not one of them has ever got out, either alive or dead! To-morrow I shall visit you, and bring you food—for I do not wish you to die of hunger; I will endeavor to protract, not shorten your life, so that I may longer enjoy the pleasure of torturing you. To-morrow, perhaps, you shall receive your first lesson in my methods of torture. Adieu—come, comrades, let's leave him the lamp, that he may contemplate the horrors of the place—for darkness here is bliss.'

The three villains ascended the steps and left the dungeon, having first carefully locked the door.

Poor Sydney fell upon his knees on the cold, damp floor, and prayed earnestly for either a safe deliverance from that awful place, or a speedy death. Somewhat comforted by the appeal to a Supreme Being, whose existence all men acknowledge in times of peril, he arose, and taking the lamp resolved to explore the dungeon. He had not proceeded far before a spectacle met his gaze which caused him to pause in horror and affright.

Seated around a vast table, was a row of figures fantastically dressed and in every extravagant attitude. At first, Frank thought that they were living creatures; but observing that they did not move, he approached nearer, and discovered that they were skeletons. Some were dressed as males, others as females; and many of them, in fearful mockery of death, had been placed in attitudes the most obscene and indecent. Presiding over this ghastly revel, was a gigantic skeleton, arrayed in what had once been a splendid theatrical dress, and grasping in its fleshless hand a large gilt goblet; this figure was seated on a sort of throne, made of rough boards.

These were the skeletons of those who had died in the Vaults, as well as of those persons who, having fallen into the power of the band of villains, had been murdered in that dungeon, by starvation or torture. With infernal ingenuity, the Dead Man had arrayed the skeletons in fanciful costumes, which had been plundered from the wardrobe of a theatre; and placed them in the most absurd and indecent positions his hellish fancy could devise. The large skeleton, which seemed to preside over the others, was the remains of a former Captain of the band, celebrated for his many villainies and gigantic stature.

While gazing upon this figure, Sydney distinctly saw the head, or skull, nod at him. Astonished at this, yet doubting the evidence of his own eyesight, he approached nearer, and held the lamp close up to it; again it moved, so plainly as to admit of no further doubt. Our hero was not superstitious, but the strangeness of this incident almost terrified him, and he was about to make a rapid retreat to the other side of the dungeon, when the mystery was explained in a manner that would have been ludicrous under any other circumstances: a large cat leaped from the skull, where it had taken up an abode, and scampered off, to the great relief of Sydney, who was glad to find that the nod of the skeleton proceeded from such a trifling cause.

On the back of each chair whereon was seated a member of the ghostly company was written the name which he or she had borne during life. Judges, magistrates and police officers were there, who had rendered themselves obnoxious to the gang, in years past, by vigilance in detecting, or severity in passing sentences upon many of its members. These individuals had been waylaid by their ruffian enemies, and made to die a lingering death in that dungeon; their fate was never known to their friends, and their sudden and unaccountable removal from the world, was chronicled in the newspapers, at the time, under the head of *mysterious disappearance*. Ladies, whose testimony had tended to the conviction of the band, were there; but their fate had been doubly horrible, for previous to their imprisonment in the dungeon, they had been dishonored by the vile embraces of almost every ruffian in the Vaults; and even after death, they had been placed in attitudes unseemly and shameful. But the horror of Sydney, while beholding these things, was soon absorbed in a discovery which to him was ten times more horrible than all the rest; for written on the chair of a female figure, was the name of his aunt Mrs. Stevens!

It will be remembered that this lady was murdered by the Dead Man, at her residence in Grand Street; on the night of the masquerade ball, in order to prevent her giving favorable testimony at the trial of Sydney. Having been found, suspended by the neck, it was at first supposed that she committed suicide; but that belief was removed from the public mind, when it was found that a robbery had been committed in the house. It was then apparent that she had been inhumanely murdered. Her servant testified that a strange man had called on her mistress that evening whom she would not be able to recognize, his face having been concealed in the folds of his cloak. After admitting him into the house, and calling Mrs. Stevens, the girl had gone out on a short errand, and on her return, found her mistress in the situation described, and quite dead. The old lady was buried; but her murderer broke open the tomb, and carried the corpse to the dungeon of the Vaults, where he had placed her with the other victims, in the position in which Sydney, her nephew, now found her.

'It is as I suspected,' thought our hero, as he sadly viewed the remains of his poor aunt—'that villain murdered her, and now it is forever out of my power to avenge her blood. Ha! what's this?—*my name*, upon an empty chair.'

And so it was; the name, Francis Sydney, was written out on the back of an unoccupied chair; he comprehended that this was designated to be *his* seat when he should form one of that awful crew, in the chamber of Death.

Suddenly, the damp, foul air of the place extinguished the light of his lamp, and he found himself in total darkness.

CHAPTER XXIII

Showing how Sydney was tortured in the Chamber of Death, and how he made his escape through the City Sewers.

Groping his way to the extremity of the dungeon, Frank sat down upon the stone steps, his mind a prey to feelings of keenest horror and despair. His soul recoiled from the idea of suicide, as a heinous crime in the sight of Heaven, or he would have dashed his brains out against the walls of his prison, and thus put an end to his misery. Vainly he tried to forget his sorrows in sleep; no sooner would he close his eye-lids, than the band of skeletons would seem to rush towards him, and with fleshless arms beckon him to join their awful company.

Slowly, slowly passed the hours away. Numbed with cold, and paralyzed with the terrors of his situation, Sydney was at last sinking into a state of insensibility, when he was aroused by the loud noise caused by the opening of the dungeon door, and the gleam of a lantern flashed upon him. He staggered to his feet, and saw that his visitors were the two villains, Maggot and Bloodhound. One of them came down the steps and deposited upon the floor a small basket and a lamp.

'Here,' said he—'is some *grub* for you, and a light to scare away the ghosts. Eat your fill—you will need it; for in an hour from this time, our captain will visit you to commence his tortures, in which I and my comrade will be obliged to help him.'

'Why will you aid that wretch in his cruelties?' asked Sydney—'I never injured you; pray act like a man of heart and feeling, and release me from this dreadful place.'

'*Release you!*' cried the man—'I dare not. True, I have no animosity against you, young man; but our Captain has, and were I to let you go, life would not be worth a minute's purchase. I'd not incur that man's wrath for a million of money. No, no, make up your mind to the worst—you can never go out of this dungeon.'

With this consoling assurance, the man and his comrade took their departure. On examining the contents of the basket, our hero found an ample supply of good, wholesome food, and a jug of water; and while heartily partaking of these necessities, (of which he stood in great need,) he could not help comparing his situation with that of an animal being fattened for slaughter!

An hour elapsed; the dungeon was again opened, and the Dead Man entered, followed by Maggot and Bloodhound. The two latter worthies carried between them an apparatus of singular appearance and construction.

'Well, dog,' cried the Dead Man, 'how do you like your new kennel? Not so comfortable, I'll swear, as your fine house on Broadway! Faith, a fine prayer you made last night, after we left you; you called on God to help you—ha, ha! Fool—*he* cannot help you!—*I* alone can do it. Down, then, on your marrow bones and worship me!'

And saying this, he raised his right arm, and with it struck his victim heavily on his head; the extremity of the arm, where the hand had been cut off, had been furnished with a piece of iron like a sledge-hammer, to enable the ruffian to possess the means of attack and defence. Fortunate it was that the blow did not fracture Sydney's skull.

Meanwhile Maggot and Bloodhound had placed the machine which they had brought with them upon the floor and began to prepare it for use. The vaults of the Spanish Inquisition never contained a more horrible instrument of torture. It was a box made of iron and shaped like a coffin; the sides and bottom were covered with sharp nails, firmly fixed with their points outwards; beneath the box was a sort of furnace, filled with shavings and charcoal. This apparatus was called by the ruffians—*The Bed of Ease*.

Sydney was made to strip himself entirely naked, and lie down in the box; then the cover was fastened on. The points of the nails penetrated his flesh, causing him the most excruciating torture; blood started profusely from all parts of his body, and he could scarce repress groans of the most heart-felt anguish. But this was nothing to what he was doomed to endure; for the demons in human shape kindled a fire beneath him, and when nature could hold out no longer, and he screamed with agony, his tormentors roared with laughter.

They released him when a cessation of his cries warned them that he could hold out no longer without endangering his life—for they wished him to live to endure future torments. He was truly a pitiable object when taken from the box—his flesh torn and bleeding, and horribly burnt. They rubbed him with oil, assisted him to dress and laid him upon a heap of straw which one of them brought. They then left him, after assuring him that, as soon as he was healed, they had tortures in store for him much more severe than the one just inflicted. The iron box they left behind them in the dungeon, probably intending to use it again on some future occasion.

In what a deplorable situation did poor Sydney now find himself placed! Nearly dead with the torments which he had just undergone, his mind was harassed by the dread of other and more severe tortures yet in store for him. How gladly would he have bared his bosom to the deadly stroke of the knife, or the fatal discharge of the pistol!

But exhausted nature could hold out no longer, and he fell into a deep sleep, from which he was awakened by the entrance of some person into the dungeon. Starting up, he was confronted by the dark and menacing visage of the Dead Man. The villain was alone and held in his left hand a large knife; Sydney perceived, by his unsteady gait, his wildly rolling eyes, and his thick, indistinct utterance, that he was much intoxicated.

'I am come, dog,' said he, with a look that a demon might have envied—'to feast upon your heart, and drink your blood. My soul is hungry. I wish you had a thousand lives for me to take. Sit up, and let me dig out your eyes, and cut off your nose, ears and fingers—for you must die by inches! Get up, I say!'

'The monster is drunk,' thought Sydney; 'had I a weapon and sufficient strength, I might perhaps overcome him; but alas! I am weak and sore—'

'Get up!' again roared the ruffian, 'that I may sacrifice ye upon the flaming altar of Satan, my deity. My heart is a coal of fire; it burns me, and blood alone can quench it!'

With the howl of a wild beast, he threw himself upon his victim.

But ere he could strike the deadly blow, he was writhing and struggling in the powerful grasp of a tall, stout man, who at that crisis rushed into the dungeon.

'Now, reptile, I have thee!' muttered the Doctor, (for it was he) as with mighty and resistless strength he dashed the miscreant to the floor and deprived him of his knife.

But the Dead Man struggled with all the fury of desperation; with his *iron hand* he made rapid and savage passes at the head of his assailant, knowing that a single well-directed blow would stun him. But the Doctor's science in pugilism enabled him to keep off the blows with ease, while he punished his antagonist in the most thorough and satisfactory manner. Finding himself likely to be overcome, the villain yelled at the top of his voice—'Treason! murder! help!'

'Your handkerchief, Mr. Sydney—quick!' cried the Doctor. Frank, who had already arisen from his bed of straw, handed his gallant protector the article he had called for—and, though very weak, assisted in gagging the vanquished ruffian, who, breathless and exhausted, could now offer but a slight resistance.

'Into the box with him!' exclaimed the Doctor, and the next minute the Dead Man was stretched upon the points of the sharp nails; the lid was closed upon him, the fire was lighted beneath, and he writhed in all the torture he had inflicted upon poor Sydney.

Suddenly, the Doctor assumed a listening attitude, and whispered to his companion—

'By heavens, the band is aroused, and the Knights are coming to the rescue. If they capture us, we are lost! There is but one way for us to escape—and that is *through the sewers*, a dreadful avenue! Will you dare it?'

'I will dare anything, to escape from this earthly hell!' cried our hero, vigor returning to his frame as he thought of liberty.

'Follow me, then,' said the Doctor, taking up the lamp, and hurrying up the dungeon steps; he led the way, at a rapid pace, up another high flight of steps, to a point which overlooked the city sewers. By the dim light of the lamp, Frank saw, twenty feet below, the dark, sluggish and nauseous stream of the filthy drainings of the vast city overhead, which, running thro' holes under the edges of the sidewalk, collect in these immense subterranean reservoirs, and are slowly discharged into the river.

'Leap boldly after me—you will land in the mud, and break no bones,' said the Doctor—'our enemies are at our heels!' A fact that was demonstrated by the sound of many footsteps hurrying rapidly towards them.

The Doctor leaped into the dark and terrible abyss. Sydney heard the splash of his fall into the muddy water, and nerving himself for the deed, jumped in after him; he sank up to his chin in the loathsome pool. His friend grasped his hand, and whispered—'We are now safe from our pursuers, unless they follow us, which is hardly probable; for I confess these sewers are so full of horrors, that even those villains would hesitate to pass through them, unless under circumstances as desperate as ours.' Frank shuddered. 'Will they not fire upon us?' he asked. The Doctor answered:—

'No, they dare not; for the noise of fire-arms would be heard in the streets above, and people might be led to inquire into the cause of such a phenomena. Fortunately my lamp is not extinguished, and as the mud is not over our heads, we may make our way out of this infernal trap, provided we are not devoured by rats and reptiles, which swarm here. Ah, by Jupiter, there are our pursuers!'

And as he spoke, some fifteen or twenty men appeared above them, on the point from which they had jumped. On seeing the fugitives, they set up a shout of surprise and anger.

'A pretty trick you've served us, Doctor,' called out the fellow known as Bloodhound—'you've nearly roasted the Dead Man, and carried off his prisoner; however, we rescued our Captain just in time to save his life. You had better come back, or we'll blow your brains out!'—and he levelled a pistol.

'Blow and be d——d,' coolly remarked the Doctor, who knew very well that he dare not fire—'come, Mr. Sydney, follow me, and leave these fellows to talk to the empty air.'

With much difficulty the two fugitives began to move off through the mud and water.

'What, cowards, will you let them escape before your eyes?' roared the Dead Man, as he rushed up to the brink of the chasm, and glared after Sydney and his friend with flaming eyes. 'Plunge in after them, and bring them back, or by G—— every man of you shall die the death of a dog!'

Not a man stirred to obey the order; and the miscreant would have leaped into the sewers himself, had they not forcibly held him back.

'No, no, Captain,' cried Maggot—'the Doctor's too much for you; you've only got one hand now, and you'd be no match for him, for he's the devil's pup at a tussle. Let them both slide this time; you may catch them napping before long. As it is, they've got but a devilish small chance of escape, for it rains terribly overhead, which will fill up the sewers, and drown them like kittens.'

Meanwhile, Frank and his brave deliverer struggled manfully through the foul waters which encompassed them. Soon an angle in the wall concealed them from their enemies; and they entered a passage of vast extent, arched overhead with immense blocks of stone. This section of the sewers was directly under Canal street, and pursued a course parallel with that great avenue, until its contents were emptied into the North river. Our subterranean travellers could distinctly hear the rumbling of the carts and carriages in the street above them, like the rolling of thunder.

It was an awful journey, through that dark and loathsome place. At every few steps they encountered the putrid carcase of some animal, floating on the surface of the sickening stream. As they advanced, hundreds of gigantic rats leaped from crevices in the wall, and plunged into the water. Their lamp cast its dim rays upon the green, slimy stone-work on either side of them; and their blood curdled with horror as they saw, clinging there, hideous reptiles, of prodigious size, engendered and nourished there. They imagined that at every step they took, they could feel those monsters crawl and squirm beneath their feet—and they trembled lest the reptiles should twine around their limbs, and strike deadly venom to their blood. But a new terror came to increase their fears; the water was growing deeper every instant, and threatened to overwhelm them. Sydney overcome by the awful effluvia, grew too sick and faint to proceed further; he requested the Doctor to leave him to his fate—but the gallant man raised his sinking form in his powerful arms, and struggled bravely on. 'Courage, my friend,' cried the Doctor—'we are near the river, for I see a light ahead, glimmering like a star of hope!' In ten minutes more they emerged from the sewers, and plunged into the clear waters of the North river.

Without much difficulty they got on board of a sloop which lay moored at the wharf; and as Sydney had money, he easily procured a change of raiment for himself and friend, from the skipper, who was too lazy to ask any questions, and who was very well satisfied to sell them two suits of clothes at five times their value. Frank took the Doctor to his home, resolved never to part with so faithful and gallant a friend, whose faults had been the faults of unfortunate circumstances, but whose heart, he felt assured, was 'in the right place.'

Poor Clinton, the dumb boy, welcomed his master and his old acquaintance the Doctor, with mute eloquence. Dennis, the Irish footman, was almost crazy with delight at Mr. Sydney's safe return, swearing that he thought him 'murthered and kilt intirely.'

That awful night was so indelibly stamped upon the memory of our hero, that often, in after times, it haunted him in his dreams.

CHAPTER XXIV

The Marriage—The intoxicated Rector—Miseries of an aged Bridegroom on his Wedding Night.

Mrs. Belmont was seated in the elegant parlor of her residence in Reade street. It was the evening appointed for her marriage with Mr. Hedge, and she was dressed in bridal attire—a spotless robe of virgin white well set off her fine form and rich complexion, while a chaplet of white roses made a beautiful contrast with the dark, luxuriant hair on which it rested.

A superb French clock on the marble mantel piece proclaimed in silvery tones, the hour of seven.

'He will soon be here,' she murmured—'to carry me to the house of the clergyman, there to be made his wife. How little the fond, foolish old man suspects the snare in which he is about to fall! How admirably have my artifices deceived him! And the other evening when in the heat of passion, he pressed me to grant him a certain favor in advance of our marriage, how well I affected indignation, and made him beg for forgiveness! Oh, he thinks me the most virtuous of my sex—but there is his carriage; now for the consummation of my hopes!'

Mr. Hedge entered the room, and raising her jewelled hand to his lips, kissed it with rapture. The old gentleman was dressed in a style quite juvenile;—his coat was of the most modern cut, his vest and gloves white, and his cambric handkerchief fragrant with *eau de cologne*. To make himself look as young as possible, he had dyed his gray hair to a jet black, and his withered cheeks had been slightly tinged with *rouge*, to conceal the wrinkles, and give him a youthful, fresh appearance. He certainly looked twenty years younger than ever, but he could not disguise his infirm gait and the paralytic motions of his body.

But let not the reader suppose that he was either a superannuated coxcomb or a driveling dotard. He was a man of sense and feeling, but his passion for Julia had, for the time, changed all his manner and habits.—He saw that she was a young and lovely woman, about to give herself to the arms of a man thrice her age; and he wished to render the union less repugnant to her, by appearing to be as youthful as possible himself. Therefore, he had made up his toilet as we have described, not from personal vanity, but from a desire to please his intended bride.

We wish not to disguise the fact that Mr. Hedge was an exceedingly amorous old gentleman; and that in taking Julia to his matrimonial embrace, he was partially actuated by the promptings of the flesh. But in justice to him we will state that these were not the only considerations which had induced him to marry her; he wanted a companion and friend—one whose accomplishments and buoyancy of spirits would serve to dispel the loneliness and *ennui* of his solitary old age. Such a person he fancied he had found in the young, beautiful 'widow,' Mrs. Belmont.

'Sweetest Julia,' said the aged bridegroom, enclosing her taper waist with her arm—'the carriage is at the door, and all is in readiness to complete our felicity. To-night we will revel in the first joys of our union in my own house—to-morrow, as you have requested, we depart for Boston.'

'Ah, dearest,' murmured Julia, as her ripe lips were pressed to his—'you make me so happy! How young you look tonight! What raptures I anticipate in your arms! Feel how my heart beats with the wildness of passion!'

She placed his hand into her fair, soft bosom, and he felt that her heart was indeed throbbing violently; yet 'twas not with amorous passion, as she had said; no, 'twas with fierce triumph at the success of her schemes.

The contact of his hand with her voluptuous charms, inflamed him with impatient desire.

'Come,' cried he,—'let us no longer defer the blissful hour that gives you to my arms.'

In a few minutes Julia was ready; and the happy pair, seating themselves in the carriage, were driven to the abode of Dr. Sinclair, who was to perform the marriage ceremony.

We said *happy* pair—yes, they were indeed so; the old gentleman was happy in the prospect of having such a beautiful creature to share his fortune and bed; and the young lady was happy in the certainty of having secured a husband whose wealth would enable her to live in luxury and splendor.

They arrive at the rector's residence, and are ushered into a spacious apartment. Everything is handsome and costly, yet everything is in disorder; judging from appearances one would suppose that the place was occupied by a gentleman of intemperate habits—not by a minister of the gospel. The rich carpet is disfigured with many stains, which look marvelously like the stains produced by the spilling of port wine. The mirror is cracked; the sofa is daubed with mud; a new hat lies crushed beneath an overturned chair. An open Bible is upon the table, but on it stand a decanter and a wine-glass; and the sacred page is stained with the blood-red juice of the grape. On the mantle-piece are books, thrown in a confused pile; the collection embraces all sorts—Watts' hymn book reposes at the side of the 'Frisky Songsters,' the Pilgrim's Progress plays hide-and-seek with the last novel of Paul de Kock; while 'Women of Noted Piety' are in close companionship with the 'Voluptuous Turk.'

Soon the rector enters, and there is something in his appearance peculiar, if not suspicious. His disordered dress corresponds with his disordered room. His coat is soiled and torn, his cravat is put on awry, and his linen is none of the cleanest. He salutes Brother Hedge and his fair intended, in an unsteady voice, while his eyes wander vacantly around the apartment, and he leans against a chair for support.

'How very strangely he looks and acts,' whispered Julia to her frosty bridegroom—'surely he can't be *tipsy?*'

'Of course not,' replied Mr. Hedge—'such a supposition with reference to our beloved pastor would be sacrilege. He is only somewhat agitated; he is extremely sensitive, and deep study has doubtless operated to the injury of his nervous system. My dear Brother Sinclair, we are waiting for you to perform the ceremony,' he added, in a louder tone.

'Waiting—ceremony—'said the rector, abstractedly, gazing upward at the ceiling—'Oh, marriage ceremony, you mean? Ah, yes, I had forgotten. Certainly. Quite right, Brother Hedge, or Ditch—ha, ha! Excuse me. All ready.'

We shall not attempt to imitate the rector, in his manner of performing the ceremony, as we deem the matter to be too serious for jest; but we will say, never before was ceremony performed in so strange a manner. However, to all intents and purposes, they were married; and at the conclusion of the service, the bridegroom slipped a fifty-dollar note into the rector's hand, and then conducted his lovely bride to the carriage, in which they were soon driven to Mr. Hedge's residence in Hudson street.

In explanation of the singular conduct of Dr. Sinclair, we will state that he became a wine-bibber and a drunkard. Remorse for his amorous follies with Josephine, and horror at her crimes, had driven him to drown such painful remembrances in the bottle. The very next day after he had accused the mother and daughter of the murder, he drank himself into a state of intoxication, and each subsequent day witnessed a renewal of the folly. On the Sabbath, he managed to preserve a tolerably decent degree of sobriety, but his appearance plainly indicated a recent debauch, and his style of preaching was tame and irregular. His congregation viewed him with suspicion and distrust privately; but as yet, no public charge had been made against him. He knew very well that he could not long continue in his own unworthy course, and be a minister of the gospel; he plainly saw the precipice over which he hung—but with mad infatuation he heeded not the danger, and rushed onwards to his ruin. His house became the scene of disorder and revelry. His servants neglected their duties when he so far forgot himself as to make them familiar associates of his orgies. The voice of prayer was no longer heard in his dwelling: the Bible was cast aside. Blasphemy had supplanted the one and obscene books had taken the place of the other. We shall see how rapid was his downfall, and to what a state of degradation he sunk at last.

But we return for the present to Mr. Hedge and his newly-made wife. They alighted at the old gentleman's princely mansion in Hudson street and entered a magnificent apartment in which a bridal supper had been prepared for them. Julia, as the mistress of the house, was received with the most profound respect by half a score of domestics, clad in plain but costly livery. Everything betokened unbounded wealth, and the repast was served on a scale of splendid luxury—every article of plate being of massive silver. Viands the most *recherche* graced the board, and wines the most rare added zest to the feast. There, sparkling like the bright waters of the Castalian fountain, flowed the rich Greek wine—a classic beverage, fit for the gods; there, too, was the delicate wine of Persia, fragrant with the spices of the East; and the diamond-crested champagne, inspiring divinities of poesy and Love.

'Drink, my Julia,' cried the happy bridegroom—'one cup to Hymen, and then let us seek his joys in each other's arms. I have a chamber prepared for us, which I have dedicated to Venus and to Cupid; there hath Love spread his wing, and beneath it shall we enjoy extatic repose. Come, dearest.'

He took her hand, and preceded by a female domestic bearing candles, conducted her up a broad marble staircase; they entered an apartment sumptuously furnished—it was the bridal chamber. The footstep fell noiseless upon the thick and yielding carpet; each chair was a gilded throne, and each sofa a luxurious divan, cushioned with purple velvet. Vast paintings, on subjects chiefly mythological, were reflected in immense mirrors, reaching from floor to ceiling. The bed was curtained with white satin, spangled with silver stars; and a wilderness of flowers, in exquisite vases, enriched the atmosphere with their perfume.

The old gentleman kissed his bride, whispered a few words in her ear, and left the chamber, followed by the domestic. Then Julia was waited upon by two young ladies, dressed in white, who saluted her respectfully, and signified their desire to assist her in disrobing.

'We are only servants, madam,' said they, modestly,—'we perform the duties of housekeepers for Mr. Hedge, and are highly honored if we can be of service to his lady.'

But the truth is, these young ladies were the illegitimate daughters of the old gentleman. Tho' Julia was his first wife, in his young days he had formed an attachment for a poor but lovely young woman; circumstances would not admit of his marrying her, and as she loved him in return, they tasted the joys of Venus without lighting the torch of Hymen. The young woman became *enciente*, and died in giving birth to twins—both daughters. Mr. Hedge brought these children up under his own roof, and educated them liberally; yet while he treated them with the most indulgent kindness, he never acknowledged himself to be their father, fearing that if the fact became known, it would injure his reputation as a man and a Christian, he being a zealous church member. The girls themselves were ignorant of their parentage, and only regarded Mr. Hedge as their generous benefactor. They had been taught to believe that they had been abandoned by their parents in their infancy, and that the old gentleman had taken them under his protection from motives of charity. They were of a gentle disposition, beloved by all who knew them, and by none more so than by Mr. Hedge, who maintained them as ladies although he suffered them to superintend the affairs of his extensive bachelor establishment. Their names were Emma and Lucy.

While these young ladies are engaged in disrobing the fair (but *not* blushing) bride, let us seek the newly-elected husband, in the privacy of his library.

A library—How we love to linger in such a place, amid the thousands of volumes grown dingy with the accumulated dust of years!—We care not for one of your modern libraries, with its spruce shelves, filled with the sickly effusions of romantic triflers—the solemn, philosophical nonsense of Arthur, the dandified affectation of Willis, and the clever but wearisome twittle-twattle of Dickens—once great in himself, now living on the fading reputation of past greatness; we care not to enter a library made up of such works, all faultlessly done up in the best style of binder. No—we love to pass long solitary hours in one of those old depositories of choice literature made venerable by the rich mellowing of time, and the sombre tapestry of cobwebs which are undisturbed by the intrusive visitation of prim housemaids. There, amid antique volumes, caskets of thought more precious than gems, how delightful to commune with the bright spirit of dead authors, whose inspired pens have left behind them the glorious scintillations of immortal genius, which sparkle on every page! When the soft light of declining day steals gently into the dusky room, and dim shadows hover in every nook, the truly contemplative mind pores with a quiet rapture over the sublime creations of Shakespeare, the massive grandeur of Scott, and the glowing beauties of Byron. Then are the dull realities of life forgotten, and the soul revels in a new and almost celestial existence.

In such a place do we now find Mr. Hedge, but he is not feasting on the delicacies of an elevated literature. Far differently is he engaged: he is entirely undressed, and reclining at full length in a portable bath, which is one-third full of *wine*. Such luxurious bathing is often resorted to by wealthy and superannuated gentlemen, who desire to infuse into their feeble limbs a degree of youthful activity and strength, which temporarily enables them to accomplish gallantries under the banner of Venus, of which they are ordinarily incapable.

'Oh that I were young!' ejaculated the bridegroom, as with a melancholy air he contemplated his own wasted frame. 'Would that thro' my veins, as in days of yore, there leaped the fiery current of vigorous youth! Alas seventy winters have chilled my blood and while my wishes are as ardent as ever, my physical organization is old, and weak, and shattered—and I fear me, cannot carry out the warm promptings of my enamored soul. How gladly would I give all my wealth, for a new lease of life, that I might revel in the joys of youth again!'

He rang a small bell, and a valet entered, bearing a dish containing a highly nutritious broth, which he had caused to be prepared on account of its invigorating properties. After partaking of this rich and savory mess, and having drank a glass of a certain cordial celebrated for its renovating influence, he arose, and his valet rubbed him vigorously with a coarse towel, then slipping on a few garments and a dressing-gown, he repaired to the bridal chamber with a beating heart.

The two young ladies, having performed their task, had retired, and Julia was on the couch awaiting her husband's coming. As he entered, she partly rose from her recumbent posture, with a smile of tender invitation lighting up her charming face; and rushing forward, he strained her passionately to his breast.

Then came a torrent of eager kisses, and a thousand whispered words of tenderness and love—sincere on the part of the old gentleman, but altogether affected on the part of Julia, who felt not the slightest degree of amorous inclination towards him. Yet he imagined her to be, like himself, fired with passion, and full of desire. His eyes feasted upon the beauties of her glorious form, which, so seductively voluptuous, was liberally exposed to his gaze; and his trembling hand wandered amid the treasures of her swelling bosom, so luxuriant in its ripened fullness.

Soon the withered form of the aged bridegroom is encircled by the plump, soft arms of his beautiful young bride. There are kisses, and murmurings, and sighs— but there is a heavy load of disappointment on the heart of the husband, who curses the three score and ten years that bind his warm wishes with a chain of ice; and he prays in vain for the return—even the temporary return—of glad youth, with its vigor, and its joys.

Julia comprehends all, and secretly congratulates herself on his imbecility which releases her from embraces that are repugnant to her, though she assumes an air of tender concern at his distress. Maddened at a failure so mortifying, Mr. Hedge half regrets his marriage.

Oh, why does weak tottering age seek to unite itself with warm, impetuous youth! The ice of winter is no congenial mate for the fresh, early flower of spring. How often do we see old, decrepit men wooing and wedding young girls, purchased by wealth from mercenary parents! Well have such sacrifices to Lust and Mammon, been termed *legalized prostitution*. And does not such a system excuse, if not justify, infidelity on the part of the wife? An old, drivelling dotard takes to his home and bed a virgin in her teens, whom he has purchased, but as he has gone through a formal ceremony, law and the world pronounce her wife. His miserable physical incapacity provokes without satisfying the passions of his victim; and in the arms of a lover she secretly enjoys the solace which she cannot derive from her legal owner. Then, if she is detected, how the world holds up its ten thousand hands in pious horror!—Wives who have *young* husbands are eloquent in their censure; old women who have long passed the rubicon of love and feeling, denounce her a *shameless hussey*; while the old reprobate who calls himself her husband, says to his indignant and sympathizing friends—'I took her from a low station in life; I raised her to a position of wealth and rank, and see how ungrateful she is.'

Irritated by the disappointment, he arose, threw on his garments, and muttering a confused apology, left the chamber, taking with him a light. As he closed the door behind him, Julia burst into a gay silvery laugh.

'Poor old man!' she said to herself,—'how disconcerted he is!' I could scarce keep myself from laughing. Well, he is not likely to prove very troublesome to me as a husband, and I'm glad of it, for really, the pawings, and kisses, and soft nonsense of such an old man are disgusting to me. Heigho! when we get to Boston, I must look out for a lover or two, to atone for the lamentable deficiencies of that withered cypher.'

When Mr. Hedge quitted the chamber, he went directly to his library, and rang the bell violently. In a few minutes the summons was answered by his valet. This man was of middle age, and rather good-looking, but possessed what is generally called a wicked eye.

'Brown,' said his master—'make a fire in this room, and bring up some wine and refreshments. I shall pass the night here.'

'The devil!' thought Brown, as he sat about obeying these orders—'master going to pass the night in his library, and just married to a woman so handsome that one's mouth waters to look at her! They've either had a quarrel, or else the old man has found himself mistaken in some of his calculations. I'm a fool if I don't turn things to my advantage. I see it all; she has cheated old Hedge into marrying her, although she has a husband already. She did not know me, in this livery; but she soon shall know me. Why, she's in my power completely, and if she don't do just as I want her to, d——n me if I don't *blow* on her, and spoil all her fun!'

We may as well enter into an explanation at once. This valet, called Brown, was no other than Davis—Frank Sydney's former butler—who had been sent to the State Prison for the term of five years, for his participation in the attempt to rob his master's house. In less than a month after his removal to Sing Sing, he was pardoned out by the Governor, who, being a good-natured man, could not refuse to grant the request of the prisoner's friends. On being set at liberty, Davis assumed the name of Brown, and entered the service of Mr. Hedge as valet. He had instantly recognized in the newly-made wife of his master, his former mistress, Mrs. Sydney;—but she knew him not, as his appearance was greatly changed. Being a shrewd fellow, he saw through the whole affair, and understanding her exact position, was resolved to take advantage of it, as soon as a proper opportunity should present itself.

The fire was made, the refreshments were brought, and the valet stood as if awaiting further orders.

'Sit down, Brown,' said his master, 'and take a glass of wine. You know that I was married to-night to a young lady—you saw her. Ah, she's a beautiful creature; and yet she might as well be a stick or a stone, for I am too old and worn-out to enjoy her charms. I did wrong to marry her; she's an estimable lady, and deserves a husband capable of affording her the satisfaction which I cannot—Yet I'll do my utmost to make her happy; I know that she will be faithful to me. Hereafter we will occupy separate chambers; and as I cannot discharge the duties of a husband, I will become a father to her. To-morrow we depart for Boston; and as I still need the services of a valet, you can go with me if you choose.'

'Thank'ee, sir; I shall be glad to go with you,' said Brown.

'Then that matter is settled,' rejoined Mr. Hedge—'you can leave me now; I shall not want you again to-night. I will stretch myself upon this sofa, and try to sleep.'

The valet bade his master good night, and left the library; but instead of going to his own room, he crept stealthily towards the chamber of Julia, now Mrs. Hedge. At the door he paused and listened; but hearing nothing, he softly opened the door, and glided in with noiseless steps, but with a palpitating heart, for it was a bold step he was taking—he, a low menial, to venture at midnight into the bed-chamber of his master's wife! Yet he was a daring fellow, lustful and reckless; and he fancied that his knowledge of the lady's true history, and her fear of exposure, would render her willing to yield her person to his wishes.

He approached the bed, and found that she was sleeping. The atmosphere of the room was warm and heavy with voluptuous perfumes; and the dying light of the wax candles shed but a dim and uncertain ray upon the gorgeous furniture, the showy drapery of the bed, and the denuded form of the fair sleeper; denuded of everything but one slight garment, whose transparent texture imperfectly concealed charms we dare not describe. How gently rose and fell that distracting bosom, with its prominent pair of luscious *twin sisters*, like two polished globes of finest alabaster! A soft smile parted her rosy lips, disclosing the pearly teeth; and her clustering hair lay in rich masses upon the pillow. So angelic was her appearance, and so soft her slumbers that a painter would have taken her as a model for a picture of Sleeping Innocence. Yet, within that beautiful exterior, dwelt a soul tarnished with guilty passion, and void of the exalted purity which so ennobles the exquisite nature of woman.

Long gazed the bold intruder upon that magnificent woman; and the sight of her ravishing charms made his breath come fast and thick, and his blood rushed madly through his veins. Trembling with eager wishes and a thousand fears, he bent over her and, almost touching his lips to hers, inhaled the fragrance of her breath, which came soft as a zephyr stirring the leaves of a rose. Then he laid his hand upon her bosom, and passed it daringly over the swelling and luxuriant outlines. Julia partially awoke, and mistaking the disturber of her slumbers for Mr. Hedge, languidly opened her eyes, and murmured—'Ah, dearest, have you returned?'

The valet replied by imprinting a hot kiss upon her moist, red lips; but at that moment the lady saw that it was not her husband who had ravished the kiss. Starting up in bed she exclaimed, in mingled surprise and alarm—

'Good heavens, who is this?—Fellow, what do you want, how dare you enter this chamber?'

'Why, ma'am,' said Brown, doggedly—'I knew that master is old, and no fit companion for such a lively young woman as you be, and I thought—'

'No more words, sir!' cried Julia, indignantly—'leave this room instantly—go at once, and I am willing to attribute your insolence to intoxication—but linger a moment, and I will alarm the house, and give you up to the anger of your master!'

'Oh, no missus,' said the fellow, coolly—'If *that* be your game, I can play one worth two of it. Give the alarm—rouse up the servants—bring your husband here—and I'll expose you before them all as the wife of Mr. Sydney, turned out by him, for a nasty scrape with a negro footman! Missus you don't remember me, but I've lived in your house once, and know *you* well enough. I am Davis, the butler, very much at your service.'

'I recollect you now,' rejoined Julia, scornfully—'You are the scoundrel who treacherously admitted burglars into the house, and who was captured and sent to the State Prison, from which you were pardoned, as I saw stated in the newspapers. You are mistaken if you think that a dread of exposure will induce me to submit to be outraged by you. Heavens, I will not yield my person to every ruffian who comes to me with threats of exposure! Vile menial, I will dare ruin and death sooner than become the slave of your lust!'

As she uttered these words with a tone and air of indignant scorn, she looked more superbly beautiful than ever—her dark eyes sparkled, her cheeks glowed, and her uncovered bosom heaved with excitement and anger.

But Brown was a determined ruffian, and resolved to accomplish his purpose even if obliged to resort to force. Grasping the lady by both arms, he said, in a stern whisper—

'Missus, I am stronger than you be—keep quiet, and let me have my way and you shan't be hurt; but if you go to kicking up a rumpus, why d——n me if I won't use you rather roughly.'

He forced her back upon the bed, and placed his heavy hand over her mouth, to prevent her from screaming. Holding her in such a position that she could not move, he covered her face, neck and breasts with lecherous kisses; and was preparing to complete the outrage, when the report of a pistol thundered through the chamber, and the ruffian fell upon the carpet, weltering in his blood. His body had been perforated by a ball from a revolver, in the hands of Mr. Hedge.

'Die, you d——d treacherous villain,' cried the old gentleman, swearing for the first time in his life.

The dying wretch turned his malignant eyes upon Julia, and gasped, faintly—

'Mr. Hedge—your wife—false—negro—Sydney—'

He could say no more, for the hand of death was upon him; and gnashing his teeth with rage and despair, he expired.

Mr. Hedge had paid no attention to the ruffian's dying words; for he had caught Julia in his arms, and was inquiring anxiously if she were hurt.

'No, dearest,' she replied—'only frightened. But how came you to arrive so opportunely to my rescue?'

'I was endeavoring to get some sleep on the sofa in my library,' answered the old gentleman—'when suddenly I fancied I heard a noise in your chamber. Thinking that robbers might have got into the house, I grasped a pistol, and cautiously approached the door of this room. Pausing a moment to listen, I heard the villain threaten you with violence in case you resisted; the door being open a little, I stepped into the room without making any noise, and saw him preparing to accomplish the outrage. Then I raised my pistol with unerring aim, and put a ball through his infernal carcass. Thank heaven, I have reserved my Julia from a fate worse than death.'

Fortunately for Julia, he had not heard what had passed between her and the valet, in reference to her exposure. He believed her to be the most virtuous of her sex; while she was beyond measure rejoiced that Davis, who might have ruined her, was now dead.

The next day the newly-married pair left New York for the city of Boston, according to previous arrangement. Arrived in that great metropolis, they took up their quarters at the most fashionable hotel, there to remain until Mr. Hedge should purchase a suitable house in which to take up their permanent residence.

Julia had not neglected to bring her maid Susan with her, as that discreet abigail might be of service to her in any little matter of intrigue she might engage in. Nero, the black, she had discharged from her service.

Her greatest happiness now arose from the belief that she had now escaped from the persecutions of the Dead Man.

CHAPTER XXV

Servants' Frolics—a Footman in Luck—a Spectre—a Footman out of Luck— the Torture—the Murder, and Destruction of Franklin House.

We left Franklin House in charge of Simon, the favorite footman of Mrs. Franklin, who was to take care of the house until it should be sold, and then join his mistress in Boston.

Now, although Simon was an honorable, faithful fellow enough, he soon grew intolerably lonesome, and heartily tired of being all alone in that great mansion. To beguile his time, he often invited other servants of his acquaintance to come and sup with him; and regardless of the orders of his mistress, several of his visitors were females. These guests he would entertain in the most sumptuous manner; and Franklin House became the scene of reckless dissipation and noisy revels, such as it had seldom witnessed before.

One evening Simon invited a goodly number of his friends to a 'grand banquet,' as he pompously termed it; and there assembled in the spacious parlor about twenty male and female domestics from various houses in the neighborhood. The males included fat butlers, gouty coachman, lean footmen and sturdy grooms; and among the females were buxom cooks, portly laundresses and pretty ladies' maids. Simon had well nigh emptied the cellar of its choice contents, in order to supply wine to his guests; and towards midnight the party became uproarious in the extreme.

We shall not attempt to sketch the toasts that were offered, nor the speeches that were made; neither shall we enter too minutely into the particulars of the game of 'hide-and-seek,' in which they indulged—or tell how our handsome footman chased some black-eyed damsel into a dark and distant chamber, and there tussled her upon the carpet, or tumbled her upon the bed, or perpetrated other little pleasantries of a similar nature. Suffice it to say, all these amusements were gone through with by the company, until tired of the sport, they reassembled in the parlor, and gathering around the fire, began to converse on ghosts.

Reader, have you ever, at the solemn hour of midnight, while listening to the recital of some fearful visitation from the land of spirits, felt your hair to bristle, and your flesh to creep, and your blood to chill with horror, as you imagined that some terrible being was at that moment standing outside the door, ready to glide into the room and stand beside your chair? Did you not then dread to look behind you as you drew close to your companions, and became almost breathless with painful interest in the story?

Solemn feeling prevailed among Simon's guests, as Toby Tunk, the fat coachman, who had been relating his experience in ghosts uttered the following words:—

'Well, I was sitting by the coffin, looking at the corpse, when the door slowly opened, and—'

Toby was fearfully interrupted, for the door of that room DID slowly open and there entered a being of so terrible an aspect, that all the assembled guests recoiled from its presence with horror and affright. It advanced towards the fireplace, seated itself in an unoccupied chair, and surveyed the company with menacing eyes.

The form of the spectre was tall, and its countenance was ghastly and awful to behold; it was enveloped in a cloak, and where its right hand should have been, was a massive piece of iron which joined the wrist.

At length, after an interval, during which all the guests came near dying with fear, it spoke in a harsh and threatening tone:—

'Those of ye that belong not in this house, depart instantly, on peril of your lives; and if any there be who *do* belong here, let them remain, and stir not!'

All, with the exception of poor Simon, tremblingly left the room and the house, resolved never again to cross the threshold of a place visited by such fearful beings. The spectre then turned to the affrighted footman, and said, with a hideous frown—

'Now, rascal, tell me what has become of your mistress and her daughter—where have they gone—speak!'

But Simon, imagining that he had to do with a being from the other world, fell upon his knees and began to mutter a prayer.

'Accursed fool!' cried the supposed spectre, striking him with his iron hand—'does *that* feel like the touch of a shadowy ghost? Get up, and answer me; I am no ghost, but a living man—living, though known as the Dead Man. Where have the two Franklin ladies gone?'

Now Simon, convinced that his visitor was indeed no ghost, was beginning to regain his natural shrewdness: and remembering the injunctions of his mistress, not to reveal where she had gone, with her daughter, he replied, in accordance with the instructions which he had received—

'The ladies have gone to Philadelphia.'

'Liar!' cried the Dead Man—'you betray yourself; had you answered with more hesitation, I might have believed you—the readiness of your reply proves its falsehood. Now, by hell! tell me correctly where the ladies have gone, or I'll murder you!'

'Not so fast, old dead face,' cried Simon, who was a brave fellow, and had by this time recovered all his courage—'perhaps you mightn't find it so easy to murder me, as you imagine. Once for all, I'll see you d——d before I will tell you where the ladies have gone.'

The Dead Man smiled grimly as he surveyed the slight form of the footman; then, in a fierce tone, he demanded—

'Are you mad?—Do you want to rush on headlong to ruin and death? Do you know me? I am one whose awful presence inspires fear in my friends, consternation in my foes. Puny wretch, will you give me the required information, ere I crush you as a worm?'

'No!' replied Simon, decidedly.

'Bah! I shall have work here,' said the other, calmly: then he sprung upon the footman, who, altogether unprepared for so sudden an attack, could make but a feeble resistance, especially in the grasp of a man who possessed more than twice his strength.

The struggle was brief, for the Dead Man handled him as easily as if he were a child. Soon he was gagged and bound fast to a chair;—then the miscreant, with a diabolical grin, thrust the poker into the fire, and when it became red-hot, he drew it forth, saying—

'I have found a way to loosen your tongue, d——n you! When you get ready to answer my question, nod your head, and the torture shall cease.'

The monster applied the iron to various parts of his victim's body, burning through the clothes, and deep into the flesh. Simon winced with intense torture, yet he did not give the designated sign in token of submission until the skin was entirely burnt from his face, by the fiery ordeal.

Then the Dead Man removed the gag from his mouth, and asked—

'Where have the Franklin ladies gone, you infernal, obstinate fool?'

'To Boston,' gasped the miserable young man, and fainted. Ah! Simon, thy faithfulness to thy worthless mistress was worthy of a better cause!

'Boston, hey?' growled the villain—'then, by G——, I must go to Boston, too. Ah, I'm not at all surprised at their selecting that city for their place of refuge—for it is the abode of hypocrisy and lust; and they no doubt anticipate reaping a rich harvest there. But ere I depart for that virtuous and Christian city, I must finish my business here. And first to silence this fool's tongue forever!'

He drew forth his deadly knife, and plunged it up to the hilt in his victim's throat.

With scarce a groan or struggle, poor Simon yielded his spirit into the hands of his Maker.

The murderer viewed his appalling work with satisfaction. His eyes seemed to feast upon the purple stream that gushed from the wound, and stained the carpet. It seemed as if, in the ferocity of his soul, he could have *drank* the gory flood!

'Would that the human race had but one single throat, and I could cut it at a stroke,' he cried, adopting the sentiment of another: then, taking a lamp, he left the room, with the intention of exploring the house.

One apartment he found carefully locked; and he was obliged to exert all his strength to break in the door. This room was furnished in a style of extravagant luxury; it was of great extent, and adorned with a multitude of paintings and statues, all the size of life.

A silken curtain, suspended across the further end of the room, bore in large gilt letters, the words 'Sanctuary of the Graces.' And behind the curtain were collected a large number of figures, exquisitely made of wax, representing males and females, large as life, and completely nude, in every imaginable variety of posture, a few classical, others voluptuous, and many positively obscene.

In this curious apartment—a perfect gallery of amorous conceptions—Josephine and her mother were in the habit of consummating those intrigues which they wished to invest with extraordinary *eclat* and voluptuousness. Here they loved to feed their impure tastes by contemplating every phase of licentious dalliance; and here they indulged in extravagant orgies which will admit of no description.

The intruder into this singular scene noticed a small iron apparatus attached to the wall; a sudden idea struck him—advancing, he touched a spring, and instantly every wax figure was in motion, imitating the movements of real life with wonderful fidelity! A closet in one corner contained the machinery of these automatons; and the whole affair was the invention of an ingenious German, whose talents had been misapplied to its creation. It had formerly constituted a private exhibition; but, after the murder of her husband, Mrs. Franklin had purchased it at a large cost.

'By Satan!' cried the Dead Man—'those Franklins are ladies after my own heart; lecherous, murderous and abandoned, they are meet companions for me. What a splendid contrivance! It needs but the additions of myself and the superb Josephine, to render it complete!'

He left the room, and entered an elegant bed-chamber which adjoined it. It was the chamber of Josephine; and her full-length portrait hung upon the wall; there was her proud brow, her wanton eyes, her magnificent bust, uncovered, and seeming to swell with lascivious emotions. Everything was sumptuous, yet everything lacked that beautiful propriety with is so charming a characteristic of the arrangements of a virtuous woman—one whose purity of soul is mirrored in all that surrounds her. The bed, gorgeous though it was, seemed, in its shameless disorder, to have been a nest of riotous harlotry. Costly garments lay trampled under foot; a bird in a golden-wired prison, was gasping and dying for want of nourishment; splendidly-bound books, with obscene contents, were scattered here and there, and a delicate white slipper, which Cinderella might have envied, was stuffed full with letters. The Dead Man examined the documents; and among them was a paper, in the handwriting of Josephine, which we shall take the liberty of transcribing:—

'PRIVATE JOURNAL.—'Monday. Passed last evening with Signor Pacci, the handsome Italian Opera singer. Was rather disappointed in my expectations; he is impetuous, but* * * *.'

'Tuesday. Have just made an appointment with ——— the actor; he came to my box last night, between the acts, and made a thousand tender pretensions. *Mem.*— must try and get rid of Tom the coachman—am tired of him; besides it is *outre* to permit liberties to a menial.'

'Thursday. Am bored to death with the persecutions of Rev. Mr. ———. I cannot endure him, he is so ugly. *Mem.* —His son is a charming youth of sixteen; must try and get him.'

'Saturday. Dreadfully provoked with mother for her disgraceful *liaison* with her new coachman. She promised to discharge the fellow—did not perceive my drift. *Mem.*-—Am to admit him to-night to my chamber.'

'Sunday. Heard Mr. ——— preach; he visits me to-night.'

Having perused this precious *morceau*, the Dead Man thrust it into his pocket, and then, after a moment's reflection, deliberately applied the flame of the lamp to the curtains of the bed; and having waited to see the fire fairly started, he ran rapidly down stairs, and escaped from the house.

Within a quarter of an hour afterwards, Franklin House was entirely enveloped in flames; and notwithstanding every effort was made to save the building, it was completely destroyed. In one short hour that magnificent and stately pile was reduced to a heap of smoking ruins.

The destruction of this house and the property contained in it, brought Mrs. Franklin and her daughter to absolute poverty. When the news of the event reached them in Boston they were far from supposing that it was caused by the hideous ruffian whom they had so much reason to fear; they attributed the conflagration to the carelessness of Simon, and knew nothing of his having been murdered, but thought that, being intoxicated, he had perished in the flames.

The mother and daughter held a long consultation as to the best means of retrieving their ruined fortunes; and the result was, they determined to send for Sophia, in order to make use of her in a damnable plot, which, while it would supply them abundantly with cash, would forever ruin the peace and happiness of that innocent and pure-minded girl.

In answer to the summons, Sophia left the home of her relative in New Jersey, and joined her mother and sister in Boston. They received her with every demonstration of affection; and little did she suspect that an infamous scheme had been concocted between them, to sacrifice her upon the altars of avarice and lust.

CHAPTER XXVI

Scene on Boston Common—George Radcliff—the Rescue—Two Model Policemen—Innocence protected—the Duel, and the Death—the Unknown.

After Frank Sydney's escape from the Dark Vaults, through the City Sewers, he did not deem it prudent to remain longer in New York. Accordingly, accompanied by the Doctor, the dumb boy Clinton, and his faithful servant Dennis, he left the city, to take up his abode elsewhere. None of his friends knew the place of his destination; some supposed that he had gone to Europe; others thought that he had emigrated to the 'far West'; while many persons imagined that he had exhausted his fortune, and been obliged to leave by the persecutions of creditors. Those who had been accustomed to borrow money from him, regretted his departure; but those who had been afflicted with jealousy at his good looks and popularity with *la belle sex*, expressed themselves as 'devilish glad he'd gone.'

But, in truth, Frank had neither gone to Europe, nor to the far West, neither had he been driven away by creditors; his fortune was still ample, and adequate to all his wants, present and to come. Where, then, was our hero flown? impatiently demands the reader. Softly, and you shall know in good time.

It was a beautiful afternoon, in spring, and Boston Common was thronged with promenaders of both sexes and all conditions. Here was the portly speculator of State street, exulting over the success of his last *shave*; here was the humble laborer, emancipated for a brief season from the drudgery of his daily toil; here was the blackleg, meditating on future gains; and here the pickpocket, on the alert for a victim. Then there were ladies of every degree, from the poor, decent wife of the respectable mechanic, with her troop of rosy children, down to the languishing lady of fashion, with her silks, her simperings, and her look of *hauteur*. Nor was there wanting, to complete the variety, the brazen-faced courtezan, with her 'nods,' and becks, and wreathed smiles, tho' to class *her* with ladies of any grade, would be sacrilege.

The weather was delicious; a soft breeze gently stirred the trees, which were beginning to assume the fair livery of spring, and the mild rays of the declining sun shone cheerily over the noble enclosure. In the principal mall a young lady was slowly walking with an air pensive and thoughtful.

She could scarce have been over sixteen years of age—a beautiful blonde, with golden hair and eyes of that deep blue wherein dwells a world of expression. In complexion she was divinely fair; her cheeks were suffused with just enough of a rich carnation to redeem her angelic countenance from an unbecoming paleness. Her figure, *petite* and surpassingly graceful, had scarce yet attained the matured fullness of womanhood; yet it was of exquisite symmetry.—Her dress was elegant without being gaudy, and tasteful without being ostentatious.

Have you noticed, reader, while perusing this narrative, that nearly all the characters introduced have been more less tainted with crime?—Even Sydney, good, generous and noble as he was, had his faults and weaknesses. Alas! human excellence is so very scarce, that had we taken *it* as the principal ingredient of our book, we should have made a slim affair of it, indeed.

But you may remember, that in the former portions of our story, we made a slight allusion to one Sophia Franklin. *She*, excellent young lady! shall redeem us from the imputation of total depravity. Her virtue and goodness shall illumine our dark pages with a celestial light—even though her mother and sister were *murderesses!*

Sophia Franklin it was, then, whom we have introduced as walking on the Common, with thoughtful and pensive air, on that fine afternoon in early spring.

But *why* thoughtful, and *why* pensive? Surely she must be happy.—There certainly cannot exist a creature made in God's glorious image, who would plant the thorn of unhappiness in the pure breast of that gentle girl?

There is. Her worst enemies are her nearest relatives. Her mother and sister are plotting to sacrifice her to the lust of a rich villain, for gold.

Oh, GOLD! —Great dragon that doth feed on human tears, and human honor, and human blood! Thou art the poor man's phantom—the rich man's curse. Magic is thy power, thou yellow talisman; thou canst cause men and women to forget themselves, their neighbors, their God! See yon grey-headed fool, who hugs gold to his breast as a mother hugs her first born; he builds houses—he accumulates money—he dabbles in railroads. A great man, forsooth, is that miserly old wretch, who stoops from manhood to indulge the dirty promptings of a petty avarice. But is he happy? NO; how can such a thing be happy, even tho' he possess thousands accumulated by his detestable meanness—when men spit on him with contempt; decency kicks him, dishonorable care will kill him, infamy will rear his monument, and the devil will roast him on the hottest gridiron in hell—*and he knows it!*

But to resume. Slowly did Sophia pursue her walk to the end of the mall, and as slowly did she retrace her steps; then, crossing a narrow path, she approached the venerable old elm, whose antique trunk is a monument of time. She had scarcely made two circuits around this ancient tree, when a gentleman who had espied her from a distance, advanced and greeted her with a familiar air. On seeing him, she became much agitated, and would have walked rapidly away, had he not caught her by the arm and forcibly detained her.

This gentleman was a person of distinguished appearance, tall, graceful figure, and fashionably dressed.—His countenance though eminently handsome, was darkly tinged with Southern blood, and deeply marked with the lines of dissipation and care. He wore a jet-black mustache and imperial and his air was at once noble and commanding. 'My pretty Sophia,' said the stranger, in a passionate tone—'why do you fly from me thus? By heavens, I love you to distraction, and have sworn a solemn oath that you shall be mine, though a legion of fiends oppose me!'

'Pray let me go, Mr. Radcliff,' said the young girl entreatingly—'you wish me to do wrong, and I cannot consent to it, indeed I cannot. As you are a gentleman, do not persecute me any more.'

'Persecute you—*never!*' exclaimed the libertine; 'become mine, and you shall have the devotion of my life-time to repay you for the sacrifice. Consent, sweet girl.'

'Never!' said Sophia, firmly; 'had you honorably solicited me to become your wife, I might have loved you; but you seek my ruin, and I despise, detest you. Let me go, sir, I implore—I command you!'

'Command *me!*' exclaimed the libertine, his eyes sparkling with rage—'silly child, it is George Radcliff who stands before you; a man whom none dare presume to command, but whom all are accustomed to *obey*! I am a monarch among women, and they bow submissive to my wishes. Listen, Sophia; I have for years plucked the fairest flowers in the gardens of female beauty, but I am sated with their intoxicating perfume, and sick of their gaudy hues. Your luxurious mother and fiery sister were acceptable to me for a time, and I enjoyed their voluptuous caresses with delight; but the devil! the conquest was too easily achieved. I soon grew tired of them and was about to withdraw my patronage, when to retain it, they mentioned *you*, describing you to be a creature of angelic loveliness; my passions were fired by the description, and I longed to add so fair and sweet a lily to the brilliant bouquet of my conquests. They sent for you to New Jersey; you came, and surpassed my highest anticipations. I paid your mother and sister a large sum for you, promising to double the amount as soon as you should become mine. I have so far failed in my efforts; unwilling to use violence, I have tried to accomplish my object by entreaty. —Now, since you will not listen to my entreaties, I shall resort to force.—This very night I have arranged to visit you, and then—and *then*, sweet one—'

He drew the shrinking girl towards him, and in spite of her resistance, profaned her pure lips with unholy kisses. During the conversation just related, day had softly melted into dim twilight, and the loungers on the Common had mostly taken their departure; very few were in the vicinity of Radcliff and Sophia—and there was but one person who saw the scene of kissing and struggling that we have described. That person was a young and handsome man, well-dressed, and possessing an open, generous and manly countenance. Observing what was going on between the pair, and seeing that the young lady was suffering violence from her companion, he silently approached, nobly resolved to protect the weaker party, at all hazards.

Sophia had partially escaped from the grasp of Radcliff, and he was about to seize her again, when the young man just mentioned stepped forward, and said, calmly—

'Come, sir, you have abused that young lady enough; molest her no further.'

'And who the devil may you be, who presumes thus to interfere with a gentleman's private amusements?' demanded the libertine, with savage irony: but the bold eyes of the other quailed not before his fierce glance.

'It matters not particularly who I am,' replied the young man, sternly—'suffice it for you to know that I am one who is bound to protect a lady against the assaults of a ruffian, even if that ruffian is clad in the garb of a gentleman.'

'Oh, sir,' said Sophia, bursting into tears—'God will reward you for rescuing me from the power of that bad man.'

Radcliff's eyes literally blazed with fury as he strode towards the young lady's protector.

'You called me a ruffian,' said he, 'take *that* for your impudence,' and he attempted to strike the young man—but the blow was skillfully warded off, and he found himself extended on the grass in a twinkling.

Two policeman now ran up and demanded the cause of the fracas. The young man related everything that had occurred, whereupon the officers took Radcliff into custody.

'Fellow,' said the individual, haughtily addressing his antagonist,—'you are, I presume, nothing more than a shopman or common mechanic, beneath my notice; you therefore may hope to escape the just punishment of your insolence to-night.'

'You are a liar,' calmly responded the other—'I am neither a shopman nor a mechanic, and if I were, I should be far superior to such a scoundrel as you. I am a gentleman; your equal in birth and fortune—your superior in manhood and in honor. If you desire satisfaction for my conduct to-night, you will find me at the Tremont House, at any time. My name is Francis Sydney. I shall see this lady in safety to her residence.'

Radcliff was led away by the two officers. They had proceeded but a short distance, when he thus addressed them—

'My good fellow, it is scarcely worth while to trouble yourselves to detain me on account of this trifling affair. Here's five dollars a piece for you—will that do?'

'Why, sir,' said one of the fellows, pocketing his V, and giving the other to his companion—'we can't exactly let you go, but if you tip us over and run for it, perhaps we shan't be able to overtake you.'

'I understand you,' said Radcliff, and he gave each of those *faithful* officers a slight push, scarce sufficient to disturb the equilibrium of a feather, whereupon one of them reeled out into the street to a distance of twenty feet, while the other fell down flat on the sidewalk in an apparently helpless condition, and the prisoner walked away at a leisurely pace, without the slightest molestation.

Meanwhile, Frank Sydney escorted Sophia to the door of her residence in Washington street. The young lady warmly thanked her deliverer, as she termed him.

'No thanks are due me, miss,' said Frank—'I have but done my duty, in protecting you from the insults of a villain. I now leave you in safety with your friends.'

'Friends!' said the fair girl, with a deep sigh—'alas, I have no friends on earth.'

The tone and manner of these words went to the heart of our hero; he turned for a moment to conceal a tear—then raised her hand respectfully to his lips, bade her farewell, and departed.

Sophia entered the house, and found her mother and sister in the parlor. They greeted her with smiles.

'My darling Soph,' said Mrs. Franklin—'that charming fellow was much disappointed to find that you had gone out. We told him that you had probably gone to walk on the Common, and he went in search of you.'

Sophia related all that had occurred to her during her absence. She complained of the libertine's treatment of her with mingled indignation and grief.

'Pooh! sis,' exclaimed Josephine, —'you mustn't think so hard of Mr. Radcliff's attentions. You must encourage him, for he is very rich, and *we need money.*'

'Must you have money at the expense of my honor?' demanded Sophia, with unwonted spirit.

'And why not?' asked her mother in a severe tone. 'Must we starve on account of your silly notions about virtue, and such humbug? Your sister and I have long since learned to dispose of our persons for pecuniary benefit, as well as for our sensual gratification—for it is as pleasurable as profitable; and you must do the same, now that you are old enough.'

'Never—never!' solemnly exclaimed Sophia—'my poor, dead father—'

'What of him?' eagerly demanded both mother and daughter, in the same breath.

'He seems to look down on me from Heaven, and tell me to commit no sin,' replied the young girl.

'Nonsense,' cried the mother—'but go now to your chamber, and retire to bed; to-night at least, you shall rest undisturbed.'

Sophia bade them a mournful good night, and left the room. When the door closed upon her, Josephine glanced at her mother with a look of satisfaction.

'Radcliff will be here to-night at twelve,' said she—'according to his appointment, for he will find no difficulty in procuring his discharge from custody. Once introduced into Sophia's chamber, he will gain his object with little trouble; then he will pay us the remaining thousand, as agreed upon.'

'And which we need most desperately,' rejoined her mother—'how unfortunate about the burning of our house! It has reduced us almost to our last penny.'

'The loss is irreparable,' sighed Josephine—'what divine raptures we used to enjoy in the 'Sanctuary of the Graces!' And there, too, was my elegant wardrobe and that heavenly French bed!'

These two abandoned women then retired to their respective chambers, to await the coming of Radcliff. At midnight he came. He was admitted into the house by Mrs. Franklin, and conducted to the chamber of Sophia, which he entered by means of a duplicate key furnished him by the perfidious mother.

The libertine had not observed, on entering the house, that he was followed by a man at a short distance. He was too intent upon the accomplishment of his vile desire, to notice the close proximity of one who was determined to oppose him in its execution. Sydney had expected that Radcliff would be liberated, and felt assured that he would seek his victim again that night. He comprehended that the poor girl resided with those who would not protect her, and he nobly resolved to constitute himself her friend. He had lingered around the house for hours, and when he saw the libertine approaching, followed him to the very door, at which he stationed himself, and listened.

Soon a piercing shriek proceeding from an upper chamber, told him that the moment for his aid had arrived. The street door was fortunately not locked, and was only secured by a night latch; this he broke by one vigorous push, and rushing through the hall, mounted the stairs, and entered the chamber from which he judged the cry of distress had issued.

Then what a sight presented itself! Sophia, in her night dress, her hair in wild disorder, struggling in the arms of the villain Radcliff, whose fine countenance was rendered hideous by rage and passion.

'What!' he exclaimed—'*you* here? By G——, you shall rue your interference with my schemes. How is it that you start up before me just at the very moment when my wishes are about to be crowned with success?'

'I will not parley with you,' replied Frank—'the chamber of this young lady is no fitting place for a dispute between us. As you claim to be a gentleman, follow me hence.'

'Lead on, then,' cried the libertine, foaming with rage. 'I desire nothing better than an opportunity to punish your presumption.'

As they descended the stairs, Josephine and her mother, alarmed by the noise of the dispute, issued from their rooms, and when Frank had given them a hasty explanation, the latter angrily demanded how he dared intrude into that house, and interfere in a matter with which he had no business.

'Madam,' replied our hero—'you are, I presume, the mother of that much abused young lady up stairs. I see that you countenance the ruin of your daughter. I tell you to beware—for I shall take proper measures to expose your vileness, and have *her* placed beyond the reach of your infernal schemes.'

He then left the house followed by Radcliff. After proceeding a short distance, the latter paused, and said—

'We can do nothing to-night, for we have no weapons, and to fight otherwise would scarce comport with the dignity of gentlemen. Meet me to-morrow morning, at the hour of six, upon this spot; bring with you a friend, and pistols; we will then repair to some secluded place, and settle our difficulty in honorable combat.'

'But what assurance have I that you will keep the appointment?' demanded Sydney; 'how do I know that this is not a mere subterfuge to escape me?'

'Young man, you do not know me,' rejoined Radcliff, and his breast swelled proudly. 'Do you think I'd resort to a base lie? Do you think that I *fear* you? I confess I am a libertine, but I am a man of honor—and that honor I now pledge you that I will keep the appointment; for, let me tell you, that I desire this meeting as much as you do.'

Strange inconsistency of terms!—'A libertine—but a man of *honor!*' This creed is preached by thousands of honorable adulterers. A seducer is of necessity a liar and a scoundrel—yet, forsooth, he is a man of *honor!*

'Very well, sir,' said Sydney—'I have no doubt you will come.' And with a cool 'good night,' they separated.

The next morning early, at a secluded spot in Roxbury neck, four men might have been seen, whose operations were peculiar. Two of them were evidently preparing to settle a dispute by the 'code of honor.' The other two (the seconds) were engaged in measuring off the distance—ten paces.

The morning was dark and cloudy, and a drizzling rain was falling. It was a most unpleasant season to be abroad, especially to execute such business as those four men had in hand.

Sydney had chosen for his second 'the Doctor'; while Radcliff had brought with him a tall individual, whose countenance was mostly concealed by an enormous coat collar and muffler, and a slouched hat. Two cases of pistols had been brought, and as 'the Doctor' was an accomplished surgeon, it was deemed unnecessary to have the attendance of another.

At length all was ready, and the antagonists took their places, with their deadly weapons in their hands. Both men were cool and collected; Radcliff was a most accomplished duelist, having been engaged in many similar encounters; and his countenance was expressive of confidence and unconcern. Sydney had never before fought a duel, yet, feeling assured of the justice of his cause, he had no apprehension as to the result. It may be asked why he so interested himself in a young lady he had never before seen, as to engage in a bloody encounter for her sake. We answer, he was prompted so to do by the chivalry of his disposition, and by a desire to vindicate the purity of his motives, and the sincerity of his conduct. He wished to let that unprincipled libertine see that he was no coward, and that he was prepared to defend the rights of a helpless woman with his life.

The word was given to fire, and both pistols were discharged at once. Sydney was wounded slightly in the arm; but Radcliff fell, mortally wounded—his antagonist's ball had pierced his breast.

Sydney bent over the dying man with deep concern; his intention had been merely to wound him—he had no desire to kill him; and when he saw that his shot had taken a fatal effect, he was sincerely grieved. He could not deny to himself that he felt a deep interest in the splendid libertine, whose princely wealth, prodigal generosity, magnificent person, and many amours, and rendered him the hero of romance, and the most celebrated man of the day. He knew that Radcliff's many vices were in a slight degree palliated by not a few excellent qualities which he possessed; and he sighed as he thought that such a brilliant intellect and such a happy combination of rare personal advantages should cease to exist, ere the possessor could repent of the sins of his past life.

Radcliff's second, the tall man with the shrouded countenance, walked to a short distance from the melancholy group, with a gloomy and abstracted air. While the Doctor made vain efforts to alleviate the sufferings of Radcliff, that unhappy man raised his dying eyes to Sydney's face, and said, faintly:—

'Young man, my doom is just.—Continue to be kind to Sophia Franklin, whom I would have wronged but for your timely interference; but beware of her mother and sister—they are devils in the shape of women. They would have sold her to me for gold—wretches that they were, and villain that I was!'

'Can I do anything for you?' asked Frank, gently.

'Nothing—but listen to me; the pains of death are upon me, and my time is short. You see my second—that tall, mysterious-looking person? I have known him, for many years—he is a villain of the deepest dye—one whom I formerly employed to kidnap young girls for my base uses. Last night I met him for the first time for a long period; I told him that I was to fight a person named Sydney this morning; he started at the mention of your name, and eagerly desired to act as my second. I consented. He is your most inveterate enemy, and thirsts for your blood. He seeks but an opportunity to kill you. *He fears your second*, and that prevents him from attacking you at once. Beware of him, for he is—is—is—the—'

Radcliff could not finish the sentence, for the agonies of death were upon him. His eyes glazed, his breath grew fainter and fainter; and in a few moments he expired.

Thus perished George Radcliff—the elegant *roue*—the heartless libertine—the man of pleasure—brilliant in intellect, beautiful in person, generous in heart—but how debased in soul!

They laid the corpse down upon the smooth, green sward, and spread a handkerchief over the pale, ghastly features. Then they turned to look for the mysterious second; he was seated, at some distance, upon a large rock, and they beckoned him to approach. He complied, with some hesitation; and the Doctor said to him—

'Sir, you seem to manifest very little interest in the fate of your friend; you see he is dead.'

'I care not,' was the reply—'his death causes me no grief, nor pleasure; he was no enemy of mine, and as for friends, I have none. Grief and friendship are sentiments which have long since died in my breast.'

'By heavens!' exclaimed the Doctor—'I know that voice! The right hand jealously thrust into your breast—your face so carefully concealed—the dying words of Radcliff—tell me that you are—'

'The Dead Man!' cried the stranger, uncovering his face—'you are right—I am he! Doctor, I did not expect to find you with Sydney, or I should not have ventured. I came to execute vengeance—but your presence restrains me; crippled as I am, I fear you. No matter; other chances will offer, when you are absent. That escape of yours through the sewers was done in masterly style. Doctor, you are a brave fellow, and your courage inspires me with admiration; you are worthy to follow my reckless fortunes. Let the past be forgotten; abandon this whining, preaching Sydney, and join me in my desperate career. Give me your hand, and let us be friends.'

The Doctor hesitated a moment, and, to Sydney's unutterable amazement, grasped the Dead Man's hand, and said—

'Oh, Captain, I will re-enlist under your banner; I am tired of a life of inactivity, and long for the excitement and dangers of an outlaw's career! We are friends, henceforth and forever.'

The Dead Man grinned with delight; but poor Sydney was thunderstruck.

'Good God!' he exclaimed—'is it possible that you, Doctor, will desert me, after swearing to me an eternal friendship? You, whom I once benefitted—you, who have since benefitted me—you, whom I thought to be one of the best, bravest, and most faithful men under the sun—notwithstanding your former faults—to prove traitor to me now, and league yourself with my worst enemy? Oh, is there such a thing as honesty or truth on earth?'

The Doctor was silent; the Dead Man whispered to him—

'Let us kill Sydney—he is no friend to either of us, and why should he live?'

'No,' said the Doctor, decidedly—'we will harm him not, at least for the present. At some future time you may do with him as you will. Let us go.'

And they went, leaving our hero in a frame of mind almost distracted with remorse and sorrow—remorse, that he had killed a fellow creature—sorrow, that a man whom he had regarded as a friend, should prove so perfidious.

He retraced his way to the city, and returned to his hotel. The body of poor Radcliff was shortly afterwards found by several laborers, who conveyed it to the city, where an inquest was held over it. A verdict of *suicide* was rendered by the jury, who, short-sighted souls, comprehended not the mysteries of duelling; and the 'rash act' was attributed by the erudite city newspapers to 'temporary insanity'!

For three or four days after these events, Sydney was confined to his bed by illness. His wounded arm pained him much, and he had caught a severe cold upon the wet, drizzly morning of the duel. Clinton, the dumb boy, attended him with the most assiduous care. This poor youth had learned the 'dumb alphabet,' or language of signs, to perfection; and as his master had also learned it, they could converse together with considerable facility. Sydney was beginning to recover from his indisposition, when one evening Clinton came into his room, and communicated to him a piece of information that astounded him. It was, that Julia, his wife, was then stopping at that very same hotel, as the wife of an old gentleman named Mr. Hedge—that she was dressed superbly, glittering with diamonds, appeared to be in the most buoyant spirits, and looked as beautiful as ever.

CHAPTER XXVII

The Ruined Rector—Misery and Destitution—the All Night House—
A Painful Scene—Inhospitality—the Denouement.

We now return to Dr. Sinclair, whom we left on the downward path to ruin. The unfortunate man was now no longer the rector of St. Paul's; a committee of the congregation had paid him an official visit, at which he had been dismissed from all connection with the church. His place was supplied by a clergyman of far less talent, but much greater integrity.

Mr. Sinclair (for such we shall hereafter call him,) was not possessed of wealth— for though he had lived in luxury, he had depended entirely upon his salary for subsistence; and now that he was turned from his sacred occupation, dishonored and disgraced, he found himself almost penniless. He had no friends to whom he could apply for assistance, for his conduct had been noised abroad, and those who formerly had loved and reverenced him, now turned their backs upon him with cold contempt.

Instead of endeavouring to retrieve his fallen reputation by repentance and good conduct, he no sooner found himself shorn of his clerical honors, than he abandoned himself to every species of degraded dissipation. In two weeks after his removal from the church he was without a home; then he became the associate of the most vile. Occasionally he would venture to the house of some one of his former congregation, and in abject tones implore the gift of some trifling sum; moved by his miserable appearance, though disgusted by his follies, the gentleman would perhaps hand him a dollar or two, and sternly bid him come there no more. Sinclair would then hasten to the low pot house in Water Street which he made his resort, and amid his vagabond companions expend the money in the lowest debauchery.

Perhaps the reader may say the thing is impossible—no man could fall so rapidly from a high and honorable position, as to become in a few short weeks the degraded creature Sinclair is now represented to be. But we maintain that there is nothing exaggerated in the picture we have drawn. Here is a church congregation eminently aristocratic, wealthy, and rigidly particular in the nicest points of propriety. The pastor proves himself unworthy of his sacred trust; he disgraces himself and them by indulgence in vice, which is betrayed by his looks and actions. Too haughty and too impatient to take the erring brother by the hand, and endeavor to reclaim him, they at once cast him off with disgust, and fill his place with a more faithful pastor. Humbled and degraded, rendered desperate by his unhappy situation, the miserable man abandons himself yet more recklessly to the vice; his self-respect is gone, the finger of scorn is pointed at him, and to drown all consciousness of his downfall, he becomes a constant tipple and an irreclaimable sot.

The low groggery in Water street where poor Sinclair made his temporary home, was extensively known as the 'All Night House,' from the fact of its being kept open night and day. As this establishment was quite a feature in itself, we shall devote a brief space to a description of it.

It was situated on the corner of Catherine street, opposite the Catherine Market—a region remarkable for a very 'ancient and fish-like smell.' This Market was a large, rotten old shanty, devoted to the sale of stale fish, bad beef, dubious sausages, suspicious oysters, and dog's meat. Beneath its stalls at night, many a 'lodger' often slumbered; and every Sunday morning it was the theatre of a lively and amusing scene, wherein was performed the renowned pastime of 'niggers dancing for eels.' All the unsavory fish that had been accumulated during the week, was thus disposed of, being given to such darkies as won the most applause in the science of the 'heel and toe.' The sport used to attract hundreds of spectators, and the rum shops in the vicinity did a good business.

Suppose it to be midnight; let us enter the All Night House, and take a view. We find the place crowded with about forty men and boys, of all ages, conditions and complexions. Here is the veteran loafer, who had not slept in a bed for years—his clothes smelling of the grease and filth of the market stalls; here is the runaway apprentice, and here the dissipated young man who has been 'locked out,' and has come here to take lodgings. The company are all seated upon low stools; some are bending forward in painful attitudes of slumber; others are vainly trying to sit upright, but, overcome by sleep, they pitch forward, and recover themselves just in time to avoid falling on the floor.

Notice in particular this young man who is seated like the rest, and is nodding in an uneasy slumber. His clothes are of broadcloth, and were once fashionable and good, but now they are torn to rags, and soiled with filth. His hands are small and white; his hair, luxuriant and curling naturally, is uncombed; his features are handsome, but bruised and unwashed. This is Sinclair!

The bar-keeper of this place is quite a character in his way. He rejoices in the title of 'Liverpool Jack,' and is the *bully of Water street*—that is, he is considered able to thrash any man that travels in that region. He is a blustering, ruffianly fellow, full of 'strange oaths.' He wears a red flannel shirt and tarpaulin hat; and possesses a bull-dog countenance expressive of the utmost ferocity.

'Hello, you fellers,' cries Liverpool Jack, savagely surveying the slumbering crowd—'yer goin' to set there all night and not paternize de *bar*—say? Vake up, or by de big Jerusalem cricket I'm bound to dump yer all off de stools!'

Some of the poor devils arouse themselves, and rub their eyes; but the majority slumbered on. Liverpool Jack becomes exasperated, and rushing among them, seizes the legs of the stools, and dumps every sleeper upon the floor. Having accomplished this feat, he resumes his place behind the bar.

The door opens, and a party of young bloods enter, who are evidently 'bound on a time.'—They are all fashionably dressed; and one of them, drawing a well-filled purse from his pocket, invites all hands up to drink—which invitation, it is needless to say, was eagerly accepted. Sinclair crowded up to the bar, with the others and one of the new comers, observing him, cries out—

'By jingo, here's parson Sinclair! Give us a sermon, parson, and you shall have a pint of red-eye!'

'A sermon—a sermon!' exclaimed the others. Sinclair is placed upon a stool, and begins a wild, incoherent harangue, made up of eloquence, blasphemy and obscenity. His hearers respond in loud 'amens,' and one of the young bloods, being facetiously inclined, procures a rotten egg, and throws it at the unhappy man, deviling his face with the nauseous missile. This piece of ruffianism is immediately followed by another; the stool on which he stands is suddenly jerked from beneath him, and he falls violently to the floor, bruising his face and head shockingly.

Roars of laughter follow this deed of cruelty; poor Sinclair is raised from the floor by Liverpool Jack, who thrusts him forth into the street with a curse, telling him to come there no more.

It is raining—a cold, drizzly rain, which penetrates through the garments and strikes chill to the bones. On such a night as this, Sinclair was wont to be seated in his comfortable study, before a blazing fire, enveloped in a luxurious dressing gown, as he perused some interesting volume, or prepared his Sabbath sermon; then, he had but to ring a silver bell, and a well-dressed servant brought in a tray containing his late supper—the smoking tea urn, the hot rolls, the fresh eggs, the delicious bacon, the delicate custard, and the exquisite preserves. Then, he had but to pass through a warm and well-lighted passage, to reach his own chamber; the comfortable bed, with its snowy drapery and warm, thick coverlid, invited to repose; and his dreams were disturbed by no visions of horror or remorse. All was purity, and happiness, and peace.

Now, how different! Houseless, homeless, shelterless—ragged, dirty, starving—diseased, degraded, desperate! Unhappy Sinclair, that was a fatal moment when thou did'st yield to the fascinations of that beautiful Josephine Franklin!

It was near one o'clock, and the storm had increased to a perfect hurricane. The miserable man had eaten nothing that day; he tottered off with weakness, and was numbed with the cold. By an irresistible impulse he wandered in the direction of his former home in Broadway. He found the house brilliantly illuminated—strains of heavenly music issued from it—lovely forms flitted past the windows, and peals of silvery laughter mingled with the howling of the tempest. A grand party was given there that night; the occupant of the house was a man of fashion and pleasure, and he was celebrating the eighteenth birth-day of his beautiful daughter.

Sinclair lingered long around the house—it seemed as if some invisible power attracted him there. From the basement there arose the grateful, savory odor of extensive cooking.

'I am starving,' said he to himself—'and they have plenty here. I will go to the door, like a beggar, and implore a morsel of food.'

With feeble steps he descended to the basement, and with a trembling hand he knocked at the door. It was opened by a fat, well-fed servant, in livery, who demanded, in a surly tone, what he wanted?

'In heaven's name, give me food, for I am starving.'

'Ugh—a beggar!' said the servant, with disgust—'get you gone, we've nothing for you; master never encourages vagrants.'

The door was shut in Sinclair's face; with an aching heart he crawled up the steps, and then, as if suddenly nerved with a desperate resolve, he approached the front door, and rang the bell. The door was opened by a footman, who stared at the intruder with surprise and suspicion.

'Tell your master,' said Sinclair, faintly, 'that a person is here who must speak with him. It is a matter of life and death.'

The servant did as requested; in a few minutes he returned and said:

'Master says that if your business is particular you must come into the drawing room; he's not coming out here in the cold.'

He followed the servant thro' the hall; and in a moment more found himself standing in the brilliantly lighted drawing-room, in the presence of a numerous party of ladies and gentlemen. His miserable appearance created quite a sensation in that fashionable circle.

'Aw, 'pon my honor,' lisped a dandy, raising his eye-glass and taking a deliberate survey of the intruder, 'what have we heah? quite a natural curiosity, dem me!'

'Oh, what an odious creature;' exclaimed a young lady with bare arms, naked shoulders, and the reddest possible hair.

'Quite shocking!' responded her admirer, a bottle-nosed specimen of monkeyism.

'I shall positively faint,' cried an old tabby, in a large turban; but as nobody noticed her, she didn't faint.

The host himself now advanced, and said, sternly,

'Well, fellow, what d'ye want?—Speak quickly and begone, for this is no place for you. You d——d stupid scoundrel,' (to the servant,) 'how dare you bring such a scare-crow here?'

'I wish to speak with you alone, sir,' said Sinclair, humbly.

The host motioned him to step out into the hall, followed him there, and commanded him to be as brief as possible.

Sinclair told him who he was, and the circumstances of misery and destitution in which he was placed. His listener shook his head incredulously, saying,

'It is a good game, my fine fellow, that you are trying to play off; you are an excellent talker, but you will find it hard to make people believe that you are Dr. Sinclair. In one word, you're an impostor. What, *you* a clergyman! Pooh, nonsense!—There, not another word, but clear out instantly. John, show this fellow the door, and never admit him again!'

As poor Sinclair passed out of the door, he heard the company laugh long and loud at the supposed imposition he had attempted to practise upon Mr. Grump, the 'worthy host.' Now be it known that this Mr. Grump was one of the most arrant scoundrels that ever went unhung. Low-bred and vulgar, he had made a fortune by petty knavery and small rascalities. He was a master printer; one of those miserable whelps who fatten on the unpaid labor of those in their employ. An indignant 'jour' once told him, with as much truth as sarcasm, that 'every hair on his head was a fifty-six pound weight of sin and iniquity!' He well knew that the poor wretch who had applied to him for relief, was no imposter; for he had heard Dr. Sinclair preach a hundred times, and he had recognized him instantly, notwithstanding his altered aspect. But he had pretended to believe him an impostor, in order that he might have a good excuse for withholding assistance from the unfortunate man.

Rudely did the servant thrust forth poor Sinclair into the inhospitable street and the fearful storm. The rain now fell in torrents; and the darkness was so intense, that the hapless wanderer cou'd only grope his way along, slowly and painfully.—Upon one corner of the street the foundation for a house had recently been dug, forming a deep and dangerous pit, lying directly in Sinclair's path: no friendly lantern warned him of the peril—no enclosure was there to protect him from falling. Unconscious of the danger, he slowly approached the brink of the pit; now he stood upon the extreme edge, and the next instant *he fell!* There was a dull, dead sound— then a stifled groan—and all was still!

Morning dawned, bright and clear, the storm had subsided during the night, and the glorious sun arose in a cloudless sky. A crowd was collected on the corner of Broadway and one of the narrow streets which cross its lower section. They were gazing at a terrible spectacle: the body of a man lay in a deep pit below them, shockingly mangled; he had fallen upon a heap of stones—his brains were dashed out, and his blood scattered all around. Among the spectators was a portly, well-dressed man, who looked at the body steadfastly for some time, and then muttered to himself—

'By G——, it is Dr. Sinclair, and no mistake! Too bad—too bad!— When he came to my house last night, I little thought to see him dead this morning! Plague on it, I ought to have given the poor devil sixpence or a shilling. No matter—he's better off now. He was a talented fellow—great pity, but can't be helped.'

Yes, it *could* have been helped, Mr. Grump; had you kindly taken that poor unfortunate by the hand, and afforded him food and shelter for a brief season, he never would have met that tragical end, but might have lived to reform, and lead a life of usefulness and honor; yes, he might have lived to bless you for that timely aid.

Reader, 'speak gently to the erring.' Do not too hastily or too harshly condemn the follies or faults of others. A gentle word, spoken in kindness to an erring brother, may do much towards winning him back to the path of rectitude and right. Harsh words and stern reproofs may drive him on to ruin.

But let us return to the crowd collected around the mangled body of Sinclair.

'It's a sin and a shame,' said a stout man, in working clothes, 'that there wasn't some kind of a fence put around this infernal trap. Where was the Alderman of this ward, that *he* didn't attend to it?'

'Be careful what you say, fellow,' said Mr. Grump, turning very red in the face, 'I'd have you to know that *I* am the Alderman of this ward!'

'Are you?—then let me tell you,' said the man, contemptuously, 'that you bear the name of being a mean, dirty old scamp; and if it was not for fear of the law, I'd give you a d——d good thrashing!'

Alderman Grump beat a hasty retreat while the crowd set up a loud shout of derision—for he was universally hated and despised.

The Coroner arrived—the inquest was held; and a 'verdict rendered in accordance with the facts.' The body was taken to the 'Dead House;' and as no friend or relative appeared to claim it, it was the next day conveyed to Potter's Field, and there interred among city paupers, felons and nameless vagrants.

CHAPTER XXVIII

The Disguised Husband—the False Wife—the Murder— the Disclosure, and Suicide.

Reader, let thy fancy again wing its flight from New York to our own city of Boston.

It was a strange coincidence that Frank Sydney and his wife Julia should tarry again beneath the same roof; yet they were not destined to meet under that roof—for the next day after Frank made the discovery, Mr. Hedge and the young lady removed from the Hotel to a splendid house which had been fitted up for them in the most aristocratic quarter of the city.

'I must see Julia once again,' said Frank to himself, when informed of her departure; —'I must see and converse with her again, for I am anxious to see if she has really reformed, since her marriage with this Mr. Hedge, whom I have heard spoken of as a very respectable old man. Of course, he can know nothing of her former character; and if I find her disposed to be faithful to her present husband, Heaven forbid that I should ruin her by exposure! But I must so disguise myself that she shall not recognise me; this I can easily do, for I am well acquainted with the art of disguise. I shall have no difficulty in meeting her on some of the fashionable promenades of the city; then my ingenuity will aid me in forming her acquaintance. My plan shall be put into immediate execution. '

Our hero felt considerable uneasiness in the knowledge that the Dead Man was then in the city; and when he reflected that the Doctor had joined that arch miscreant, he knew not what infernal plot might be concocted against his liberty or life. He puzzled his brain in vain to account for the Doctor's singular conduct in deserting him for the friendship of a villain; and he was forced to arrive at the unwelcome conclusion, that the Doctor was a man whose natural depravity led him to prefer the companionship of crime to the society of honesty and honor.

Sydney never ventured abroad without being thoroughly armed; and he was determined, if attacked by his enemies, to sell his life as dearly as possible.

He had called once upon Miss Sophia Franklin, since the night he had rescued her from the designs of the libertine Radcliff; Josephine and her mother plainly evinced by their looks that they did not relish his visit; but the fair Sophia received him with every demonstration of gratitude and pleasure. She could not deny to herself that she felt a deep and growing interest in the handsome young stranger, who had so gallantly defended her honor: while on his part, he sympathized with her unfortunate situation, on account of her unprincipled relatives, and admired her for her beauty and goodness. He sighed as he thought that his abandoned wife was a barrier to any hopes which he might entertain in reference to Sophia; for he felt that he could joyfully make the young lady his bride, and thus preserve her from her mother and sister, were there no obstacle in the way. When he contrasted her purity and virtue with the vices of Julia, he cursed his destiny that had placed so great a prize beyond his grasp.

Sophia, as yet, knew nothing of Frank's history, and was of course ignorant that he had a wife. Sweet hopes swelled the maiden's bosom, when the thought arose in her pure heart that she might be beloved by one whom she knew was worthy of her tenderest regard.

It was with a high degree of satisfaction that Julia now found herself, by the liberality of Mr. Hedge, mistress of a splendid establishment.—Her dresses, her jewelry, her furniture were of the most magnificent kind; her husband placed no restraint upon her whatever, he slept in a separate chamber, and never annoyed her with his impotent embraces; each morning he was accustomed to meet her in the breakfast parlor, and partake with her the only meal they took together during the day; after the repast, he would usually present her with money sufficient to do her fashionable 'shopping;' then he would kiss her rosy cheek, bid her adieu, and leave her to pass the day as her fancy or caprice might dictate.

Enjoying such a life of luxurious ease, Julia was almost perfectly happy. Yet her cup was not quite full; there was one thing wanting to complete the list of her pleasures—and this deficiency occupied her thoughts by day, and her dreams by night. Not to keep the reader in suspense, she longed for a handsome and agreeable lover—yet none could she find suited to her taste or wishes. True, she might have selected one from among the many gentlemen of leisure 'about town,' who are always ready to dangle at the heels of any woman who will clothe and feed them for their 'services.'—But she preferred a lover of a more exalted grade; one whose personal beauty was set off by mental graces, and superior manners. And he must be poor; for then he would be more dependent upon her, and consequently, more devoted and more constant.

Time passed, and still Julia had no lover.—Mr. Hedge mentally gave her credit for the most virtuous fidelity; yet the amorous fair one was constantly on the *qui vive* to catch in her silken meshes some desirable man with whom she might in secret pass the hours of her voluptuous leisure.

One day, while promenading Tremont street, her eyes rested upon a gentleman whose appearance sent a thrill of admiration and desire through every fibre of her frame. His figure, of medium height, was erect and well-built; his gait was dignified and graceful; his dress, in exact accordance with the *mode*, was singularly elegant and rich—but a superb waistcoat, a gorgeous cravat in which glittered a diamond pin, and salmon-colored gloves, were the least attractive points in his appearance; for his countenance was eminently handsome and striking. His hair fell in rich masses over a fine, thoughtful brow; his eyes were dark, piercing, and full of expression and fire; and the lower part of his face was almost completely hidden by a luxuriant growth of whiskers, imperial and moustache. Whatever of foppishness there might be in his dress, was qualified by the dignified grace of his manner.

'He is a charming creature, and I must catch him,' thought Julia. So, on the next day when she met him again, and at the moment when his eyes were fixed admiringly upon her countenance, she smiled, then blushed in the most engaging manner, and passed on in sweet confusion. The gallant gentleman, encouraged by the smile and blush, turned and followed her. She walked on as far as the Common, entered, and regardless of her satin dress, seated herself upon one of the sheet-iron covered benches. The gentleman (bold fellow!) seated himself upon the same bench, though at a respectful distance. Julia blushed again, and cast down her beautiful eyes.

You know very well, reader, how two persons, who are not acquainted, always begin a conversation. The weather is the topic first touched upon;—and that hackneyed subject merges easily and naturally into more agreeable discourse. So it was with Julia and her gallant; in less than half an hour after seating themselves on that bench, they were sociably and unrestrainedly conversing on the theatres, the opera, the last novel, and other matters and things pertaining to the world of fashion and amusement. The lady judged her companion, by a slight peculiarity in his accent, to be a foreigner—a circumstance that raised him still more in her estimation, for our amorous American ladies adore foreigners. He was also a man of wit, education and talent; and Julia became completely fascinated with him. He proposed an exchange of cards; she assented, and found her new friend to be the 'Signor Montoni'; and he subsequently informed her that he was an Italian teacher of languages—a piece of information that gave her pleasure, as his following a profession was a pretty certain indication that he was poor.

When Julia returned home, the Italian accompanied her to the door. The next day they met again, and the next; and the intimacy between them increased so rapidly, that within a week after their confidential chat on the Common, Montoni called on Julia at her residence. But the lady noticed that he had suddenly grown reserved and bashful; and he made this and their other interviews provokingly short. She had hoped to have found in him an impetuous and impassioned lover—one who needed but the opportunity to pluck the ripe fruit so temptingly held out to him; but she found him, instead, an apparently cold and passionless man, taking no advantage of his intimacy with her, and treating her with a distant respect that precluded all hope in her bosom of a successful amour.

In vain did the beautiful wanton assail him with inviting glances and seductive smiles; in vain did she, while in his presence, recline upon the sofa in attitudes of the most voluptuous abandonment; in vain did she, as if unconsciously, display to his gaze charms which might have moved an anchorite—a neck and shoulders of exquisite proportions, and a bosom glowing and swelling with a thousand suppressed fires. He withstood all these attacks, and remained calm and unmoved. When she gave him her hand to kiss at parting, he would merely raise it to his lips, and leave her with a cold 'adieu.'

'He is cold—senseless—unworthy of my regard; I will see him no more,' said Julia to herself. Yet when the image of the handsome Italian arose before her, so calmly noble, so proudly composed, her resolution forsook her, and she felt that he held her, heart and soul, under some strange and magical fascination.

'Yes, I love him,' she cried, bursting into a passionate flood of tears—'devotedly, madly love him. Oh, why am I the suppliant slave of this cold stranger? why cannot I entice him to my arms? Distraction: my most consummate art fails to kindle in his icy breast a single spark of the raging fire that is consuming me!'

It may be proper to mention that Mr. Hedge knew nothing of the Italian's visits to his wife; for Julia received him in a private parlor of her own, and there was no danger of interruption. The old gentleman passed most of his evenings in his library; and having implicit faith in the integrity of his wife, he allowed her to spend her evenings as she chose.

One evening Signor Montoni visited Julia rather earlier than usual; and she resolved that evening to make a desperate effort to conquer him, even if obliged to make known her wishes in words.

During the evening she exerted herself, as usual, to captivate him, and bring him to her feet. She sang—she played—she liberally displayed the graces of her person, and the charms of her accomplished mind, but still in vain.—There he sat, with folded arms, in deep abstraction, gazing at the elaborate figures on the gorgeous carpet.

At nine o'clock, Montoni arose, and took the lady's hand to bid her adieu. She gently detained him, and drew him towards her upon the sofa.

'Listen to me, Montoni;' said she, gazing into his eyes with an expression of deep fondness—'listen to me, and I will speak calmly if I can, though my heart is beating in wild tumult. Call me unwomanly, bold, wanton if you will, for making this declaration—*but I love you!*—God only knows how ardently, how passionately. The first moment I saw you, your image impressed itself indelibly upon my heart; in person, you were my *beau ideal* of manhood—and in mind I found you all that I could wish. I have sought to make you my lover—for my husband is old and impotent, and my passions are strong. Look at me, Montoni; am I ugly or repulsive? Nay, the world calls me beautiful, yet I seek to be beautiful only in your eyes, my beloved. Why, then, have you despised my advances, disregarded my mute invitations, and left me to pine with disappointment and with hope deferred? Why will you not take me in your arms, cover me with kisses, and breathe into my ear the melody of your whispered love?'

The lady paused, and the Italian gazed at her with admiration. Ah, how beautiful she looked! and yet how like a fiend in the shape of a lovely woman, tempting a man to ruin!

'Lady,' said Montoni, as a shade of sadness passed over his fine features—'you have mentioned your husband, and the recollection that you *have* a husband forbids that I should take advantage of your preference for me. God forbid that I should be the cause of a wife's infidelity! Pardon me, lady—you are very beautiful; the Almighty never created so fair a sanctuary to become the dwelling place of sin; be advised, therefore, to suppress this guilty passion, and remain faithful to your husband, who, old though he be, has claims upon your constancy.'

'I long for the declarations of a lover, not the reasonings of a philosopher,' cried Julia passionately. —'Thou man of ice, nothing can melt you?'

'Remember your duty to your husband,' said Montoni, gravely, as he arose to depart. 'I will see you to-morrow evening—adieu.'

He left her to her reflections.—Wild, tumultuous thoughts arose in her mind; and from the chaos of her bewildered brain, came a Hideous Whisper, prompting her to a bloody crime.

She thought of her husband as an obstacle to her happiness with Montoni; and she began to hate the old man with the malignity of a fiend.

'Curses on the old dotard!' she cried, in a paroxysm of rage—'were it not for *him*, I might revel in the arms of my handsome Italian, whose unaccountable scruples will not permit him to enjoy the bliss of love with me, while I have a husband.— Were that husband DEAD—'

Then, like a Mighty Shadow, came that dark thought over her soul. Myriads of beautiful demons, all bearing the semblance of Montoni, seemed to gather around her, and urge her to perpetrate a deed of—*murder!*

But then a fair vision spread itself before her wandering fancy. There was her girlhood's home—far, far away in a green, flowery spot, where she had dwelt ere her life had been cast amid the follies and vices of cities. Then she thought of her mother—that gentle mother, whose heart she had broken, and who was sleeping in the old church-yard of her native village.—A tear dim'd her brilliant eye as these better feelings of her nature gained a temporary ascendancy: but she dashed her tear away, and suppressed the emotions of her heart, when the image of the fascinating Italian arose before her.

'He must be mine! I swear it by everything in heaven, earth or hell—he must be mine! Yes, though I stain my soul with the blackest crime—though remorse and misery be my lot on earth—though eternal torment be my portion in the world to come—he must and shall be mine! Aid me, ye powers of hell, in this my scheme—make my heart bold, my hand firm, my brain calm; for the deed is full of horror, and the thought of it chills my blood; I shudder and turn sick and dizzy—yet, for thy sake, Montoni, I WILL DO IT!'

That night the wretched woman slept not; but in the solitude of her chamber employed her mind in endeavoring to form some plan by which to accomplish her fell purpose with secrecy and safety. Ere morning dawned, she had arranged the *programme* of the awful drama in which she was to play the part of a murderess.

When Mr. Hedge met her at breakfast, he noticed that she appeared feverish and unwell; and with almost parental solicitude, he gently chided her for neglecting to take proper care of her health.

'My dear Julia,' said he—'you must not pour out the golden sands of youth too fast. If you will suffer me to offer you advice, you will go less abroad, and endeavor to seek recreation at home. You know my ardent affection for you alone prompts me to make this suggestion.'

Julia slightly curled her lip, but said nothing. The kindness of her husband's manner did not in the least affect her, or alter the abominable purpose of her heart. Mr. Hedge did not notice her contemptuous look; he gave her a sum of money, as usual, kissed her and bade her adieu.

When he had gone, she dressed herself in her plainest attire, and going into an obscure part of the city, entered an apothecary's shop and purchased some arsenic. She then retraced her steps to her residence, and found that Mr. Hedge, contrary to his usual custom, had returned, and would dine at home. This arrangement afforded her much satisfaction.

'The fates are propitious,' said she—'to-night Montoni shall find me without a husband.'

Mr. Hedge and Julia dined alone; dispensing with the attendance of a servant, they never were more sociable or more affectionate together.

The old gentleman was in high spirits. 'My dear,' said he, 'your presence to-day inspires me with an unusual degree of happiness—and egad, I feel younger than ever. Pledge me in a bumper of good old port.'

'I cannot endure port,' said Julia—'sparkling champagne for me. I will ring for some.'

'By your leave, madam,' said her husband, with an air of gallantry; and rising, he walked across the room, and rang the bell.

Quick as lightning, Julia took a small paper parcel from her bosom, and breaking it open, poured a white powder into her husband's glass, which was nearly full of port wine.

Mr. Hedge resumed his seat, and raising the fatal glass to his lips, slowly drained it to the dregs. Just then the butler entered, in answer to the summons; and in obedience to Julia's order, he brought in a bottle of champagne, and withdrew.

'I am very unwell,' said the old gentleman—'my love, will you assist me to my chamber?' He arose with difficulty, and with her aid reached his chamber, and lay down upon the bed. Instantly he closed his eyes, and seemed to fall into a deep slumber.

'He will wake in another world,' murmured the guilty woman, as she saw the hue of death beginning to overspread his features. No repentance, no remorse, touched her vile heart; calmly she surveyed her victim for a few moments—then, not wishing to witness his dying agonies, she left the chamber, having carefully locked the door.

That afternoon she went out and purchased a new and magnificent set of jewels. If for a moment the recollection of her horrible crime obtruded itself upon her mind, she banished it by thinking of her adored Montoni. Hers was a kind of mental intoxication, under the influence of which she could have perpetrated the most enormous crimes, blindly and almost unconsciously.

Returning home she prepared her toilet with the most elaborate care. A French 'artist,' (all barbers are *artists*, by the way,) was sent for, who arranged her beautiful hair in the latest *mode;* and when arrayed in her superb evening dress of white satin with her fair neck, her wrist and her lovely brow blazing with jewels, she looked like some queen of Oriental romance, waiting to receive the homage of her vassals.

And when, as the clock struck eight, the Signor Montoni entered, who can wonder that he thought her divinely lovely, as he glanced at her face radiant with smiles, her cheek suffused with the rich hues of health and happiness, and her eyes sparking with delight at seeing him?

We said *happiness*—'twas not the deep, quiet happiness of the heart, but the wild, delirious joy of the intoxicated brain.

'Dear Montoni,' she cried, embracing and kissing him—'your presence never gave more pleasure. I have waited for your coming with impatience. You are mine now, you cannot deny me—the obstacle is removed.—Oh, my God, what happiness!'

'Lady,' replied the Italian, in his usual cold and respectful tone, as he disengaged himself from her embrace, 'what means this agitation? You speak of an *obstacle* as being removed; pray explain the enigma.'

'Signor Montoni,' cried Julia, her eyes flashing almost fearfully—'when I spoke to you of love last night, you preached to me of my husband, and my duty to him. The recollection that I *had* a husband, you said, forbade that you should take advantage of my preference for you. Rejoice with me, Montoni—come to my arms—my husband is no more!'

'How—what mean you?' demanded the Italian, in breathless astonishment.

'Follow me,' she said; and taking a lamp, she led the way to the chamber of Mr. Hedge. She unlocked the door, they entered, and she beckoned her companion to approach the bed.

Montoni advanced, and gazed upon the swollen, disfigured face of a corpse!

'Your husband—dead!' cried the Italian. 'By heaven there has been foul play here. Woman, can it be possible—'

'Yes, all things are possible to Love!' exclaimed Julia, laughing hysterically;—
' 'twas I did the deed, Montoni; for *your* dear sake I killed him!'

'Murderess!' cried Montoni, recoiling from her with horror, 'has it come to this?—Then indeed it is time that this wretched farce should end!'

He tore off the wig, the false whiskers, imperial and moustache—and Frank Sydney stood before her! With a wild shriek she fell senseless upon the carpet.

'God of heaven!' exclaimed Frank—'what infernal crimes blot thy fair creation! Let me escape from this house, for the atmosphere is thick with guilt, and will suffocate me if I remain longer!'

And without casting one look at the ghastly corpse, or the swooning murderess upon the floor, he rushed from the house, and fled rapidly from it, as though it were the abode of the pestilence.

Miserable Julia! She awoke to a full consciousness of her guilt and wretchedness. The intoxication of her senses was over; her delirium was past, and horrible remorse usurped the place of passion in her breast.—She arose, and gazed fearfully around her; there lay the body of her murdered victim, its stony eyes turned towards her, and seeming to reproach her for the deed. She could not remain in that awful chamber, in the presence of that accusing corpse, whose blood seemed to cry out for vengeance; she ran from it, and at every step imagined that her dead husband was pursuing her, to bring her back.

Not for worlds would she have remained that night in the house; hastily throwing on a bonnet and shawl, she issued forth into the street. She cared not where she went, so long as she escaped from the vicinity of that scene of murder. In a state of mind bordering on distraction, the wretched woman wandered about the streets until a late hour; the disorder of her dress, the wildness of her appearance, induced many whom she met to suppose her to be intoxicated; and several riotous young men, returning from a theatre, believing her to be a courtezan, treated her with the utmost rudeness, at the same time calling her by the most opprobrious names, until a gentleman who was passing rescued her from their brutality.

Midnight came, and still was the unhappy Julia a wanderer through the streets. At length she found herself upon Charlestown bridge; and being much fatigued, she paused and leaned against the railing, uncertain what to do or where to go. That hour was the most wretched of her life; her brain was dizzy with excitement—her heart racked with remorse—her limbs weak with fatigue, and numbed with cold. The spirit of Mr. Hedge seemed to emerge from the water, and invite her with outstretched arms to make the fatal plunge; and when she thought of his unvaried kindess to her, his unbounded generosity, and implicit faith in her honor, how bitterly she reproached herself for her base ingratitude and abominable crime! Oh, how gladly would she have given up her miserable life, could she but have undone that fearful deed! And even in that wretched hour she cursed Frank Sydney, as being the cause of her crime and its attendant misery.

'May the lightning of heaven's wrath sere his brain and scorch his heart!' she said—'had he not, disguised as the Italian, won my love and driven me to desperation, I now should be happy and comparatively guiltless. But, by his infernal means, I have become a murderess and an outcast—perhaps doomed to swing upon the scaffold! But no, no;—sooner than die *that* death, I would end my misery in the dark waters of this river, which flows so calmly beneath my feet!'

She heard the sound of approaching footsteps, and saw two men advancing on the opposite foot-path of the bridge. She crouched down to avoid observation; and as they passed, she distinctly heard their conversation.

'Have you heard,' said one, 'of the case of murder in —— street?'

'No; how was it?' demanded the other.

'Why, a rich old fellow named Hedge was found this evening in his chamber, stone dead, having been poisoned by his wife, who they say is a young and handsome woman. It is supposed she did it on account of a lover, or some such thing; and since the murder, she has disappeared—but the police are on her track, and they won't be long in finding her. 'Twill be a bad job for her.'

The men passed on out of sight and hearing; but the words struck terror to the heart of Julia. She started up and gazed wildly around her, expecting every moment to see the myrmidons of the law approaching, to drag her away to prison. Then she looked down upon the calm river, on whose placid breast reposed the soft moonlight.

'Why should I live?' she murmured, sadly—'earth has no longer any charms for me; the past brings remorse, the present is most wretched, the future full of impending horror! Death is my only refuge; the only cure for all my sorrows. Take me to thy embrace, thou peaceful river; thou canst end my earthly woes, but thou canst not wash off the stains of guilt from my soul! There may be a hell, but its torments cannot exceed those of this world—'

She mounted upon the topmost rail of the bridge, clasped her hands, muttered a brief prayer, and leaped into the river. There was a splash—a gurgling sound—and then profound and solemn silence resumed its reign.

*   *   *   *   *

One more unfortunate,
Weary of breath,
Rashly importunate,
Gone to her death!

*   *   *   *   *

The bleak wind of March
Made her tremble and shiver;
But not the dark arch
Of the black flowing river;
Mad from life's history,

Glad to death's mystery,
Swift to be hurl'd—
Any where, any where
Out of the world!

In she plunged boldly,
No matter how coldly
The rough river ran—
Over the brink of it,
Picture it—think of it, Dissolute Man!

*   *   *   *   *

Owning her weakness,
Her evil behaviour!
And leaving, with meekness,
Her sins to her Saviour!

CHAPTER XXIX

Wherein one of the Characters in this Drama maketh a sudden and rapid exit from the stage.

In an upper apartment of an old, rickety wooden building in Ann street, two men were seated at a rough deal table, engaged in smoking long pipes and discussing the contents of a black bottle. Not to keep the reader in suspense, we may as well state at once that these two individuals were no other than our old acquaintances, the Dead Man and the Doctor.

The room was dusky, gloomy, and dirty, with a multitude of cob-webs hanging from the ceiling, and the broken panes in the windows stuffed full of rags. The smoke-dried walls were covered with rude inscriptions and drawings, representing deeds of robbery and murder; and a hanging scene was not the least prominent of these interesting specimens of the 'fine arts.' The house was a noted resort for thieves, and the old harridan who kept it was known to the police as a 'fence,' or one who purchased stolen goods.

'Yes, Doctor,' cried the Dead Man, with an oath, as he slowly removed the pipe from his lips, and blew a cloud which curled in fantastic wreaths to the ceiling—'this state of affairs won't answer: we must have money. And money we *will* have, this very night, if our spy, Stuttering Tom, succeeds in finding out where those Franklin ladies live. The bottle's out—knock for another pint of *lush*.'

The Doctor obeyed, and in answer to the summons an old, wrinkled, blear-eyed hag made her appearance with the liquor. This old wretch was the 'landlady' of the house; she had been a celebrated and beautiful courtezan in her day, but age and vice had done their work, and she was now an object hideous to look upon. Though tottering upon the verge of the grave (she was over eighty,) an inordinate love of money, and an equal partiality for 'the ardent,' were her characteristics; but stranger than all, the miserable old creature affected still to retain, undiminished, those amorous propensities which had distinguished her in her youth! This horrible absurdity made her act in a manner at once ludicrous and disgusting; and the Dead Man, being facetiously inclined, resolved to humor her weakness, and enjoy a laugh at her expense by pretending to have fallen in love with her.

'By Satan!' he cried, clasping the old crone around the waist—'you look irresistible to-night, mother: I've half a mind to ravish a kiss from ye—ha, ha, ha!'

'Have done, now!' exclaimed the hag, in a cracked tone, at the same time vainly endeavoring to contort her toothless jaws into an engaging simper, while the Doctor nearly burst with laughter—'have done now, or I'll slap ye for your impudence. But, faith, ye are such a pleasant gentleman, that I don't mind bestowing a kiss or two upon ye!'

'You're a gay old lass,' said the Dead Man, without availing himself of the old lady's kind permission—'you have been a 'high one' in your time, but your day is nearly over.'

'No, no!' shrieked the old wretch, while her head and limbs quivered with palsy—'don't say that—I'm young as ever, only a little *shakey*, or so—I'm not going to die for many, many years to come—ha, ha, ha! a kiss, love, a kiss—'

The old woman fell to the floor in a paralytic fit, and when they raised her up, they found that she was dead!

'Devil take the old fool!' cried the Dead Man, throwing the corpse contemptuously to the floor—'I meant to have strangled her some day, but I now am cheated of the sport. No matter; drink, Doctor!'

The dead body was removed by several of the wretched inmates of the house, just as Stuttering Tom entered to announce the result of his search for the Franklin ladies.

Tom was a short, dumpy specimen of humanity, with red hair, freckled face, nose of the pug order, and goggle eyes. His dress was picturesque, if not ragged: his coat and pants were so widely apart, at the waist, as to reveal a large track of very incorrect linen; and the said coat had been deprived of one of its tails, an unfortunate occurrence, as the loss exposed a large compound fracture in the rear of the young gentleman's trowsers, whereby he was subjected to the remark that he had 'a letter in the post office.' His name was derived from an inveterate habit of stuttering with which he was afflicted; and he related the issue of his search somewhat in the following manner:

'You see, I ha-ha-happened to be l-loafing down Wa-Wa-Washington street, this evening, quite pro-miscus like, ven I seed two vim-vimmen, as vos gallus ha-handsum, and dr-dressed to kill, a valking along, vich puts me in m-m-mind of the F-F-Franklin vimmen, as you hired me to f-f-find out. So I up and f-follers 'em, and by-and-by a f-fellers meets 'em and says, says he, 'Good evening, Missus and Miss

F-F-Franklin.' These is the werry victims, says I to myself; and I f-f-foller them till they goes into a house in Wa-Washington street—and here I am.'

'You have done well, Tom,' said the Dead Man, approvingly—'you must now conduct us to the house in Washington street which the ladies entered: it is nine o'clock, and time that we should be up and doing.'

Stuttering Tom led the way, and the three issued from the house. Ann street was 'all alive' at that hour; from every cellar came forth the sound of a fiddle, and the side-walks were crowded with a motley throng of Hibernians, Ethiopians, and Cyprians of an inferior order. Talk of Boston being a moral city! There is villainy, misery and vice enough in Ann street alone, to deserve for the whole place the fate of Sodom and Gomorrah.

The Dead Man and the Doctor, under the guidance of Stuttering Tom, soon reached the house in Washington street where Josephine and her mother had taken up their residence. The guide was then rewarded and dismissed; the two adventurers ascended the steps, and one of them rang the door-bell.

A servant girl answered the summons, and in reply to their inquiries informed them that the ladies were both in the parlor.

'Show us up there,' said the Dead Man, in a commanding tone, as he concealed his hideous face behind his upturned coat-collar. The girl obeyed, and having conducted them up a flight of stairs, ushered them into an apartment where Josephine and her mother were seated, engaged there in playing *ecarte*.

Their confusion and terror may easily be imagined, when turning to see who their visitors were, their eyes rested upon the awful lineaments of the DEAD MAN!

'Your humble servant, ladies,' said the villain, with a triumphant laugh—'you see you cannot hide from me, or escape me. Fair Josephine, you look truly charming—will you oblige me with a private interview?'

'It will be useless,' said Josephine coldly, as she recovered some portion of her composure—'we have no more money to give you.'

'You can give me something more acceptable than *money*,' rejoined the other, with a horrible leer—'at our last interview I told you what I should require at our next. Doctor, I leave you with the voluptuous mother, while I make court to the beautiful daughter.'

He grasped Josephine violently by the arm, and dragged her from the room, forced her into an adjoining apartment, and thrust her brutally upon a sofa, saying with a fearful oath—

'Dare to resist me, and I'll spoil your beauty, miss! Why do you act the prude with me—*you*, a shameless hussey, who has numbered more amours than years?'

'Odious ruffian!' exclaimed Josephine, no longer able to control her indignation—'I view you with contempt and loathing. Sooner than submit to your filthy embraces, I will dare exposure, and death itself! Think not to force me to a compliance with your wishes—I will resist you while life animates my frame. I fear you not, low villain that you are.'

The Dead Man raised his *iron hand* as if to dash out her brains for her temerity.— But he checked himself, and surveyed her with a sort of calm ferocity, as he said—

'Young lady, since you are determined to oppose my wishes, I will not force you. Neither will I kill you; yet my vengeance shall be more terrible than death. You are beautiful and you pride yourself upon that beauty—but I will deprive you of your loveliness. You call me hideous—I will make you hideous as I am. Your cheeks shall become ghastly, your complexion livid, and your brilliant eyes shall become sightless orbs—for the curse of *blindness* shall be added to your other miseries. Obstinate girl, bid an eternal farewell to eyesight and beauty, for from this moment you are deprived of both, forever!'

He drew from his pocket a small phial, and with the quickness of lightning dashed it in the face of the unfortunate Josephine. It was shattered in a hundred pieces, and the contents—VITRIOL—ran in her eyes and down her face, burning her flesh in the most horrible manner. She shrieked with agony the most intense, and the Doctor rushed into the room, followed by Mrs. Franklin. They both stood aghast when they beheld the awful spectacle.

The Doctor was the first to recover his presence of mind; he rushed to the aid of the burning wretch, and saved her life, though he could not restore her lost eyesight, or remove the horrible disfigurement of her burned and scarred visage. Mrs. Franklin was so overcome at her daughter's misfortune and sufferings that she fell upon the floor insensible.

At that moment the door of the apartment was violently thrown open, and a young gentleman entered. The Dead Man and the Doctor turned, and in the new-comer recognised Frank Sydney!

It will be necessary to explain the mystery of Frank's sudden appearance at that emergency. A day or two after the suicide of Julia, the body of that wretched woman was picked up by some fisherman, and conveyed to the city, where it was immediately recognized as the lady of Mr. Hedge. The circumstance of her death soon came to the knowledge of our hero; and while he could not help shedding a tear as he thought of her melancholy fate (she had once been his wife, and he had once loved her,) he could not deny to himself that he derived a secret joy from the thought, that now his hopes with reference to Sophia Franklin were not without some foundation. Acting upon this impulse, he had taken the earliest opportunity to call upon the young lady; and at that interview, he had with his customary frankness, related to her his entire history, and concluded his narrative by making her an offer of his hand and heart—and, reader, that honorable offer was accepted with the same frankness with which it was made. On the evening in question, Frank was enjoying one of those charming *tete-a-tetes* with his Sophia, which all lovers find so delightful, when the agonizing screams of the suffering Josephine brought him to the room, as we have seen, and he found himself, to his astonishment, standing face to face with the Dead Man and the Doctor.

'Why, blood and fury!' cried the former, a gleam of pleasure passing over his horrid features—'here is the very man of all men upon earth, whom I most desired to see. Sydney, you are welcome.'

'What damnable villainy have you been at now?' demanded Frank, recovering his courage and presence of mind, altho' he had reason to believe that he had fallen into the power of his worst enemy in the world.

'What business is that of yours?' growled the Dead Man—'Suffice it for you to know that my *next* act of villainy will be your assassination.'

Our hero drew a revolver from his pocket, and levelled it at the villain's head, saying—

'Advance but a step towards me, and you are a *dead man* indeed—Scoundrel! I am no longer a prisoner in your dungeon vaults, but free, and able to protect myself against your brutal cruelty. Though you are aided by the Doctor, whom I once thought my friend, I fear you not, but dare you to do your worst.'

'You are brave, Sydney,' said the Dead Man, with something like a grim of admiration—'but I hate you, and you must die. From the first moment when I met you in the Dark Vaults, to the present time, I have observed something in you that inspires me with a kind of *fear*—a moral superiority over my malice and hatred that inflames me with jealous rage. Even when you were in my power, undergoing my trials and tortures, I have observed contempt upon your lip and scorn in your eye. I once called you coward—but you are a man of doubtless courage, and by Satan! I have half a mind to shake hands with you and call you friend.'

During this harangue, Frank had unconsciously lowered his pistol, not suspecting that the long speech was merely a ruse of the Dead Man to spring upon him unawares. While he stood in an attitude poorly calculated for defence, the miscreant suddenly, with the quickness of lightning, sprang upon him, and with irresistible force hurled him to the floor.

But our hero received an aid which was as unexpected as it was welcome; for the Doctor threw himself upon the Dead Man, grappled him by the throat, and nearly strangled him. In vain the ruffian struggled—he was in the grasp of an adversary too powerful and too intrepid to be successfully resisted by him. Panting and breathless, he was soon vanquished by his ancient enemy, who, having tied his arms behind him with a strong cord, regarded him with a look of hatred and contempt.

'Why, Doctor, what means this?' demanded the villain, in astonishment at having been so desperately attacked by one whom he had lately regarded as a friend.

'It means, d——n you,' coolly replied the other—'you have been deceived and foiled. In deserting Mr. Sydney to join *your* bloody standard, I acted in accordance with a plan which I had formed to entrap and conquer you. I know that as long as I remained the professed friend of Mr. Sydney, you would view me with distrust and fear, and consequently, that you would be always on the alert to guard against any attempt of mine to wreak my vengeance on you. So I professed to become your friend, and pretended to attach myself to your interest, knowing that a good opportunity would thereby be afforded me to frustrate any scheme you might form against the life or safety of Mr. Sydney. You see how well I have succeeded; you are completely in my power, and by G——d, this night shall witness the termination of your bloody and infamous career.'

'You surely will not murder me,' said the Dead Man, frightened by the determined tone and manner of a man whose vengeance he had reason to dread.

'To take your accursed life will be no murder,' replied the Doctor—'you are a thousand times worse than a poisonous reptile or a beast of prey, and to kill you would be but an act of justice. Yet do not flatter yourself with the prospect of an easy and comparatively painless death; I have sworn that you shall die a death of lingering torture, and you will see how well I'll keep my oath. My knowledge as a physician, and natural ingenuity, have furnished me with a glorious method of tormenting you; and although you are a master in the art of torture, you will see how far I have surpassed you.'

'You have, by serving me this trick, proved yourself to be both a liar and a traitor,' remarked the Dead Man, bitterly.

'Any means,' rejoined the Doctor, calmly—'are justifiable in overthrowing such an infernal villain as you are; but I see the motive of your sneer—you wish to enrage me, that I may stab you to the heart at once, and place you beyond the reach of protracted torment. You shall fail in this, for I am cool as ice. Before commencing operations upon you, I must attend professionally to those ladies.'

Mrs. Franklin was easily recovered from her fainting fit;—and the suffering Josephine received at the skillful hands of the Doctor every care and attention which her lamentable case demanded. He pronounced her life in no danger; but alas! her glorious beauty was gone forever—her face was horribly burnt and disfigured, and her brilliant eyes were destroyed; she was stone blind!

Thus it is that the wicked are often the instruments of each other's punishment in this world, as devils are said to torment each other in the next.

The mother and daughter having been properly looked after, Frank Sydney took the Doctor aside, and warmly thanked him for his timely and acceptable aid.

'You have proved yourself to be a true and faithful man,' said he grasping his friend's hand—'and my unjust opinions in regard to you have given place to the highest confidence in your integrity and honor. You have saved my life tonight, and not for the first time. I owe you a debt of gratitude; and from this moment we are sworn friends. You shall share my fortune, and move in a sphere of respectability and worth.'

'Mr. Sydney,' said the Doctor, much affected—'do you remember that night I met you in the Park, and would have robbed you? I was then moneyless and starving. I will not now stop to relate how I became reduced to such abject wretchedness, but I must do myself the justice to say that my downfall was produced by the rascalities of others. Your liberality to me upon that night was an evidence to my mind that the world was not entirely heartless and unjust; and tho' I did not immediately forsake the evil of my ways, yet your kindness softened me, and laid the foundation of my present reformation.—Noble young man, I accept the offer of your friendship with gratitude, but I will not share your fortune. No—my ambition is, to build up a fortune of my own, by laboring in my profession, in which I am skilled. By following a course of strict honor and integrity, I may partially retrieve the errors of my past life.'

'I cannot but commend your resolution,' remarked Frank—'but you must not refuse to accept from me such pecuniary aid as will be necessary to establish you in a respectable and creditable manner.—But in regard to this miscreant here; you actually intend to kill him by slow torture?'

'I do,' replied the Doctor, in a determined manner—'and my only regret is that

I cannot protract his sufferings a year. Do not think me cold-blooded or cruel, my dear friend; that villain merits the worst death that man can inflict upon him. If we were to hand him over to the grasp of the law, for his numerous crimes, his infernal ingenuity might enable him to escape. Our only security lies in crushing the reptile while we have him in our trap.'

'I shall not interfere with you in your just punishment of the villain,' said our hero—'but I must decline being present. The enormous crimes he had committed, and the wrongs which I have sustained at his hands, will not allow me to say a single word in his behalf—yet I will not witness his torments.'

'I understand and respect your scruples; I being a physician, such a spectacle cannot affect my nerves.—You will please assist me to place the *subject* upon this table, and then you can retire.'

They raised the Dead Man from the floor, and placed him on a large table which stood in the centre of the room. Frank then bade the Doctor a temporary farewell, and passing through the hall was about to leave the house, when a servant informed him that Miss Sophia Franklin wished to see him. He joyfully obeyed the summons, and found the young lady in deep distress at the condition of her sister Josephine, and very anxious for an explanation of the terrible cause. Frank stated all he knew of the matter, and we leave him to the task of consoling her, while we witness the operations of the Doctor upon his living *subject*.

In the first place, he tied the Dead Man down upon the table so firmly, that he could not move a hair's breadth. During this process, the miserable victim, losing all his customary bravado and savage insolence, begged hard to be killed at once, rather than undergo the torments which he dreaded. But the Doctor only laughed, and drew from his pocket a case of surgical instruments; he then produced a small phial, which he held close to his victim's eyes, and bade him examine it narrowly.

'You see,' said he, 'this little phial?—it contains a slow poison of peculiar and fearful power. You shall judge of its effects yourself presently. I will infuse it into your blood, and it will cause you greater agony than melted lead poured upon your heart.'

'For God's sake, Doctor,' cried the wretch,—'spare me *that*! I have heard you tell of it before. Will nothing move you? Show me mercy, and I will reveal to you many valuable and astounding secrets, known only to me. I will tell you where, within twenty miles of Boston, I have buried over twenty thousand dollars in gold and silver; I will myself lead you to the spot and you shall have it all—all! I will furnish you with a list of fashionable drinking houses in the city, where is sold liquor impregnated with a slow but deadly poison, which in two years will bring on a lingering disease, generally thought to be consumption; this disease always terminates in death, and the whole matter is arranged by physicians, who thus get a constant and extensive practice. I will take you to rooms where persons, under the name of 'secret societies,' privately meet to indulge in the most unnatural and beastly licentiousness. I will prove to you, by ocular demonstration, that in *certain cities* of the Union, not a letter passes through the post offices, that is not broken open and read, and then re-sealed by a peculiar process—by which means much private information is gained by the police, and the most tremendous secrets often leak out, to the astonishment of the parties concerned. I will communicate to you a method by which the most virtuous and chaste woman can be made wild with desire, and easily overcome. I will show you how to make a man drop dead in the street, without touching him, or using knife or pistol—and not a mark will be found on his person. I will—'

'That'll do,' said the Doctor, dryly—'the matters you have mentioned are mostly no secrets to me; and if your object was to gain time and dissuade me from my purpose, you have signally failed. Villain! your long career of crime is now about to receive its reward. Prayers and entreaties shall not avail you; and to put an end to them, as well as to prevent you from yelling out in your agony—by which people would be attracted hither—I will take the liberty to *gag* you.'

In forcing the jaws of the Dead Man widely apart, in order to accomplish that purpose, the victim contrived to get one of his tormentor's fingers between his teeth, and it was nearly bitten off ere it could be disengaged. This enraged the Doctor so that he was about to kill his enemy instantly, but he checked himself; and having effectually gagged him, he prepared to commence the terrible ordeal.

Taking a lancet from the case, he made an incision in the subject's right arm; then, in the wound, he poured a few drops of the contents of the phial. The effects were instantaneous and terrible; the poison became infused in every vein of the sufferer's body, and his blood seemed changed to liquid fire; he writhed in mighty agony—his heart leaped madly in his breast, in the intensity of his torment—his brain swam in a sea of fire—his eyes started from their sockets, and blood oozed from every pore of his body.

These awful results were produced by a wonderful chemical preparation, known to but few, and first discovered in the days of the Spanish Inquisition. It was then termed the 'Ordeal of Fire;' and the infernal vengeance of hell itself could not have produced torment more intense or protracted; for though it racked every nerve and sinew in the body, filling the veins with a flood like molten lead, it was comparatively slow in producing death, and kept the sufferer for several hours writhing in all the tortures of the damned.

For two mortal hours the miserable wretch endured the torment; while the Doctor stood over him, viewing him with a fixed gaze and an unmoved heart. Then he removed the gag from the sufferer's mouth, and poured a glass of water down his throat, which temporarily assuaged his agony.

'Doctor,' gasped the dying wretch—'for God's sake stab me to the heart, and end my misery! I am in hell—I am floating in an ocean of fire—my murdered victims are pouring rivers of blazing blood upon me—my soul is in flames—my *heart* is RED HOT! Ah, kill me—kill me!'

The Doctor, after a moment's deliberation, again took an instrument from his case, and skillfully divided the flesh in the region of the abdomen, making an incision of considerable extent. He then produced a small flask of gunpowder, in the neck of which he inserted a straw filled with the same combustible; and in the end of the straw he fastened a small slip of paper which he had previously prepared with saltpetre. Having made these arrangements, he placed the powder flask completely in the victim's abdomen, leaving the slow match to project slightly from the wound. The Dead Man was perfectly conscious during this horrible process, notwithstanding he suffered the most excruciating pain.

'You are going to blow me to atoms, Doctor,' he with difficulty articulated, as a ghastly smile spread over his hideous features—'I thank you for it; although I hate and curse you in this my dying hour. Grant me a moment longer; if the spirits of the dead are allowed to re-visit the earth, *my* spirit shall visit you! Ha, ha, ha! In a few seconds, I shall be free from the power of your torture—free to follow you like a shadow through life, free to preside in ghastly horror over your midnight slumbers and to breathe constantly in your ear, curses—curses—curses!'

'Miserable devil, your blood-polluted spirit will be too strongly bound to hell, to wander on earth,' said the Doctor, with a contempt not unmingled with pity. 'Farewell, thou man of many crimes; for the wrongs you have done me, I forgive you, but human and divine justice have demanded this sacrifice.'

He ignited a match, touched it to the paper at the end of the straw, and hastily retreated to the further extremities of the room.

It was an awful moment; slowly the paper burnt towards the straw—so slowly, that the victim of this awful sacrifice had time to vent his dying rage in malignant curses, on himself, his tormentor, and his Maker! The straw is reached—the fire runs down to the powder flask with a low hiss—and then—

Awful was the explosion that followed; the wretch was torn into a hundred pieces; his limbs, his brains, his blood were scattered all about. A portion of the mangled carcass struck the Doctor; the lamp was broken by the shock and darkness prevailed in the room.

The inmates of the house, frightened at the noise, rushed to the scene of the catastrophe with lights. Frank Sydney, Sophia and Mrs. Franklin, as well as several other male and female domestics, entering the apartment, stood aghast at the shocking spectacle presented to their gaze. There stood the Doctor, with folded arms and his face stained with blood; here an arm, here, a blackened mass of flesh; and here, the most horrible object of all, the mutilated and ghastly head, with the same expression of malignant hate upon its hideous features as when those livid lips had last uttered curses!

'The deed is done,' said the Doctor, addressing Sydney, with a grim smile—'justice has its due at last, and the diabolical villain has gone to his final account. Summon some scavenger to collect the vile remains, and bury them in a dung-hill. To give them Christian, decent burial would be treason to man, sacrilege to the Church, and impiety to God!'

Thus perished the 'Dead Man,' a villain so stupendous, so bloodthirsty and so desperate that it may well be doubted whether such a monster ever could have existed. But this diabolical character is not entirely drawn from the author's imagination; neither is it highly exaggerated;—for the annals of crime will afford instances of villainy as deep and as monstrous as any that characterized the career of the 'Dead Man' of our tale. What, for example, can be more awful or incredible than the hideous deed of a noted criminal in France, who, having ensnared a peasant girl in a wood, brutally murdered her, then outraged the corpse, and afterwards *ate a part of it*? Yet no one will presume to doubt the fact, as it forms a portion of the French criminal records. Humanity shudders at such instances of worse than devilish depravity.

Moreover, to show that we have indulged in no improbabilities in portraying the chief villain of our tale, we assert that a person bearing that name and the same disfigurement of countenance, *really existed* not two years ago. He was renowned for his many crimes, and was murdered by a former accomplice, in a manner not dissimilar to the death we have assigned to him in the story.

But we turn from a contemplation of such villains, to pursue a different and somewhat more agreeable channel.

CHAPTER XXX

Showing that a man should never marry a woman before he sees her face—
The Disappointed Bridegroom—Final Catastrophe.

Two months passed away. Two months!—how short a space of time, and yet, perchance, how pregnant with events affecting the happiness and the destiny of millions! Within that brief span—the millionth fraction of a single sand in Time's great hour-glass—thousands have begun their existence, to pursue through life a career of honor, of profit, of ambition, or of crime!—and thousands, too, have ceased their existence, and their places are filled by others in the great race of human life.

But a truce to moralizing.—Two months passed away, and it was now the season of summer—that delicious season, fraught with more voluptuous pleasures than virgin spring, gloomy autumn or hoary winter. It was in rather an obscure street of Boston—in a modest two-story wooden house—and in an apartment plainly, even humbly furnished, that two ladies were seated, engaged in an earnest conversation.

One of these ladies was probably near forty years of age, and had evidently once been extremely handsome; her countenance still retained traces of great beauty—but time, and care, and perhaps poverty, were beginning to mar it. Her figure was good, though perhaps rather too full for grace; and her dress was very plain yet neat, and not without some claims to taste.

Her companion was probably much younger, and was attired with considerable elegance; yet a strange peculiarity in her costume would have instantly excited the surprise of an observer—for although the day was excessively warm, she wore a thick veil, which reached to her waist, and effectually concealed her face. She conversed in a voice of extraordinary melody; and the refined language of both ladies evinced that they had been accustomed to move in a higher sphere of society than that in which we now find them.

'At what time do you expect him here?' asked the oldest lady, in continuation of the discourse in which they had previously been engaged.

'At eight o'clock this evening,' replied the other. 'He is completely fascinated with me; and notwithstanding I have assured him, over and over again, that my countenance is horribly disfigured, and that I am entirely blind, he persists in believing that I am beautiful, and that I have perfect eye-sight, attributing my concealment of face to a whim.'

'Which opinion you have artfully encouraged, Josephine,' said Mrs. Franklin.— The reader has probably already guessed the identity of the two ladies; this was the mother and her once beautiful, but now hideous and blind daughter. They were reduced to the most abject poverty, and had been forced to leave their handsome residence in Washington street, and take up their abode in an humble and cheap tenement. Entirely destitute of means, they were obliged to struggle hard to keep themselves above absolute want. Josephine, being a superb singer, had obtained an engagement to sing in one of the fashionable churches; but as she always appeared closely veiled, the fact of her being so terribly disfigured was unsuspected. The beauty of her voice and the graceful symmetry of her figure had attracted the attention and won the admiration of a wealthy member of the church, who was also attached to the choir; and as she was always carefully conducted in and out of the church by her mother this gentleman never suspected that she was blind. He had framed an excuse to call upon her at her residence; and, tho' astonished to find her veiled, at home—and tho' he had never seen her face—he was charmed with her brilliant conversation, and resolved to win her, if possible. The very mystery of her conduct added to the intensity of his passion.

Mr. Thurston, (the church member,) continued his visits to Josephine, but never saw her face. When he grew more familiar, he ventured upon one occasion to inquire why she kept herself so constantly veiled; whereupon she informed him that her face had been disfigured by being scalded during her infancy, which accident had also deprived her of sight. But when he requested her to raise her veil, and allow him to look at her face, she refused with so much good-humored animation, that he began to suspect the young lady of having playfully deceived him.

'This interesting creature,' thought he, 'is trying to play me a trick. —She hides her face and pretends to be a fright, while the coquetry of her manners and the perfect ease of her conversation, convince me that she cannot be otherwise than beautiful.—What, the owner of that superb voice and that elegant form, *ugly*? Impossible! Now I can easily guess her object in trying to play off this little piece of deception upon me: I have read somewhere of a lady who kept her face constantly veiled, and proclaimed herself to be hideously ugly, which was universally believed, notwithstanding which she secured an admirer, who loved her for her graces of mind; he offered her his hand, and she agreed to marry him, provided that he would not seek to behold her face until after the performance of the ceremony—adding, that if he saw how ugly she was, he would certainly never marry her. 'I love you for your mind, and care not for the absence of beauty,' cried the lover. They were married; they retired to their chamber. 'Now prepare yourself for an awful sight,'—

said the bride, slowly raising her veil. The husband could not repress a shudder—
he gazed for the first time upon the face of his wife—when lo and behold! instead
of an ugly and disfigured face, he saw before him a countenance radiant with
celestial beauty! 'Dear husband,' said the lovely wife, casting her arms around her
astonished and happy lord, 'you loved me truly, although you thought me ugly;
such devotion and such disinterested love well merit the prize of beauty.'

'Now, I feel assured,' said Mr. Thurston to himself, pursuing the current of his
thoughts—'that this young lady, Miss Franklin, is trying to deceive me in a similar
manner, in order to test the sincerity of my affection; and should I marry her, I
would find her to be a paragon of beauty. Egad, she is so accomplished and
bewitching, that I've more than half a mind to propose, and make her Mrs. T.'

The worthy deacon (for such he was,) being a middle-aged man of very good
looks, and moreover very rich, Josephine was determined to 'catch him' if she
could; she therefore took advantage of his disbelief in her deformity, and, while she
persisted in her assurances that she was hideously ugly, she made those assurances
in a manner so light and playful, that Mr. T. would have taken his oath that she was
beautiful, and he became more and more smitten with the mysterious veiled lady,
whose face he had never seen.

Josephine, with consummate art, was resolved, if possible, to entice him into
matrimony; and once his wife, she knew that in case he refused to live with her on
discovering her awful deformity, he would liberally provide for her support, and
thus her mother and herself would be enabled again to live in luxury. As for Sophia,
she no longer lived with them—the fair, innocent girl had gone to occupy a position
to be stated hereafter.

We now resume the conversation between Mrs. Franklin and her daughter,
which we interrupted by the above necessary explanation.—'Which opinion you
have artfully encouraged, Josephine,' said Mrs. Franklin—'and you will of course
suffer him to enjoy that opinion, until after your marriage with him, which event
is, I think, certain; then you can reveal your true condition to him, and if he casts
you off, he will be obliged to afford you a sufficient income, which we both so much
need; for he cannot charge you with having deceived him, as you represent to him
your real condition, and if he chooses to disbelieve you, that is his own affair, not
yours.'

'True, mother; and the marriage must be speedily accomplished, for we are sadly
in need of funds, and all my best dresses are at the pawnbroker's. Alas, that my
beauty should be destroyed—that beauty which would have captured the hearts
and purses of so many rich admirers! I am almost inclined to rejoice that my eye-
sight is gone, for I cannot see my deformity. Am I very hideous, mother?'

'My poor, afflicted child,' said Mrs. Franklin, shedding tears—'do not question
me on that subject. Oh, Josephine, had I, your mother, set you an example of purity
and virtue, and trained you up in the path of rectitude, we never should have
experienced our past and present misery, and you, my once beautiful child, would
not now be deformed and blind. Alas, I have much to reproach myself for.'

'Tut, mother; you have grown puritanical of late. Let us try to forget the past,
and cherish hope for the future.—How very warm it is!'

She retired from the window to avoid the observation of the passers-by, and removed her veil. Good God! —Can she be the once lovely Josephine! Ah, terrible punishment of sin!

Her once radiant countenance was of a ghastly yellow hue, save where deep purple streaks gave it the appearance of a putrefying corpse. Her once splendid eyes, that had so oft flashed with indignant scorn, glowed with the pride of her imperial beauty, or sparkled with the fires of amorous passion, had been literally burned out of her head! That once lofty and peerless brow was disfigured by hideous scars, and a wig supplied the place of her once clustering and luxuriant hair.—She was as loathsome to look upon as had been her destroyer, the Dead Man. Oh, it was a pitiful sight to see that talented and accomplished young lady thus stricken with the curses of deformity and blindness, through her own wickedness— to see that temple which God had made so beautiful and fair to look upon, thus shattered and defiled by the ravages of sin!

Evening came, and with it brought Mr. Thurston. Josephine, seated on a sofa and impenetrably veiled, received him with a courteous welcome;—and comported herself so admirably and artfully, that the most critical observer would not have imagined her to be blind, but would have supposed her to be wearing a veil merely out of caprice, or from some trifling cause. —When she spoke to her lover, or was addressed by him, she invariably turned her face towards him, as if unconsciously; and the gentleman chuckled inwardly, as he thought he saw in that simple act an evidence of her being possessed of the faculty of sight.

But one incident occurred which doubly confirmed him in his belief; it was an artful contrivance of Josephine and her mother. Previous to Mr. Thurston's arrival, a rose had been placed upon the carpet, close to Josephine's feet; and during a pause in the conversation, while apparently in an abstracted mood, she leaned forward, took it up by the stem, and began slowly to pick it to pieces, scattering the leaves all about her.

'By Jupiter, I have her now!' said the lover to himself, triumphantly—and then he abruptly said—

'How now, Josephine! If you are blind, how saw you that rose upon the carpet?'

Josephine, affecting to be much confused, stammered out something about her having discovered the rose to be near her by its fragrance; but Mr. Thurston laughed and said—

'It won't do, my dear Miss Franklin; it is evident that you can see as well as I can. Come, end this farce at once, and let me see your face.'

'No, you shall not, for I have vowed that the first man who beholds my face shall be my husband.'

'Then hear me, Josephine,' cried her lover, raising her fair had to his lips—'I know not what singular whim has prompted you in your endeavors to make me think you ugly and blind, but this I know, you have inspired me with ardent love. I *know* you to be beautiful and free from imperfection of sight—nay, do not speak— but I will not again allude to the subject, nor press you to raise your veil, until after our marriage—that is, if you will accept me. Speak, Josephine.'

'Mr. Thurston, if, after my many solemn assurances to you that I am afflicted in the manner I have so often described, you ask me to become your wife—here is my hand.'

'A thousand thanks, my beautiful, mysterious, veiled lady!' exclaimed the enraptured lover—'as to your being afflicted—ha, ha! —I'll risk it, I'll risk it! Naughty Josephine, I'll punish you hereafter for your attempt to deceive me!'

The poor man little suspected how egregiously she *was* deceiving him!—He was a person of no natural penetration, and could no more see thro' her designs, than through the veil which covered her face.

Midnight came, and found Josephine and her victim still seated upon the sofa in the little parlor, her head reposing upon his shoulder, and his arm encircling her waist. He felt as happy as any man can feel, who imagines he has won the love of a beautiful woman; but had he known the blackness of her heart, and seen the awful hideousness of her face, how he would have cast her from him with contempt and loathing!

When about to take his leave, he lingered in the entry and begged her to grant him a kiss; she consented, on condition that it should be a 'kiss in the dark.' The candle was extinguished, she raised her veil, and he pressed his lips to hers. Could he have seen her ghastly cheek, her eyeless sockets, and the livid lips which he so rapturously kissed, his soul would have grown sick with horror. But he departed, in blissful ignorance of her deformity of body and impurity of soul.

We hasten to the final catastrophe. They were married. The eager bridegroom conducted his veiled and trembling bride to the nuptial chamber.—Josephine was much agitated; for the grand crisis had arrived, which would either raise her to a comfortable independence, or hurl her into the dark abyss of despair.

'Is it very light here?' she asked. 'Yes, dearest,' replied the husband—'I have caused this our bridal chamber to be illuminated, in order that I may the better be enabled to feast my eyes upon your beauty, so long concealed from my gaze.'

'Prepare yourself,' murmured Josephine, 'for a terrible disappointment. I have not deceived you. —Behold your bride!'

She threw up her veil.

LETTER FROM MRS. SOPHIA SYDNEY TO A LADY.

You cannot imagine, my dearest Alice, what a life of calm felicity I enjoy with my beloved Francis, in our new home among the majestic mountains of Vermont. Had you the faintest conception of the glorious scenery which surrounds the little rustic cottage which we inhabit, (our ark of safety—poor, wearied doves that we are!) you would willingly abandon your abode in the noisy, crowded metropolis, to join us in our beautiful and secluded retreat.

Our dwelling is situated on the margin of a clear and quiet lake, whose glassy surface mirrors each passing cloud, and at night reflects a myriad of bright stars. We have procured a small but elegant pleasure barge, in which we often gently glide over those placid waters, when Evening darkens our mountain home with the shadow of her wing, and when the moon gilds our liquid path with soft radiance. Then, while my Francis guides the little vessel, I touch my guitar and sing some simple melody; and as we approach the dark, mysterious shore, my imagination oft conjures up a troop of fairy beings with bright wings, stealing away into the dim recesses of the shadowy forest. And often, when the noon-day sun renders the air oppressive with his heat, I wander into the depths of that forest, where the giant trees, forming a vast arch overhead, exclude the glare of summer, and produce a soft, delicious twilight. My favorite resting place is upon a mossy bank, near which flows a crystal brook whose dancing waters murmur with a melody almost as sweet as the low breathings of an Aeolian harp.—Here, with a volume of philosophic Cowper or fascinating Scott, I sometimes linger until twilight begins to deepen into darkness, and then return to meet with smiles the playful chidings of my husband, for my protracted absence—an offence he can easily forgive, if I present him with a bouquet of wild flowers gathered during my ramble; although he laughingly calls the floral offering a bribe.

We have almost succeeded in banishing the remembrance of our past sorrows, and look forward to the future with trustful hope. I am happy, Alice—very, very happy; and oh! may no care or trouble ever o'ershadow our tranquil home.

CONCLUSION

'So on your patience evermore attending,
New joy wait on you—here our play has ending.'
[SHAKESPEARE]

Reader, our task is done. Thou hast kindly accompanied us through our rambling narrative, until the end; and now it but remains for us to dispose of the *dramatis personae* who have figured in the various scenes, and then bid thee farewell.

Frank Sydney and his beautiful Sophia were united in marriage, and are now residing in one of the most romantic spots to be found in all New England. Sophia has long since ceased all correspondence with her wretched and abandoned mother, who has become the keeper (under an assumed name) of a celebrated and fashionable brothel in West Cedar street.

Josephine Franklin terminated her miserable existence by poison (procured for her by her own mother,) on the day after her marriage with Mr. Thurston, who, when he beheld the hideous deformity of his bride, instead of the beauty which he expected, recoiled with horror—and after bitterly reproaching her, drove her from his presence, bidding her never to let him see her again, and refusing to make the smallest provision for her support. A few days after Josephine's death, Mr. Thurston, overcome with mortification, shot himself through the heart.

The Doctor has become one of the most respectable physicians, in Boston, and enjoys a lucrative and extensive practice. He is married to an amiable lady, and has named his first son after Sydney, his generous benefactor. He has received into his office, as a student of medicine, Clinton Romaine, the dumb boy, who bids fair to become a skilful and useful physician.

Nero, the African, who has played no inconsiderable part in our drama, finally came to Boston, and now follows the respectable occupation of barber, in the vicinity of the Maine Railroad Depot.

In conclusion, if the foregoing pages have in the least degree contributed to the reader's entertainment, or initiated him into any mystery of CITY CRIMES heretofore unknown—and if this tale, founded on fact, has served to illustrate the truth of the ancient proverbs that 'honesty is the best policy' and 'virtue is its own reward'—then is the author amply repaid for his time and toil, and he tenders to the indulgent public his most respectful parting salutations.

[THE END.]

My Life:

OR

THE ADVENTURES OF GEO. THOMPSON.
BEING THE AUTO-BIOGRAPHY OF AN
AUTHOR. WRITTEN BY HIMSELF.

Why rove in *Fiction's* shadowy land,
  And seek for treasures there,
When *Truth's* domain, so near at hand,
  Is filled with things most rare—
When every day brings something new,
Some great, stupendous change,
Something exciting, wild and *true*,
Most wonderful and strange!

[ORIGINAL.]

{First published 1854}

MY LIFE:

OR THE

ADVENTURES OF

GEO. THOMPSON.

BEING THE

Auto-Biography of an Author.

WRITTEN BY HIMSELF.

BOSTON:
PUBLISHED BY FEDERHEN & CO.,
9 & 13 COURT STREET.

1854.

Yellow Cover of Thompson's *My Life*. Original size 6 x 9⅛". Courtesy, American Antiquarian Society.

INTRODUCTION

In which the author defineth his position.

It having become the fashion of distinguished novelists to write their own lives—or, in other words, to blow their own trumpets,—the author of these pages is induced, at the solicitation of numerous friends, whose bumps of inquisitiveness are strongly developed, to present his autobiography to the public—in so doing which, he but follows the example of Alexandre Dumas, the brilliant French novelist, and of the world-renowned Dickens, both of whom are understood to be preparing their personal histories for the press.

Now, in comparing myself with the above great worthies, who are so deservedly distinguished in the world of literature, I shall be accused of unpardonable presumption and ridiculous egotism—but I care not what may be said of me, inasmuch as a total independence of the opinions, feelings and prejudices of the world, has always been a prominent characteristic of mine—and that portion of the world and the "rest of mankind" which does not like me, has my full permission to go to the devil as soon as it can make all the necessary arrangements for the journey.

I shall be true and candid, in these pages. I shall not seek to conceal one of my numerous faults which I acknowledge and deplore; and, if I imagine that I possess one solitary merit, I shall not be backward in making that merit known. Those who know me personally, will never accuse me of entertaining one single atom of that despicable quality, self-conceit; those who do not know me, are at liberty to think what they please. —Heaven knows that had I possessed a higher estimation of myself, a more complete reliance upon my own powers, and some of that universal commodity known as "cheek," I should at this present moment have been far better off in fame and fortune. But I have been unobtrusive, unambitious, retiring—and my friends have blamed me for this a thousand times. I have seen writers of no talent at all—petty scribblers, wasters of ink and spoilers of paper, who could not write six consecutive lines of English grammar, and whose short paragraphs for the newspapers invariably had to undergo revision and correction—I have seen such fellows causing themselves to be invited to public banquets and other festivals, and forcing their unwelcome presence into the society of the most distinguished men of the day.

I have spoken of my friends—now a word or two in regard to my enemies. Like most men who have figured before the public, in whatever capacity, I have secured the hatred of many persons, who, jealous of my humble fame, have lost no opportunity of spitting out their malice and opposing my progress. The friendship of such persons is a misfortune—their enmity is a blessing.

313

I assure them that their hatred will never cause me to lose a fraction of my appetite, or my nightly rest. They may consider themselves very fortunate, if, in the following pages, they do not find themselves immortalized by my notice, although they are certainly unworthy of so great a distinction. I enjoy the friendship of men of letters, and am therefore not to be put down by the opposition of a parcel of senseless blockheads, without brain, or heart, or soul.

I shall doubtless find it necessary to make allusions to local places, persons, incidents, &c. Those will add greatly to the interest of the narrative. Many portraits will be readily recognized, especially those whose originals reside in Boston, where the greater portion of my literary career has been passed.

The life of an author, must necessarily be one of peculiar and absorbing interest, for he dwells in a world of his own creation, and his tastes, habits, and feelings are different from those of other people. How little is he understood—how imperfectly is he appreciated, by a cold, unsympathising world! his eccentricities are ridiculed—his excesses are condemned by unthinking persons, who cannot comprehend the fact that a writer, whose mind is weary, naturally longs for physical excitement of some kind of other, and too often seeks for a temporary mental oblivion in the intoxicating bowl. Under any and every circumstance, the author is certainly deserving of some degree of charitable consideration, because he labors hard for the public entertainment, and draws heavily on the treasures of his imagination, in order to supply the continual demands of the reading community. When the author has led a life of stirring adventure, his history becomes one of extraordinary and thrilling interest. I flatter myself that this narrative will be found worthy of the reader's perusal.

And now a few words concerning my personal identity. Many have insanely supposed me to be George Thompson, the celebrated English abolitionist and member of the British Parliament, but such cannot be the case, that individual having returned to his own country. Again—others have taken me for George Thompson, the pugilist; but by far the greater part of the performers in this interesting "Comedy of Errors" have imagined me to be no less a personage than the celebrated "*One-eyed Thompson,*" and they long continued in this belief, even after that talented but most unfortunate man had committed suicide in New York, and in spite of the fact that his name was William H., and not George. Two circumstances, however, seemed to justify the belief before the man's death:—he, like myself, had the great misfortune to be deprived of an eye. How the misfortune happened to *me*, I shall relate in the proper place. I have written many works of fiction, but I have passed through adventures quite as extraordinary as any which I have drawn from the imagination.

In order to establish my claim to the title of "author," I will enumerate a few of the works which I have written:—

Gay Girls of New York, Dissipation, The Housekeeper, Venus in Boston, Jack Harold, Criminal, Outlaw, Road to Ruin, Brazen Star, Kate Castleton, Redcliff, The Libertine, City Crimes, The Gay Deceiver, Twin Brothers, Demon of Gold, Dashington, Lady's Garter, Harry Glindon, Catharine and Clara.

In addition to these works—which have all met with a rapid sale and most extensive circulation—I have written a sufficient quantity of tales, sketches, poetry, essays and other literary stock of every description, to constitute half a dozen cart loads. My adventures, however, and not my productions must employ my pen; and begging the reader's pardon for this rather lengthy, but very necessary, introduction, I begin my task.

CHAPTER I

In which I begin to Acquire a Knowledge of the World.

I have always thought, and still think, that it matters very little where or when a man is born—it is sufficient for him to know that he is *here*, and that he had better adapt himself, as far as possible, to the circumstances by which he is surrounded, provided that he wishes to toddle through the world with comfort and credit to himself and to the approbation of others. But still, in order to please all classes of readers, I will state that some thirty years ago a young stranger struggled into existence in the city of New York; and I will just merely hint that the twenty-eighth day of August, in the year of our Lord one thousand eight hundred and twenty-three, should be inserted in the next (comic) almanac as having been the birth-day of a great man— for when an individual attains a bodily weight of two hundred pounds and over, may he not be styled *great?*

My parents were certainly respectable people, but they both inconsiderately died at a very early period of my life, leaving me a few hundred dollars and a thickheaded uncle, to whom was attached an objectionable aunt, the proprietress of a long nose and a shrewish temper. The nose was adapted to the consumption of snuff, and the temper was effective in the destruction of my happiness and peace of mind. The worthy couple, with a prophetic eye, saw that I was destined to become, in future years, somewhat of a *gourmand*, unless care should be taken to prevent such a melancholy fate; therefore, actuated by the best motives, and in order to teach me the luxury of abstinence, they began by slow but sure degrees to starve me. Good people, how I reverence their memory!

One night I committed burglary upon a closet, and feloniously carried off a chunk of bread and meat, which I devoured in the cellar.

"Oh, my prophetic soul—*my uncle!*" That excellent man caught me in the act of eating the provender, and—my bones ache at this very moment as I think of the licking I got! I forgot to mention that I had a rather insignificant brother, four years older than myself, who became my uncle's apprentice, and who joined that gentleman in his persecutions against me. My kind relatives were rather blissful people in the way of ignorance, and they hated me because they imagined that I regarded myself as their superior—a belief that was founded on the fact that I shunned their society and passed the greater portion of my time in reading and writing.

I lived at that time in Thomas street, very near the famous brothel of Rosina

Townsend, in whose house that dreadful murder was committed which the New York public will still remember with a thrill of horror. I allude to the murder of the celebrated courtezan Ellen Jewett. Her lover, Richard P. Robinson, was tried and acquitted of the murder, through the eloquence of his talented counsel, Ogden Hoffman, Esq. The facts of the case are briefly these:—Robinson was a clerk in a wholesale store, and was the paramour of Ellen, who was strongly attached to him. Often have I seen them walking together, both dressed in the height of fashion, the beautiful Ellen leaning upon the arm of the dashing Dick, while their elegant appearance attracted universal attention and admiration. But all this soon came to a bloody termination. Dick was engaged to be married to a young lady of the highest respectability, the heiress of wealth and the possessor of surpassing loveliness. He informed Ellen that his connection with her must cease in consequence of his matrimonial arrangements, whereupon Ellen threatened to expose him to his "intended" if he abandoned her. Embarrassed by the critical nature of his situation, Dick, then, in an evil hour, resolved to kill the courtezan who threatened to destroy his anticipated happiness. One Saturday night he visited her as usual; and after a splendid supper, they returned to her chamber. Upon that occasion, as was afterwards proved on the trial, Dick wore an ample cloak, and several persons noticed that he seemed to have something concealed beneath it. His manner towards Ellen and also his words, were that night unusually caressing and affectionate. What passed in that chamber, and who perpetrated that murder the Almighty knows—*and, perhaps, Dick Robinson, if he is still alive, also knows!** The next morning (Sunday,) at a very early hour, smoke was seen to proceed from Ellen's chamber, and the curtains of her bed were found to have been set on fire. The flames were with difficulty extinguished, and there in the half consumed bed, was found the mangled corpse of Ellen Jewett, having on the side of her head an awful wound, which had evidently been inflicted by a hatchet. Dick Robinson was nowhere to be found, but in the garden, near a fence, were discovered his cloak and a bloody hatchet. With many others, I entered the room in which lay the body of Ellen, and never shall I forget the horrid spectacle that met my gaze! There, upon that couch of sin, which had been scathed by fire, lay blackened the half-burned remains of a once-beautiful woman, whose head exhibited the dreadful wound which had caused her death. It had plainly been the murderer's intention to burn down the house in order to destroy the ghastly evidence of his crime; but fate ordained that the fire should be discovered and extinguished before the *fatal wound* became obliterated. Robinson, as I said before, was tried and pronounced guiltless of the crime, through the ingenuity of his counsel, who termed him an *"innocent boy."* The public, however, firmly believed in his guilt; and the question arises—"If Dick Robinson did not kill Ellen Jewett, *who did?*" I do not believe that ever before was presented so shameful an instance of perverted justice, or so striking an illustration of the "glorious uncertainty of the law." It is rather singular that

---

* The last that was heard of Robinson, he was in Texas, and it was reported that he was married and wealthy, his right arm he had lost in some battle, the name of which I do not remember.

Furlong, a grocer, who swore to an *alibi* in favor of Robinson, and who was the chief instrument employed to effect the acquittal of that young man, some time afterwards committed suicide by drowning, having first declared that his conscience reproached him for the part which he played at the trial!

The Sabbath upon which this murder was brought to light was a dark, stormy day, and I have reason to remember it well, for, in the afternoon, that good old pilgrim—my uncle, of course,—discovered that I had played truant from Sunday School in the morning, and for that atrocious crime, he, in his holy zeal for my spiritual and temporal welfare, resolved to bestow upon me a wholesome and severe flogging, being aided and abetted in the formation of that laudable resolution by my religious aunt and my sanctimonious brother, the latter of whom had turned *informer* against me. Sweet relatives? how I love to think of them—and never do I fail to remember them in my prayers. Well, I was lugged up into the garret, which was intended to be the scene of my punishment. If I recollect rightly, I was then about twelve years of age, and rather a stout youth considering my years. I determined to rebel against the authority of my beloved kindred, assert my independence, and defend myself to the best of my ability. "I have suffered enough;" said I to myself, "and now I'm *going in.*"

"Sabbath-breaker, strip off your jacket," mildly remarked by dear uncle as he savagely flourished a cowhide of most formidable aspect and alarming suppleness.

My reply was brief, but expressive:

"I'll see you d——d first," said I.

My uncle turned pale, my aunt screamed, and my brother rolled up the white of his eyes and groaned.

"What, what did you say?" demanded my uncle, who could not believe the evidence of his own senses, for up to that moment I had always tamely submitted to the good man's amiable treatment of me, and he found it impossible to imagine that I was capable of resisting him. Well, if there ever *was* an angel on earth, that uncle of mine was that particular angel. Saints in general are provided with pinched noses, green eyes, and voices like unto the wailings of a small pig, which is suffering the agonies of death beneath a cart-wheel. And, if there ever was a cherub, my brother *was* certainly that individual cherub, although, in truth, my pious recollections do not furnish me with the statement that cherubs are remarkable for swelled heads and bandy legs.

"I say," was my reply to my uncle's astonished inquiry, "that I ain't going to stand any more abuse and beatings. I've stood bad treatment long enough from the whole pack of you. I'm almost starved, and I'm kicked about like a dog. Let any of you three tyrants touch me, and I'll show you what is to get desperate. I disown you all as relatives, and hereafter I'm going to live where I please, and do as I please."

Furious with rage, my sweet-tempered uncle raised the cowhide and with it struck me across the face. I immediately pitched into that portion of his person where he was accustomed to stow away his Sabbath beans, and the excellent man fell head over heels down the garret stairs, landing securely at the bottom and failing to pick himself up, for the simple reason that he had broken his leg. What a pity it would have been, and what a loss society would have sustained, if, instead of his leg, the holy man had broken his *neck!*

My dear brother, accompanied by my affectionate aunt, now choked me, but I was not to be conquered just then, for "thrice is he armed who hath his quarrel just." The lady I landed in a tub of impure water that happened to be standing near; and she presented quite an interesting appearance, kicking up her heels and squalling like a cat in difficulties. My other assailant I hurled into a heap of ashes, and the way he blubbered was a caution to a Nantucket whaleman. Rushing down the stairs, I passed over the prostrate form of my crippled uncle, who requested me to come back, so that he might kick me with his serviceable foot; but, brute that I was, I disregarded him—requested him to go to a place which shall be nameless—and then left the house as expeditiously as possible, fully determined never to return, whatever might be the consequences.

"I am now old enough, and big enough," I mentally reflected, "to take care of myself; and to-morrow I'll look for work, and try to get a chance to learn a trade. Where shall I sleep to-night? It's easy enough to ask that question, but deuced hard to answer it. I wish to-day wasn't Sunday!"

Rather an impious wish, but quite natural under the circumstances. I felt in my pockets, to see if I was the proprietor of any loose change; my search was magnificently successful, for I discovered that I had a sixpence!

Yes, reader, a new silver sixpence, that glittered in my hand like a bright star of hope, urging me on to enterprise—to exertions. So fearful was I of losing the precious coin, that I continued to grasp it tightly in my hand. I never had been allowed any pocket money, even on the Fourth of July; and this large sum had come into my possession through the munificence of a neighbor, as a reward for performing an errand.

Not knowing where else to go, I went down on the Battery, and sheltered myself under a tree from the rain, which fell in torrents. Rather an interesting situation for a youth of twelve—homeless, friendless, almost penniless! I was wet through to the skin, and as night came on, I became desperately hungry, for I had eaten no dinner that day, and even my breakfast had been of the *phantom* order—something like the pasteboard meals which are displayed upon the stage of the theatre. However, I did not despair, for I was young and active, full of the hope so natural to a youth ere rough contact with the world has crushed his spirit. I was well aware of the fact that I was no fool, although I had often been called one by my hostile and unappreciating relatives, whose opinions I had ever held in most supreme contempt. As I stood under that tree to shelter myself from the rain, I felt quite happy, for a feeling of independence had arisen within me. I was now my own master, and the consciousness that I must solely rely upon myself, was to me a source of gratification and pride. I had not the slightest doubt of being able to dig my way through the world in some way or other.

Night came on at last, black as the brow of a Congo nigger, and starless as a company of travelling actors. I could not remain under the tree all night, that was certain; and so I left it, although I could scarcely see my hand before me. That hand, by the way, still tenaciously grasped the invaluable sixpence. Groping my way out of the Battery, and guided by a light, I entered the bar-room of a respectable hotel, where a large number of well-dressed gentlemen were assembled, who were seeking shelter from the storm, and at the same time indulging their convivial propensities. Much noise and confusion prevailed; and two gentlemen, who, as I afterwards learned, were officers belonging to a Spanish vessel then in port, fell into a dispute and got into a fight, during which one of them stabbed the other with a dirk-knife, inflicting a mortal wound.

Officers were sent for, the murderer and his victim were removed, and comparative quiet prevailed. I was seated in an obscure corner of the bar-room, wondering how I should get through the night, when I was unceremoniously accosted by a lad of about my own age. He was a rakish looking youth, quite handsome withal, dressed in the height of fashion, and was smoking a cigar with great vigor and apparent relish. It will be seen hereafter that I have reason to remember this individual to the very last day of my life. Would to heaven that I had never met him!

This youth slapped me familiarly on the shoulder, and said—

"Hallo, bub! why, you're wet as a drowned rat! Come and take a brandy cocktail—it will warm you up!"

I had never drank a drop of liquor in my life, and I hadn't the faintest idea of what a brandy cocktail was, and so I told my new friend, who laughed immoderately as he exclaimed—

"How jolly green you are, to be sure; why, you're a regular *greenhorn*, and I'm going to call you by that name hereafter. Have you got any tin?"

I knew that he meant money, and so I told him that I had but a sixpence in the world.

"Bah!" cried my friend, as he drew his cigar from his mouth and salivated in the most fashionable manner, "who are you, what are you and what are you doing here? Come, tell me all about yourself, and it may perhaps be in my power to do you a service."

His frank, off-hand manner won my confidence. I told him my whole story, without any reserve; and he laughed uproariously when I told him how I had pitched my tyrannical uncle down stairs.

"It served the old chap right," said he approvingly—"you are a fellow of some spirit, and I like you. Come take a drink, and we can afterwards talk over what is best to be done."

I objected to drink, because I had formed a strong prejudice against ardent spirits, having often been a witness of its deplorable effects in depriving men—and women, too—of their reason, and reducing them to the condition of brute beasts. So, in declining my friend's invitation, I told him my reasons for so doing, whereupon he laughed louder than ever, as he remarked—

"Why, *Greenhorn*, you'd make an excellent temperance lecturer. But perhaps you think I haven't got any money to pay the rum. Look here—what do you think of *that?*"

He displayed a large roll of bank bills, and flourished them triumphantly. I had never before seen so much money, except in the broker's windows; and my friend was immediately established in my mind as a *millionaire*, whose wealth was inexhaustible. I suddenly conceived for him the most profound respect, and would not have offended him for the world. How could I persist in refusing to drink with a young gentleman of such wealth, and (as a necessary consequence) such distinction? Besides, I suddenly felt quite a curiosity to drink some liquor, just to see how it tasted. After all, it was only very low people who got drunk and wallowed in the mire. *Gentlemen* (I thought) never get drunk, and they always seem so happy and joyous after they have been drinking! How they shake hands, and swear eternal friendship, and seem generously willing to lend or give away all they have in the world! So thought I, as my mind was made up to accept the invitation of my friend. It is singular that I had forgotten all about the murder which had just taken place in that bar-room, and which had been directly produced by intemperance.

"The fact is, my dear *Greenhorn*," said my friend, impressively, as he flourished his hand after the manner of some aged, experience and eloquent orator, "the fact is, the *use* of liquor, and its *abuse*, are two very different things. A man (here he drew himself up) can drink like a gentleman, or he can swill like a loafer, or a beast. Now *I* prefer the gentlemanly portion of the argument, and therefore we'll go up and take a gentlemanly drink. I shall be happy, young man, to initiate you into the divine joys and mysteries of Bacchus—ahem!"

I looked at my friend with increased wonder, for he displayed an assurance, a self-possession, an elegant *nonchalance*, that were far beyond his years, for he was only about twelve years old—my own age exactly. And then what language he used—so refined, glowing, and indicative of a knowledge of the world! I longed to be like him—to equal him in his many perfections—to sport as much money as he did, and to wear as good "*harness*." I forgot to mention that he carried a splendid gold watch, and that several glittering rings adorned his fingers. "Who can he be?" was the question which I asked myself; and of course, I could not find an answer.

"Felix," said my friend, addressing the bar-keeper in a style of patronizing condescension, as we approached the bar, "Felix, my good fellow, just mix us a couple of brandy cocktails, will you, and make them *strong*, d'ye hear, for the night is wet, and I and my verdant friend here, are about to travel in search of amusement, even as the Caliph and his Vizier used to perambulate the streets of Baghdad. Come, hurry up!"

The bar-keeper grinned, mixed the liquor, and handed us the tumblers. My friend knocked his glass against mine, and remarked "here's luck," a ceremony and an observation which both somewhat surprised me at the time, although I have long since become thoroughly acquainted with what was then a mystery. Many of my readers—indeed, I may say the greater portion of them—will require no explanation of this matter; and as for those who are in ignorance of it, I will simply say, long may they keep so!

My friend tossed off his cocktail with the air of one who is used to it, and rather liked it than otherwise; but I was not quite so successful, for being wholly unacquainted with the science of drinking, the strength of the liquor nearly choked me, to the intense amusement of my more experienced friend, who advised me to try again. I *did* try again, and more successfully; the liquor went the way of all rum, and soon produced the usual effects. Of course its influence on me was exceedingly powerful, I being entirely unaccustomed to its use. A very agreeable feeling of exhilaration stole over me—I thought I was worth just one hundred thousand dollars—I embraced my friend and swore he was a "trump"—I then noticed, with mild surprise, that he had been multiplied into two individuals—there were two barkeepers now, although just before I drank, there was but one—an additional chandelier had just stepped in to visit the solitary one which had lighted the room— to speak plainly, I saw double; and to sum the whole matter up in a few words, I was, for the first time in my life, most decidedly and incontestably *drunk*.

As nearly as I can remember, my friend linked his arm within mine, and we passed out into the street—he partially supporting me, and keeping me from falling. Two precious youths, of twelve years of age, we certainly were—one staggering and trying to fall down, and the other laughing, and holding him up!

The rain had ceased falling, and the stars were shining as if nothing had happened. The cool air sobered me, and my friend congratulated me on my recovery from a state of inebriety.

"After a little practice at the bar," said he—"it will take a good many *tods* to *floor* you. Let me give you a few hints as regards drinking. Never mix your liquor— always stick to one kind. After every glass, eat a cracker—or, what is better, a pickle. Plain drinks are always the best—far preferable to fancy drinks, which contain sugar, and lemons, and mint, and other trash; although a mixed drink may be taken on a stormy night, such as this has been. Drink ale, or beer, sparingly, and only after dinner—for, taken in large quantities, it is apt to bloat a person, and it plays the very devil with his internal arrangements. Besides, it is filthy stuff, at best, being made of the most repulsive materials and in the dirtiest manner. Always drink *good liquor*, which will not hurt you, while the vile stuff which is sold in the different bar-rooms will soon send you to your grave. If you pass a day or two in drinking freely, do not miss eating a single meal, and if you do not feel inclined to eat, *force* yourself to do it; for, if you neglect your food, that terrible fiend, *Delirium Tremens*, will have you in his savage grasp before you know it. Every morning after a *spree*, take a good stiff horn of brandy, and soon afterwards a glass of plain soda, which will cool you off. Never drink gin—it is vulgar stuff, not fit to be used by gentlemen.—When you desire to reform from drinking, never break off abruptly, which is dangerous; but *taper off* gradually—three glasses to-day, two to-morrow, and one the next day. Never drink with low people, under any circumstances, for it brings you down to their level. When you go to a drinking party, or to a fashionable dinner, sit with your back toward the sun—confine yourself to one kind of liquor—take an occasional sip of vinegar—and the very devil himself cannot drink you under the table! Now do you understand me, my dear *greenhorn?*"

Such language and advice, emanating from a boy of twelve, astonished me, and hurried me to the conclusion that he must be a very *"fast"* youth indeed. I took a more particular survey of my new friend. He was not remarkable handsome, but his face was flushing not with health, but with drinking. A rosy tint suffused his full cheeks, and a delicate vermillion colored the top of his well-formed nose. His form was somewhat slighter than mine, but he looked vigorous and active. His closely buttoned jacket developed a full breast, and a pair of muscular arms. His small feet were encased in patent-leather boots. Upon his head was a jaunty cloth cap, from beneath which flowed a quantity of fine, curly hair. I really envied him his good looks, as also his mental endowments. He saw that I admired him; and he liked me for it.

Such was *Jack Slack*, I may as well give his name at once, for I hate the trickery of authors who keep the curiosity of their readers painfully excited to the end of their narratives for the purpose of producing an *effect*. My professional habits as a writer prompt me to do the same; but I must not forget that I am writing my own history, and not an effusion of my imagination, which seems to be a prolific mother, for it hath produced many children, and (if I live) may produce many more.

While I now write, the Sabbath bells are ringing in sweet harmony, and through my open window comes the cool but mild breath of an autumnal morning. Yes, it is Sunday, and all the holy associations of the sacred day crowd upon me. I can almost see the village church, and the throng of worshippers within it, listening to the fervent remarks and exhortations of their pastor. Then I can fancy the gorgeous cathedral, with its stained windows, its elaborate carvings, its pealing organs, and its fashionable assembly of superficial worshippers. While others are praying, pleasuring and sleeping, I am rushing my iron pen over the spotless paper, and wishing that my penmanship could keep pace with my thought.—This is a digression; but the reader will pardon it. There is *one* dear creature, I know, who, when her eyes scan these pages, will understand me. But she, alas! is far away.

Where was I? Oh, speaking of Jack Slack. How well do I remember the night upon which first I met him! I can see him now, with his mischievous smiles, his eyes full of deviltry—his scornful lips—I can almost hear his mocking laugh. Yes, although eighteen years have passed since then, the remembrance of that night is fresh within me, as if its occurrence were but things of yesterday.

May perdition seize the circumstances which led me to encounter him! He was the foundation of my misfortunes in life. But for him, I might have led a happy, tranquil life; unknown, it is true, but still happy. But, poor fellow! he is dead now. He died by my hand, and I do not regret the act, nor would I recall it, had I the power. But of this the reader shall know hereafter.

That was my first night of dissipation—that was the occasion of my initiation into the mysteries of debauchery. I had previously led a necessarily regular and abstemious life—to bed at eight, up at six, at school by nine, and so on. (By the way, I never learned any thing at school—the master pronounced me the most stupid rascal in the concern; and flogged me accordingly—good old man! All I ever learned was acquired in a *printing office*.) Well, here was I at the age of twelve, fairly launched upon the sea of city life, without a guide, protector, or friend. What wonder is it that I became a reckless, dissipated individual, careless of myself, my interests, my fame and fortune?

Jack Slack and I, arm-in-arm, entered Broadway, and proceeded at a leisurely pace up that noble avenue. Many a courtezan did we meet, and many a watchman did we salute with the compliments of the season. (There were no *Brazen Stars,** nor *M.P.'s,* then.) One lady of the pave, whom my companion addressed in terms of complimentary gallantry, said—"Little boy, go home to your mother and tell her she wants you!"

I am now about to make a humiliating confession, but I must not shrink from it, inasmuch as I sat down with the determination of writing "the truth, the whole truth, and nothing but the truth." I allowed Jack to persuade me to accompany him on a visit to a celebrated establishment in Leonard street—a house occupied by accommodating ladies of great personal attractions, who were not especially virtuous. That was of course my first visit to a house of ill-fame; and without exactly comprehending the nature of the place and its arrangements, I was deeply impressed with the strangeness and novelty of every thing that surrounded me. The costly and elegant furniture—the brilliant chandeliers—the magnificent but rather *loose* French prints and paintings—the universal luxury that prevailed—the voluptuous ladies, with their bare shoulders, painted cheeks, and free-and-easy manners—the buxom, bustling landlady, who was dressed with almost regal splendor and wore a profusion of jewelry—the crowd of half-drunken gentlemen who were drinking wine and laughing uproariously—all these things astonished and bewildered me. My friend Jack appeared to be well known to the inmates of the house, with whom he seemed to be an immense favorite. Having—much to my dissatisfaction and disgust—introduced me to a lady, he took possession of another one, and called for a couple of bottles of wine. Jack and his lady were evidently upon the most intimate and affectionate terms, while my female companion seemed inclined to be very loving, but I did not appreciate her advances, being altogether unaccustomed to such things. The champagne was brought, and I was persuaded to drink freely of it. The consequence was that I soon became helplessly intoxicated. I can indistinctly remember the dancing lights, the popping of champagne corks—the noise, the confusion, the thrumming of a piano, and the boisterous laughter—and then I fell into a condition of complete insensibility.

When I awoke, I was astonished at my situation and naturally enough, for I was in a strange apartment and snugly stowed away in a strange but decidedly luxuriant bed. The room was handsomely furnished, but to my additional surprise, many female garments were scattered about, indicating that the regular inhabitant of the place was a lady. This mystery was soon solved, for I was not the only inmate of the couch. My companion was the lady to whom I had been introduced by Jack Slack. Pitying my helpless condition—and, doubtless, prompted by the mischievous Jack—she had carried me to bed, and had also retired herself, being actuated by a benevolent anxiety for my safety. What a delicate situation for a modest youth to be placed in! Having, to my no small satisfaction, ascertained that the lady was fast

---

* I have just written a story under this title, full of fact and fun, and containing more truth than poetry. The reader can have it by applying to the publisher of this work. It is well worthy of perusal.

asleep, I arose so carefully and noiselessly as not to awaken her. In truth, I was disgusted with the whole concern, and determined to leave it as speedily as possible. A light was fortunately burning in the room, which enabled me to move about with safety. A gold watch which lay upon the table informed me that it was nearly midnight.—Leaving the chamber and its sleeping inmate, I crept down stairs, and, on passing the door of the principal sitting-room, the voice of Jack Slack, who was singing a comic song amid the most enthusiastic applause, convinced me that my interesting friend was still rendering himself a source of amusement and an object of admiration. Without stopping to compliment him upon the excellence of his performance, I approached the front door, turned the key which was in the lock, unfastened the chain, and passed out into the street, just as the clock of a neighboring steeple was proclaiming the hour of twelve.

My head ached terribly after the champagne which I had so profusely drank, and besides, I felt heavy and sleepy to an extraordinary degree. Unable to resist the overpowering influence of my feelings, I sat down upon the steps of a house and was fast asleep in less than a minute. Then I dreamed of being seized in the powerful grasp of some gigantic demon, and hurried away to the bottomless pit. I certainly felt conscious of being moved about, but my oblivious condition would not admit of arriving at any definite understanding of what was happening to me. When I finally awoke, I found myself in an apartment that was far different in its aspect from the luxurious chamber I had just quitted. The floor, walls and ceiling of the apartment were of stone; there were no windows, but a narrow aperture, high up in the wall, admitted the feeble glimmer of daylight. There was an iron door, and a water-pipe, and platform on which I lay, and on which reposed several gentlemen of seedy raiment and unwholesome appearance. The place and the company, as dimly revealed by the uncertain morning light, inspired me with emotions of horror; and in my inexperience and ignorance, I said to myself—

"I must leave this place at once. How I came here is a mystery, but it is certain that I cannot remain."

I arose from my hard couch, and approached the iron door with the confident expectation of being able to pass out without any difficulty, for I imagined that I had fallen into one of those cheap and wretched lodging houses with which the city abounds. (By the way, I may hereafter have something to say with reference to these cheap lodging-houses. Some rich development may be made, which will rather astonish the unsophisticated reader.)

To my surprise, I found that the door could not be opened; and then one of my fellow-lodgers, who had been observing my movements, exclaimed:

"Are you going to leave us, my lad? Then leave us your card, or a lock of your hair to remember you by."

"Will you be kind enough to tell me what place this is?" said I.

The man laughed loudly, as he replied—

"Why, don't you know? What an innocent youth you are, to be sure! How the devil could you come here, without knowing anything about it? But I suppose that you were drunk, which is a great pity for a boy like you. Well, not to keep you in suspense, I must inform you that you are in the *watch-house of the Tombs!*"

This information appalled me. To be in confinement—to be a prisoner—to be associated with a company of outcasts, thieves and perhaps murderers—was to me the height of horror. I looked particularly at the man with whom I had been conversing. He was a savage-looking individual, with a beard like that of a pirate, and an eye that spoke of blood and outrage. He was roughly dressed, in a garb that announced him to be a mariner.

In the course of a conversation that we fell into, he informed me that he had committed a murder on the preceding evening, and that he expected to be hung.

"We quarrelled at cards," said he, "and he gave me the lie—whereupon I drew my death-knife and stabbed him to the heart. He died instantly; the police rushed in, and here I am. My neck will be stretched, but I don't care. What matters it how a man dies? When my time comes, I shall go forth as readily and as cheerfully as if I were going to take a drink."

(I will here remark that I afterwards saw this man hung in the yard of the *Tombs*. His history is in my possession, and I shall hereafter write it.)*

At nine o'clock I was taken before the magistrate, who, after severely reprimanding me for my misconduct, discharged me from custody, with the remark that if I were brought there again he would be obliged to commit me to the Tombs for the term of five days. Delighted at having obtained my liberty, I posted out of the court room and found myself in Centre street. My debauch of the preceding night had not spoiled my appetite, by any means; and, as I still had in my possession the sixpence alluded to before, I resolved to produce some breakfast forthwith. Aware that my limited finances would not admit of my obtaining a very sumptuous repast, and fully appreciating the necessity of economy, I entered the shop of a baker and purchased three rolls at the rate of one cent per copy. Thus provided, I repaired to a neighboring street pump, and made a light but wholesome breakfast.

It was thus, reader, that your humble servant began to acquire a knowledge of the world.

CHAPTER II

In which I become a Printer, and am introduced into certain mysteries of connubial life.

Having breakfasted to my entire satisfaction and also to my great bodily refreshment, I entered the Park, seated myself upon the steps of the City Hall, and thought "what is best to be done?"—It was Monday morning, and the weather was excellently fine. It was an excellent time to search for employment. A sign on an old building in Chatham street attracted my notice; upon it were inscribed the words, "Book and Job Printing."

"Good!" was my muttered exclamation, as I left the Park and crossed over

* This work is now in active course of preparation. To the lovers of exciting tales, this story will be one of particular attraction. It will be issued by the publisher of this narrative.

towards the old building in question—"I'll be a printer! Franklin was one, and he, like myself, was fond of rolls, because he entered Philadelphia with one under each arm. Yes, I'll be a printer."

Entering the printing office, I found it to be a very small concern, containing but one press and a rather limited assortment of type. The proprietor of the office, whom I shall call Mr. Romaine, was a rather intellectual looking man, of middle age. Being very industrious, he did the principal portion of his work himself, occasionally, however, hiring a journeyman when work was unusually abundant. As I entered he looked up from his case and inquired, with an air of benevolence—

"Well, my lad, what can I do for *you* this morning?"

"If you please, sir, I want to learn to be a printer," replied I, boldly.

"Ah, indeed! Well, I was just thinking of taking an apprentice. But give an account of yourself—how old are you, and who are you?"

I frankly communicated to Mr. Romaine all that he desired to know concerning me, and he expressed himself as being perfectly satisfied. He immediately set me to "learning the boxes" of a case of type; and in half an hour I had accomplished the task, which was not very difficult, it being merely an effort of memory.

It having been arranged that I should take up my abode in the house of Mr. Romaine, I accompanied that gentleman home to dinner. He lived in William street and his wife kept a fashionable boarding-house for merchants, professional men, &c. Several of these gentlemen were married men and had their wives with them. Mrs. Romaine, the wife of my employer, was one of the finest-looking women I ever saw—tall, voluptuous, and truly beautiful. She was about twenty-five years of age, and her manners were peculiarly fascinating and agreeable. She was always dressed in a style of great elegance, and was admirably adapted to the station which she filled as landlady of an establishment like that. I will remark that although she had been the wife of Mr. Romaine for a number of years, she had not been blessed with offspring, which was doubtless to her a source of great disappoint-ment, to say nothing of the *chagrin* which a married woman naturally feels when she fails in due time to add to the population of her country.

Accustomed as I had been to the economical scantiness of my uncle's table, I was both surprised and delighted with the luxurious abundance that greeted me on sitting down to dinner at Mrs. Romaine's. I was equally well pleased with the sprightliness, intelligence and good-humor of the conversation in which the ladies and gentlemen engaged, and also with their refined and courteous bearing towards each other. I congratulated myself on having succeeded in getting not only into business, but also into good society.

"If my dearly-beloved relatives," thought I, "could see me now, they might not be well pleased at my situation and prospects. Let them go to Beelzebub! I will get on in the world, in spite of them!"

In a few days I began to be very useful about the printing office, for I had learned to set type and to *roll* behind the press; I also performed all the multifarious duties of *devil*, and was so fortunate as to secure the good will of my employer, who generously purchased for me a fine new suit of clothes, and seemed anxious to make me as comfortable as possible. His wife, also, treated me very kindly; but there was something mysterious about this lady, which for a time, puzzled me extremely. One discovery which I made rather astonished me, young as I was, and caused me to do a "devil of a thinking." Mr. Romaine and his wife occupied separate sleeping apartments, and there seemed to be an aversion between them, although they treated each other with the most formal and scrupulous politeness. But my readers will agree with me that mere *politeness* is not the only sentiment which should exist between a husband and his wife. There was evidently something "rotten in Denmark" between Mr. and Mrs. Romaine, and I determined, if possible, to penetrate the mystery.

Mr. Romaine, who was professedly a pious man, was particularly in favor of "remembering the Sabbath day to keep it holy," and he therefore directed me to be very punctual in attendance at church and Sunday school, and I obeyed his praiseworthy request until visions of literary greatness and renown began to dawn upon me, whereupon, prompted by gingerbread and ambition, and being moreover aided and abetted by another printer's devil of tender years and literary aspirations, I, one Sunday morning, entered the printing office, (of which I kept the key,) and assisted by my companion, set up and worked off one hundred copies of a diminutive periodical just six inches square, containing a *very* brief abstract of the news of the day, a *very* indifferent political leader, and a few *rather* partial theatrical criticisms. This extensive newspaper we issued on three successive Sundays, circulating it among our juvenile friends at the moderate rate of one cent a copy. On the fourth Sunday we were caught in the act of printing our journal by Mr. Romaine himself, who, although he with difficulty refrained from laughing at the fun of the thing, gave us a long lecture on the crime of Sabbath-breaking, and then made us distribute the type, forgetting that we were breaking the Sabbath as much by taking our form to pieces as by putting it together.

Mr. Romaine was also strongly opposed to theatres, but, nevertheless, I visited the "little Frankin" four or five times every week, to see John and Bill Sefton in the "Golden Farmer," and other thrilling melo-dramas, a convenient ally, a garden and a shed enabled me to enter my chamber at any hour during the night, without my employer's becoming aware of my absence from home.

One night after having been to my favorite place of amusement, I returned home about midnight. On entering the garden, I discovered to my surprise a light streaming from the kitchen windows—a very unusual occurrence. I crept softly up to one of the windows, and looking into the kitchen, a scene met my gaze that filled me with astonishment.

Mrs. Romaine, arrayed in her night-dress only, was seated at a table, and at her side was a young gentleman named Anderson, who boarded in the house, and who was a prosperous merchant. His arm was around the lady's waist, and her head rested affectionately upon his shoulder. She looked uncommonly beautiful and voluptuous that night, I thought, young as I was, I wondered not at the look of passionate admiration with which Anderson regarded his fair companion, upon whose sensual countenance there rested an expression of gratified love. Upon the table were the remains of a supper of which they had evidently partaken; there were also a bottle of wine and two glasses, partially filled. Mrs. Romaine sipped her wine occasionally, as well as her paramour; and the guilty pair seemed to be enjoying themselves highly. It was plain that the lady was resolved to lose nothing by her estrangement from her husband; it was equally plain that between her and Mr. Romaine there existed not the smallest particle of love. I now ceased to wonder why the wedded pair occupied separate apartments; and I came to the conclusion that disappointment in the matter of children was the cause of their mutual aversion. If I were writing a romance instead of a narrative of facts, I would here introduce an imaginary tender conversation between the pair. But as no such conversation took place I have none to describe.

"Well," said I to myself—"this is a pretty state of affairs, truly. I guess that if Mr. Romaine suspected any thing of this kind, there would be the very devil to pay, and no mistake. But it's no business of mine; and so I'll climb into my window and go to bed."

My employer was a very good sort of a man, and I sincerely pitied him on account of his unhappy connubial situation. I turned away from the kitchen window, and began to mount the shed in order to reach my chamber. I had nearly gained the roof of the shed, when a board gave way and I was precipitated to the ground, a distance of about ten feet. Fortunately I sustained no injury; but the noise aroused and alarmed the loving couple in the kitchen. Mrs. Romaine, in her terror and dread of discovery, gave utterance to a slight scream; while Mr. Anderson rushed forth and seized me in a rather powerful grasp. I struggled, and kicked, and strove to extricate myself, but it was all of no use. With many a muttered imprecation Anderson dragged me into the kitchen, and swore that if I did not remain quiet he would stab me to the heart with a dirk-knife that he produced from his pocket.

"You young rascal," said he "who employed you to play the part of a spy? Did Mr. Romaine direct you to watch us? Is he lurking outside, in the garden? If so, let him beware, for I am a desperate man, one not to be trifled with!"

I explained everything to the entire satisfaction of both the gentleman and lady, whose countenances brightened when they found that matters were far from being as bad as they expected.

"Now, my boy," said Anderson, "just do keep perfectly dark about this business, and I'll make your fortune. You shall never want a dollar while I live. As an earnest of what I may hereafter do for you, accept this trifle, which will enable you to gratify your theatre-going propensities to your heart's content."

The "trifle" was a ten dollar gold piece. I had never before possessed so much money; and no millionaire ever felt richer than I did at that moment. Delightful visions of dramatic treats arose before me, and I was happy.

Mr. Anderson made me drink a couple of glasses of wine, which tasted very good, and caused me to feel quite elevated. Then he told me that I had better go to bed, and I fully agreed with him. So, bidding the enamoured couple a patronizing good night and facetiously wishing them a pleasant time together—the wine had made me bold and saucy—I left the kitchen and began to ascend the stairs towards my own room with all the silence and caution of which I was capable.

I was destined that night to make another astonishing discovery. Being quite tipsy, I was deprived of my usual judgement, and suffered myself to stumble against a table that stood upon one of the landings opposite the chamber door of a young and particularly pretty widow named Mrs. Raymond, who boarded in the house. She possessed a snug independent fortune, and led a life of elegant leisure. Although demure in her looks and reverend in her deportment, there was a whole troop of dancing devils in her eyes that proclaimed the fact that her nature was not exactly as cold as ice.

My collision with the table caused me to recoil, and I fell violently against Mrs. Raymond's door, which burst open, and down I landed in the very centre of the apartment.

I heard a scream, and then a curse. The scream was the performance of the fair widow; the curse was the production of Mr. Romaine, my pious, Sabbath-venerating and theatre-opposing employer, who, springing up from the sofa upon which he had been seated by the side of the widow, seized me by the throat and demanded how the devil I came there?

My wits had not entirely deserted me, and I managed to tell quite a plausible story. I candidly confessed that I had been to the theatre and stated that I had got into the house through the kitchen window. Of course I said nothing about Anderson and Mrs. Romaine.

"You have been drinking," said Mr. Romaine, in a tone that was by no means severe, "but I forgive you for that, and also for having disobeyed me by going to the theatre. Be a good boy in future, and you shall never want a friend while I live."

While he was speaking, I looked about the room. It was exquisitely furnished with the most refined and elegant taste. Mrs. Raymond, who still sat upon the sofa, blushed deeply as her eyes encountered mine. She was *en deshabille*, and looked charming. I could not help admiring the divine perfections of her form, as *revealed* by the deliciously careless attire which she wore. I did not wonder that my respected presence confused her, for she had always held herself up as the very pink and pattern of female propriety, and besides, she often lectured me severely upon the enormity of some of my juvenile offences, which came to her knowledge.

Mr. Romaine continued to address me, thus:

"If you will solemnly promise to say nothing about having seen me in this room, I will reward you handsomely."

I readily gave the required promise, whereupon my pious employer presented me with a five-dollar bill, which I received with all the nonchalance in the world. I then withdrew, and reached my own room without encountering any more adventures. Sleep did not visit me that night, for my thoughts were too busily engaged with the discoveries which I had made; and besides, the blissful consciousness of being the possessor of the princely sum of fifteen dollars, would have kept me awake, independent of anything else.

A day of two after these occurrences, while looking over one of the morning newspapers, I saw an advertisement signed by my uncle, in which that worthy man offered a reward for my apprehension. The notice contained a minute description of my personal appearance and the clothes which I had on when I "ran away."

Although my garments had been entirely changed, I was fearful that some one might recognize my person, and carry me back to my uncle's house, where I had every reason to expect far worse treatment than I had ever received before. But Mr. Romaine, to whom I showed the advertisement, told me not to be at all alarmed, as he would protect me at any risk. This assurance made me feel much easier. I was never molested in consequence of that advertisement.

After the night on which I had detected the intrigue of my employer and his wife, I began to live emphatically "in clover," and accumulated money tolerably fast. All the parties concerned treated me with the utmost consideration and respect. Mr. Romaine suffered me to do pretty much as I pleased in the printing office, and so I enjoyed a very agreeable and leisurely time of it, doing as much Sunday printing on my own account as I desired, and going to the theatre as often as I wished. Mr. Anderson would occasionally slip a five dollar note into my hand, at the same time enjoining me to "keep mum;" Mrs. Romaine, with her own fair hands, made me a dozen superb shirts, supplied me with handkerchiefs, stockings and fancy cravats innumerable, and so arranged it that when I returned from the theatre at night, a nice little supper awaited me in the kitchen. These repasts she would sometimes share with me, for, like a sensible woman, she was fond of all the good things of this life, including good eating and drinking. Anderson would join us occasionally, and a snug, cosy little party we made. Mrs. Raymond, the pretty widow, was not backward in testifying to me how grateful she was for my silence with reference to her frailty. She made me frequent presents of money, and gave me an elegant and valuable ring, which I wore until the "intervention of unfortunate circumstance" compelled me to consign it to the custody of "my uncle"—not my beloved relative of Thomas street, (peace to his memory, for he has gone the way of all pork,) —but that accommodating uncle of mine and everybody else, Mr. Simpson, who dwelleth in the *Rue de Chatham*, and whose mansion is decorated with three gilded balls. Kind, convenient Uncle Simpson!

Ah! those were my halcyon days, when not a single care cast its shadow o'er my soul. As I think of that season of unalloyed happiness, I involuntarily exclaim, in the words of a fine popular song—

"I would I were a boy again!"

Three years passed away, unmarked by the occurrence of any event of sufficient importance to merit a place in this narrative. When I reached my fifteenth year, the fashionable boarding-house of Mrs. Romaine became the scene of a tragedy so bloody, so awful and so appalling, that even now, while I think and write about it, my blood runs cold in my veins. That terrible affair can no more be obliterated form my memory than can the sun be effaced from the arch of heaven; and to my dying day, its recollection will continue to haunt me like a hideous spectre.

But I must devote a separate chapter to the details of that sanguinary event. I would gladly escape from the task of describing it; but, of course, were I to omit it, this narrative would be incomplete. Therefore the unwelcome duty must be performed.

CHAPTER III

In which is enacted a bloody tragedy.

I began to observe with considerable uneasiness, that Mr. Romaine stealthily regarded his wife with looks of intense hatred and malignant ferocity; then he would transfer his gaze from her to Mr. Anderson, who was altogether unconscious of the scrutiny. My employer was usually a very quiet man, but I knew that his passions were very violent, and that, when once thoroughly aroused, he was capable of perpetrating almost any act of savage vengeance. I began to fear that he suspected the intimacy which existed between his adulterous wife and her paramour. By the way it may be as well to remark that I had never told either Anderson or Mrs. Romaine of the intrigue between Mr. Romaine and the widow, Mrs. Raymond; and it is scarcely necessary to observe that I was equally discreet in withholding from my employer and his "ladye love" all knowledge of the state of affairs between the other parties.

I communicated my fears to Mr. Anderson, but he laughed at them saying—

"Nonsense, my dear boy—why should Romaine suspect anything of the kind? I and Harriet (Mrs. Romaine) have always been very discreet and careful. Our intimacy began three or four years ago; and as it has lasted that length of time without discovery, it is scarcely likely to be detected *now*. You are quite sure that you have given Romaine no hint of the affair?"

"Do you think me capable of such base treachery?" I demanded, with an offended air.

"Forgive me," said Anderson, "I did wrong to doubt you. Believe me, your fears are groundless; however, I thank you for the caution, and shall hereafter exercise additional care, so as to prevent the possibility of discovery. Here is a ticket for the opera to-night; when you return, which will be about midnight, come to Harriet's room, and we three will sup like two kings and a queen."

Having dressed myself with unusual care, I went to the opera. While listening to the divine strains of a celebrated *prima donna*, my attention was attracted by a group occupying one of the most conspicuous boxes. This group consisted of a youth apparently about my own age, and two showy looking females whose dresses were cut so low as to reveal much more of their busts than decency could sanction, even among an opera audience. There could be no doubt as to the character of these two women. I examined their youthful cavalier with attention; and soon recognized my *quondam* friend and pitcher—JACK SLACK. Jack was magnificently dressed, and his appearance was truly superb. The most fastidious Parisian exquisite—even the great Count D'Orsay himself might have envied him the arrangement of his hair, the tie of his cravat, the spotlessness of his white kids. He flourished a glittering, jeweled *lorgnette*, and the way the fellow put on "French airs" must have been a caution to the proudest scion of aristocracy in the house.

After a little while Jack saw me; and, having taken a good long stare at me through his opera-glass, he beckoned me to come to him, at the same time pointing

331

significantly at one of his "lady" companions, as if to intimate that she was entirely at my disposal. But I shook my head, and did not stir, for I had no desire to resume my acquaintance with that fascinating but mysterious youth. Perhaps I entertained a presentiment that he was destined to become, to both of us, the cause of a great misfortune.

Jack looked angry and disappointed, at my refusal to accept of his hospitable invitation. He directed the attention of his women towards me, and I saw that they were attempting to titter and sneer at my expense;—but the effort was a total failure, for there was not a better-dressed person in the house than I was. Having honored the envious party with a smile of scorn,—which, I flattered myself, was perfectly successful,—I turned towards the stage, and did not indulge in another look at Jack or his friends during the remainder of the opera. I am convinced that from that hour, Jack Slack became my mortal foe.

At the conclusion of the performances, I left the house and saw Jack getting into a carriage with the two courtezans. He observed me, and uttered a decisive shout, to which I paid no attention, but hurried home, anxious to make one of the little party in the apartment of Mrs. Romaine, and quite ready to partake of the delicacies which, I knew, would be provided.

On my arrival home, I immediately repaired to Mrs. Romaine's private room, where I found that good lady in company with Mr. Anderson. We three sat down to supper in the highest possible spirits. Alas! how little did we anticipate the terrible catastrophe that was so soon to follow!

The more substantial portion of the banquet having been disposed of, the sparkling wine-cup was circulated freely, and we became very gay and jovial. Unrestrained by my presence, and exhilarated by the rosy beverage of jolly Bacchus, the lovers indulged in many little acts of tender dalliance. Always making it a point to mind my own business, I applied myself diligently to the bottle, for the wine was excellent and the sardines had made me thirsty. I had just lighted a cigar, and was resigning myself to the luxurious and deliciously soothing influence of the weed, when the door was thrown violently open, and Mr. Romaine rushed into the room.

His appearance was frightful! his face was dreadfully pale, and his eyes glared with the combined fires of jealousy and rage. Intense excitement caused him to quiver in every limb. In one hand he grasped a pistol, and in the other a bowie knife of the largest and most formidable kind.

It was but too evident that my fears had been well founded, and that Mr. Romaine had discovered the intimacy between Anderson and his wife.

The reader will agree with me that the "injured husband" was equally culpable on account of his intrigue with the young and handsome widow, Mrs. Raymond.— How prone are many people to lose sight of their own imperfections while they censure and severely punish the failings of those who are not a whit more guilty than themselves! The swinish glutton condemns the drunkard—the villainous seducer reproves the frequenter of brothels—the arch hypocrite takes to task the open, undisguised sinner—and the rich, miserly old reprobate, whose wealth places him above the possibility of ever coming to want, who would sooner "hang the guiltless than eat his mutton cold," and who would not bestow a cent upon a poor devil to keep him from starving—that old rascal, perhaps, in his capacity as a magistrate, sentences to jail an unfortunate man whom hunger has driven into the "crime" of stealing a loaf of bread! Bah! ladies and gentlemen, take the *beams* out of your own eyes before you allude to the *motes* in the optics of your fellow beings. That's *my* advice, free of charge.

On seeing her husband enter in that furious and threatening manner, Mrs. Romaine, overcome with fear and shame—for she well knew that her guilt had been detected—fell to the floor insensible. Anderson, confused and not knowing what to say, sat motionless as a statue;—while I awaited, with almost trembling anxiety, the issue of this most extraordinary state of affairs.

Romaine was the first to break the silence, and he spoke in a tone of voice that was singularly calm considering his physical agitation.

"Well, sir," said he, addressing Anderson—"you are enjoying yourself finely—drinking my wine, devouring my provisions, and making love to my wife in her own bed-chamber. Anderson, for some time past I have suspected you and Harriet of being guilty of criminal intimacy. I have noticed your secret signs, and have read and interpreted the language of your eyes, whenever you and she have exchanged glances in my presence. You both took me to be a weak fool, too blind and imbecile to detect your adulterous intercourse; but I have now come to convince you that I am a man capable of avenging his ruined conjugal honor!"

Anderson, recovering some degree of his usual self-possession, remarked,

"Your accusation, sir, is unjust. Your wife and myself are friends, and nothing more. She invited me to sup with her here to-night and that is all about it. If our intentions were criminal, would we have courted the presence of a third party?"

With these words, Anderson pointed towards me, but Romaine, without observing me at all, continued to address the paramour of his wife.

"Anderson, you are a liar, and the falsehoods which you have uttered, only serve to increase your guilt, and confirm me in my resolution to sacrifice both you and that guilty woman who lies yonder. Can I disbelieve the evidence of my own eyes? Must I go into particulars, and say that last night, at about this hour, in the kitchen—ha! you turn pale—you tremble—your guilt is confessed. I would have killed you last night, Anderson, but I had not the weapons. This knife and pistol I purchased to-day, *and I shall use them!*

"Try and revive that *harlot*, for I would speak with her ere she dies!"

Anderson mechanically obeyed. Placing the insensible form of Mrs. Romaine upon a sofa, he sprinkled water upon her face, and she was soon restored to a state of consciousness. For a few moments she gazed about her wildly; and then, when her eyes settled upon her husband, and she saw the terrible weapons with which he was armed, she covered her face with her hands and trembled in an agony of terror, for she knew that her life was in the greatest possible danger.

Romaine now addressed his wife in a tone of calmness which was, under the circumstances, far more terrible than the most violent outburst of passion:

"Harriet," said he—"I now fully comprehend your reasons for requesting to be allowed to occupy a separate apartment. You desired an opportunity to gratify your licentious propensities without any restraint. Woman, why have you used me thus? Have I deserved this infamous treatment? Have I ever used you unkindly, or spoken a harsh word to you? Do you think that I will tamely wear the horns which you and your paramour have planted upon my brow? Do you think that I will suffer myself to be made an object of scorn, and allow myself to be pointed at and ridiculed by a sneering community?"

"Forgive me," murmured the unhappy wife—"I will not offend again. I acknowledge that I have committed a grievous sin; but Heaven only knows how sincerely I repent of it!"

"Your repentance comes too late," said Romaine, hoarsely—"Heaven may forgive you, but *I* shall not! You say that you will not offend again. Having forever destroyed my happiness, my peace of mind, and my honor, *you will not offend again!* You shall not have the opportunity, wretched woman. You shall no longer survive your infamy. You and the partner of your guilt must die!"

With these words, Romaine cocked his pistol and approached his wife, saying, in a low, savage tone that evinced the desperate purpose of his heart—

"Take your choice, madam; do you prefer to die by *lead* or by *steel?*"

The miserable woman threw herself upon her knees, exclaiming—

"Mercy, husband—mercy! Do not kill me, for I am not prepared to die!"

"You call me husband *now*—you, who have so long refused to receive me as a husband. Come—I am impatient to shed your blood, and that of your paramour. Breathe a short prayer to Heaven, for mercy and forgiveness, and then resign your body to death and your soul to eternity!"

So saying the desperate and half-crazy man raised on high the glittering knife. Poor Mrs. Romaine uttered a shriek, and, before she could repeat it, the knife descended with the swiftness of lightning, and penetrated her heart. Her blood spouted all over her white dress, and she sank down at the murderer's feet, a lifeless corpse!

Paralyzed with horror, I could neither move nor speak. Anderson also stood motionless, like a bird which is subjected to the fascinating gaze of a serpent. Notwithstanding the terrible danger in which he was placed, he seemed to be rooted to the spot and incapable of making a single effort to save himself by either resistance or flight.

The scene was most extraordinary, thrilling and awful. The luxurious chamber—the failing lamp—the murderer, holding in his hand the bloody knife—the doomed Anderson, whose soul was quivering on the brink of the dread abyss of eternity; all these combined to form a spectacle of the most strange and appalling character.

Romaine now raised his pistol and took deliberate aim at Anderson, saying,

"My work is but half done; it is *your* turn now! Are you ready?"

"Do not shoot me like a dog," implored the unfortunate young man, who, to do him justice, possessed a considerable amount of courage—"give me, at least, *some* chance for my life. If I have wronged you, and I candidly confess that I have, I am ready to give you the satisfaction of a gentleman. Give me a pistol, place me upon an equal footing with yourself, and we will settle the matter as becomes men of honor. This boy, here, will be a witness of the affair."

To this proposition, Romaine scornfully replied,

"I admire your assurance, sir.—After seducing the wife, you want a chance to shoot the husband. Well, as I am an accommodating man, it shall be as you say, for I am sick of life and care not if I am killed. But I have no other pistol. Stay!—suppose we *toss up* a coin, and thus decide which of us shall have this weapon, with the privilege of using it. Here is a quarter of a dollar; I will throw it up in the air, and when it falls upon the floor, if the *head* is uppermost, the pistol is *mine;* but if the *tail* is uppermost, the pistol shall be *yours.* I warn you that if I win, I shall show you no mercy; and, if you win, I shall expect none from you. Do you agree to this?"

"I do," replied Anderson, firmly, "and I thank you for your fairness."

Romaine threw up the coin, which spun around in the air and landed upon the carpet. How strange that it should have become the province of that insignificant coin to decide which of those two men must die!

Romaine calmly took the dim lamp from the table, and knelt down upon the carpet in a pool of his wife's blood.

"Watch me closely, and see that I do not touch the coin," said he, as he bent eagerly over the life-deciding quarter of a dollar.

How my heart beat at that moment, and what must have been the sensation of poor Anderson!

"*The head is uppermost, and I have won!*" said Romaine, in a hoarse whisper—"come and see for yourself."

"I am satisfied, your word is sufficient," said Anderson, with a shudder, as he folded his arms across his breast and seemed to abandon himself to profound despair.

Romaine's pale face assumed an expression of savage delight, as he raised the pistol and pointed it at the head of his intended victim, saying—

"Then, sir, nothing remains but for me to avail myself of the favor which fortune has conferred upon me. Young man, in five seconds I shall fire!"

"Hold!" cried Anderson, "I have a favor to ask, which I am sure you will not refuse to grant me. Before I die, let me write a couple of letters, and make a few notes of the manner in which I wish my property to be disposed of. It is the last request of a dying man."

"It is granted," said Romaine, "there, upon that *escritoire*, are writing materials. But make haste, for I am impatient to finish this disagreeable business."

Anderson sat down, and began to write rapidly. I longed to rush out and give the alarm, so that the impending tragedy might be averted; but I feared that any movement on my part might result in the passage of a bullet through my brain, and therefore I remained quiet, for which I am sure, no sensible reader will blame me.

Poor Anderson! tears gushed from his eyes and streamed down his cheeks while he was writing one of the letters, which, as I afterwards ascertained, was addressed to a young lady to whom he was engaged to be married. He wrote two letters, folded, sealed and directed them; these he handed to me, saying—

"Have the kindness to deliver these letters to the persons to whom they are addressed. Will you faithfully promise to do this?"

I promised, of course; he shook hands with me, and bade me farewell; then, calmly turning towards Romaine, he announced his readiness to die. Up to that moment, I had tried to persuade myself that Anderson's life would be spared, thinking that Romaine must have had enough of blood after slaying his wife in that barbarous manner. But I was doomed to be terribly disappointed. Scarcely had Anderson muttered the words, "I am ready to die," when Romaine pulled the trigger of the upraised pistol, and the young merchant fell dead upon the floor, the bullet having penetrated his brain.

"Now I am satisfied, for I have had my revenge," said the murderer, coolly, as he wiped the perspiration from his pallid brow.

"Blood-thirsty villain!" exclaimed I, unable longer to restrain my indignation— "you will swing upon the gallows for this night's work!"

"Not so," rejoined Romaine, calmly, "for I do not intend to survive this wholesale butchery, and did not, from the first. I was determined that Anderson should die, at all events. *He won the pistol*, for the coin fell with the tail uppermost. Had he stooped to examine it, I would have blown out his brains, just the same. But hark! the boarders and inmates of the house have been aroused by the report of the pistol, and they are hastening here. The gallows—no, no, I must avoid *that!* They shall not take me alive. Now, may heaven have mercy upon my guilty soul!"

With these words the unhappy man seized the Bowie knife and plunged it into his heart, thus adding the crime of suicide to the two atrocious murders which he had just committed.

Scarcely had this crowning point of the fearful tragedy been enacted, when a crowd of people, half-dressed and excited, rushed into the room. Among them was the beautiful widow, Mrs. Raymond. On seeing the bleeding corpse of Romaine stretched upon the floor, she gave utterance to a piercing scream and fell down insensible.

In the horror and confusion that prevailed, I was unnoticed. I determined to leave the house, never to return, for I dreaded being brought before the public, as a witness, being a great hater of notoriety in any shape. (The reader may smile at this last remark; but I assure him, or her, that my frequent appearance before the public as a writer, has been the result of necessity—not of inclination.)

Accordingly, I left the house unobserved, and took lodgings for the remainder of the night at a hotel. But sleep visited me not, for my mind was too deeply engrossed with the bloody scenes which I had witnessed, to suffer the approach of "tired nature's sweet restorer." In the morning I arose early, and investigated the condition of my finances. The result of this examination was highly satisfactory, for I found that I was the possessor of a considerable sum of money.

I walked about the city until noon, uncertain how to act. I felt a strong disposition to travel, and see the world;—but I could not make up my mind in what direction to go. After a sumptuous dinner at Sandy Welch's "Terrapin Lunch,"—one of the most famous *restaurants* of the day—I indulged in a contemplative walk up Broadway. Such thoughts as these ran through my mind:—"I cannot help contrasting my present situation with the position I was in, three years ago. Then I was almost penniless, and gladly breakfasted on dry bread at a street pump; now I have three hundred dollars in my pocket, and have just dined like an epicurean prince. Then I was clad in garments that were coarse and cheap; now I am dressed in the finest raiment that money could procure. Then I had no trade; now I have a profession which will be to me an unfailing means of support. But, alas! then I was comparatively innocent, and ignorant of the wicked ways of the world; now, although only fifteen years of age, I am too thoroughly posted up on all the mysteries of city follies and vices. No matter: there's nothing like experience, after all."

Comforting myself with this philosophical reflection, I strolled on. A newsboy came along, bawling out, at the top of his voice—"Here's the extra *Sun*, with a full account of the two murders and suicide in William street last night—only one cent!" Of course I purchased a copy; and, upon perusing the account, I could not help smiling at the ludicrous and absurd exaggerations which it contained. It was a perfect modern tragedy of *Othello*, with Romaine as the Moor, Mrs. Romaine as Desdemona, and Anderson as a sort of cross between Iago and Michael Cassio. I was not alluded to in any way whatever, which caused me to rejoice exceedingly.*

Suddenly remembering the two letters which had been confided to my care by the unfortunate Anderson, I resolved to deliver them immediately. One was directed to a Mr. Sargent, in Pine street. I soon found the place, which was a large mercantile establishment. Over the door was the sign *"Anderson & Sargent."* This had been poor Anderson's place of business, and Sargent had been his partner. I entered, found Mr. Sargent in the counting-room, and delivered to him the letter. He opened it, read it through coolly, shrugged his shoulders, and said—

"I have already been made acquainted with the full particulars of this melancholy affair. Anderson was a clever fellow, and I'm sorry he's gone, although his death will certainly promote my interests. He gives me, in this letter, every necessary instruction as to the disposition of his property, and he also directs me to present you with the sum of two hundred dollars, both as an acknowledgement of your services and as a token of his friendship. I will fill out a check for the amount immediately."

This instance of Anderson's kindness and generosity, almost at the very moment of his death, deeply affected me; and, at the same time, I could not help feeling disgusted with the heartlessness displayed by Sargent, who regarded the tragical death of his partner merely as an event calculated to advance his own interests.

Having received the check, I withdrew from the august presence of Mr. Sargent, who was a tall, thin, hook-nosed personage, of unwholesome aspect and abrupt

* Many of my New York readers will remember the "William Street Tragedy," to which I have alluded. The bloody event created the most intense excitement at the time of its occurrence. Having witnessed the horrible affair, I have truly related all the facts concerning it.

manners. I drew the money at the bank, and then hastened to deliver the other letter, which was addressed to Miss Grace Arlington, whose residence was designated as being situated in one of the fashionable squares uptown. I had no difficulty in finding the house, which was of the most elegant and aristocratic appearance. My appeal to the doorbell was responded to by a smart-looking female domestic, who, on learning my errand, ushered me into the presence of her mistress. Miss Grace Arlington was a very lovely and delicate young lady, whose soft eyes beamed with tenderness and sensibility, whose voice was as sweet as the music of an angel's harp, while her step was as light as the tread of a fairy whose tiny feet will not crush the leaves of a rose. When I handed her the letter, and she recognized the well known handwriting, she bestowed upon me a winning and grateful smile which I shall never forget. My heart misgave me as she opened the missive, for I could well divine its contents; and I almost reproached myself for being the messenger of such evil tidings. I watched her closely as she read. She was naturally somewhat pale, but I saw her face grow ghastly white before she had read two lines. When she had finished the perusal of the fatal letter, she pressed her hand upon her breast, murmured "Oh God!" and would have fallen to the floor if I had not caught her in my arms.

"Curses on my stupidity!" I muttered, as I placed her insensible form upon a sofa—"I ought to have prepared her gradually for the terrible announcement which I knew that letter to contain!"

I rang the bell furiously, and the almost deafening summons was answered by half-a-dozen female servants, who, on seeing the condition of their young Mistress, set up a loud chorus of screams. The uproar brought Mr. Arlington, the father of the young lady, to the scene. He was a fine-looking old gentleman, a retired merchant and a *millionaire*. I hastened to explain to him all that had occurred, and Anderson's letter, which lay upon the floor, confirmed my statements. Mr. Arlington was horror-struck, for he, as well as his daughter, had until that moment been in happy ignorance of the bloody affair. The old gentleman had first established Anderson in business, and he had always cherished for that unfortunate young man the warmest friendship. No wonder, then, that he was overpowered when he became aware of the tragical end of him whom he had expected so shortly to become his son-in-law.

A celebrated physician, who resided next door, was sent for. He happened to be at home, and arrived almost instantly. He knelt down beside the broken-hearted girl, and, as his fingers touched her wrist, a look of profound grief settled upon his benevolent face.

"Well, Doctor," exclaimed Mr. Arlington, breathlessly, "what is the matter with my child? She will recover soon, will she not? It is merely a fainting fit produced by the reception of unwelcome news."

"Alas, sir!" replied the Doctor, in a tone of deep sympathy, as he brushed away the tears from his eyes—"I may as well tell you the melancholy truth at once. The sudden shock caused by the unwelcome news you speak of, has proved fatal; your daughter is dead!"

Poor old Arlington staggered to a seat, covered his face with his hands, and moaned in the agony of his spirits. Notwithstanding all his wealth, how I pitied him!

Seeing that I could be of no service whatever, I left the house of mourning and walked down town in a very thoughtful mood. I had already begun to enter upon an experience such as few youths of fifteen are ever called upon to encounter; and I wondered what the dim, uncertain Future had in store for me.

However, as the reader will see in the next chapter, I did not long suffer my mind to be intruded upon by melancholy reflections.

CHAPTER IV

In which I set forth upon my travels, and met with a great misfortune.

Having plenty of means at my disposal, I determined to enjoy myself to the full extent of my physical and intellectual capacity, for I remembered the graceful words of the charming poet who sung—

> "Go it while you're young:
> For, when you get old, you can't!"

Behold me, at the age of fifteen, fairly launched upon all the dissipations of a corrupt and licentious city! It is not without a feeling of shame that I make these confessions; but truth compels me to do so. I soon became thoroughly initiated into all the mysteries of high and low life in New York. In my daily and nightly peregrinations I frequently encountered my old friend Jack Slack; we never spoke, but on the contrary regarded each other with looks of enmity and defiance. Stronger and stronger within me grew the presentiment that this mysterious youth was destined to become my evil genius and the cause of a great misfortune. Therefore, whenever I met him, I could not help shuddering with dread.

Three years passed away in this manner, and I had reached the age of eighteen, with an unimpaired constitution and a firm belief that I was destined to exist for ever. I had lived luxuriously upon the earnings of my pen, for I was a regular contributor to the Knickerbroker Magazine and other popular periodicals. Having accumulated considerable money, notwithstanding my extravagance, I resolved to take a Southern tour, visiting Philadelphia, Washington, and other cities of note. Accordingly, one fine day, I found myself established in comfortable quarters, at the most fashionable hotel in the "city of brotherly love." I became a regular frequenter of the theatres and other places of amusement, and formed the acquaintance of many actors and literary people. It was here that I had the honor of being introduced to Booth, the great tragedian, now dead; to "Ned Forrest," the American favorite; to "Uncle" J.R. Scott, as fine a man as ever drank a noggin of ale or ate a "dozen raw," and to Major Richardson, the author of "Wacousta," and the "Monk Knight of St. John," the latter being one of the most voluptuous works ever written. Poor Major! his was a melancholy end. He was formerly a Major in the British army, and was a gentleman by birth, education and principle. Possessing a fine person, a generous heart and the most winning manners, he was a general favorite with his associates. He became the victim of rapacious publishers, and grew poor. Too proud to accept of assistance from his friends, he retired to obscure lodgings and there endeavored to support himself by the productions of his pen. But his spirit was broken and his intellect crushed by the base ingratitude of those who should have been his warmest friends. Often have I visited him in his garret— for he actually occupied one; and, with a bottle of whiskey before us, we have condemned the world as being full of selfishness, ingratitude and villainy. Winter came on, and the Major had no fuel, nor the means of procuring any. I have repeatedly called upon him and found him sitting in the intensely cold atmosphere of his miserable apartment, wrapped in a blanket and busily engaged in writing with a hand that was blue and trembled with the cold. He firmly refused to receive aid, in any shape, from his friends; and they were obliged to witness his gradual decay with sad hearts. The gallant Major always persisted in denying that he needed anything; he swore his garret was the most comfortable place in the world, and that the introduction of a fire would have been preposterous; he always affirmed with a round military oath, that he "lived like a fighting-cock," and was never without his bottle of wine at dinner; yet I once came upon him rather unexpectedly, and found him dining upon a crust of bread and a red herring. Sometimes, but rarely, he appeared at the theatres, and, upon such occasions, he was always scrupulously well-dressed, for Major Richardson would never appear abroad otherwise than as a gentleman. Want, privation and disappointment finally conquered him; he grew thin, and haggard, and melancholy, and reserved, and discouraged the visits of his friends who used to love to assemble at his humble lodgings and avail themselves of his splendid conversational powers, or listen to his personal reminiscences and racy anecdotes of military life. One morning he was found dead in his bed; and his death caused the most profound grief in the breasts of all who knew him as he deserved to be known, and who respected him for his many excellent qualities of head and heart. His remains received a handsome and appropriate burial; and many a tear was shed o'er the grave of him who had been a gallant soldier and a celebrated author, but a truly wronged and most unfortunate man.

The reader will, I am sure, pardon this digression, for I was anxious to do justice to the memory of a much-valued friend and literary brother. I now resume the direct course of my narrative, and come to the darkest portion of my career.

One night, in a billiard room, I had a very unpleasant encounter with an old acquaintance. I observed, at one of the tables, a young man whose countenance seemed strangely familiar to me, although I did not immediately recognize him. He was dressed in the extreme of fashion, and his upper lip was darkened by an incipient moustache—the result, doubtless, of many months of industrious culti-vation. A cigar was in his mouth, and a billiard-cue was in his hand; and he profusely adorned his conversation with the most extravagant oaths. Altogether, he seemed to be a very "fast" young man; and I puzzled my brain in endeavoring to remember where I had met him before.

Suddenly, he raised his eyes, and their gaze encountered mine; then I wondered that I had not before recognized "my old friend," Jack Slack!

"This fellow is my evil genius; he follows me everywhere," thought I, turning to leave the saloon. Would to heaven that I had never entered it! But regrets are useless now.

Jack stepped after me, and detained me. I instantly saw that trouble was about to come.

"Greenhorn," said Jack, with an air of angry reproach, as he laid his hand upon my shoulder—"why do you so continually avoid me? What in the devil's name have I ever done to deserve this treatment? Have I ever injured you in any way? Damn it, we are equal in age, and in disposition—let us be friends. I can put you in a way, in this city, to enjoy the tallest kind of sport. Give me your hand, and let's go up to the bar and take a social drink."

"Jack," said I, seriously and very calmly—"I will shake hands with you in friendship, but I candidly confess that I do not like you; and I believe that it will be better for us both not to associate together at all. Observe me! —I have no hard feelings against you;—you are a clever fellow, and generous to a fault; but something whispers to me that we must not be companions, and I therefore respectfully desire you not to speak to me again. Good night."*

I turned to go, but Jack placed himself directly in my path, and said, in a voice that was hoarse with passion—

"Stay and hear me. We must not part in this way. Do you think that I will tamely submit to be *cut* in a manner so disgraceful? Do you think that I am going to remain the object of an unfounded and ridiculous prejudice? Explain yourself, and apologize, or by G——, it will be the worse for you!"

"Explain myself—apologize!" I scornfully repeated—"you are a fool, and don't know to whom you are talking. Let me go."

"No!" passionately screamed my enraged antagonist, who was somewhat intoxicated—"you must stay and hear me out. I may as well throw off the mask at once. Know, then, that I hate you like hell-fire, and that, the very first time I saw you, I resolved to make you as bad as myself. Therefore did I induce you to drink, and visit disreputable places. The cool contempt with which you have always treated me, had increased my hatred ten-fold. I thirst for vengeance, and *I'll fix you yet!*"

"Do your worst," said I, contemptuously; and again did I essay to take my departure. Meanwhile, during the quarrel, the frequents of the saloon had gathered around and appeared to enjoy the scene highly.

"If he has given you any cause of offence, Jack, why don't you pitch into him?" suggested a half-drunken fellow who bore the enviable reputation of being a most expert pickpocket.

Jack unfortunately adopted the suggestion, and struck me with all his force. I of

* It is singular, but it is true, that a few nights prior to the tragical occurrences which I am about to relate, I saw, in a dream, a perfect and exact fore-shadow of the whole melancholy affair! Who can explain this mystery?

course returned the blow, with very tolerable effect.—Had the row commenced and terminated in mere *fisticuffs* all would have been well, and I should not now be called upon to write down the details of a bloody tragedy.

Drawing a dirk-knife from his breast, Jack attacked me with the utmost fury. I then did what any other person, situated as I was, would have done—I acted in my own defence. "Self-defence" is universally acknowledged to be the "first law of nature." There was I, a stranger, savagely attacked by a young man armed with a dangerous weapon, and surrounded by his friends and associates—a desperate set, who seemed disposed to assist in the task of demolishing me.

I quickly drew from my pocket a pistol, without which, at that time, I never travelled. Before, however, I could cock and level it, my infuriated enemy dashed his dirk-knife into my face, and the point entered my right eye. It was fortunate that the weapon did not penetrate the brain, and cause my instant death.

Maddened by the horrible pain which I suffered, and believing myself to be mortally wounded, I raised the pistol and discharged it. Jack Slack fell to the floor, a corpse, his head being shattered to pieces. *I never regretted the act.*

A cry of horror and dismay burst from the lips of all present, on witnessing this dreadful but justifiable deed of retribution.

"Gentlemen," said I, as the blood was trickling down my face—"I call upon you all to witness that I slew this young man in self-defence. He drove me to commit the deed, and I could not avoid it. I am willing and anxious to abide the decision of a jury of my countrymen; therefore, send for an officer, and I will voluntarily surrender myself into his custody."

Scarcely had I uttered these words, when the excruciating torment which I suffered caused me to faint away. When I recovered, I found myself in a prison-cell, with a bandage over my damaged optic, and a physician feeling my pulse.

"Ah!" said I, looking around, "I am in *limbo*, I see. Well, I do not fear the result. But, doctor, am I seriously injured—am I likely to kick the bucket?"

"Not at all," was the doctor's encouraging reply—"but you have lost the sight of your eye."

"Oh, is *that* all?" said I with a laugh—"well, I believe that it is said in the Bible somewhere, that it is better to enter the kingdom of heaven with one eye than to go to the devil with two."

The physician departed for his home, and I departed for the land of dreams. The pain of my wound had considerably mitigated, and I slept quite comfortably.

I have always been somewhat of a philosopher in the way of enduring the ills of life, and I tried to reconcile myself to my misfortune and situation with as good a grace as possible. In this I succeeded much better than might have been expected. When a person loses an eye and is at the same time imprisoned for killing another individual, it is certainly natural for that unfortunate person to yield to despair; but, seeing the uselessness of grief, I resolved to "face the music" with all the courage of which I was possessed.

Two or three days passed away, and I became almost well—for, to use a common expression, I owned the constitution of a horse. The newspapers which I was allowed to send out and purchase, made me acquainted with something that rather surprised me, for they communicated to me the information that Jack Slack, the young gentleman to whom I had presented a ticket of admission to the other world, was a person whose *real* name was John Shaffer, *alias* Slippery Jack, *alias* Jack Slack. His profession was that of a pickpocket, in which avocation he had always been singularly expert. He was well known to the police, and had been frequently imprisoned. I was gratified to see that the newspapers all justified me in what I had done, and predicted my honorable discharge from custody. That prediction proved correct; for, after I had been in confinement a week, the Grand Jury failed to bring a bill of indictment against me, and I was consequently set at liberty.

Tired of Philadelphia, I went to Washington. A New York member of Congress, with whom I was well acquainted, volunteered to show me the "lions;" and I had the honor of a personal introduction to Mr. Van Buren and other distinguished official personages. Some people would be surprised if they did but know of the splendid dissipation that prevails among the "dignitaries of the nation" at Washington.

I have seen more than one member of the United States Senate staggering through the streets, from what cause the reader will have no difficulty in judging. I have seen a great statesman, since deceased, carried from an after-dinner table to his chamber. I have seen the honorable Secretary of one of the National departments engaged in a brawl in a brothel. I have seen Representatives fighting in a bar-room like so many rowdies, and I have heard them use language that would disgrace a beggar in his drink. I need not allude to the many outrageous scenes which have been enacted in the councils of the nation; for the newspapers have already given them sufficient publicity.

Leaving Washington, I journeyed South, and, after many adventures which the limits of this work will not permit me to describe, I arrived in the City of New Orleans. I had no difficulty in procuring a lucrative situation as reporter on a popular daily newspaper; and enjoyed free access to all the theatres and other places of amusement.—I remained in New Orleans just one year; but, not liking the climate,—and finding, moreover, that I was living too *"fast,"* and accumulating no money,—I resolved to "pull up stakes" and start in a Northerly direction. Accordingly, I returned to Philadelphia.

It would have been much better for me had I remained in New Orleans, for the hardest kind of times prevailed in the "Quaker City," on my arrival there. It was almost impossible to obtain employment of any description; and many actors, authors and artists, as well as mechanics, were most confoundedly "hard up." I soon exhausted the contents of my purse; and, like the Prodigal Son, "began to be in want."

One fine day, in a very disconsolate mood, I was wandering through an obscure street, when I encountered a former lady acquaintance, whom, I trust, the reader has not forgotten.

But the particulars of that unexpected encounter, and the details of what subsequently transpired, are worthy of a separate chapter.

CHAPTER V

*I encountered a lady acquaintance, and, like a knight errant of old,
became the champion of beauty.*

A musical voice pronounced my name; and looking up, I saw a very handsome woman seated at the window of a rather humble wooden tenement, the first floor of which was occupied as a cheap grocery. I immediately recognised my old acquaintance, Mrs. Raymond, the pretty widow of the fashionable boarding-house in William street, New York—she who had carried on an intrigue with Mr. Romaine. I have, in a former chapter, described the terrible affair in which Romaine slew his wife and Anderson her paramour—and then killed himself.

I need scarcely say that this encounter with Mrs. Raymond, under such peculiar circumstances, rather astonished me. I had known her as a lady of wealth, and the most elegant and fastidious tastes; and yet here I found her living in an obscure and disreputable portion of the city, and occupying a house which none but the victims of poverty would ever have consented to dwell in.

"Wait until I come down and conduct you up stairs," said Mrs. Raymond; and she disappeared from the window.

In a few moments she opened the door leading to the upper part of the house; and having warmly shaken hands with me, she desired me to follow her. I complied, and was shown into an apartment on the second floor.

"This is my room, and my only one; don't laugh at it," said Mrs. Raymond, with a melancholy smile.

I looked around me. The room was small, but scrupulously clean; and, notwithstanding the scantiness and humility of the furniture, a certain air of refinement prevailed. I have often remarked that it is impossible for a person who has been accustomed to the elegancies of life, to become so low, in fortune or character, as to entirely lose every trace of former superiority.

"You may break, you may ruin the vase, if you will,
But the scent of the roses will cling 'round it still!"

Mrs. Raymond's apartment merely contained a fine table, two or three common chairs, a closet, a bed, and a harp—the relic of better and happier days. The uncarpeted floor was almost as white as snow—and certainly no snow could be purer or whiter than the drapery of her unpretending couch.

We sat down—I and my beautiful hostess—and entered into earnest conversation. I examined the lady with attention. She had lost none of her former radiant beauty, and I fancied that a shade of melancholy rather enhanced her charms. Her dress was coarse and plain, but very neat, like everything else around her. Never before, in the course of my rather extensive experience, had I beheld a more interesting and fascinating woman; and never shall I forget that day, as we sat together in her little room, with the soft sunlight of a delightful May afternoon pouring in through the windows.

344

"It haunts me still, though many a year has fled,
Like some wild melody."

"My dear friend," said Mrs. Raymond, accompanying her words with a look of
the deepest sympathy, "I see that you have met with a great misfortune. Pardon me,
if—"

"You shall know all," said I; and then I proceeded to make her acquainted with
all that had happened to me since the occurrence of the William street tragedy. Of
course, I did not omit to give her the full particulars of my fatal affray with Jack
Slack, as that accounted for the "great misfortune" to which she had alluded. When
I had finished my narration, the lady sighed deeply and said—

"Ah, my friend, we have both been made the victims of cruel misfortune. You
see me to-day penniless and destitute; I, formerly so rich, courted and admired.
Have you the time and patience to listen to my melancholy story?"

I eagerly answered in the affirmative; and Mrs. Raymond spoke as follows:—

"After that terrible affair in William street—the recollection of which still
curdles my blood with horror—I took up my abode in a private family at the lower
end of Broadway. I soon formed the acquaintance of a gentleman of fine appearance, and agreeable address, named Livingston, who enjoyed the enviable reputation of being a person of wealth and a man of honor. I was pleased with him, and
noticing my partiality, he made violent love to me. Tired of living the life of a single
woman—desirous of securing a protection, and wishing to become an honorable
wife instead of a mistress—I did not reject him, for he moved in the very highest
circles, and seemed to be in every way unobjectionable. I will not weary you with
the details of our courtship; suffice it to say that we were married. We took an
elegant house in one of the up-town avenues; and, for a time, all went well. After
a while, I discovered that my husband had no fortune whatever; but I loved him too
well to reproach him—and besides, he had never represented himself to me as
being a man of wealth; it was the circle in which he moved which had bestowed
upon him that reputation. Also, I considered that my fortune was sufficient for us
both. Therefore, the discovery of his poverty did not in the least diminish my
regard for him. It was not long before the extensive demands which he kept
constantly making upon my purse, alarmed me; I feared that he had fallen into
habits of gambling; and I ventured to remonstrate with him upon his extravagance.
He confessed his fault, entreated my forgiveness, and promised amendment. Of
course, I forgave him; for a loving wife can forgive anything in her husband but
infidelity. But he did *not* reform; he continued his ruinous career; and my fortune
melted away like snow beneath the rays of the sun. The man possessed such an
irresistible influence over me, that I never could refuse an application on his part
for money. I believed that he sincerely loved me, and that was enough for me—I
asked for no more. I entertained romantic notions of 'love in a cottage.'

"At length my fortune was all gone—irrevocably gone. 'No matter,' I thought—
'I have still my dear husband left; nothing can ever take him away from me. I will
share poverty with him, and we shall be happy together.' We gave up our splendid
mansion, and sold our magnificent furniture, and rented a small but respectable

house. And now my blood boils to relate how that villain Livingston served me—
for he was a villain, a cool, deliberate, black-hearted one. He deserted me, carrying
off with him what little money and the few jewels I still possessed, thus leaving me
entirely destitute. But what added to my affliction,—nay, I should rather say my
maddening rage, was a note which the base scoundrel had written and left behind
him, in which he mockingly begged to be excused for his absence, and stated that
he had other wives to attend to in other cities. 'I never loved you,' he wrote in that
infamous letter, every word of which is branded upon my heart as with a pen of
fire—'I never loved you, and my only object in marrying you was to enjoy your
fortune; I have no further use for you. It may console you to know that the principal
portion of the large sums of money which you gave me from time to time, was
applied, not as you imagined to the payment of gambling debts, but to the support
of two voluptuous mistresses of mine, whom I kept in separate establishments that
were furnished with almost regal splendor. Thus did you unconsciously contribute
to the existence of two rivals, who received a greater share of my attentions than
you did. In conclusion, as you are now without resources, I would advise you to sell
your charms to the highest bidder. There are many wealthy and amorous gentlemen in New York, who will pay you handsomely for your smiles and kisses. I shall
not be jealous of their attentions to my *sixth wife!* I intend to marry six more within
the next six months. Yours truly, LIVINGSTON.' Thus wrote the accursed
wretch, for whom I had sacrificed everything—fortune, position in society, and
friends; for who among my fashionable acquaintances, would associate with an
impoverished and deserted wife? Not one. Furious at Livingston's treatment of me,
I resolved to follow him, even unto the end of the earth, in order to avenge my
wrongs. By careful inquiry, I learned that he had taken his departure for the western
part of the state of Pennsylvania. You will hardly credit it, but it is God's truth, that
being without money to pay travelling expenses, I actually set out *on foot*, and
travelled through New Jersey until I reached this city. I subsisted on the road by
soliciting the hospitality of the farmers, which was in most cases grudgingly and
scantily bestowed, for *benevolence* is not a prominent characteristic of the New
Jersey people,* and besides, there was certainly something rather suspicious in the
idea of a well-dressed woman travelling on foot, and alone. On my arrival here in
Philadelphia, I found myself worn out and exhausted by the fatiguing journey
which I had performed. Having called upon some kind Quaker ladies of whose
goodness I had often heard, I told them my sad history, which aroused their
warmest sympathies. They placed me in this apartment, paid a month's rent in
advance, purchased for me the articles of furniture which you see, and obtained for
me some light employment. I worked industriously, and almost cheerfully, my
object being to earn money enough to carry me to Pittsburg, in Western
Pennsylvania, where, I have reason to believe, the villain has located himself.

"In my moments of leisure, I longed for some means of recreation; for I saw no
company, and was very lonesome. So I wrote on to New York, and through the

---

* Some people imagine that New Jersey belongs to the United States. That opinion I hold to be
erroneous.

agency of a kind friend, had my harp sent out to me here, the rest of my poor furniture being presented to that friend. Then did the divine charm of music lighten the burden of my sorrows. One circumstance rather discouraged me: I found that with the utmost industry I could not earn more than sufficient to pay my rent and other necessary expenses, although I lived frugally, almost on bread and water, except on Sundays, when I would manage to treat myself to a cup of tea. You may smile at these trifling details, my dear friend, but I mention them to show you the hardships and privations to which poor women are often exposed. My landlady, who keeps the grocery store down stairs, is a coarse, vulgar, hard-hearted woman; and, when I was thrown out of employment in consequence of the hardness of the times, and could not pay her rent, she not only abused me dreadfully, but annoyed me by making the most infamous suggestions, proposing that I should embrace a life of prostitution, and offering to procure me plenty of 'patrons.' I, of course, indignantly repelled the horrible proposals—but, would you believe it? she actually introduced into my apartment an old, gray-haired and well-dressed libertine, for a purpose which you can easily imagine. The old villain, however, decamped when I displayed a small dagger, and declared that I would kill myself rather than become his victim. This conduct of mine still further incensed my landlady against me; and I expect every moment to be turned out into the street. It is true that I might raise a small sum of money by the sale of my harp, which is a very superior instrument, but as it was the gift of my first husband, I cannot endure the thought of parting with it, for there are associated with it some of the fondest recollections of my life. I am sure that if those kind Quaker ladies had known the character of this house and the neighborhood around it, they would not have placed me here. Heaven only knows what I have suffered, and still suffer. I live in constant dread that some ruffian, instigated by my landlady, who wishes to gratify both her avarice and malignity, may break in upon me some time when I am off my guard, and make me the victim of a brutal outrage. This fear keeps me awake nights, and makes my days miserable. Nor is this all; I have not tasted food since the day before yesterday."

"Good God!" I exclaimed—"is it possible? Oh, accursed be the circumstances which have made us both so misfortunate; and doubly accursed be that scoundrel Livingston, the author of all your sorrows. By heavens! I will seek him out, and terribly punish him for his base conduct towards you. Yes, my dear Mrs. Raymond—for such I shall continue to call you, notwithstanding your marriage to that monster Livingston—rest assured that your wrongs shall be avenged.—The villain shall rue the day when he made a play-thing of a woman's heart, robbed her of her fortune, and then left her to poverty and despair!"

[This language of mine may seem rather theatrical and romantic; but the reader will please to remember that I was only nineteen years of age at the time of its utterance—a period of life not remarkable for sobriety of language or discretion of conduct. Were that interview to take place *to-day*, I should probably thus express myself: —"My dear Mrs. Raymond, I advise you to forget the d——d rascal and put on the tea-kettle, while I rush out and negotiate for some *grub!*"]

Mrs. Raymond gratefully pressed my hand, and said—

"I thank you for thus espousing my cause; —but, my dear friend, *mine* must be the task of punishing the villain. No other hand but *mine* shall strike the blow that will send his black, polluted soul into eternity!"

These fierce words, which were pronounced with the strongest emphasis, caused me to look at my fair hostess with some degree of astonishment; and no wonder—for the quiet, elegant lady had been suddenly transferred into the enraged and revenge-thirsting woman. She looked superbly beautiful at that moment; —her cheeks glowed, her eyes sparkled, and her bosom heaved like the waves of a stormy sea.

"Well," said I—"we will discuss that matter hereafter. Have the goodness to excuse my absence for a few minutes. I have a little errand to perform."

She smiled, for she knew the nature of my errand. I went down stairs and walked up the street, in the greatest perplexity; for—let me whisper it into your ear, reader, I had not a sufficient amount of the current coin of the realm in my pockets to create a gingle upon a tomb-stone.

"What the devil shall I do?" said I to myself—"here I have constituted myself the champion and protector of a hungry lady, and haven't enough money to purchase a salt herring! Shall I *show up* my satin waistcoat? No, d——n it, that won't do, for I *must* keep up appearances. Can't I borrow a trifle from some of my friends? No, curse them, they are all as poverty-stricken as I am! I have it!—I'll test the benevolence of some *gospel-wrestler*, and borrow the devil's impudence for the occasion."

I walked rapidly into a more fashionable quarter of the city, looking attentively at every door-plate. At last I saw the name, *"Reverend Phineas Porkley."** That was enough. Without a moment's hesitation I mounted the steps and rang the bell savagely. The door was opened by a fat old flunkey with a red nose of an alarming aspect. I rushed by him into the hall, dashed my hat recklessly upon the table, and shouted—

"Where's Brother Porkley? Show me to him instantly! Don't dare say he's out, for I know that he's at home! It's a matter of life and death! Woman dying—children starving—and the devil to pay generally. Wake Snakes, you fat porpoise, and conduct me to your master!"

The flunkey's red nose grew pale with astonishment and fear; yet he managed to stammer out—

" 'Pon my life, sir—really, sir—Mr. Porkley, sir—he's at home, certainly, sir—in his library, sir—writing his next Sunday's sermons, sir—can't see any one, sir—"

"Catiff, conduct me to his presence!" I exclaimed, in a deep voice, after the manner of the dissatisfied brigand who desires to "mub" the false duke in his own ancestral halls.

Not daring to disobey, the trembling flunkey led the way up one flight of stairs and pointed to a door, which I abruptly opened. There, in his library, sat Brother

---

* In this, as in several other cases, I have used a fictitious name, inasmuch as a number of the persons alluded to in this narrative are still living.

Porkley, a monstrously fat man with a pale, oily face that contained about as much expression as the surface of a cheese.

But how was Brother Porkley engaged when I intruded upon him? Was he writing a sermon, or attentively perusing some good theological work? Neither. Oh, then perhaps the excellent man was at prayer. Wrong again. He was merely smoking a short pipe and sipping a glass of brandy and water, like a sensible man— for is it not better to take one's comfort than to play the part of a hypocrite? *I* think so.

"My dear Brother Porkley," cried I, rushing forward and grasping the astonished parson by the hand, which I shook with tremendous violence, "I come on a mission of Charity and Love! I come as a messenger of Benevolence! I come as a dove of Peace with the olive branch in my claw! Porkley, greatest philanthropist of the age, *come down*, for suffering humanity requires your assistance!"

"What do you mean, sir?" demanded the reverend Falstaff, as he vainly strove to extricate his hand from my affectionate grasp, "who are you and what do you want?"

"Brother," said I, in a broken voice, as I dashed an imaginary tear from the tip end of my nose, "in the next street there dwells a poor but pious family, consisting of a widow woman and her twelve small children. They live in a cellar, sir, one hundred feet below the surface of the earth, in the midst of darkness, horror and bull-frogs, which animals they are compelled to eat in a raw state, in order to exist. Yes *sir!*"

"But what is all this to me?"

"Much, sir, you are a Christian—a clergyman—and a trump. If you do not assist that distressed family, your reputation for benevolence will not be worth the first red cent. Those children are howling for food—bull-frogs being scarce—and that fond mother is dying of small-pox."

"Small-pox!"

"Yes *sir!* I have attended her during the last five nights, and fear that I am infected with the disease; but I am willing to lose my life in the holy cause of charity."

"Good God, sir! You will communicate the disease to *me!* Let go my hand, sir, and leave this house before you load the air with pestilence!"

"No, *sir!* I couldn't think of leaving until you have done something for the relief of that distressed widow and her twelve small children."

"D——n the distressed widow and—bless my soul! what am I saying? My good young man, what will satisfy you?"

"Five dollars, reverend sir."

"Here, then, here is the money. Now go, go quickly. Every moment that you remain here is pregnant with evil. Pray make haste!"

"But won't you come and pray with the distressed widow and her—"

"No! If I do may I be—blessed! *Will* you go!"

"I'm off, old Porkhead!"

With these words I bolted out of the library, stumbled over a corpulent cat that was quietly reposing on the landing, descended the stairs in two leaps, upset the fat flunkey in the hall, and gained the street in safety with my booty—a five dollar city bill. I hastened back towards the residence of Mrs. Raymond, but stopped at an eating-saloon on the way and loaded myself with provisions ready cooked. I did not forget to purchase two bottles of excellent wine. Thus provided, I entered the apartment of Mrs. Raymond, who received me with a smile of gratitude and joy which I shall never forget.

We sat down to the table with sharp appetites, and did full justice to the repast, which was really most excellent. The wine raised our spirits, and, forgetting our misfortunes, merrily did we chat about old times in New York, carefully omitting the slightest allusion to the bloody affair in William street. When we had finished one bottle, Mrs. Raymond favored me with an air upon her harp, which she played with exquisite skill. After executing a brilliant Italian waltz, she played and sang that plaintive song:

> "The light of other days have faded,
> And all their glory's past."

Just as the song was finished, there came a loud knocking at the door.

"It is my landlady," said Mrs. Raymond, in a low tone, "conceal yourself, and you will see how she treats me."

I stepped into the closet; but through a crevice in the door I could see all that transpired.

A fat, vulgar-looking woman entered with a consequential air, and a face inflamed by drink, gave her a peculiarly repulsive appearance. Of course she was utterly unconscious of my presence in the house. Taking up her position in the middle of the apartment, she placed her hands upon her hips, and said, in a hoarse and angry voice—

"Come up out o' that! *You're* a pretty one to be playing and singing, when you owe me for two months' rent. You have been feasting, too, I see. Where did you get the money? Why didn't you pay it to *me*? Have you any money left?"

"No I have not."

"Come up out o' that! Why the devil don't you sell that humstrum of yours, that harp, I mean, and raise the wind? It will bring a good ten dollars, I'll be sworn. And why don't you take my advice and earn money as other women do? You are handsome, the men would run after you like mad. That nice, rich old gentleman, Mr. Letcher, that I brought to see you, would have given you any amount of money if you had only treated him kindly—but you frightened him away. Come up out o' that! Now, what do you mean to do? I can't let you stay here any longer unless you raise some money. This evening I'll fetch another nice gentleman here; and if you cut up any of your *tantrums* with *him*, I'll bundle you out into the street this very night."

"If you bring any man here to molest me," said Mrs. Raymond, spiritedly—"I will stab him to the heart, and then kill myself."

"Come out o' that," screamed the landlady, approaching Mrs. Raymond with a threatening look, "don't think to frighten me with your tragical airs. I must have my money, and so I'll take this harp and sell it, in spite of you!"

She seized upon the instrument and was about to carry it off, when I rushed forth from my place of concealment, exclaiming—

"Come up out o' that! Drop that instrument, you old harridan, or I'll drop *you!* Do not imagine that this lady is entirely friendless. I am here to protect her."

The astounded landlady put down the harp and began to mutter many apologies, for I was extremely well dressed, and she probably believed me to be some person of consequence who had become the protector and patron of Mrs. Raymond.

"Oh, sir—I'm sure, sir—I didn't mean, sir—if I had known, sir—I beg a thousand pardons, sir—"

"Come up out o' that!" cried I, "leave the room, instantly."

The landlady vanished with a celerity that was rather remarkable, considering her extreme corpulence.

After a short pause, Mrs. Raymond said to me—

"You see to what abuse my circumstances subject me."

"Would to God my circumstances were such as to render you that assistance you so much need; would that I could raise you from such unendurable misery! But to speak without equivocation, my condition is as penniless as your own."

"Then you can, indeed, sympathize with my distress."

"Most sincerely; but you must not go alone in quest of that villainous husband; —and money will be necessary."

"This harp will—"

"Oh, no—you can never part with it."

"I must."

"Then let it be but temporarily. There is a pawnbroker's shop on the next square, there we can redeem it—if you can for a time endure to have it removed from your sight."

"No matter," said my heroine, undauntedly, "a wronged woman can endure anything when she is in pursuit of vengeance. The weather is delicious; we will travel leisurely, and have a very pleasant time. Should our money become exhausted, we will solicit the hospitality of the good old Pennsylvania farmers, who are renowned for their kindness to travellers, and who will not refuse a bite and a sup, or a night's shelter, to two poor wanderers. If you refuse to accompany me, I will go alone."

"I will go with you to the end of the earth!" I exclaimed, with enthusiasm, for I could not help admiring the noble courage of that beautiful woman, whose splendid countenance now glowed with all the animation of anticipated vengeance.

She pressed my hand warmly, in acknowledgement of my devotion; and then, having put on her bonnet and shawl, she announced herself as being in readiness to set out.

"I have no valuables of any kind," said she, "and the landlady is welcome to this furniture, which will discharge my indebtedness to her. I shall return to this house no more."

I shouldered the harp, and we left the house without encountering the amiable landlady.

To reach the nearest pawnbroker's, it was necessary to pass through one of the principal streets. To my dismay a crowd of actors, reporters and others were assembled upon the steps of a hotel. The rascals spied me out before I could cross over; and so, putting on as bold a front as possible, I walked on pretending not to notice them, while a "running commentary," something like the following, was kept up until I was out of hearing:

"*Stag his knibbs,*"* said the "heavy man" of the Arch street theatre.

"Thompson, give us a tune!" bawled out a miserable wretch of a light comedian, or "walking gentleman."

"Jem Baggs, the *Wandering Minstrel*, by G——!" yelled a pitiful demon of a newspaper reporter.

"Who is that magnificent woman accompanying him?" inquired a dandy editor, raising his eye-glass and surveying my fair companion with an admiring gaze.

"Egad! she's a beauty!" cried all the fellows, in a chorus. Mrs. Raymond blushed and smiled. It was evident that these expressions of admiration were not displeasing to her.

"Excuse those gentlemen," said I to her, apologetically—"they are all particular friends of mine."

"I am not offended; indeed they are very complimentary," responded the lady, with a gay laugh. She had the most musical laugh in the world, and the most beautiful one to *look at*, for it displayed her fine, pearly teeth to the most charming advantage.

We reached the pawnbroker's and I went boldly in while Mrs. Raymond waited for me outside the door, for I did not wish her to be exposed to the mortification of being stared at by those who might be in the shop.

The pawnbroker was a gentleman of Jewish persuasion, and possessed a nose like the beak of an eagle. He took the instrument and examined it carefully,

"Vat is dish?" said he, "a harp? Oh, dat is no use. We have tousands such tings offered every day. Dere is no shecurity in mushical instruments. Vat do you want for it?"

"Ten dollars," I replied, in a tone of decision.

"Can't give it," said the Israelite—"it ish too moosh. Give you eight."

"No," said I, taking up the harp and preparing to depart.

"Here, den," said *my uncle*, "I will give you ten, but only shust to *oblishe* you—mind dat."

I duly thanked him for his willingness to *oblige* me. Uncle Moses gave me the ticket and money; and I left the shop and rejoined Mrs. Raymond, to whom I handed over the duplicate and the X.

---

* It is not generally known among "outsiders," that circus people and actors are in the habit of using among themselves a sort of flash language which enables them to converse about professional and other affairs without being understood by outside listeners. If I had room, I could relate many amusing anecdotes under this head. "*Stag his knibbs*" signifies "*Look at him.*"

"I will take the ticket," said she, smiling—"but you shall keep the money, for I appoint you my cashier."

At the suggestion of my fair friend we now sought out a cheap second-hand clothing establishment, which, fortunately, was kept by a woman, who, when matters were confidentially explained to her, readily entered into our plan. Mrs. Raymond and the woman retired into a rear apartment, while I remained in the shop.

Half or three-quarters of an hour passed away. At last the door of the inner apartment was opened and there entered the shop a young person whom I did not immediately recognize. This person seemed to be a very beautiful boy, neatly dressed in a cloth jacket and cap, and possessing a from of the most exquisite symmetry. This pretty and interesting lad approached me, and tapping me playfully upon the cheek, said—

"My dear fellow, how do you like me now? Have I not made a change for the better? How queenly I feel in this strange rig!"

It was of course Mrs. Raymond who addressed me. Her disguise was perfect; never before had I seen so complete a transformation, even upon the stage. No one would have suspected her to be otherwise than what she seemed, a singularly delicate and handsome boy, apparently about sixteen years of age.

I congratulated the lady upon the admirable appearance which she made in her newly adopted costume, but expressed my regret that she should have been compelled to part with her magnificent hair.

"There was no help for it," said she, laughing. "I confess that I experienced some regret when I felt my hair tumbling from my shoulders; but the loss was unavoidable, for those tresses would have betrayed my sex. This good woman, here, proved to be a very expert barber." Reflecting that a coarse suit of clothes would be just as good and better, for a dusty road, than a fine suit of broadcloth, I made a bargain with the proprietress of the shop to exchange my garments for coarse ones of fustian, she giving me a reasonable sum to counter-balance the great superiority of my wardrobe. This arrangement was speedily completed, and I found myself suddenly transformed into a rustic looking individual, who, in appearance, certainly deserved the title of a perfect "greenhorn."

All parties begin satisfied, I and my fair companion departed. In the evening, having supped, we went to the theatre, where I revenged myself upon the "heavy man," and the "light comedian," who had in the afternoon made merry at my expense for carrying the harp, by getting up a hiss for the former gentleman, who knew not one single word of his part, and by hitting the latter individual upon the nose with an apple, for which latter feat (as the actor was a great favorite,) I was hounded out of the theatre, and narrowly escaped being carried to the watch-house. I and my fair friend then took lodgings for the night at a neighboring hotel.

CHAPTER VI

In which is introduced a celebrated Comedian from the Theatre Royal,
Drury Lane, London.

The next morning, bright and early, "two travellers might have been seen" crossing one of the ponderous bridges that lead over the Schuylkill from Philadelphia to the opposite shore. The one was a stout young cavalier, arrayed in fustian brown; the other was a pretty youth, attired in broadcloth blue, and brilliant was his flashing eye, and coal-black was his hair. By my troth, good masters, a fairer youth ne'er touched the light guitar within the boudoir of my lady.

"Now, by my knightly oath," quoth he in fustian brown, "my soul expands in the soft beauty of this rosy morn, my blood dances merrily through every vein, and I feel like eating a thundering good breakfast at the next hostelrie. —What sayest *thou*, fair youth?"

"Of a truth, Sir George," quoth he in broadcloth blue, in a voice of liquid melody, "I am hungered, and would gladly sit me down before a flagon of coffee, and a goodly platter of ham and eggs."

"Bravely spoken," quoth the stout young cavalier, with watering mouth; and then, relapsing into silence, the train journeyed onward.

Soon they paused before a goodly hostelrie, which bore upon its swinging sign-board the device of "The Pig and the Snuffers."

"What ho, within there! House, house, I say!" hastily roared the youth in fustian brown, as he vigorously applied his cowhide boot to the door of the inn.

Forth came mine host of the Pig and Snuffers—a jovial knave and a right merry one, I ween, with mighty paunch and nose of ruby red. Now, by the rood! a funnier knight than this same Rupert Harmon, ne'er drew a foaming tankard of nut-brown ale, or blew a cloud from a short pipe in a chimney corner.

"Welcome, my masters—a right good welcome," quoth the fat host of the Pig and Snuffers.

"Bestir thyself, knave," quoth the cove in fustian brown, as he entered the inn followed by the pretty youth in broadcloth blue—"beshrew me, I am devilish hungry, and athirst likewise. Knave, a stoup of sack, and then let ham, eggs and coffee smoke upon the festive board!"

"To hear is to obey," said he of the Pig and Snuffers, as he waddled out of the room in order to give the necessary instructions for breakfast.

It came! Ha, ha! Shall I attempt to describe that breakfast? Nay—my powers are inadequate to the task.

But, dropping the style of my friend, G.P.R. James, the great English novelist, I shall continued my narrative in my own humble way.

We breakfasted, and cheerfully set out upon our journey. The weather was delightful; the odor of spring flowers perfumed the air, and the soft breeze made music amid the branches of the trees. On every side of us were the evidences of agricultural prosperity—fine, spacious farm-houses, immense barns, vast orchards, and myriads of thriving domestic animals. Sturdy old Dutch farmers, jogging leisurely along in their great wagons to and from the city, saluted us with a hearty "good morrow;" and one jolly old fellow who was returning home after having disposed of a quantity of produce, insisted upon giving us a "lift" in his wagon. So we got in, and about dark reached the farmer's home—a substantial and comfortable mansion that indicated its owner to be a man of considerable wealth.

I was surprised at the powers of endurance exhibited by my fair friend, who after a pretty hard day's journey, exhibited not the slightest symptom of fatigue. She kept up a most exuberant flow of spirits, and seemed delighted with the novelty of the journey which we had commenced. She was truly a charming companion, full of wit, sentiment and intelligence; and I look back upon those days with a sigh of regret—for such unalloyed happiness I shall never see again.

The good old farmer, with characteristic hospitality, declared that we should go not further that night; and we gladly availed ourselves of his kindness. He introduced us to his wife—a fine old lady, and a famous knitter of stockings—and also to his only daughter, a plump, rosy, girl about eighteen years old. This damsel surveyed my disguised companion with a look of the most intense admiration; and I saw at once that she had actually fallen in love with Mrs. Raymond!

"There will be some fun here," said I to myself—"I must keep dark and watch the movements. The idea of a woman falling love with one of her own sex, is rather rich!"

After a capital supper—ye gods, what German sausages!— I accepted the old farmer's invitation to inspect his barn, cattle, &c. My fair friend was taken possession of by the amorous Dutch damsel, who seemed to be particularly anxious to display the beauties of her *dairy*, which is always the pride of a farmer's daughter. I could not help laughing at the look of comical embarrassment which poor Mrs. Raymond assumed, when the buxom young lady seized her and dragged her off.

I of course praised the farmer's barn and stock with the air of a judge of such matters, and we returned to the house, where I applied myself to the task of entertaining the old lady, and in this I succeeded so well, that she presented me with a nice pair of stockings of her own knitting.

After a while, my fair friend and the farmer's daughter returned;—and I noticed that Mrs. Raymond looked exceedingly annoyed and perplexed, while the countenance of the Dutch damsel exhibited anger and disappointment. I could easily guess how matters stood; but, of course, I said nothing.

During the evening, my fair friend had an opportunity of speaking to me in private; and she said to me, with a deep blush, although she could not help smiling as she spoke—

"I have something to tell you which is really very awkward and ridiculous, yet you can't think how it vexes me. Now don't laugh at me in that provoking manner, but listen. That great, silly Dutch girl, after showing me her dairy, which is really a very pretty affair and well worth seeing, suddenly made the most furious love to me—supposing me, of course, to be what I seem, a boy. I was terribly confused and frightened, and knew not what to say, nor how to act. Throwing her fat arms around me, she declared that I was so handsome that she could not resist me, and that I must become her lover. I told her that I was too young to know anything about love; and then the creature volunteered to teach me all about it. Then I intimated that I could not think of marrying at present, as I was too poor to support a wife; but she laughed at the idea of matrimony, and said that she only wanted me to be her little lover. Finally I effected my release by promising to meet her about midnight, in the orchard by the gate. Now, is not all this very dreadful—to be persecuted by a big, unrelenting Dutch girl in this manner?"

I roared with laughter. It was rude and ungallant, I confess; but how could I help it? Mrs. Raymond made a desperate effort to become angry; but so ludicrous was the whole affair, that she could not resist the contagious influence of my mirth; and she, too, almost screamed with laughter.

When our mirth had somewhat subsided, I inquired—

"Well, are you going to keep an appointment with the Dutch Venus?"

"What an absurd question! Of course not! She may wait by the orchard gate all night, for what *I* care—the great, lubbery fool!"

"What do you say to *my* meeting her at the appointed time and place? I will act as your representative, and make every satisfactory explanation."

"You shall do no such thing. How dare you make such a proposition? I am perfectly astonished at your impudence!"

The next morning, after breakfast, we prepared to depart. I saw that the farmer's daughter regarded my fair friend with a ferocious look. The damsel had probably passed two or three hours in the night air, waiting for her "faithless swain."

Having thanked the good old farmer for his hospitality, and received his blessing in return, we departed.

It is not my intention to weary the reader with the details of each day's travel; indeed, my limited space would not admit of such particularity. I shall, however, as briefly as possible, relate such incidents of the journey as I may deem especially worthy of mention. When we reached Lancaster, we discovered that our funds had entirely given out, for we had lived expensively at taverns on the way, instead of exercising a judicious economy. How to raise a fresh supply of money was now the question, and one most difficult to be answered. But an unexpected stroke of good fortune was in store for us. Strolling into the bar-room of the principal hotel, I saw a play-bill stuck up on the wall. This I read with avidity; and then, to my great satisfaction, I became aware of the fact that an old friend of mine, one Bill Pratt, a travelling actor and manager, had "just arrived in Lancaster with a talented company of comedians, who would that evening have the honor of appearing before the ladies and gentlemen of the above named place in a series of entertainments at once Moral, Chaste, Instructive and Classical, at the Town Hall. Admission—twelve-and-a-half cents."

So read the play-bill. I and my fair friend immediately posted to the Town Hall, and there I found Brother Pratt busily engaged in arranging his stage, putting up his scenery, &c. He was prodigiously glad to see me.* Among his company I recognized several old acquaintances. I introduced my travelling companion to the

* All who have the good fortune to know Bill Pratt *alias* "The Original Beader," will acknowledge that a wittier, funnier or better man never breathed.

ladies and gentlemen of the profession; and I do not think that any of them suspected her true sex. We all dined together at the hotel; and a merry party we certainly were, "within the limits of becoming mirth." Wit sparkled, conundrums puzzled, bad puns checked, and rich jokes awoke the laughing echoes of the old dining-hall. Happy people are those travelling actors—happy because they are careless, and, in the enjoyment of to-day, think not of the morrow. Are they not true philosophers?

> "Oh, what's the use of sighing,
> Since time is on the wing—
> To-morrow we'll be dying,
> So merrily, merrily sing—
> Tra, la, la!"

After dining in company with Brother Pratt I seated myself upon the piazza; and, while we smoked our cheroots, we recalled the past, dwelt upon the present, and anticipated the future.

After a considerable amount of desultory conversation, the Brother suddenly asked me—

"Who is that handsome little fellow with whom you are travelling?"

"Oh, he ran away from home in order to see something of the world, as well as to avoid being apprenticed to a laborious trade," was my reply, for I did not consider it at all necessary to let my friend into the secret.

"He's a lad of spirit, and I like him," rejoined the Brother. "If he went upon the stage, what a splendid court page he'd make! But where are you going? Tell me all about it."

I told the Brother all that was necessary for him to know.

"And so," said he, reflectively, "you are entirely out of funds. That's bad. We must raise you some cash, in some way or other. I will immediately cause bills to be printed, announcing that 'the manager has the pleasure of informing his numerous patrons that he has, at enormous expense, succeeded in effecting a brief engagement with Mr. George Thompson, the celebrated comedian from the Theatre Royal, Drury Lane, London, who will make his first appearance in his celebrated character of Robert Macaire, in the great drama of that name, as performed by him upwards of two hundred nights before crowded and fashionable audiences including the royalty, nobility and gentry of England, who greeted him with the most terrific and enthusiastic yells of applause, and Her Majesty the Queen was so delighted with the masterly and brilliant representation, that she presented Mr. Thompson with a magnificent diamond ring valued at five thousand pounds sterling, which ring will be exhibited to the audience at the conclusion of the performance.' How will *that* do, my boy? We'll raise the price of admission to twenty-five cents on account of the extra attraction. I'll play Jaques Strop, the house will be crammed, and you will go on your way rejoicing, with a full pocket."

"I say, old fellow," I gravely remarked—"are you not laying it on a *little too thick?*"

"Not at all," coolly replied the brother as he carefully knocked the ashes off the end of his cigar, "not at all. Humbug is the order of the day. I'll get a flashy ring to represent the one presented to you by the queen. You know enough about stage business to play the part of Robert Macaire very respectably and you also know that I am not very slow in Jaques Strop. You'll make a hit, depend on it. I'll get you the book, and you can look over the part. What you don't learn you can gag.* I'll announce you for to-morrow night. Leave all to me; I'll arrange everything. Let's go in and drink!"

I was soon master of the part; and, at the end of the next day's rehearsal, I was found to be "dead letter perfect." The manager and the members of his company congratulated me on the success which I was sure to meet with. Meanwhile, the town had been flooded with bills, which made the same extravagant announcement that Brother Pratt had suggested to me. Public expectation and curiosity were worked up to the highest pitch; and a crowd of excited people assembled in front of the principal hotel, in anticipation of the sudden arrival of the "distinguished comedian" in a splendid coach drawn by four superb white horses, and attended by a retinue of servants in magnificent livery.

Evening came, and the large hall was crowded almost to suffocation, although the price of tickets had been doubled. I was full of confidence, having fortified myself by imbibing several glasses of brandy and water. Just before going on the stage Brother Pratt was, to use a common expression, "pretty well over the bay." Well, to make a long story as short as possible, I went on at the proper time, followed by Jaques Strop. My appearance was greeted with a perfect whirlwind of applause, which lasted four or five minutes. Taking off my dilapidated beaver, I gracefully bowed my thanks and then began the part which commences thus:

"Come along, comrade, put your best leg foremost. What are you afraid of? We are out of danger now, and shall soon reach the frontier."

I may say without egotism, that I got through the part remarkably well, and I certainly kept the audience in a continual roar of laughter. Mrs. Raymond occupied a front seat; —and her encouraging smile sustained me throughout the play. When the piece was over, I was loudly called for.

"Now, my boy," said Brother Pratt to me, "go in front of the curtain and make a rip-staving speech—I know you can do it. Say that at the urgent solicitation of the manager, you have consented to appear to-morrow night as Jem Baggs, in the Wandering Minstrel."

"Very good," said I, "but these people will now want to see the ring which Queen Victoria presented to me. How shall I manage that?"

"Easy enough," replied the Brother, as he drew from his pocket and handed me a big brass ring ornamented with a piece of common glass about the size of a hen's egg.

Out I stepped in front of the curtain. A bouquet as large as a cabbage struck me in the face, and fell at my feet. The giver of this delicate compliment was an ancient female very youthfully dressed. I picked up the bouquet, and pressed it to my heart. This was affecting, it melted the audience to tears. Silence having been obtained,

* This word, in theatrical parlance, signifies "to employ language which the author of the play never wrote."

I made a bombastic speech, which Brother Pratt afterwards declared to be the best he had ever heard delivered in front of the "green baize." I spoke of being a stranger in a strange land, of the warm welcome which I received, of eternal gratitude, of bearing with me beyond the ocean the remembrance of their kindness, admitted that I was closely allied to the British aristocracy, but declared that my sentiments were purely republican and in favor of the "Star-Spangled Banner."

Here there was a tempest of applause and when it had subsided, the orchestra, consisting of a fiddle and a bass-drum, struck up the favorite national air which my words had suggested. Then I exhibited the diamond ring which had been presented to me by the Queen of England; and, as the spectators viewed the royal gift, the most profound silence prevailed among them. When I had sufficiently gratified them by displaying the lump of brass and glass, I remarked that I would appear on the next evening as Jem Baggs in the Wandering Minstrel. This announcement was received with shouts of approbation; and bowing almost to the foot-lights, I withdrew.

The next night, the audience was equally large and enthusiastic, and my "farewell speech" was so deeply affecting, that there was not a dry eye in the house.

Brother Pratt urged me to become a regular member of his company; but, although he offered me a good salary, and glowingly depicted the pleasant life of a strolling player, I declined, not having any ambition in that way. Besides, it was my duty to get on to Pittsburg with Mrs. Raymond, without any unnecessary delay.

Having received nearly fifty dollars as my share of the proceeds, I took my leave of Brother Pratt and his company; and, accompanied, of course, by my fair friend, resumed my journey.

I wish I had sufficient time and space to describe all the adventures through which we passed, prior to our arrival in Pittsburg. But such details would occupy too much room, and I must make the most of the few pages that are left for me to occupy.

We crossed the Alleghanies, and, taking the canal at Johnstown, soon reached Pittsburg. Here we made some essential improvements in our garments, and put up at a respectable hotel, Mrs. Raymond still sustaining her masculine character.

By diligent inquiry, we learned that the villain, Livingston, was in the city; and my fair friend prepared to avenge the base wrongs which he had inflicted upon her.

CHAPTER VII

A deed of blood and horror.

We had no difficulty in ascertaining the place of Livingston's abode; for he was well known in the city. He resided in a handsome house situated on one of the principal streets; and we discovered that the lawless rascal was actually engaged in the practice of the law!

"My dear friend," said Mrs. Raymond to me one day, as we were strolling along the banks of the river, "I will not suffer you to involve yourself in any trouble on my account. You must have nothing to do with this Livingston. You must remain entirely in the back-ground. To me belongs the task of punishing him. I tell you frankly that I shall kill the man. He is not fit to live, and he must not be permitted to continue his career of villainy. Whatever may be my fate, do not, I entreat you, by unhappy on my account. When I have shed the heart's blood of Livingston, I shall be willing to die upon the scaffold. To the very last moment of my life, I shall cherish for you a sentiment of the most affectionate gratitude; you sacrificed all your own plans in order to accompany me here, and, throughout the entire long journey, you have treated me with a degree of kindness and attention, which I can never forget while life remains. But a truce to melancholy; let us change the subject."

"With all my heart," said I; and leaving the river side, we walked up into the centre of the city.

We passed an elegant dwelling-house on the door of which was a silver plate bearing the name "Livingston." This was the residence of the villain who ruined Mrs. Raymond.

A carriage drove up before the door, and from it leaped a tall, fine-looking man, dressed in the height of fashion. He assisted a beautiful and elegantly attired lady to alight from the vehicle, and conducted her into the house.

"That man is Livingston, and that woman must be *one of his wives*," said Mrs. Raymond, with a bitter smile, as she placed her hand in her bosom, where, I knew, she carried a dirk-knife.

"My friend," resumed she, after a pause, "leave me; I may as well perform my bloody task now, as at any other time. I will invent some pretext for requesting an interview with Livingston, and then, without uttering a single word, I will stab him to the heart. Farewell, forget me, and be happy!"

"Stay," said I—"you must not leave me thus. Let me persuade you to abandon, at least for the present, your terrible design with reference to Livingston. You are agitated, excited; wait until you are cool, and capable of sober reflections."

Mrs. Raymond regarded me with a look of anger, as she said, passionately—

"And was it for the purpose of giving me such advice as *this*, that you accompanied me from Philadelphia to this city? You knew, all the while, the object of my journey; and yet now, in the eleventh hour, when an excellent opportunity presents itself for the accomplishment of that object, you seek to dissuade me from my purpose. Have I entirely mistaken your character? Are you really as weak-minded, and as devoid of courage and spirit, as your language would seem to indicate? When that young ruffian mutilated you in Philadelphia, didn't you consider that you acted perfectly right? Well, this Livingston has destroyed the happiness of my life, and transformed me from a lady of wealth into a penniless beggar. Say does he not deserve to *die?*"

"Why—yes," was my reluctant reply—"but then it seems to terrible to go about the horrible business deliberately, and in cold blood."

"He coolly and deliberately planned and effected the ruin of my peace, happiness and fortune," rejoined Mrs. Raymond, in a tone of fixed determination—"and it is therefore but just that he should be coolly and deliberately slain. Once more, farewell; by everything sacred, I swear that you shall not turn me from my purpose. My regard for you is great—but, if you seek to detain me by force, your heart shall be made acquainted with the point of my knife!"

"I have no idea of using force," said I, reproachfully—"but, if I *had*, no such threat as the one which you have just now made, would deter me. Go, my friend, go—do as you will; but I will go with you, for I swear that I will not leave you."

This announcement deeply affected Mrs. Raymond, who embraced me and begged my pardon for the language which she had used.

"Forgive me, my best, my only friend," said she—"the loyalty and devotion which you have always manifested towards me should have prompted different expressions.—If you are *determined* to accompany me, and see me through this business, *follow me.*"

I obeyed, hoping to be able to prevent the perpetration of the terrible deed which she meditated.

She rang the bell at the door, which was opened by a servant.

"I wish to see your master, instantly, on particular business," said the disguised woman.

"What name, sir?" demanded the servant.

"It matters not. Say to Mr. Livingston that two gentlemen wish to see him on business of the greatest importance."

The servant disappeared, but soon returned, saying that she would conduct us to her master.

We followed her into a handsomely furnished library, where Mr. Livingston was seated, looking over some letters. He glanced at us carelessly, and said—

"Well, young gentlemen, what can I do for you to-day? Do you wish to consult me on any matter of law? I am entirely at your service."

It was evident that the villain did not recognize the woman whom he had so basely wronged.

Mrs. Raymond uttered not one single word, but, thrusting her hand into her bosom, she slowly approached the author of her ruin, who still continued to peruse his letters in entire unconsciousness of the terrible danger that hung over him.

I watched Mrs. Raymond with the closest attention, fully determined to spring forward at the critical moment and prevent the desperate woman from accomplishing her deadly purpose.

It was a deeply interesting and thrilling scene, and one which I shall never forget. There sat the intended victim, whose soul was hovering on the awful precincts of an endless eternity; there stood the avenger of her own wrongs, her right hand nervously grasping the hilt of the weapon in her bosom, her face deadly pale, and her eyes flashing with wild excitement. And there I stood, trembling with agitation, and ready to spring forward at the proper time to prevent the consummation of a bloody tragedy.

Mr. Livingston suddenly looked up from his letters, and started when he beheld the pale and wrathful countenance of Mrs. Raymond, whose eyes were fixed upon him with an expression of the most deadly hatred.

"Your face seems strongly familiar to me; have we not met before?" asked Livingston.

"Yes," calmly replied Mrs. Raymond—"we *have* met before."

"That voice!" cried the doomed villain—"surely I know it. Who are you, and what want you with me?"

"I am the victim of your treacherous villainy, and I want revenge!" screamed Mrs. Raymond, as, with the quickness of lightning, and before I could prevent her, she drew her weapon and plunged it into the heart of Livingston, who fell from his chair to the floor and died instantly.

"Now I am satisfied," said the woman, as she coolly wiped the blood from the blade of her knife.

Language cannot depict the horror which the contemplation of this bloody deed caused within me. True, I had myself slain a human being—but then it was done in self-defence, and amid all the heat and excitement of a personal contest. *This* deed, on the contrary, had been committed, coolly and deliberately; and, although Mrs. Raymond's wrongs were undoubtedly very great, I really could not find it in my heart to justify her in what she had done.

How bitterly I reproached myself for not having adopted some effectual means of hindering the performance of that appalling deed, even at the risk of incurring Mrs. Raymond's severe and eternal displeasure! I felt myself to be in some measure an accessory to the crime; and I feared the law would, at all events, consider me as such.

"What is done cannot be helped now," said I to Mrs. Raymond, who stood calmly surveying the body of her victim—"come let us leave the house and seek safety in flight. We may possibly escape the consequence of this bloody act."

"No," said the woman—"*I* shall not stir an inch. I have relieved the world of a monster, and now I am ready to receive my reward, even if it be the scaffold. But go, my friend—go, and secure your own safety."

"No, I will not leave you, even if I have to share your fate," was my reply. That was a very foolish determination, I admit; for how could my remaining with her, do her any good? I was merely placing myself in a position of the utmost peril. But I thought it wrong to desert Mrs. Raymond in that dark and trying hour; and therefore, as she refused to escape, I resolved to remain with her.

Some one softly opened the door, and a female voice said—

"My dear, are you particularly engaged? May I come in?"

Hearing no reply, the fair speaker entered with a smile on her rosy lips. This lady was the newly-made wife of Livingston. She had been, of course, in happy ignorance of his true character, and of the fact that he was already the husband of several wives.

On seeing us, she evinced surprise, for she knew not of her husband having visitors. Suddenly, her eyes fell upon Livingston's bleeding corpse, which lay upon the floor. On seeing this horrid spectacle, she gave utterance to a piercing scream, and fell down insensible.

That shrill, agonizing scream penetrated every part of the house, and brought all the inmates to the library, to see what had happened. Horror took possession of the group, as they gazed upon the awful scene. For a few minutes, there reigned the most profound silence. This was at last broken by one of the male servants, who demanded—

"Who has done this?"

"I did it," replied Mrs. Raymond, calmly, "I alone am guilty. Here is the weapon with which I did the deed. This young man here is entirely innocent; he tried to prevent the act, but I was too quick for him. Let me be conveyed at once to prison."

Officers being sent for, soon arrived and took us both into custody, notwithstanding the passionate protestations of Mrs. Raymond that I had no hand whatever in the affair.

"That must be shown to the satisfaction of higher authorities than we are," said one of the officers. "At all events, it is our duty to secure this young man as a witness. If he is innocent, he will doubtless be able to prove it."

Half an hour afterwards, I was an inmate of the Pittsburg jail, in an apartment adjoining that occupied by Mrs. Raymond, whose real sex still remained undiscovered.

CHAPTER VIII

An Escape, and a Triumph.

After a few weeks' incarceration, Mrs. Raymond, in accordance with my advice, made known the secret of her sex to the chief officer of the prison, to whom she also communicated the great wrongs which she had suffered at the hand of Livingston. The officer, who was a good and humane man, was deeply affected by this narrative. He immediately placed Mrs. Raymond in a more comfortable room and caused her to be provided with an abundance of female garments, which she now resumed. Her story, of course, was given in all the newspapers; and it excited the deepest sympathy in her behalf. One editor boldly asserted that no jury could be found to convict the fair prisoner under the circumstances. As regarded my case, the propriety of my immediate discharge from custody was strongly urged, an opinion in which I fully concurred.

I shall dwell upon these matters as briefly as possible. I was first brought to trial, and the jury acquitted me without leaving their seats; Mrs. Raymond was merely convicted of manslaughter in the fourth degree, so great was the sympathy that existed in her behalf, and the judge sentenced her to be imprisoned during the term of two years. Although I considered her particularly fortunate in receiving a punishment so comparatively light, I resolved to effect her liberation in some way or other.

I may as well here remark that the last wife and victim of Livingston never survived the blow. She soon died of a broken heart.

My first step was to repair to Harrisburg, the capitol city of the State, in order to solicit Mrs. Raymond's pardon from Governor Porter, who was renowned, and by some parties strongly condemned, for his constant willingness to bestow executive clemency upon prisoners convicted of the most serious offences.* I easily obtained an interview with his Excellency, whom I found to be a very clever sort of personage. Having made known my errand, and related all the particulars of Mrs. Raymond's case, I urged her claims to mercy with all the eloquence of which I was master.

The Governor listened to me with attention; and, when I had concluded, he said—

"My inclination strongly prompts me to pardon this most unfortunate lady; but I have recently pardoned so many convicted prisoners, that the press and the people generally are down on me, and I really dare not grant any more pardons at present. I will, however, commute the lady's sentence from two years to one."

With this partial concession I was obliged to be contented. The necessary documents were made out, and with them I posted back to Pittsburg. When I entered the cell of my fair friend and told her what I had effected in her behalf, she burst into tears of gratitude and joy. One long year taken off her sentence, was certainly something worth considering.

"Courage, my friend!" said I, "even if you are obliged to serve out the remnant of your sentence, which I trust will not be the case, a year will soon pass away. I shall not leave Pittsburg until you are free. You will see me often; and I will take care that you are abundantly provided with everything that can contribute to your comfort. Keep up a good heart; you have at least one friend who will never desert you."

Three months passed away, during which time I gained an excellent subsistence by writing for various newspapers and magazines. Three times every week I had an interview with Mrs. Raymond, whom I caused to be supplied with every comfort and luxury allowed by the rules of the prison. She had just nine months to serve, when one day I was unexpectedly enabled to effect her liberation in the following manner.

I had called upon her, as usual. After an interview of about half an hour's duration, I bade her adieu and left her apartment. To gain the street, it was necessary to pass through the office of the prison. In that office were generally seated three of four turnkeys, one of whom always went and locked Mrs. Raymond's door after my leaving her.

Upon entering the office on the occasion to which I now refer, I found but one turnkey there, and he was *fast asleep*. I instantly resolved to take advantage of the lucky circumstance which good fortune had thrown in my way.

Hastening back to Mrs. Raymond's cell, I briefly told her the state of affairs and bade her follow me. She obeyed, as might be supposed, without much reluctance.

* It is related of Governor Porter as an illustration of his pardoning propensities, that once, after his term of office had expired, a gentleman accidentally ran against him in the street. "I beg your pardon," said the gentleman. "I cannot grant it," said Mr. Porter, "for I am no longer Governor."

We passed through the office and out into the street; but, before departing, I transferred the key from the inside to the outside of the door and locked the sleeping turnkey in, so that there could be no possibility of his immediately pursuing us, when he should awaken and discover the flight of his prisoner.

I was tolerably well furnished with cash, and my fair friend, at my suggestion, purchased an elegant bonnet and shawl—for, it will be remembered, she had resumed the garments appropriate to the female sex. As for myself, I was exceedingly well dressed, and no alteration in my costume was necessary, in order to present a respectable appearance.

I entertained no serious apprehensions of any great effort being made to capture the fugitive, she having had but nine months to serve, and being therefore a person of but little importance when viewed as a prisoner. Moreover, I hoped that the kind-hearted chief officer of the prison would charitably refrain from making any extraordinary exertions in the matter. But these considerations did not prevent me from exercising a reasonable degree of caution.

We left Pittsburg that evening, for Philadelphia, where we arrived in due season. I immediately sought and procured employment as a writer, at a liberal salary. A few days after our arrival in Philadelphia, Mrs. Raymond said to me—

"My dear friend, I am not going to remain a burden to you. Listen to the plan which I have to propose. I think of going upon the stage."

"What, and becoming an actress?"

"Yes. I flatter myself that my voice and figure are both passable; and I really think that I possess some talent for the theatrical profession. A respectable actress always receives a good salary. If the plan meets with your approbation, I shall place myself under the tuition of some competent teacher; and my *debut* shall be made as soon as advisable."

I did not attempt to dissuade Mrs. Raymond from carrying out this plan, which I thought, in fact, to be a very excellent idea. Once successfully brought out upon the stage, she would have a profession which would be to her an unfailing means of support.

According to the best of my judgment, she possessed every mental and physical qualification necessary to constitute a good actress. Beautiful and sprightly, talented and accomplished—possessing, too, the most exquisite taste and skill as a vocalist and musician, I saw no reason why she should not succeed upon the stage as well, and far better, than many women a thousand times less talented. Therefore, encouraged by my cordial approbation of her plan, and acting in accordance with my recommendation, the fair aspirant to dramatic honors placed herself under the instructions of a popular and well-known actor, who was fully capable of the task which he had undertaken.

A few months passed away, and my fair friend announced herself as being nearly in readiness to make her first appearance. I was delighted with the rapid and satisfactory progress which she had made. The recitations with which she occasionally favored me, were delivered in the highest style of the elocutionary art, and convinced me that she was destined to meet with the most unbounded success.

She proposed making her *debut* as *Beatrice*, in Shakespeare's glorious comedy, "Much Ado About Nothing,"—a character well calculated to display her arch vivacity and charming sprightliness. I saw her rehearse the part, and was satisfied that she *must* achieve a brilliant triumph,—an opinion that was fully concurred in by her gratified instructor, and also by the manager and several of the leading actors and actresses of the theatre.

The eventful evening came at last, and the house was crowded in every part. Seating myself in a private box in company with the actor who had instructed Mrs. Raymond, I awaited her appearance with the utmost confidence. The curtain arose, and the play commenced. When *Beatrice* came on, a perfect storm of applause saluted her. Her appearance, in her elegant and costly stage costume, was really superb. Perfectly self-possessed, and undaunted by the sea of faces spread out before her, she went on with her part, and was frequently interrupted by deafening shouts of approval. The *Benedict* of the evening being a very fine actor, and the *Dogberry* being as funny a dog as ever created a broad grin or a hearty laugh—the entire comedy passed off in the most admirable manner; and, at its conclusion, my fair friend being loudly called for, she was led out in front of the curtain by *Benedict*. A shower of bouquets now saluted her; and, having gracefully acknowledged the kindness of the audience, she retired.

This decided success caused the manager to engage Mrs. Raymond at a liberal salary. She subsequently appeared with equal success in a round of the best characters; and the press, and every tongue, became eloquent in her praise. She was now in a fair way to acquire a fortune as great as the one which she had lost through the villainy of Livingston.

Thinking her worthy of a higher position than that of a mere stock actress, I advised her, after a year's sojourn in Philadelphia, to travel as a *star*. To this she eagerly assented, and accordingly I accompanied her to New York, where she was immediately engaged by the late Thomas S. Hamblin, of the Bowery Theatre.*
Her success at this popular establishment was unprecedented in the annals of dramatic triumphs. Night after night was she greeted by crowded, enthusiastic and enraptured audiences. In short, she became one of the most celebrated actresses of the day.

CHAPTER IX

An accident—a suicide—and a change of residence.

A dreadful accident abruptly terminated Mrs. Raymond's brilliant professional career. One night, while she was dressing in her private room at the theatre, a camphene lamp exploded and her face was shockingly burned. Her beauty was

---

* I have not, for reasons that will be easily understood, given the name which Mrs. Raymond assumed, after her adoption of the dramatic profession.

destroyed forever, and her career upon the stage was ended. Thus was the public deprived of a most delightful source of entertainment, and thus was a popular actress thrown out of the profession just as she had reached the pinnacle of fame, and just as she was in a fair way to acquire a handsome fortune.

It would be impossible for me to describe the grief, consternation and horror of the unfortunate lady, on account of this melancholy accident. In vain did I attempt to console her, she refused to be comforted. She abandoned herself to despair; and I caused her to be closely and constantly watched, fearing that she might attempt to commit suicide.

The play-going public soon found a new idol, and poor Mrs. Raymond was forgotten. Her face was terribly disfigured, and it was very fortunate that her sight was not destroyed. When she became well enough, she endeavored to gain a situation as a teacher of music; but she was unceremoniously rejected by every person to whom she applied, on account of the repulsiveness of her countenance. This of course, still further increased the dark despair that overshadowed her soul.

"My friend," said she to me one day, "I shall not long survive this terrible misfortune. My heart is breaking, and death will ere long put an end to my sufferings."

"Come, come," said I, "where is your philosophy? Have you not passed through trials as great as this? While there is life, there is hope; and you will be happy yet."

I uttered these commonplace expressions because I knew not what else to say. Mrs. Raymond replied, with a mournful smile—

"Ah! with all your knowledge of the world, you know not how a woman feels when she has been suddenly deprived of her beauty. The miser who loses his wealth—the fond mother from whom death snatches away her darling child; these bereaved ones do not feel their losses more acutely than does a once lovely woman feel the loss of her charms. Do not talk to me of philosophy, for such language is mockery."

I visited my unfortunate and no longer fair friend very often, but all my attempts to cheer her up signally failed. She persisted in declaring that she was not long for this world; and I began to believe so myself, for she failed rapidly. I saw that she was provided with every comfort; but alas! happiness was beyond her reach forever.

One evening I set out to pay her a visit. On my arrival at the house in which she had taken apartments, the landlady informed me that she had not seen Mrs. Raymond during the whole of that day.

"It is very singular," remarked the woman, "I knocked five or six times at the door of her chamber, but she gave me no answer, although I know she has not gone out."

These words caused a dreadful misgiving to seize me. Fearing that something terrible had happened, I rushed up stairs, and knocked loudly upon the door of Mrs. Raymond's chamber. No answer being returned, I burst open the door, and my worst fears were realized, for there, upon the floor lay the lifeless form of that most unfortunate woman. She had committed suicide by taking arsenic.

This dreadful event afflicted me more deeply than any other occurrence of my life. I had become attached to Mrs. Raymond on account of a certain congeniality of disposition between us. We had travelled far together, and shared great dangers. That was another link to bind us together. Besides I admired her for her talent, and more particularly for her heroic resolution. She was, altogether, a most extraordinary woman, and, under the circumstances, it was no wonder that her tragical end should have caused within me a feeling of the most profound sorrow.

Having followed her remains to their last resting-place, I did something that I was very accustomed to do—I sat down to indulge in a little serious reflection, the result of which was that I determined to go to Boston, for New York had become wearisome to me. Besides, I knew that Boston was the grand storehouse of American literature—the "Athens of America," and I doubted not my ability to achieve both fame and money there.

To Boston I accordingly went. On the first day of my arrival, I crossed over to Charlestown for the purpose of viewing the Bunker Hill Monument. Having satisfied my curiosity, I strolled into a printing office, fell into conversation with the proprietor, and the result was that I found myself engaged at a moderate salary to edit and take the entire charge of a long-established weekly newspaper of limited circulation, entitled the "Bunker Hill Aurora and Boston Mirror." This journal soon began to increase both in reputation and circulation, for I filled it with good original tales and with sprightly editorials. Yet no credit was awarded to me, for my name never appeared in connection with my productions, and people imagined that W——, the proprietor, was the author of the improvements which had taken place.

"Egad!" the subscribers to the *Aurora* would say—"old W—— has waked up at last. His paper is now full of tip-top reading, whereas it was formerly not worth house-room!"

How many instances of this kind have I seen—of writers toiling with their pens and brains for the benefit and credit of ungrateful wretches without intellect, or soul, or honor, or common humanity! Charlestown is probably the meanest and most contemptible place in the whole universe—totally unfit to be the dwelling-place of any man who calls himself *white*. The inhabitants all belong to the *Paul Pry* family. A stranger goes among them, and forthwith inquisitive whispers concerning him begin to float about like feathers in the air. "Who is he? What is he? Where did he come from? What's his business? *Has he got any money?* (Great emphasis is laid on this question.) Is he married, or single? What are his habits? Is he a temperance man? Does he smoke—does he drink—does he chew? Does he go to meeting on Sundays? What religious denomination does he belong to? What are his politics? Does he use profane language? What time does he got to bed—and what time does he get up? Wonder what he had for dinner to-day?" &c., &c., &c.

During my residence in Charlestown, where I lived three years, I became acquainted with the celebrated editor and wit, Corporal Streeter, who was my next-door neighbor. I dwelt, by the way, in an old-fashioned house situated on Wood street. Two ancient pear trees sadly waved their branches in front of the house, and they are still there, unless some despoiling hand has cut them down—which Heaven forbid! If ever I re-visit that place, I shall gaze with reverence at the old house—for in it I passed some of the happiest days of my life. The antique edifice I christened "The Hermitage." The squalling cats of that neighborhood afforded me a fine opportunity for pistol practice.

At the end of three years, I had a slight "misunderstanding" with Mr. W——, the proprietor of the Aurora, one of the most stupendously mean men it was ever my misfortune to encounter. He was worthy of being the owner of the only newspaper in Charlestown, alias, "Hogtown." Having civilly requested Mr. W— to go to the devil at his earliest convenience, I left him and his rookery in disgust, and shifted my quarters over to Boston.

Here I engaged largely in literary pursuits, and began to write a series of novels. These were well received by the public, as every Bostonian will recollect.

In my next chapter, I shall tell the reader how a gentleman got into difficulties.

CHAPTER X

Six weeks in Leverett Street Jail.

A popular actor who was a personal friend of mine* took a farewell benefit at the National Theatre. At his invitation, and just before the close of the evening's performances, I attempted to enter the stage door for his purpose of seeing him in his dressing-room, as he intended to sup with me and several friends. A half-drunken Irishman attached to the stage department in some menial capacity, stopped me and insolently ordered me out. I treated the Greek, of course, with the contempt which he merited, whereupon he called another overgrown bog-trotter to his assistance, and the twain forthwith attacked me with great fury. Finding myself in danger of receiving rather rough treatment, I drew a small pocket pistol and aimed at their shins, being determined that one of them, at least, should hobble around upon crutches for a short time. The cap on the pistol, however, refused to explode, and the two vagabonds immediately caused me to be arrested, charging me with "assault and battery with the intent to kill!" I was forthwith accommodated with a private apartment in Leverett Street jail, where I remained six weeks, during which time I enjoyed myself tolerably well, being amply provided with good dinners, not prison fare, but from the outside, candles, newspapers, books, writing materials, &c. During my imprisonment, I wrote "The Gay Deceiver," and "Venus in Boston." My next door neighbor was no less a personage than Dr. John W. Webster, who was afterwards executed for the murder of Dr. Parkman. Webster was a great glutton, and thought of nothing but his stomach, even up to the very hour of his death. On account of his "position in society," (!) every officer of the prison became his waiter; and a certain ruffianly turnkey, who was in the habit of abusing poor prisoners in the most outrageous manner, would fawn to the Doctor like a hungry dog to a benevolent butcher.

* I allude to Mr. W. G. Jones, now deceased.

Webster was very polite to me, frequently sending me books and newspapers—favors which I as often reciprocated. He once sent me a jar of preserves, a box of sardines and a bottle of wine. The latter gift I highly appreciated, wines and liquors of every kind being prohibited luxuries. That night I became very happy and jovial; but I did not leave the house.

Dr. Webster was confident of being acquitted; but the result proved how terribly he was mistaken. Probably, in the annals of criminal jurisprudence, there never was seen a more striking instance of equal and exact justice, than was afforded by the trial, conviction and execution of John W. Webster. Money, influential friends, able counsel, prayers, petitions, the *prestige* of a scientific reputation failed to save him from that fate which he merited as well as if he had been the most obscure individual in existence.

After six weeks imprisonment, I was brought to trial before Chief Justice Wells. I was defended by a very tolerable lawyer, to whom I paid twenty-five dollars in consideration of his conversing five minutes with a jury of my peers, the said jury consisting of twelve hungry individuals who wanted to go out to dinner. When my legal adviser had made a few well-meaning remarks, the jury retired to talk the matter over among themselves; and, after about fifteen minutes absence, they returned and expressed their opinion that I was "not guilty." This opinion induced me to believe that they were very sensible fellows indeed. Not for a moment did I think of demanding a new trial; that would have been impertinent, as doubting the sagacity of the jury. My two Irish prosecutors left the court-room in a rage; and two more chop-fallen disappointed and mortified Greeks were never seen. The Judge took his departure, the spectators dispersed, and I crossed the street and dined sumptuously at Parker's, with a large party of friends.

Very many of my Boston readers will remember a long series of articles which I wrote and published about that time, in the columns of one of the newspapers, entitled "Mysteries of Leverett Street Jail." In those sketches I gave the arrangements of the Jail, and its officers, "particular fits;" and the manner in which the fellows writhed under the inflictions, was a caution to petty tyrants generally. The startling revelations which I made created great excitement throughout the whole community; and I have good reason to believe that those exposures were the means of producing a far better state of affairs in the interior of the "stone jug."

I have thus, very briefly, given the extent of my experience with reference to the old Leverett Street Jail. Unlawful ladies and gentlemen are now accommodated in an elegant establishment in Cambridge street, for the old Jail has been levelled to the ground to make room for "modern improvements." —I visited it just before the commencement of its destruction, and gazed at my old apartment "more in sorrow than in anger." There were my name and a few verses, which I had written upon the wall. There was the rude table, upon which I had penned two novels, which, from their tone, seem rather to have emanated from a gilded *boudoir*. There, too, in the grated window, was a little flower-pot in which I had cultivated a solitary plant. That poor plant had withered and died long ago, for the prisoners who succeeded me probably had no taste for such "trash." I took and carefully preserved the dead remains of my floral favorite—"for," said I to myself—"they will serve to remind me of a dark spot in my existence."

And now, with the reader's permission, I will turn to matters of a more cheerful character.

CHAPTER XI

"The Uncles and Nephews."

Ring up the curtain! Room there for the Boston Players. Let them approach our presence, not as they appear upon the stage, in rouge, and spangles, and wigs, and calves and cotton pad; but as they look in broad day-light, or in the bar-room when the play is over, arrayed in garments of a modern date, wearing their own personal faces, swearing their own private oaths, and drinking real malt out of honest pewter, instead of imbibing dusty atmosphere from paste-board goblets. Room, I say!

There is an intimate connection between the press and the stage, that is a congeniality of character, habit, taste, feeling and disposition, between the writer and the actor. The press and the stage are, in a measure, dependent on each other. The newspaper looks to the theatre for light, racy and readable items, with which to adorn its columns, like festoons of flowers gracefully hung around columns of marble. The theatre looks to the newspaper for impartial criticisms and laudatory notices. Show me a convivial party of actors, and I will swear there are at least two or three professional writers among them. I know many actors who are practical printers, fellows who can wield a composing-stick as deftly as a fighting sword. Long life and prosperity to the whole of them, say I; and bless them for a careless, happy, pleasure-loving, bill-hating and beer-imbibing race of men. Amen.

There is one point of resemblance between the hero of the sock and buskin and the Knight of the quill. The former dresses up his person and adopts the language of another, in order to represent a certain character; the latter clothes his ideas in an appropriate garb of words, and puts sentiments in the mouths of his characters which are not always his own. But I was speaking of the Boston Players.

Admitting the foregoing argument to be correct, it is not to be wondered at that I became extensively acquainted among the members of the theatrical profession. My name was upon the free list of every theatre in the city; and every night I visited one or more of the houses—not to see the play, but to chat in the saloons with the actors and literary people who in those places most did congregate. After the play was over, we all used to assemble in an ale-house near the principal theatre; and day-light would often surprise us in the midst of our "devotions." A curious mixed-up set we were to be sure! I will try to recollect the most prominent members of our club. First of all there was the argumentative and positive Jim Prior, who might properly be regarded as President of the club. Then came H. W. Fenno, Esq., the gentlemanly Treasurer of the National. He, however, seldom tarried after having once "put the party through." The eccentric "Old Spear" was generally present, seated in an obscure corner smoking a solitary cigar. Comical S.D. Johnson and his hopeful son George were usually on hand to enliven the scene; and so was Jim Ring, alias J. Henry, the best negro performer, next to Daddy Rice, in the United States. Chunkey Monroe, who did the villains at the National; and, towering above him might be seen his cousin, Lengthy Monroe, who enacted the hard old codgers at the same establishment. That fine fellow, Ned Sandford, must not be forgotten; neither must Sam Lake, the clever little dancer. Rube Meer was invariably to be found in company with a pot of malt; and he was usually assisted by P. Jones, a personage who never allowed himself to be funny until he had consumed four pints. Charley Saunders, the comedian and dramatist, the author of "Rosina Meadows" and many other popular plays—kept the "table in a roar," by his wit and also by his excruciatingly bad puns. Bird, of "Pea-nut Palace" notoriety, held forth in nasal accents to Bill Colwell, the husband of the pretty and accomplished Anna Cruise. Big Sam Johnson, a heavy actor, a gallant Hibernian and a splendid fellow, discussed old Jamaica with his friend and boon companion, Sam Palmer, alias "Chucks." The mysterious Frank Whitman captures his brother-actor at the Museum, Jack Adams, and imprisoning him in a corner from which there was no escape, imparts to him the most tremendous secrets. Ned Wilkings—one of the best reporters in the city—tells the last "funny thing" to John Young; while Joe Bradley, proprietor of the Mail, touches glasses with Jim McKinney. Meanwhile, the two waiters, Handiboe and Abbott, circulate around with the greatest activity, fetching on the liquors and removing the dirty glasses, from which they slyly contrive to drain a few drops now and then, for their bodily refreshment. As an instance of the "base uses" to which genius may "come at last," I will state that Handiboe, whom we now find in such a menial position, was once quite a literary character; while poor Abbott, to whom I now throw a few small coins in charity, was a setter of type. The rest of the party is made up of Pete Cunningham, Sam Glenn, Bill Dimond, Jim Brand, Bill Donaldson, Dan Townsend, Jack Weaver, Cal Smith, and a host of others whom it would puzzle the very devil himself to remember.

Such was the "Uncle and Nephew Club," of which I had the honor to be a prominent member. Almost every man belonging to it was a wit, a punster or a humorist of some kind; and I will venture to say, that had some industrious individual taken the pains to preserve and publish one-half the good things that were said at our meetings, a large volume might be formed that would be no contemptible specimen of genius. Whenever a member had the audacity to perpetrate some shocking bad pun, and such enormities were frequent, the offender was sentenced to undergo some ludicrous punishment; and the utmost good-humor and hilarity always prevailed.

I will now relate a rather amusing adventure in which I participated with others of the "Uncles and Nephews."

One night we were assembled, as usual, at our head-quarters. The Fourth of July was to "come off" the next day, and we determined to have some fun. Accordingly, a couple of stout messengers were despatched to the theatre, armed with the necessary authority and keys, and they soon returned laden with dresses from the wardrobe. These garments the party proceeded to assume; and we were quickly transformed into as picturesque-looking a crowd as any that ever figured at a masquerade ball. As for myself, I made a very tolerable representation of Falstaff; while Richard, Othello, Macbeth, Hamlet, Shylock, and other gentlemen of Shakespeare's creation, gave variety to the procession. Then there was a clown in full circus costume, accompanied by Harlequin in his glittering shape-dress. We sadly longed for a sprightly Columbine; but then we consoled ourselves with Pantaloon, admirably rendered by P. Jones.

Our "music" consisted of a bass-drum, which was tortured by the clown; a fish-horn beautifully played upon by Sam Palmer; a dinner-bell whose din was extracted by Jack Adams. Having formed the procession on the side-walk, the music struck up, and we marched.

Our first halting-place was at the saloon of Peter Brigham, at the head of Hanover street. Here we filed in, and great excitement did our extraordinary appearance create. A mob soon collected before the door, attracted by our grotesque costumes as well as by the infernal noise of our "musical" instruments, upon which we continue to perform with undiminished vigor. Peter Brigham was in agonies, and rushed about the saloon like an insane fly in a tar barrel. The frightened waiters abandoned their posts and fled. The mob outside cheered vociferously; and Harlequin began to belabor poor Pantaloon with his gilded lath to the immense amusement of the spectators.

Peter Brigham at length mounted a chair, and said—

"Gentlemen, will you hear me? (Hoarse growl from the bass-drum.) I cannot suffer this noise and racket to go on in my house. (Blast of defiance from the fish-horn.) You know I have always tried to keep a decent and respectable place. (Peal of sarcastic laughter from the dinner bell.) I have a proposition to make.—(Hear! hear!) If you will promise to leave the house quietly, I will treat you all to as much champagne as you can drink." (Yell of acceptance from the bass-drum, fish-horn and dinner-bell! Great excitement generally.)

The wine was produced, and the facility with which it was disposed of, caused Mr. Brigham to stare. He endured its consumption, however, with the most philosophical fortitude, until we began to drink toasts, make speeches, and exhibit other indications of a design on our part to "tarry yet awhile." Peter then reminded us of our promise; and, as gentlemen of honor, we fulfilled the same by immediately falling into procession and marching out of the saloon. Away we went down Hanover street, followed by the admiring and hooting crowd. We entered the establishment of Theodore Johnson, and were hospitably received by the prince of good fellows, who, assisted by Chris Anderson, "did the honors" with the utmost liberality. Sam Palmer and P. Jones, here favored the company with a broad-sword combat; after which I, as Falstaff, gave a few recitations—the performances concluded with Abbott as *Jocks*, the Brazilian ape. Our next visit was to the Pemberton House, then under the control of Uriah W. Carr, a very small man,

both physically and morally. Uriah received us very churlishly, and peremptorily
refused to "come down" with the hospitality of the season. He was particularly
down on me for having once written and published some verses concerning him.
The following is all that I can recollect of that interesting production:—

> "Tis comical, indeed it is
> To see him mix a punch—
> He puts two drops of liquor in,
> And then he eyes the *lunch;*
> He struts about most pompously,
> Then stands before the fire,
> Just like a little bantam-cock,
> This comical Uriah!"

Inasmuch as Uriah refused to bring on the "bush" for either love or money, we
determined to help ourselves. Therefore, every man appointed himself a bar-
keeper *pro tem.* Wines, liquors and cigars were disposed of with marvelous celerity,
and poor little Uriah danced about and tore his hair in the agony of his spirits.
Meanwhile, a large number of actors and others, boarding at the Pemberton, joined
us, being ushered in by Charles Dibden Pitt, a performer of great elegance and
power, then playing a brilliant star engagement—at the Museum. This gentleman
is decidedly "one of the boys," and goes in for a "good time." At his suggestion, a
committee was appointed to descend to the kitchen and bring up provisions. Ned
Abbot and Bill Ball performed this duty in the most admirable and satisfactory
manner. They departed for the lower regions, and soon returned laden both with
substantials and delicacies. Then, such a feast!—or, rather, such a banquet!
Champagne flowed like water, for we had discovered a closet filled with baskets of
the foaming beverage. The whole company was of course soon in a state of glorious
elevation. The song and jest went round unceasingly, and peals of jovial laughter
trooped away like merry elves upon the midnight air. We were in excellent humor
to adopt the prayer of the following who said—

> "Oh, let us linger late to-night,
> Nor part while wit and song are bright;
> And, Joshua, make the sun stand still,
> That we of joy may have our fill!"

There was one gentleman who refused to participate in the festivities of the
occasion. This was little Uriah, the landlord, who gazed upon the progress of the
banquet with a troubled brow; yet he did not dare to openly remonstrate, through
fear of offending Mr. Pitt, and other valuable boarders.

Unfortunately for the harmony of the festival, a party of drunken students from
Cambridge dropped in, and I instantly saw that a row was inevitable. After
unceremoniously helping themselves to drink, the students gazed at our strange-
looking company superciliously, and one of them remarked with a sneer—

"What fools are these, dressed up in this absurd manner? Oh, they must be monkies, the property of some enterprising organ-grinder. Let them dance before me, for my soul is heavy, and I would be gay!"

Here little Billy Eaton, the writer, who was one of our party, fired up and obligingly offered to fight and whip the man with the heavy soul, for and in consideration of the trifling sum of one cent. This handsome offer was accepted; but, before the gentlemen could strip for the combat, a general collision took place between all the hostile parties. Chairs were brandished, canes were flourished and decanters were hurled, to the great destruction of mirrors and other fragile property. The bar was overturned, and the din of battle was awful to hear. Notwithstanding the uproar and confusion that prevailed, I could not help noticing poor Uriah, who, in the dimly-lighted hall, was quietly dancing an insane polka, accompanying his movements by low howls of despair. The little man had temporarily lost his few wits, that was plain. The combat raged with undiminished fury. Our clown attacked a student with his bass-drum, one end of which burst in, imprisoning the representative of the seat of learning, who found it impossible to extricate himself from his musical predicament. Sam Palmer, with his fish-horn, did tremendous execution; while Jack Adams was equally effective with his dinner-bell which, at every blow, sounded forth a note of warning. The heroic P. Jones performed prodigies of valor, and covered himself with glory. This wonderful young man, having planted himself behind a rampart of chairs, placed himself in the position of a pugilistic frog, and boldly defied his enemies to "come on and be punched." At the commencement of the fight, Abbott coiled himself up under the table, and was seen no more; while Handiboe fled for safety to the cole-hole. The battle was at its height, and the bird of victory seemed about to perch upon the banner of the "Uncles and Nephews," when some reckless, hardened individual turned off the gas, thus producing total darkness. This made matters ten times worse than ever, for it was impossible to distinguish friends from foes. Suddenly, in rushed a posse of watchmen, headed by the renowned Marshal Tukey, and bearing torches. Many of the combatants were arrested, and but few contrived to make their escape. I had the honor of figuring among the unlucky ones; and, with my companions passed the night in durance vile. In the morning, when day light feebly penetrated our gloomy dungeon, what a strange-looking spectacle presented itself! Stretched upon the floor in every imaginable picturesque attitude, were about a score of men, the majority of them arrayed in the soiled and torn theatrical dresses. These unhappy individuals afforded a most melancholy sight, as many of them had black eyes, bruised noses and battered visages.

"D——d pretty fools we've made of ourselves," said Macbeth, one of whose optics had been highly discolored.

"Yes," groaned Othello, whose black eyes were only partially concealed by the yellow color which he had smeared over his face—"and here we are in the jug, where we shall be compelled to remain all day, and lose all the fun of the Fourth of July."

"That isn't the worst of it," sighed Hamlet, whose royal frontispiece had received severe damage—"I am on the bills to play twice this afternoon and once this evening, and my being absent will cause me to be *forfeited*, if not discharged.

D——n those college students! What the devil became of them? They all got clear, I suppose."

"No," said I—"they are in a separate apartment. Of course the officers would not put them in with us, for that would be encouraging a renewal of the fight."

"My head aches horribly," remarked Richard, Duke of Gloster—"I would give my kingdom for a drink!"

"And I," observed Shylock—"would like a pound of flesh, providing it were beefsteak, for I am almost famished."

"Hah! what a hog!" growled Cardinal Richelieu, one side of whose face had been "cove in" most dreadfully—"to think of *eating* at such a time as this!"

"Hark," said Claude Melnott, whose handsome countenance had been knocked completely out of shape, and who looked as if he had just returned from the wars rather the worse for wear; "hark! Don' t you hear the sound of artillery, and of music? The ceremonies and festivities of the glorious day have commenced. Would to Heaven that I were with Pauline, in our palace on the lake of Como!"

"Dry up, you fool!" angrily exclaimed the aged and venerable King Lear, whose nasal organ exhibited signs of its having sustained a violent contusion—"I haven't closed an eye during the whole night, and now you keep me awake with your infernal jabbering. Shut up, I say!"

"Oh, shut up be blowed!" said P. Jones—"how can a man shut up when he thinks of the good *budge* (rum) he loses by being shut up here? Rube Meer, isn't this too bad?"

"Worse than the time when I sent on a fishing excursion with Jim Morse," groaned poor Rube, as he fumbled in his pocket for a match with which to light his pipe, "has anybody got a rope with which a fellow could contrive to hang himself?"

"I say, Jack Adams," said Sam Palmer, who was dressed as Don Caesar de Bezas, "what will Harry Smith and old Kimball say, when we don't make our appearance to-day, the busiest day in the whole year?"

"I care not," replied Jack, as he fondly pressed the portrait of his Katy to his lips, "so long as this blessed consolation is left me, the world may do its worst! Frown on, ye fiends of misfortune! I defy ye all, so long as my Katy Darling remains but true!"

"That's the one!" shouted the bold Dick Brown, as "usher" at the National Theatre, "let us have the song of Katy Darling, and all join in the chorus."

This was done; and from the depths of that gloomy dungeon rolled forth the words, in tones of thunder—

"Did they tell thee I was false, Katy Darling?"

Suddenly, to our great joy, the ponderous iron door of the dungeon was unlocked and thrown open, and an officer announced that he had orders to release us all, provided that we would engage to satisfy the landlord of the Pemberton House for the damage he had sustained. This we of course agreed to do, it being understood that the college students should be compelled to pay one-half the amount, which was certainly no more than right, as they had perpetrated half the damage, and had commenced the row in the first place. The landlord having received sufficient security that his damages would be made whole, we were all set at liberty, to our most intense delight, for we had anticipated being imprisoned during the whole of that glorious day.

We left the house of bondage, and, as we passed through the already crowded streets, our fantastic dresses and strange appearance generally, collected a mob at our heels, which, in broad daylight, was certainly rather annoying. However, we soon reached the theatre, and resumed our own proper habiliments.

It was announced upon the bills of the theatre that a certain actor would that evening deliver an original Fourth of July poem. That poem I had engaged to write, yet not a single line had I committed to paper. The actor was in a terrible quandary, and swore that his failure to recite the poem, as announced, would render him unpopular with the public and ruin him forever. Telling him to keep cool and call again in two hours, I sat down to my writing-desk and dashed off a poem of considerable length. My pen flew with the rapidity of lightning, words and ideas crowded upon me in overwhelming numbers, and in three-quarters of an hour my work was done! I sent for the actor who was astonished at the brief space of time in which I had performed the task. Having heard me read the poem, he declared himself to be delighted with it; and, with all due humility and modesty, I must say that the production did possess considerable merit. I had avoided the usual stereotyped allusions to the "star spangled banner," to the "Ameri-eagle," to the "blood of our forefathers," &c.;—and had dwelt principally upon the sublime moral spectacle afforded by an oppressed people arising in their might to throw off the yoke of bondage and assert their independence as a nation. The actor soon committed the poem to memory; and, having rehearsed it over to me and found himself perfect, he departed. That night he recited it from the stage to a dense audience; and, during its delivery and at its conclusion, I had the satisfaction of listening to the most delicious music that an author's ears can ever know, the clapping of hands, and deafening peals of applause.

CONCLUSION

My Parting Bow.

Several years have passed since the date of the events last narrated. Those years have been crowded with adventures full as extraordinary as those already detailed; but alas! neither time nor space will at present, admit of my giving them to the public. Perhaps, at some future time, I may make up for this deficiency, if my life is spared.

The reader may rest assured of one thing: —that *not one single word of fiction or exaggeration has been introduced into these pages.* Why should I wander in the realms of romance, when there are more startling facts at my command than I can possibly make use of? Is not truth stranger than fiction? Every day's experience proves such to be the case.

I cannot close up these pages without availing myself of the opportunity to return my thanks in this public manner, to several gentlemen from whom I have received courtesies and acts of kindness. First and foremost, there is Jerry Etheridge, a man of great political influence and historical learning. To this distinguished gentleman I am indebted for an act of generosity that rescued me from a serious embarrassment. I am not the only recipient of his bounty, for I know many others who have applied to him in times of need, and who have left him, encouraged by his cheering words and relieved by his liberality. He is one of those true philanthropists who never publish their good deeds to others. I consider that when one man befriends another and then tells of it, all obligation ceases to exist between the parties, and no gratitude is due the one who confers the benefit, which he bestows, perhaps just on purpose to acquire a reputation for whole-souled benevolence, and not out of any particular good-will to the other. I am also under obligation to Mr. W. R. GOODALL, the promising young American actor, who will one day, I predict, occupy a most elevated position in the profession which he has adopted, and for which he is peculiarly qualified. Who that ever heard his famous imitations, as Jeremiah Clip, will hesitate to admit that he is a young man of the most extraordinary talent? NED SANDFORD and JIM LANERGAN, both of whom are now while I write this, playing at the Broadway Theatre, I return my most sincere thanks for favors received; and I trust that they will pardon me for making this public allusion to them. Finally, to every person who has, through disinterested motive, treated me with kindness and consideration, I would say—friends, your goodness shall never be forgotten while life remains.

I have many bitter enemies, and they will, I presume, continue to snarl at my heels like mongrel curs. Their miserable attempts to injure me will only rebound back upon themselves. I am above the reach of their malignity, and shall pursue my own independent course regardless of their spleen.

Nearly one year has now elapsed since I left Boston—a place that I cannot but regard with some degree of affectionate remembrance; for, with all its faults, I like it still.

It is possible that I may hereafter continue to write tales for the public amusement. Should I conclude to continue in my business as a writer, I shall always, as heretofore, labor to produce that which is interesting, exciting and founded on truth, and entirely unobjectionable in a moral point of view. Unlike many so-called writers who throw off a quantity of trash and care not how it fills up space, I am always willing to bestow time and toil upon my work, for the sake of my own credit, for the purpose of securing the rapid and extensive sale of the book—and in order to give the public perfect satisfaction.

Reader, fare thee well! We may never meet again; but I thank thee for accompanying me from the beginning to

THE END

BIBLIOGRAPHY

WORKS BY GEORGE THOMPSON

Explanation of Notations

With the exception of the three works reprinted in this volume, Thompson's works can be read today only in rare book rooms or in Lyle Wright's microfilm series, *American Fiction*. To aid future researchers, we have sought to determine the locations and first publication dates of as many of the texts as possible. The list of Thompson's works, which may of course still be incomplete, is annotated as follows.

1. For works available on the Wright microfilm, the Wright number is indicated in brackets, preceded by W and a volume number: [W Vol. I, 2480]. Volume I corresponds to the years 1776–1850; Volume II corresponds to 1851–75.

2. For works reprinted in part in Henry Spencer Ashbee's *Bibliography of Prohibited Books* (see "Secondary Literature below"), the relevant pages of the 1962 edition are indicated in brackets: [Ashbee 203–209].

3. For works serialized or excerpted in newspapers, surviving issues that contain installments of the work are indicated in brackets: [*Belle*, October 15, 1855].

4. For works that we know to be held in rare book rooms (either because we have read them there, because the librarians in question confirmed their holdings for us as we prepared this manuscript for publication, or, in a few cases, because we found them in the libraries' online catalogs), locations are indicated in normal type, according to the following key:

AAS   American Antiquarian Society
BP   Boston Public Library
C   Columbia University
D   Duke University
HEH   Henry E. Huntington Library, San Marino, California
KEmT Kansas State Teachers' College, Emporia
LC   Library of Congress
MnU   University of Minnesota
N   Newberry Library, Chicago
NH   New Hampshire State Library
NYH   New-York Historical Society
NYP   New York Public Library (*note:* works listed are held in the general research collection, not in the rare book room)

NYU   Fales Library at New York University
T   Tulane University
UP   University of Pennsylvania
UV   University of Virginia, Charlottesville
Y   Yale University

5. In a very few cases in which works are listed in the National Union Catalog of Pre-1956 Imprints or the Lyle Wright bibliography as belonging to a library, but we were not able to confirm the availability of the book, locations are abbreviated according to the same key, but are printed in italics. The same is true of several works that are listed in the Wright bibliography but do not appear on the set of the Wright microfilm available to the editors.

6. When the approximate date of first publication of a novel (or, in the case of lost works, the fact that it was written by Thompson at all) can be inferred from the fact that it was included in a list of the author's previous works on the title page of another novel, the earliest relevant title page and its date are listed in brackets. For example, our listing for *Dissipation*, which reads, " [Title page of *City Crimes*, 1849]," indicates that the title page is the earliest one we found in which *Dissipation* is listed as one of the author's prior works.

Unless otherwise noted, we attribute the works in this list to Thompson because they were published either under his name or under his primary pseudonym, "Greenhorn."

Surviving Works by George Thompson

"Absurdities of the Drama." [This is an essay that appeared in *Life in Boston and New England Police Gazette*, April 27, 1850. Held by AAS.]

Adolene Wellmont; or the Female Adventurer. New York: George W. Hill, 1853. AAS. [Advertised as by Thompson in the *Belle* of October 15, 1855.]

Adventures of Lola Montes. New York, 1857. [Ashbee attributes this work to Thompson; it is also listed on the title page of *Mysteries of Bond Street*. It was serialized with the name "Eugene de Orsay" as author in *Venus' Miscellany*. Installments survive in the June 6, June 20, June 27, July 4, and July 11, 1857, issues of that paper.]

Adventures of a Pickpocket, or, Life at a Fashionable Watering Place. New York, n.d. *[W Vol. I 2581a]*, UV. [An installment also appears in the September 1, 1849, issue of *Life in Boston Sporting Chronicle, and Lights and Shadows of New England Morals*.]

Anna Mowbray, or Tales of the Harem. New York: H. R. J. Barkley, n.d. [W Vol. II 2477, incomplete]. D [incomplete].

Autobiography of Petite Bunkum, the Great Yankee Showman. New York: P. H. Harris, 1855. AAS.

The Brazen Star, or, the Adventures of a New York M.P.: A True Tale of the Times We Live In. New York: G. W. Hill, 1853. [W Vol. II 2478], UP.

The Bridal Chamber, and its Mysteries: or, Life at our Fashionable Hotels. New York, 1856. *[W Vol II 2479]*, [Ashbee 218]. [Chapter 5 of the novel was printed along with a review in the *New York Atlas* of Sunday January 7, 1855, p. 4 (held at AAS).]

The Brigands; or, the Maiden in Search of Her Father. New York: Frederic A. Brady, [n.d., but Jack Harold series, of which this was no. 7, was probably published between 1870 and 1873]. AAS, C, HEH, *MnU*, NYP, UV, Y.

Catherine and Clara, or the Double Suicide: A True Tale of Disappointed Love. Boston:

Federhen, 1854. [W Vol. II 2480], *NH*, NYP [NYP has two copies: one bound with its copy of *Harry Glindon*, one listed under its own call number], NYU.

City Crimes; or Life in New York and Boston. Boston: W. Berry, 1849. [W Vol. I 2582, incomplete], N, T [incomplete].

The Countess, or Memoirs of Women of Leisure. Boston: Berry & Wright, 1849. [W Vol. I 2583], Y.

The Criminal; or, the Adventures of Jack Harold. Being a Sequel to the Tale of "Jack Harold, or, the Criminal's Career." Boston: W. Berry, 1851. [The Wright bibliography lists this work at Vol. II 2481 but the book to which it is a sequel is what actually appears on the microfilm under this number. See below, *Jack Harold*.] AAS, *KEmT*, UP. [An installment also appears in *Life in Boston and New England Police Gazette*, January 4, 1851.]

Dashington; or, the Mysteries of a Private Mad House. New York: F. H. Brady, n.d. [Possibly 1855: it is advertised on the title page of *The Locket*, 1855, as well as in the *Belle* of October 15, 1855.] H.

The Delights of Love; or the Lady Libertine. Being the Adventures of an Amorous Widow. New York: H. Farrell, n.d. [W Vol. II 2482], [Ashbee 203–209].

The Demon of Death; or, the Bandit's Oath!!! [This is a play. Act I appears in the *Belle* of January 1, 1885; Act II in the *Belle* of January 22, 1855.]

The Demon of Gold. Boston, 1853. HEH.

Facts, Theories, and Parallel Cases, Concerning the Mysteries of Bond Street. New York: 1857. AAS [This is a small section at the end of the AAS copy of *The Mysteries of Bond Street*, not a separate volume. Ashbee, however, lists it as a separate title, and it may have appeared on its own.]

Fanny Greeley; or, Confessions of a Free-love Sister Written by Herself. New York: Henry S. G. Smith, n.d. [Ashbee 210–217].

The Gay Girls of New York, or Life on Broadway. New York, 1853. [W Vol. II 2483], UV.

The G'hals of Boston; or, Pen and Pencil Sketches of Celebrated Courtesans. Boston: William Berry & Co., n.d. NYP.

Grace Willard: or, the High and the Low. New York: Frederic A. Brady, [n.d., but Jack Harold series, of which this was no. 11, was probably published between 1870 and 1873]. AAS.

Harry Glindon, or, the Man of Many Crimes: A Startling Narrative of the Career of a Desperate Villain. New York, 1854. [W Vol. II 2484], NYP.

The House Breaker; or, the Mysteries of Crime. Boston: W. L. Bradbury, 1848. [W Vol. I 2584], C, *KEmT*, NYP.

Iniquities of New York. [The first two pages, containing Chapter I, "The Magdalens of New York," are bound with the AAS copy of *New York Life*, ca.1849.]

Jack Harold, or the Criminal's Career. Boston: W. Berry, 1850. [W Vol. II 2481]. [Note: The Wright bibliography lists this work under W Vol. I 2584a, but nothing appears on the microfilm there. Jack Harold actually appears under the number allocated to its sequel, "The Criminal," W Vol. II 2481.] AAS, HEH, LC. [Installments of this work were also published in surviving issues of *Life in Boston and New England Police Gazette* from May 18 and August 10, 1850.]

Kate Castleton, the Beautiful Milliner; or, the Wife and Widow of a Day. New York: George W. Hill, 1853. [Wright lists this work at Vol. II 2485; what actually appears on microfilm under this number is the German translation of it, listed below as *Merkwürdige Geschichte von Käthchen Castleton*.] H.

The Ladies' Garter. New York: Howland & Co., n.d. [W Vol. II 2486], AAS, HEH, UV. [This work must have appeared by the early 1850s, since it is listed on the title page of *The Brazen Star*, published in 1853. It is sometimes listed as *Lady's Garter*.]

Life and Exploits of "Bristol Bill." Boston: Willis Little & Co., 1851. [W Vol. II 2487], AAS, HEH, LC, NYH, UV.

The Locket: A Romance of New York. New York: P. F. Harris, 1855. [W Vol. II 2488], AAS, LC.

The Loves of Cleopatra or, Mark Anthony and His Concubines; A Historical Tale of the Nile. [Under the pseudonym "Appollonius of Gotham." The initial installment survives in the July 11, 1857 issue of *Venus' Miscellany*.]

The Magic Cloak, or the Demon of the Bottle. [*Belle*, November 8, 1858.]

The Magic Night Cap: A Story for Husbands and Wives. [*Belle*, January 29 and March 12, 1855. May have been continued in another paper published by P. F. Harris (which to our knowledge has not survived) called *The Bowery Boy*.]

Merkwürdige Geschichte von Käthchen Castleton, die schöne Putzmacherin, oder, die Schicksale eines jungen Mädchens im niederen Lebensstande, die an einem Tage zugleich Frau und Witwe wurde. New York: Holbrook, 1853. [W Vol. II 2485. The Wright bibliography lists the English original of this work, *Kate Castleton*, at this number, but the German translation appears on the microfilm under it.] AAS, LC.

My Life: or the Adventures of Geo. Thompson. Boston: Federhen, 1854. AAS.

Mysteries and Miseries of Philadephia, by a Member of the Philadelphia Bar. New York: Williams, n.d. [W Vol. II 2488a], HEH, *N*, UV.

The Mysteries of Bond-Street: or, the Seraglios of Upper Tendom. New York, 1857. [*W Vol. II 2489*], AAS. [Known to be Thompson's because the title page says it is by the author of *Anna Mowbray*, *Bridal Chamber*, and *Kate Montrose, Amorous Adventures of Lola Montes, Marie de Clairville*, and *Confessions of a Sofa*, all of which appeared either under Thompson's name or under "Greenhorn," or are attributed to him by Ashbee (see individual entries). Serialized in *Venus' Miscellany* under the pseudonym "Appollonius." The concluding installment has survived in the May 9, 1857, issue of the paper, and the May 16, 1857, issue advertises its availability in book form.]

Mysteries of Leverett Street Jail. [*Life in Boston and New England Police Gazette*, April 6, 1850, AAS.]

New York Life: or, The Mysteries of Upper-Tendom Revealed. New York: Charles S. Atwood, n.d. [This book appears under the pseudonym "Charles Paul de Kock," but is known to be Thompson's because it is said to be by the author of (among other things) *The Lady's Garter*, which was published under the name "Greenhorn." Although it is not dated, this book probably appeared in the first four months of 1849. Chapter XXIII is a satire on Ned Buntline, titled "Bob Towline; or some revelations of a Reformer." Thompson refers to Towline's plan, announced "not long since," to travel by boat and correspond with his newspaper: this announcement was made in *Ned Buntline's Own* on December 2, 1848. Although he mocks and critiques him in a number of ways, moreover, Thompson makes no mention of his alleged involvement in the Astor Place riot of May 10, 1849, leading one to believe the book was written before that date.] AAS.

The Outlaw, or, the Felon's Fortunes. New York: F. A. Brady, 1851. [W Vol. II 2490], AAS, HEH, UP, UV, *Y*.

The Road to Ruin: or, the Felon's Doom. New York: F. A. Brady, ca.1851. [W Vol. II 2491],

HEH, UP. [An installment appears in *Life and Boston and New England Police Gazette* of June 23, 1850.]

The Shop Girls of New York. [*Belle*, November 8, 1858. Thompson is said to be continuing the serial, which was begun by another author.]

Ten Days in the Tombs, or a Key to the Modern Bastile. New York: P. F. Harris, 1855. [Under the pseudonym "John McGinn."] [*Belle*, October 15 and November 26, 1855], C.

Tom De Lacy, or the Convict's Revenge [*Belle*, September 3, 10, 24, October 1 and 8 (conclusion), 1855.]

The Twin Brothers: or the Fatal Resemblance. New York, Perry & Co., 185—. [The title page has no last digit in the year.] AAS.

Venus in Boston; A Romance of City Life. New York, 1849. [W Vol. I 2585], BP, Y. [An installment appeared in the September 1, 1849 issue of *Life in Boston Sporting Chronicle, and Lights and Shadows of New England Morals.*]

Also by Thompson

To the best of our knowledge, no copies of the following works survive. As indicated below, we know they once existed because they are either listed on the title pages of surviving works as previous works by Thompson, advertised on separate pages of those works or in newspapers for which he wrote, or included in Ashbee's list of additional works by Thompson.

The Actress; or, A Peep Behind the Curtain. [Advertised in *My Life*, 1854.]

Adventures of a Libertine. [Title page of *Anna Mowbray.*]

Alice Wade; or Guilt and Retribution. [Advertised in surviving issues of publisher Frederic A. Brady's Jack Harold series, a set of 12 Thompson novels that appeared sometime between 1870 and 1873. *Alice Wade* was no. 12.]

Asmodeus. [Title page of *New York Life*, 1849.]

The California Widow; or Love, Intrigue, Crime and Fashionable Dissipation. [Ashbee.]

Confessions of a Sofa (probably the same work as *Adventures of a Sofa; or Drawing-room Intrigues*). [Ashbee attributes this work to Thompson. It is also listed on the title page of *The Mysteries of Bond Street*. The January 31, 1857, issue of *Venus' Miscellany* announced that it would be available to the trade by February 15; the May 1857 issues advertised it as "now ready."]

The Coquette of Chestnut Street. [Ashbee.]

Dissipation; or Crime and Its Consequences. [Title page of *City Crimes*, 1849. Full title from list of books advertised in 1857 issues of *Venus' Miscellany.*]

Fast Life in London and Paris. [Advertised in surviving issues of publisher Frederic A. Brady's Jack Harold series, a set of 12 Thompson novels that appeared sometime between 1870 and 1873. *Fast Life* was no. 10.]

The Gay Deceiver; or, Man's Perfidy and Woman's Frailty. [Title page of *The House Breaker*, 1848; full title listed in Ashbee.]

Julia King: or, The Follies of a Beautiful Courtesan. [Title page of *Anna Mowbray*; also advertised as "now ready" in *Life in Boston and New England Police Gazette* of April 6, 1850.]

Julia Maxwell, or the Mysteries of Brooklyn. [Advertised in *Mysteries and Miseries of Philadelphia.*]

Kate Montrose; or, the Maniac's Daughter. [Title page of *Anna Mowbray*; full title listed in Ashbee.]

Lady Dashington. [Title page of *The Ladies' Garter.*]

La Tour de Nesle; or the Amours of Margurite [sic] of Burgundy. [Ashbee attributes this work to Thompson. The July 4, 1857 issue of *Venus' Miscellany* attributes it to "Appollonius of Gotham," a pseudonym for Thompson. The May 9, 1857, issue of *Venus' Miscellany* announces that the novel is now available in book form, and refers to its serialization in "the first numbers" of the paper. Since the May 9 issue is no. 26, and the paper was a weekly, the novel may have appeared in the paper beginning about six months earlier, in mid-November 1856.]

The Life of Kate Hastings. [Ashbee.]

Marie de Clairville: or, the Confessions of a Boarding School Miss. [Ashbee attributes this work to Thompson. The June 27, 1857, issue of *Venus' Miscellany* advertises this work as "now ready."]

Radcliff; or, the Adventures of a Libertine. [Title page of *The House Breaker*, 1848; full title listed in Ashbee.]

The Spaniard's Crime. [Title page of *Jack Harold*, 1850.]

The Virgin Wife; or, the High and the Low. New York: F. A. Brady, n.d. [In a volume held at the New York Public Library, the cover of this work, which is said to be by Greenhorn, is bound together with another work published by Brady, *The Virgin Wife: A Thrilling Tale* by M. Rabeau. It is unclear whether Rabeau is a pseudonym for Thompson. *The Virgin Wife* is also advertised as No. 9 in the Jack Harold series issued by Brady between 1870 and 1873.]

Possibly by Thompson

The following works were advertised in newspapers that published Thompson's work, and were said to be by the French novelist Paul de Kock. Thompson definitely used the name de Kock for *New York Life: or, the Mysteries of Upper-Tendom Revealed.* In that case, it is clear that the work is his because de Kock is said to be the author of other works published under "Greenhorn" or Thompson's name. This leads one to believe that the following may be his works as well.

Advertised in July 23, 1851, issue of *Life in Boston and New England Police Gazette:*
Confessions of a Lady's Maid
The Evil Genius
Harriet Wilson
Madeline the Avenger
Paul the Profligate
Adventures of a Country Girl
Simon the Radical

Advertised in April 11, 1857, issue of *Life in Boston and New York:*
Memoirs of an Old Man of Twenty-Five
The Child of Nature Improved by Chance
Tales by Twilight
Brother James, or the Libertine
History of a Rake
The Intrigues of Three Days
The Misteries [sic] of Venus, or Lessons of Love

The following, published under the name of "Asmodeus," may also be Thompson's. Asmodeus, originally a biblical demon, had been described by the 19th-century authors Le Sage and Carlyle as a creature who could see through the roofs of a city's houses. Thompson invokes Asmodeus in *New York Life* as a figure who can see and expose hidden wickedness; also, an illustration to Chapter V of *Venus in Boston*, serialized in the *Life in Boston Sporting Chronicle* issue of September 1, 1849, depicted a broadside on the wall of a pub which read "Lyceum: Asmodeus in Boston."

The Lame Devil, or Asmodeus in Boston. [Advertised in January 4, 1851, issue of *Life in Boston and New England Police Gazette.*]

Sharps and Flats; or the Perils of City Life. Being the Adventures of one who Lived by his Wits. By Asmodeus. [Installments of this work survive in the *Life in Boston and New England Police Gazette* of April 6, 1850 and May 18, 1850.]

Edited by Thompson

The Broadway Belle. As discussed in the introduction to this volume, the title, format and editors of the paper varied somewhat over the course of its run. The following institutions hold the indicated issues of the paper.

American Antiquarian Society, Worcester, Massachusetts

January 1, 1855	February 19, 1855	September 10, 1855
January 8, 1855	February 26, 1855	September 17, 1855
January 22, 1855	March 5, 1855	September 24, 1855
January 29, 1855	March 12, 1855	October 1, 1855
February 12, 1855	September 3, 1855	November 8, 1858

New York Public Library, New York

October 8, 1855
October 15, 1855
October 22, 1855
October 29, 1855

New York Historical Society, New York
November 26, 1855

Papers in Which Thompson's Works Appeared

Issues held at the American Antiquarian Society in Worcester, Massachusetts

Life in Boston and New England Police Gazette
April 6, 1850
April 27, 1850
May 18, 1850
August 10, 1850
January 4, 1851
June 23, 1851

Life in Boston and New York
  May 13, 1854
  April 14, 1855
  Nov. 22, 1855
  April 11, 1857

Life in Boston Sporting Chronicle, and Lights and Shadows of New England Morals
  September 1, 1849

Venus' Miscellany
  January 31, 1857
  May 23, 1857

Issues held at the Boston Public Library
(We have not had the opportunity to examine these issues, but did confirm their existence.)

Life in Boston Sporting Chronicle, and Lights and Shadows of New England Morals
  February 10, 1849
  February 2, 1856

Issues held in the rare book room at Princeton's Firestone Library

Venus' Miscellany

May 9, 1857	May 30, 1857	June 27, 1857
May 16, 1857	June 6, 1857	July 4, 1857
May 23, 1857	June 20, 1857	July 11, 1847

SECONDARY LITERATURE

Ashbee, Henry Spencer. *Bibliography of Prohibited Books.* 1880. Reprint, New York: Jack Brussel, 1962.

Ashwill, Gary. "The Mysteries of Capitalism in George Lippard's City Novels. " *ESQ: A Journal of the American Renaissance,* 40 (4th quarter 1994): 293–317.

Barker-Benfield, G. J. *Horrors of the Half-Known Life: Male Attitudes Toward Women and Sexuality in Nineteenth-Century America.* New York: Harper and Row, 1976.

Baym, Nina. *Women's Fiction: A Guide to Novels by and about Women in America, 1820–1870.* Ithaca: Cornell University Press, 1978.

Benjamin, Walter. "On Some Motifs in Baudelaire." In *Illuminations,* edited by Hannah Arendt, 155-200. New York: Shocken, 1968.

Bergmann, Hans. *God in the Street: New York Writing from the Penny Press to Melville.* Philadelphia: Temple University Press, 1995.

Blumin, Stuart M. "George G. Foster and the Emerging Metropolis." Introduction to Foster's *New York by Gas-Light.* 1850. Reprint, Berkeley: University of California Press, 1990. Pp. 1–61.

Bode, Carl, ed. *Anatomy of Popular Culture, 1840–1861.* Berkeley: University of California Press, 1959.

Bouton, John Bell. *The Life and Choice Writings of George Lippard.* New York: H. H. Randall, 1855.

Boyle, Thomas. *Black Swine in the Sewers of Hampstead: Beneath the Surface of Victorian Sensationalism.* New York: Viking, 1989.

Brand, Dana. *The Spectator and the City in Nineteenth-Century American Literature.* New York: Cambridge University Press, 1991.

Brown, Herbert Ross. *The Sentimental Novel in America, 1789–1869.* Durham: Duke University Press, 1940.

Buckley, Peter G. "The Case against Ned Buntline: The 'Words, Signs, and Gestures' of Popular Authorship." *Prospects,* 13 (1988): 249–72.

Burr, C. Chauncey. Introduction to George Lippard's *Washington and His Generals.* Philadelphia: T. B. Peterson, 1847. Pp. i–xxvii.

Burrows, Edwin G., and Mike Wallace. *Gotham: A History of New York City to 1898.* New York: Oxford University Press, 1999.

Butterfield, Roger: "George Lippard and His Secret Brotherhood." *Pennsylvania Magazine of History and Biography,* 79 (1955): 285.

Charvat, William. *Literary Publishing in America, 1790–1850.* 1959. Reprint, Amherst: University of Massachusetts Press, 1993.

Clarker, Graham, ed. *The American City: Literary and Cultural Perspectives.* London: Vision Press, 1988.

Cohen, Daniel A. *Pillars of Salt, Monuments of Grace: New England Crime Literature and the Origins of American Popular Culture, 1674–1860.* New York: Oxford University Press, 1981.

Cohen, Patricia Cline. *The Murder of Helen Jewett: The Life and Death of a Prostitute in Nineteenth-Century New York.* New York: Alfred A. Knopf, 1998.

Comstock, Anthony. *Frauds Exposed; or, How the People are Deceived and Robbed, and Youth Corrupted, Being a Full Exposure of Various Schemes Operated through the Mails, and Unearthed by the Author in a Seven Years' Service as a Special Agent of the Post Office Department and Secretary and Chief Agent of the New York Society for the Suppression of Vice.* New York: J. H. Brown, 1880.

———. *Traps for the Young.* Ed. Robert Bremner. 1884. Reprint, Cambridge, Mass.: Harvard University Press, 1967.

Cott, Nancy F. *The Bonds of Womanhood: Woman's Sphere in New England, 1780–1835.* New Haven: Yale University Press, 1977.

———. "Passionlessness: An Interpretation of Victorian Sexual Ideology, 1790–1850." *Signs,* 4 (1978): 210–36.

Cowie, Alexander. *The Rise of the American Novel.* New York: American Book Co., 1948.

Craig, Alec. *The Banned Books of England and Other Countries: A Study of the Conception of Literary Obscenity.* London, Allen and Unwin, 1962.

———. *Suppressed Books: A History of the Conception of Literary Obscenity.* Cleveland: World Publishing, 1963.

Curtis, Julia. "Philadelphia in an Uproar: The Monks of Monk Hall, 1844." *Theatre History Studies,* 5 (1985): 41–47.

Daniels, Christine, and Michael Kennedy, eds. *Over the Threshold: Intimate Violence in Early America, 1640–1865.* New York: Routledge, 1999.

Davidson, Cathy N. *Revolution and the Word: The Rise of the Novel in America.* New York: Oxford University Press, 1986.

Davis, David Brion. *Homicide in American Fiction.* Ithaca: Cornell University Press, 1957.

Degler, Carl N. *At Odds: Women and the Family in America from the Revolution to the Present*. New York: Oxford University Press, 1980.

De Grazia, Emilio. "Edgar Allan Poe, George Lippard, and the Walnut-Coffin Papers." *Papers of the Bibliographical Society of America*, 66 (1972): 58–60.

———. "Poe's Devoted Democrat, George Lippard." *Poe Studies*, 6 (June 1973): 6–8.

D'Emilio, John, and Estelle B. Freedman. *Intimate Matters: A History of Sexuality in America*. New York: Harper and Row, 1988.

Denning, Michael. *Mechanic Accents: Dime Novels and Working-Class Culture in America*. London: Verso, 1987.

Douglas, Ann. *The Feminization of American Culture*. New York: Knopf, 1977.

Ehrlich, Heyward. "The 'Mysteries' of Philadelphia: Lippard's *The Quaker City* and 'Urban' Gothic." *ESQ: A Journal of the American Renaissance*, 66 (1st quarter 1972): 50–65.

Fiedler, Leslie. *Love and Death in the American Novel*. Revised edition. New York: Stein and Day, 1966.

———. "The Male Novel." *Partisan Review*, 37 (1970): 74–89. Expanded and reprinted as the introduction to Fiedler's edition of George Lippard's *The Monks of Monk Hall*. New York: Odyssey Press, 1970.

Friedman, Stephen. *City Moves: A User's Guide to the Way Cities Work*. New York: McGraw-Hill, 1989.

Gelfant, Blanche Housman. *The American City Novel*. Norman: University of Oklahoma Press, 1970.

Gienapp, William E. *The Origins of the Republican Party, 1852–1856*. New York: Oxford University Press, 1987.

Gilfoyle, Timothy J. *City of Eros: New York City, Prostitution, and the Commercialization of Sex, 1790–1920*. New York: W. W. Norton, 1992.

Goulemot, Jean Marie. *Forbidden Texts: Erotic Literature and Its Readers in Eighteenth-Century France*. Translated by James Simpson. Philadelphia: University of Pennsylvania Press, 1994.

Haight, A. Lynn. *Banned Books: Informal Notes on Some Books Banned for Various Reasons at Various Times and Various Places*. New York: Bowker, 1935.

Halttunen, Karen. *Murder Most Foul: The Killer and the American Gothic Imagination*. Cambridge, Mass.: Harvard University Press, 1998.

Harris, Neil. *Humbug: The Art of P. T. Barnum*. Boston: Little, Brown, 1973.

Hart, James D. *The Popular Book: A History of America's Literary Tastes*. Berkeley: University of California Press, 1950.

Hughes, Winifred. *The Maniac in the Cellar: Sensation Novels of the 1860s*. Princeton: Princeton University Press, 1980.

Hunt, Lynn, ed. *The Invention of Pornography: Obscenity and the Origins of Modernity, 1500–1800*. 1993. Reprint, New York: Zone Books, 1996.

Ivy, Randolph Woods. "The Victorian Sensation Novel: A Study in Formula Fiction." Ph.D. diss., University of Chicago, 1974.

Jackson, Joseph. "George Lippard: Misunderstood Man of Letters." *Pennsylvania Magazine of History and Biography*, 59 (1930): 376–91.

Jay, Michael C., and Ann C. Watts, eds. *Literature and the Urban Experience*. New Brunswick, N.J.: Rutgers University Press, 1981.

Kammen, Michael. *American Culture, American Tastes: Social Change and the Twentieth Century*. New York: Knopf, 1999.

Kasson, John F. *Rudeness and Civility: Manners in Nineteenth-Century Urban America.* New York: Hill and Wang, 1990.

Kendrick, Walter. *The Secret Museum: Pornography in Modern Culture.* New York: Viking, 1988.

Kipnis, Laura. *Bound and Gagged: Pornography and the Politics of Fantasy in America.* New York: Grove Press, 1996.

Levine, Lawrence W. *Highbrow/Lowbrow: The Emergence of Cultural Hierarchy in America.* Cambridge, Mass.: Harvard University Press, 1988.

Looby, Christopher. "George Thompson's 'Romance of the Real': Transgression and Taboo in American Sensation Fiction." *American Literature,* 65 (December 1993): 651–672.

Loth, David Goldsmith. *The Erotic in Literature: A Historical Survey of Pornography as Delightful as It Is Indiscreet.* New York: J. Messner, 1961.

Lott, Eric. *Love and Theft: Blackface Minstrelsy and the American Working Class.* New York: Oxford University Press, 1993.

Machor, James L. *Pastoral Cities: Urban Ideals and the Symbolic Landscape of America.* Madison: University of Wisconsin Press, 1987.

Marcus, Steven. *The Other Victorians: A Study of Sexuality and Pornography in Mid-Nineteenth-Century England.* New York: Basic Books, 1966.

Mott, Frank Luther. *Golden Multitudes: The Story of Best Sellers in the United States.* New York: Macmillan, 1947.

Mintz, Steven. *A Prison of Expectations: The Family in Victorian Culture.* New York: New York University Press, 1983.

Monaghan, Jay. *The Great Rascal: The Life and Adventures of Ned Buntline.* Boston: Little, Brown, 1952.

Mumford, Lewis. *The City in History: Its Origins, Its Transformations, and Its Prospects.* New York: Harcourt Brace, 1961.

Nasaw, David. *Going Out: The Rise and Fall of Public Amusements.* New York: Basic Books, 1993.

Noel, Mary. *Villains Galore: The Heyday of the Popular Story Weekly.* New York: Macmillan, 1954.

Nye, Russell B. *The Unembarrassed Muse: The Popular Arts in America.* New York: Dial, 1970.

Papashvily, Helen. *All the Happy Endings: A Study of the Domestic Novel in the Nineteenth Century.* New York: Harper, 1956.

Papke, David Ray. *Framing the Criminal: Crime, Cultural Work, and the Loss of Critical Perspective, 1830–1900.* Hamden, Conn.: Archon, 1987.

Pleck, Elizabeth. *Domestic Tyranny: The Making of Social Policy against Family Violence from Colonial Times to the Present.* New York: Oxford University Press, 1987.

Poirier, Richard. *A World Elsewhere: The Place of Style in American Literature.* New York: Oxford University Press, 1966.

Pollin, Burton R. "More on Lippard and Poe." *Poe Studies,* 7, no.1 (June 1974): 22–23.

Reynolds, David S. *Beneath the American Renaissance: The Subversive Imagination in the Age of Emerson and Melville.* New York: Knopf, 1988.

———. *Faith in Fiction: The Emergence of Religious Literature in America.* Cambridge, Mass.: Harvard University Press, 1981.

———. *George Lippard.* Boston: G. K. Hall, 1982.

————. Introduction to George Lippard's *The Quaker City: or, The Monks of Monk Hall*. Amherst: University of Massachusetts Press, 1995.

————. *Walt Whitman's America: A Cultural Biography*. New York: Knopf, 1995.

Reynolds, David S., ed. *George Lippard, Prophet of Protest: Writings of an American Radical, 1822–1854*. New York: Peter Lang, 1986.

Ridgely, J. V. "George Lippard's *The Quaker City*: The World of American Porno-Gothic." *Studies in the Literary Imagination*, 8 (Spring 1974): 77–94.

Ringe, Donald A. *American Gothic: Imagination and Reason in Nineteenth-Century Fiction*. Lexington: University Press of Kentucky, 1982.

Rothman, Ellen K. *Hands and Hearts: A History of Courtship in America*. New York: Basic Books, 1984.

Sears, Hal D. *The Sex Radicals: Free Love in High Victorian America*. Lawrence: Regents Press of Kansas, 1977.

Seecamp, Carsten E. "The Chapter of Perfection: A Neglected Influence on George Lippard." *Pennsylvania Magazine of History and Biography*, 94 (April 1970): 192–212.

Siegel, Adrienne. "Brothels, Bets, and Bars: Popular Literature as Guidebook to the Urban Underground, 1840–1870." *North Dakota Quarterly*, 44 (Spring 1976): 5–22.

————. *The Image of the American City in Popular Literature, 1820–1870*. Port Washington, N.Y.: Kennikat Press, 1981.

A Sketch of Events in the Life of George Law, Published in Advance of his Biography. Also, Extracts from the Public Journals. New York: J. C. Derby, 1855.

Smith-Rosenberg, Carroll. *Disorderly Conduct: Visions of Gender in Victorian America*. New York: Oxford University Press, 1985.

Snyder, Robert W. *The Voice of the City: Vaudeville and Popular Culture in New York*. New York: Oxford University Press, 1989.

Spurlock, John C. *Free Love: Marriage and Middle-Class Radicalism in America, 1825–1860*. New York: New York University Press, 1988.

Srebnick, Amy Gilman. *The Mysterious Death of Mary Rogers: Sex and Culture in Nineteenth-Century New York*. New York: Oxford University Press, 1995.

Stern, Madeline B. *Heads and Headlines: The Phrenological Fowlers*. Norman: University of Oklahoma Press, 1971.

Stewart, David M. "Cultural Work, City Crime, Reading, Pleasure." *American Literary History*, 9 (Winter 1997): 676–701.

Still, Bayrd. *Mirror for Gotham: New York as Seen by Contemporaries from Dutch Days to the Present*. New York: New York University Press, 1956.

Stout, Janis P. *Sodoms in Eden: The City in American Fiction before 1860*. Westport, Conn.: Greenwood Press, 1976.

Streeby, Shelley. "Haunted Houses: George Lippard, Nathaniel Hawthorne, and Middle-Class America." *Criticism*, 38 (Summer 1996): 443–72.

Taylor, George Rogers. "Gaslight Foster: A New York 'Journeyman Journalist' at Mid-Century." *New York History*, 58 (July 1977): 297–312.

————. "Philadelphia in Slices: by George G. Foster." *Pennsylvania Magazine of History and Bibliography*, 93 (January 1969): 23–72.

Toll, Robert C. *Blacking Up: The Minstrel Show in Nineteenth-Century America*. New York: Oxford University Press, 1974.

Tompkins, Jane. *Sensational Designs: The Cultural Work of American Fiction, 1790–1860*. New York: Oxford University Press, 1985.

Wagner, Peter. *Eros Revived: Erotica of the Enlightenment in England and America.* London: Secker and Warburg, 1988.

Welter, Barbara. "The Cult of True Womanhood, 1820–1860." *American Quarterly*, 18 (1966): 131–75.

——. *Dimity Convictions: The American Woman in the Nineteenth Century.* Columbus: Ohio State University Press, 1976.

Widmer, Edward L. *Young America: The Flowering of Democracy in New York City.* New York: Oxford University Press, 1999.

Wishy, Bernard. *The Child and the Republic: The Dawn of Modern American Child Nurture.* Philadelphia: University of Pennsylvania Press, 1968.

Wright, Lyle Henry. *American Fiction, 1774–1875: A Contribution to a Bibliography.* San Marino, Calif.: Huntington Library, 1957.

Wyld, Lionel D. "George Lippard: Gothicism and Social Consciousness in the Early American Novel." *Four Quarters*, 5 (1956): 6–12.

Zboray, Ronald. *A Fictive People: Antebellum Economic Development and the American Reading Public.* New York: Oxford University Press, 1993.

Ziff, Larzer. *Literary Democracy: The Declaration of Cultural Independence in America.* New York: Viking, 1981.

DAVID S. REYNOLDS is Distinguished Professor of English at Baruch College and the Graduate School of the City University of New York. He is the author of *Beneath the American Renaissance: The Subversive Imagination in the Age of Emerson and Melville* (winner of the Christian Gauss Award) and *Walt Whitman's America: A Cultural Biography* (winner of the Bancroft Prize and the Ambassador Book Award; finalist for the National Book Critics Circle Award).

KIMBERLY R. GLADMAN is an independent scholar with a particular interest in nineteenth-century popular culture. She received her Ph.D. in comparative literature from New York University in 2001.